The Castle

and

The Trial

Franz Kafka

Must Have Books
503 Deerfield Place
Victoria, BC
V9B 6G5
Canada

ISBN 9781773238609

Copyright 2022 – Must Have Books

All rights reserved in accordance with international law. No part of this book may be reproduced or transmitted in any form or by any means, electronic or mechanical, including photocopying, recording, or by any information storage or retrieval system, except in the case of excerpts by a reviewer who may quote brief passages in an article or review, without written permission from the publisher.

CONTENTS

The Trial 4

The Castle 128

THE TRIAL

Chapter One Arrest - Conversation with Mrs. Grubach - Then Miss Bürstner

Someone must have been telling lies about Josef K., he knew he had done nothing wrong but, one morning, he was arrested. Every day at eight in the morning he was brought his breakfast by Mrs. Grubach's cook - Mrs. Grubach was his landlady - but today she didn't come. That had never happened before. K. waited a little while, looked from his pillow at the old woman who lived opposite and who was watching him with an inquisitiveness quite unusual for her, and finally, both hungry and disconcerted, rang the bell. There was immediately a knock at the door and a man entered. He had never seen the man in this house before. He was slim but firmly built, his clothes were black and close-fitting, with many folds and pockets, buckles and buttons and a belt, all of which gave the impression of being very practical but without making it very clear what they were actually for. "Who are you?" asked K., sitting half upright in his bed. The man, however, ignored the question as if his arrival simply had to be accepted, and merely replied, "You rang?" "Anna should have brought me my breakfast," said K. He tried to work out who the man actually was, first in silence, just through observation and by thinking about it, but the man didn't stay still to be looked at for very long. Instead he went over to the door, opened it slightly, and said to someone who was clearly standing immediately behind it, "He wants Anna to bring him his breakfast." There was a little laughter in the neighbouring room, it was not clear from the sound of it whether there were several people laughing. The strange man could not have learned anything from it that he hadn't known already, but now he said to K., as if making his report "It is not possible." "It would be the first time that's happened," said K., as he jumped out of bed and quickly pulled on his trousers. "I want to see who that is in the next room, and why it is that Mrs. Grubach has let me be disturbed in this way." It immediately occurred to him that he needn't have said this out loud, and that he must to some extent have acknowledged their authority by doing so, but that didn't seem important to him at the time. That, at least, is how the stranger took it, as he said, "Don't you think you'd better stay where you are?" "I want neither to stay here nor to be spoken to by you until you've introduced yourself." "I meant it for your own good," said the stranger and opened the door, this time without being asked. The next room, which K. entered more slowly than he had intended, looked at first glance exactly the same as it had the previous evening. It was Mrs. Grubach's living room, over-filled with furniture, tablecloths, porcelain and photographs. Perhaps there was a little more space in there than usual today, but if so it was not immediately obvious, especially as the main difference was the presence of a man sitting by the open window with a book from which he now looked up. "You should have stayed in your room! Didn't Franz tell you?" "And what is it you want, then?" said K., looking back and forth between this new acquaintance and the one named Franz, who had remained in the doorway. Through the open window he noticed the old woman again, who had come close to the window opposite so that she could continue to see everything. She was showing an inquisitiveness that really made it seem like she was going senile. "I want to see Mrs. Grubach ...," said K., making a movement as if tearing himself away from the two men - even though they were standing well away from him - and wanted to go. "No," said the man at the window, who threw his book down on a coffee table and stood up. "You can't go away when you're under arrest." "That's how it seems," said K. "And why am I under arrest?" he then asked. "That's something we're not allowed to tell you. Go into your room and wait there. Proceedings are underway and you'll learn about everything all in good time. It's not really part of my job to be friendly towards you like this, but I hope no-one, apart from Franz, will hear about it, and he's been more friendly towards you than he should have been, under the rules, himself. If you carry on having as much good luck as you have been with your arresting officers then you can reckon on things going well with you." K. wanted to sit down, but then he saw that, apart from the chair by the window, there was nowhere anywhere in the room where he could sit. "You'll get the chance to see for yourself how true all this is," said Franz and both men then walked up to K. They were significantly bigger than him, especially the second man, who frequently slapped him on the shoulder. The two of them felt K.'s nightshirt, and said he would now have to wear one that was of much lower quality, but that they would keep the nightshirt along with his other underclothes and return them to him if his case turned out well. "It's better for you if you give us the things than if you leave them in the storeroom," they said. "Things have a tendency to go missing in the storeroom, and after a certain amount of time they sell things off, whether the case involved has come to an end or not. And cases like this can last a long time, especially the ones that have been coming up lately. They'd give you the money they got for them, but it wouldn't be very much as it's not what they're offered for them when they sell them that counts, it's how much they get slipped on the side, and things like that lose their value anyway when they get passed on from hand to hand, year after year." K. paid hardly any attention to what they were saying, he did not place much value on what he may have still possessed or on who decided what happened to them. It was much more important to him to get a clear understanding of his position, but he could not think clearly while these people were here, the second policeman's belly - and they could only be policemen - looked friendly enough, sticking out towards him, but when K. looked up and saw his dry, boney face it did not seem to fit with the body. His strong nose twisted to one side as if ignoring K. and sharing an understanding with the other policeman. What sort of people were these? What were they talking about? What office did they belong to? K. was living in a free country, after all, everywhere was at peace, all laws were decent and were upheld, who was it who dared accost him in his own home? He was always inclined to take life as lightly as he could, to cross bridges when he came to them, pay no heed for the future, even when everything seemed under threat. But here that did not seem the right thing to do. He could have taken it all as a joke, a big joke set up by his colleagues at the bank for some unknown reason, or also perhaps because today was his thirtieth birthday, it was all possible of course, maybe all he had to do was laugh in the policemen's face in some way and they would laugh with him, maybe they were tradesmen from the corner of the street, they looked like they might be - but he was nonetheless determined, ever since he first caught sight of the one called Franz, not to lose any slight advantage he might have had over these people. There was a very slight risk that people would later say he couldn't understand a joke, but - although he wasn't normally in the habit of learning from experience - he might also have had a few unimportant occasions in mind when, unlike his more cautious friends, he had acted with no thought at all for what might follow and had been made to suffer for it. He didn't want that to happen again, not this time at least; if they were play-acting he would act along with them.

He still had time. "Allow me," he said, and hurried between the two policemen through into his room. "He seems sensible enough," he heard them say behind him. Once in his room, he quickly pulled open the drawer of his writing desk, everything in it was very tidy but in his agitation he was unable to find the identification documents he was looking for straight away. He finally found his bicycle permit and was about to go back to the policemen with it when it seemed to him too petty, so he carried on searching until he found his birth certificate. Just as he got back in the adjoining room the door on the other side opened and Mrs. Grubach was about to enter. He only saw her for an instant, for as soon as she recognised K. she was clearly embarrassed, asked for forgiveness and disappeared, closing the door behind her very carefully. "Do come in," K. could have said just then. But now he stood in the middle of the room with his papers in his hand and still looking at the door which did not open again. He stayed like that until he was startled out of it by the shout of the policeman who sat at the little table at the open window and, as K. now saw, was eating his breakfast. "Why didn't she come in?" he asked. "She's not allowed to," said the big policeman. "You're under arrest, aren't you." "But how can I be under arrest? And how come it's like this?" "Now you're starting again," said the policeman, dipping a piece of buttered bread in the honeypot. "We don't answer questions like that." "You will have to answer them," said K. "Here are my identification papers, now show me yours and I certainly want to see the arrest warrant." "Oh, my God!" said the policeman. "In a position like yours, and you think you can start giving orders, do you? It won't do you any good to get us on the wrong side, even if you think it will - we're probably more on your side that anyone else you know!" "That's true, you know, you'd better believe it," said Franz, holding a cup of coffee in his hand which he did not lift to his mouth but looked at K. in a way that was probably meant to be full of meaning but could not actually be understood. K. found himself, without intending it, in a mute dialogue with Franz, but then slapped his hand down on his papers and said, "Here are my identity documents." "And what do you want us to do about it?" replied the big policeman, loudly. "The way you're carrying on, it's worse than a child. What is it you want? Do you want to get this great, bloody trial of yours over with quickly by talking about ID and arrest warrants with us? We're just coppers, that's all we are. Junior officers like us hardly know one end of an ID card from another, all we've got to do with you is keep an eye on you for ten hours a day and get paid for it. That's all we are. Mind you, what we can do is make sure that the high officials we work for find out just what sort of person it is they're going to arrest, and why he should be arrested, before they issue the warrant. There's no mistake there. Our authorities as far as I know, and I only know the lowest grades, don't go out looking for guilt among the public; it's the guilt that draws them out, like it says in the law, and they have to send us police officers out. That's the law. Where d'you think there'd be any mistake there?" "I don't know this law," said K. "So much the worse for you, then," said the policeman. "It's probably exists only in your heads," said K., he wanted, in some way, to insinuate his way into the thoughts of the policemen, to re-shape those thoughts to his benefit or to make himself at home there. But the policeman just said dismissively, "You'll find out when it affects you." Franz joined in, and said, "Look at this, Willem, he admits he doesn't know the law and at the same time insists he's innocent." "You're quite right, but we can't get him to understand a thing," said the other. K. stopped talking with them; do I, he thought to himself, do I really have to carry on getting tangled up with the chattering of base functionaries like this? - and they admit themselves that they are of the lowest position. They're talking about things of which they don't have the slightest understanding, anyway. It's only because of their stupidity that they're able to be so sure of themselves. I just need few words with someone of the same social standing as myself and everything will be incomparably clearer, much clearer than a long conversation with these two can make it. He walked up and down the free space in the room a couple of times, across the street he could see the old woman who, now, had pulled an old man, much older than herself, up to the window and had her arms around him. K. had to put an end to this display, "Take me to your superior," he said. "As soon as he wants to see you. Not before," said the policeman, the one called Willem. "And now my advice to you," he added, "is to go into your room, stay calm, and wait and see what's to be done with you. If you take our advice, you won't tire yourself out thinking about things to no purpose, you need to pull yourself together as there's a lot that's going to required of you. You've not behaved towards us the way we deserve after being so good to you, you forget that we, whatever we are, we're still free men and you're not, and that's quite an advantage. But in spite of all that we're still willing, if you've got the money, to go and get you some breakfast from the café over the road."

Without giving any answer to this offer, K. stood still for some time. Perhaps, if he opened the door of the next room or even the front door, the two of them would not dare to stand in his way, perhaps that would be the simplest way to settle the whole thing, by bringing it to a head. But maybe they would grab him, and if he were thrown down on the ground he would lose all the advantage he, in a certain respect, had over them. So he decided on the more certain solution, the way things would go in the natural course of events, and went back in his room without another word either from him or from the policemen.

He threw himself down on his bed, and from the dressing table he took the nice apple that he had put there the previous evening for his breakfast. Now it was all the breakfast he had and anyway, as he confirmed as soon as he took his first, big bite of it, it was far better than a breakfast he could have had through the good will of the policemen from the dirty café. He felt well and confident, he had failed to go into work at the bank this morning but that could easily be excused because of the relatively high position he held there. Should he really send in his explanation? He wondered about it. If nobody believed him, and in this case that would be understandable, he could bring Mrs. Grubach in as a witness, or even the old pair from across the street, who probably even now were on their way over to the window opposite. It puzzled K., at least it puzzled him looking at it from the policemen's point of view, that they had made him go into the room and left him alone there, where he had ten different ways of killing himself. At the same time, though, he asked himself, this time looking at it from his own point of view, what reason he could have to do so. Because those two were sitting there in the next room and had taken his breakfast, perhaps? It would have been so pointless to kill himself that, even if he had wanted to, the pointlessness would have made him unable. Maybe, if the policemen had not been so obviously limited in their mental abilities, it could have been supposed that they had come to the same conclusion and saw no danger in leaving him alone because of it. They could watch now, if they wanted, and see how he went over to the cupboard in the wall where he kept a bottle of good schnapps, how he first emptied a glass of it in place of his breakfast and how he then took a second glassful in order to give himself courage, the last one just as a precaution for the unlikely chance it would be needed.

Then he was so startled by a shout to him from the other room that he struck his teeth against the glass. "The supervisor wants to see you!" a voice said. It was only the shout that startled him, this curt, abrupt, military shout, that he would not have expected from the policeman called Franz. In itself, he found the order very welcome. "At last!" he called back, locked the cupboard and, without delay, hurried into the next room. The two policemen were standing there and chased him back into his bedroom as if that were a matter of course. "What d'you think you're doing?" they cried. "Think you're going to see the supervisor dressed in just your shirt, do you? He'd see to it you got a right thumping, and us and all!" "Let go of me for God's sake!" called K., who had already been pushed back as far as his wardrobe, "if you accost me when I'm still in bed you can't expect to find me in my evening dress." "That won't help you," said the policemen, who always became very quiet, almost sad, when K. began to shout, and in that way confused him or, to some extent, brought him to his senses. "Ridiculous formalities!" he grumbled, as he lifted his coat from the chair and kept it in both his hands for a little while, as if holding it out for the policemen's inspection. They shook their heads. "It's got to be a black coat," they said. At that, K. threw the coat to the floor and said - without knowing even himself what he meant by it - "Well it's not going to be the main trial, after all." The policemen laughed, but continued to insist, "It's got to be a black coat." "Well that's alright by me if it makes things go any faster," said K. He opened the wardrobe himself, spent a long time searching through all the clothes, and chose his best black suit which had a short jacket that had greatly surprised those who knew him, then he also pulled out a fresh shirt and began, carefully, to get dressed. He secretly told himself that he had succeeded in speeding things up by letting the policemen forget to make him have a bath. He watched them to see if they might remember after all, but of course it never occurred to them, although Willem did not forget to send Franz up to the supervisor with the message saying that K. was getting dressed.

Once he was properly dressed, K. had to pass by Willem as he went through the next room into the one beyond, the door of which was already wide open. K. knew very well that this room had recently been let to a typist called 'Miss Bürstner'. She was in the habit of going out to work very early and coming back home very late, and K. had never exchanged more than a few words of greeting with her. Now, her bedside table had been pulled into the middle of the room to be used as a desk for these proceedings, and the supervisor sat behind it. He had his legs crossed, and had thrown one arm over the backrest of the chair.

In one corner of the room there were three young people looking at the photographs belonging to Miss Bürstner that had been put into a piece of fabric on the wall. Hung up on the handle of the open window was a white blouse. At the window across the street, there was the old pair again, although now their number had increased, as behind them, and far taller than they were, stood a man with an open shirt that showed his chest and a reddish goatee beard which he squeezed and twisted with his fingers. "Josef K.?" asked the supervisor, perhaps merely to attract K.'s attention as he looked round the room. K. nodded. "I daresay you were quite surprised by all that's been taking place this morning," said the supervisor as, with both hands, he pushed away the few items on the bedside table - the candle and box of matches, a book and a pin cushion which lay there as if they were things he would need for his own business. "Certainly," said K., and he began to feel relaxed now that, at last, he stood in front of someone with some sense, someone with whom he would be able to talk about his situation. "Certainly I'm surprised, but I'm not in any way very surprised." "You're not very surprised?" asked the supervisor, as he positioned the candle in the middle of the table and the other things in a group around it. "Perhaps you don't quite understand me," K. hurriedly pointed out. "What I mean is ..." here K. broke off what he was saying and looked round for somewhere to sit. "I may sit down, mayn't I?" he asked. "That's not usual," the supervisor answered. "What I mean is...," said K. without delaying a second time, "that, yes, I am very surprised but when you've been in the world for thirty years already and had to make your own way through everything yourself, which has been my lot, then you become hardened to surprises and don't take them too hard. Especially not what's happened today." "Why especially not what's happened today?" "I wouldn't want to say that I see all of this as a joke, you seem to have gone to too much trouble making all these arrangements for that. Everyone in the house must be taking part in it as well as all of you, that would be going beyond what could be a joke. So I don't want to say that this is a joke." "Quite right," said the supervisor, looking to see how many matches were left in the box. "But on the other hand," K. went on, looking round at everyone there and even wishing he could get the attention of the three who were looking at the photographs, "on the other hand this really can't be all that important. That follows from the fact that I've been indicted, but can't think of the slightest offence for which I could be indicted. But even that is all beside the point, the main question is: Who is issuing the indictment? What office is conducting this affair? Are you officials? None of you is wearing a uniform, unless what you are wearing" - here he turned towards Franz - "is meant to be a uniform, it's actually more of a travelling suit. I require a clear answer to all these questions, and I'm quite sure that once things have been made clear we can take our leave of each other on the best of terms." The supervisor slammed the box of matches down on the table. "You're making a big mistake," he said. "These gentlemen and I have got nothing to do with your business, in fact we know almost nothing about you. We could be wearing uniforms as proper and exact as you like and your situation wouldn't be any the worse for it. As to whether you're on a charge, I can't give you any sort of clear answer to that, I don't even know whether you are or not. You're under arrest, you're quite right about that, but I don't know any more than that. Maybe these officers have been chit-chatting with you, well if they have that's all it is, chit- chat. I can't give you an answer to your questions, but I can give you a bit of advice: You'd better think less about us and what's going to happen to you, and think a bit more about yourself. And stop making all this fuss about your sense of innocence; you don't make such a bad impression, but with all this fuss you're damaging it. And you ought to do a bit less talking, too. Almost everything you've said so far has been things we could have taken from your behaviour, even if you'd said no more than a few words. And what you have said has not exactly been in your favour."

K. stared at the supervisor. Was this man, probably younger than he was, lecturing him like a schoolmaster? Was he being punished for his honesty with a telling off? And was he to learn nothing about the reasons for his arrest or those who were arresting him? He became somewhat cross and began to walk up and down. No-one stopped him doing this and he pushed his sleeves back, felt his chest, straightened his hair, went over to the three men, said, "It makes no sense," at which these three turned round to face him and came towards him with serious expressions. He finally came again to a halt in front of the supervisor's desk. "State Attorney Hasterer is a good friend of mine," he said, "can I telephone him?" "Certainly," said the supervisor, "but I don't know what the point of that will be, I suppose you must have some private matter you want to discuss with him." "What the point is?" shouted K., more disconcerted that cross. "Who do you think you are? You want to see some point in it while you're carrying out something as pointless as it could be? It's enough to make you cry! These gentlemen first accost me, and now they sit or stand about in here and let me be hauled up in front of you. What point there would be, in telephoning a state attorney when I'm ostensibly under arrest? Very well, I won't make the telephone call." "You can call him if you want to," said the supervisor, stretching his hand out towards the outer room where the telephone was, "please, go on, do make your phone call." "No, I don't want to any more," said K., and went over to the window. Across the street, the people were still there at the window, and it was only now that K. had gone up to his window that they seemed to become uneasy about quietly watching what was going on. The old couple wanted to get up but the man behind them calmed them down. "We've got some kind of audience over there," called K. to the supervisor, quite loudly, as he pointed out with his forefinger. "Go away," he then called across to them. And the three of them did immediately retreat a few steps, the old pair even found themselves behind the man who then concealed them with the breadth of his body and seemed, going by the movements of his mouth, to be saying something incomprehensible into the distance. They did not disappear entirely, though, but seemed to be waiting for the moment when they could come back to the window without being noticed. "Intrusive, thoughtless people!" said K. as he turned back into the room. The supervisor may have agreed with him, at least K. thought that was what he saw from the corner of his eye. But it was just as possible that he had not even been listening as he had his hand pressed firmly down on the table and seemed to be comparing the length of his fingers. The two policemen were sitting on a chest covered with a coloured blanket, rubbing their knees. The three young people had put their hands on their hips and were looking round aimlessly. Everything was still, like in some office that has been forgotten about. "Now, gentlemen," called out K., and for a moment it seemed as if he was carrying all of them on his shoulders, "it looks like your business with me is over with. In my opinion, it's best now to stop wondering about whether you're proceeding correctly or incorrectly, and to bring the matter to a peaceful close with a mutual handshake. If you are of the same opinion, then please…" and he walked up to the supervisor's desk and held out his hand to him. The supervisor raised his eyes, bit his lip and looked at K.'s outstretched hand; K still believed the supervisor would do as he suggested. But instead, he stood up, picked up a hard round hat that was laying on Miss Bürstner's bed and put it carefully onto his head, using both hands as if trying on a new hat. "Everything seems so simple to you, doesn't it," he said to K. as he did so, "so you think we should bring the matter to a peaceful close, do you. No, no, that won't do. Mind you, on the other hand I certainly wouldn't want you to think there's no hope for you. No, why should you think that? You're simply under arrest, nothing more than that. That's what I had to tell you, that's what I've done and now I've seen how you've taken it. That's enough for one day and we can take our leave of each other, for the time being at least. I expect you'll want to go in to the bank now, won't you." "In to the bank?" asked K., "I thought I was under arrest." K. said this with a certain amount of defiance as, although his handshake had not been accepted, he was feeling more independent of all these people, especially since the supervisor had stood up. He was playing with them. If they left, he had decided he would run after them and offer to let them arrest him. That's why he even repeated, "How can I go in to the bank when I'm under arrest?" "I see you've misunderstood me," said the supervisor who was already at the door. "It's true that you're under arrest, but that shouldn't stop you from carrying out your job. And there shouldn't be anything to stop you carrying on with your usual life." "In that case it's not too bad, being under arrest," said K., and went up close to the supervisor. "I never meant it should be anything else," he replied. "It hardly seems to have been necessary to notify me of the arrest in that case," said K., and went even closer. The others had also come closer. All of them had gathered together into a narrow space by the door. "That was my duty," said the supervisor. "A silly duty," said K., unyielding. "Maybe so," replied the supervisor, "only don't let's waste our time talking on like this. I had assumed you'd be wanting to go to the bank. As you're paying close attention to every word I'll add this: I'm not forcing you to go to the bank, I'd just assumed you wanted to. And to make things easier for you, and to let you get to the bank with as little fuss as possible I've put these three gentlemen, colleagues of yours, at your disposal." "What's that?" exclaimed K., and looked at the three in astonishment. He could only remember seeing them in their group by the photographs, but these characterless, anaemic young people were indeed officials from his bank, not colleagues of his, that was putting it too high and it showed a gap in the omniscience of the supervisor, but they were nonetheless junior members of staff at the bank. How could K. have failed to see that? How occupied he must have been with the supervisor and the policemen not to have recognised these three! Rabensteiner, with his stiff demeanour and swinging hands, Kullich, with his blonde hair and deep-set eyes, and Kaminer, with his involuntary grin caused by chronic muscle spasms. "Good morning," said K. after a while, extending his hand to the gentlemen as they bowed correctly to him. "I didn't recognise you at all. So, we'll go into work now, shall we?" The gentlemen laughed and nodded enthusiastically, as if that was what they had been waiting for all the time, except that K. had left his hat in his room so they all dashed, one after another, into the room to fetch it, which caused a certain amount of embarrassment. K. stood where he was and watched them through the open double doorway, the last to go, of course, was the apathetic Rabensteiner who had broken into no more than an elegant trot. Kaminer got to the hat and K., as he often had to do at the bank, forcibly reminded himself that the grin was not deliberate, that he in fact wasn't able to grin deliberately. At that moment Mrs. Grubach opened the door from the hallway into the living room where all the people were. She did not seem to feel guilty about anything at all, and K., as often before, looked down at the belt of her apron which, for no reason, cut so deeply into her hefty body. Once downstairs, K., with his watch in his hand, decided to take a taxi - he had already been delayed by half an hour and there was no need to make the delay any longer. Kaminer ran to the corner to summon it, and the two others were making obvious efforts to keep K. diverted when Kullich pointed to the doorway of the house on the other side of the street where the large man with the blonde goatee beard appeared and, a little embarrassed at first at letting himself be seen in his full height, stepped back to the wall and leant against it. The old couple were probably still on the stairs. K. was cross with Kullich for pointing out this man whom he had already seen himself, in fact whom he had been expecting. "Don't look at him!" he snapped, without noticing how odd it was to speak to free men in this way. But there was no explanation needed anyway as just then the taxi arrived, they sat inside and set off. Inside the taxi, K. remembered that he had not noticed the supervisor and the policemen leaving - the supervisor had stopped him noticing the three bank staff and now the three bank staff had stopped him noticing the supervisor. This showed that K. was not very attentive, and he resolved to watch himself more carefully in this respect. Nonetheless, he gave it no thought as he twisted himself round and leant over onto the rear shelf of the car to catch sight of the supervisor and the policemen if he could. But he turned back round straight away and leant comfortably into the corner of the taxi without even having made the effort to see anyone. Although it did not seem like it, now was just the time when he needed some encouragement, but the gentlemen seemed tired just then, Rabensteiner looked out of the car to the right, Kullich to the left and only Kaminer was there with his grin at K.'s service. It would have been inhumane to make fun of that.

That spring, whenever possible, K. usually spent his evenings after work - he usually stayed in the office until nine o'clock - with a short walk, either by himself or in the company of some of the bank officials, and then he would go into a pub where he would sit at the regulars' table with mostly older men until eleven. There were, however, also exceptions to this habit, times, for instance, when K. was invited by the bank's manager (whom he greatly respected for his industry and trustworthiness) to go with him for a ride in his car or to eat dinner with him at his large house. K. would also go, once a week, to see a girl called Elsa who worked as a waitress in a wine bar through the night until late in the morning. During the daytime she only received visitors while still in bed.

That evening, though, - the day had passed quickly with a lot of hard work and many respectful and friendly birthday greetings - K. wanted to go straight home. Each time he had any small break from the day's work he considered, without knowing exactly what he had in mind, that Mrs. Grubach's flat seemed to have been put into great disarray by the events of that morning, and that it was up to him to put it back into order. Once order had been restored, every trace of those events would have been erased and everything would take its previous course once more. In particular, there was nothing to fear from the three bank officials, they had immersed themselves back into their paperwork and there was no alteration to be seen in them. K. had called each of them, separately or all together, into his office that day for no other reason than to observe them; he was always satisfied and had always been able to let them go again.

At half past nine that evening, when he arrived back in front of the building where he lived, he met a young lad in the doorway who was standing there, his legs apart and smoking a pipe. "Who are you?" immediately asked K., bringing his face close to the lad's, as it was hard to see in the half light of the landing. "I'm the landlord's son, sir," answered the lad, taking the pipe from his mouth and stepping to one side. "The landlord's son?" asked K., and impatiently knocked on the ground with his stick. "Did you want anything, sir? Would you like me to fetch my father?" "No, no," said K., there was something forgiving in his voice, as if the boy had harmed him in some way and he was excusing him. "It's alright," he said then, and went on, but before going up the stairs he turned round once more.

He could have gone directly to his room, but as he wanted to speak with Mrs. Grubach he went straight to her door and knocked. She was sat at the table with a knitted stocking and a pile of old stockings in front of her. K. apologised, a little embarrassed at coming so late, but Mrs. Grubach was very friendly and did not want to hear any apology, she was always ready to speak to him, he knew very well that he was her best and her favourite tenant. K. looked round the room, it looked exactly as it usually did, the breakfast dishes, which had been on the table by the window that morning, had already been cleared away. "A woman's hands will do many things when no-one's looking," he thought, he might himself have smashed all the dishes on the spot but certainly would not have been able to carry it all out. He looked at Mrs. Grubach with some gratitude. "Why are you working so late?" he asked. They were now both sitting at the table, and K. now and then sank his hands into the pile of stockings. "There's a lot of work to do," she said, "during the day I belong to the tenants; if I'm to sort out my own things there are only the evenings left to me." "I fear I may have caused you some exceptional work today." "How do you mean, Mr. K.?" she asked, becoming more interested and leaving her work in her lap. "I mean the men who were here this morning." "Oh, I see," she said, and went peacefully back to what she was doing, "that was no trouble, not especially." K. looked on in silence as she took up the knitted stocking once more. She seems surprised at my mentioning it, he thought, she seems to think it's improper for me to mention it. All the more important for me to do so. An old woman is the only person I can speak about it with. "But it must have caused some work for you," he said then, "but it won't happen again." "No, it can't happen again," she agreed, and smiled at K. in a way that was almost pained. "Do you mean that seriously?" asked K. "Yes," she said, more gently, "but the important thing is you mustn't take it too hard. There are so many awful things happening in the world! As you're being so honest with me, Mr. K., I can admit to you that I listened to a little of what was going on from behind the door, and that those two policemen told me one or two things as well. It's all to do with your happiness, and that's something that's quite close to my heart, perhaps more than it should be as I am, after all, only your landlady. Anyway, so I heard one or two things but I can't really say that it's about anything very serious. No. You have been arrested, but it's not in the same way as when they arrest a thief. If you're arrested in the same way as a thief, then it's bad, but an arrest like this ... . It seems to me that it's something very complicated - forgive me if I'm saying something stupid - something very complicated that I don't understand, but something that you don't really need to understand anyway."

"There's nothing stupid about what you've said, Mrs. Grubach, or at least I partly agree with you, only, the way I judge the whole thing is harsher than yours, and think it's not only not something complicated but simply a fuss about nothing. I was just caught unawares, that's what happened. If I had got up as soon as I was awake without letting myself get confused because Anna wasn't there, if I'd got up and paid no regard to anyone who might have been in my way and come straight to you, if I'd done something like having my breakfast in the kitchen as an exception, asked you to bring my clothes from my room, in short, if I had behaved sensibly then nothing more would have happened, everything that was waiting to happen would have been stifled. People are so often unprepared. In the bank, for example, I am well prepared, nothing of this sort could possibly happen to me there, I have my own assistant there, there are telephones for internal and external calls in front of me on the desk, I continually receive visits from people, representatives, officials, but besides that, and most importantly, I'm always occupied with my work, that's to say I'm always alert, it would even be a pleasure for me to find myself faced with something of that sort. But now it's over with, and I didn't really even want to talk about it any more, only I wanted to hear what you, as a sensible woman, thought about it all, and I'm very glad to hear that we're in agreement. But now you must give me your hand, an agreement of this sort needs to be confirmed with a handshake."

Will she shake hands with me? The supervisor didn't shake hands, he thought, and looked at the woman differently from before, examining her. She stood up, as he had also stood up, and was a little self-conscious, she hadn't been able to understand everything that K. said. As a result of this self consciousness she said something that she certainly did not intend and certainly was not appropriate. "Don't take it so hard, Mr. K.," she said, with tears in her voice and also, of course, forgetting the handshake. "I didn't know I was taking it hard," said K., feeling suddenly tired and seeing that if this woman did agree with him it was of very little value.

Before going out the door he asked, "Is Miss Bürstner home?" "No," said Mrs. Grubach, smiling as she gave this simple piece of information, saying something sensible at last. "She's at the theatre. Did you want to see her? Should I give her a message?" "I, er, I just wanted to have a few words with her." "I'm afraid I don't know when she's coming in; she usually gets back late when she's been to the theatre." "It really doesn't matter," said K. his head hanging as he turned to the door to leave, "I just wanted to give her my apology for taking over her room today." "There's no need for that, Mr. K., you're too conscientious, the young lady doesn't know anything about it, she hasn't been home since early this morning and everything's been tidied up again, you can see for yourself." And she opened the door to Miss Bürstner's room. "Thank you, I'll take your word for it," said K, but went nonetheless over to the open door. The moon shone quietly into the unlit room. As far as could be seen, everything was indeed in its place, not even the blouse was hanging on the window handle. The pillows on the bed looked remarkably plump as they lay half in the moonlight. "Miss Bürstner often comes home late," said K., looking at Mrs. Grubach as if that were her responsibility. "That's how young people are!" said Mrs. Grubach to excuse herself. "Of course, of course," said K., "but it can be taken too far." "Yes, it can be," said Mrs. Grubach, "you're so right, Mr. K. Perhaps it is in this case. I certainly wouldn't want to say anything nasty about Miss Bürstner, she is a good, sweet girl, friendly, tidy, punctual, works hard, I appreciate all that very much, but one thing is true, she ought to have more pride, be a bit less forthcoming. Twice this month already, in the street over the way, I've seen her with a different gentleman. I really don't like saying this, you're the only one I've said this to, Mr. K., I swear to God, but I'm going to have no choice but to have a few words with Miss Bürstner about it myself. And it's not the only thing about her that I'm worried about." "Mrs. Grubach, you are on quite the wrong track," said K., so angry that he was hardly able to hide it, "and you have moreover misunderstood what I was saying about Miss Bürstner, that is not what I meant. In fact I warn you quite directly not to say anything to her, you are quite mistaken, I know Miss Bürstner very well and there is no truth at all in what you say. And what's more, perhaps I'm going to far, I don't want to get in your way, say to her whatever you see fit. Good night." "Mr. K.," said Mrs. Grubach as if asking him for something and hurrying to his door which he had already opened, "I don't want to speak to Miss Bürstner at all, not yet, of course I'll continue to keep an eye on her but you're the only one I've told what I know. And it is, after all something that everyone who lets rooms has to do if she's to keep the house decent, that's all I'm trying to do." "Decent!" called out K. through the crack in the door, "if you want to keep the house decent you'll first have to give me notice." Then he slammed the door shut, there was a gentle knocking to which he paid no more attention.

He did not feel at all like going to bed, so he decided to stay up, and this would also give him the chance to find out when Miss Bürstner would arrive home. Perhaps it would also still be possible, even if a little inappropriate, to have a few words with her. As he lay there by the window, pressing his hands to his tired eyes, he even thought for a moment that he might punish Mrs. Grubach by persuading Miss Bürstner to give in her notice at the same time as he would. But he immediately realised that that would be shockingly excessive, and there would even be the suspicion that he was moving house because of the incidents of that morning. Nothing would have been more nonsensical and, above all, more pointless and contemptible.

When he had become tired of looking out onto the empty street he slightly opened the door to the living room so that he could see anyone who entered the flat from where he was and lay down on the couch. He lay there, quietly smoking a cigar, until about eleven o'clock. He wasn't able to hold out longer than that, and went a little way into the hallway as if in that way he could make Miss Bürstner arrive sooner. He had no particular desire for her, he could not even remember what she looked like, but now he wanted to speak to her and it irritated him that her late arrival home meant this day would be full of unease and disorder right to its very end. It was also her fault that he had not had any dinner that evening and that he had been unable to visit Elsa as he had intended. He could still make up for both of those things, though, if he went to the wine bar where Elsa worked. He wanted to do so even later, after the discussion with Miss Bürstner.

It was already gone half past eleven when someone could be heard in the stairway. K., who had been lost in his thoughts in the hallway, walking up and down loudly as if it were his own room, fled behind his door. Miss Bürstner had arrived. Shivering, she pulled a silk shawl over her slender shoulders as she locked the door. The next moment she would certainly go into her room, where K. ought not to intrude in the middle of the night; that meant he would have to speak to her now, but, unfortunately, he had not put the electric light on in his room so that when he stepped out of the dark it would give the impression of being an attack and would certainly, at the very least, have been quite alarming. There was no time to lose, and in his helplessness he whispered through the crack of the door, "Miss Bürstner." It sounded like he was pleading with her, not calling to her. "Is there someone there?" asked Miss Bürstner, looking round with her eyes wide open. "It's me," said K. and came out. "Oh, Mr. K.!" said Miss Bürstner with a smile. "Good Evening," and offered him her hand. "I wanted to have a word with you, if you would allow me?" "Now?" asked Miss Bürstner, "does it have to be now? It is a little odd, isn't it?" "I've been waiting for you since nine o'clock." "Well, I was at the theatre, I didn't know anything about you waiting for me." "The reason I need to speak to you only came up today" "I see, well I don't see why not, I suppose, apart from being so tired I could drop. Come into my room for a few minutes then. We certainly can't talk out here, we'd wake everyone up and I think that would be more unpleasant for us than for them. Wait here till I've put the light on in my room, and then turn the light down out here." K. did as he was told, and then even waited until Miss Bürstner came out of her room and quietly invited him, once more, to come in. "Sit down," she said, indicating the ottoman, while she herself remained standing by the bedpost despite the tiredness she had spoken of; she did not even take off her hat, which was small but decorated with an abundance of flowers. "What is it you wanted, then? I'm really quite curious." She gently crossed her legs. "I expect you'll say," K. began, "that the matter really isn't all that urgent and we don't need to talk about it right now, but ..." "I never listen to introductions," said Miss Bürstner. "That makes my job so much easier," said K. "This morning, to some extent through my fault, your room was made a little untidy, this happened because of people I did not know and against my will but, as I said, because of my fault; I wanted to apologise for it." "My room?" asked Miss Bürstner, and instead of looking round the room scrutinised K. "It is true," said K., and now, for the first time, they looked each other in the eyes, "there's no point in saying exactly how this came about." "But that's the interesting thing about it," said Miss Bürstner. "No," said K. "Well then," said Miss Bürstner, "I don't want to force my way into any secrets, if you insist that it's of no interest I won't insist. I'm quite happy to forgive you for it, as you ask, especially as I can't see anything at all that's been left untidy." With her hand laid flat on her lower hip, she made a tour around the room. At the mat where the photographs were she stopped. "Look at this!" she cried. "My photographs really have been put in the wrong places. Oh, that's horrible. Someone really has been in my room without permission." K. nodded, and quietly cursed Kaminer who worked at his bank and who was always active doing things that had neither use nor purpose. "It is odd," said Miss Bürstner, "that I'm forced to forbid you to do something that you ought to have forbidden yourself to do, namely to come into my room when I'm not here." "But I did explain to you," said K., and went over to join her by the photographs, "that it wasn't me who interfered with your photographs; but as you don't believe me I'll have to admit that the investigating committee brought along three bank employees with them, one of them must have touched your photographs and as soon as I get the chance I'll ask to have him dismissed from the bank. Yes, there was an investigating committee here," added K., as the young lady was looking at him enquiringly. "Because of you?" she asked. "Yes," answered K. "No!" the lady cried with a laugh. "Yes, they were," said K., "you believe that I'm innocent then, do you?" "Well now, innocent ..." said the lady, "I don't want to start making any pronouncements that might have serious consequences, I don't really know you after all, it means they're dealing with a serious criminal if they send an investigating committee straight out to get him. But you're not in custody now - at least I take it you've not escaped from prison considering that you seem quite calm - so you can't have committed any crime of that sort." "Yes," said K., "but it might be that the investigating committee could see that I'm innocent, or not so guilty as had been supposed." "Yes, that's certainly a possibility," said Miss Bürstner, who seemed very interested. "Listen," said K., "you don't have much experience in legal matters." "No, that's true, I don't," said Miss Bürstner, "and I've often regretted it, as I'd like to know everything and I'm very interested in legal matters. There's something peculiarly attractive about the law, isn't there? But I'll certainly be perfecting my knowledge in this area, as next month I start work in a legal office." "That's very good," said K., "that means you'll be able to give me some help with my trial." "That could well be," said Miss Bürstner, "why not? I like to make use of what I know." "I mean it quite seriously," said K., "or at least, half seriously, as you do. This affair is too petty to call in a lawyer, but I could make good use of someone who could give me advice." "Yes, but if I'm to give you advice I'll have to know what it's all about," said Miss Bürstner. "That's exactly the problem," said K., "I don't know that myself." "So you have been making fun of me, then," said Miss Bürstner exceedingly disappointed, "you really ought not to try something like that on at this time of night." And she stepped away from the photographs where they had stood so long together. "Miss Bürstner, no," said K., "I'm not making fun of you. Please believe me! I've already told you everything I know. More than I know, in fact, as it actually wasn't even an investigating committee, that's just what I called them because I don't know what else to call them. There was no cross questioning at all, I was merely arrested, but by a committee." Miss Bürstner sat on the ottoman and laughed again. "What was it like then?" she asked. "It was terrible" said K., although his mind was no longer on the subject, he had become totally absorbed by Miss Bürstner's gaze who was supporting her chin on one hand - the elbow rested on the cushion of the ottoman - and slowly stroking her hip with the other. "That's too vague," said Miss Bürstner. "What's too vague?" asked K. Then he remembered himself and asked, "Would you like me to show you what it was like?" He wanted to move in some way but did not want to leave. "I'm already tired," said Miss Bürstner. "You arrived back so late," said K. "Now you've started telling me off. Well I suppose I deserve it as I shouldn't have let you in here in the first place, and it turns out there wasn't even any point." "Oh, there was a point, you'll see now how important a point it was," said K. "May I move this table away from your bedside and put it here?" "What do you think you're doing?" said Miss Bürstner. "Of course you can't!" "In that case I can't show you," said K., quite upset, as if Miss Bürstner had committed some incomprehensible offence against him. "Alright then, if you need it to show what you mean, just take the bedside table then," said Miss Bürstner, and after a short pause added in a weak voice, "I'm so tired I'm allowing more than I ought to." K. put the little table in the middle of the room and sat down behind it. "You have to get a proper idea of where the people were situated, it is very interesting. I'm the supervisor, sitting over there on the chest are two policemen, standing next to the photographs there are three young people. Hanging on the handle of the window is a white blouse - I just mention that by the way. And now it begins. Ah yes, I'm forgetting myself, the most important person of all, so I'm standing here in front of the table. The supervisor is sitting extremely comfortably with his legs crossed and his arm hanging over the backrest here like some layabout. And now it really does begin. The supervisor calls out as if he had to wake me up, in fact he shouts at me, I'm afraid, if I'm to make it clear to you, I'll have to shout as well, and it's nothing more than my name that he shouts out." Miss Bürstner, laughing as she listened to him, laid her forefinger on her mouth so that K. would not shout, but it was too late. K. was too engrossed in his role and slowly called out, "Josef K.!". It was not as loud as he had threatened, but nonetheless, once he had suddenly called it out, the cry seemed gradually to spread itself all round the room.

There was a series of loud, curt and regular knocks at the door of the adjoining room. Miss Bürstner went pale and laid her hand on her heart. K. was especially startled, as for a moment he had been quite unable to think of anything other than the events of that morning and the girl for whom he was performing them. He had hardly pulled himself together when he jumped over to Miss Bürstner and took her hand. "Don't be afraid," he whispered, "I'll put everything right. But who can it be? It's only the living room next door, nobody sleeps in there." "Yes they do," whispered Miss Bürstner into K.'s ear, "a nephew of Mrs. Grubach's, an captain in the army, has been sleeping there since yesterday. There's no other room free. I'd forgotten about it too. Why did you have to shout like that? You've made me quite upset." "There is no reason for it," said K., and, now as she sank back onto the cushion, kissed her forehead. "Go away, go away," she said, hurriedly sitting back up, "get out of here, go, what is it you want, he's listening at the door he can hear everything. You're causing me so much trouble!" "I won't go," said K., "until you've calmed down a bit. Come over into the other corner of the room, he won't be able to hear us there." She let him lead her there. "Don't forget," he said, "although this might be unpleasant for you you're not in any real danger. You know how much esteem Mrs. Grubach has for me, she's the one who will make all the decisions in this, especially as the captain is her nephew, but she believes everything I say without question. What's more, she has borrowed a large sum of money from me and that makes her dependent on me. I will confirm whatever you say to explain our being here together, however inappropriate it might be, and I guarantee to make sure that Mrs. Grubach will not only say she believes the explanation in public but will believe it truly and sincerely. You will have no need to consider me in any way. If you wish to let it be known that I have attacked you then Mrs. Grubach will be informed of such and she will believe it without even losing her trust in me, that's how much respect she has for me." Miss Bürstner looked at the floor in front of her, quiet and a little sunk in on herself. "Why would Mrs. Grubach not believe that I've attacked you?" added K. He looked at her hair in front of him, parted, bunched down, reddish and firmly held in place. He thought she would look up at him, but without changing her manner she said, "Forgive me, but it was the suddenness of the knocking that startled me so much, not so much what the consequences of the captain being here might be. It was all so quiet after you'd shouted, and then there was the knocking, that's was made me so shocked, and I was sitting right by the door, the knocking was right next to me. Thank you for your suggestions, but I won't accept them. I can bear the responsibility for anything that happens in my room myself, and I can do so with anyone. I'm surprised you don't realise just how insulting your suggestions are and what they imply about me, although I certainly acknowledge your good intentions. But now, please go, leave me alone, I need you to go now even more than I did earlier. The couple of minutes you asked for have grown into half an hour, more than half an hour now." K. took hold of her hand, and then of her wrist, "You're not cross with me, though?" he said. She pulled her hand away and answered, "No, no, I'm never cross with anyone." He grasped her wrist once more, she tolerated it now and, in that way, lead him to the door. He had fully intended to leave. But when he reached the door he came to a halt as if he hadn't expected to find a door there, Miss Bürstner made use of that moment to get herself free, open the door, slip out into the hallway and gently say to K. from there, "Now, come along, please. Look," she pointed to the captain's door, from under which there was a light shining, "he's put a light on and he's laughing at us." "Alright, I'm coming," said K., moved forward, took hold of her, kissed her on the mouth and then over her whole face like a thirsty animal lapping with its tongue when it eventually finds water. He finally kissed her on her neck and her throat and left his lips pressed there for a long time. He did not look up until there was a noise from the captain's room. "I'll go now," he said, he wanted to address Miss Bürstner by her Christian name, but did not know it. She gave him a tired nod, offered him her hand to kiss as she turned away as if she did not know what she was doing, and went back into her room with her head bowed. A short while later, K. was lying in his bed. He very soon went to sleep, but before he did he thought a little while about his behaviour, he was satisfied with it but felt some surprise that he was not more satisfied; he was seriously worried about Miss Bürstner because of the captain.

Chapter Two First Cross-examination

K. was informed by telephone that there would be a small hearing concerning his case the following Sunday. He was made aware that these cross examinations would follow one another regularly, perhaps not every week but quite frequently. On the one hand it was in everyone's interest to bring proceedings quickly to their conclusion, but on the other hand every aspect of the examinations had to be carried out thoroughly without lasting too long because of the associated stress. For these reasons, it had been decided to hold a series of brief examinations following on one after another. Sunday had been chosen as the day for the hearings so that K. would not be disturbed in his professional work. It was assumed that he would be in agreement with this, but if he wished for another date then, as far as possible, he would be accommodated. Cross-examinations could even be held in the night, for instance, but K. would probably not be fresh enough at that time. Anyway, as long as K. made no objection, the hearing would be left on Sundays. It was a matter of course that he would have to appear without fail, there was probably no need to point this out to him. He would be given the number of the building where he was to present himself, which was in a street in a suburb well away from the city centre which K. had never been to before.

Once he had received this notice, K. hung up the receiver without giving an answer; he had decided immediately to go there that Sunday, it was certainly necessary, proceedings had begun and he had to face up to it, and this first examination would probably also be the last. He was still standing in thought by the telephone when he heard the voice of the deputy director behind him - he wanted to use the telephone but K. stood in his way. "Bad news?" asked the deputy director casually, not in order to find anything out but just to get K. away from the device. "No, no," said K., he stepped to one side but did not go away entirely. The deputy director picked up the receiver and, as he waited for his connection, turned away from it and said to K., "One question, Mr. K.: Would you like to give me the pleasure of joining me on my sailing boat on Sunday morning? There's quite a few people coming, you're bound to know some of them. One of them is Hasterer, the state attorney. Would you like to come along? Do come along!" K. tried to pay attention to what the deputy director was saying. It was of no small importance for him, as this invitation from the deputy director, with whom he had never got on very well, meant that he was trying to improve his relations with him. It showed how important K. had become in the bank and how its second most important official seemed to value his friendship, or at least his impartiality. He was only speaking at the side of the telephone receiver while he waited for his connection, but in giving this invitation the deputy director was humbling himself. But K. would have to humiliate him a second time as a result, he said, "Thank you very much, but I'm afraid I will have no time on Sunday, I have a previous obligation." "Pity," said the deputy director, and turned to the telephone conversation that had just been connected. It was not a short conversation, but K., remained standing confused by the instrument all the time it was going on. It was only when the deputy director hung up that he was shocked into awareness and said, in order to partially excuse his standing there for no reason, "I've just received a telephone call, there's somewhere I need to go, but they forgot to tell me what time." "Ask them then," said the deputy director. "It's not that important," said K., although in that way his earlier excuse, already weak enough, was made even weaker. As he went, the deputy director continued to speak about other things. K. forced himself to answer, but his thoughts were mainly about that Sunday, how it would be best to get there for nine o'clock in the morning as that was the time that courts always start work on weekdays.

  The weather was dull on Sunday. K. was very tired, as he had stayed out drinking until late in the night celebrating with some of the regulars, and he had almost overslept. He dressed hurriedly, without the time to think and assemble the various plans he had worked out during the week. With no breakfast, he rushed to the suburb he had been told about. Oddly enough, although he had little time to look around him, he came across the three bank officials involved in his case, Rabensteiner, Kullich and Kaminer. The first two were travelling in a tram that went across K.'s route, but Kaminer sat on the terrace of a café and leant curiously over the wall as K. came over. All of them seemed to be looking at him, surprised at seeing their superior running; it was a kind of pride that made K. want to go on foot, this was his affair and the idea of any help from strangers, however slight, was repulsive to him, he also wanted to avoid asking for anyone's help because that would initiate them into the affair even if only slightly. And after all, he had no wish at all to humiliate himself before the committee by being too punctual. Anyway, now he was running so that he would get there by nine o'clock if at all possible, even though he had no appointment for this time.

He had thought that he would recognise the building from a distance by some kind of sign, without knowing exactly what the sign would look like, or from some particular kind of activity outside the entrance. K. had been told that the building was in Juliusstrasse, but when he stood at the street's entrance it consisted on each side of almost nothing but monotonous, grey constructions, tall blocks of flats occupied by poor people. Now, on a Sunday morning, most of the windows were occupied, men in their shirtsleeves leant out smoking, or carefully and gently held small children on the sills. Other windows were piled up with bedding, above which the dishevelled head of a woman would briefly appear. People called out to each other across the street, one of the calls provoked a loud laugh about K. himself. It was a long street, and spaced evenly along it were small shops below street level, selling various kinds of foodstuffs, which you reached by going down a few steps. Women went in and out of them or stood chatting on the steps. A fruitmonger, taking his goods up to the windows, was just as inattentive as K. and nearly knocked him down with his cart. Just then, a gramophone, which in better parts of town would have been seen as worn out, began to play some murderous tune.

K. went further into the street, slowly, as if he had plenty of time now, or as if the examining magistrate were looking at him from one of the windows and therefore knew that K. had found his way there. It was shortly after nine. The building was quite far down the street, it covered so much area it was almost extraordinary, and the gateway in particular was tall and long. It was clearly intended for delivery wagons belonging to the various warehouses all round the yard which were now locked up and carried the names of companies some of which K. knew from his work at the bank. In contrast with his usual habits, he remained standing a while at the entrance to the yard taking in all these external details. Near him, there was a bare-footed man sitting on a crate and reading a newspaper. There were two lads swinging on a hand cart. In front of a pump stood a weak, young girl in a bedjacket who, as the water flowed into her can, looked at K. There was a piece of rope stretched between two windows in a corner of the yard, with some washing hanging on it to dry. A man stood below it calling out instructions to direct the work being done.

K. went over to the stairway to get to the room where the hearing was to take place, but then stood still again as besides these steps he could see three other stairway entrances, and there also seemed to be a small passageway at the end of the yard leading into a second yard. It irritated him that he had not been given more precise directions to the room, it meant they were either being especially neglectful with him or especially indifferent, and he decided to make that clear to them very loudly and very unambiguously. In the end he decided to climb up the stairs, his thoughts playing on something that he remembered the policeman, Willem, saying to him; that the court is attracted by the guilt, from which it followed that the courtroom must be on the stairway that K. selected by chance.

As he went up he disturbed a large group of children playing on the stairs who looked at him as he stepped through their rows. "Next time I come here," he said to himself, "I must either bring sweets with me to make them like me or a stick to hit them with." Just before he reached the first landing he even had to wait a little while until a ball had finished its movement, two small lads with sly faces like grown-up scoundrels held him by his trouser-legs until it had; if he were to shake them off he would have to hurt them, and he was afraid of what noise they would make by shouting.

On the first floor, his search began for real. He still felt unable to ask for the investigating committee, and so he invented a joiner called Lanz - that name occurred to him because the captain, Mrs. Grubach's nephew, was called Lanz - so that he could ask at every flat whether Lanz the joiner lived there and thus obtain a chance to look into the rooms. It turned out, though, that that was mostly possible without further ado, as almost all the doors were left open and the children ran in and out. Most of them were small, one-windowed rooms where they also did the cooking. Many women held babies in one arm and worked at the stove with the other. Half grown girls, who seemed to be dressed in just their pinafores worked hardest running to and fro. In every room, the beds were still in use by people who were ill, or still asleep, or people stretched out on them in their clothes. K. knocked at the flats where the doors were closed and asked whether Lanz the joiner lived there. It was usually a woman who opened the door, heard the enquiry and turned to somebody in the room who would raise himself from the bed. "The gentleman's asking if a joiner called Lanz, lives here." "A joiner, called Lanz?" he would ask from the bed." "That's right," K. would say, although it was clear that the investigating committee was not to be found there, and so his task was at an end. There were many who thought it must be very important for K. to find Lanz the joiner and thought long about it, naming a joiner who was not called Lanz or giving a name that had some vague similarity with Lanz, or they asked neighbours or accompanied K. to a door a long way away where they thought someone of that sort might live in the back part of the building or where someone would be who could advise K. better than they could themselves. K. eventually had to give up asking if he did not want to be led all round from floor to floor in this way. He regretted his initial plan, which had at first seemed so practical to him. As he reached the fifth floor, he decided to give up the search, took his leave of a friendly, young worker who wanted to lead him on still further and went down the stairs. But then the thought of how much time he was wasting made him cross, he went back again and knocked at the first door on the fifth floor. The first thing he saw in the small room was a large clock on the wall which already showed ten o'clock. "Is there a joiner called Lanz who lives here?" he asked. "Pardon?" said a young woman with black, shining eyes who was, at that moment, washing children's underclothes in a bucket. She pointed her wet hand towards the open door of the adjoining room.

K. thought he had stepped into a meeting. A medium sized, two windowed room was filled with the most diverse crowd of people - nobody paid any attention to the person who had just entered. Close under its ceiling it was surrounded by a gallery which was also fully occupied and where the people could only stand bent down with their heads and their backs touching the ceiling. K., who found the air too stuffy, stepped out again and said to the young woman, who had probably misunderstood what he had said, "I asked for a joiner, someone by the name of Lanz." "Yes," said the woman, "please go on in." K. would probably not have followed her if the woman had not gone up to him, taken hold of the door handle and said, "I'll have to close the door after you, no-one else will be allowed in." "Very sensible," said K., "but it's too full already." But then he went back in anyway. He passed through between two men who were talking beside the door - one of them held both hands far out in front of himself making the movements of counting out money, the other looked him closely in the eyes - and someone took him by the hand. It was a small, red-faced youth. "Come in, come in," he said. K. let himself be led by him, and it turned out that there was - surprisingly in a densely packed crowd of people moving to and fro - a narrow passage which may have been the division between two factions; this idea was reinforced by the fact that in the first few rows to the left and the right of him there was hardly any face looking in his direction, he saw nothing but the backs of people directing their speech and their movements only towards members of their own side. Most of them were dressed in black, in old, long, formal frock coats that hung down loosely around them. These clothes were the only thing that puzzled K., as he would otherwise have taken the whole assembly for a local political meeting.

At the other end of the hall where K. had been led there was a little table set at an angle on a very low podium which was as overcrowded as everywhere else, and behind the table, near the edge of the podium, sat a small, fat, wheezing man who was talking with someone behind him. This second man was standing with his legs crossed and his elbows on the backrest of the chair, provoking much laughter. From time to time he threw his arm in the air as if doing a caricature of someone. The youth who was leading K. had some difficulty in reporting to the man. He had already tried twice to tell him something, standing on tip-toe, but without getting the man's attention as he sat there above him. It was only when one of the people up on the podium drew his attention to the youth that the man turned to him and leant down to hear what it was he quietly said. Then he pulled out his watch and quickly looked over at K. "You should have been here one hour and five minutes ago," he said. K. was going to give him a reply but had no time to do so, as hardly had the man spoken than a general muttering arose all over the right hand side of the hall. "You should have been here one hour and five minutes ago," the man now repeated, raising his voice this time, and quickly looked round the hall beneath him. The muttering also became immediately louder and, as the man said nothing more, died away only gradually. Now the hall was much quieter than when K. had entered. Only the people up in the gallery had not stopped passing remarks. As far as could be distinguished, up in the half-darkness, dust and haze, they seemed to be less well dressed than those below. Many of them had brought pillows that they had put between their heads and the ceiling so that they would not hurt themselves pressed against it.

K. had decided he would do more watching than talking, so he did not defend himself for supposedly having come late, and simply said, "Well maybe I have arrived late, I'm here now." There followed loud applause, once more from the right hand side of the hall. Easy people to get on your side, thought K., and was bothered only by the quiet from the left hand side which was directly behind him and from which there was applause from only a few individuals. He wondered what he could say to get all of them to support him together or, if that were not possible, to at least get the support of the others for a while.

"Yes," said the man, "but I'm now no longer under any obligation to hear your case" - there was once more a muttering, but this time it was misleading as the man waved the people's objections aside with his hand and continued - "I will, however, as an exception, continue with it today. But you should never arrive late like this again. And now, step forward!" Someone jumped down from the podium so that there would be a place free for K., and K. stepped up onto it. He stood pressed closely against the table, the press of the crowd behind him was so great that he had to press back against it if he did not want to push the judge's desk down off the podium and perhaps the judge along with it.

The judge, however, paid no attention to that but sat very comfortably on his chair and, after saying a few words to close his discussion with the man behind him, reached for a little note book, the only item on his desk. It was like an old school exercise book and had become quite misshapen from much thumbing. "Now then," said the judge, thumbing through the book. He turned to K. with the tone of someone who knows his facts and said, "you are a house painter?" "No," said K., "I am the chief clerk in a large bank." This reply was followed by laughter among the right hand faction down in the hall, it was so hearty that K. couldn't stop himself joining in with it. The people supported themselves with their hands on their knees and shook as if suffering a serious attack of coughing. Even some of those in the gallery were laughing. The judge had become quite cross but seemed to have no power over those below him in the hall, he tried to reduce what harm had been done in the gallery and jumped up threatening them, his eyebrows, until then hardly remarkable, pushed themselves up and became big, black and bushy over his eyes.

The left hand side of the hall was still quiet, though, the people stood there in rows with their faces looking towards the podium listening to what was being said there, they observed the noise from the other side of the hall with the same quietness and even allowed some individuals from their own ranks, here and there, to go forward into the other faction. The people in the left faction were not only fewer in number than the right but probably were no more important than them, although their behaviour was calmer and that made it seem like they were. When K. now began to speak he was convinced he was doing it in the same way as them.

"Your question, My Lord, as to whether I am a house painter - in fact even more than that, you did not ask at all but merely imposed it on me - is symptomatic of the whole way these proceedings against me are being carried out. Perhaps you will object that there are no proceedings against me. You will be quite right, as there are proceedings only if I acknowledge that there are. But, for the moment, I do acknowledge it, out of pity for yourselves to a large extent. It's impossible not to observe all this business without feeling pity. I don't say things are being done without due care but I would like to make it clear that it is I who make the acknowledgement."

K. stopped speaking and looked down into the hall. He had spoken sharply, more sharply than he had intended, but he had been quite right. It should have been rewarded with some applause here and there but everything was quiet, they were all clearly waiting for what would follow, perhaps the quietness was laying the ground for an outbreak of activity that would bring this whole affair to an end. It was somewhat disturbing that just then the door at the end of the hall opened, the young washerwoman, who seemed to have finished her work, came in and, despite all her caution, attracted the attention of some of the people there. It was only the judge who gave K. any direct pleasure, as he seemed to have been immediately struck by K.'s words. Until then, he had listened to him standing, as K.'s speech had taken him by surprise while he was directing his attention to the gallery. Now, in the pause, he sat down very slowly, as if he did not want anyone to notice. He took out the notebook again, probably so that he could give the impression of being calmer.

"That won't help you, sir," continued K., "even your little book will only confirm what I say." K. was satisfied to hear nothing but his own quiet words in this room full of strangers, and he even dared casually to pick up the examining judge's notebook and, touching it only with the tips of his fingers as if it were something revolting, lifted it in the air, holding it just by one of the middle pages so that the others on each side of it, closely written, blotted and yellowing, flapped down. "Those are the official notes of the examining judge," he said, and let the notebook fall down onto the desk. "You can read in your book as much as you like, sir, I really don't have anything in this charge book to be afraid of, even though I don't have access to it as I wouldn't want it in my hand, I can only touch it with two fingers." The judge grabbed the notebook from where it had fallen on the desk - which could only have been a sign of his deep humiliation, or at least that is how it must have been perceived - tried to tidy it up a little, and held it once more in front of himself in order to read from it.

The people in the front row looked up at him, showing such tension on their faces that he looked back down at them for some time. Every one of them was an old man, some of them with white beards. Could they perhaps be the crucial group who could turn the whole assembly one way or the other? They had sunk into a state of motionlessness while K. gave his oration, and it had not been possible to raise them from this passivity even when the judge was being humiliated. "What has happened to me," continued K., with less of the vigour he had had earlier, he continually scanned the faces in the first row, and this gave his address a somewhat nervous and distracted character, "what has happened to me is not just an isolated case. If it were it would not be of much importance as it's not of much importance to me, but it is a symptom of proceedings which are carried out against many. It's on behalf of them that I stand here now, not for myself alone."

Without having intended it, he had raised his voice. Somewhere in the hall, someone raised his hands and applauded him shouting, "Bravo! Why not then? Bravo! Again I say, Bravo!" Some of the men in the first row groped around in their beards, none of them looked round to see who was shouting. Not even K. thought him of any importance but it did raise his spirits; he no longer thought it at all necessary that all of those in the hall should applaud him, it was enough if the majority of them began to think about the matter and if only one of them, now and then, was persuaded.

"I'm not trying to be a successful orator," said K. after this thought, "that's probably more than I'm capable of anyway. I'm sure the examining judge can speak far better than I can, it is part of his job after all. All that I want is a public discussion of a public wrong. Listen: ten days ago I was placed under arrest, the arrest itself is something I laugh about but that's beside the point. They came for me in the morning when I was still in bed. Maybe the order had been given to arrest some house painter - that seems possible after what the judge has said - someone who is as innocent as I am, but it was me they chose. There were two police thugs occupying the next room. They could not have taken better precautions if I had been a dangerous robber. And these policemen were unprincipled riff-raff, they talked at me till I was sick of it, they wanted bribes, they wanted to trick me into giving them my clothes, they wanted money, supposedly so that they could bring me my breakfast after they had blatantly eaten my own breakfast in front of my eyes. And even that was not enough. I was led in front of the supervisor in another room. This was the room of a lady who I have a lot of respect for, and I was forced to look on while the supervisor and the policemen made quite a mess of this room because of me, although not through any fault of mine. It was not easy to stay calm, but I managed to do so and was completely calm when I asked the supervisor why it was that I was under arrest. If he were here he would have to confirm what I say. I can see him now, sitting on the chair belonging to that lady I mentioned - a picture of dull-witted arrogance. What do you think he answered? What he told me, gentlemen, was basically nothing at all; perhaps he really did know nothing, he had placed me under arrest and was satisfied. In fact he had done more than that and brought three junior employees from the bank where I work into the lady's room; they had made themselves busy interfering with some photographs that belonged to the lady and causing a mess. There was, of course, another reason for bringing these employees; they, just like my landlady and her maid, were expected to spread the news of my arrest and damage my public reputation and in particular to remove me from my position at the bank. Well they didn't succeed in any of that, not in the slightest, even my landlady, who is quite a simple person - and I will give you here her name in full respect, her name is Mrs. Grubach - even Mrs. Grubach was understanding enough to see that an arrest like this has no more significance than an attack carried out on the street by some youths who are not kept under proper control. I repeat, this whole affair has caused me nothing but unpleasantness and temporary irritation, but could it not also have had some far worse consequences?"

K. broke off here and looked at the judge, who said nothing. As he did so he thought he saw the judge use a movement of his eyes to give a sign to someone in the crowd. K. smiled and said, "And now the judge, right next to me, is giving a secret sign to someone among you. There seems to be someone among you who is taking directions from above. I don't know whether the sign is meant to produce booing or applause, but I'll resist trying to guess what its meaning is too soon. It really doesn't matter to me, and I give his lordship the judge my full and public permission to stop giving secret signs to his paid subordinate down there and give his orders in words instead; let him just say "Boo now!," and then the next time "Clap now!".

Whether it was embarrassment or impatience, the judge rocked backwards and forwards on his seat. The man behind him, whom he had been talking with earlier, leant forward again, either to give him a few general words of encouragement or some specific piece of advice. Below them in the hall the people talked to each other quietly but animatedly. The two factions had earlier seemed to hold views strongly opposed to each other but now they began to intermingle, a few individuals pointed up at K., others pointed at the judge. The air in the room was fuggy and extremely oppressive, those who were standing furthest away could hardly even be seen through it. It must have been especially troublesome for those visitors who were in the gallery, as they were forced to quietly ask the participants in the assembly what exactly was happening, albeit with timid glances at the judge. The replies they received were just as quiet, and given behind the protection of a raised hand.

"I have nearly finished what I have to say," said K., and as there was no bell available he struck the desk with his fist in a way that startled the judge and his advisor and made them look up from each other. "None of this concerns me, and I am therefore able to make a calm assessment of it, and, assuming that this so-called court is of any real importance, it will be very much to your advantage to listen to what I have to say. If you want to discuss what I say, please don't bother to write it down until later on, I don't have any time to waste and I'll soon be leaving."

There was immediate silence, which showed how well K. was in control of the crowd. There were no shouts among them as there had been at the start, no-one even applauded, but if they weren't already persuaded they seemed very close to it.

K was pleased at the tension among all the people there as they listened to him, a rustling rose from the silence which was more invigorating than the most ecstatic applause could have been. "There is no doubt," he said quietly, "that there is some enormous organisation determining what is said by this court. In my case this includes my arrest and the examination taking place here today, an organisation that employs policemen who can be bribed, oafish supervisors and judges of whom nothing better can be said than that they are not as arrogant as some others. This organisation even maintains a high-level judiciary along with its train of countless servants, scribes, policemen and all the other assistance that it needs, perhaps even executioners and torturers - I'm not afraid of using those words. And what, gentlemen, is the purpose of this enormous organisation? Its purpose is to arrest innocent people and wage pointless prosecutions against them which, as in my case, lead to no result. How are we to avoid those in office becoming deeply corrupt when everything is devoid of meaning? That is impossible, not even the highest judge would be able to achieve that for himself. That is why policemen try to steal the clothes off the back of those they arrest, that is why supervisors break into the homes of people they do not know, that is why innocent people are humiliated in front of crowds rather than being given a proper trial. The policemen only talked about the warehouses where they put the property of those they arrest, I would like to see these warehouses where the hard won possessions of people under arrest is left to decay, if, that is, it's not stolen by the thieving hands of the warehouse workers."

K. was interrupted by a screeching from the far end of the hall, he shaded his eyes to see that far, as the dull light of day made the smoke whitish and hard to see through. It was the washerwoman whom K. had recognised as a likely source of disturbance as soon as she had entered. It was hard to see now whether it was her fault or not. K. could only see that a man had pulled her into a corner by the door and was pressing himself against her. But it was not her who was screaming, but the man, he had opened his mouth wide and looked up at the ceiling. A small circle had formed around the two of them, the visitors near him in the gallery seemed delighted that the serious tone K. had introduced into the gathering had been disturbed in this way. K.'s first thought was to run over there, and he also thought that everyone would want to bring things back into order there or at least to make the pair leave the room, but the first row of people in front of him stayed were they were, no-one moved and no-one let K. through. On the contrary, they stood in his way, old men held out their arms in front of him and a hand from somewhere - he did not have the time to turn round - took hold of his collar. K., by this time, had forgotten about the pair, it seemed to him that his freedom was being limited as if his arrest was being taken seriously, and, without any thought for what he was doing, he jumped down from the podium. Now he stood face to face with the crowd. Had he judged the people properly? Had he put too much faith in the effect of his speech? Had they been putting up a pretence all the time he had been speaking, and now that he come to the end and to what must follow, were they tired of pretending? What faces they were, all around him! Dark, little eyes flickered here and there, cheeks drooped down like on drunken men, their long beards were thin and stiff, if they took hold of them it was more like they were making their hands into claws, not as if they were taking hold of their own beards. But underneath those beards - and this was the real discovery made by K. - there were badges of various sizes and colours shining on the collars of their coats. As far as he could see, every one of them was wearing one of these badges. All of them belonged to the same group, even though they seemed to be divided to the right and the left of him, and when he suddenly turned round he saw the same badge on the collar of the examining judge who calmly looked down at him with his hands in his lap. "So," called out K, throwing his arms in the air as if this sudden realisation needed more room, "all of you are working for this organisation, I see now that you are all the very bunch of cheats and liars I've just been speaking about, you've all pressed yourselves in here in order to listen in and snoop on me, you gave the impression of having formed into factions, one of you even applauded me to test me out, and you wanted to learn how to trap an innocent man! Well, I hope you haven't come here for nothing, I hope you've either had some fun from someone who expected you to defend his innocence or else - let go of me or I'll hit you," shouted K. to a quivery old man who had pressed himself especially close to him - "or else that you've actually learned something. And so I wish you good luck in your trade." He briskly took his hat from where it lay on the edge of the table and, surrounded by a silence caused perhaps by the completeness of their surprise, pushed his way to the exit. However, the examining judge seems to have moved even more quickly than K., as he was waiting for him at the doorway. "One moment," he said. K. stood where he was, but looked at the door with his hand already on its handle rather than at the judge. "I merely wanted to draw your attention," said the judge, "to something you seem not yet to be aware of: today, you have robbed yourself of the advantages that a hearing of this sort always gives to someone who is under arrest." K. laughed towards the door. "You bunch of louts," he called, "you can keep all your hearings as a present from me," then opened the door and hurried down the steps. Behind him, the noise of the assembly rose as it became lively once more and probably began to discuss these events as if making a scientific study of them.

Chapter Three In the empty Courtroom - The Student - The Offices

Every day over the following week, K. expected another summons to arrive, he could not believe that his rejection of any more hearings had been taken literally, and when the expected summons really had not come by Saturday evening he took it to mean that he was expected, without being told, to appear at the same place at the same time. So on Sunday, he set out once more in the same direction, going without hesitation up the steps and through the corridors; some of the people remembered him and greeted him from their doorways, but he no longer needed to ask anyone the way and soon arrived at the right door. It was opened as soon as he knocked and, paying no attention to the woman he had seen last time who was standing at the doorway, he was about to go straight into the adjoining room when she said to him "There's no session today". "What do you mean; no session?" he asked, unable to believe it. But the woman persuaded him by opening the door to the next room. It was indeed empty, and looked even more dismal empty than it had the previous Sunday. On the podium stood the table exactly as it had been before with a few books laying on it. "Can I have a look at those books?" asked K., not because he was especially curious but so that he would not have come for nothing. "No," said the woman as she re-closed the door, "that's not allowed. Those books belong to the examining judge." "I see," said K., and nodded, "those books must be law books, and that's how this court does things, not only to try people who are innocent but even to try them without letting them know what's going on." "I expect you're right," said the woman, who had not understood exactly what he meant. "I'd better go away again, then," said K. "Should I give a message to the examining judge?" asked the woman. "Do you know him, then?" asked K. "Of course I know him," said the woman, "my husband is the court usher." It was only now that K. noticed that the room, which before had held nothing but a wash-tub, had been fitted out as a living room. The woman saw how surprised he was and said, "Yes, we're allowed to live here as we like, only we have to clear the room out when the court's in session. There's lots of disadvantages to my husband's job." "It's not so much the room that surprises me," said K., looking at her crossly, "it's your being married that shocks me." "Are you thinking about what happened last time the court was in session, when I disturbed what you were saying?" asked the woman. "Of course," said K., "it's in the past now and I've nearly forgotten about it, but at the time it made me furious. And now you tell me yourself that you are a married woman." "It wasn't any disadvantage for you to have your speech interrupted. The way they talked about you after you'd gone was really bad." "That could well be," said K., turning away, "but it does not excuse you." "There's no-one I know who'd hold it against me," said the woman. "Him, who put his arms around me, he's been chasing after me for a long time. I might not be very attractive for most people, but I am for him. I've got no protection from him, even my husband has had to get used to it; if he wants to keep his job he's got to put up with it as that man's a student and he'll almost certainly be very powerful later on. He's always after me, he'd only just left when you arrived." "That fits in with everything else," said K., "I'm not surprised." "Do you want to make things a bit better here?" the woman asked slowly, watching him as if she were saying something that could be as dangerous for K. as for herself. "That's what I thought when I heard you speak, I really liked what you said. Mind you, I only heard part of it, I missed the beginning of it and at the end I was lying on the floor with the student - it's so horrible here," she said after a pause, and took hold of K.'s hand. "Do you believe you really will be able to make things better?" K. smiled and twisted his hand round a little in her soft hands. "It's really not my job to make things better here, as you put it," he said, "and if you said that to the examining judge he would laugh at you or punish you for it. I really would not have become involved in this matter if I could have helped it, and I would have lost no sleep worrying about how this court needs to be made better. But because I'm told that I have been arrested - and I am under arrest - it forces me to take some action, and to do so for my own sake. However, if I can be of some service to you in the process I will, of course, be glad to do so. And I will be glad to do so not only for the sake of charity but also because you can be of some help to me." "How could I help you, then?" said the woman. "You could, for example, show me the books on the table there." "Yes, certainly," the woman cried, and pulled K. along behind her as she rushed to them. The books were old and well worn, the cover of one of them had nearly broken through in its middle, and it was held together with a few threads. "Everything is so dirty here," said K., shaking his head, and before he could pick the books up the woman wiped some of the dust off with her apron. K. took hold of the book that lay on top and threw it open, an indecent picture appeared. A man and a woman sat naked on a sofa, the base intent of whoever drew it was easy to see but he had been so grossly lacking in skill that all that anyone could really make out were the man and the woman who dominated the picture with their bodies, sitting in overly upright postures that created a false perspective and made it difficult for them to approach each other. K. didn't thumb through that book any more, but just threw open the next one at its title page, it was a novel with the title, What Grete Suffered from her Husband, Hans. "So this is the sort of law book they study here," said K., "this is the sort of person sitting in judgement over me." "I can help you," said the woman, "would you like me to?" "Could you really do that without placing yourself in danger? You did say earlier on that your husband is wholly dependent on his superiors." "I still want to help you," said the woman, "come over here, we've got to talk about it. Don't say any more about what danger I'm in, I only fear danger where I want to fear it. Come over here." She pointed to the podium and invited him to sit down on the step with her. "You've got lovely dark eyes," she said after they had sat down, looking up into K.'s face, "people say I've got nice eyes too, but yours are much nicer. It was the first thing I noticed when you first came here. That's even why I came in here, into the assembly room, afterwards, I'd never normally do that, I'm not really even allowed to." So that's what all this is about, thought K., she's offering herself to me, she's as degenerate as everything else around here, she's had enough of the court officials, which is understandable I suppose, and so she approaches any stranger and makes compliments about his eyes. With that, K. stood up in silence as if he had spoken his thoughts out loud and thus explained his action to the woman. "I don't think you can be of any assistance to me," he said, "to be of any real assistance you would need to be in contact with high officials. But I'm sure you only know the lower employees, and there are crowds of them milling about here. I'm sure you're very familiar with them and could achieve a great deal through them, I've no doubt of that, but the most that could be done through them would have no bearing at all on the final outcome of the trial. You, on the other hand, would lose some of your friends as a result, and I have no wish of that. Carry on with these people in the same way as you have been, as it does seem to me to be something you cannot do without. I have no regrets in saying this as, in return for your compliment to me, I also find you rather attractive, especially when you look at me as sadly as you are now, although you really have no reason to do so. You belong to the people I have to combat, and you're very comfortable among them, you're even in love with the student, or if you don't love him you do at least prefer him to your husband. It's easy to see that from what you've been saying." "No!" she shouted, remained sitting where she was and grasped K.'s hand, which he failed to pull away fast enough. "You can't go away now, you can't go away when you've misjudged me like that! Are you really capable of going away now? Am I really so worthless that you won't even do me the favour of staying a little bit longer?" "You misunderstand me," said K., sitting back down, "if it's really important to you for me to stay here then I'll be glad to do so, I have plenty of time, I came here thinking there would be a trial taking place. All I meant with what I said just now was to ask you not to do anything on my behalf in the proceedings against me. But even that is nothing for you to worry about when you consider that there's nothing hanging on the outcome of this trial, and that, whatever the verdict, I will just laugh at it. And that's even presupposing it ever even reaches any conclusion, which I very much doubt. I think it's much more likely that the court officials will be too lazy, too forgetful, or even too fearful ever to continue with these proceedings and that they will soon be abandoned if they haven't been abandoned already. It's even possible that they will pretend to be carrying on with the trial in the hope of receiving a large bribe, although I can tell you now that that will be quite in vain as I pay bribes to no-one. Perhaps one favour you could do me would be to tell the examining judge, or anyone else who likes to spread important news, that I will never be induced to pay any sort of bribe through any stratagem of theirs - and I'm sure they have many stratagems at their disposal. There is no prospect of that, you can tell them that quite openly. And what's more, I expect they have already noticed themselves, or even if they haven't, this affair is really not so important to me as they think. Those gentlemen would only save some work for themselves, or at least some unpleasantness for me, which, however, I am glad to endure if I know that each piece of unpleasantness for me is a blow against them. And I will make quite sure it is a blow against them. Do you actually know the judge?" "Course I do," said the woman, "he was the first one I thought of when I offered to help you. I didn't know he's only a minor official, but if you say so it must be true. Mind you, I still think the report he gives to his superiors must have some influence. And he writes so many reports. You say these officials are lazy, but they're certainly not all lazy, especially this examining judge, he writes ever such a lot. Last Sunday, for instance, that session went on till the evening. Everyone had gone, but the examining judge, he stayed in the hall, I had to bring him a lamp in, all I had was a little kitchen lamp but he was very satisfied with it and started to write straight away. Meantime my husband arrived, he always has the day off on Sundays, we got the furniture back in and got our room sorted out and then a few of the neighbours came, we sat and talked for a bit by a candle, in short, we forgot all about the examining judge and went to bed. All of a sudden in the night, it must have been quite late in the night, I wakes up, next to the bed, there's the examining judge shading the lamp with his hand so that there's no light from it falls on my husband, he didn't need to be as careful as that, the way my husband sleeps the light wouldn't have woken him up anyway. I was quite shocked and nearly screamed, but the judge was very friendly, warned me I should be careful, he whispered to me he's been writing all this time, and now he's brought me the lamp back, and he'll never forget how I looked when he found me there asleep. What I mean, with all this, I just wanted to tell you how the examining judge really does write lots of reports, especially about you as questioning you was definitely one of the main things on the agenda that Sunday. If he writes reports as long as that they must be of some importance. And besides all that, you can see from what happened that the examining judge is after me, and it's right now, when he's first begun to notice me, that I can have a lot of influence on him. And I've got other proof I mean a lot to him, too. Yesterday, he sent that student to me, the one he really trusts and who he works with, he sent him with a present for me, silk stockings. He said it was because I clear up in the courtroom but that's only a pretence, that job's no more than what I'm supposed to do, it's what my husband gets paid for. Nice stockings, they are, look," - she stretched out her leg, drew her skirt up to her knee and looked, herself, at the stocking - "they are nice stockings, but they're too good for me, really."

  She suddenly interrupted herself and lay her hand on K.'s as if she wanted to calm him down, and whispered, "Be quiet, Berthold is watching us." K. slowly looked up. In the doorway to the courtroom stood a young man, he was short, his legs were not quite straight, and he continually moved his finger round in a short, thin, red beard with which he hoped to make himself look dignified. K. looked at him with some curiosity, he was the first student he had ever met of the unfamiliar discipline of jurisprudence, face to face at least, a man who would even most likely attain high office one day. The student, in contrast, seemed to take no notice of K. at all, he merely withdrew his finger from his beard long enough to beckon to the woman and went over to the window, the woman leant over to K. and whispered, "Don't be cross with me, please don't, and please don't think ill of me either, I've got to go to him now, to this horrible man, just look at his bent legs. But I'll come straight back and then I'll go with you if you'll take me, I'll go wherever you want, you can do whatever you like with me, I'll be happy if I can be away from here for as long as possible, it'd be best if I could get away from here for good." She stroked K.'s hand once more, jumped up and ran over to the window. Before he realised it, K. grasped for her hand but failed to catch it. He really was attracted to the woman, and even after thinking hard about it could find no good reason why he should not give in to her allure. It briefly crossed his mind that the woman meant to entrap him on behalf of the court, but that was an objection he had no difficulty in fending off. In what way could she entrap him? Was he not still free, so free that he could crush the entire court whenever he wanted, as least where it concerned him? Could he not have that much confidence in himself? And her offer of help sounded sincere, and maybe it wasn't quite worthless. And maybe there was no better revenge against the examining judge and his cronies than to take this woman from him and have her for himself. Maybe then, after much hard work writing dishonest reports about K., the judge would go to the woman's bed late one night and find it empty. And it would be empty because she belonged to K., because this woman at the window, this lush, supple, warm body in its sombre clothes of rough, heavy material belonged to him, totally to him and to him alone. Once he had settled his thoughts towards the woman in this way, he began to find the quiet conversation at the window was taking too long, he rapped on the podium with his knuckles, and then even with his fist. The student briefly looked away from the woman to glance at K. over his shoulder but did allow himself to be disturbed, in fact he even pressed himself close to the woman and put his arms around her. She dropped her head down low as if listening to him carefully, as she did so he kissed her right on the neck, hardly even interrupting what he was saying. K. saw this as confirmation of the tyranny the student held over the woman and which she had already complained about, he stood up and walked up and down the room. Glancing sideways at the student, he wondered what would be the quickest possible way to get rid of him, and so it was not unwelcome to him when the student, clearly disturbed by K.'s to-ing and fro-ing which K. had now developed into a stamping up and down, said to him, "You don't have to stay here, you know, if you're getting impatient. You could have gone earlier, no-one would have missed you. In fact you should have gone, you should have left as quickly as possible as soon as I got here." This comment could have caused all possible rage to break out between them, but K. also bore in mind that this was a prospective court official speaking to a disfavoured defendant, and he might well have been taking pride in speaking in this way. K. remained standing quite close to him and said with a smile, "You're quite right, I am impatient, but the easiest way to settle this impatience would be if you left us. On the other hand, if you've come here to study - you are a student, I hear - I'll be quite happy to leave the room to you and go away with the woman. I'm sure you'll still have a lot of study to do before you're made into a judge. It's true that I'm still not all that familiar with your branch of jurisprudence but I take it it involves a lot more than speaking roughly - and I see you have no shame in doing that extremely well." "He shouldn't have been allowed to move about so freely," said the student, as if he wanted to give the woman an explanation for K.'s insults, "that was a mistake. I've told the examining judge so. He should at least have been detained in his room between hearings. Sometimes it's impossible to understand what the judge thinks he's doing." "You're wasting your breath," said K., then he reached his hand out towards the woman and said, "come with me." "So that's it," said the student, "oh no, you're not going to get her," and with a strength you would not have expected from him, he glanced tenderly at her, lifted her up on one arm and, his back bent under the weight, ran with her to the door. In this way he showed, unmistakeably, that he was to some extent afraid of K., but he nonetheless dared to provoke him still further by stroking and squeezing the woman's arm with his free hand. K. ran the few steps up to him, but when he had reached him and was about to take hold of him and, if necessary, throttle him, the woman said, "It's no good, it's the examining judge who's sent for me, I daren't go with you, this little bastard…" and here she ran her hand over the student's face, "this little bastard won't let me." "And you don't want to be set free!" shouted K., laying his hand on the student's shoulder, who then snapped at it with his teeth. "No!" shouted the woman, pushing K. away with both hands, "no, no don't do that, what d'you think you're doing!? That'd be the end of me. Let go of him, please just let go of him. He's only carrying out the judge's orders, he's carrying me to him." "Let him take you then, and I want to see nothing more of you," said K., enraged by his disappointment and giving the student a thump in the back so that he briefly stumbled and then, glad that he had not fallen, immediately jumped up all the higher with his burden. K. followed them slowly. He realised that this was the first unambiguous setback he had suffered from these people. It was of course nothing to worry about, he accepted the setback only because he was looking for a fight. If he stayed at home and carried on with his normal life he would be a thousand times superior to these people and could get any of them out of his way just with a kick. And he imagined the most laughable scene possible as an example of this, if this contemptible student, this inflated child, this knock-kneed redbeard, if he were kneeling at Elsa's bed wringing his hands and begging for forgiveness. K. so enjoyed imagining this scene that he decided to take the student along to Elsa with him if ever he should get the opportunity.

    K. was curious to see where the woman would be taken and he hurried over to the door, the student was not likely to carry her through the streets on his arm. It turned out that the journey was far shorter. Directly opposite the flat there was a narrow flight of wooden steps which probably led up to the attic, they turned as they went so that it was not possible to see where they ended. The student carried the woman up these steps, and after the exertions of running with her he was soon groaning and moving very slowly. The woman waved down at K. and by raising and lowering her shoulders she tried to show that she was an innocent party in this abduction, although the gesture did not show a lot of regret. K. watched her without expression like a stranger, he wanted to show neither that he was disappointed nor that he would easily get over his disappointment.

The two of them had disappeared, but K. remained standing in the doorway. He had to accept that the woman had not only cheated him but that she had also lied to him when she said she was being taken to the examining judge. The examining judge certainly wouldn't be sitting and waiting in the attic. The wooden stairs would explain nothing to him however long he stared at them. Then K. noticed a small piece of paper next to them, went across to it and read, in a childish and unpractised hand, "Entrance to the Court Offices". Were the court offices here, in the attic of this tenement, then? If that was how they were accommodated it did not attract much respect, and it was some comfort for the accused to realise how little money this court had at its disposal if it had to locate its offices in a place where the tenants of the building, who were themselves among the poorest of people, would throw their unneeded junk. On the other hand, it was possible that the officials had enough money but that they squandered it on themselves rather than use it for the court's purposes. Going by K.'s experience of them so far, that even seemed probable, except that if the court were allowed to decay in that way it would not just humiliate the accused but also give him more encouragement than if the court were simply in a state of poverty. K. also now understood that the court was ashamed to summon those it accused to the attic of this building for the initial hearing, and why it preferred to impose upon them in their own homes. What a position it was that K. found himself in, compared with the judge sitting up in the attic! K., at the bank, had a big office with an ante-room, and had an enormous window through which he could look down at the activity in the square. It was true, though, that he had no secondary income from bribes and fraud, and he couldn't tell a servant to bring him a woman up to the office on his arm. K., however, was quite willing to do without such things, in this life at least. K. was still looking at the notice when a man came up the stairs, looked through the open door into the living room where it was also possible to see the courtroom, and finally asked K. whether he had just seen a woman there. "You're the court usher, aren't you?" asked K. "That's right," said the man, "oh, yes, you're defendant K., I recognise you now as well. Nice to see you here." And he offered K. his hand, which was far from what K. had expected. And when K. said nothing, he added, "There's no court session planned for today, though." "I know that," said K. as he looked at the usher's civilian coat which, beside its ordinary buttons, displayed two gilded ones as the only sign of his office and seemed to have been taken from an old army officer's coat. "I was speaking with your wife a little while ago. She is no longer here. The student has carried her off to the examining judge." "Listen to this," said the usher, "they're always carrying her away from me. It's Sunday today, and it's not part of my job to do any work today, but they send me off with some message which isn't even necessary just to get me away from here. What they do is they send me off not too far away so that I can still hope to get back on time if I really hurry. So off I go running as fast as I can, shout the message through the crack in the door of the office I've been sent to, so out of breath they'll hardly be able to understand it, run back here again, but the student's been even faster than I have - well he's got less far to go, he's only got to run down the steps. If I wasn't so dependent on them I'd have squashed the student against the wall here a long time ago. Right here, next to the sign. I'm always dreaming of doing that. Just here, just above the floor, that's where he's crushed onto the wall, his arms stretched out, his fingers spread apart, his crooked legs twisted round into a circle and blood squirted out all around him. It's only ever been a dream so far, though." "Is there nothing else you do?" asked K. with a smile. "Nothing that I know of," said the usher. "And it's going to get even worse now, up till now he's only been carrying her off for himself, now he's started carrying her off for the judge and all, just like I'd always said he would." "Does your wife, then, not share some of the responsibility?" asked K. He had to force himself as he asked this question, as he, too, felt so jealous now. "Course she does," said the usher, "it's more her fault than theirs. It was her who attached herself to him. All he did, he just chases after any woman. There's five flats in this block alone where he's been thrown out after working his way in there. And my wife is the best looking woman in the whole building, but it's me who's not even allowed to defend himself." "If that's how things are, then there's nothing that can be done," said K. "Well why not?" asked the usher. "He's a coward that student, if he wants to lay a finger on my wife all you'd have to do is give him such a good hiding he'd never dare do it again. But I'm not allowed to do that, and nobody else is going to do me the favour as they're all afraid of his power. The only one who could do it is a man like you." "What, how could I do it?" asked K. in astonishment. "Well you're facing a charge, aren't you," said the usher. "Yes, but that's all the more reason for me to be afraid. Even if he has no influence on the outcome of the trial he probably has some on the initial examination." "Yes, exactly," said the usher, as if K.'s view had been just as correct as his own. "Only we don't usually get any trials heard here with no hope at all." "I am not of the same opinion", said K., "although that ought not to prevent me from dealing with the student if the opportunity arises." "I would be very grateful to you," said the usher of the court, somewhat formally, not really seeming to believe that his highest wish could be fulfilled. "Perhaps," continued K., "perhaps there are some other officials of yours here, perhaps all of them, who would deserve the same." "Oh yes, yes," said the usher, as if this was a matter of course. Then he looked at K. trustingly which, despite all his friendliness, he had not done until then, and added, "they're always rebelling." But the conversation seemed to have become a little uncomfortable for him, as he broke it off by saying, "now I have to report to the office. Would you like to come with me?" "There's nothing for me to do there," said K. "You'd be able to have a look at it. No-one will take any notice of you." "Is it worth seeing then?" asked K. hesitatingly, although he felt very keen to go with him. "Well," said the usher, "I thought you'd be interested in it." "Alright then," said K. finally, "I'll come with you." And, quicker than the usher himself, he ran up the steps.

At the entrance he nearly fell over, as behind the door there was another step. "They don't show much concern for the public," he said. "They don't show any concern at all," said the usher, "just look at the waiting room here." It consisted of a long corridor from which roughly made doors led out to the separate departments of the attic. There was no direct source of light but it was not entirely dark as many of the departments, instead of solid walls, had just wooden bars reaching up to the ceiling to separate them from the corridor. The light made its way in through them, and it was also possible to see individual officials through them as they sat writing at their desks or stood up at the wooden frameworks and watched the people on the corridor through the gaps. There were only a few people in the corridor, probably because it was Sunday. They were not very impressive. They sat, equally spaced, on two rows of long wooden benches which had been placed along both sides of the corridor. All of them were carelessly dressed although the expressions on their faces, their bearing, the style of their beards and many details which were hard to identify showed that they belonged to the upper classes. There were no coat hooks for them to use, and so they had placed their hats under the bench, each probably having followed the example of the others. When those who were sitting nearest the door saw K. and the usher of the court they stood up to greet them, and when the others saw that, they also thought they had to greet them, so that as the two of them went by all the people there stood up. None of them stood properly upright, their backs were bowed, their knees bent, they stood like beggars on the street. K. waited for the usher, who was following just behind him. "They must all be very dispirited," he said. "Yes," said the usher, "they are the accused, everyone you see here has been accused." "Really!" said K. "They're colleagues of mine then." And he turned to the nearest one, a tall, thin man with hair that was nearly grey. "What is it you are waiting for here?" asked K., politely, but the man was startled at being spoken to unexpectedly, which was all the more pitiful to see because the man clearly had some experience of the world and elsewhere would certainly have been able to show his superiority and would not have easily given up the advantage he had acquired. Here, though, he did not know what answer to give to such a simple question and looked round at the others as if they were under some obligation to help him, and as if no-one could expect any answer from him without this help. Then the usher of the court stepped forward to him and, in order to calm him down and raise his spirits, said, "The gentleman here's only asking what it is you're waiting for. You can give him an answer." The voice of the usher was probably familiar to him, and had a better effect than K.'s. "I'm ... I'm waiting ..." he began, and then came to a halt. He had clearly chosen this beginning so that he could give a precise answer to the question, but now he didn't know how to continue. Some of the others waiting had come closer and stood round the group, the usher of the court said to them, "Get out the way, keep the gangway free." They moved back slightly, but not as far as where they had been sitting before. In the meantime, the man whom K. had first approached had pulled himself together and even answered him with a smile. "A month ago I made some applications for evidence to be heard in my case, and I'm waiting for it to be settled." "You certainly seem to be going to a lot of effort," said K. "Yes," said the man, "it is my affair after all." "Not everyone thinks the same way as you do," said K. "I've been indicted as well but I swear on my soul that I've neither submitted evidence nor done anything else of the sort. Do you really think that's necessary?" "I don't really know, exactly," said the man, once more totally unsure of himself; he clearly thought K. was joking with him and therefore probably thought it best to repeat his earlier answer in order to avoid making any new mistakes. With K. looking at him impatiently, he just said, "as far as I'm concerned, I've applied to have this evidence heard." "Perhaps you don't believe I've been indicted?" asked K. "Oh, please, I certainly do," said the man, stepping slightly to one side, but there was more anxiety in his answer than belief. "You don't believe me then?" asked K., and took hold of his arm, unconsciously prompted by the man's humble demeanour, and as if he wanted to force him to believe him. But he did not want to hurt the man and had only taken hold of him very lightly. Nonetheless, the man cried out as if K. had grasped him not with two fingers but with red hot tongs. Shouting in this ridiculous way finally made K. tired of him, if he didn't believe he was indicted then so much the better; maybe he even thought K. was a judge. And before leaving, he held him a lot harder, shoved him back onto the bench and walked on. "These defendants are so sensitive, most of them," said the usher of the court. Almost all of those who had been waiting had now assembled around the man who, by now, had stopped shouting and they seemed to be asking him lots of precise questions about the incident. K. was approached by a security guard, identifiable mainly by his sword, of which the scabbard seemed to be made of aluminium. This greatly surprised K., and he reached out for it with his hand. The guard had come because of the shouting and asked what had been happening. The usher of the court said a few words to try and calm him down but the guard explained that he had to look into it himself, saluted, and hurried on, walking with very short steps, probably because of gout.

K. didn't concern himself long with the guard or these people, especially as he saw a turning off the corridor, about half way along it on the right hand side, where there was no door to stop him going that way. He asked the usher whether that was the right way to go, the usher nodded, and that is the way that K. went. The usher remained always one or two steps behind K, which he found irritating as in a place like this it could give the impression that he was being driven along by someone who had arrested him, so he frequently waited for the usher to catch up, but the usher always remained behind him. In order to put an end to his discomfort, K. finally said, "Now that I've seen what it looks like here, I'd like to go." "You haven't seen everything yet," said the usher ingenuously. "I don't want to see everything," said K., who was also feeling very tired, "I want to go, what is the way to the exit?" "You haven't got lost, have you?" asked the usher in amazement, "you go down this way to the corner, then right down the corridor straight ahead as far as the door." "Come with me," said K., "show me the way, I'll miss it, there are so many different ways here." "It's the only way there is," said the usher, who had now started to sound quite reproachful, "I can't go back with you again, I've got to hand in my report, and I've already lost a lot of time because of you as it is." "Come with me!" K. repeated, now somewhat sharper as if he had finally caught the usher out in a lie. "Don't shout like that," whispered the usher, "there's offices all round us here. If you don't want to go back by yourself come on a bit further with me or else wait here till I've sorted out my report, then I'll be glad to go back with you again." "No, no," said K., "I will not wait and you must come with me now." K. had still not looked round at anything at all in the room where he found himself, and it was only when one of the many wooden doors all around him opened that he noticed it. A young woman, probably summoned by the loudness of K.'s voice, entered and asked, "What is it the gentleman wants?" In the darkness behind her there was also a man approaching. K. looked at the usher. He had, after all, said that no-one would take any notice of K., and now there were two people coming, it only needed a few and everyone in the office would become aware of him and asking for explanations as to why he was there. The only understandable and acceptable thing to say was that he was accused of something and wanted to know the date of his next hearing, but this was an explanation he did not want to give, especially as it was not true - he had only come out of curiosity. Or else, an explanation even less usable, he could say that he wanted to ascertain that the court was as revolting on the inside as it was on the outside. And it did seem that he had been quite right in this supposition, he had no wish to intrude any deeper, he was disturbed enough by what he had seen already, he was not in the right frame of mind just then to face a high official such as might appear from behind any door, and he wanted to go, either with the usher of the court or, if needs be, alone.

But he must have seemed very odd standing there in silence, and the young woman and the usher were indeed looking at him as if they thought he would go through some major metamorphosis any second which they didn't want to miss seeing. And in the doorway stood the man whom K. had noticed in the background earlier, he held firmly on to the beam above the low door swinging a little on the tips of his feet as if becoming impatient as he watched. But the young woman was the first to recognise that K.'s behaviour was caused by his feeling slightly unwell, she brought a chair and asked, "Would you not like to sit down?" K. sat down immediately and, in order to keep his place better, put his elbows on the armrests. "You're a little bit dizzy, aren't you?" she asked him. Her face was now close in front of him, it bore the severe expression that many young women have just when they're in the bloom of their youth. "It's nothing for you to worry about," she said, "that's nothing unusual here, almost everyone gets an attack like that the first time they come here. This is your first time is it? Yes, it's nothing unusual then. The sun burns down on the roof and the hot wood makes the air so thick and heavy. It makes this place rather unsuitable for offices, whatever other advantages it might offer. But the air is almost impossible to breathe on days when there's a lot of business, and that's almost every day. And when you think that there's a lot of washing put out to dry here as well - and we can't stop the tenants doing that - it's not surprising you started to feel unwell. But you get used to the air alright in the end. When you're here for the second or third time you'll hardly notice how oppressive the air is. Are you feeling any better now?" K. made no answer, he felt too embarrassed at being put at the mercy of these people by his sudden weakness, and learning the reason for feeling ill made him feel not better but a little worse. The girl noticed it straight away, and to make the air fresher for K., she took a window pole that was leaning against the wall and pushed open a small hatch directly above K.'s head that led to the outside. But so much soot fell in that the girl had to immediately close the hatch again and clean the soot off K.'s hands with her handkerchief, as K. was too tired to do that for himself. He would have liked just to sit quietly where he was until he had enough strength to leave, and the less fuss people made about him the sooner that would be. But then the girl said, "You can't stay here, we're in people's way here ..." K. looked at her as if to ask whose way they were impeding. "If you like, I can take you to the sick room," and turning to the man in the doorway said, "please help me". The man immediately came over to them, but K. did not want to go to the sick room, that was just what he wanted to avoid, being led further from place to place, the further he went the more difficult it must become. So he said, "I am able to walk now," and stood up, shaking after becoming used to sitting so comfortably. But then he was unable to stay upright. "I can't manage it," he said shaking his head, and sat down again with a sigh. He remembered the usher who, despite everything, would have been able to lead him out of there but who seemed to have gone long before. K. looked out between the man and the young woman who were standing in front of him but was unable to find the usher. "I think," said the man, who was elegantly dressed and whose appearance was made especially impressive with a grey waistcoat that had two long, sharply tailored points, "the gentleman is feeling unwell because of the atmosphere here, so the best thing, and what he would most prefer, would be not to take him to the sick room but get him out of the offices altogether." "That's right," exclaimed K., with such joy that he nearly interrupted what the man was saying, "I'm sure that'll make me feel better straight away, I'm really not that weak, all I need is a little support under my arms, I won't cause you much trouble, it's not such a long way anyway, lead me to the door and then I'll sit on the stairs for a while and soon recover, as I don't suffer from attacks like this at all, I'm surprised at it myself. I also work in an office and I'm quite used to office air, but here it seems to be too strong, you've said so yourselves. So please, be so kind as to help me on my way a little, I'm feeling dizzy, you see, and it'll make me ill if I stand up by myself." And with that he raised his shoulders to make it easier for the two of them to take him by the arms.

The man, however, didn't follow this suggestion but just stood there with his hands in his trouser pockets and laughed out loud. "There, you see," he said to the girl, "I was quite right. The gentleman is only unwell here, and not in general." The young woman smiled too, but lightly tapped the man's arm with the tips of her fingers as if he had allowed himself too much fun with K. "So what do you think, then?" said the man, still laughing, "I really do want to lead the gentleman out of here." "That's alright, then," said the girl, briefly inclining her charming head. "Don't worry too much about him laughing," said the girl to K., who had become unhappy once more and stared quietly in front of himself as if needing no further explanation. "This gentleman - may I introduce you?" - (the man gave his permission with a wave of the hand) - "so, this gentleman's job is to give out information. He gives all the information they need to people who are waiting, as our court and its offices are not very well known among the public he gets asked for quite a lot. He has an answer for every question, you can try him out if you feel like it. But that's not his only distinction, his other distinction is his elegance of dress. We, that's to say all of us who work in the offices here, we decided that the information-giver would have to be elegantly dressed as he continually has to deal with the litigants and he's the first one they meet, so he needs to give a dignified first impression. The rest of us I'm afraid, as you can see just by looking at me, dress very badly and old-fashioned; and there's not much point in spending much on clothes anyway, as we hardly ever leave the offices, we even sleep here. But, as I said, we decided that the information-giver would have to have nice clothes. As the management here is rather peculiar in this respect, and they would get them for us, we had a collection - some of the litigants contributed too - and bought him these lovely clothes and some others besides. So everything would be ready for him to give a good impression, except that he spoils it again by laughing and frightening people." "That's how it is," said the man, mocking her, "but I don't understand why it is that you're explaining all our intimate facts to the gentleman, or rather why it is that you're pressing them on him, as I'm sure he's not all interested. Just look at him sitting there, it's clear he's occupied with his own affairs." K. just did not feel like contradicting him. The girl's intention may have been good, perhaps she was under instructions to distract him or to give him the chance to collect himself, but the attempt had not worked. "I had to explain to him why you were laughing," said the girl. "I suppose it was insulting." "I think he would forgive even worse insults if I finally took him outside." K. said nothing, did not even look up, he tolerated the two of them negotiating over him like an object, that was even what suited him best. But suddenly he felt the information-giver's hand on one arm and the young woman's hand on the other. "Up you get then, weakling," said the information-giver. "Thank you both very much," said K., pleasantly surprised, as he slowly rose and personally guided these unfamiliar hands to the places where he most needed support. As they approached the corridor, the girl said quietly into K.'s ear, "I must seem to think it's very important to show the information-giver in a good light, but you shouldn't doubt what I say, I just want to say the truth. He isn't hard-hearted. It's not really his job to help litigants outside if they're unwell but he's doing it anyway, as you can see. I don't suppose any of us is hard-hearted, perhaps we'd all like to be helpful, but working for the court offices it's easy for us to give the impression we are hard-hearted and don't want to help anyone. It makes me quite sad." "Would you not like to sit down here a while?" asked the information-giver, there were already in the corridor and just in front of the defendant whom K. had spoken to earlier. K. felt almost ashamed to be seen by him, earlier he had stood so upright in front of him and now he had to be supported by two others, his hat was held up by the information-giver balanced on outstretched fingers, his hair was dishevelled and hung down onto the sweat on his forehead. But the defendant seemed to notice nothing of what was going on and just stood there humbly, as if wanting to apologise to the information-giver for being there. The information-giver looked past him. "I know," he said, "that my case can't be settled today, not yet, but I've come in anyway, I thought, I thought I could wait here anyway, it's Sunday today, I've got plenty of time, and I'm not disturbing anyone here." "There's no need to be so apologetic," said the information-giver, "it's very commendable for you to be so attentive. You are taking up space here when you don't need to but as long as you don't get in my way I will do nothing to stop you following the progress of your case as closely as you like. When one has seen so many people who shamefully neglect their cases one learns to show patience with people like you. Do sit down." "He's very good with the litigants," whispered the girl. K. nodded, but started to move off again when the information-giver repeated, "Would you not like to sit down here a while?" "No," said K., "I don't want to rest." He had said that as decisively as he could, but in fact it would have done him a lot of good to sit down. It was as if he were suffering sea-sickness. He felt as if he were on a ship in a rough sea, as if the water were hitting against the wooden walls, a thundering from the depths of the corridor as if the torrent were crashing over it, as if the corridor were swaying and the waiting litigants on each side of it rising and sinking. It made the calmness of the girl and the man leading him all the more incomprehensible. He was at their mercy, if they let go of him he would fall like a board. Their little eyes glanced here and there, K. could feel the evenness of their steps but could not do the same, as from step to step he was virtually being carried. He finally noticed they were speaking to him but he did not understand them, all he heard was a noise that filled all the space and through which there seemed to be an unchanging higher note sounding, like a siren. "Louder," he whispered with his head sunk low, ashamed at having to ask them to speak louder when he knew they had spoken loudly enough, even if it had been, for him, incomprehensible. At last, a draught of cool air blew in his face as if a gap had been torn out in the wall in front of him, and next to him he heard someone say, "First he says he wants to go, and then you can tell him a hundred times that this is the way out and he doesn't move." K. became aware that he was standing in front of the way out, and that the young woman had opened the door. It seemed to him that all his strength returned to him at once, and to get a foretaste of freedom he stepped straight on to one of the stairs and took his leave there of his companions, who bowed to him. "Thank you very much," he repeated, shook their hands once more and did not let go until he thought he saw that they found it hard to bear the comparatively fresh air from the stairway after being so long used to the air in the offices. They were hardly able to reply, and the young woman might even have fallen over if K. had not shut the door extremely fast. K. then stood still for a while, combed his hair with the help of a pocket mirror, picked up his hat from the next stair - the information-giver must have thrown it down there - and then he ran down the steps so fresh and in such long leaps that the contrast with his previous state nearly frightened him. His normally sturdy state of health had never prepared him for surprises such as this. Did his body want to revolt and cause him a new trial as he was bearing the old one with such little effort? He did not quite reject the idea that he should see a doctor the next time he had the chance, but whatever he did - and this was something on which he could advise himself - he wanted to spend all Sunday mornings in future better than he had spent this one.

Chapter Four Miss Bürstner's Friend

For some time after this, K. found it impossible to exchange even just a few words with Miss Bürstner. He tried to reach her in many and various ways but she always found a way to avoid it. He would come straight home from the office, remain in her room without the light on, and sit on the sofa with nothing more to distract him than keeping watch on the empty hallway. If the maid went by and closed the door of the apparently empty room he would get up after a while and open it again. He got up an hour earlier than usual in the morning so that he might perhaps find Miss Bürstner alone as she went to the office. But none of these efforts brought any success. Then he wrote her a letter, both to the office and the flat, attempting once more to justify his behaviour, offered to make whatever amends he could, promised never to cross whatever boundary she might set him and begged merely to have the chance to speak to her some time, especially as he was unable to do anything with Mrs. Grubach either until he had spoken with Miss Bürstner, he finally informed her that the following Sunday he would stay in his room all day waiting for a sign from her that there was some hope of his request being fulfilled, or at least that she would explain to him why she could not fulfil it even though he had promised to observe whatever stipulations she might make. The letters were not returned, but there was no answer either. However, on the following Sunday there was a sign that seemed clear enough. It was still early when K. noticed, through the keyhole, that there was an unusual level of activity in the hallway which soon abated. A French teacher, although she was German and called Montag, a pale and febrile girl with a slight limp who had previously occupied a room of her own, was moving into Miss Bürstner's room. She could be seen shuffling through the hallway for several hours, there was always another piece of clothing or a blanket or a book that she had forgotten and had to be fetched specially and brought into the new home.

When Mrs. Grubach brought K. his breakfast - ever since the time when she had made K. so cross she didn't trust the maid to do the slightest job - he had no choice but to speak to her, for the first time in five days. "Why is there so much noise in the hallway today?" he asked as she poured his coffee out, "Can't something be done about it? Does this clearing out have to be done on a Sunday?" K. did not look up at Mrs. Grubach, but he saw nonetheless that she seemed to feel some relief as she breathed in. Even sharp questions like this from Mr. K. she perceived as forgiveness, or as the beginning of forgiveness. "We're not clearing anything out, Mr. K.," she said, "it's just that Miss Montag is moving in with Miss Bürstner and is moving her things across." She said nothing more, but just waited to see how K. would take it and whether he would allow her to carry on speaking. But K. kept her in uncertainty, took the spoon and pensively stirred his coffee while he remained silent. Then he looked up at her and said, "What about the suspicions you had earlier about Miss Bürstner, have you given them up?" "Mr. K.," called Mrs. Grubach, who had been waiting for this very question, as she put her hands together and held them out towards him. "I just made a chance remark and you took it so badly. I didn't have the slightest intention of offending anyone, not you or anyone else. You've known me for long enough, Mr. K., I'm sure you're convinced of that. You don't know how I've been suffering for the past few days! That I should tell lies about my tenants! And you, Mr. K., you believed it! And said I should give you notice! Give you notice!" At this last outcry, Mrs. Grubach was already choking back her tears, she raised her apron to her face and blubbered out loud.

"Oh, don't cry Mrs. Grubach," said K., looking out the window, he was thinking only of Miss Bürstner and how she was accepting an unknown girl into her room. "Now don't cry," he said again as he turned his look back into the room where

Mrs. Grubach was still crying. "I meant no harm either when I said that. It was simply a misunderstanding between us. That can happen even between old friends sometimes." Mrs. Grubach pulled her apron down to below her eyes to see whether K. really was attempting a reconciliation. "Well, yes, that's how it is," said K., and as Mrs. Grubach's behaviour indicated that the captain had said nothing he dared to add, "Do you really think, then, that I'd want to make an enemy of you for the sake of a girl we hardly know?" "Yes, you're quite right, Mr. K.," said Mrs. Grubach, and then, to her misfortune, as soon as she felt just a little freer to speak, she added something rather inept. "I kept asking myself why it was that Mr. K. took such an interest in Miss Bürstner. Why does he quarrel with me over her when he knows that any cross word from him and I can't sleep that night? And I didn't say anything about Miss Bürstner that I hadn't seen with my own eyes." K. said nothing in reply, he should have chased her from the room as soon as she had opened her mouth, and he didn't want to do that. He contented himself with merely drinking his coffee and letting Mrs. Grubach feel that she was superfluous. Outside, the dragging steps of Miss Montag could still be heard as she went from one side of the hallway to the other. "Do you hear that?" asked K. pointing his hand at the door. "Yes," said Mrs. Grubach with a sigh, "I wanted to give her some help and I wanted the maid to help her too but she's stubborn, she wants to move everything in herself. I wonder at Miss Bürstner. I often feel it's a burden for me to have Miss Montag as a tenant but Miss Bürstner accepts her into her room with herself." "There's nothing there for you to worry about" said K., crushing the remains of a sugar lump in his cup. "Does she cause you any trouble?" "No," said Mrs. Grubach, "in itself it's very good to have her there, it makes another room free for me and I can let my nephew, the captain, occupy it. I began to worry he might be disturbing you when I had to let him live in the living room next to you over the last few days. He's not very considerate." "What an idea!" said K. standing up, "there's no question of that. You seem to think that because I can't stand this to-ing and fro-ing of Miss Montag that I'm over-sensitive - and there she goes back again." Mrs. Grubach appeared quite powerless. "Should I tell her to leave moving the rest of her things over till later, then, Mr. K.? If that's what you want I'll do it immediately." "But she has to move in with Miss Bürstner!" said K. "Yes," said Mrs. Grubach, without quite understanding what K. meant. "So she has to take her things over there." Mrs. Grubach just nodded. K. was irritated all the more by this dumb helplessness which, seen from the outside, could have seemed like a kind of defiance on her part. He began to walk up and down the room between the window and the door, thus depriving Mrs. Grubach of the chance to leave, which she otherwise probably would have done.

Just as K. once more reached the door, someone knocked at it. It was the maid, to say that Miss Montag would like to have a few words with Mr. K., and therefore requested that he come to the dining room where she was waiting for him. K. heard the maid out thoughtfully, and then looked back at the shocked Mrs. Grubach in a way that was almost contemptuous. His look seemed to be saying that K. had been expecting this invitation for Miss Montag for a long time, and that it was confirmation of the suffering he had been made to endure that Sunday morning from

Mrs. Grubach's tenants. He sent the maid back with the reply that he was on his way, then he went to the wardrobe to change his coat, and in answer to Mrs. Grubach's gentle whining about the nuisance Miss Montag was causing merely asked her to clear away the breakfast things. "But you've hardly touched it," said Mrs. Grubach. "Oh just take it away!" shouted K. It seemed to him that Miss Montag was mixed up in everything and made it repulsive to him.

As he went through the hallway he looked at the closed door of Miss Bürstner's room. But it wasn't there that he was invited, but the dining room, to which he yanked the door open without knocking.

The room was long but narrow with one window. There was only enough space available to put two cupboards at an angle in the corner by the door, and the rest of the room was entirely taken up with the long dining table which started by the door and reached all the way to the great window, which was thus made almost inaccessible. The table was already laid for a large number of people, as on Sundays almost all the tenants ate their dinner here at midday.

When K. entered, Miss Montag came towards him from the window along one side of the table. They greeted each other in silence. Then Miss Montag, her head unusually erect as always, said, "I'm not sure whether you know me." K. looked at her with a frown. "Of course I do," he said, "you've been living here with Mrs. Grubach for quite some time now." "But I get the impression you don't pay much attention to what's going on in the lodging house," said Miss Montag. "No," said K. "Would you not like to sit down?" said Miss Montag. In silence, the two of them drew chairs out from the farthest end of the table and sat down facing each other. But Miss Montag stood straight up again as she had left her handbag on the window sill and went to fetch it; she shuffled down the whole length of the room. When she came back, the handbag lightly swinging, she said, "I'd like just to have a few words with you on behalf of my friend. She would have come herself, but she's feeling a little unwell today. Perhaps you'll be kind enough to forgive her and listen to me instead. There's anyway nothing that she could have said that I won't. On the contrary, in fact, I think I can say even more than her because I'm relatively impartial. Would you not agree?" "What is there to say, then?" answered K., who was tired of Miss Montag continuously watching his lips. In that way she took control of what he wanted to say before he said it. "Miss Bürstner clearly refuses to grant me the personal meeting that I asked her for." "That's how it is," said Miss Montag, "or rather, that's not at all how it is, the way you put it is remarkably severe. Generally speaking, meetings are neither granted nor the opposite. But it can be that meetings are considered unnecessary, and that's how it is here. Now, after your comment, I can speak openly. You asked my friend, verbally or in writing, for the chance to speak with her. Now my friend is aware of your reasons for asking for this meeting - or at least I suppose she is - and so, for reasons I know nothing about, she is quite sure that it would be of no benefit to anyone if this meeting actually took place. Moreover, it was only yesterday, and only very briefly, that she made it clear to me that such a meeting could be of no benefit for yourself either, she feels that it can only have been a matter of chance that such an idea came to you, and that even without any explanations from her, you will very soon come to realise yourself, if you have not done so already, the futility of your idea. My answer to that is that although it may be quite right, I consider it advantageous, if the matter is to be made perfectly clear, to give you an explicit answer. I offered my services in taking on the task, and after some hesitation my friend conceded. I hope, however, also to have acted in your interests, as even the slightest uncertainty in the least significant of matters will always remain a cause of suffering and if, as in this case, it can be removed without substantial effort, then it is better if that is done without delay." "I thank you," said K. as soon as Miss Montag had finished. He stood slowly up, looked at her, then across the table, then out the window - the house opposite stood there in the sun - and went to the door. Miss Montag followed him a few paces, as if she did not quite trust him. At the door, however, both of them had to step back as it opened and Captain Lanz entered. This was the first time that K. had seen him close up. He was a large man of about forty with a tanned, fleshy face. He bowed slightly, intending it also for K., and then went over to Miss Montag and deferentially kissed her hand. He was very elegant in the way he moved. The courtesy he showed towards Miss Montag made a striking contrast with the way she had been treated by K. Nonetheless, Miss Montag did not seem to be cross with K. as it even seemed to him that she wanted to introduce the captain. K. however, did not want to be introduced, he would not have been able to show any sort of friendliness either to Miss Montag or to the captain, the kiss on the hand had, for K., bound them into a group which would keep him at a distance from Miss Bürstner whilst at the same time seeming to be totally harmless and unselfish. K. thought, however, that he saw more than that, he thought he also saw that Miss Montag had chosen a means of doing it that was good, but two-edged. She exaggerated the importance of the relationship between K. and Miss Bürstner, and above all she exaggerated the importance of asking to speak with her and she tried at the same time to make out that K. was exaggerating everything. She would be disappointed, K. did not want to exaggerate anything, he was aware that Miss Bürstner was a little typist who would not offer him much resistance for long. In doing so he deliberately took no account of what Mrs. Grubach had told him about Miss Bürstner. All these things were going through his mind as he left the room with hardly a polite word. He wanted to go straight to his room, but a little laugh from Miss Montag that he heard from the dining room behind him brought him to the idea that he might prepare a surprise for the two of them, the captain and Miss Montag. He looked round and listened to find out if there might be any disturbance from any of the surrounding rooms, everywhere was quiet, the only thing to be heard was the conversation from the dining room and Mrs. Grubach's voice from the passage leading to the kitchen. This seemed an opportune time, K. went to Miss Bürstner's room and knocked gently. There was no sound so he knocked again but there was still no answer in reply. Was she asleep? Or was she really unwell? Or was she just pretending as she realised it could only be K. knocking so gently? K. assumed she was pretending and knocked harder, eventually, when the knocking brought no result, he carefully opened the door with the sense of doing something that was not only improper but also pointless. In the room there was no-one. What's more, it looked hardly at all like the room K. had known before. Against the wall there were now two beds behind one another, there were clothes piled up on three chairs near the door, a wardrobe stood open. Miss Bürstner must have gone out while Miss Montag was speaking to him in the dining room. K. was not greatly bothered by this, he had hardly expected to be able to find Miss Bürstner so easily and had made this attempt for little more reason than to spite Miss Montag. But that made it all the more embarrassing for him when, as he was closing the door again, he saw Miss Montag and the captain talking in the open doorway of the dining room. They had probably been standing there ever since K. had opened the door, they avoided seeming to observe K. but chatted lightly and followed his movements with glances, the absent minded glances to the side such as you make during a conversation. But these glances were heavy for K., and he rushed alongside the wall back into his own room.

Chapter Five The whip-man

One evening, a few days later, K. was walking along one of the corridors that separated his office from the main stairway - he was nearly the last one to leave for home that evening, there remained only a couple of workers in the light of a single bulb in the dispatch department - when he heard a sigh from behind a door which he had himself never opened but which he had always thought just led into a junk room. He stood in amazement and listened again to establish whether he might not be mistaken. For a while there was silence, but then came some more sighs. His first thought was to fetch one of the servitors, it might well have been worth having a witness present, but then he was taken by an uncontrollable curiosity that make him simply yank the door open. It was, as he had thought, a junk room. Old, unusable forms, empty stone ink-bottles lay scattered behind the entrance. But in the cupboard-like room itself stood three men, crouching under the low ceiling. A candle fixed on a shelf gave them light. "What are you doing here?" asked K. quietly, but crossly and without thinking. One of the men was clearly in charge, and attracted attention by being dressed in a kind of dark leather costume which left his neck and chest and his arms exposed. He did not answer. But the other two called out, "Mr. K.! We're to be beaten because you made a complaint about us to the examining judge." And now, K. finally realised that it was actually the two policemen, Franz and Willem, and that the third man held a cane in his hand with which to beat them. "Well," said K., staring at them, "I didn't make any complaint, I only said what took place in my home. And your behaviour was not entirely unobjectionable, after all." "Mr. K.," said Willem, while Franz clearly tried to shelter behind him as protection from the third man, "if you knew how badly we get paid you wouldn't think so badly of us. I've got a family to feed, and Franz here wanted to get married, you just have to get more money where you can, you can't do it just by working hard, not however hard you try. I was sorely tempted by your fine clothes, policemen aren't allowed to do that sort of thing, course they aren't, and it wasn't right of us, but it's tradition that the clothes go to the officers, that's how it's always been, believe me; and it's understandable too, isn't it, what can things like that mean for anyone unlucky enough to be arrested? But if he starts talking about it openly then the punishment has to follow." "I didn't know about any of this that you've been telling me, and I made no sort of request that you be punished, I was simply acting on principle." "Franz," said Willem, turning to the other policeman, "didn't I tell you that the gentleman didn't say he wanted us to be punished? Now you can hear for yourself, he didn't even know we'd have to be punished." "Don't you let them persuade you, talking like that," said the third man to K., "this punishment is both just and unavoidable." "Don't listen to him," said Willem, interrupting himself only to quickly bring his hand to his mouth when it had received a stroke of the cane, "we're only being punished because you made a complaint against us. Nothing would have happened to us otherwise, not even if they'd found out what we'd done. Can you call that justice? Both of us, me especially, we'd proved our worth as good police officers over a long period - you've got to admit yourself that as far as official work was concerned we did the job well - things looked good for us, we had prospects, it's quite certain that we would've been made whip-men too, like this one, only he had the luck not to have anyone make a complaint about him, as you really don't get many complaints like that. Only that's all finished now, Mr. K., our careers are at an end, we're going to have to do work now that's far inferior to police work and besides all this we're going to get this terrible, painful beating." "Can the cane really cause so much pain, then?" asked K., testing the cane that the whip-man swang in front of him. "We're going to have to strip off totally naked," said Willem. "Oh, I see," said K., looking straight at the whip-man, his skin was burned brown like a sailor's, and his face showed health and vigour. "Is there then no possibility of sparing these two their beating?" he asked him. "No," said the whip-man, shaking his head with a laugh. "Get undressed!" he ordered the policemen. And to K. he said, "You shouldn't believe everything they tell you, it's the fear of being beaten, it's already made them a bit weak in the head. This one here, for instance," he pointed at Willem, "all that he told you about his career prospects, it's just ridiculous. Look at him, look how fat he is - the first strokes of the cane will just get lost in all that fat. Do you know what it is that's made him so fat? He's in the habit of, everyone that gets arrested by him, he eats their breakfast. Didn't he eat up your breakfast? Yeah, I thought as much. But a man with a belly like that can't be made into a whip-man and never will be, that is quite out of the question." "There are whip-men like that," Willem insisted, who had just released the belt of this trousers. "No," said the whip-man, striking him such a blow with the cane on his neck that it made him wince, "you shouldn't be listening to this, just get undressed." "I would make it well worth your while if you would let them go," said K., and without looking at the whip-man again - as such matters are best carried on with both pairs of eyes turned down - he pulled out his wallet. "And then you'd try and put in a complaint against me, too," said the whip-man, "and get me flogged. No, no!" "Now, do be reasonable," said K., "if I had wanted to get these two punished I would not now be trying to buy their freedom, would I. I could simply close the door here behind me, go home and see or hear nothing more of it. But that's not what I'm doing, it really is of much more importance to me to let them go free; if I had realised they would be punished, or even that they might be punished, I would never have named them in the first place as they are not the ones I hold responsible. It's the organisation that's to blame, the high officials are the ones to blame." "That's how it is!" shouted the policemen, who then immediately received another blow on their backs, which were by now exposed. "If you had a senior judge here beneath your stick," said K., pressing down the cane as he spoke to stop it being raised once more, "I really would do nothing to stop you, on the contrary, I would even pay you money to give you all the more strength." "Yeah, that's all very plausible, what you're saying there," said the whip-man, "only I'm not the sort of person you can bribe. It's my job to flog people, so I flog them." Franz, the policeman, had been fairly quiet so far, probably in expectation of a good result from K.'s intervention, but now he stepped forward to the door wearing just his trousers, knelt down hanging on to K.'s arm and whispered, "Even if you can't get mercy shown for both of us, at least try and get me set free. Willem is older than me, he's less sensitive than me in every way, he even got a light beating a couple of years ago, but my record's still clean, I only did things the way I did because Willem led me on to it, he's been my teacher both for good and bad. Down in front of the bank my poor bride is waiting for me at the entrance, I'm so ashamed of myself, it's pitiful." His face was flowing over with tears, and he wiped it dry on K.'s coat. "I'm not going to wait any longer," said the whip-man, taking hold of the cane in both hands and laying in to Franz while Willem cowered back in a corner and looked on secretly, not even daring to turn his head. Then, the sudden scream that shot out from Franz was long and irrevocable, it seemed to come not from a human being but from an instrument that was being tortured, the whole corridor rang with it, it must have been heard by everyone in the building. "Don't shout like that!", called out K., unable to prevent himself, and, as he looked anxiously in the direction from which the servitor would come, he gave Franz a shove, not hard, but hard enough for him to fall down unconscious, clawing at the ground with his hands by reflex; he still did not avoid being hit; the rod still found him on the floor; the tip of the rod swang regularly up and down while he rolled to and fro under its blows. And now one of the servitors appeared in the distance, with another a few steps behind him. K. had quickly thrown the door shut, gone over to one of the windows overlooking the yard and opened it. The screams had completely stopped. So that the servitor wouldn't come in, he called out, "It's only me!" "Good evening, chief clerk," somebody called back. "Is there anything wrong?" "No, no," answered K., "it's only a dog yelping in the yard." There was no sound from the servitors so he added, "You can go back to what you were doing." He did not want to become involved with a conversation with them, and so he leant out of the window. A little while later, when he looked out in the corridor, they had already gone. Now, K. remained at the window, he did not dare go back into the junk room, and he did not want to go home either. The yard he looked down into was small and rectangular, all around it were offices, all the windows were now dark and only those at the very top caught a reflection of the moon. K tried hard to see into the darkness of one corner of the yard, where a few handcarts had been left behind one another. He felt anguish at not having been able to prevent the flogging, but that was not his fault, if Franz had not screamed like that - clearly it must have caused a great deal of pain but it's important to maintain control of oneself at important moments - if Franz had not screamed then it was at least highly probable that K. would have been able to dissuade the whip-man. If all the junior officers were contemptible why would the whip-man, whose position was the most inhumane of all, be any exception, and K. had noticed very clearly how his eyes had lit up when he saw the banknotes, he had obviously only seemed serious about the flogging to raise the level of the bribe a little. And K. had not been ungenerous, he really had wanted to get the policemen freed; if he really had now begun to do something against the degeneracy of the court then it was a matter of course that he would have to do something here as well. But of course, it became impossible for him to do anything as soon as Franz started screaming. K. could not possibly have let the junior bank staff, and perhaps even all sorts of other people, come along and catch him by surprise as he haggled with those people in the junk room. Nobody could really expect that sort of sacrifice of him. If that had been his intention then it would almost have been easier, K. would have taken his own clothes off and offered himself to the whip-man in the policemen's place. The whip-man would certainly not have accepted this substitution anyway, as in that way he would have seriously violated his duty without gaining any benefit. He would most likely have violated his duty twice over, as court employees were probably under orders not to cause any harm to K. while he was facing charges, although there may have been special conditions in force here. However things stood, K. was able to do no more than throw the door shut, even though that would still do nothing to remove all the dangers he faced. It was regrettable that he had given Franz a shove, and it could only be excused by the heat of the moment.

In the distance, he heard the steps of the servitors; he did not want them to be too aware of his presence, so he closed the window and walked towards the main staircase. At the door of the junk room he stopped and listened for a little while. All was silent. The two policemen were entirely at the whip-man's mercy; he could have beaten them to death. K. reached his hand out for the door handle but drew it suddenly back. He was no longer in any position to help anyone, and the servitors would soon be back; he did, though, promise himself that he would raise the matter again with somebody and see that, as far as it was in his power, those who really were guilty, the high officials whom nobody had so far dared point out to him, received their due punishment. As he went down the main stairway at the front of the bank, he looked carefully round at everyone who was passing, but there was no girl to be seen who might have been waiting for somebody, not even within some distance from the bank. Franz's claim that his bride was waiting for him was thus shown to be a lie, albeit one that was forgivable and intended only to elicit more sympathy.

The policemen were still on K.'s mind all through the following day; he was unable to concentrate on his work and had to stay in his office a little longer than the previous day so that he could finish it. On the way home, as he passed by the junk room again, he opened its door as if that had been his habit. Instead of the darkness he expected, he saw everything unchanged from the previous evening, and did not know how he should respond. Everything was exactly the same as he had seen it when he had opened the door the previous evening. The forms and bottles of ink just inside the doorway, the whip-man with his cane, the two policemen, still undressed, the candle on the shelf, and the two policemen began to wail and call out "Mr. K.!" K. slammed the door immediately shut, and even thumped on it with his fists as if that would shut it all the firmer. Almost in tears, he ran to the servitors working quietly at the copying machine. "Go and get that junk room cleared out!" he shouted, and, in amazement, they stopped what they were doing. "It should have been done long ago, we're sinking in dirt!" They would be able to do the job the next day, K. nodded, it was too late in the evening to make them do it there and then as he had originally intended. He sat down briefly in order to keep them near him for a little longer, looked through a few of the copies to give the impression that he was checking them and then, as he saw that they would not dare to leave at the same time as himself, went home tired and with his mind numb.

Chapter Six K.'s uncle - Leni

One afternoon - K. was very busy at the time, getting the post ready - K.'s Uncle Karl, a small country land owner, came into the room, pushing his way between two of the staff who were bringing in some papers. K. had long expected his uncle to appear, but the sight of him now shocked K. far less than the prospect of it had done a long time before. His uncle was bound to come, K. had been sure of that for about a month. He already thought at the time he could see how his uncle would arrive, slightly bowed, his battered panama hat in his left hand, his right hand already stretched out over the desk long before he was close enough as he rushed carelessly towards K. knocking over everything that was in his way. K.'s uncle was always in a hurry, as he suffered from the unfortunate belief that he had a number of things to do while he was in the big city and had to settle all of them in one day - his visits were only ever for one day - and at the same time thought he could not forgo any conversation or piece of business or pleasure that might arise by chance. Uncle Karl was K.'s former guardian, and so K. was duty-bound to help him in all of this as well as to offer him a bed for the night. 'I'm haunted by a ghost from the country', he would say.

As soon as they had greeted each other - K. had invited him to sit in the armchair but Uncle Karl had no time for that - he said he wanted to speak briefly with K. in private. "It is necessary," he said with a tired gulp, "it is necessary for my peace of mind." K. immediately sent the junior staff from the room and told them to let no-one in. "What's this that I've been hearing, Josef?" cried K.'s uncle when they were alone, as he sat on the table shoving various papers under himself without looking at them to make himself more comfortable. K. said nothing, he knew what was coming, but, suddenly relieved from the effort of the work he had been doing, he gave way to a pleasant lassitude and looked out the window at the other side of the street. From where he sat, he could see just a small, triangular section of it, part of the empty walls of houses between two shop windows. "You're staring out the window!" called out his uncle, raising his arms, "For God's sake, Josef, give me an answer! Is it true, can it really be true?" "Uncle Karl," said K., wrenching himself back from his daydreaming, "I really don't know what it is you want of me." "Josef," said his uncle in a warning tone, "as far as I know, you've always told the truth. Am I to take what you've just said as a bad sign?" "I think I know what it is you want," said K. obediently, "I expect you've heard about my trial." "That's right," answered his uncle with a slow nod, "I've heard about your trial." "Who did you hear it from, then?" asked K. "Erna wrote to me," said his uncle, "she doesn't have much contact with you, it's true, you don't pay very much attention to her, I'm afraid to say, but she learned about it nonetheless. I got her letter today and, of course, I came straight here. And for no other reason, but it seems to me that this is reason enough. I can read you out the part of the letter that concerns you." He drew the letter out from his wallet. "Here it is. She writes; 'I have not seen Josef for a long time, I was in the bank last week but Josef was so busy that they would not let me through; I waited there for nearly an hour but then I had to go home as I had my piano lesson. I would have liked to have spoken to him, maybe there will be a chance another time. He sent me a big box of chocolates for my name-day, that was very nice and attentive of him. I forgot to tell you about it when I wrote, and I only remember now that you ask me about it. Chocolate, as I am sure you are aware, disappears straight away in this lodging house, almost as soon as you know somebody has given you chocolate it is gone. But there is something else I wanted to tell you about Josef. Like I said, they would not let me through to see him at the bank because he was negotiating with some gentleman just then. After I had been waiting quietly for quite a long time I asked one of the staff whether his meeting would last much longer. He said it might well do, as it was probably about the legal proceedings, he said, that were being conducted against him. I asked what sort of legal proceedings it was that were being conducted against the chief clerk, and whether he was not making some mistake, but he said he was not making any mistake, there were legal proceedings underway and even that they were about something quite serious, but he did not know any more about it. He would have liked to have been of some help to the chief clerk himself, as the chief clerk was a gentleman, good and honest, but he did not know what it was he could do and merely hoped there would be some influential gentlemen who would take his side. I'm sure that is what will happen and that everything will turn out for the best in the end, but in the mean time things do not look at all good, and you can see that from the mood of the chief clerk himself. Of course, I did not place too much importance on this conversation, and even did my best to put the bank clerk's mind at rest, he was quite a simple man. I told him he was not to speak to anyone else about this, and I think it is all just a rumour, but I still think it might be good if you, Dear Father, if you looked into the matter the next time you visit. It will be easy for you to find out more detail and, if it is really necessary, to do something about it through the great and influential people you know. But if it is not necessary, and that is what seems most likely, then at least your daughter will soon have the chance to embrace you and I look forward to it.' - She's a good child," said K.'s uncle when he had finished reading, and wiped a few tears from his eyes. K. nodded. With all the different disruptions he had had recently he had completely forgotten about Erna, even her birthday, and the story of the chocolates had clearly just been invented so that he wouldn't get in trouble with his aunt and uncle. It was very touching, and even the theatre tickets, which he would regularly send her from then on, would not be enough to repay her, but he really did not feel, now, that it was right for him to visit her in her lodgings and hold conversations with a little, eighteen year old schoolgirl. "And what do you have to say about that?" asked his uncle, who had forgotten all his rush and excitement as he read the letter, and seemed to be about to read it again. "Yes, Uncle," said K., "it is true." "True!" called out his uncle. "What is true? How can this be true? What sort of trial is it? Not a criminal trial, I hope?" "It's a criminal trial," answered K. "And you sit quietly here while you've got a criminal trial round your neck?" shouted his uncle, getting ever louder. "The more calm I am, the better it will be for the outcome," said K. in a tired voice, "don't worry." "How can I help worrying?!" shouted his uncle, "Josef, my Dear Josef, think about yourself, about your family, think about our good name! Up till now, you've always been our pride, don't now become our disgrace. I don't like the way you're behaving," he said, looking at K. with his head at an angle, "that's not how an innocent man behaves when he's accused of something, not if he's still got any strength in him. Just tell me what it's all about so that I can help you. It's something to do with the bank, I take it?" "No," said K. as he stood up, "and you're speaking too loud, Uncle, I expect one of the staff is listening at the door and I find that rather unpleasant. It's best if we go somewhere else, then I can answer all your questions, as far as I can. And I know very well that I have to account to the family for what I do." "You certainly do!" his uncle shouted, "Quite right, you do. Now just get a move on, Josef, hurry up now!" "I still have a few documents I need to prepare," said K., and, using the intercom, he summoned his deputy who entered a few moments later. K.'s uncle, still angry and excited, gestured with his hand to show that K. had summoned him, even though there was no need whatever to do so. K. stood in front of the desk and explained to the young man, who listened calm and attentive, what would need to be done that day in his absence, speaking in a calm voice and making use of various documents. The presence of K.'s uncle while this was going on was quite disturbing; he did not listen to what was being said, but at first he stood there with eyes wide open and nervously biting his lips. Then he began to walk up and down the room, stopped now and then at the window, or stood in front of a picture always making various exclamations such as, "That is totally incomprehensible to me!" or "Now just tell me, what are you supposed to make of that?!" The young man pretended to notice nothing of this and listened to K.'s instructions through to the end, he made a few notes, bowed to both K. and his uncle and then left the room. K.'s uncle had turned his back to him and was looking out the window, bunching up the curtains with his outstretched hands. The door had hardly closed when he called out, "At last! Now that he's stopped jumping about we can go too!" Once they were in the front hall of the bank, where several members of staff were standing about and where, just then, the deputy director was walking across, there was unfortunately no way of stopping K.'s uncle from continually asking questions about the trial. "Now then, Josef," he began, lightly acknowledging the bows from those around them as they passed, "tell me everything about this trial; what sort of trial is it?" K. made a few comments which conveyed little information, even laughed a little, and it was only when they reached the front steps that he explained to his uncle that he had not wanted to talk openly in front of those people. "Quite right," said his uncle, "but now start talking." With his head to one side, and smoking his cigar in short, impatient draughts, he listened. "First of all, Uncle," said K., "it's not a trial like you'd have in a normal courtroom." "So much the worse," said his uncle. "How's that?" asked K., looking at him. "What I mean is, that's for the worse," he repeated. They were standing on the front steps of the bank; as the doorkeeper seemed to be listening to what they were saying K. drew his uncle down further, where they were absorbed into the bustle of the street. His uncle took K.'s arm and stopped asking questions with such urgency about the trial, they walked on for a while in silence. "But how did all this come about?" he eventually asked, stopping abruptly enough to startle the people walking behind, who had to avoid walking into him. "Things like this don't come all of a sudden, they start developing a long time beforehand, there must have been warning signs of it, why didn't you write to me? You know I'd do anything for you, to some extent I am still your guardian, and until today that's something I was proud of. I'll still help you, of course I will, only now, now that the trial is already underway, it makes it very difficult. But whatever; the best thing now is for you to take a short holiday staying with us in the country. You've lost weight, I can see that now. The country life will give you strength, that will be good, there's bound to be a lot of hard work ahead of you. But besides that it'll be a way of getting you away from the court, to some extent. Here they've got every means of showing the powers at their disposal and they're automatically bound to use them against you; in the country they'll either have to delegate authority to different bodies or just have to try and bother you by letter, telegram or telephone. And that's bound to weaken the effect, it won't release you from them but it'll give you room to breathe." "You could forbid me to leave," said K., who had been drawn slightly into his uncle's way of thinking by what he had been saying. "I didn't think you would do it," said his uncle thoughtfully, "you won't suffer too much loss of power by moving away." K. grasped his uncle under the arm to prevent him stopping still and said, "I thought you'd think all this is less important than I do, and now you're taking it so hard." "Josef," called his uncle trying to disentangle himself from him so that he could stop walking, but K. did not let go, "you've completely changed, you used to be so astute, are you losing it now? Do you want to lose the trial? Do you realise what that would mean? That would mean you would be simply destroyed. And that everyone you know would be pulled down with you or at the very least humiliated, disgraced right down to the ground. Josef, pull yourself together. The way you're so indifferent about it, it's driving me mad. Looking at you I can almost believe that old saying: 'Having a trial like that means losing a trial like that'." "My dear Uncle," said K., "it won't do any good to get excited, it's no good for you to do it and it'd be no good for me to do it. The case won't be won by getting excited, and please admit that my practical experience counts for something, just as I have always and still do respect your experience, even when it surprises me. You say that the family will also be affected by this trial; I really can't see how, but that's beside the point and I'm quite willing to follow your instructions in all of this. Only, I don't see any advantage in staying in the country, not even for you, as that would indicate flight and a sense of guilt. And besides, although I am more subject to persecution if I stay in the city I can also press the matter forward better here." "You're right," said his uncle in a tone that seemed to indicate they were finally coming closer to each other, "I just made the suggestion because, as I saw it, if you stay in the city the case will be put in danger by your indifference to it, and I thought it was better if I did the work for you. But will you push things forward yourself with all your strength, if so, that will naturally be far better." "We're agreed then," said K. "And do you have any suggestions for what I should do next?" "Well, naturally I'll have to think about it," said his uncle, "you must bear in mind that I've been living in the country for twenty years now, almost without a break, you lose your ability to deal with matters like this. But I do have some important connections with several people who, I expect, know their way around these things better than I do, and to contact them is a matter of course. Out there in the country I've been getting out of condition, I'm sure you're already aware of that. It's only at times like this that you notice it yourself. And this affair of yours came largely unexpected, although, oddly enough, I had expected something of the sort after I'd read Erna's letter, and today when I saw your face I knew it with almost total certainty. But all that is by the by, the important thing now is, we have no time to lose." Even while he was still speaking, K.'s uncle had stood on tiptoe to summon a taxi and now he pulled K. into the car behind himself as he called out an address to the driver. "We're going now to see Dr. Huld, the lawyer," he said, "we were at school together. I'm sure you know the name, don't you? No? Well that is odd. He's got a very good reputation as a defence barrister and for working with the poor. But I esteem him especially as someone you can trust." "It's alright with me, whatever you do," said K., although he was made uneasy by the rushed and urgent way his uncle was dealing with the matter. It was not very encouraging, as the accused, be to taken to a lawyer for poor people. "I didn't know," he said, "that you could take on a lawyer in matters like this." "Well of course you can," said his uncle, "that goes without saying. Why wouldn't you take on a lawyer? And now, so that I'm properly instructed in this matter, tell me what's been happening so far." K. instantly began telling his uncle about what had been happening, holding nothing back - being completely open with him was the only way that K. could protest at his uncle's belief that the trial was a great disgrace. He mentioned Miss Bürstner's name just once and in passing, but that did nothing to diminish his openness about the trial as Miss Bürstner had no connection with it. As he spoke, he looked out the window and saw how, just then, they were getting closer to the suburb where the court offices were. He drew this to his uncle's attention, but he did not find the coincidence especially remarkable. The taxi stopped in front of a dark building. K.'s uncle knocked at the very first door at ground level; while they waited he smiled, showing his big teeth, and whispered, "Eight o'clock; not the usual sort of time to be visiting a lawyer, but Huld won't mind it from me." Two large, black eyes appeared in the spy-hatch in the door, they stared at the two visitors for a while and then disappeared; the door, however, did not open. K. and his uncle confirmed to each other the fact that they had seen the two eyes. "A new maid, afraid of strangers," said K.'s uncle, and knocked again. The eyes appeared once more. This time they seemed almost sad, but the open gas flame that burned with a hiss close above their heads gave off little light and that may have merely created an illusion. "Open the door," called K.'s uncle, raising his fist against it, "we are friends of Dr. Huld, the lawyer!" "Dr. Huld is ill," whispered someone behind them. In a doorway at the far end of a narrow passage stood a man in his dressing gown, giving them this information in an extremely quiet voice. K.'s uncle, who had already been made very angry by the long wait, turned abruptly round and retorted, "Ill? You say he's ill?" and strode towards the gentleman in a way that seemed almost threatening, as if he were the illness himself. "They've opened the door for you, now," said the gentleman, pointing at the door of the lawyer. He pulled his dressing gown together and disappeared. The door had indeed been opened, a young girl - K. recognised the dark, slightly bulging eyes - stood in the hallway in a long white apron, holding a candle in her hand. "Next time, open up sooner!" said K.'s uncle instead of a greeting, while the girl made a slight curtsey. "Come along, Josef," he then said to K. who was slowly moving over towards the girl. "Dr. Huld is unwell," said the girl as K.'s uncle, without stopping, rushed towards one of the doors. K. continued to look at the girl in amazement as she turned round to block the way into the living room, she had a round face like a puppy's, not only the pale cheeks and the chin were round but the temples and the hairline were too. "Josef!" called his uncle once more, and he asked the girl, "It's trouble with his heart, is it?" "I think it is, sir," said the girl, who by now had found time to go ahead with the candle and open the door into the room. In one corner of the room, where the light of the candle did not reach, a face with a long beard looked up from the bed. "Leni, who's this coming in?" asked the lawyer, unable to recognise his guests because he was dazzled by the candle. "It's your old friend, Albert," said K.'s uncle. "Oh, Albert," said the lawyer, falling back onto his pillow as if this visit meant he would not need to keep up appearances. "Is it really as bad as that?" asked K.'s uncle, sitting on the edge of the bed. "I don't believe it is. It's a recurrence of your heart trouble and it'll pass over like the other times." "Maybe," said the lawyer quietly, "but it's just as much trouble as it's ever been. I can hardly breathe, I can't sleep at all and I'm getting weaker by the day." "I see," said K.'s uncle, pressing his panama hat firmly against his knee with his big hand. "That is bad news. But are you getting the right sort of care? And it's so depressing in here, it's so dark. It's a long time since I was last here, but it seemed to me friendlier then. Even your young lady here doesn't seem to have much life in her, unless she's just pretending." The maid was still standing by the door with the candle; as far as could be made out, she was watching K. more than she was watching his uncle even while the latter was still speaking about her. K. leant against a chair that he had pushed near to the girl. "When you're as ill as I am," said the lawyer, "you need to have peace. I don't find it depressing." After a short pause he added, "and Leni looks after me well, she's a good girl." But that was not enough to persuade K.'s uncle, he had visibly taken against his friend's carer and, even though he did not contradict the invalid, he persecuted her with his scowl as she went over to the bed, put the candle on the bedside table and, leaning over the bed, made a fuss of him by tidying the pillows. K.'s uncle nearly forgot the need to show any consideration for the man who lay ill in bed, he stood up, walked up and down behind the carer, and K. would not have been surprised if he had grabbed hold of her skirts behind her and dragged her away from the bed. K. himself looked on calmly, he was not even disappointed at finding the lawyer unwell, he had been able to do nothing to oppose the enthusiasm his uncle had developed for the matter, he was glad that this enthusiasm had now been distracted without his having to do anything about it. His uncle, probably simply wishing to be offensive to the lawyer's attendant, then said, "Young lady, now please leave us alone for a while, I have some personal matters to discuss with my friend." Dr. Huld's carer was still leant far over the invalid's bed and smoothing out the cloth covering the wall next to it, she merely turned her head and then, in striking contrast with the anger that first stopped K.'s uncle from speaking and then let the words out in a gush, she said very quietly, "You can see that Dr. Huld is so ill that he can't discuss any matters at all." It was probably just for the sake of convenience that she had repeated the words spoken by K.'s uncle, but an onlooker might even have perceived it as mocking him and he, of course, jumped up as if he had just been stabbed. "You damned …," in the first gurglings of his excitement his words could hardly be understood, K. was startled even though he had been expecting something of the sort and ran to his uncle with the intention, no doubt, of closing his mouth with both his hands. Fortunately, though, behind the girl, the invalid raised himself up, K.'s uncle made an ugly face as if swallowing something disgusting and then, somewhat calmer, said, "We have naturally not lost our senses, not yet; if what I am asking for were not possible I would not be asking for it. Now please, go!" The carer stood up straight by the bed directly facing K.'s uncle, K. thought he noticed that with one hand she was stroking the lawyer's hand. "You can say anything in front of Leni," said the invalid, in a tone that was unmistakably imploring. "It's not my business," said K.'s uncle, "and it's not my secrets." And he twisted himself round as if wanting to go into no more negotiations but giving himself a little more time to think. "Whose business is it then?" asked the lawyer in an exhausted voice as he leant back again. "My nephew's," said K.'s uncle, "and I've brought him along with me." And he introduced him, "Chief Clerk Josef K." "Oh!" said the invalid, now with much more life in him, and reached out his hand towards K. "Do forgive me, I didn't notice you there at all." Then he then said to his carer, "Leni, go," stretching his hand out to her as if this were a farewell that would have to last for a long time. This time the girl offered no resistance. "So you," he finally said to K.'s uncle, who had also calmed down and stepped closer, "you haven't come to visit me because I'm ill but you've come on business." The lawyer now looked so much stronger that it seemed the idea of being visited because he was ill had somehow made him weak, he remained supporting himself of one elbow, which must have been rather tiring, and continually pulled at a lock of hair in the middle of his beard. "You already look much better," said K.'s uncle, "now that that witch has gone outside." He interrupted himself, whispered, "I bet you she's listening!" and sprang over to the door. But behind the door there was no-one, K.'s uncle came back not disappointed, as her not listening seemed to him worse than if she had been, but probably somewhat embittered. "You're mistaken about her," said the lawyer, but did nothing more to defend her; perhaps that was his way of indicating that she did not need defending. But in a tone that was much more committed he went on, "As far as your nephew's affairs are concerned, this will be an extremely difficult undertaking and I'd count myself lucky if my strength lasted out long enough for it; I'm greatly afraid it won't do, but anyway I don't want to leave anything untried; if I don't last out you can always get somebody else. To be honest, this matter interests me too much, and I can't bring myself to give up the chance of taking some part in it. If my heart does totally give out then at least it will have found a worthy affair to fail in." K. believed he understood not a word of this entire speech, he looked at his uncle for an explanation but his uncle sat on the bedside table with the candle in his hand, a medicine bottle had rolled off the table onto the floor, he nodded to everything the lawyer said, agreed to everything, and now and then looked at K. urging him to show the same compliance. Maybe K.'s uncle had already told the lawyer about the trial. But that was impossible, everything that had happened so far spoke against it. So he said, "I don't understand ..." "Well, maybe I've misunderstood what you've been saying," said the lawyer, just as astonished and embarrassed as K. "Perhaps I've been going too fast. What was it you wanted to speak to me about? I thought it was to do with your trial." "Of course it is," said K.'s uncle, who then asked K., "So what is it you want?" "Yes, but how is it that you know anything about me and my case?" asked K. "Oh, I see," said the lawyer with a smile. "I am a lawyer, I move in court circles, people talk about various different cases and the more interesting ones stay in your mind, especially when they concern the nephew of a friend. There's nothing very remarkable about that." "What is it you want, then?" asked K.'s uncle once more, "You seem so uneasy about it" "You move in this court's circles?" asked K. "Yes," said the lawyer. "You're asking questions like a child," said K.'s uncle. "What circles should I move in, then, if not with members of my own discipline?" the lawyer added. It sounded so indisputable that K. gave no answer at all. "But you work in the High Court, not that court in the attic," he had wanted to say but could not bring himself to actually utter it. "You have to realise," the lawyer continued, in a tone as if he were explaining something obvious, unnecessary and incidental, "you have to realise that I also derive great advantage for my clients from mixing with those people, and do so in many different ways, it's not something you can keep talking about all the time. I'm at a bit of a disadvantage now, of course, because of my illness, but I still get visits from some good friends of mine at the court and I learn one or two things. It might even be that I learn more than many of those who are in the best of health and spend all day in court. And I'm receiving a very welcome visit right now, for instance." And he pointed into a dark corner of the room. "Where?" asked K., almost uncouth in his surprise. He looked round uneasily; the little candle gave off far too little light to reach as far as the wall opposite. And then, something did indeed begin to move there in the corner. In the light of the candle held up by K.'s uncle an elderly gentleman could be seen sitting beside a small table. He had been sitting there for so long without being noticed that he could hardly have been breathing. Now he stood up with a great deal of fuss, clearly unhappy that attention had been drawn to him. It was as if, by flapping his hands about like short wings, he hoped to deflect any introductions and greetings, as if he wanted on no account to disturb the others by his presence and seemed to be exhorting them to leave him back in the dark and forget about his being there. That, however, was something that could no longer be granted him. "You took us by surprise, you see," said the lawyer in explanation, cheerfully indicating to the gentleman that he should come closer, which, slowly, hesitatingly, looking all around him, but with a certain dignity, he did. "The office director - oh, yes, forgive me, I haven't introduced you - this is my friend Albert K., this is his nephew, the chief clerk Josef K., and this is the office director - so, the office director was kind enough to pay me a visit. It's only possible to appreciate just how valuable a visit like this is if you've been let into the secret of what a pile of work the office director has heaped over him. Well, he came anyway, we were having a peaceful chat, as far as I was able when I'm so weak, and although we hadn't told Leni she mustn't let anyone in as we weren't expecting anyone, we still would rather have remained alone, but then along came you, Albert, thumping your fists on the door, the office director moved over into the corner pulling his table and chair with him, but now it turns out we might have, that is, if that's what you wish, we might have something to discuss with each other and it would be good if we can all come back together again. - Office director …," he said with his head on one side, pointing with a humble smile to an armchair near the bed. "I'm afraid I'll only be able to stay a few minutes more," smiled the office director as he spread himself out in the armchair and looked at the clock. "Business calls. But I wouldn't want to miss the chance of meeting a friend of my friend." He inclined his head slightly toward K.'s uncle, who seemed very happy with his new acquaintance, but he was not the sort of person to express his feelings of deference and responded to the office director's words with embarrassed, but loud, laughter. A horrible sight! K. was able to quietly watch everything as nobody paid any attention to him, the office director took over as leader of the conversation as seemed to be his habit once he had been called forward, the lawyer listened attentively with his hand to his ear, his initial weakness having perhaps only had the function of driving away his new visitors, K.'s uncle served as candle-bearer - balancing the candle on his thigh while the office director frequently glanced nervously at it - and was soon free of his embarrassment and was quickly enchanted not only by the office director's speaking manner but also by the gentle, waving hand-movements with which he accompanied it. K., leaning against the bedpost, was totally ignored by the office director, perhaps deliberately, and served the old man only as audience. And besides, he had hardly any idea what the conversation was about and his thoughts soon turned to the care assistant and the ill treatment she had suffered from his uncle. Soon after, he began to wonder whether he had not seen the office director somewhere before, perhaps among the people who were at his first hearing. He may have been mistaken, but thought the office director might well have been among the old gentlemen with the thin beards in the first row.

There was then a noise that everyone heard from the hallway as if something of porcelain were being broken. "I'll go and see what's happened," said K., who slowly left the room as if giving the others the chance to stop him. He had hardly stepped into the hallway, finding his bearings in the darkness with his hand still firmly holding the door, when another small hand, much smaller than K.'s own, placed itself on his and gently shut the door. It was the carer who had been waiting there. "Nothing has happened," she whispered to him, "I just threw a plate against the wall to get you out of there." "I was thinking about you, as well," replied K. uneasily. "So much the better," said the carer. "Come with me". A few steps along, they came to a frosted glass door which the carer opened for him. "Come in here," she said. It was clearly the lawyer's office, fitted out with old, heavy furniture, as far as could be seen in the moonlight which now illuminated just a small, rectangular section of the floor by each of the three big windows. "This way," said the carer, pointing to a dark trunk with a carved, wooden backrest. When he had sat down, K. continued to look round the room, it was a large room with a high ceiling, the clients of this lawyer for the poor must have felt quite lost in it. K. thought he could see the little steps with which visitors would approach the massive desk. But then he forgot about all of this and had eyes only for the carer who sat very close beside him, almost pressing him against the armrest. "I did think," she said "you would come out here to me by yourself without me having to call you first. It was odd. First you stare at me as soon as you come in, and then you keep me waiting. And you ought to call me Leni, too," she added quickly and suddenly, as if no moment of this conversation should be lost. "Gladly," said K. "But as for its being odd, Leni, that's easy to explain. Firstly, I had to listen to what the old men were saying and couldn't leave without a good reason, but secondly I'm not a bold person, if anything I'm quite shy, and you, Leni, you didn't really look like you could be won over in one stroke, either." "That's not it," said Leni, laying one arm on the armrest and looking at K., "you didn't like me, and I don't suppose you like me now, either." "Liking wouldn't be very much," said K., evasively. "Oh!" she exclaimed with a smile, thus making use of K.'s comment to gain an advantage over him. So K. remained silent for a while. By now, he had become used to the darkness in the room and was able to make out various fixtures and fittings. He was especially impressed by a large picture hanging to the right of the door, he leant forward in order to see it better. It depicted a man wearing a judge's robes; he was sitting on a lofty throne gilded in a way that shone forth from the picture. The odd thing about the picture was that this judge was not sitting there in dignified calm but had his left arm pressed against the back and armrest, his right arm, however, was completely free and only grasped the armrest with his hand, as if about to jump up any moment in vigorous outrage and make some decisive comment or even to pass sentence. The accused was probably meant to be imagined at the foot of the steps, the top one of which could be seen in the picture, covered with a yellow carpet. "That might be my judge," said K., pointing to the picture with one finger. "I know him," said Leni looking up at the picture, "he comes here quite often. That picture is from when he was young, but he can never have looked anything like it, as he's tiny, minute almost. But despite that, he had himself made to look bigger in the picture as he's madly vain, just like everyone round here. But even I'm vain and that makes me very unhappy that you don't like me." K. replied to that last comment merely by embracing Leni and drawing her towards him, she lay her head quietly on his shoulder. To the rest of it, though, he said, "What rank is he?" "He's an examining judge," she said, taking hold of the hand with which K. held her and playing with his fingers. "Just an examining judge once again," said K. in disappointment, "the senior officials keep themselves hidden. But here he is sitting on a throne." "That's all just made up," said Leni with her face bent over K.'s hand, "really he's sitting on a kitchen chair with an old horse blanket folded over it. But do you have to be always thinking about your trial?" she added slowly. "No, not at all," said K., "I probably even think too little about it." "That's not the mistake you're making," said Leni, "you're too unyielding, that's what I've heard." "Who said that?" asked K., he felt her body against his chest and looked down on her rich, dark, tightly-bound hair. "I'd be saying too much if I told you that," answered Leni. "Please don't ask for names, but do stop making these mistakes of yours, stop being so unyielding, there's nothing you can do to defend yourself from this court, you have to confess. So confess to them as soon as you get the chance. It's only then that they give you the chance to get away, not till then. Only, without help from outside even that's impossible, but you needn't worry about getting this help as I want to help you myself." "You understand a lot about this court and what sort of tricks are needed," said K. as he lifted her, since she was pressing in much too close to him, onto his lap. "That's alright, then," she said, and made herself comfortable on his lap by smoothing out her skirt and adjusting her blouse. Then she hung both her arms around his neck, leant back and took a long look at him. "And what if I don't confess, could you not help me then?" asked K. to test her out. I'm accumulating women to help me, he thought to himself almost in amazement, first Miss Bürstner, then the court usher's wife, and now this little care assistant who seems to have some incomprehensible need for me. The way she sits on my lap as if it were her proper place! "No," answered Leni, slowly shaking her head, "I couldn't help you then. But you don't want my help anyway, it means nothing to you, you're too stubborn and won't be persuaded." Then, after a while she asked, "Do you have a lover?" "No," said K. "Oh, you must have," she said. "Well, I have really," said K. "Just think, I've even betrayed her while I'm carrying her photograph with me." Leni insisted he show her a photograph of Elsa, and then, hunched on his lap, studied the picture closely. The photograph was not one that had been taken while Elsa was posing for it, it showed her just after she had been in a wild dance such as she liked to do in wine bars, her skirt was still flung out as she span round, she had placed her hands on her firm hips and, with her neck held taut, looked to one side with a laugh; you could not see from the picture whom her laugh was intended for. "She's very tightly laced," said Leni, pointing to the place where she thought this could be seen. "I don't like her, she's clumsy and crude. But maybe she's gentle and friendly towards you, that's the impression you get from the picture. Big, strong girls like that often don't know how to be anything but gentle and friendly. Would she be capable of sacrificing herself for you, though?" "No," said K., "she isn't gentle or friendly, and nor would she be capable of sacrificing herself for me. But I've never yet asked any of those things of her. I've never looked at this picture as closely as you." "You can't think much of her, then," said Leni. "She can't be your lover after all." "Yes she is," said K., "I'm not going to take my word back on that." "Well she might be your lover now, then," said Leni, "but you wouldn't miss her much if you lost her or if you exchanged her for somebody else, me for instance." "That is certainly conceivable," said K. with a smile, "but she does have one major advantage over you, she knows nothing about my trial, and even if she did she wouldn't think about it. She wouldn't try to persuade me to be less unyielding." "Well that's no advantage," said Leni. "If she's got no advantage other than that, I can keep on hoping. Has she got any bodily defects?" "'Bodily defects'?" asked K. "Yeah," said Leni, "as I do have a bodily defect, just a little one. Look." She spread the middle and ring fingers of her right hand apart from each other. Between those fingers the flap of skin connecting them reached up almost as far as the top joint of the little finger. In the darkness, K. did not see at first what it was she wanted to show him, so she led his hand to it so that he could feel. "What a freak of nature," said K., and when he had taken a look at the whole hand he added, "What a pretty claw!" Leni looked on with a kind of pride as K. repeatedly opened and closed her two fingers in amazement, until, finally, he briefly kissed them and let go. "Oh!" she immediately exclaimed, "you kissed me!" Hurriedly, and with her mouth open, she clambered up K.'s lap with her knees. He was almost aghast as he looked up at her, now that she was so close to him there was a bitter, irritating smell from her, like pepper, she grasped his head, leant out over him, and bit and kissed his neck, even biting into his hair. "I've taken her place!" she exclaimed from time to time. "Just look, now you've taken me instead of her!" Just then, her knee slipped out and, with a little cry, she nearly fell down onto the carpet, K. tried to hold her by putting his arms around her and was pulled down with her. "Now you're mine," she said. Her last words to him as he left were, "Here's the key to the door, come whenever you want", and she planted an undirected kiss on his back. When he stepped out the front door there was a light rain falling, he was about to go to the middle of the street to see if he could still glimpse Leni at the window when K.'s uncle leapt out of a car that K., thinking of other things, had not seen waiting outside the building. He took hold of K. by both arms and shoved him against the door as if he wanted to nail him to it. "Young man," he shouted, "how could you do a thing like that?! Things were going well with this business of yours, now you've caused it terrible damage. You slip off with some dirty, little thing who, moreover, is obviously the lawyer's beloved, and stay away for hours. You don't even try to find an excuse, don't try to hide anything, no, you're quite open about it, you run off with her and stay there. And meanwhile we're sitting there, your uncle who's going to such effort for you, the lawyer who needs to be won over to your side, and above all the office director, a very important gentleman who is in direct command of your affair in its present stage. We wanted to discuss how best to help you, I had to handle the lawyer very carefully, he had to handle the office director carefully, and you had most reason of all to at least give me some support. Instead of which you stay away. Eventually we couldn't keep up the pretence any longer, but these are polite and highly capable men, they didn't say anything about it so as to spare my feelings but in the end not even they could continue to force themselves and, as they couldn't speak about the matter in hand, they became silent.

We sat there for several minutes, listening to see whether you wouldn't finally come back. All in vain. In the end the office director stood up, as he had stayed far longer than he had originally intended, made his farewell, looked at me in sympathy without being able to help, he waited at the door for a long time although it's more than I can understand why he was being so good, and then he went. I, of course, was glad he'd gone, I'd been holding my breath all this time. All this had even more affect on the lawyer lying there ill, when I took my leave of him, the good man, he was quite unable to speak. You have probably contributed to his total collapse and so brought the very man who you are dependent on closer to his death. And me, your own uncle, you leave me here in the rain - just feel this, I'm wet right through - waiting here for hours, sick with worry."

Chapter Seven Lawyer - Manufacturer - Painter

One winter morning - snow was falling in the dull light outside - K. was sitting in his office, already extremely tired despite the early hour. He had told the servitor he was engaged in a major piece of work and none of the junior staff should be allowed in to see him, so he would not be disturbed by them at least. But instead of working he turned round in his chair, slowly moved various items around his desk, but then, without being aware of it, he lay his arm stretched out on the desk top and sat there immobile with his head sunk down on his chest.

He was no longer able to get the thought of the trial out of his head. He had often wondered whether it might not be a good idea to work out a written defence and hand it in to the court. It would contain a short description of his life and explain why he had acted the way he had at each event that was in any way important, whether he now considered he had acted well or ill, and his reasons for each. There was no doubt of the advantages a written defence of this sort would have over relying on the lawyer, who was anyway not without his shortcomings. K. had no idea what actions the lawyer was taking; it was certainly not a lot, it was more than a month since the lawyer had summoned him, and none of the previous discussions had given K. the impression that this man would be able to do much for him. Most importantly, he had asked him hardly any questions. And there were so many questions here to be asked. Asking questions were the most important thing. K. had the feeling that he would be able to ask all the questions needed here himself. The lawyer, in contrast, did not ask questions but did all the talking himself or sat silently facing him, leant forward slightly over the desk, probably because he was hard of hearing, pulled on a strand of hair in the middle of his beard and looked down at the carpet, perhaps at the very spot where K. had lain with Leni. Now and then he would give K. some vague warning of the sort you give to children. His speeches were as pointless as they were boring, and K. decided that when the final bill came he would pay not a penny for them. Once the lawyer thought he had humiliated K. sufficiently, he usually started something that would raise his spirits again. He had already, he would then say, won many such cases, partly or in whole, cases which may not really have been as difficult as this one but which, on the face of it, had even less hope of success. He had a list of these cases here in the drawer - here he would tap on one or other of the drawers in his desk - but could, unfortunately, not show them to K. as they dealt with official secrets. Nonetheless, the great experience he had acquired through all these cases would, of course, be of benefit to K. He had, of course, begun work straight away and was nearly ready to submit the first documents. They would be very important because the first impression made by the defence will often determine the whole course of the proceedings. Unfortunately, though, he would still have to make it clear to K. that the first documents submitted are sometimes not even read by the court. They simply put them with the other documents and point out that, for the time being, questioning and observing the accused are much more important than anything written. If the applicant becomes insistent, then they add that before they come to any decision, as soon as all the material has been brought together, with due regard, of course, to all the documents, then these first documents to have been submitted will also be checked over. But unfortunately, even this is not usually true, the first documents submitted are usually mislaid or lost completely, and even if they do keep them right to the end they are hardly read, although the lawyer only knew about this from rumour. This is all very regrettable, but not entirely without its justifications. But K. should not forget that the trial would not be public, if the court deems it necessary it can be made public but there is no law that says it has to be. As a result, the accused and his defence don't have access even to the court records, and especially not to the indictment, and that means we generally don't know - or at least not precisely - what the first documents need to be about, which means that if they do contain anything of relevance to the case it's only by a lucky coincidence. If anything about the individual charges and the reasons for them comes out clearly or can be guessed at while the accused is being questioned, then it's possible to work out and submit documents that really direct the issue and present proof, but not before. Conditions like this, of course, place the defence in a very unfavourable and difficult position. But that is what they intend. In fact, defence is not really allowed under the law, it's only tolerated, and there is even some dispute about whether the relevant parts of the law imply even that. So strictly speaking, there is no such thing as a counsel acknowledged by the court, and anyone who comes before this court as counsel is basically no more than a barrack room lawyer. The effect of all this, of course, is to remove the dignity of the whole procedure, the next time K. is in the court offices he might like to have a look in at the lawyers' room, just so that he's seen it. He might well be quite shocked by the people he sees assembled there. The room they've been allocated, with its narrow space and low ceiling, will be enough to show what contempt the court has for these people. The only light in the room comes through a little window that is so high up that, if you want to look out of it, you first have to get one of your colleagues to support you on his back, and even then the smoke from the chimney just in front of it will go up your nose and make your face black. In the floor of this room - to give yet another example of the conditions there - there is a hole that's been there for more than a year, it's not so big that a man could fall through, but it is big enough for your foot to disappear through it. The lawyers' room is on the second floor of the attic; if your foot does go through it will hang down into the first floor of the attic underneath it, and right in the corridor where the litigants are waiting. It's no exaggeration when lawyers say that conditions like that are a disgrace. Complaints to the management don't have the slightest effect, but the lawyers are strictly forbidden to alter anything in the room at their own expense. But even treating the lawyers in this way has its reasons. They want, as far as possible, to prevent any kind of defence, everything should be made the responsibility of the accused. Not a bad point of view, basically, but nothing could be more mistaken than to think from that that lawyers are not necessary for the accused in this court. On the contrary, there is no court where they are less needed than here. This is because proceedings are generally kept secret not only from the public but also from the accused. Only as far as that is possible, of course, but it is possible to a very large extent. And the accused doesn't get to see the court records either, and it's very difficult to infer what's in the court records from what's been said during questioning based on them, especially for the accused who is in a difficult situation and is faced with every possible worry to distract him. This is when the defence begins. Counsel for the defence are not normally allowed to be present while the accused is being questioned, so afterwards, and if possible still at the door of the interview room, he has to learn what he can about it from him and extract whatever he can that might be of use, even though what the accused has to report is often very confused. But that is not the most important thing, as there's really not a lot that can be learned in this way, although in this, as with anything else, a competent man will learn more than another. Nonetheless, the most important thing is the lawyer's personal connections, that's where the real value of taking counsel lies. Now K. will most likely have already learned from his own experience that, among its very lowest orders, the court organisation does have its imperfections, the court is strictly closed to the public, but staff who forget their duty or who take bribes do, to some extent, show where the gaps are. This is where most lawyers will push their way in, this is where bribes are paid and information extracted, there have even, in earlier times at least, been incidents where documents have been stolen. There's no denying that some surprisingly favourable results have been attained for the accused in this way, for a limited time, and these petty advocates then strut to and fro on the basis of them and attract new clients, but for the further course of the proceedings it signifies either nothing or nothing good. The only things of real value are honest personal contacts, contacts with higher officials, albeit higher officials of the lower grades, you understand. That is the only way the progress of the trial can be influenced, hardly noticeable at first, it's true, but from then on it becomes more and more visible. There are, of course, not many lawyers who can do this, and K. has made a very good choice in this matter. There were probably no more than one or two who had as many contacts as Dr. Huld, but they don't bother with the company of the lawyers' room and have nothing to do with it. This means they have all the less contact with the court officials. It is not at all necessary for Dr. Huld to go to the court, wait in the ante-rooms for the examining judges to turn up, if they turn up, and try to achieve something which, according to the judges' mood is usually more apparent than real and most often not even that. No, K. has seen for himself that the court officials, including some who are quite high up, come forward without being asked, are glad to give information which is fully open or at least easy to understand, they discuss the next stages in the proceedings, in fact in some cases they can be won over and are quite willing to adopt the other person's point of view. However, when this happens, you should never trust them too far, as however firmly they may have declared this new point of view in favour of the defendant they might well go straight back to their offices and write a report for the court that says just the opposite, and might well be even harder on the defendant than the original view, the one they insist they've been fully dissuaded from. And, of course, there's no way of defending yourself from this, something said in private is indeed in private and cannot then be used in public, it's not something that makes it easy for the defence to keep those gentlemen's favour. On the other hand, it's also true that the gentlemen don't become involved with the defence - which will of course be done with great expertise - just for philanthropic reasons or in order to be friendly, in some respects it would be truer to say that they, too, have it allocated to them. This is where the disadvantages of a court structure that, right from the start, stipulates that all proceedings take place in private, come into force. In normal, mediocre trials its officials have contact with the public, and they're very well equipped for it, but here they don't; normal trials run their course all by themselves, almost, and just need a nudge here and there; but when they're faced with cases that are especially difficult they're as lost as they often are with ones that are very simple; they're forced to spend all their time, day and night, with their laws, and so they don't have the right feel for human relationships, and that's a serious shortcoming in cases like this. That's when they come for advice to the lawyer, with a servant behind them carrying the documents which normally are kept so secret. You could have seen many gentlemen at this window, gentlemen of whom you would least expect it, staring out this window in despair on the street below while the lawyer is at his desk studying the documents so that he can give them good advice. And at times like that it's also possible to see how exceptionally seriously these gentlemen take their professions and how they are thrown into great confusion by difficulties which it's just not in their natures to overcome. But they're not in an easy position, to regard their positions as easy would be to do them an injustice. The different ranks and hierarchies of the court are endless, and even someone who knows his way around them cannot always tell what's going to happen. But even for the junior officials, the proceedings in the courtrooms are usually kept secret, so they are hardly able to see how the cases they work with proceed, court affairs appear in their range of vision often without their knowing where they come from and they move on further without their learning where they go. So civil servants like this are not able to learn the things you can learn from studying the successive stages that individual trials go through, the final verdict or the reasons for it. They're only allowed to deal with that part of the trial which the law allocates them, and they usually know less about the results of their work after it's left them than the defence does, even though the defence will usually stay in contact with the accused until the trial is nearly at its end, so that the court officials can learn many useful things from the defence. Bearing all this in mind, does it still surprise K. that the officials are irritated and often express themselves about the litigants in unflattering ways - which is an experience shared by everyone. All the officials are irritated, even when they appear calm. This causes many difficulties for the junior advocates, of course. There is a story, for instance, that has very much the ring of truth about it. It goes like this: One of the older officials, a good and peaceful man, was dealing with a difficult matter for the court which had become very confused, especially thanks to the contributions from the lawyers. He had been studying it for a day and a night without a break - as these officials are indeed hard working, no-one works as hard as they do. When it was nearly morning, and he had been working for twenty-four hours with probably very little result, he went to the front entrance, waited there in ambush, and every time a lawyer tried to enter the building he would throw him down the steps. The lawyers gathered together down in front of the steps and discussed with each other what they should do; on the one hand they had actually no right to be allowed into the building so that there was hardly anything that they could legally do to the official and, as I've already mentioned, they would have to be careful not to set all the officials against them. On the other hand, any day not spent in court is a day lost for them and it was a matter of some importance to force their way inside. In the end, they agreed that they would try to tire the old man out. One lawyer after another was sent out to run up the steps and let himself be thrown down again, offering what resistance he could as long as it was passive resistance, and his colleagues would catch him at the bottom of the steps. That went on for about an hour until the old gentleman, who was already exhausted from working all night, was very tired and went back to his office. Those who were at the bottom of the steps could not believe it at first, so they sent somebody out to go and look behind the door to see if there really was no-one there, and only then did they all gather together and probably didn't even dare to complain, as it's far from being the lawyers' job to introduce any improvements in the court system, or even to want to. Even the most junior lawyer can understand the relationship there to some extent, but one significant point is that almost every defendant, even very simple people, begins to think of suggestions for improving the court as soon as his proceedings have begun, many of them often even spend time and energy on the matter that could be spent far better elsewhere. The only right thing to do is to learn how to deal with the situation as it is. Even if it were possible to improve any detail of it - which is anyway no more than superstitious nonsense - the best that they could achieve, although doing themselves incalculable harm in the process, is that they will have attracted the special attention of the officials for any case that comes up in the future, and the officials are always ready to seek revenge. Never attract attention to yourself! Stay calm, however much it goes against your character! Try to gain some insight into the size of the court organism and how, to some extent, it remains in a state of suspension, and that even if you alter something in one place you'll draw the ground out from under your feet and might fall, whereas if an enormous organism like the court is disrupted in any one place it finds it easy to provide a substitute for itself somewhere else. Everything is connected with everything else and will continue without any change or else, which is quite probable, even more closed, more attentive, more strict, more malevolent. So it's best to leave the work to the lawyers and not to keep disturbing them. It doesn't do much good to make accusations, especially if you can't make it clear what they're based on and their full significance, but it must be said that K. caused a great deal of harm to his own case by his behaviour towards the office director, he was a very influential man but now he might as well be struck off the list of those who might do anything for K. If the trial is mentioned, even just in passing, it's quite obvious that he's ignoring it. These officials are in many ways just like children. Often, something quite harmless - although K.'s behaviour could unfortunately not be called harmless - will leave them feeling so offended that they will even stop talking with good friends of theirs, they turn away when they see them and do everything they can to oppose them. But then, with no particular reason, surprisingly enough, some little joke that was only ever attempted because everything seemed so hopeless will make them laugh and they'll be reconciled. It's both difficult and hard at the same time to deal with them, and there's hardly any reason for it. It's sometimes quite astonishing that a single, average life is enough to encompass so much that it's at all possible ever to have any success in one's work here. On the other hand, there are also dark moments, such as everyone has, when you think you've achieved nothing at all, when it seems that the only trials to come to a good end are those that were determined to have a good end from the start and would do so without any help, while all the others are lost despite all the running to and fro, all the effort, all the little, apparent successes that gave such joy. Then you no longer feel very sure of anything and, if asked about a trial that was doing well by its own nature but which was turned for the worse because you assisted in it, would not even dare deny that. And even that is a kind of self- confidence, but then it's the only one that's left. Lawyers are especially vulnerable to fits of depression of that sort - and they are no more than fits of depression of course - when a case is suddenly taken out of their hands after they've been conducting it satisfactorily for some time. That's probably the worst that can happen to a lawyer. It's not that the accused takes the case away from him, that hardly ever happens, once a defendant has taken on a certain lawyer he has to stay with him whatever happens. How could he ever carry on by himself after he's taken on help from a lawyer? No, that just doesn't happen, but what does sometimes happen is that the trial takes on a course where the lawyer may not go along with it. Client and trial are both simply taken away from the lawyer; and then even contact with the court officials won't help, however good they are, as they don't know anything themselves. The trial will have entered a stage where no more help can be given, where it's being processed in courts to which no-one has any access, where the defendant cannot even be contacted by his lawyer. You come home one day and find all the documents you've submitted, which you've worked hard to create and which you had the best hopes for, lying on the desk, they've been sent back as they can't be carried through to the next stage in the trial, they're just worthless scraps of paper. It doesn't mean that the case has been lost, not at all, or at least there is no decisive reason for supposing so, it's just that you don't know anything more about the case and won't be told anything of what's happening. Well, cases like that are the exceptions, I'm glad to say, and even if K.'s trial is one of them, it's still, for the time being, a long way off. But there was still plenty of opportunity for lawyers to get to work, and K. could be sure they would be made use of. As he had said, the time for submitting documents was still in the future and there was no rush to prepare them, it was much more important to start the initial discussions with the appropriate officials, and they had already taken place. With varying degrees of success, it must be said. It was much better not to give away any details before their time, as in that way K. could only be influenced unfavourably and his hopes might be raised or he might be made too anxious, better just to say that some individuals have spoken very favourably and shown themselves very willing to help, although others have spoken less favourably, but even they have not in any way refused to help. So all in all, the results are very encouraging, only you should certainly not draw any particular conclusions as all preliminary proceedings begin in the same way and it was only the way they developed further that would show what the value of these preliminary proceedings has been. Anyway, nothing has been lost yet, and if we can succeed in getting the office director, despite everything, on our side - and several actions have been undertaken to this end - then everything is a clean wound, as a surgeon would say, and we can wait for the results with some comfort.

When he started talking on in this way the lawyer was quite tireless. He went through it all again every time K. went to see him. There was always some progress, but he could never be told what sort of progress it was. The first set of documents to be submitted were being worked on but still not ready, which usually turned out to be a great advantage the next time K. went to see him as the earlier occasion would have been a very bad time to put them in, which they could not then have known. If K., stupefied from all this talking, ever pointed out that even considering all these difficulties progress was very slow, the lawyer would object that progress was not slow at all, but that they might have progressed far further if K. had come to him at the right time. But he had come to him late and that lateness would bring still further difficulties, and not only where time was concerned. The only welcome interruption during these visits was always when Leni contrived to bring the lawyer his tea while K. was there. Then she would stand behind K. - pretending to watch the lawyer as he bent greedily over his cup, poured the tea in and drank - and secretly let K. hold her hand. There was always complete silence. The lawyer drank. K. squeezed Leni's hand and Leni would sometimes dare to gently stroke K.'s hair. "Still here, are you?" the lawyer would ask when he was ready. "I wanted to take the dishes away," said Leni, they would give each other's hands a final squeeze, the lawyer would wipe his mouth and then start talking at K. again with renewed energy.

Was the lawyer trying to comfort K. or to confuse him? K. could not tell, but it seemed clear to him that his defence was not in good hands. Maybe everything the lawyer said was quite right, even though he obviously wanted to make himself as conspicuous as possible and probably had never even taken on a case as important as he said K.'s was. But it was still suspicious how he continually mentioned his personal contacts with the civil servants. Were they to be exploited solely for K.'s benefit? The lawyer never forgot to mention that they were dealing only with junior officials, which meant officials who were dependent on others, and the direction taken in each trial could be important for their own furtherment. Could it be that they were making use of the lawyer to turn trials in a certain direction, which would, of course, always be at the cost of the defendant? It certainly did not mean that they would do that in every trial, that was not likely at all, and there were probably also trials where they gave the lawyer advantages and all the room he needed to turn it in the direction he wanted, as it would also be to their advantage to keep his reputation intact. If that really was their relationship, how would they direct K.'s trial which, as the lawyer had explained, was especially difficult and therefore important enough to attract great attention from the very first time it came to court? There could not be much doubt about what they would do. The first signs of it could already be seen in the fact that the first documents still had not been submitted even though the trial had already lasted several months, and that, according to the lawyer, everything was still in its initial stages, which was very effective, of course, in making the defendant passive and keeping him helpless. Then he could be suddenly surprised with the verdict, or at least with a notification that the hearing had not decided in his favour and the matter would be passed on to a higher office.

It was essential that K. take a hand in it himself. On winter's mornings such as this, when he was very tired and everything dragged itself lethargically through his head, this belief of his seemed irrefutable. He no longer felt the contempt for the trial that he had had earlier. If he had been alone in the world it would have been easy for him to ignore it, although it was also certain that, in that case, the trial would never have arisen in the first place. But now, his uncle had already dragged him to see the lawyer, he had to take account of his family; his job was no longer totally separate from the progress of the trial, he himself had carelessly - with a certain, inexplicable complacency - mentioned it to acquaintances and others had learned about it in ways he did not know, his relationship with Miss Bürstner seemed to be in trouble because of it. In short, he no longer had any choice whether he would accept the trial or turn it down, he was in the middle of it and had to defend himself. If he was tired, then that was bad.

But there was no reason to worry too much before he needed to. He had been capable of working himself up to his high position in the bank in a relatively short time and to retain it with respect from everyone, now he simply had to apply some of the talents that had made that possible for him to the trial, and there was no doubt that it had to turn out well. The most important thing, if something was to be achieved, was to reject in advance any idea that he might be in any way guilty. There was no guilt. The trial was nothing but a big piece of business, just like he had already concluded to the benefit of the bank many times, a piece of business that concealed many lurking dangers waiting in ambush for him, as they usually did, and these dangers would need to be defended against. If that was to be achieved then he must not entertain any idea of guilt, whatever he did, he would need to look after his own interests as closely as he could. Seen in this way, there was no choice but to take his representation away from the lawyer very soon, at best that very evening. The lawyer had told him, as he talked to him, that that was something unheard of and would probably do him a great deal of harm, but K. could not tolerate any impediment to his efforts where his trial was concerned, and these impediments were probably caused by the lawyer himself. But once he had shaken off the lawyer the documents would need to be submitted straight away and, if possible, he would need to see to it that they were being dealt with every day. It would of course not be enough, if that was to be done, for K. to sit in the corridor with his hat under the bench like the others. Day after day, he himself, or one of the women or somebody else on his behalf, would have to run after the officials and force them to sit at their desks and study K.'s documents instead of looking out on the corridor through the grating. There could be no let-up in these efforts, everything would need to be organised and supervised, it was about time that the court came up against a defendant who knew how to defend and make use of his rights.

But when K. had the confidence to try and do all this the difficulty of composing the documents was too much for him. Earlier, just a week or so before, he could only have felt shame at the thought of being made to write out such documents himself; it had never entered his head that the task could also be difficult. He remembered one morning when, already piled up with work, he suddenly shoved everything to one side and took a pad of paper on which he sketched out some of his thoughts on how documents of this sort should proceed. Perhaps he would offer them to that slow-witted lawyer, but just then the door of the manager's office opened and the deputy-director entered the room with a loud laugh. K. was very embarrassed, although the deputy-director, of course, was not laughing at K.'s documents, which he knew nothing about, but at a joke he had just heard about the stock-exchange, a joke which needed an illustration if it was to be understood, and now the deputy-director leant over K.'s desk, took his pencil from his hand, and drew the illustration on the writing pad that K. had intended for his ideas about his case.

K. now had no more thoughts of shame, the documents had to be prepared and submitted. If, as was very likely, he could find no time to do it in the office he would have to do it at home at night. If the nights weren't enough he would have to take a holiday. Above all, he could not stop half way, that was nonsense not only in business but always and everywhere. Needless to say, the documents would mean an almost endless amount of work. It was easy to come to the belief, not only for those of an anxious disposition, that it was impossible ever to finish it. This was not because of laziness or deceit, which were the only things that might have hindered the lawyer in preparing it, but because he did not know what the charge was or even what consequences it might bring, so that he had to remember every tiny action and event from the whole of his life, looking at them from all sides and checking and reconsidering them. It was also a very disheartening job. It would have been more suitable as a way of passing the long days after he had retired and become senile. But now, just when K. needed to apply all his thoughts to his work, when he was still rising and already posed a threat to the deputy-director, when every hour passed so quickly and he wanted to enjoy the brief evenings and nights as a young man, this was the time he had to start working out these documents. Once more, he began to feel resentment. Almost involuntarily, only to put an end to it, his finger felt for the button of the electric bell in the ante-room. As he pressed it he glanced up to the clock. It was eleven o'clock, two hours, he had spent a great deal of his costly time just dreaming and his wits were, of course, even more dulled than they had been before. But the time had, nonetheless, not been wasted, he had come to some decisions that could be of value. As well as various pieces of mail, the servitors brought two visiting cards from gentlemen who had already been waiting for K. for some time. They were actually very important clients of the bank who should not really have been kept waiting under any circumstances. Why had they come at such an awkward time, and why, the gentlemen on the other side of the closed door seemed to be asking, was the industrious K. using up the best business time for his private affairs? Tired from what had gone before, and tired in anticipation of what was to follow, K. stood up to receive the first of them.

He was a short, jolly man, a manufacturer who K. knew well. He apologised for disturbing K. at some important work, and K., for his part, apologised for having kept the manufacturer waiting for so long. But even this apology was spoken in such a mechanical way and with such false intonation that the manufacturer would certainly have noticed if he had not been fully preoccupied with his business affairs. Instead, he hurriedly pulled calculations and tables out from all his pockets, spread them out in front of K., explained several items, corrected a little mistake in the arithmetic that he noticed as he quickly glanced over it all, and reminded K. of a similar piece of business he'd concluded with him about a year before, mentioning in passing that this time there was another bank spending great effort to get his business, and finally stopped speaking in order to learn K.'s opinion on the matter. And K. had indeed, at first, been closely following what the manufacturer was saying, he too was aware of how important the deal was, but unfortunately it did not last, he soon stopped listening, nodded at each of the manufacturer's louder exclamations for a short while, but eventually he stopped doing even that and did no more than stare at the bald head bent over the papers, asking himself when the manufacturer would finally realise that everything he was saying was useless. When he did stop talking, K. really thought at first that this was so that he would have the chance to confess that he was incapable of listening. Instead, seeing the anticipation on the manufacturer's face, obviously ready to counter any objections made, he was sorry to realise that the business discussion had to be continued. So he bent his head as if he'd been given an order and began slowly to move his pencil over the papers, now and then he would stop and stare at one of the figures. The manufacturer thought there must be some objection, perhaps his figures weren't really sound, perhaps they weren't the decisive issue, whatever he thought, the manufacturer covered the papers with his hand and began once again, moving very close to K., to explain what the deal was all about. "It is difficult," said K., pursing his lips. The only thing that could offer him any guidance were the papers, and the manufacturer had covered them from his view, so he just sank back against the arm of the chair. Even when the door of the manager's office opened and revealed not very clearly, as if through a veil, the deputy director, he did no more than look up weakly. K. thought no more about the matter, he merely watched the immediate effect of the deputy director's appearance and, for him, the effect was very pleasing; the manufacturer immediately jumped up from his seat and hurried over to meet the deputy director, although K. would have liked to make him ten times livelier as he feared the deputy director might disappear again. He need not have worried, the two gentlemen met each other, shook each other's hand and went together over to K.'s desk. The manufacturer said he was sorry to find the chief clerk so little inclined to do business, pointing to K. who, under the view of the deputy director, had bent back down over the papers. As the two men leant over the desk and the manufacturer made some effort to gain and keep the deputy director's attention, K. felt as if they were much bigger than they really were and that their negotiations were about him. Carefully and slowly turning his eyes upwards, he tried to learn what was taking place above him, took one of the papers from his desk without looking to see what it was, lay it on the flat of his hand and raised it slowly up as he rose up to the level of the two men himself. He had no particular plan in mind as he did this, but merely felt this was how he would act if only he had finished preparing that great document that was to remove his burden entirely. The deputy director had been paying all his attention to the conversation and did no more than glance at the paper, he did not read what was written on it at all as what was important for the chief clerk was not important for him, he took it from K.'s hand saying, "Thank you, I'm already familiar with everything", and lay it calmly back on the desk. K. gave him a bitter, sideways look. But the deputy director did not notice this at all, or if he did notice it it only raised his spirits, he frequently laughed out loud, one time he clearly embarrassed the manufacturer when he raised an objection in a witty way but drew him immediately back out of his embarrassment by commenting adversely on himself, and finally invited him into his office where they could bring the matter to its conclusion. "It's a very important matter," said the manufacturer. "I understand that completely. And I'm sure the chief clerk …" - even as he said this he was actually speaking only to the manufacturer - "will be very glad to have us take it off his hands. This is something that needs calm consideration. But he seems to be over-burdened today, there are even some people in the room outside who've been waiting there for hours for him." K. still had enough control of himself to turn away from the deputy director and direct his friendly, albeit stiff, smile only at the manufacturer, he made no other retaliation, bent down slightly and supported himself with both hands on his desk like a clerk, and watched as the two gentlemen, still talking, took the papers from his desk and disappeared into the manager's office. In the doorway, the manufacturer turned and said he wouldn't make his farewell with K. just yet, he would of course let the chief clerk know about the success of his discussions but he also had a little something to tell him about.

    At last, K. was by himself. It did not enter his head to show anyone else into his office and only became vaguely aware of how nice it was that the people outside thought he was still negotiating with the manufacturer and, for this reason, he could not let anyone in to see him, not even the servitor. He went over to the window, sat down on the ledge beside it, held firmly on to the handle and looked down onto the square outside. The snow was still falling, the weather still had not brightened up at all.

    He remained a long time sitting in this way, not knowing what it actually was that made him so anxious, only occasionally did he glance, slightly startled, over his shoulder at the door to the outer room where, mistakenly, he thought he'd heard some noise. No-one came, and that made him feel calmer, he went over to the wash stand, rinsed his face with cold water and, his head somewhat clearer, went back to his place by the window. The decision to take his defence into his own hands now seemed more of a burden than he had originally assumed. All the while he had left his defence up to the lawyer his trial had had little basic affect on him, he had observed it from afar as something that was scarcely able to reach him directly, when it suited him he looked to see how things stood but he was also able to draw his head back again whenever he wanted. Now, in contrast, if he was to conduct his defence himself, he would have to devote himself entirely to the court - for the time being, at least - success would mean, later on, his complete and conclusive liberation, but if he was to achieve this he would have to place himself, to start with, in far greater danger than he had been in so far. If he ever felt tempted to doubt this, then his experience with the deputy director and the manufacturer that day would be quite enough to convince him of it. How could he have sat there totally convinced of the need to do his own defence? How would it be later? What would his life be like in the days ahead? Would he find the way through it all to a happy conclusion? Did a carefully worked out defence - and any other sort would have made no sense - did a carefully worked out defence not also mean he would need to shut himself off from everything else as much as he could? Would he survive that? And how was he to succeed in conducting all this at the bank? It involved much more than just submitting some documents that he could probably prepare in a few days' leave, although it would have been great temerity to ask for time off from the bank just at that time, it was a whole trial and there was no way of seeing how long it might last. This was an enormous difficulty that had suddenly been thrown into K.'s life!

And was he supposed to be doing the bank's work at a time like this? He looked down at his desk. Was he supposed to let people in to see him and go into negotiations with them at a time like this? While his trial trundled on, while the court officials upstairs in the attic room sat looking at the papers for this trial, should he be worrying about the business of the bank? Did this not seem like a kind of torture, acknowledged by the court, connected with the trial and which followed him around? And is it likely that anyone in the bank, when judging his work, would take any account of his peculiar situation? No- one and never. There were those who knew about his trial, although it was not quite clear who knew about it or how much. But he hoped rumours had not reached as far as the deputy director, otherwise he would obviously soon find a way of making use of it to harm K., he would show neither comradeship nor humaneness. And what about the director? It was true that he was well disposed towards K., and as soon as he heard about the trial he would probably try to do everything he could to make it easier for him, but he would certainly not devote himself to it. K. at one time had provided the counter-balance to what the deputy director said but the director was now coming more and more under his influence, and the deputy director would also exploit the weakened condition of the director to strengthen his own power. So what could K. hope for? Maybe considerations of this sort weakened his power of resistance, but it was still necessary not to deceive oneself and to see everything as clearly as it could be seen at that moment.

For no particular reason, just to avoiding returning to his desk for a while, he opened the window. It was difficult to open and he had to turn the handle with both his hands. Then, through the whole height and breadth of the window, the mixture of fog and smoke was drawn into the room, filling it with a slight smell of burning. A few flakes of snow were blown in with it. "It's a horrible autumn," said the manufacturer, who had come into the room unnoticed after seeing the deputy director and now stood behind K. K. nodded and looked uneasily at the manufacturer's briefcase, from which he would now probably take the papers and inform K. of the result of his negotiations with the deputy director. However, the manufacturer saw where K. was looking, knocked on his briefcase and without opening it said, "You'll be wanting to hear how things turned out. I've already got the contract in my pocket, almost. He's a charming man, your deputy director - he's got his dangers, though." He laughed as he shook K.'s hand and wanted to make him laugh with him. But to K., it once more seemed suspicious that the manufacturer did not want to show him the papers and saw nothing about his comments to laugh at. "Chief clerk," said the manufacturer, "I expect the weather's been affecting your mood, has it? You're looking so worried today." "Yes," said K., raising his hand and holding the temple of his head, "headaches, worries in the family." "Quite right," said the manufacturer, who was always in a hurry and could never listen to anyone for very long, "everyone has his cross to bear." K. had unconsciously made a step towards the door as if wanting to show the manufacturer out, but the manufacturer said, "Chief clerk, there's something else I'd like to mention to you. I'm very sorry if it's something that'll be a burden to you today of all days but I've been to see you twice already, lately, and each time I forgot all about it. If I delay it any longer it might well lose its point altogether. That would be a pity, as I think what I've got to say does have some value." Before K. had had the time to answer, the manufacturer came up close to him, tapped his knuckle lightly on his chest and said quietly, "You've got a trial going on, haven't you?" K. stepped back and immediately exclaimed, "That's what the deputy director's been telling you!" "No, no," said the manufacturer, "how would the deputy director know about it?" "And what about you?" asked K., already more in control of himself. "I hear things about the court here and there," said the manufacturer, "and that even applies to what it is that I wanted to tell you about." "There are so many people who have connections with the court!" said K. with lowered head, and he led the manufacturer over to his desk. They sat down where they had been before, and the manufacturer said, "I'm afraid it's not very much that I've got to tell you about. Only, in matters like this, it's best not to overlook the tiniest details. Besides, I really want to help you in some way, however modest my help might be. We've been good business partners up till now, haven't we? Well then." K. wanted to apologise for his behaviour in the conversation earlier that day, but the manufacturer would tolerate no interruption, shoved his briefcase up high in his armpit to show that he was in a hurry, and carried on. "I know about your case through a certain Titorelli. He's a painter, Titorelli's just his artistic name, I don't even know what his real name is. He's been coming to me in my office for years from time to time, and brings little pictures with him which I buy more or less just for the sake of charity as he's hardly more than a beggar. And they're nice pictures, too, moorland landscapes and that sort of thing. We'd both got used to doing business in this way and it always went smoothly. Only, one time these visits became a bit too frequent, I began to tell him off for it, we started talking and I became interested how it was that he could earn a living just by painting, and then I learned to my amazement that his main source of income was painting portraits. 'I work for the court,' he said, 'what court?' said I. And that's when he told me about the court. I'm sure you can imagine how amazed I was at being told all this. Ever since then I learn something new about the court every time he comes to visit, and so little by little I get to understand something of how it works. Anyway, Titorelli talks a lot and I often have to push him away, not only because he's bound to be lying but also, most of all, because a businessman like me who's already close to breaking point under the weight of his own business worries can't pay too much attention to other people's. But all that's just by the by. Perhaps - this is what I've been thinking - perhaps Titorelli might be able to help you in some small way, he knows lots of judges and even if he can't have much influence himself he can give you some advice about how to get some influential people on your side. And even if this advice doesn't turn out to make all the difference I still think it'll be very important once you've got it. You're nearly a lawyer yourself. That's what I always say, Mr. K. the chief clerk is nearly a lawyer. Oh I'm sure this trial of yours will turn out all right. So do you want to go and see Titorelli, then? If I ask him to he'll certainly do everything he possibly can. I really do think you ought to go. It needn't be today, of course, just some time, when you get the chance. And anyway - I want to tell you this too - you don't actually have to go and see Titorelli, this advice from me doesn't place you under any obligation at all. No, if you think you can get by without Titorelli it'll certainly be better to leave him completely out of it. Maybe you've already got a clear idea of what you're doing and Titorelli could upset your plans. No, if that's the case then of course you shouldn't go there under any circumstances! And it certainly won't be easy to take advice from a lad like that. Still, it's up to you. Here's the letter of recommendation and here's the address."

Disappointed, K. took the letter and put it in his pocket. Even at best, the advantage he might derive from this recommendation was incomparably smaller than the damage that lay in the fact of the manufacturer knowing about his trial, and that the painter was spreading the news about. It was all he could manage to give the manufacturer, who was already on his way to the door, a few words of thanks. "I'll go there," he said as he took his leave of the manufacturer at the door, "or, as I'm very busy at present, I'll write to him, perhaps he would like to come to me in my office some time." "I was sure you'd find the best solution," said the manufacturer. "Although I had thought you'd prefer to avoid inviting people like this Titorelli to the bank and talking about the trial here. And it's not always a good idea to send letters to people like Titorelli, you don't know what might happen to them. But you're bound to have thought everything through and you know what you can and can't do." K. nodded and accompanied the manufacturer on through the ante-room. But despite seeming calm on the outside he was actually very shocked; he had told the manufacturer he would write to Titorelli only to show him in some way that he valued his recommendations and would consider the opportunity to speak with Titorelli without delay, but if he had thought Titorelli could offer any worthwhile assistance he would not have delayed. But it was only the manufacturer's comment that made K. realise what dangers that could lead to. Was he really able to rely on his own understanding so little? If it was possible that he might invite a questionable character into the bank with a clear letter, and ask advice from him about his trial, separated from the deputy director by no more than a door, was it not possible or even very likely that there were also other dangers he had failed to see or that he was even running towards? There was not always someone beside him to warn him. And just now, just when he would have to act with all the strength he could muster, now a number of doubts of a sort he had never before known had presented themselves and affected his own vigilance! The difficulties he had been feeling in carrying out his office work; were they now going to affect the trial too? Now, at least, he found himself quite unable to understand how he could have intended to write to Titorelli and invite him into the bank.

He shook his head at the thought of it once more as the servitor came up beside him and drew his attention to the three gentlemen who were waiting on a bench in the ante-room. They had already been waiting to see K. for a long time. Now that the servitor was speaking with K. they had stood up and each of them wanted to make use of the opportunity to see K. before the others. It had been negligent of the bank to let them waste their time here in the waiting room, but none of them wanted to draw attention to this. "Mr. K., ..." one of them was saying, but K. had told the servitor to fetch his winter coat and said to the three of them, as the servitor helped him to put it on, "Please forgive me, gentlemen, I'm afraid I have no time to see you at present. Please do forgive me but I have some urgent business to settle and have to leave straight away. You've already seen yourselves how long I've been delayed. Would you be so kind as to come back tomorrow or some time? Or perhaps we could settle your affairs by telephone? Or perhaps you would like to tell me now, briefly, what it's about and I can then give you a full answer in writing. Whatever, the best thing will be for you to come here again." The gentlemen now saw that their wait had been totally pointless, and these suggestions of K.'s left them so astounded that they looked at each other without a word. "That's agreed then, is it?" asked K., who had turned toward the servitor bringing him his hat. Through the open door of K.'s office they could see that the snowfall outside had become much heavier. So K. turned the collar of his coat up and buttoned it up high under his chin. Just then the deputy director came out of the adjoining room, smiled as he saw K. negotiating with the gentlemen in his winter coat, and asked, "Are you about to go out?" "Yes," said K., standing more upright, "I have to go out on some business." But the deputy director had already turned towards the gentlemen. "And what about these gentlemen?" he asked. "I think they've already been waiting quite a long time." "We've already come to an understanding," said K. But now the gentlemen could be held back no longer, they surrounded K. and explained that they would not have been waiting for hours if it had not been about something important that had to be discussed now, at length and in private. The deputy director listened to them for a short while, he also looked at K. as he held his hat in his hand cleaning the dust off it here and there, and then he said, "Gentlemen, there is a very simple way to solve this. If you would prefer it, I'll be very glad to take over these negotiations instead of the chief clerk. Your business does, of course, need to be discussed without delay. We are businessmen like yourselves and know the value of a businessman's time. Would you like to come this way?" And he opened the door leading to the ante-room of his own office.

The deputy director seemed very good at appropriating everything that K. was now forced to give up! But was K. not giving up more than he absolutely had to? By running off to some unknown painter, with, as he had to admit, very little hope of any vague benefit, his renown was suffering damage that could not be repaired. It would probably be much better to take off his winter coat again and, at the very least, try to win back the two gentlemen who were certainly still waiting in the next room. If K. had not then glimpsed the deputy director in his office, looking for something from his bookshelves as if they were his own, he would probably even have made the attempt. As K., somewhat agitated, approached the door the deputy director called out, "Oh, you've still not left!" He turned his face toward him - its many deep folds seemed to show strength rather than age - and immediately began once more to search. "I'm looking for a copy of a contract," he said, "which this gentleman insists you must have. Could you help me look for it, do you think?" K. made a step forward, but the deputy director said, "thank you, I've already found it," and with a big package of papers, which certainly must have included many more documents than just the copy of the contract, he turned and went back into his own office.

"I can't deal with him right now," K. said to himself, "but once my personal difficulties have been settled, then he'll certainly be the first to get the effect of it, and he certainly won't like it." Slightly calmed by these thoughts, K. gave the servitor, who had already long been holding the door to the corridor open for him, the task of telling the director, when he was able, that K. was going out of the bank on a business matter. As he left the bank he felt almost happy at the thought of being able to devote more of himself to his own business for a while.

He went straight to the painter, who lived in an outlying part of town which was very near to the court offices, although this area was even poorer, the houses were darker, the streets were full of dirt that slowly blew about over the half-melted snow. In the great gateway to the building where the painter lived only one of the two doors was open, a hole had been broken open in the wall by the other door, and as K. approached it a repulsive, yellow, steaming liquid shot out causing some rats to scurry away into the nearby canal. Down by the staircase there was a small child lying on its belly crying, but it could hardly be heard because of the noise from a metal-workshop on the other side of the entrance hall, drowning out any other sound. The door to the workshop was open, three workers stood in a circle around some piece of work that they were beating with hammers. A large tin plate hung on the wall, casting a pale light that pushed its way in between two of the workers, lighting up their faces and their work-aprons. K. did no more than glance at any of these things, he wanted to get things over with here as soon as possible, to exchange just a few words to find out how things stood with the painter and go straight back to the bank. Even if he had just some tiny success here it would still have a good effect on his work at the bank for that day. On the third floor he had to slow down his pace, he was quite out of breath - the steps, just like the height of each floor, were much higher than they needed to be and he'd been told that the painter lived right up in the attic. The air was also quite oppressive, there was no proper stairwell and the narrow steps were closed in by walls on both sides with no more than a small, high window here and there. Just as K. paused for a while some young girls ran out of one of the flats and rushed higher up the stairs, laughing. K. followed them slowly, caught up with one of the girls who had stumbled and been left behind by the others, and asked her as they went up side by side, "Is there a painter, Titorelli, who lives here?" The girl, hardly thirteen years old and somewhat hunchbacked, jabbed him with her elbow and looked at him sideways. Her youth and her bodily defects had done nothing to stop her being already quite depraved. She did not smile once, but looked at K. earnestly, with sharp, acquisitive eyes. K. pretended not to notice her behaviour and asked, "Do you know Titorelli, the painter?" She nodded and asked in reply, "What d'you want to see him for?" K. thought it would be to his advantage quickly to find out something more about Titorelli. "I want to have him paint my portrait," he said. "Paint your portrait?" she asked, opening her mouth too wide and lightly hitting K. with her hand as if he had said something extraordinarily surprising or clumsy, with both hands she lifted her skirt, which was already very short, and, as fast as she could, she ran off after the other girls whose indistinct shouts lost themselves in the heights. At the next turn of the stairs, however, K. encountered all the girls once more. The hunchbacked girl had clearly told them about K.'s intentions and they were waiting for him. They stood on both sides of the stairs, pressing themselves against the wall so that K. could get through between them, and smoothed their aprons down with their hands. All their faces, even in this guard of honour, showed a mixture of childishness and depravity. Up at the head of the line of girls, who now, laughing, began to close in around K., was the hunchback who had taken on the role of leader. It was thanks to her that K. found the right direction without delay - he would have continued up the stairs straight in front of him, but she showed him that to reach Titorelli he would need to turn off to one side. The steps that led up to the painter were especially narrow, very long without any turning, the whole length could be seen in one glance and, at the top, at Titorelli's closed door, it came to its end. This door was much better illuminated than the rest of the stairway by the light from a small skylight set obliquely above it, it had been put together from unpainted planks of wood and the name 'Titorelli' was painted on it in broad, red brushstrokes. K. was no more than half way up the steps, accompanied by his retinue of girls, when, clearly the result of the noise of all those footsteps, the door opened slightly and in the crack a man who seemed to be dressed in just his nightshirt appeared. "Oh!" he cried, when he saw the approaching crowd, and vanished. The hunchbacked girl clapped her hands in glee and the other girls crowded in behind K. to push him faster forward.

They still had not arrived at the top, however, when the painter up above them suddenly pulled the door wide open and, with a deep bow, invited K. to enter. The girls, on the other hand, he tried to keep away, he did not want to let any of them in however much they begged him and however much they tried to get in - if they could not get in with his permission they would try to force their way in against his will. The only one to succeed was the hunchback when she slipped through under his outstretched arm, but the painter chased after her, grabbed her by the skirt, span her once round and set her down again by the door with the other girls who, unlike the first, had not dared to cross the doorstep while the painter had left his post. K. did not know what he was to make of all this, as they all seemed to be having fun. One behind the other, the girls by the door stretched their necks up high and called out various words to the painter which were meant in jest but which K. did not understand, and even the painter laughed as the hunchback whirled round in his hand. Then he shut the door, bowed once more to K., offered him his hand and introduced himself, saying, "Titorelli, painter". K. pointed to the door, behind which the girls were whispering, and said, "You seem to be very popular in this building." "Ach, those brats!" said the painter, trying in vain to fasten his nightshirt at the neck. He was also bare-footed and, apart from that, was wearing nothing more than a loose pair of yellowish linen trousers held up with a belt whose free end whipped to and fro. "Those kids are a real burden for me," he continued. The top button of his nightshirt came off and he gave up trying to fasten it, fetched a chair for K. and made him sit down on it. "I painted one of them once - she's not here today - and ever since then they've been following me about. If I'm here they only come in when I allow it, but as soon as I've gone out there's always at least one of them in here. They had a key made to my door and lend it round to each other. It's hard to imagine what a pain that is. Suppose I come back home with a lady I'm going to paint, I open the door with my own key and find the hunchback there or something, by the table painting her lips red with my paintbrush, and meanwhile her little sisters will be keeping guard for her, moving about and causing chaos in every corner of the room. Or else, like happened yesterday, I might come back home late in the evening - please forgive my appearance and the room being in a mess, it is to do with them - so, I might come home late in the evening and want to go to bed, then I feel something pinching my leg, look under the bed and pull another of them out from under it. I don't know why it is they bother me like this, I expect you've just seen that I do nothing to encourage them to come near me. And they make it hard for me to do my work too, of course. If I didn't get this studio for nothing I'd have moved out a long time ago." Just then, a little voice, tender and anxious, called out from under the door, "Titorelli, can we come in now?" "No," answered the painter. "Not even just me, by myself?" the voice asked again. "Not even just you," said the painter, as he went to the door and locked it.

Meanwhile, K. had been looking round the room, if it had not been pointed out it would never have occurred to him that this wretched little room could be called a studio. It was hardly long enough or broad enough to make two steps. Everything, floor, walls and ceiling, was made of wood, between the planks narrow gaps could be seen. Across from where K. was, the bed stood against the wall under a covering of many different colours. In the middle of the room a picture stood on an easel, covered over with a shirt whose arms dangled down to the ground. Behind K. was the window through which the fog made it impossible to see further than the snow covered roof of the neighbouring building.

The turning of the key in the lock reminded K. that he had not wanted to stay too long. So he drew the manufacturer's letter out from his pocket, held it out to the painter and said, "I learned about you from this gentleman, an acquaintance of yours, and it's on his advice that I've come here". The painter glanced through the letter and threw it down onto the bed. If the manufacturer had not said very clearly that Titorelli was an acquaintance of his, a poor man who was dependent on his charity, then it would really have been quite possible to believe that Titorelli did not know him or at least that he could not remember him. This impression was augmented by the painter's asking, "Were you wanting to buy some pictures or did you want to have yourself painted?" K. looked at the painter in astonishment. What did the letter actually say? K. had taken it as a matter of course that the manufacturer had explained to the painter in his letter that K. wanted nothing more with him than to find out more about his trial. He had been far too rash in coming here! But now he had to give the painter some sort of answer and, glancing at the easel, said, "Are you working on a picture currently?" "Yes," said the painter, and he took the shirt hanging over the easel and threw it onto the bed after the letter. "It's a portrait. Quite a good piece of work, although it's not quite finished yet." This was a convenient coincidence for K., it gave him a good opportunity to talk about the court as the picture showed, very clearly, a judge. What's more, it was remarkably similar to the picture in the lawyer's office, although this one showed a quite different judge, a heavy man with a full beard which was black and bushy and extended to the sides far up the man's cheeks. The lawyer's picture was also an oil painting, whereas this one had been made with pastel colours and was pale and unclear. But everything else about the picture was similar, as this judge, too, was holding tightly to the arm of his throne and seemed ominously about to rise from it. At first K. was about to say, "He certainly is a judge," but he held himself back for the time being and went closer to the picture as if he wanted to study it in detail. There was a large figure shown in middle of the throne's back rest which K. could not understand and asked the painter about it. That'll need some more work done on it, the painter told him, and taking a pastel crayon from a small table he added a few strokes to the edges of the figure but without making it any clearer as far as K. could make out. "That's the figure of justice," said the painter, finally. "Now I see," said K., "here's the blindfold and here are the scales. But aren't those wings on her heels, and isn't she moving?" "Yes," said the painter, "I had to paint it like that according to the contract. It's actually the figure of justice and the goddess of victory all in one." "That is not a good combination," said K. with a smile. "Justice needs to remain still, otherwise the scales will move about and it won't be possible to make a just verdict." "I'm just doing what the client wanted," said the painter. "Yes, certainly," said K., who had not meant to criticise anyone by that comment. "You've painted the figure as it actually appears on the throne." "No," said the painter, "I've never seen that figure or that throne, it's all just invention, but they told me what it was I had to paint." "How's that?" asked K. pretending not fully to understand what the painter said. "That is a judge sitting on the judge's chair, isn't it?" "Yes," said the painter, "but that judge isn't very high up and he's never sat on any throne like that." "And he has himself painted in such a grand pose? He's sitting there just like the president of the court." "Yeah, gentlemen like this are very vain," said the painter. "But they have permission from higher up to get themselves painted like this. It's laid down quite strictly just what sort of portrait each of them can get for himself. Only it's a pity that you can't make out the details of his costume and pose in this picture, pastel colours aren't really suitable for showing people like this." "Yes," said K., "it does seem odd that it's in pastel colours." "That's what the judge wanted," said the painter, "it's meant to be for a woman." The sight of the picture seemed to make him feel like working, he rolled up his shirtsleeves, picked up a few of the crayons, and K. watched as a reddish shadow built up around the head of the judge under their quivering tips and radiated out the to edges of the picture. This shadow play slowly surrounded the head like a decoration or lofty distinction. But around the figure of Justice, apart from some coloration that was barely noticeable, it remained light, and in this brightness the figure seemed to shine forward so that it now looked like neither the God of Justice nor the God of Victory, it seemed now, rather, to be a perfect depiction of the God of the Hunt. K. found the painter's work more engrossing than he had wanted; but finally he reproached himself for staying so long without having done anything relevant to his own affair. "What's the name of this judge?" he asked suddenly. "I'm not allowed to tell you that," the painter answered. He was bent deeply over the picture and clearly neglecting his guest who, at first, he had received with such care. K. took this to be just a foible of the painter's, and it irritated him as it made him lose time. "I take it you must be a trustee of the court," he said. The painter immediately put his crayons down, stood upright, rubbed his hands together and looked at K. with a smile. "Always straight out with the truth," he said. "You want to learn something about the court, like it says in your letter of recommendation, but then you start talking about my pictures to get me on your side. Still, I won't hold it against you, you weren't to know that that was entirely the wrong thing to try with me. Oh, please!" he said sharply, repelling K.'s attempt to make some objection. He then continued, "And besides, you're quite right in your comment that I'm a trustee of the court." He made a pause, as if wanting to give K. the time to come to terms with this fact. The girls could once more be heard from behind the door. They were probably pressed around the keyhole, perhaps they could even see into the room through the gaps in the planks. K. forewent the opportunity to excuse himself in some way as he did not wish to distract the painter from what he was saying, or else perhaps he didn't want him to get too far above himself and in this way make himself to some extent unattainable, so he asked, "Is that a publicly acknowledged position?" "No," was the painter's curt reply, as if the question prevented him saying any more. But K. wanted him to continue speaking and said, "Well, positions like that, that aren't officially acknowledged, can often have more influence than those that are." "And that's how it is with me," said the painter, and nodded with a frown. "I was talking about your case with the manufacturer yesterday, and he asked me if I wouldn't like to help you, and I answered: 'He can come and see me if he likes', and now I'm pleased to see you here so soon. This business seems to be quite important to you, and, of course, I'm not surprised at that. Would you not like to take your coat off now?" K. had intended to stay for only a very short time, but the painter's invitation was nonetheless very welcome. The air in the room had slowly become quite oppressive for him, he had several times looked in amazement at a small, iron stove in the corner that certainly could not have been lit, the heat of the room was inexplicable. As he took off his winter overcoat and also unbuttoned his frock coat the painter said to him in apology, "I must have warmth. And it is very cosy here, isn't it. This room's very good in that respect." K. made no reply, but it was actually not the heat that made him uncomfortable but, much more, the stuffiness, the air that almost made it more difficult to breathe, the room had probably not been ventilated for a long time. The unpleasantness of this was made all the stronger for K. when the painter invited him to sit on the bed while he himself sat down on the only chair in the room in front of the easel. The painter even seemed to misunderstand why K. remained at the edge of the bed and urged K. to make himself comfortable, and as he hesitated he went over to the bed himself and pressed K. deep down into the bedclothes and pillows. Then he went back to his seat and at last he asked his first objective question, which made K. forget everything else. "You're innocent, are you?" he asked. "Yes," said K. He felt a simple joy at answering this question, especially as the answer was given to a private individual and therefore would have no consequences. Up till then no-one had asked him this question so openly. To make the most of his pleasure he added, "I am totally innocent." "So," said the painter, and he lowered his head and seemed to be thinking. Suddenly he raised his head again and said, "Well if you're innocent it's all very simple." K. began to scowl, this supposed trustee of the court was talking like an ignorant child. "My being innocent does not make things simple," said K. Despite everything, he couldn't help smiling and slowly shook his head. "There are many fine details in which the court gets lost, but in the end it reaches into some place where originally there was nothing and pulls enormous guilt out of it." "Yeah, yeah, sure," said the painter, as if K. had been disturbing his train of thought for no reason. "But you are innocent, aren't you?" "Well of course I am," said K. "That's the main thing," said the painter. There was no counter-argument that could influence him, but although he had made up his mind it was not clear whether he was talking this way because of conviction or indifference. K., then, wanted to find out and said therefore, "I'm sure you're more familiar with the court than I am, I know hardly more about it than what I've heard, and that's been from many very different people. But they were all agreed on one thing, and that was that when ill thought-out accusations are made they are not ignored, and that once the court has made an accusation it is convinced of the guilt of the defendant and it's very hard to make it think otherwise." "Very hard?" the painter asked, throwing one hand up in the air. "It's impossible to make it think otherwise. If I painted all the judges next to each other here on canvas, and you were trying to defend yourself in front of it, you'd have more success with them than you'd ever have with the real court." "Yes," said K. to himself, forgetting that he had only gone there to investigate the painter.

One of the girls behind the door started up again, and asked, "Titorelli, is he going to go soon?" "Quiet!" shouted the painter at the door, "Can't you see I'm talking with the gentleman?" But this was not enough to satisfy the girl and she asked, "You going to paint his picture?" And when the painter didn't answer she added, "Please don't paint him, he's an 'orrible bloke." There followed an incomprehensible, interwoven babble of shouts and replies and calls of agreement. The painter leapt over to the door, opened it very slightly - the girls' clasped hands could be seen stretching through the crack as if they wanted something - and said, "If you're not quiet I'll throw you all down the stairs. Sit down here on the steps and be quiet." They probably did not obey him immediately, so that he had to command, "Down on the steps!" Only then it became quiet.

"I'm sorry about that," said the painter as he returned to K. K. had hardly turned towards the door, he had left it completely up to the painter whether and how he would place him under his protection if he wanted to. Even now, he made hardly any movement as the painter bent over him and, whispering into his ear in order not to be heard outside, said, "These girls belong to the court as well." "How's that?" asked K., as he leant his head to one side and looked at the painter. But the painter sat back down on his chair and, half in jest, half in explanation, "Well, everything belongs to the court." "That is something I had never noticed until now," said K. curtly, this general comment of the painter's made his comment about the girls far less disturbing. Nonetheless, K. looked for a while at the door, behind which the girls were now sitting quietly on the steps. Except, that one of them had pushed a drinking straw through a crack between the planks and was moving it slowly up and down. "You still don't seem to have much general idea of what the court's about", said the painter, who had stretched his legs wide apart and was tapping loudly on the floor with the tip of his foot. "But as you're innocent you won't need it anyway. I'll get you out of this by myself." "How do you intend to do that?" asked K. "You did say yourself not long ago that it's quite impossible to go to the court with reasons and proofs." "Only impossible for reasons and proofs you take to the court yourself" said the painter, raising his forefinger as if K. had failed to notice a fine distinction. "It goes differently if you try to do something behind the public court, that's to say in the consultation rooms, in the corridors or here, for instance, in my studio." K. now began to find it far easier to believe what the painter was saying, or rather it was largely in agreement with what he had also been told by others. In fact it was even quite promising. If it really was so easy to influence the judges through personal contacts as the lawyer had said then the painter's contacts with these vain judges was especially important, and at the very least should not be undervalued. And the painter would fit in very well in the circle of assistants that K. was slowly gathering around himself. He had been noted at the bank for his talent in organising, here, where he was placed entirely on his own resources, would be a good opportunity to test that talent to its limits. The painter observed the effect his explanation had had on K. and then, with a certain unease, said, "Does it not occur to you that the way I'm speaking is almost like a lawyer? It's the incessant contact with the gentlemen of the court has that influence on me. I gain a lot by it, of course, but I lose a lot, artistically speaking." "How did you first come into contact with the judges, then?" asked K., he wanted first to gain the painter's trust before he took him into his service. "That was very easy," said the painter, "I inherited these contacts. My father was court painter before me. It's a position that's always inherited. They can't use new people for it, the rules governing how the various grades of officials are painted are so many and varied, and, above all, so secret that no- one outside of certain families even knows them. In the drawer there, for instance, I've got my father's notes, which I don't show to anyone. But you're only able to paint judges if you know what they say. Although, even if I lost them no-one could ever dispute my position because of all the rules I just carry round in my head. All the judges want to be painted like the old, great judges were, and I'm the only one who can do that." "You are to be envied," said K., thinking of his position at the bank. "Your position is quite unassailable, then?" "Yes, quite unassailable," said the painter, and he raised his shoulders in pride. "That's how I can even afford to help some poor man facing trial now and then." "And how do you do that?" asked K., as if the painter had not just described him as a poor man. The painter did not let himself be distracted, but said, "In your case, for instance, as you're totally innocent, this is what I'll do." The repeated mention of K.'s innocence was becoming irksome to him. It sometimes seemed to him as if the painter was using these comments to make a favourable outcome to the trial a precondition for his help, which of course would make the help itself unnecessary. But despite these doubts K. forced himself not to interrupt the painter. He did not want to do without the painter's help, that was what he had decided, and this help did not seem in any way less questionable than that of the lawyer. K. valued the painter's help far more highly because it was offered in a way that was more harmless and open.

    The painter had pulled his seat closer to the bed and continued in a subdued voice: "I forgot to ask you; what sort of acquittal is it you want? There are three possibilities; absolute acquittal, apparent acquittal and deferment. Absolute acquittal is the best, of course, only there's nothing I could do to get that sort of outcome. I don't think there's anyone at all who could do anything to get an absolute acquittal. Probably the only thing that could do that is if the accused is innocent. As you are innocent it could actually be possible and you could depend on your innocence alone. In that case you won't need me or any other kind of help."

    At first, K. was astonished at this orderly explanation, but then, just as quietly as the painter, he said, "I think you're contradicting yourself." "How's that?" asked the painter patiently, leaning back with a smile. This smile made K. feel as if he were examining not the words of the painter but seeking out inconsistencies in the procedures of the court itself. Nonetheless, he continued unabashed and said, "You remarked earlier that the court cannot be approached with reasoned proofs, you later restricted this to the open court, and now you go so far as to say that an innocent man needs no assistance in court. That entails a contradiction. Moreover, you said earlier that the judges can be influenced personally but now you insist that an absolute acquittal, as you call it, can never be attained through personal influence. That entails a second contradiction." "It's quite easy to clear up these contradictions," said the painter. "We're talking about two different things here, there's what it says in the law and there's what I know from my own experience, you shouldn't get the two confused. I've never seen it in writing, but the law does, of course, say on the one hand that the innocent will be set free, but on the other hand it doesn't say that the judges can be influenced. But in my experience it's the other way round. I don't know of any absolute acquittals but I do know of many times when a judge has been influenced. It's possible, of course, that there was no innocence in any of the cases I know about. But is that likely? Not a single innocent defendant in so many cases? When I was a boy I used to listen closely to my father when he told us about court cases at home, and the judges that came to his studio talked about the court, in our circles nobody talks about anything else; I hardly ever got the chance to go to court myself but always made use of it when I could, I've listened to countless trials at important stages in their development, I've followed them closely as far as they could be followed, and I have to say that I've never seen a single acquittal." "So. Not a single acquittal," said K., as if talking to himself and his hopes. "That confirms the impression I already have of the court. So there's no point in it from this side either. They could replace the whole court with a single hangman." "You shouldn't generalise," said the painter, dissatisfied, "I've only been talking about my own experience." "Well that's enough," said K., "or have you heard of any acquittals that happened earlier?" "They say there have been some acquittals earlier," the painter answered, "but it's very hard to be sure about it. The courts don't make their final conclusions public, not even the judges are allowed to know about them, so that all we know about these earlier cases are just legends. But most of them did involve absolute acquittals, you can believe that, but they can't be proved. On the other hand, you shouldn't forget all about them either, I'm sure there is some truth to them, and they are very beautiful, I've painted a few pictures myself depicting these legends." "My assessment will not be altered by mere legends," said K. "I don't suppose it's possible to cite these legends in court, is it?" The painter laughed. "No, you can't cite them in court," he said. "Then there's no point in talking about them," said K., he wanted, for the time being, to accept anything the painter told him, even if he thought it unlikely or contradicted what he had been told by others. He did not now have the time to examine the truth of everything the painter said or even to disprove it, he would have achieved as much as he could if the painter would help him in any way even if his help would not be decisive. As a result, he said, "So let's pay no more attention to absolute acquittal, but you mentioned two other possibilities." "Apparent acquittal and deferment. They're the only possibilities," said the painter. "But before we talk about them, would you not like to take your coat off? You must be hot." "Yes," said K., who until then had paid attention to nothing but the painter's explanations, but now that he had had the heat pointed out to him his brow began to sweat heavily. "It's almost unbearable." The painter nodded as if he understood K.'s discomfort very well. "Could we not open the window?" asked K. "No," said the painter. "It's only a fixed pane of glass, it can't be opened." K. now realised that all this time he had been hoping the painter would suddenly go over to the window and pull it open. He had prepared himself even for the fog that he would breathe in through his open mouth. The thought that here he was entirely cut off from the air made him feel dizzy. He tapped lightly on the bedspread beside him and, with a weak voice, said, "That is very inconvenient and unhealthy." "Oh no," said the painter in defence of his window, "as it can't be opened this room retains the heat better than if the window were double glazed, even though it's only a single pane. There's not much need to air the room as there's so much ventilation through the gaps in the wood, but when I do want to I can open one of my doors, or even both of them." K. was slightly consoled by this explanation and looked around to see where the second door was. The painter saw him do so and said, "It's behind you, I had to hide it behind the bed." Only then was K. able to see the little door in the wall. "It's really much too small for a studio here," said the painter, as if he wanted to anticipate an objection K. would make. "I had to arrange things as well as I could. That's obviously a very bad place for the bed, in front of the door. For instance when the judge I'm painting at present comes he always comes through the door by the bed, and I've even given him a key to this door so that he can wait for me here in the studio when I'm not home. Although nowadays he usually comes early in the morning when I'm still asleep. And of course, it always wakes me up when I hear the door opened beside the bed, however fast asleep I am. If you could hear the way I curse him as he climbs over my bed in the morning you'd lose all respect for judges. I suppose I could take the key away from him but that'd only make things worse. It only takes a tiny effort to break any of the doors here off their hinges." All the time the painter was speaking, K. was considering whether he should take off his coat, but he finally realised that, if he didn't do so, he would be quite unable to stay here any longer, so he took off his frock coat and lay it on his knee so that he could put it back on again as soon as the conversation was over. He had hardly done this when one of the girls called out, "Now he's taken his coat off!" and they could all be heard pressing around the gaps in the planks to see the spectacle for themselves. "The girls think I'm going to paint your portrait," said the painter, "and that's why you're taking your coat off." "I see," said K., only slightly amused by this, as he felt little better than he had before even though he now sat in his shirtsleeves. With some irritation he asked, "What did you say the two other possibilities were?" He had already forgotten the terms used. "Apparent acquittal and deferment," said the painter. "It's up to you which one you choose. You can get either of them if I help you, but it'll take some effort of course, the difference between them is that apparent acquittal needs concentrated effort for a while and that deferment takes much less effort but it has to be sustained. Now then, apparent acquittal. If that's what you want I'll write down an assertion of your innocence on a piece of paper. The text for an assertion of this sort was passed down to me from my father and it's quite unassailable. I take this assertion round to the judges I know. So I'll start off with the one I'm currently painting, and put the assertion to him when he comes for his sitting this evening. I'll lay the assertion in front of him, explain that you're innocent and give him my personal guarantee of it. And that's not just a superficial guarantee, it's a real one and it's binding." The painter's eyes seemed to show some reproach of K. for wanting to impose that sort of responsibility on him. "That would be very kind of you", said K. "And would the judge then believe you and nonetheless not pass an absolute acquittal?" "It's like I just said," answered the painter. "And anyway, it's not entirely sure that all the judges would believe me, many of them, for instance, might want me to bring you to see them personally. So then you'd have to come along too. But at least then, if that happens, the matter is half way won, especially as I'd teach you in advance exactly how you'd need to act with the judge concerned, of course. What also happens, though, is that there are some judges who'll turn me down in advance, and that's worse. I'll certainly make several attempts, but still, we'll have to forget about them, but at least we can afford to do that as no one judge can pass the decisive verdict. Then when I've got enough judges' signatures on this document I take it to the judge who's concerned with your case. I might even have his signature already, in which case things develop a bit quicker than they would do otherwise. But there aren't usually many hold ups from then on, and that's the time that the defendant can feel most confident. It's odd, but true, that people feel more confidence in this time than they do after they've been acquitted. There's no particular exertion needed now. When he has the document asserting the defendant's innocence, guaranteed by a number of other judges, the judge can acquit you without any worries, and although there are still several formalities to be gone through there's no doubt that that's what he'll do as a favour to me and several other acquaintances. You, however, walk out the court and you're free." "So, then I'll be free," said K., hesitantly. "That's right," said the painter, "but only apparently free or, to put it a better way, temporarily free, as the most junior judges, the ones I know, they don't have the right to give the final acquittal. Only the highest judge can do that, in the court that's quite out of reach for you, for me and for all of us. We don't know how things look there and, incidentally, we don't want to know. The right to acquit people is a major privilege and our judges don't have it, but they do have the right to free people from the indictment. That's to say, if they're freed in this way then for the time being the charge is withdrawn but it's still hanging over their heads and it only takes an order from higher up to bring it back into force. And as I'm in such good contact with the court I can also tell you how the difference between absolute and apparent acquittal is described, just in a superficial way, in the directives to the court offices. If there's an absolute acquittal all proceedings should stop, everything disappears from the process, not just the indictment but the trial and even the acquittal disappears, everything just disappears. With an apparent acquittal it's different. When that happens, nothing has changed except that the case for your innocence, for your acquittal and the grounds for the acquittal have been made stronger. Apart from that, proceedings go on as before, the court offices continue their business and the case gets passed to higher courts, gets passed back down to the lower courts and so on, backwards and forwards, sometimes faster, sometimes slower, to and fro. It's impossible to know exactly what's happening while this is going on. Seen from outside it can sometimes seem that everything has been long since forgotten, the documents have been lost and the acquittal is complete. No-one familiar with the court would believe it. No documents ever get lost, the court forgets nothing. One day - no-one expects it - some judge or other picks up the documents and looks more closely at them, he notices that this particular case is still active, and orders the defendant's immediate arrest. I've been talking here as if there's a long delay between apparent acquittal and re-arrest, that is quite possible and I do know of cases like that, but it's just as likely that the defendant goes home after he's been acquitted and finds somebody there waiting to re-arrest him. Then, of course, his life as a free man is at an end." "And does the trial start over again?" asked K., finding it hard to believe. "The trial will always start over again," said the painter, "but there is, once again as before, the possibility of getting an apparent acquittal. Once again, the accused has to muster all his strength and mustn't give up." The painter said that last phrase possibly as a result of the impression that K., whose shoulders had dropped somewhat, gave on him. "But to get a second acquittal," asked K., as if in anticipation of further revelations by the painter, "is that not harder to get than the first time?" "As far as that's concerned," answered the painter, "there's nothing you can say for certain. You mean, do you, that the second arrest would have an adverse influence on the judge and the verdict he passes on the defendant? That's not how it happens. When the acquittal is passed the judges are already aware that re-arrest is likely. So when it happens it has hardly any effect. But there are countless other reasons why the judges' mood and their legal acumen in the case can be altered, and efforts to obtain the second acquittal must therefore be suited to the new conditions, and generally just as vigorous as the first." "But this second acquittal will once again not be final," said K., shaking his head. "Of course not," said the painter, "the second acquittal is followed by the third arrest, the third acquittal by the fourth arrest and so on. That's what is meant by the term apparent acquittal." K. was silent. "You clearly don't think an apparent acquittal offers much advantage," said the painter, "perhaps deferment would suit you better. Would you like me to explain what deferment is about?" K. nodded. The painter had leant back and spread himself out in his chair, his nightshirt was wide open, he had pushed his hand inside and was stroking his breast and his sides. "Deferment," said the painter, looking vaguely in front of himself for a while as if trying to find a perfectly appropriate explanation, "deferment consists of keeping proceedings permanently in their earliest stages. To do that, the accused and those helping him need to keep in continuous personal contact with the court, especially those helping him. I repeat, this doesn't require so much effort as getting an apparent acquittal, but it probably requires a lot more attention. You must never let the trial out of your sight, you have to go and see the appropriate judge at regular intervals as well as when something in particular comes up and, whatever you do, you have to try and remain friendly with him; if you don't know the judge personally you have to influence him through the judges you do know, and you have to do it without giving up on the direct discussions. As long as you don't fail to do any of these things you can be reasonably sure the trial won't get past its first stages. The trial doesn't stop, but the defendant is almost as certain of avoiding conviction as if he'd been acquitted. Compared with an apparent acquittal, deferment has the advantage that the defendant's future is less uncertain, he's safe from the shock of being suddenly re-arrested and doesn't need to fear the exertions and stress involved in getting an apparent acquittal just when everything else in his life would make it most difficult. Deferment does have certain disadvantages of its own though, too, and they shouldn't be under-estimated. I don't mean by this that the defendant is never free, he's never free in the proper sense of the word with an apparent acquittal either. There's another disadvantage. Proceedings can't be prevented from moving forward unless there are some at least ostensible reasons given. So something needs to seem to be happening when looked at from the outside. This means that from time to time various injunctions have to be obeyed, the accused has to be questioned, investigations have to take place and so on. The trial's been artificially constrained inside a tiny circle, and it has to be continuously spun round within it. And that, of course, brings with it certain unpleasantnesses for the accused, although you shouldn't imagine they're all that bad. All of this is just for show, the interrogations, for instance, they're only very short, if you ever don't have the time or don't feel like going to them you can offer an excuse, with some judges you can even arrange the injunctions together a long time in advance, in essence all it means is that, as the accused, you have to report to the judge from time to time." Even while the painter was speaking those last words K. had laid his coat over his arm and had stood up. Immediately, from outside the door, there was a cry of 'He's standing up now!'. "Are you leaving already?" asked the painter, who had also stood up. "It must be the air that's driving you out. I'm very sorry about that. There's still a lot I need to tell you. I had to put everything very briefly but I hope at least it was all clear." "Oh yes," said K., whose head was aching from the effort of listening. Despite this affirmation the painter summed it all up once more, as if he wanted to give K. something to console him on his way home. "Both have in common that they prevent the defendant being convicted," he said. "But they also prevent his being properly acquitted," said K. quietly, as if ashamed to acknowledge it. "You've got it, in essence," said the painter quickly. K. placed his hand on his winter overcoat but could not bring himself to put it on. Most of all he would have liked to pack everything together and run out to the fresh air. Not even the girls could induce him to put his coat on, even though they were already loudly telling each other that he was doing so. The painter still had to interpret K.'s mood in some way, so he said, "I expect you've deliberately avoided deciding between my suggestions yet. That's good. I would even have advised against making a decision straight away. There's no more than a hair's breadth of difference between the advantages and disadvantages. Everything has to be carefully weighed up. But the most important thing is you shouldn't lose too much time." "I'll come back here again soon," said K., who had suddenly decided to put his frock coat on, threw his overcoat over his shoulder and hurried over to the door behind which the girls now began to scream. K. thought he could even see the screaming girls through the door. "Well, you'll have to keep your word," said the painter, who had not followed him, "otherwise I'll come to the bank to ask about it myself." "Will you open this door for me," said K. pulling at the handle which, as he noticed from the resistance, was being held tightly by the girls on the other side. "Do you want to be bothered by the girls?" asked the painter. "It's better if you use the other way out," he said, pointing to the door behind the bed. K. agreed to this and jumped back to the bed. But instead of opening that door the painter crawled under the bed and from underneath it asked K., "Just a moment more, would you not like to see a picture I could sell to you?" K. did not want to be impolite, the painter really had taken his side and promised to help him more in the future, and because of K.'s forgetfulness there had been no mention of any payment for the painter's help, so K. could not turn him down now and allowed him to show him the picture, even though he was quivering with impatience to get out of the studio. From under the bed, the painter withdrew a pile of unframed paintings. They were so covered in dust that when the painter tried to blow it off the one on top the dust swirled around in front of K.'s eyes, robbing him of breath for some time. "Moorland landscape," said the painter passing the picture to K. It showed two sickly trees, well separated from each other in dark grass. In the background there was a multi-coloured sunset. "That's nice," said K. "I'll buy it." K. expressed himself in this curt way without any thought, so he was glad when the painter did not take this amiss and picked up a second painting from the floor. "This is a counterpart to the first picture," said the painter. Perhaps it had been intended as a counterpart, but there was not the slightest difference to be seen between it and the first picture, there were the trees, there the grass and there the sunset. But this was of little importance to K. "They are beautiful landscapes," he said, "I'll buy them both and hang them in my office." "You seem to like this subject," said the painter, picking up a third painting, "good job I've still got another, similar picture here." The picture though, was not similar, rather it was exactly the same moorland landscape. The painter was fully exploiting this opportunity to sell off his old pictures. "I'll take this one too," said K. "How much do the three paintings cost?" "We can talk about that next time," said the painter. "You're in a hurry now, and we'll still be in contact. And besides, I'm glad you like the paintings, I'll give you all the paintings I've got down here. They're all moorland landscapes, I've painted a lot of moorland landscapes. A lot of people don't like that sort of picture because they're too gloomy, but there are others, and you're one of them, who love gloomy themes." But K. was not in the mood to hear about the professional experiences of this painter cum beggar. "Wrap them all up!" he called out, interrupting the painter as he was speaking, "my servant will come to fetch them in the morning." "There's no need for that," said the painter. "I expect I can find a porter for you who can go with you now." And, at last, he leant over the bed and unlocked the door. "Just step on the bed, don't worry about that," said the painter, "that's what everyone does who comes in here." Even without this invitation, K. had shown no compunction in already placing his foot in the middle of the bed covers, then he looked out through the open door and drew his foot back again. "What is that?" he asked the painter. "What are you so surprised at?" he asked, surprised in his turn. "Those are court offices. Didn't you know there are court offices here? There are court offices in almost every attic, why should this building be any different? Even my studio is actually one of the court offices but the court put it at my disposal." It was not so much finding court offices even here that shocked K., he was mainly shocked at himself, at his own naïvety in court matters. It seemed to him that one of the most basic rules governing how a defendant should behave was always to be prepared, never allow surprises, never to look, unsuspecting, to the right when the judge stood beside him to his left - and this was the very basic rule that he was continually violating. A long corridor extended in front of him, air blew in from it which, compared with the air in the studio, was refreshing. There were benches set along each side of the corridor just as in the waiting area for the office he went to himself. There seemed to be precise rules governing how offices should be equipped. There did not seem to be many people visiting the offices that day. There was a man there, half sitting, half laying, his face was buried in his arm on the bench and he seemed to be sleeping; another man was standing in the half-dark at the end of the corridor. K. now climbed over the bed, the painter followed him with the pictures. They soon came across a servant of the court - K. was now able to recognise all the servants of the court from the gold buttons they wore on their civilian clothes below the normal buttons - and the painter instructed him to go with K. carrying the pictures. K. staggered more than he walked, his handkerchief pressed over his mouth. They had nearly reached the exit when the girls stormed in on them, so K. had not been able to avoid them. They had clearly seen that the second door of the studio had been opened and had gone around to impose themselves on him from this side. "I can't come with you any further!" called out the painter with a laugh as the girls pressed in. "Goodbye, and don't hesitate too long!" K. did not even look round at him. Once on the street he took the first cab he came across. He now had to get rid of the servant, whose gold button continually caught his eye even if it caught no-one else's. As a servant, the servant of the court was going to sit on the coach-box. But K. chased him down from there. It was already well into the afternoon when K. arrived in front of the bank. He would have liked to leave the pictures in the cab but feared there might be some occasion when he would have to let the painter see he still had them. So he had the pictures taken to his office and locked them in the lowest drawer of his desk so that he could at least keep them safe from the deputy director's view for the next few days.

Chapter Eight Block, the businessman - Dismissing the lawyer

K. had at last made the decision to withdraw his defence from the lawyer. It was impossible to remove his doubts as to whether this was the right decision, but this was outweighed by his belief in its necessity. This decision, on the day he intended to go to see the lawyer, took a lot of the strength he needed for his work, he worked exceptionally slowly, he had to remain in his office a long time, and it was already past ten o'clock when he finally stood in front of the lawyer's front door. Even before he rang he considered whether it might not be better to give the lawyer notice by letter or telephone, a personal conversation would certainly be very difficult. Nonetheless, K. did not actually want to do without it, if he gave notice by any other means it would be received in silence or with a few formulated words, and unless Leni could discover anything K. would never learn how the lawyer had taken his dismissal and what its consequences might be, in the lawyer's not unimportant opinion. But sitting in front of him and taken by surprise by his dismissal, K. would be able easily to infer everything he wanted from the lawyer's face and behaviour, even if he could not be induced to say very much. It was not even out of the question that K. might, after all, be persuaded that it would be best to leave his defence to the lawyer and withdraw his dismissal.

As usual, there was at first no response to K.'s ring at the door. "Leni could be a bit quicker," thought K. But he could at least be glad there was nobody else interfering as usually happened, be it the man in his nightshirt or anyone else who might bother him. As K. pressed on the button for the second time he looked back at the other door, but this time it, too, remained closed. At last, two eyes appeared at the spy-hatch in the lawyer's door, although they weren't Leni's eyes. Someone unlocked the door, but kept himself pressed against it as he called back inside, "It's him!", and only then did he open the door properly. K. pushed against the door, as behind him he could already hear the key being hurriedly turned in the lock of the door to the other flat. When the door in front of him finally opened, he stormed straight into the hallway. Through the corridor which led between the rooms he saw Leni, to whom the warning cry of the door opener had been directed, still running away in her nightshirt. He looked at her for a moment and then looked round at the person who had opened the door. It was a small, wizened man with a full beard, he held a candle in his hand. "Do you work here?" asked K. "No," answered the man, "I don't belong here at all, the lawyer is only representing me, I'm here on legal business." "Without your coat?" asked K., indicating the man's deficiency of dress with a gesture of his hand. "Oh, do forgive me!" said the man, and he looked at himself in the light of the candle he was holding as if he had not known about his appearance until then. "Is Leni your lover?" asked K. curtly. He had set his legs slightly apart, his hands, in which he held his hat, were behind his back. Merely by being in possession of a thick overcoat he felt his advantage over this thin little man. "Oh God," he said and, shocked, raised one hand in front of his face as if in defence, "no, no, what can you be thinking?" "You look honest enough," said K. with a smile, "but come along anyway." K. indicated with his hat which way the man was to go and let him go ahead of him. "What is your name then?" asked K. on the way. "Block. I'm a businessman," said the small man, twisting himself round as he thus introduced himself, although K. did not allow him to stop moving. "Is that your real name?" asked K. "Of course it is," was the man's reply, "why do you doubt it?" "I thought you might have some reason to keep your name secret," said K. He felt himself as much at liberty as is normally only felt in foreign parts when speaking with people of lower standing, keeping everything about himself to himself, speaking only casually about the interests of the other, able to raise him to a level above one's own, but also able, at will, to let him drop again. K. stopped at the door of the lawyer's office, opened it and, to the businessman who had obediently gone ahead, called, "Not so fast! Bring some light here!" K. thought Leni might have hidden in here, he let the businessman search in every corner, but the room was empty. In front of the picture of the judge K. took hold of the businessman's braces to stop him moving on. "Do you know him?" he asked, pointing upwards with his finger. The businessman lifted the candle, blinked as he looked up and said, "It's a judge." "An important judge?" asked K., and stood to the side and in front of the businessman so that he could observe what impression the picture had on him. The businessman was looking up in admiration. "He's an important judge." "You don't have much insight," said K. "He is the lowest of the lowest examining judges." "I remember now," said the businessman as he lowered the candle, "that's what I've already been told." "Well of course you have," called out K., "I'd forgotten about it, of course you would already have been told." "But why, why?" asked the businessman as he moved forwards towards the door, propelled by the hands of K. Outside in the corridor K. said, "You know where Leni's hidden, do you?" "Hidden?" said the businessman, "No, but she might be in the kitchen cooking soup for the lawyer." "Why didn't you say that immediately?" asked K. "I was going to take you there, but you called me back again," answered the businessman, as if confused by the contradictory commands. "You think you're very clever, don't you," said K, "now take me there!" K. had never been in the kitchen, it was surprisingly big and very well equipped. The stove alone was three times bigger than normal stoves, but it was not possible to see any detail beyond this as the kitchen was at the time illuminated by no more than a small lamp hanging by the entrance. At the stove stood Leni, in a white apron as always, breaking eggs into a pot standing on a spirit lamp. "Good evening, Josef," she said with a glance sideways. "Good evening," said K., pointing with one hand to a chair in a corner which the businessman was to sit on, and he did indeed sit down on it. K. however went very close behind Leni's back, leant over her shoulder and asked, "Who is this man?" Leni put one hand around K. as she stirred the soup with the other, she drew him forward toward herself and said, "He's a pitiful character, a poor businessman by the name of Block. Just look at him." The two of them looked back over their shoulders. The businessman was sitting on the chair that K. had directed him to, he had extinguished the candle whose light was no longer needed and pressed on the wick with his fingers to stop the smoke. "You were in your nightshirt," said K., putting his hand on her head and turning it back towards the stove. She was silent. "Is he your lover?" asked K. She was about to take hold of the pot of soup, but K. took both her hands and said, "Answer me!" She said, "Come into the office, I'll explain everything to you." "No," said K., "I want you to explain it here." She put her arms around him and wanted to kiss him. K., though, pushed her away and said, "I don't want you to kiss me now." "Josef," said Leni, looking at K. imploringly but frankly in the eyes, "you're not going to be jealous of Mr. Block now, are you? Rudi," she then said, turning to the businessman, "help me out will you, I'm being suspected of something, you can see that, leave the candle alone." It had looked as though Mr. Block had not been paying attention but he had been following closely. "I don't even know why you might be jealous," he said ingenuously. "Nor do I, actually," said K., looking at the businessman with a smile. Leni laughed out loud and while K. was not paying attention took the opportunity of embracing him and whispering, "Leave him alone, now, you can see what sort of person he is. I've been helping him a little bit because he's an important client of the lawyer's, and no other reason. And what about you? Do you want to speak to the lawyer at this time of day? He's very unwell today, but if you want I'll tell him you're here. But you can certainly spend the night with me. It's so long since you were last here, even the lawyer has been asking about you.

Don't neglect your case! And I've got some things to tell you that I've learned about. But now, before anything else, take your coat off!" She helped him off with his coat, took the hat off his head, ran with the things into the hallway to hang them up, then she ran back and saw to the soup. "Do you want me to tell him you're here straight away or take him his soup first?" "Tell him I'm here first," said K. He was in a bad mood, he had originally intended a detailed discussion of his business with Leni, especially the question of his giving the lawyer notice, but now he no longer wanted to because of the presence of the businessman. Now he considered his affair too important to let this little businessman take part in it and perhaps change some of his decisions, and so he called Leni back even though she was already on her way to the lawyer. "Bring him his soup first," he said, "I want him to get his strength up for the discussion with me, he'll need it." "You're a client of the lawyer's too, aren't you," said the businessman quietly from his corner as if he were trying to find this out. It was not, however, taken well. "What business is that of yours?" said K., and Leni said, "Will you be quiet. - I'll take him his soup first then, shall I?" And she poured the soup into a dish. "The only worry then is that he might go to sleep soon after he's eaten." "What I've got to say to him will keep him awake," said K., who still wanted to intimate that he intended some important negotiations with the lawyer, he wanted Leni to ask him what it was and only then to ask her advice. But instead, she just promptly carried out the order he had given her. When she went over to him with the dish she deliberately brushed against him and whispered, "I'll tell him you're here as soon as he's eaten the soup so that I can get you back as soon as possible." "Just go," said K., "just go." "Be a bit more friendly," she said and, still holding the dish, turned completely round once more in the doorway.

K. watched her as she went; the decision had finally been made that the lawyer was to be dismissed, it was probably better that he had not been able to discuss the matter any more with Leni beforehand; she hardly understood the complexity of the matter, she would certainly have advised him against it and perhaps would even have prevented him from dismissing the lawyer this time, he would have remained in doubt and unease and eventually have carried out his decision after a while anyway as this decision was something he could not avoid. The sooner it was carried out the more harm would be avoided. And moreover, perhaps the businessman had something to say on the matter.

K. turned round, the businessman hardly noticed it as he was about to stand up. "Stay where you are," said K. and pulled up a chair beside him. "Have you been a client of the lawyer's for a long time?" asked K. "Yes," said the businessman, "a very long time." "How many years has he been representing you so far, then?" asked K. "I don't know how you mean," said the businessman, "he's been my business lawyer - I buy and sell cereals - he's been my business lawyer since I took the business over, and that's about twenty years now, but perhaps you mean my own trial and he's been representing me in that since it started, and that's been more than five years. Yes, well over five years," he then added, pulling out an old briefcase, "I've got everything written down; I can tell you the exact dates if you like. It's so hard to remember everything. Probably, my trial's been going on much longer than that, it started soon after the death of my wife, and that's been more than five and a half years now." K. moved in closer to him. "So the lawyer takes on ordinary legal business, does he?" he asked. This combination of criminal and commercial business seemed surprisingly reassuring for K. "Oh yes," said the businessman, and then he whispered, "They even say he's more efficient in jurisprudence than he is in other matters." But then he seemed to regret saying this, and he laid a hand on K.'s shoulder and said, "Please don't betray me to him, will you." K. patted his thigh to reassure him and said, "No, I don't betray people." "He can be so vindictive, you see," said the businessman. "I'm sure he won't do anything against such a faithful client as you," said K. "Oh, he might do," said the businessman, "when he gets cross it doesn't matter who it is, and anyway, I'm not really faithful to him." "How's that then?" asked K. "I'm not sure I should tell you about it," said the businessman hesitantly. "I think it'll be alright," said K. "Well then," said the businessman, "I'll tell you about some of it, but you'll have to tell me a secret too, then we can support each other with the lawyer." "You are very careful," said K., "but I'll tell you a secret that will set your mind completely at ease. Now tell me, in what way have you been unfaithful to the lawyer?" "I've ..." said the businessman hesitantly, and in a tone as if he were confessing something dishonourable, "I've taken on other lawyers besides him." "That's not so serious," said K., a little disappointed. "It is, here," said the businessman, who had had some difficulty breathing since making his confession but who now, after hearing K.'s comment, began to feel more trust for him. "That's not allowed. And it's allowed least of all to take on petty lawyers when you've already got a proper one. And that's just what I have done, besides him I've got five petty lawyers." "Five!" exclaimed K., astonished at this number, "Five lawyers besides this one?" The businessman nodded. "I'm even negotiating with a sixth one." "But why do you need so many lawyers?" asked K. "I need all of them," said the businessman. "Would you mind explaining that to me?" asked K. "I'd be glad to," said the businessman. "Most of all, I don't want to lose my case, well that's obvious. So that means I mustn't neglect anything that might be of use to me; even if there's very little hope of a particular thing being of any use I can't just throw it away. So everything I have I've put to use in my case. I've taken all the money out of my business, for example, the offices for my business used to occupy nearly a whole floor, but now all I need is a little room at the back where I work with one apprentice. It wasn't just using up the money that caused the difficulty, of course, it was much more to do with me not working at the business as much as I used to. If you want to do something about your trial you don't have much time for anything else." "So you're also working at the court yourself?" asked K. "That's just what I want to learn more about." "I can't tell you very much about that," said the businessman, "at first I tried to do that too but I soon had to give it up again. It wears you out too much, and it's really not much use. And it turned out to be quite impossible to work there yourself and to negotiate, at least for me it was. It's a heavy strain there just sitting and waiting. You know yourself what the air is like in those offices." "How do you know I've been there, then?" asked K. "I was in the waiting room myself when you went through." "What a coincidence that is!" exclaimed K., totally engrossed and forgetting how ridiculous the businessman had seemed to him earlier. "So you saw me! You were in the waiting room when I went through. Yes, I did go through it one time." "It isn't such a big coincidence," said the businessman, "I'm there nearly every day." "I expect I'll have to go there quite often myself now," said K., "although I can hardly expect to be shown the same respect as I was then. They all stood up for me. They must have thought I was a judge." "No," said the businessman, "we were greeting the servant of the court. We knew you were a defendant. That sort of news spreads very quickly." "So you already knew about that," said K., "the way I behaved must have seemed very arrogant to you. Did you criticise me for it afterwards?" "No," said the businessman, "quite the opposite. That was just stupidity." "What do you mean, 'stupidity'?" asked K. "Why are you asking about it?" said the businessman in some irritation. "You still don't seem to know the people there and you might take it wrong. Don't forget in proceedings like this there are always lots of different things coming up to talk about, things that you just can't understand with reason alone, you just get too tired and distracted for most things and so, instead, people rely on superstition. I'm talking about the others, but I'm no better myself. One of these superstitions, for example, is that you can learn a lot about the outcome of a defendant's case by looking at his face, especially the shape of his lips. There are lots who believe that, and they said they could see from the shape of your lips that you'd definitely be found guilty very soon. I repeat that all this is just a ridiculous superstition, and in most cases it's completely disproved by the facts, but when you live in that society it's hard to hold yourself back from beliefs like that. Just think how much effect that superstition can have. You spoke to one of them there, didn't you? He was hardly able to give you an answer. There are lots of things there that can make you confused, of course, but one of them, for him, was the appearance of your lips. He told us all later he thought he could see something in your lips that meant he'd be convicted himself." "On my lips?" asked K., pulling out a pocket mirror and examining himself. "I can see nothing special about my lips. Can you?" "Nor can I," said the businessman, "nothing at all." "These people are so superstitious!" exclaimed K. "Isn't that what I just told you?" asked the businessman. "Do you then have that much contact with each other, exchanging each other's opinions?" said K. "I've kept myself completely apart so far." "They don't normally have much contact with each other," said the businessman, "that would be impossible, there are so many of them. And they don't have much in common either. If a group of them ever thinks they have found something in common it soon turns out they were mistaken. There's nothing you can do as a group where the court's concerned. Each case is examined separately, the court is very painstaking. So there's nothing to be achieved by forming into a group, only sometimes an individual will achieve something in secret; and it's only when that's been done the others learn about it; nobody knows how it was done. So there's no sense of togetherness, you meet people now and then in the waiting rooms, but we don't talk much there. The superstitious beliefs were established a long time ago and they spread all by themselves." "I saw those gentlemen in the waiting room," said K., "it seemed so pointless for them to be waiting in that way." "Waiting is not pointless," said the businessman, "it's only pointless if you try and interfere yourself. I told you just now

I've got five lawyers besides this one. You might think - I thought it myself at first - you might think I could leave the whole thing entirely up to them now. That would be entirely wrong. I can leave it up to them less than when I had just the one. Maybe you don't understand that, do you?" "No," said K., and to slow the businessman down, who had been speaking too fast, he laid his hand on the businessman's to reassure him, "but I'd like just to ask you to speak a little more slowly, these are many very important things for me, and I can't follow exactly what you're saying." "You're quite right to remind me of that," said the businessman, "you're new to all this, a junior. Your trial is six months old, isn't it? Yes, I've heard about it. Such a new case! But I've already thought all these things through countless times, to me they're the most obvious things in the world." "You must be glad your trial has already progressed so far, are you?" asked K., he did not wish to ask directly how the businessman's affairs stood, but received no clear answer anyway. "Yes, I've been working at my trial for five years now," said the businessman as his head sank, "that's no small achievement." Then he was silent for a while. K. listened to hear whether Leni was on her way back. On the one hand he did not want her to come back too soon as he still had many questions to ask and did not want her to find him in this intimate discussion with the businessman, but on the other hand it irritated him that she stayed so long with the lawyer when K. was there, much longer than she needed to give him his soup. "I still remember it exactly," the businessman began again, and K. immediately gave him his full attention, "when my case was as old as yours is now. I only had this one lawyer at that time but I wasn't very satisfied with him." Now I'll find out everything, thought K., nodding vigorously as if he could thereby encourage the businessman to say everything worth knowing. "My case," the businessman continued, "didn't move on at all, there were some hearings that took place and I went to every one of them, collected materials, handed all my business books to the court - which I later found was entirely unnecessary - I ran back and forth to the lawyer, and he submitted various documents to the court too ..." "Various documents?" asked K. "Yes, that's right," said the businessman. "That's very important for me," said K., "in my case he's still working on the first set of documents. He still hasn't done anything. I see now that he's been neglecting me quite disgracefully." "There can be lots of good reasons why the first documents still aren't ready," said the businessman, "and anyway, it turned out later on that the ones he submitted for me were entirely worthless. I even read one of them myself, one of the officials at the court was very helpful. It was very learned, but it didn't actually say anything. Most of all, there was lots of Latin, which I can't understand, then pages and pages of general appeals to the court, then lots of flattery for particular officials, they weren't named, these officials, but anyone familiar with the court must have been able to guess who they were, then there was self-praise by the lawyer where he humiliated himself to the court in a way that was downright dog-like, and then endless investigations of cases from the past which were supposed to be similar to mine. Although, as far as I was able to follow them, these investigations had been carried out very carefully. Now, I don't mean to criticise the lawyer's work with all of this, and the document I read was only one of many, but even so, and this is something I will say, at that time I couldn't see any progress in my trial at all." "And what sort of progress had you been hoping for?" asked K. "That's a very sensible question," said the businessman with a smile, "it's only very rare that you see any progress in these proceedings at all. But I didn't know that then. I'm a businessman, much more in those days than now, I wanted to see some tangible progress, it should have all been moving to some conclusion or at least should have been moving on in some way according to the rules. Instead of which there were just more hearings, and most of them went through the same things anyway; I had all the answers off pat like in a church service; there were messengers from the court coming to me at work several times a week, or they came to me at home or anywhere else they could find me; and that was very disturbing of course (but at least now things are better in that respect, it's much less disturbing when they contact you by telephone), and rumours about my trial even started to spread among some of the people I do business with, and especially my relations, so I was being made to suffer in many different ways but there was still not the slightest sign that even the first hearing would take place soon. So I went to the lawyer and complained about it. He explained it all to me at length, but refused to do anything I asked for, no-one has any influence on the way the trial proceeds, he said, to try and insist on it in any of the documents submitted - like I was asking - was simply unheard of and would do harm to both him and me. I thought to myself: What this lawyer can't or won't do another lawyer will. So I looked round for other lawyers. And before you say anything: none of them asked for a definite date for the main trial and none of them got one, and anyway, apart from one exception which I'll talk about in a minute, it really is impossible, that's one thing this lawyer didn't mislead me about; but besides, I had no reason to regret turning to other lawyers. Perhaps you've already heard how Dr. Huld talks about the petty lawyers, he probably made them sound very contemptible to you, and he's right, they are contemptible. But when he talks about them and compares them with himself and his colleagues there's a small error running through what he says, and, just for your interest, I'll tell you about it. When he talks about the lawyers he mixes with he sets them apart by calling them the 'great lawyers'. That's wrong, anyone can call himself 'great' if he wants to, of course, but in this case only the usage of the court can make that distinction. You see, the court says that besides the petty lawyers there are also minor lawyers and great lawyers. This one and his colleagues are only minor lawyers, and the difference in rank between them and the great lawyers, who I've only ever heard about and never seen, is incomparably greater than between the minor lawyers and the despised petty lawyers." "The great lawyers?" asked K. "Who are they then? How do you contact them?" "You've never heard about them, then?" said the businessman. "There's hardly anyone who's been accused who doesn't spend a lot of time dreaming about the great lawyers once he's heard about them. It's best if you don't let yourself be misled in that way. I don't know who the great lawyers are, and there's probably no way of contacting them. I don't know of any case I can talk about with certainty where they've taken any part. They do defend a lot of people, but you can't get hold of them by your own efforts, they only defend those who they want to defend. And I don't suppose they ever take on cases that haven't already got past the lower courts. Anyway, it's best not to think about them, as if you do it makes the discussions with the other lawyers, all their advice and all that they do manage to achieve, seem so unpleasant and useless, I had that experience myself, just wanted to throw everything away and lay at home in bed and hear nothing more about it. But that, of course, would be the stupidest thing you could do, and you wouldn't be left in peace in bed for very long either." "So you weren't thinking about the great lawyers at that time?" asked K. "Not for very long," said the businessman, and smiled again, "you can't forget about them entirely, I'm afraid, especially in the night when these thoughts come so easily. But I wanted immediate results in those days, so I went to the petty lawyers."

"Well look at you two sat huddled together!" called Leni as she came back with the dish and stood in the doorway. They were indeed sat close together, if either of them turned his head even slightly it would have knocked against the other's, the businessman was not only very small but also sat hunched down, so that K. was also forced to bend down low if he wanted to hear everything. "Not quite yet!" called out K., to turn Leni away, his hand, still resting on the businessman's hand, twitching with impatience. "He wanted me to tell him about my trial," said the businessman to Leni. "Carry on, then, carry on," she said. She spoke to the businessman with affection but, at the same time, with condescension. K. did not like that, he had begun to learn that the man was of some value after all, he had experience at least, and he was willing to share it. Leni was probably wrong about him. He watched her in irritation as Leni now took the candle from the businessman's hand - which he had been holding on to all this time - wiped his hand with her apron and then knelt beside him to scratch off some wax that had dripped from the candle onto his trousers. "You were about to tell me about the petty lawyers," said K., shoving Leni's hand away with no further comment. "What's wrong with you today?" asked Leni, tapped him gently and carried on with what she had been doing. "Yes, the petty lawyers," said the businessman, putting his hand to his brow as if thinking hard. K. wanted to help him and said, "You wanted immediate results and so went to the petty lawyers." "Yes, that's right," said the businessman, but did not continue with what he'd been saying. "Maybe he doesn't want to speak about it in front of Leni," thought K., suppressing his impatience to hear the rest straight away, and stopped trying to press him.

"Have you told him I'm here?" he asked Leni. "Course I have," she said, "he's waiting for you. Leave Block alone now, you can talk to Block later, he'll still be here." K. still hesitated. "You'll still be here?" he asked the businessman, wanting to hear the answer from him and not wanting Leni to speak about the businessman as if he weren't there, he was full of secret resentment towards Leni today. And once more it was only Leni who answered. "He often sleeps here." "He sleeps here?" exclaimed K., he had thought the businessman would just wait there for him while he quickly settled his business with the lawyer, and then they would leave together to discuss everything thoroughly and undisturbed. "Yes," said Leni, "not everyone's like you, Josef, allowed to see the lawyer at any time you like. Don't even seem surprised that the lawyer, despite being ill, still receives you at eleven o'clock at night. You take it far too much for granted, what your friends do for you. Well, your friends, or at least

I do, we like to do things for you. I don't want or need any more thanks than that you're fond of me." "Fond of you?" thought K. at first, and only then it occurred to him, "Well, yes, I am fond of her." Nonetheless, what he said, forgetting all the rest, was, "He receives me because I am his client. If I needed anyone else's help I'd have to beg and show gratitude whenever I do anything." "He's really nasty today, isn't he?" Leni asked the businessman. "Now it's me who's not here," thought K., and nearly lost his temper with the businessman when, with the same rudeness as Leni, he said, "The lawyer also has other reasons to receive him. His case is much more interesting than mine. And it's only in its early stages too, it probably hasn't progressed very far so the lawyer still likes to deal with him. That'll all change later on." "Yeah, yeah," said Leni, looking at the businessman and laughing. "He doesn't half talk!" she said, turning to face K. "You can't believe a word he says. He's as talkative as he is sweet. Maybe that's why the lawyer can't stand him. At least, he only sees him when he's in the right mood. I've already tried hard to change that but it's impossible. Just think, there are times when I tell him Block's here and he doesn't receive him until three days later. And if Block isn't on the spot when he's called then everything's lost and it all has to start all over again. That's why I let Block sleep here, it wouldn't be the first time Dr. Huld has wanted to see him in the night. So now Block is ready for that. Sometimes, when he knows Block is still here, he'll even change his mind about letting him in to see him." K. looked questioningly at the businessman. The latter nodded and, although he had spoken quite openly with K. earlier, seemed to be confused with shame as he said, "Yes, later on you become very dependent on your lawyer." "He's only pretending to mind," said Leni. "He likes to sleep here really, he's often said so." She went over to a little door and shoved it open. "Do you want to see his bedroom?" she asked. K. went over to the low, windowless room and looked in from the doorway. The room contained a narrow bed which filled it completely, so that to get into the bed you would need to climb over the bedpost. At the head of the bed there was a niche in the wall where, fastidiously tidy, stood a candle, a bottle of ink, and a pen with a bundle of papers which were probably to do with the trial. "You sleep in the maid's room?" asked K., as he went back to the businessman. "Leni's let me have it," answered the businessman, "it has many advantages." K. looked long at him; his first impression of the businessman had perhaps not been right; he had experience as his trial had already lasted a long time, but he had paid a heavy price for this experience. K. was suddenly unable to bear the sight of the businessman any longer. "Bring him to bed, then!" he called out to Leni, who seemed to understand him. For himself, he wanted to go to the lawyer and, by dismissing him, free himself from not only the lawyer but also from Leni and the businessman. But before he had reached the door the businessman spoke to him gently. "Excuse me, sir," he said, and K. looked round crossly. "You've forgotten your promise," said the businessman, stretching his hand out to K. imploringly from where he sat. "You were going to tell me a secret." "That is true," said K., as he glanced at Leni, who was watching him carefully, to check on her. "So listen; it's hardly a secret now anyway. I'm going to see the lawyer now to sack him." "He's sacking him!" yelled the businessman, and he jumped up from his chair and ran around the kitchen with his arms in the air. He kept on shouting, "He's sacking his lawyer!" Leni tried to rush at K. but the businessman got in her way so that she shoved him away with her fists. Then, still with her hands balled into fists, she ran after K. who, however, had been given a long start. He was already inside the lawyer's room by the time Leni caught up with him. He had almost closed the door behind himself, but Leni held the door open with her foot, grabbed his arm and tried to pull him back. But he put such pressure on her wrist that, with a sigh, she was forced to release him. She did not dare go into the room straight away, and K. locked the door with the key.

"I've been waiting for you a very long time," said the lawyer from his bed. He had been reading something by the light of a candle but now he laid it onto the bedside table and put his glasses on, looking at K. sharply through them. Instead of apologising K. said, "I'll be leaving again soon." As he had not apologised the lawyer ignored what K. said, and replied, "I won't let you in this late again next time." "I find that quite acceptable," said K. The lawyer looked at him quizzically. "Sit down," he said. "As you wish," said K., drawing a chair up to the bedside table and sitting down. "It seemed to me that you locked the door," said the lawyer. "Yes," said K., "it was because of Leni." He had no intention of letting anyone off lightly. But the lawyer asked him, "Was she being importunate again?" "Importunate?" asked K. "Yes," said the lawyer, laughing as he did so, had a fit of coughing and then, once it had passed, began to laugh again. "I'm sure you must have noticed how importunate she can be sometimes," he said, and patted K.'s hand which K. had rested on the bedside table and which he now snatched back. "You don't attach much importance to it, then," said the lawyer when K. was silent, "so much the better. Otherwise I might have needed to apologise to you. It is a peculiarity of Leni's. I've long since forgiven her for it, and I wouldn't be talking of it now, if you hadn't locked the door just now. Anyway, perhaps I should at least explain this peculiarity of hers to you, but you seem rather disturbed, the way you're looking at me, and so that's why I'll do it, this peculiarity of hers consists in this; Leni finds most of the accused attractive. She attaches herself to each of them, loves each of them, even seems to be loved by each of them; then she sometimes entertains me by telling me about them when I allow her to. I am not so astonished by all of this as you seem to be. If you look at them in the right way the accused really can be attractive, quite often. But that is a remarkable and to some extent scientific phenomenon. Being indicted does not cause any clear, precisely definable change in a person's appearance, of course. But it's not like with other legal matters, most of them remain in their usual way of life and, if they have a good lawyer looking after them, the trial doesn't get in their way. But there are nonetheless those who have experience in these matters who can look at a crowd, however big, and tell you which among them is facing a charge. How can they do that, you will ask. My answer will not please you. It is simply that those who are facing a charge are the most attractive. It cannot be their guilt that makes them attractive as not all of them are guilty - at least that's what I, as a lawyer, have to say - and nor can it be the proper punishment that has made them attractive as not all of them are punished, so it can only be that the proceedings levelled against them take some kind of hold on them. Whatever the reason, some of these attractive people are indeed very attractive. But all of them are attractive, even Block, pitiful worm that he is." As the lawyer finished what he was saying, K. was fully in control of himself, he had even nodded conspicuously at his last few words in order to confirm to himself the view he had already formed; that the lawyer was trying to confuse him, as he always did, by making general and irrelevant observations, and thus distract him from the main question of what he was actually doing for K.'s trial. The lawyer must have noticed that K. was offering him more resistance than before, as he became silent, giving K. the chance to speak himself, and then, as K. also remained silent, he asked, "Did you have a particular reason for coming to see me today?" "Yes," said K., putting his hand up to slightly shade his eyes from the light of the candle so that he could see the lawyer better, "I wanted to tell you that I'm withdrawing my representation from you, with immediate effect." "Do I understand you rightly?" asked the lawyer as he half raised himself in his bed and supported himself with one hand on the pillow. "I think you do," said K., sitting stiffly upright as if waiting in ambush. "Well we can certainly discuss this plan of yours," said the lawyer after a pause. "It's not a plan any more," said K. "That may be," said the lawyer, "but we still mustn't rush anything." He used the word 'we', as if he had no intention of letting K. go free, and as if, even if he could no longer represent him, he could still at least continue as his adviser. "Nothing is being rushed," said K., standing slowly up and going behind his chair, "everything has been well thought out and probably even for too long. The decision is final." "Then allow me to say a few words," said the lawyer, throwing the bed cover to one side and sitting on the edge of the bed. His naked, white-haired legs shivered in the cold. He asked K. to pass him a blanket from the couch. K. passed him the blanket and said, "You are running the risk of catching cold for no reason." "The circumstances are important enough," said the lawyer as he wrapped the bed cover around the top half of his body and then the blanket around his legs. "Your uncle is my friend and in the course of time I've become fond of you as well. I admit that quite openly. There's nothing in that for me to be ashamed of." It was very unwelcome for K. to hear the old man speak in this touching way, as it forced him to explain himself more fully, which he would rather have avoided, and he was aware that it also confused him even though it could never make him reverse his decision. "Thank you for feeling so friendly toward me," he said, "and I also realise how deeply involved you've been in my case, as deeply as possible for yourself and to bring as much advantage as possible to me. Nonetheless, I have recently come to the conviction that it is not enough. I would naturally never attempt, considering that you are so much older and more experienced than I am, to convince you of my opinion; if I have ever unintentionally done so then I beg your forgiveness, but, as you have just said yourself, the circumstances are important enough and it is my belief that my trial needs to be approached with much more vigour than has so far been the case." "I see," said the lawyer, "you've become impatient." "I am not impatient," said K., with some irritation and he stopped paying so much attention to his choice of words. "When I first came here with my uncle you probably noticed I wasn't greatly concerned about my case, and if I wasn't reminded of it by force, as it were, I would forget about it completely. But my uncle insisted I should allow you to represent me and I did so as a favour to him. I could have expected the case to be less of a burden than it had been, as the point of taking on a lawyer is that he should take on some of its weight. But what actually happened was the opposite. Before, the trial was never such a worry for me as it has been since you've been representing me. When I was by myself I never did anything about my case, I was hardly aware of it, but then, once there was someone representing me, everything was set for something to happen, I was always, without cease, waiting for you to do something, getting more and more tense, but you did nothing. I did get some information about the court from you that I probably could not have got anywhere else, but that can't be enough when the trial, supposedly in secret, is getting closer and closer to me." K. had pushed the chair away and stood erect, his hands in the pockets of his frock coat. "After a certain point in the proceedings," said the lawyer quietly and calmly, "nothing new of any importance ever happens. So many litigants, at the same stage in their trials, have stood before me just like you are now and spoken in the same way." "Then these other litigants," said K., "have all been right, just as I am. That does not show that I'm not." "I wasn't trying to show that you were mistaken," said the lawyer, "but I wanted to add that I expected better judgement from you than from the others, especially as I've given you more insight into the workings of the court and my own activities than I normally do. And now I'm forced to accept that, despite everything, you have too little trust in me. You don't make it easy for me." How the lawyer was humiliating himself to K.! He was showing no regard for the dignity of his position, which on this point, must have been at its most sensitive. And why did he do that? He did seem to be very busy as a lawyer as well a rich man, neither the loss of income nor the loss of a client could have been of much importance to him in themselves. He was moreover unwell and should have been thinking of passing work on to others. And despite all that he held on tightly to K. Why? Was it something personal for his uncle's sake, or did he really see K.'s case as one that was exceptional and hoped to be able to distinguish himself with it, either for K.'s sake or - and this possibility could never be excluded - for his friends at the court? It was not possible to learn anything by looking at him, even though K. was scrutinizing him quite brazenly. It could almost be supposed he was deliberately hiding his thoughts as he waited to see what effect his words would have. But he clearly deemed K.'s silence to be favourable for himself and he continued, "You will have noticed the size of my office, but that I don't employ any staff to help me. That used to be quite different, there was a time when several young lawyers were working for me but now I work alone. This is partly to do with changes in the way I do business, in that I concentrate nowadays more and more on matters such as your own case, and partly to do with the ever deeper understanding that I acquire from these legal matters. I found that I could never let anyone else deal with this sort of work unless I wanted to harm both the client and the job I had taken on. But the decision to do all the work myself had its obvious result: I was forced to turn almost everyone away who asked me to represent them and could only accept those I was especially interested in - well there are enough creatures who leap at every crumb I throw down, and they're not so very far away. Most importantly, I became ill from over-work. But despite that I don't regret my decision, quite possibly I should have turned more cases away than I did, but it did turn out to be entirely necessary for me to devote myself fully to the cases I did take on, and the successful results showed that it was worth it. I once read a description of the difference between representing someone in ordinary legal matters and in legal matters of this sort, and the writer expressed it very well. This is what he said: some lawyers lead their clients on a thread until judgement is passed, but there are others who immediately lift their clients onto their shoulders and carry them all the way to the judgement and beyond. That's just how it is. But it was quite true when I said I never regret all this work. But if, as in your case, they are so fully misunderstood, well, then I come very close to regretting it." All this talking did more to make K. impatient than to persuade him. From the way the lawyer was speaking, K. thought he could hear what he could expect if he gave in, the delays and excuses would begin again, reports of how the documents were progressing, how the mood of the court officials had improved, as well as all the enormous difficulties - in short all that he had heard so many times before would be brought out again even more fully, he would try to mislead K. with hopes that were never specified and to make him suffer with threats that were never clear. He had to put a stop to that, so he said, "What will you undertake on my behalf if you continue to represent me?" The lawyer quietly accepted even this insulting question, and answered, "I should continue with what I've already been doing for you." "That's just what I thought," said K., "and now you don't need to say another word." "I will make one more attempt," said the lawyer as if whatever had been making K. so annoyed was affecting him too. "You see, I have the impression that you have not only misjudged the legal assistance I have given you but also that that misjudgement has led you to behave in this way, you seem, although you are the accused, to have been treated too well or, to put it a better way, handled with neglect, with apparent neglect. Even that has its reason; it is often better to be in chains than to be free. But I would like to show you how other defendants are treated, perhaps you will succeed in learning something from it. What I will do is I will call Block in, unlock the door and sit down here beside the bedside table." "Be glad to," said K., and did as the lawyer suggested; he was always ready to learn something new. But to make sure of himself for any event he added, "but you do realise that you are no longer to be my lawyer, don't you?" "Yes," said the lawyer. "But you can still change your mind today if you want to." He lay back down in the bed, pulled the quilt up to his chin and turned to face the wall. Then he rang.

Leni appeared almost the moment he had done so. She looked hurriedly at K. and the lawyer to try and find out what had happened; she seemed to be reassured by the sight of K. sitting calmly at the lawyer's bed. She smiled and nodded to K., K. looked blankly back at her. "Fetch Block," said the lawyer. But instead of going to fetch him, Leni just went to the door and called out, "Block! To the lawyer!" Then, probably because the lawyer had turned his face to the wall and was paying no attention, she slipped in behind K.'s chair. From then on, she bothered him by leaning forward over the back of the chair or, albeit very tenderly and carefully, she would run her hands through his hair and over his cheeks. K. eventually tried to stop her by taking hold of one hand, and after some resistance Leni let him keep hold of it. Block came as soon as he was called, but he remained standing in the doorway and seemed to be wondering whether he should enter or not. He raised his eyebrows and lowered his head as if listening to find out whether the order to attend the lawyer would be repeated. K. could have encouraged him to enter, but he had decided to make a final break not only with the lawyer but with everything in his home, so he kept himself motionless. Leni was also silent. Block noticed that at least no-one was chasing him away, and, on tiptoe, he entered the room, his face was tense, his hands were clenched behind his back. He left the door open in case he needed to go back again. K. did not even glance at him, he looked instead only at the thick quilt under which the lawyer could not be seen as he had squeezed up very close to the wall. Then his voice was heard: "Block here?" he asked. Block had already crept some way into the room but this question seemed to give him first a shove in the breast and then another in the back, he seemed about to fall but remained standing, deeply bowed, and said, "At your service, sir." "What do you want?" asked the lawyer, "you've come at a bad time." "Wasn't I summoned?" asked Block, more to himself than the lawyer. He held his hands in front of himself as protection and would have been ready to run away any moment. "You were summoned," said the lawyer, "but you have still come at a bad time." Then, after a pause he added, "You always come at a bad time." When the lawyer started speaking Block had stopped looking at the bed but stared rather into one of the corners, just listening, as if the light from the speaker were brighter than Block could bear to look at. But it was also difficult for him to listen, as the lawyer was speaking into the wall and speaking quickly and quietly. "Would you like me to go away again, sir?" asked Block. "Well you're here now," said the lawyer. "Stay!" It was as if the lawyer had not done as Block had wanted but instead threatened him with a stick, as now Block really began to shake. "I went to see," said the lawyer, "the third judge yesterday, a friend of mine, and slowly brought the conversation round to the subject of you. Do you want to know what he said?" "Oh, yes please," said Block. The lawyer did not answer immediately, so Block repeated his request and lowered his head as if about to kneel down. But then K. spoke to him: "What do you think you're doing?" he shouted. Leni had wanted to stop him from calling out and so he took hold of her other hand. It was not love that made him squeeze it and hold on to it so tightly, she sighed frequently and tried to disengage her hands from him. But Block was punished for K.'s outburst, as the lawyer asked him, "Who is your lawyer?" "You are, sir," said Block. "And who besides me?" the lawyer asked. "No-one besides you, sir," said Block. "And let there be no-one besides me," said the lawyer. Block fully understood what that meant, he glowered at K., shaking his head violently. If these actions had been translated into words they would have been coarse insults. K. had been friendly and willing to discuss his own case with someone like this! "I won't disturb you any more," said K., leaning back in his chair. "You can kneel down or creep on all fours, whatever you like. I won't bother with you any more." But Block still had some sense of pride, at least where K. was concerned, and he went towards him waving his fists, shouting as loudly as he dared while the lawyer was there. "You shouldn't speak to me like that, that's not allowed. Why are you insulting me? Especially here in front of the lawyer, where both of us, you and me, we're only tolerated because of his charity. You're not a better person than me, you've been accused of something too, you're facing a charge too. If, in spite of that, you're still a gentleman then I'm just as much a gentleman as you are, if not even more so. And I want to be spoken to as a gentleman, especially by you. If you think being allowed to sit there and quietly listen while I creep on all fours as you put it makes you something better than me, then there's an old legal saying you ought to bear in mind: If you're under suspicion it's better to be moving than still, as if you're still you can be in the pan of the scales without knowing it and be weighed along with your sins." K. said nothing. He merely looked in amazement at this distracted being, his eyes completely still. He had gone through such changes in just the last few hours! Was it the trial that was throwing him from side to side in this way and stopped him knowing who was friend and who was foe? Could he not see the lawyer was deliberately humiliating him and had no other purpose today than to show off his power to K., and perhaps even thereby subjugate K.? But if Block was incapable of seeing that, or if he so feared the lawyer that no such insight would even be of any use to him, how was it that he was either so sly or so bold as to lie to the lawyer and conceal from him the fact that he had other lawyers working on his behalf? And how did he dare to attack K., who could betray his secret any time he liked? But he dared even more than this, he went to the lawyer's bed and began there to make complaints about K. "Dr. Huld, sir," he said, "did you hear the way this man spoke to me? You can count the length of his trial in hours, and he wants to tell me what to do when I've been involved in a legal case for five years. He even insults me. He doesn't know anything, but he insults me, when I, as far as my weak ability allows, when I've made a close study of how to behave with the court, what we ought to do and what the court practices are." "Don't let anyone bother you," said the lawyer, "and do what seems to you to be right." "I will," said Block, as if speaking to himself to give himself courage, and with a quick glance to the side he kneeled down close beside the bed. "I'm kneeling now Dr. Huld, sir," he said. But the lawyer remained silent. With one hand, Block carefully stroked the bed cover. In the silence while he did so, Leni, as she freed herself from K.'s hands, said, "You're hurting me. Let go of me. I'm going over to Block." She went over to him and sat on the edge of the bed. Block was very pleased at this and with lively, but silent, gestures he immediately urged her to intercede for him with the lawyer. It was clear that he desperately needed to be told something by the lawyer, although perhaps only so that he could make use of the information with his other lawyers. Leni probably knew very well how the lawyer could be brought round, pointed to his hand and pursed her lips as if making a kiss. Block immediately performed the hand-kiss and, at further urging from Leni, repeated it twice more. But the lawyer continued to be silent. Then Leni leant over the lawyer, as she stretched out, the attractive shape of her body could be seen, and, bent over close to his face, she stroked his long white hair. That now forced him to give an answer. "I'm rather wary of telling him," said the lawyer, and his head could be seen shaking slightly, perhaps so that he would feel the pressure of Leni's hand better. Block listened closely with his head lowered, as if by listening he were breaking an order. "What makes you so wary about it?" asked Leni. K. had the feeling he was listening to a contrived dialogue that had been repeated many times, that would be repeated many times more, and that for Block alone it would never lose its freshness. "What has his behaviour been like today?" asked the lawyer instead of an answer. Before Leni said anything she looked down at Block and watched him a short while as he raised his hands towards her and rubbed them together imploringly. Finally she gave a serious nod, turned back to the lawyer and said, "He's been quiet and industrious." This was an elderly businessman, a man whose beard was long, and he was begging a young girl to speak on his behalf. Even if there was some plan behind what he did, there was nothing that could reinstate him in the eyes of his fellow man. K. could not understand how the lawyer could have thought this performance would win him over. Even if he had done nothing earlier to make him want to leave then this scene would have done so. It was almost humiliating even for the onlooker. So these were the lawyer's methods, which K. fortunately had not been exposed to for long, to let the client forget about the whole world and leave him with nothing but the hope of reaching the end of his trial by this deluded means. He was no longer a client, he was the lawyer's dog. If the lawyer had ordered him to crawl under the bed as if it were a kennel and to bark out from under it, then he would have done so with enthusiasm. K. listened to all of this, testing it and thinking it over as if he had been given the task of closely observing everything spoken here, inform a higher office about it and write a report. "And what has he been doing all day?" asked the lawyer. "I kept him locked in the maid's room all day," said Leni, "so that he wouldn't stop me doing my work. That's where he usually stays. From time to time I looked in through the spyhole to see what he was doing, and each time he was kneeling on the bed and reading the papers you gave him, propped up on the window sill. That made a good impression on me; as the window only opens onto an air shaft and gives hardly any light. It showed how obedient he is that he was even reading in those conditions." "I'm pleased to hear it," said the lawyer. "But did he understand what he was reading?" While this conversation was going on, Block continually moved his lips and was clearly formulating the answers he hoped Leni would give. "Well I can't give you any certain answer to that of course," said Leni, "but I could see that he was reading thoroughly. He spent all day reading the same page, running his finger along the lines. Whenever I looked in on him he sighed as if this reading was a lot of work for him. I expect the papers you gave him were very hard to understand." "Yes," said the lawyer, "they certainly are that. And I really don't think he understood anything of them. But they should at least give him some inkling of just how hard a struggle it is and how much work it is for me to defend him. And who am I doing all this hard work for? I'm doing it - it's laughable even to say it - I'm doing it for Block. He ought to realise what that means, too. Did he study without a pause?" "Almost without a pause," answered Leni. "Just the once he asked me for a drink of water, so I gave him a glassful through the window. Then at eight o'clock I let him out and gave him something to eat." Block glanced sideways at K., as if he were being praised and had to impress K. as well. He now seemed more optimistic, he moved more freely and rocked back and forth on his knees. This made his astonishment all the more obvious when he heard the following words from the lawyer: "You speak well of him," said the lawyer, "but that's just what makes it difficult for me. You see, the judge did not speak well of him at all, neither about Block nor about his case." "Didn't speak well of him?" asked Leni. "How is that possible?" Block looked at her with such tension he seemed to think that although the judge's words had been spoken so long before she would be able to change them in his favour. "Not at all," said the lawyer. "In fact he became quite cross when I started to talk about Block to him. 'Don't talk to me about Block,' he said. 'He is my client,' said I. 'You're letting him abuse you,' he said. 'I don't think his case is lost yet,' said I. 'You're letting him abuse you,' he repeated. 'I don't think so,' said I. 'Block works hard in his case and always knows where it stands. He practically lives with me so that he always knows what's happening. You don't always find such enthusiasm as that. He's not very pleasant personally, I grant you, his manners are terrible and he's dirty, but as far as the trial's concerned he's quite immaculate.' I said immaculate, but I was deliberately exaggerating. Then he said, 'Block is sly, that's all. He's accumulated plenty of experience and knows how to delay proceedings. But there's more that he doesn't know than he does. What do you think he'd say if he learned his trial still hasn't begun, if you told him they haven't even rung the bell to announce the start of proceedings?' Alright Block, alright," said the lawyer, as at these words Block had begun to raise himself on his trembling knees and clearly wanted to plead for some explanation. It was the first time the lawyer had spoken any clear words directly to Block. He looked down with his tired eyes, half blankly and half at Block, who slowly sank back down on his knees under this gaze. "What the judge said has no meaning for you," said the lawyer. "You needn't be frightened at every word. If you do it again I won't tell you anything else at all. It's impossible to start a sentence without you looking at me as if you were receiving your final judgement. You should be ashamed of yourself here in front of my client! And you're destroying the trust he has for me. Just what is it you want? You're still alive, you're still under my protection. There's no point in worrying! Somewhere you've read that the final judgement can often come without warning, from anyone at any time. And, in the right circumstances, that's basically true, but it's also true that I dislike your anxiety and fear and see that you don't have the trust in me you should have. Now what have I just said? I repeated something said by one of the judges. You know that there are so many various opinions about the procedure that they form into a great big pile and nobody can make any sense of them. This judge, for instance, sees proceedings as starting at a different point from where I do. A difference of opinion, nothing more. At a certain stage in the proceedings tradition has it that a sign is given by ringing a bell. This judge sees that as the point at which proceedings begin. I can't set out all the opinions opposed to that view here, and you wouldn't understand it anyway, suffice it to say that there are many reasons to disagree with him." Embarrassed, Block ran his fingers through the pile of the carpet, his anxiety about what the judge had said had let him forget his inferior status towards the lawyer for a while, he thought only about himself and turned the judges words round to examine them from all sides. "Block," said Leni, as if reprimanding him, and, taking hold of the collar of his coat, pulled him up slightly higher. "Leave the carpet alone and listen to what the lawyer is saying."

This chapter was left unfinished.

Chapter Nine In the Cathedral

A very important Italian business contact of the bank had come to visit the city for the first time and K. was given the task of showing him some of its cultural sights. At any other time he would have seen this job as an honour but now, when he was finding it hard even to maintain his current position in the bank, he accepted it only with reluctance. Every hour that he could not be in the office was a cause of concern for him, he was no longer able to make use of his time in the office anything like as well as he had previously, he spent many hours merely pretending to do important work, but that only increased his anxiety about not being in the office. Then he sometimes thought he saw the deputy director, who was always watching, come into K.'s office, sit at his desk, look through his papers, receive clients who had almost become old friends of K., and lure them away from him, perhaps he even discovered mistakes, mistakes that seemed to threaten K. from a thousand directions when he was at work now, and which he could no longer avoid. So now, if he was ever asked to leave the office on business or even needed to make a short business trip, however much an honour it seemed - and tasks of this sort happened to have increased substantially recently - there was always the suspicion that they wanted to get him out of his office for a while and check his work, or at least the idea that they thought he was dispensable. It would not have been difficult for him to turn down most of these jobs, but he did not dare to do so because, if his fears had the slightest foundation, turning the jobs down would have been an acknowledgement of them. For this reason, he never demurred from accepting them, and even when he was asked to go on a tiring business trip lasting two days he said nothing about having to go out in the rainy autumn weather when he had a severe chill, just in order to avoid the risk of not being asked to go. When, with a raging headache, he arrived back from this trip he learned that he had been chosen to accompany the Italian business contact the following day. The temptation for once to turn the job down was very great, especially as it had no direct connection with business, but there was no denying that social obligations towards this business contact were in themselves important enough, only not for K., who knew quite well that he needed some successes at work if he was to maintain his position there and that, if he failed in that, it would not help him even if this Italian somehow found him quite charming; he did not want to be removed from his workplace for even one day, as the fear of not being allowed back in was too great, he knew full well that the fear was exaggerated but it still made him anxious. However, in this case it was almost impossible to think of an acceptable excuse, his knowledge of Italian was not great but still good enough; the deciding factor was that K. had earlier known a little about art history and this had become widely known around the bank in extremely exaggerated form, and that K. had been a member of the Society for the Preservation of City Monuments, albeit only for business reasons. It was said that this Italian was an art lover, so the choice of K. to accompany him was a matter of course.

It was a very rainy and stormy morning when K., in a foul temper at the thought of the day ahead of him, arrived early at seven o'clock in the office so that he could at least do some work before his visitor would prevent him. He had spent half the night studying a book of Italian grammar so that he would be somewhat prepared and was very tired; his desk was less attractive to him than the window where he had spent far too much time sitting of late, but he resisted the temptation and sat down to his work. Unfortunately, just then the servitor came in and reported that the director had sent him to see whether the chief clerk was already in his office; if he was, then would he please be so kind as to come to his reception room as the gentleman from Italy was already there. "I'll come straight away," said K. He put a small dictionary in his pocket, took a guide to the city's tourist sites under his arm that he had compiled for strangers, and went through the deputy director's office into that of the director. He was glad he had come into the office so early and was able to be of service immediately, nobody could seriously have expected that of him. The deputy director's office was, of course, still as empty as the middle of the night, the servitor had probably been asked to summon him too but without success. As K. entered the reception room two men stood up from the deep armchairs where they had been sitting. The director gave him a friendly smile, he was clearly very glad that K. was there, he immediately introduced him to the Italian who shook K.'s hand vigorously and joked that somebody was an early riser. K. did not quite understand whom he had in mind, it was moreover an odd expression to use and it took K. a little while to guess its meaning. He replied with a few bland phrases which the Italian received once more with a laugh, passing his hand nervously and repeatedly over his blue-grey, bushy moustache. This moustache was obviously perfumed, it was almost tempting to come close to it and sniff. When they had all sat down and begun a light preliminary conversation, K. was disconcerted to notice that he understood no more than fragments of what the Italian said. When he spoke very calmly he understood almost everything, but that was very infrequent, mostly the words gushed from his mouth and he seemed to be enjoying himself so much his head shook. When he was talking in this way his speech was usually wrapped up in some kind of dialect which seemed to K. to have nothing to do with Italian but which the director not only understood but also spoke, although K. ought to have foreseen this as the Italian came from the south of his country where the director had also spent several years. Whatever the cause, K. realised that the possibility of communicating with the Italian had been largely taken from him, even his French was difficult to understand, and his moustache concealed the movements of his lips which might have offered some help in understanding what he said. K. began to anticipate many difficulties, he gave up trying to understand what the Italian said - with the director there, who could understand him so easily, it would have been pointless effort - and for the time being did no more than scowl at the Italian as he relaxed sitting deep but comfortable in the armchair, as he frequently pulled at his short, sharply tailored jacket and at one time lifted his arms in the air and moved his hands freely to try and depict something that K. could not grasp, even though he was leaning forward and did not let the hands out of his sight. K. had nothing to occupy himself but mechanically watch the exchange between the two men and his tiredness finally made itself felt, to his alarm, although fortunately in good time, he once caught himself nearly getting up, turning round and leaving. Eventually the Italian looked at the clock and jumped up. After taking his leave from the director he turned to K., pressing himself so close to him that K. had to push his chair back just so that he could move. The director had, no doubt, seen the anxiety in K.'s eyes as he tried to cope with this dialect of Italian, he joined in with this conversation in a way that was so adroit and unobtrusive that he seemed to be adding no more than minor comments, whereas in fact he was swiftly and patiently breaking into what the Italian said so that K. could understand. K. learned in this way that the Italian first had a few business matters to settle, that he unfortunately had only a little time at his disposal, that he certainly did not intend to rush round to see every monument in the city, that he would much rather - at least as long as K. would agree, it was entirely his decision - just see the cathedral and to do so thoroughly. He was extremely pleased to be accompanied by someone who was so learned and so pleasant - by this he meant K., who was occupied not with listening to the Italian but the director - and asked if he would be so kind, if the time was suitable, to meet him in the cathedral in two hours' time at about ten o'clock. He hoped he would certainly be able to be there at that time. K. made an appropriate reply, the Italian shook first the director's hand and then K.'s, then the director's again and went to the door, half turned to the two men who followed him and continuing to talk without a break. K. remained together with the director for a short while, although the director looked especially unhappy today. He thought he needed to apologise to K. for something and told him - they were standing intimately close together - he had thought at first he would accompany the Italian himself, but then - he gave no more precise reason than this - then he decided it would be better to send K. with him. He should not be surprised if he could not understand the Italian at first, he would be able to very soon, and even if he really could not understand very much he said it was not so bad, as it was really not so important for the Italian to be understood. And anyway, K.'s knowledge of Italian was surprisingly good, the director was sure he would get by very well. And with that, it was time for K. to go. He spent the time still remaining to him with a dictionary, copying out obscure words he would need to guide the Italian round the cathedral. It was an extremely irksome task, servitors brought him the mail, bank staff came with various queries and, when they saw that K. was busy, stood by the door and did not go away until he had listened to them, the deputy director did not miss the opportunity to disturb K. and came in frequently, took the dictionary from his hand and flicked through its pages, clearly for no purpose, when the door to the ante-room opened even clients would appear from the half darkness and bow timidly to him - they wanted to attract his attention but were not sure whether he had seen them - all this activity was circling around K. with him at its centre while he compiled the list of words he would need, then looked them up in the dictionary, then wrote them out, then practised their pronunciation and finally tried to learn them by heart. The good intentions he had had earlier, though, seemed to have left him completely, it was the Italian who had caused him all this effort and sometimes he became so angry with him that he buried the dictionary under some papers firmly intending to do no more preparation, but then he realised he could not walk up and down in the cathedral with the Italian without saying a word, so, in an even greater rage, he pulled the dictionary back out again.

At exactly half past nine, just when he was about to leave, there was a telephone call for him, Leni wished him good morning and asked how he was, K. thanked her hurriedly and told her it was impossible for him to talk now as he had to go to the cathedral. "To the cathedral?" asked Leni. "Yes, to the cathedral." "What do you have to go to the cathedral for?" said Leni. K. tried to explain it to her briefly, but he had hardly begun when Leni suddenly said, "They're harassing you." One thing that K. could not bear was pity that he had not wanted or expected, he took his leave of her with two words, but as he put the receiver back in its place he said, half to himself and half to the girl on the other end of the line who could no longer hear him, "Yes, they're harassing me."

By now the time was late and there was almost a danger he would not be on time. He took a taxi to the cathedral, at the last moment he had remembered the album that he had had no opportunity to give to the Italian earlier and so took it with him now. He held it on his knees and drummed impatiently on it during the whole journey. The rain had eased off slightly but it was still damp chilly and dark, it would be difficult to see anything in the cathedral but standing about on cold flagstones might well make K.'s chill much worse. The square in front of the cathedral was quite empty, K. remembered how even as a small child he had noticed that nearly all the houses in this narrow square had the curtains at their windows closed most of the time, although today, with the weather like this, it was more understandable. The cathedral also seemed quite empty, of course no-one would think of going there on a day like this. K. hurried along both the side naves but saw no-one but an old woman who, wrapped up in a warm shawl, was kneeling at a picture of the Virgin Mary and staring up at it. Then, in the distance, he saw a church official who limped away through a doorway in the wall. K. had arrived on time, it had struck ten just as he was entering the building, but the Italian still was not there. K. went back to the main entrance, stood there indecisively for a while, and then walked round the cathedral in the rain in case the Italian was waiting at another entrance. He was nowhere to be found. Could the director have misunderstood what time they had agreed on? How could anyone understand someone like that properly anyway? Whatever had happened, K. would have to wait for him for at least half an hour. As he was tired he wanted to sit down, he went back inside the cathedral, he found something like a small carpet on one of the steps, he moved it with his foot to a nearby pew, wrapped himself up tighter in his coat, put the collar up and sat down. To pass the time he opened the album and flicked through the pages a little but soon had to give up as it became so dark that when he looked up he could hardly make out anything in the side nave next to him.

In the distance there was a large triangle of candles flickering on the main altar, K. was not certain whether he had seen them earlier. Perhaps they had only just been lit. Church staff creep silently as part of their job, you don't notice them. When

K. happened to turn round he also saw a tall, stout candle attached to a column not far behind him. It was all very pretty, but totally inadequate to illuminate the pictures which were usually left in the darkness of the side altars, and seemed to make the darkness all the deeper. It was discourteous of the Italian not to come but it was also sensible of him, there would have been nothing to see, they would have had to content themselves with seeking out a few pictures with K.'s electric pocket torch and looking at them one small part at a time. K. went over to a nearby side chapel to see what they could have hoped for, he went up a few steps to a low marble railing and leant over it to look at the altar picture by the light of his torch. The eternal light hung disturbingly in front of it. The first thing that K. partly saw and partly guessed at was a large knight in armour who was shown at the far edge of the painting. He was leaning on his sword that he had stuck into the naked ground in front of him where only a few blades of grass grew here and there. He seemed to be paying close attention to something that was being played out in front of him. It was astonishing to see how he stood there without going any closer. Perhaps it was his job to stand guard. It was a long time since K. had looked at any pictures and he studied the knight for a long time even though he had continually to blink as he found it difficult to bear the green light of his torch. Then when he moved the light to the other parts of the picture he found an interment of Christ shown in the usual way, it was also a comparatively new painting. He put his torch away and went back to his place.

There seemed to be no point in waiting for the Italian any longer, but outside it was certainly raining heavily, and as it was not so cold in the cathedral as K. had expected he decided to stay there for the time being. Close by him was the great pulpit, there were two plain golden crosses attached to its little round roof which were lying almost flat and whose tips crossed over each other. The outside of the pulpit's balustrade was covered in green foliage which continued down to the column supporting it, little angels could be seen among the leaves, some of them lively and some of them still. K. walked up to the pulpit and examined it from all sides, its stonework had been sculpted with great care, it seemed as if the foliage had trapped a deep darkness between and behind its leaves and held it there prisoner, K. lay his hand in one of these gaps and cautiously felt the stone, until then he had been totally unaware of this pulpit's existence. Then K. happened to notice one of the church staff standing behind the next row of pews, he wore a loose, creased, black cassock, he held a snuff box in his left hand and he was watching K. Now what does he want? thought K. Do I seem suspicious to him? Does he want a tip? But when the man in the cassock saw that K. had noticed him he raised his right hand, a pinch of snuff still held between two fingers, and pointed in some vague direction. It was almost impossible to understand what this behaviour meant, K. waited a while longer but the man in the cassock did not stop gesturing with his hand and even augmented it by nodding his head. "Now what does he want?" asked K. quietly, he did not dare call out loud here; but then he drew out his purse and pushed his way through the nearest pews to reach the man. He, however, immediately gestured to turn down this offer, shrugged his shoulders and limped away. As a child K. had imitated riding on a horse with the same sort of movement as this limp. "This old man is like a child," thought

K., "he doesn't have the sense for anything more than serving in a church. Look at the way he stops when I stop, and how he waits to see whether I'll continue." With a smile, K. followed the old man all the way up the side nave and almost as far as the main altar, all this time the old man continued to point at something but K. deliberately avoided looking round, he was only pointing in order to make it harder for K. to follow him. Eventually, K. did stop following, he did not want to worry the old man too much, and he also did not want to frighten him away completely in case the Italian turned up after all.

When he entered the central nave to go back to where he had left the album, he noticed a small secondary pulpit on a column almost next to the stalls by the altar where the choir sat. It was very simple, made of plain white stone, and so small that from a distance it looked like an empty niche where the statue of a saint ought to have been. It certainly would have been impossible for the priest to take a full step back from the balustrade, and, although there was no decoration on it, the top of the pulpit curved in exceptionally low so that a man of average height would not be able stand upright and would have to remain bent forward over the balustrade. In all, it looked as if it had been intended to make the priest suffer, it was impossible to understand why this pulpit would be needed as there were also the other ones available which were large and so artistically decorated.

And K. would certainly not have noticed this little pulpit if there had not been a lamp fastened above it, which usually meant there was a sermon about to be given. So was a sermon to be given now? In this empty church? K. looked down at the steps which, pressed close against the column, led up to the pulpit. They were so narrow they seemed to be there as decoration on the column rather than for anyone to use. But under the pulpit - K. grinned in astonishment - there really was a priest standing with his hand on the handrail ready to climb the steps and looking at K. Then he nodded very slightly, so that K. crossed himself and genuflected as he should have done earlier. With a little swing, the priest went up into the pulpit with short fast steps. Was there really a sermon about to begin? Maybe the man in the cassock had not been really so demented, and had meant to lead K.'s way to the preacher, which in this empty church would have been very necessary. And there was also, somewhere in front of a picture of the Virgin Mary, an old woman who should have come to hear the sermon. And if there was to be a sermon why had it not been introduced on the organ? But the organ remained quiet and merely looked out weakly from the darkness of its great height.

K. now considered whether he should leave as quickly as possible, if he did not do it now there would be no chance of doing so during the sermon and he would have to stay there for as long as it lasted, he had lost so much time when he should have been in his office, there had long been no need for him to wait for the Italian any longer, he looked at his watch, it was eleven. But could there really be a sermon given? Could K. constitute the entire congregation? How could he when he was just a stranger who wanted to look at the church? That, basically, was all he was. The idea of a sermon, now, at eleven o'clock, on a workday, in hideous weather, was nonsense. The priest - there was no doubt that he was a priest, a young man with a smooth, dark face - was clearly going up there just to put the lamp out after somebody had lit it by mistake.

But there had been no mistake, the priest seemed rather to check that the lamp was lit and turned it a little higher, then he slowly turned to face the front and leant down on the balustrade gripping its angular rail with both hands. He stood there like that for a while and, without turning his head, looked around. K. had moved back a long way and leant his elbows on the front pew. Somewhere in the church - he could not have said exactly where - he could make out the man in the cassock hunched under his bent back and at peace, as if his work were completed. In the cathedral it was now very quiet! But K. would have to disturb that silence, he had no intention of staying there; if it was the priest's duty to preach at a certain time regardless of the circumstances then he could, and he could do it without K.'s taking part, and K.'s presence would do nothing to augment the effect of it. So K. began slowly to move, felt his way on tiptoe along the pew, arrived at the broad aisle and went along it without being disturbed, except for the sound of his steps, however light, which rang out on the stone floor and resounded from the vaulting, quiet but continuous at a repeating, regular pace. K. felt slightly abandoned as, probably observed by the priest, he walked by himself between the empty pews, and the size of the cathedral seemed to be just at the limit of what a man could bear. When he arrived back at where he had been sitting he did not hesitate but simply reached out for the album he had left there and took it with him. He had nearly left the area covered by pews and was close to the empty space between himself and the exit when, for the first time, he heard the voice of the priest. A powerful and experienced voice. It pierced through the reaches of the cathedral ready waiting for it! But the priest was not calling out to the congregation, his cry was quite unambiguous and there was no escape from it, he called "Josef K.!"

K. stood still and looked down at the floor. In theory he was still free, he could have carried on walking, through one of three dark little wooden doors not far in front of him and away from there. It would simply mean he had not understood, or that he had understood but chose not to pay attention to it. But if he once turned round he would be trapped, then he would have acknowledged that he had understood perfectly well, that he really was the Josef K. the priest had called to and that he was willing to follow. If the priest had called out again K. would certainly have carried on out the door, but everything was silent as K. also waited, he turned his head slightly as he wanted to see what the priest was doing now. He was merely standing in the pulpit as before, but it was obvious that he had seen K. turn his head. If K. did not now turn round completely it would have been like a child playing hide and seek. He did so, and the priest beckoned him with his finger. As everything could now be done openly he ran - because of curiosity and the wish to get it over with - with long flying leaps towards the pulpit. At the front pews he stopped, but to the priest he still seemed too far away, he reached out his hand and pointed sharply down with his finger to a place immediately in front of the pulpit. And K. did as he was told, standing in that place he had to bend his head a long way back just to see the priest. "You are Josef K.," said the priest, and raised his hand from the balustrade to make a gesture whose meaning was unclear. "Yes," said K., he considered how freely he had always given his name in the past, for some time now it had been a burden to him, now there were people who knew his name whom he had never seen before, it had been so nice first to introduce yourself and only then for people to know who you were. "You have been accused," said the priest, especially gently. "Yes," said K., "so I have been informed." "Then you are the one I am looking for," said the priest. "I am the prison chaplain." "I see," said K. "I had you summoned here," said the priest, "because I wanted to speak to you." "I knew nothing of that," said K. "I came here to show the cathedral to a gentleman from Italy." "That is beside the point," said the priest. "What are you holding in your hand? Is it a prayer book?" "No," answered K., "it's an album of the city's tourist sights." "Put it down," said the priest. K. threw it away with such force that it flapped open and rolled across the floor, tearing its pages. "Do you know your case is going badly?" asked the priest. "That's how it seems to me too," said K. "I've expended a lot of effort on it, but so far with no result. Although I do still have some documents to submit." "How do you imagine it will end?" asked the priest. "At first I thought it was bound to end well," said K., "but now I have my doubts about it. I don't know how it will end. Do you know?" "I don't," said the priest, "but I fear it will end badly. You are considered guilty. Your case will probably not even go beyond a minor court. Provisionally at least, your guilt is seen as proven." "But I'm not guilty," said K., "there's been a mistake. How is it even possible for someone to be guilty. We're all human beings here, one like the other." "That is true," said the priest, "but that is how the guilty speak." "Do you presume I'm guilty too?" asked K. "I make no presumptions about you," said the priest. "I thank you for that," said K. "but everyone else involved in these proceedings has something against me and presumes I'm guilty. They even influence those who aren't involved. My position gets harder all the time." "You don't understand the facts," said the priest, "the verdict does not come suddenly, proceedings continue until a verdict is reached gradually." "I see," said K., lowering his head. "What do you intend to do about your case next?" asked the priest. "I still need to find help," said K., raising his head to see what the priest thought of this. "There are still certain possibilities I haven't yet made use of." "You look for too much help from people you don't know," said the priest disapprovingly, "and especially from women. Can you really not see that's not the help you need?" "Sometimes, in fact quite often, I could believe you're right," said K., "but not always. Women have a lot of power. If I could persuade some of the women I know to work together with me then I would be certain to succeed. Especially in a court like this that seems to consist of nothing but woman-chasers. Show the examining judge a woman in the distance and he'll run right over the desk, and the accused, just to get to her as soon as he can." The priest lowered his head down to the balustrade, only now did the roof over the pulpit seem to press him down. What sort of dreadful weather could it be outside? It was no longer just a dull day, it was deepest night. None of the stained glass in the main window shed even a flicker of light on the darkness of the walls. And this was the moment when the man in the cassock chose to put out the candles on the main altar, one by one. "Are you cross with me?" asked

K. "Maybe you don't know what sort of court it is you serve." He received no answer. "Well, it's just my own experience," said K. Above him there was still silence. "I didn't mean to insult you," said K. At that, the priest screamed down at K.: "Can you not see two steps in front of you?" He shouted in anger, but it was also the scream of one who sees another fall and, shocked and without thinking, screams against his own will.

The two men, then, remained silent for a long time. In the darkness beneath him, the priest could not possibly have seen K. distinctly, although K. was able to see him clearly by the light of the little lamp. Why did the priest not come down? He had not given a sermon, he had only told K. a few things which, if he followed them closely, would probably cause him more harm than good. But the priest certainly seemed to mean well, it might even be possible, if he would come down and cooperate with him, it might even be possible for him to obtain some acceptable piece of advice that could make all the difference, it might, for instance, be able to show him not so much to influence the proceedings but how to break free of them, how to evade them, how to live away from them. K. had to admit that this was something he had had on his mind quite a lot of late. If the priest knew of such a possibility he might, if K. asked him, let him know about it, even though he was part of the court himself and even though, when K. had criticised the court, he had held down his gentle nature and actually shouted at K.

"Would you not like to come down here?" asked K. "If you're not going to give a sermon come down here with me." "Now I can come down," said the priest, perhaps he regretted having shouted at K. As he took down the lamp from its hook he said, "to start off with I had to speak to you from a distance. Otherwise I'm too easily influenced and forget my duty."

K. waited for him at the foot of the steps. While he was still on one of the higher steps as he came down them the priest reached out his hand for K. to shake. "Can you spare me a little of your time?" asked K. "As much time as you need," said the priest, and passed him the little lamp for him to carry. Even at close distance the priest did not lose a certain solemnity that seemed to be part of his character. "You are very friendly towards me," said K., as they walked up and down beside each other in the darkness of one of the side naves. "That makes you an exception among all those who belong to the court. I can trust you more than any of the others I've seen. I can speak openly with you." "Don't fool yourself," said the priest. "How would I be fooling myself?" asked K. "You fool yourself in the court," said the priest, "it talks about this self-deceit in the opening paragraphs to the law. In front of the law there is a doorkeeper. A man from the countryside comes up to the door and asks for entry. But the doorkeeper says he can't let him in to the law right now. The man thinks about this, and then he asks if he'll be able to go in later on. 'That's possible,' says the doorkeeper, 'but not now'. The gateway to the law is open as it always is, and the doorkeeper has stepped to one side, so the man bends over to try and see in. When the doorkeeper notices this he laughs and says, 'If you're tempted give it a try, try and go in even though I say you can't. Careful though: I'm powerful. And I'm only the lowliest of all the doormen. But there's a doorkeeper for each of the rooms and each of them is more powerful than the last. It's more than I can stand just to look at the third one.' The man from the country had not expected difficulties like this, the law was supposed to be accessible for anyone at any time, he thinks, but now he looks more closely at the doorkeeper in his fur coat, sees his big hooked nose, his long thin tartar-beard, and he decides it's better to wait until he has permission to enter. The doorkeeper gives him a stool and lets him sit down to one side of the gate. He sits there for days and years. He tries to be allowed in time and again and tires the doorkeeper with his requests. The doorkeeper often questions him, asking about where he's from and many other things, but these are disinterested questions such as great men ask, and he always ends up by telling him he still can't let him in. The man had come well equipped for his journey, and uses everything, however valuable, to bribe the doorkeeper. He accepts everything, but as he does so he says, 'I'll only accept this so that you don't think there's anything you've failed to do'. Over many years, the man watches the doorkeeper almost without a break. He forgets about the other doormen, and begins to think this one is the only thing stopping him from gaining access to the law. Over the first few years he curses his unhappy condition out loud, but later, as he becomes old, he just grumbles to himself. He becomes senile, and as he has come to know even the fleas in the doorkeeper's fur collar over the years that he has been studying him he even asks them to help him and change the doorkeeper's mind. Finally his eyes grow dim, and he no longer knows whether it's really getting darker or just his eyes that are deceiving him. But he seems now to see an inextinguishable light begin to shine from the darkness behind the door. He doesn't have long to live now. Just before he dies, he brings together all his experience from all this time into one question which he has still never put to the doorkeeper. He beckons to him, as he's no longer able to raise his stiff body. The doorkeeper has to bend over deeply as the difference in their sizes has changed very much to the disadvantage of the man. 'What is it you want to know now?' asks the doorkeeper, 'You're insatiable.' 'Everyone wants access to the law,' says the man, 'how come, over all these years, no- one but me has asked to be let in?' The doorkeeper can see the man's come to his end, his hearing has faded, and so, so that he can be heard, he shouts to him: 'Nobody else could have got in this way, as this entrance was meant only for you. Now I'll go and close it'."

"So the doorkeeper cheated the man," said K. immediately, who had been captivated by the story. "Don't be too quick," said the priest, "don't take somebody else's opinion without checking it. I told you the story exactly as it was written. There's nothing in there about cheating." "But it's quite clear," said K., "and your first interpretation of it was quite correct. The doorkeeper gave him the information that would release him only when it could be of no more use." "He didn't ask him before that," said the priest, "and don't forget he was only a doorkeeper, and as doorkeeper he did his duty." "What makes you think he did his duty?" asked K., "He didn't. It might have been his duty to keep everyone else away, but this man is who the door was intended for and he ought to have let him in." "You're not paying enough attention to what was written and you're changing the story," said the priest. "According to the story, there are two important things that the doorkeeper explains about access to the law, one at the beginning, one at the end. At one place he says he can't allow him in now, and at the other he says this entrance was intended for him alone. If one of the statements contradicted the other you would be right and the doorkeeper would have cheated the man from the country. But there is no contradiction. On the contrary, the first statement even hints at the second. You could almost say the doorkeeper went beyond his duty in that he offered the man some prospect of being admitted in the future. Throughout the story, his duty seems to have been merely to turn the man away, and there are many commentators who are surprised that the doorkeeper offered this hint at all, as he seems to love exactitude and keeps strict guard over his position. He stays at his post for many years and doesn't close the gate until the very end, he's very conscious of the importance of his service, as he says, 'I'm powerful,' he has respect for his superiors, as he says, 'I'm only the lowliest of the doormen', he's not talkative, as through all these years the only questions he asks are 'disinterested', he's not corruptible, as when he's offered a gift he says, 'I'll only accept this so that you don't think there's anything you've failed to do,' as far as fulfilling his duty goes he can be neither ruffled nor begged, as it says about the man that, 'he tires the doorkeeper with his requests', even his external appearance suggests a pedantic character, the big hooked nose and the long, thin, black tartar-beard. How could any doorkeeper be more faithful to his duty? But in the doorkeeper's character there are also other features which might be very useful for those who seek entry to the law, and when he hinted at some possibility in the future it always seemed to make it clear that he might even go beyond his duty. There's no denying he's a little simple minded, and that makes him a little conceited. Even if all he said about his power and the power of the other doorkeepers and how not even he could bear the sight of them - I say even if all these assertions are right, the way he makes them shows that he's too simple and arrogant to understand properly. The commentators say about this that, 'correct understanding of a matter and a misunderstanding of the same matter are not mutually exclusive'. Whether they're right or not, you have to concede that his simplicity and arrogance, however little they show, do weaken his function of guarding the entrance, they are defects in the doorkeeper's character. You also have to consider that the doorkeeper seems to be friendly by nature, he isn't always just an official. He makes a joke right at the beginning, in that he invites the man to enter at the same time as maintaining the ban on his entering, and then he doesn't send him away but gives him, as it says in the text, a stool to sit on and lets him stay by the side of the door. The patience with which he puts up with the man's requests through all these years, the little questioning sessions, accepting the gifts, his politeness when he puts up with the man cursing his fate even though it was the doorkeeper who caused that fate - all these things seem to want to arouse our sympathy. Not every doorkeeper would have behaved in the same way. And finally, he lets the man beckon him and he bends deep down to him so that he can put his last question. There's no more than some slight impatience - the doorkeeper knows everything's come to its end - shown in the words, 'You're insatiable'. There are many commentators who go even further in explaining it in this way and think the words, 'you're insatiable' are an expression of friendly admiration, albeit with some condescension. However you look at it the figure of the doorkeeper comes out differently from how you might think." "You know the story better than I do and you've known it for longer," said K. They were silent for a while. And then K. said, "So you think the man was not cheated, do you?" "Don't get me wrong," said the priest, "I'm just pointing out the different opinions about it. You shouldn't pay too much attention to people's opinions. The text cannot be altered, and the various opinions are often no more than an expression of despair over it. There's even one opinion which says it's the doorkeeper who's been cheated." "That does seem to take things too far," said K. "How can they argue the doorkeeper has been cheated?" "Their argument," answered the priest, "is based on the simplicity of the doorkeeper. They say the doorkeeper doesn't know the inside of the law, only the way into it where he just walks up and down. They see his ideas of what's inside the law as rather childish, and suppose he's afraid himself of what he wants to make the man frightened of. Yes, he's more afraid of it than the man, as the man wants nothing but to go inside the law, even after he's heard about the terrible doormen there, in contrast to the doorkeeper who doesn't want to go in, or at least we don't hear anything about it. On the other hand, there are those who say he must have already been inside the law as he has been taken on into its service and that could only have been done inside. That can be countered by supposing he could have been given the job of doorkeeper by somebody calling out from inside, and that he can't have gone very far inside as he couldn't bear the sight of the third doorkeeper. Nor, through all those years, does the story say the doorkeeper told the man anything about the inside, other than his comment about the other doorkeepers. He could have been forbidden to do so, but he hasn't said anything about that either. All this seems to show he doesn't know anything about what the inside looks like or what it means, and that that's why he's being deceived. But he's also being deceived by the man from the country as he's this man's subordinate and doesn't know it. There's a lot to indicate that he treats the man as his subordinate, I expect you remember, but those who hold this view would say it's very clear that he really is his subordinate. Above all, the free man is superior to the man who has to serve another. Now, the man really is free, he can go wherever he wants, the only thing forbidden to him is entry into the law and, what's more, there's only one man forbidding him to do so - the doorkeeper. If he takes the stool and sits down beside the door and stays there all his life he does this of his own free will, there's nothing in the story to say he was forced to do it. On the other hand, the doorkeeper is kept to his post by his employment, he's not allowed to go away from it and it seems he's not allowed to go inside either, not even if he wanted to. Also, although he's in the service of the law he's only there for this one entrance, therefore he's there only in the service of this one man who the door's intended for. This is another way in which he's his subordinate. We can take it that he's been performing this somewhat empty service for many years, through the whole of a man's life, as it says that a man will come, that means someone old enough to be a man. That means the doorkeeper will have to wait a long time before his function is fulfilled, he will have to wait for as long as the man liked, who came to the door of his own free will. Even the end of the doorkeeper's service is determined by when the man's life ends, so the doorkeeper remains his subordinate right to the end. And it's pointed out repeatedly that the doorkeeper seems to know nothing of any of this, although this is not seen as anything remarkable, as those who hold this view see the doorkeeper as deluded in a way that's far worse, a way that's to do with his service. At the end, speaking about the entrance he says, 'Now I'll go and close it', although at the beginning of the story it says the door to the law is open as it always is, but if it's always open - always - that means it's open independently of the lifespan of the man it's intended for, and not even the doorkeeper will be able to close it. There are various opinions about this, some say the doorkeeper was only answering a question or showing his devotion to duty or, just when the man was in his last moments, the doorkeeper wanted to cause him regret and sorrow. There are many who agree that he wouldn't be able to close the door. They even believe, at the end at least, the doorkeeper is aware, deep down, that he's the man's subordinate, as the man sees the light that shines out of the entry to the law whereas the doorkeeper would probably have his back to it and says nothing at all to show there's been any change." "That is well substantiated," said K., who had been repeating some parts of the priest's explanation to himself in a whisper. "It is well substantiated, and now I too think the doorkeeper must have been deceived. Although that does not mean I've abandoned what I thought earlier as the two versions are, to some extent, not incompatible. It's not clear whether the doorkeeper sees clearly or is deceived. I said the man had been cheated. If the doorkeeper understands clearly, then there could be some doubt about it, but if the doorkeeper has been deceived then the man is bound to believe the same thing. That would mean the doorkeeper is not a cheat but so simple-minded that he ought to be dismissed from his job immediately; if the doorkeeper is mistaken it will do him no harm but the man will be harmed immensely." "There you've found another opinion," said the priest, "as there are many who say the story doesn't give anyone the right to judge the doorkeeper. However he might seem to us he is still in the service of the law, so he belongs to the law, so he's beyond what man has a right to judge. In this case we can't believe the doorkeeper is the man's subordinate. Even if he has to stay at the entrance into the law his service makes him incomparably more than if he lived freely in the world. The man has come to the law for the first time and the doorkeeper is already there. He's been given his position by the law, to doubt his worth would be to doubt the law." "I can't say I'm in complete agreement with this view," said K. shaking his head, "as if you accept it you'll have to accept that everything said by the doorkeeper is true. But you've already explained very fully that that's not possible." "No," said the priest, "you don't need to accept everything as true, you only have to accept it as necessary." "Depressing view," said K. "The lie made into the rule of the world."

    K. said that as if it were his final word but it was not his conclusion. He was too tired to think about all the ramifications of the story, and the sort of thoughts they led him into were not familiar to him, unrealistic things, things better suited for officials of the court to discuss than for him. The simple story had lost its shape, he wanted to shake it off, and the priest who now felt quite compassionate allowed this and accepted K.'s remarks without comment, even though his view was certainly very different from K.'s.

In silence, they carried on walking for some time, K. stayed close beside the priest without knowing where he was. The lamp in his hand had long since gone out. Once, just in front of him, he thought he could see the statue of a saint by the glitter of the silver on it, although it quickly disappeared back into the darkness. So that he would not remain entirely dependent on the priest, K. asked him, "We're now near the main entrance, are we?" "No," said the priest, "we're a long way from it. Do you already want to go?" K. had not thought of going until then, but he immediately said, "Yes, certainly, I have to go. I'm the chief clerk in a bank and there are people waiting for me, I only came here to show a foreign business contact round the cathedral." "Alright," said the priest offering him his hand, "go then." "But I can't find my way round in this darkness by myself," said K. "Go to your left as far as the wall," said the priest, "then continue alongside the wall without leaving it and you'll find a way out." The priest had only gone a few paces from him, but K. was already shouting loudly, "Please, wait!" "I'm waiting," said the priest. "Is there anything else you want from me?" asked K. "No," said the priest. "You were so friendly to me earlier on," said K., "and you explained everything, but now you abandon me as if I were nothing to you." "You have to go," said the priest. "Well, yes," said K., "you need to understand that." "First, you need to understand who I am," said the priest. "You're the prison chaplain," said K., and went closer to the priest, it was not so important for him to go straight back to the bank as he had made out, he could very well stay where he was. "So that means I belong to the court," said the priest. "So why would I want anything from you? the court doesn't want anything from you. It accepts you when you come and it lets you go when you leave."

Chapter Ten End

The evening before K.'s thirty-first birthday - it was about nine o'clock in the evening, the time when the streets were quiet - two men came to where he lived. In frock coats, pale and fat, wearing top hats that looked like they could not be taken off their heads. After some brief formalities at the door of the flat when they first arrived, the same formalities were repeated at greater length at K.'s door. He had not been notified they would be coming, but K. sat in a chair near the door, dressed in black as they were, and slowly put on new gloves which stretched tightly over his fingers and behaved as if he were expecting visitors. He immediately stood up and looked at the gentlemen inquisitively. "You've come for me then, have you?" he asked. The gentlemen nodded, one of them indicated the other with the top hand now in his hand. K. told them he had been expecting a different visitor. He went to the window and looked once more down at the dark street. Most of the windows on the other side of the street were also dark already, many of them had the curtains closed. In one of the windows on the same floor where there was a light on, two small children could be seen playing with each other inside a playpen, unable to move from where they were, reaching out for each other with their little hands. "Some ancient, unimportant actors - that's what they've sent for me," said K. to himself, and looked round once again to confirm this to himself. "They want to sort me out as cheaply as they can."

K. suddenly turned round to face the two men and asked, "What theatre do you play in?" "Theatre?" asked one of the gentlemen, turning to the other for assistance and pulling in the corners of his mouth. The other made a gesture like someone who was dumb, as if he were struggling with some organism causing him trouble. "You're not properly prepared to answer questions," said K. and went to fetch his hat.

As soon as they were on the stairs the gentlemen wanted to take K.'s arms, but K. said "Wait till we're in the street, I'm not ill." But they waited only until the front door before they took his arms in a way that K. had never experienced before. They kept their shoulders close behind his, did not turn their arms in but twisted them around the entire length of K.'s arms and took hold of his hands with a grasp that was formal, experienced and could not be resisted. K. was held stiff and upright between them, they formed now a single unit so that if any one of them had been knocked down all of them must have fallen. They formed a unit of the sort that normally can be formed only by matter that is lifeless.

Whenever they passed under a lamp K. tried to see his companions more clearly, as far as was possible when they were pressed so close together, as in the dim light of his room this had been hardly possible. "Maybe they're tenors," he thought as he saw their big double chins. The cleanliness of their faces disgusted him. He could see the hands that cleaned them, passing over the corners of their eyes, rubbing at their upper lips, scratching out the creases on those chins.

When K. noticed that, he stopped, which meant the others had to stop too; they were at the edge of an open square, devoid of people but decorated with flower beds. "Why did they send you, of all people!" he cried out, more a shout than a question. The two gentleman clearly knew no answer to give, they waited, their free arms hanging down, like nurses when the patient needs to rest. "I will go no further," said K. as if to see what would happen. The gentlemen did not need to make any answer, it was enough that they did not loosen their grip on K. and tried to move him on, but K. resisted them. "I'll soon have no need of much strength, I'll use all of it now," he thought. He thought of the flies that tear their legs off struggling to get free of the flypaper. "These gentleman will have some hard work to do".

Just then, Miss Bürstner came up into the square in front of them from the steps leading from a small street at a lower level. It was not certain that it was her, although the similarity was, of course, great. But it did not matter to K. whether it was certainly her anyway, he just became suddenly aware that there was no point in his resistance. There would be nothing heroic about it if he resisted, if he now caused trouble for these gentlemen, if in defending himself he sought to enjoy his last glimmer of life. He started walking, which pleased the gentlemen and some of their pleasure conveyed itself to him. Now they permitted him to decide which direction they took, and he decided to take the direction that followed the young woman in front of them, not so much because he wanted to catch up with her, nor even because he wanted to keep her in sight for as long as possible, but only so that he would not forget the reproach she represented for him. "The only thing I can do now," he said to himself, and his thought was confirmed by the equal length of his own steps with the steps of the two others, "the only thing I can do now is keep my common sense and do what's needed right till the end. I always wanted to go at the world and try and do too much, and even to do it for something that was not too cheap. That was wrong of me. Should I now show them I learned nothing from facing trial for a year? Should I go out like someone stupid? Should I let anyone say, after I'm gone, that at the start of the proceedings I wanted to end them, and that now that they've ended I want to start them again? I don't want anyone to say that. I'm grateful they sent these unspeaking, uncomprehending men to go with me on this journey, and that it's been left up to me to say what's necessary".

Meanwhile, the young woman had turned off into a side street, but K. could do without her now and let his companions lead him. All three of them now, in complete agreement, went over a bridge in the light of the moon, the two gentlemen were willing to yield to each little movement made by K. as he moved slightly towards the edge and directed the group in that direction as a single unit. The moonlight glittered and quivered in the water, which divided itself around a small island covered in a densely-piled mass of foliage and trees and bushes. Beneath them, now invisible, there were gravel paths with comfortable benches where K. had stretched himself out on many summer's days. "I didn't actually want to stop here," he said to his companions, shamed by their compliance with his wishes. Behind K.'s back one of them seemed to quietly criticise the other for the misunderstanding about stopping, and then they went on. They went on up through several streets where policemen were walking or standing here and there; some in the distance and then some very close. One of them with a bushy moustache, his hand on the grip of his sword, seemed to have some purpose in approaching the group, which was hardly unsuspicious. The two gentlemen stopped, the policeman seemed about to open his mouth, and then K. drove his group forcefully forward. Several times he looked back cautiously to see if the policeman was following; but when they had a corner between themselves and the policeman K. began to run, and the two gentlemen, despite being seriously short of breath, had to run with him.

In this way they quickly left the built up area and found themselves in the fields which, in this part of town, began almost without any transition zone. There was a quarry, empty and abandoned, near a building which was still like those in the city. Here the men stopped, perhaps because this had always been their destination or perhaps because they were too exhausted to run any further. Here they released their hold on K., who just waited in silence, and took their top hats off while they looked round the quarry and wiped the sweat off their brows with their handkerchiefs. The moonlight lay everywhere with the natural peace that is granted to no other light.

After exchanging a few courtesies about who was to carry out the next tasks - the gentlemen did not seem to have been allocated specific functions - one of them went to K. and took his coat, his waistcoat, and finally his shirt off him. K. made an involuntary shiver, at which the gentleman gave him a gentle, reassuring tap on the back. Then he carefully folded the things up as if they would still be needed, even if not in the near future. He did not want to expose K. to the chilly night air without moving though, so he took him under the arm and walked up and down with him a little way while the other gentleman looked round the quarry for a suitable place.

When he had found it he made a sign and the other gentleman escorted him there. It was near the rockface, there was a stone lying there that had broken loose. The gentlemen sat K. down on the ground, leant him against the stone and settled his head down on the top of it. Despite all the effort they went to, and despite all the co-operation shown by K., his demeanour seemed very forced and hard to believe. So one of the gentlemen asked the other to grant him a short time while he put K. in position by himself, but even that did nothing to make it better. In the end they left K. in a position that was far from the best of the ones they had tried so far. Then one of the gentlemen opened his frock coat and from a sheath hanging on a belt stretched across his waistcoat he withdrew a long, thin, double-edged butcher's knife which he held up in the light to test its sharpness. The repulsive courtesies began once again, one of them passed the knife over K. to the other, who then passed it back over K. to the first. K. now knew it would be his duty to take the knife as it passed from hand to hand above him and thrust it into himself. But he did not do it, instead he twisted his neck, which was still free, and looked around. He was not able to show his full worth, was not able to take all the work from the official bodies, he lacked the rest of the strength he needed and this final shortcoming was the fault of whoever had denied it to him. As he looked round, he saw the top floor of the building next to the quarry. He saw how a light flickered on and the two halves of a window opened out, somebody, made weak and thin by the height and the distance, leant suddenly far out from it and stretched his arms out even further. Who was that? A friend? A good person? Somebody who was taking part? Somebody who wanted to help? Was he alone? Was it everyone? Would anyone help? Were there objections that had been forgotten? There must have been some. The logic cannot be refuted, but someone who wants to live will not resist it. Where was the judge he'd never seen? Where was the high court he had never reached? He raised both hands and spread out all his fingers.

But the hands of one of the gentleman were laid on K.'s throat, while the other pushed the knife deep into his heart and twisted it there, twice. As his eyesight failed, K. saw the two gentlemen cheek by cheek, close in front of his face, watching the result. "Like a dog!" he said, it was as if the shame of it should outlive him.

THE END

THE CASTLE

IT was late in the evening when K. arrived, The village was deep in snow. The Castle hill was hidden, veiled in mist and darkness, nor was there even a glimmer of light to show that a castle was there. On the wooden bridge leading from the main road to the village K. stood for a long time gazing into the illusory emptiness above him. Then he went on to find quarters for the night. The inn was still awake, and although the landlord could not provide a room and was upset by such a late and unexpected arrival, he was willing to let K. sleep on a bag of straw in the parlour. K. accepted the offer. Some peasants were still sitting over their beer, but he did not want to talk, and after himself fetching the bag of straw from the attic, lay down beside the stove. It was a warm corner, the peasants were quiet, and letting his weary eyes stray over them he soon fell asleep. But very shortly he was awakened. A young man dressed like a townsman, with the face of an actor, his eyes narrow and his eyebrows strongly marked, was standing beside him along with the landlord. The peasants were still in the room, and a few had turned their chairs round so as to see and hear better. The young man apologized very courteously for having awakened K., introducing himself as the son of the Castellan, and then said:

"This village belongs to the Castle, and whoever lives here or passes the night here does so in a manner of speaking in the Castle itself. Nobody may do that without the Count's permission. But you have no such permit, or at least you have produced none."

K. had half raised himself and now, smoothing down his hair and looking up at the two men, he said:

"What village is this I have wandered into? Is there a castle here?"

"Most certainly," replied the young man slowly, while here and there a head was shaken over K.'s remark, "the castle of my lord the Count West-west."

"And must one have a permit to sleep here?" asked K., as if he wished to assure himself that what he had heard was not a dream.

"One must have a permit," was the reply, and there was an ironical contempt for K. in the young man's gesture as he stretched out his arm and appealed to the others, "Or must one not have a permit?"

"Well, then, I'll have to go and get one," said K. yawning and pushing his blanket away as if to rise up.

"And from whom, pray?" asked the young man.

"From the Count," said K., "that's the only thing to be done."

"A permit from the Count in the middle of the night!" cried the young man, stepping back a pace.

"Is that impossible?" inquired K. coolly. "Then why did you waken me?"

At this the young man flew into a passion.

"None of your guttersnipe manners!" he cried, "I insist on respect for the Count's authority I I woke you up to inform you that you must quit the Count's territory at once."

"Enough of this fooling," said K. in a markedly quiet voice, laying himself down again and pulling up the blanket.

"You're going a little too far, my good fellow, and I'll have something to say tomorrow about your conduct. The landlord here and those other gentlemen will bear me out if necessary. Let me tell you that I am the Land Surveyor whom the Count is expecting. My
assistants are coming on tomorrow in a carriage with the apparatus. I did not want to miss the chance of a walk through the snow, but unfortunately lost my way several times and so arrived very late. That it was too late to present myself at the Castle I knew very well before you saw fit to inform me. That is why I have made shift with this bed for the night, where, to put it mildly, you have had the discourtesy to disturb me. That is all I have to say. Good night, gentlemen."

And K. turned over on his side towards the stove.

"Land Surveyor?" he heard the hesitating question behind his back, and then there was a general silence. But the young man soon recovered his assurance, and lowering his voice, sufficiently to appear considerate of K.'s sleep while yet speaking loud enough to be clearly heard, said to the landlord:

"I'll ring up and inquire."

So there was a telephone in this village inn? They had everything up to the mark. The particular instance surprised K., but on the whole he had really expected it. It appeared that the telephone was placed almost over his head and in his drowsy condition he had overlooked it. If the young man must needs telephone he could not, even with the best intentions, avoid disturbing K., the only question was whether K. would let him do so; he decided to allow it. In that case, however, there was no sense in pretending to sleep, and so he turned on his back again. He could see the peasants putting their heads together, the arrival of a Land Surveyor was no small event.

The door into the kitchen had been opened, and blocking the whole doorway stood the imposing figure of the landlady, to whom the landlord was advancing on tiptoe in order to tell her what was happening. And now the conversation began on the telephone. The Castellan was asleep, but an under-castellan, one of the under-castellans, a certain Herr Fritz, was available. The young man, announcing himself as Schwarzer, reported that he had found K., a disreputable-looking man in the thirties, sleeping calmly on a bag of straw with a minute rucksack for pillow and a knotty stick within reach. He had naturally suspected the fellow, and as the landlord had obviously neglected his duty he, Schwarzer, had felt bound to investigate the matter. He had roused the man, questioned him, and duly warned him off the Count's territory, all of which K. had taken with an ill grace, perhaps with some justification, as it eventually turned out, for he claimed to be a Land Surveyor engaged by the Count. Of course, to say the least of it, that was a statement which required official confirmation, and so Schwarzer begged Herr Fritz to inquire in the Central Bureau if a Land Surveyor were really expected, and to telephone the answer at once. Then there was silence while Fritz was making inquiries up there and the young man was waiting for the answer.

K. did not change his position, did not even once turn round, seemed quite indifferent and stared into space. Schwarzer's report, in its combination of malice and prudence, gave him an idea of the measure of diplomacy in which even underlings in the Castle like Schwarzer were versed. Nor were they remiss in industry, the Central Office had a night service. And apparently answered questions quickly, too, for Fritz was already ringing.

His reply seemed brief enough, for Schwarzer hung up the receiver immediately, crying angrily:

"Just what I said! Not a trace of a Land Surveyor. A common, lying tramp, and probably worse."

For a moment K. thought that all of them, Schwarzer, the peasants, the landlord and the landlady, were going to fall upon him in a body, and to escape at least the first shock of their assault he crawled right underneath the blanket. But the telephone rang again, and with a special insistence, it seemed to K. Slowly he put out his head.

Although it was improbable that this message also concerned K., they all stopped short and Schwarzer took up the receiver once more. He listened to a fairly long statement, and then said in a low voice:

"A mistake, is it? I'm sorry to hear that. The head of the department himself said so?

Very queer, very queer. How am I to explain it all to the Land Surveyor?"

K. pricked up his ears. So the Castle had recognized him as the Land Surveyor. That was unpropitious for him, on the one hand, for it meant that the Castle was well informed about him, had estimated all the probable chances, and was taking up the challenge with a smile. On the other hand, however, it was quite propitious, for if his interpretation were right they had underestimated his strength, and he would have more freedom of action than he had dared to hope. And if they expected to cow him by their lofty superiority in recognizing him as Land Surveyor, they were mistaken; it made his skin prickle a little, that was all. He waved off Schwarzer who was timidly approaching him, and refused an urgent invitation to transfer himself into the landlord's own room; he only accepted a warm drink from the landlord and from the landlady a basin to wash in, a piece of soap, and a towel. He did not even have to ask that the room should be cleared, for all the men flocked out with averted faces lest he should recognize them again next day. The lamp was blown out, and he was left in peace at last. He slept deeply until morning, scarcely disturbed by rats scuttling past once or twice. After breakfast, which, according to his host, was to be paid for by the Castle, together with all the other expenses of his board and lodging, he prepared to go out immediately into the village. But since the landlord, to whom he had been very curt because of his behaviour the preceding night, kept circling around him in dumb entreaty, he took pity on

the man and asked him to sit down for a while. "I haven't met the Count yet," said K., "but he pays well for good work, doesn't he? When a man like me travels so far from home he wants to go back with something in his pockets."

"There's no need for the gentleman to worry about that kind of thing; nobody complains of being badly paid."

"Well," said K.," I'm not one of your timid people, and can give a piece of my mind even to a Count, but of course it's much better to have everything settled up without any trouble."

The landlord sat opposite K. on the rim of the window-ledge, not daring to take a more comfortable seat, and kept on gazing at K. with an anxious look in his large brown eyes.

He had thrust his company on K. at Erst, but now it seemed that he was eager to escape.

Was he afraid of being cross-questioned about the Count? Was he afraid of some indiscretion on the part of the "gentleman" whom he took K. to be? K. must divert his attention. He looked at the clock, and said:

"My assistants should be arriving soon. Will you be able to put them up here?"

"Certainly, sir," he said, "but won't they be staying with you up at the Castle?"

Was the landlord so willing, then, to give up prospective customers, and K. in particular, whom he so unconditionally transferred to the Castle?

"That's not at all certain yet," said K. "I must first find out what work I am expected to do. If I have to work down here, for instance, it would be more sensible to lodge down here. I'm afraid, too, that the life at the Castle wouldn't suit me. I like to be my own master."

"You don't know the Castle," said the landlord quietly.

"Of course," replied K., "one shouldn't judge prematurely. All that I know at present about the Castle is that the people there know how to choose a good Land Surveyor.

Perhaps it has other attractions as well."

And he stood up in order to rid the landlord of his presence, since the man was biting his lip uneasily. His confidence was not to be lightly won. As K. was going out he noticed a dark portrait in a dim frame on the wall. He had already observed it from his couch by the stove, but from that distance he had not been able to distinguish any details and had thought that it was only a plain back to the frame. But it was a picture after all, as now appeared, the bust portrait of a man about fifty. His head was sunk so low upon his breast that his eyes were scarcely visible, and the weight of the high, heavy forehead and the strong hooked nose seemed to have borne the head down. Because of this pose the man's full beard was pressed in at the chin and spread out farther down.

His left hand was buried in his luxuriant hair, but seemed incapable of supporting the head.

"Who is that?" asked K., "the Count?"

He was standing before the portrait and did not look round at the landlord.

"No," said the latter, "the Castellan."

"A handsome castellan, indeed," said K., "a pity that he had such an ill-bred son."

"No, no," said the landlord, drawing K. a little towards him and whispering in his ear,

"Schwarzer exaggerated yesterday, his father is only an under-castellan, and one of the lowest, too."

At that moment the landlord struck K. as a very child.

"The villain!" said K. with a laugh, but the landlord instead of laughing said, "Even his father is powerful."

"Get along with you," said K., "you think everyone powerful. Me too, perhaps?"

"No," he replied, timidly yet seriously, "I don't think you powerful."

"You're a keen observer," said K., "for between you and me I'm not really powerful. And consequently I suppose I have no less respect for the powerful than you have, only I'm not so honest as you and am not always willing to acknowledge it." And K. gave the landlord a tap on the cheek to hearten him and awaken his friendliness. It made him smile a little. He was actually young, with that soft and almost beardless face of his; how had he come to have that massive, elderly wife, who could be seen through a small window bustling about the kitchen with her elbows sticking out? K. did not want to force his confidence any further, however, nor to scare away the smile he had at last evoked.

Now, he could see the Castle above him clearly defined in the glittering air, its outline made still more definite by the moulding of snow covering it in a thin layer. There seemed to be much less snow up there on the hill than down in the village, where K. found progress as laborious as on the main road the previous day. Here the heavy snowdrifts reached right up to the cottage windows and began again on the low roofs, but up on the hill everything soared light and free into the air, or at least so it appeared from down below. On the whole this distant prospect of the Castle satisfied K.'s expectations. It was neither an old stronghold nor a new mansion, but a rambling pile consisting of innumerable small buildings closely packed together and of one or two storeys; if K. had not known that it was a castle he might have taken it for a little town. There was only one tower as far as he could see, whether it belonged to a dwelling-house or a church he could not determine. Swarms of crows were circling round it. With his eyes fixed on the Castle K. went on farther, thinking of nothing else at all. But on approaching it he was disappointed in the Castle; it was after all only a wretched-looking town, a huddle of

village houses, whose sole merit, if any, lay in being built of stone, but the plaster had long since flaked off and the stone seemed to be crumbling away. K. had a fleeting recollection of his native town. It was hardly inferior to this so-called Castle, and if it were merely a question of enjoying the view it was a pity to have come so far. K.

would have done better to visit his native town again, which he had not seen for such a long time. And in his mind he compared the church tower at home with the tower above him.

The church tower, firm in line, soaring unfalteringly to its tapering point, topped with red tiles and broad in the roof, an earthly building-what else can men build? -but with a loftier goal than the humble dwellinghouses, and a clearer meaning than the muddle of everyday life. The tower above him here-the only one visible-the tower of a house, as was now apparent, perhaps of the main building, was uniformly round, part of it graciously mantled with ivy, pierced by small windows that glittered in the sun, a somewhat maniacal glitter, and topped by what looked like an attic, with battlements that were irregular, broken, fumbling, as if designed by the trembling or careless hand of a child, clearly outlined against the blue. It was as if a melancholy-mad tenant who ought to have been kept locked in the topmost chamber of his house had burst through the roof and lifted himself up to the gaze of the world.

Again K. came to a stop, as if in standing still he had more power of judgement. But he was disturbed. Behind the village church where he had stopped-it was really only a chapel widened with barn-like additions so as to accommodate the parishioners - was the school.

A long, low building, combining remarkably a look of great age with a provincial appearance, it lay behind a fenced-in garden which was now a field of snow. The children were just coming out with their teacher. They thronged round him, all gazing up at him and chattering without a break so rapidly that K. could not follow what they said. The teacher, a small young man with narrow shoulders and a very upright carriage which yet did not make him ridiculous, had already fixed K. with his eyes from the distance, naturally enough, for apart from the school-children there was not another human being in sight. Being the stranger, K. made the first advance, especially as the other was an authoritative-looking little man, and said:

"Good morning, sir."

As if by one accord the children fell silent, perhaps the master liked to have a sudden stillness as a preparation for his words.

"You are looking at the Castle?" he asked more gently than K. had expected, but with the inflexion that denoted disapproval of K.'s occupation.

"Yes," said K. "I am a stranger here, I came to the village only last night."

"You don't like the Castle?" returned the teacher quickly.

"What?" countered K., a little taken aback, and repeated the question in a modified form. "Do I like the Castle? Why do you assume that I don't like it?"

"Strangers never do," said the teacher.

To avoid saying the wrong thing K. changed the subject and asked: "I suppose you know the Count?"

"No," said the teacher turning away.

But K. would not be put off and asked again: "What, you don't know the Count?"

"Why should I?" replied the teacher in a low tone, and added aloud in French: "Please remember that there are innocent children present."

K. took this as a justification for asking: "Might I come to pay you a visit one day, sir? I am to be staying here for some time and already feel a little lonely. I don't fit in with the peasants nor, I imagine, with the Castle."

"There is no difference between the peasantry and the Castle," said the teacher.

"Maybe," said K.., "that doesn't alter my position. Can I pay you a visit one day?"

"I live in Swan Street at the butcher's."

That was assuredly more of a statement than an invitation, but K. said: "Right, I'll come."

The teacher nodded and moved on with his batch of children, who began to scream again immediately. They soon vanished in a steeply descending by-street. But K. was disconcerted, irritated by the conversation. For the first time since his arrival he felt really tired. The long journey he had made seemed at first to have imposed no strain upon him - how quietly he had sauntered through the days, step by step i - but now the consequences of his exertion were making themselves felt, and at the wrong time, too. He felt irresistibly drawn to seek out new acquaintances, but each new acquaintance only seemed to increase his weariness. If he forced himself in his present condition to go on at least as far as the Castle entrance, he would have done more than enough. So he resumed his walk, but the way proved long. For the street he was in, the main street of the village, did not lead up to the Castle hill, it only made towards it and then, as if deliberately, turned aside, and though it did not lead away from the Castle it got no nearer to it either. At every turn K. expected the road to double back to the Castle, and only because of this expectation did he go on; he was flatly unwilling, tired as he was, to leave the street, and he was also amazed at the length of the village, which seemed to have no end; again and again the same little houses, and frost-bound window-panes and snow and the entire absence of human beings-but at last he tore himself away from the obsession of the street and escaped into a small side-lane, where the snow was still deeper and the exertion of lifting one's feet clear was fatiguing; he broke into a sweat,

suddenly came to a stop, and could not go on. Well, he was not on a desert island, there were cottages to right and left of him. He made a snowball and threw it at length of the village-and there appeared an old peasant in a brown fur jacket, with his head cocked to one side, a frail and kindly figure.

"May I come into your house for a little?" asked K., " Ìm very tired."

He did not hear the old man's reply, but thankfully observed that a plank was pushed out towards him to rescue him from the snow, and in a few steps he was in the kitchen. A large kitchen, dimly lit. Anyone coming in from outside could make out nothing at first.

K. stumbled over a washing' tub, a woman's hand steadied him. The crying of children came loudly from one corner. From another steam was welling out and turning the dim light into darkness. K. stood as if in the clouds.

"He must be drunk," said somebody.

"Who are you?" cried a hectoring voice, and then obviously to the old man: "Why did you let him in? Are we to let in everybody that wanders about in the street?"

"I am the Count's Land Surveyor" said K., trying to justify himself before this still invisible personage.

"Oh, it's the Land Surveyor," said a woman's voice, and then came a complete silence.

"You know me, then?" asked K.

"Of course," said the same voice curtly.

The fact that he was known did not seem to be a recommendation. At last the steam thinned a little, and K. was able gradually to make things out. It seemed to be a general washing-day. Near the door clothes were being washed. But the steam was coming from another corner, where in a wooden tub larger than any K. had ever seen, as wide as two beds, two men were bathing in steaming water. But still more astonishing, although one could not say what was so astonishing about it, was the scene in the right-hand corner.

From a large opening, the only one in the back wall, a pale snowy light came in, apparently from the courtyard, and gave a gleam as of silk to the dress of a woman who was almost reclining in a high arm-chair. She was suckling an infant at her breast.

Several children were playing around her, peasant children, as was obvious, but she seemed to be of another class, although of course illness and weariness give even peasants a look of refinement.

"Sit down, " said one of the men, who had a full beard and breathed heavily through his mouth which always hung open, pointing-it was a funny sight-with his wet hand over the edge of the tub towards a settle, and showering drops of warm water all over K.'s face as he did so.

On the settle the old man who had admitted K. was already sitting, sunk in vacancy. K.

was thankful to find a seat at last. Nobody paid any further attention to him. The woman at the washing-tub, young, plump, and fair, sang in a low voice as she worked, the men stamped and rolled about in the bath, the children tried to get closer to them but were constantly driven back by mighty splashes of water which fell on K., too, and the woman in the arm-chair lay as if lifeless staring at the roof without even a glance towards the child at her bosom. She made a beautiful, sad, fixed picture, and K. looked at her for what must have been a long time; then he must have fallen asleep, for when a loud voice roused him he found that his head was lying on the old man's shoulder.

The men had finished with the tub-in which the children were now wallowing in charge of the fair-haired woman-and were standing fully dressed before K. It appeared that the hectoring one with the full beard was the less important of the two. The other, a still, slow-thinking man who kept his head bent, was not taller than his companion and had a much smaller beard, but he was broader in the shoulders and had a broad face as well, and he it was who said:

"You can't stay here, sir. Excuse the discourtesy."

"I don't want to stay," said K, "I only wanted to rest a little. I have rested, and now I shall go."

"You're probably surprised at our lack of hospitality," said the man, "but hospitality is not our custom here, we have no use for visitors."

Somewhat refreshed by his sleep, his perceptions somewhat quickened, K.

was pleased by the man's frankness. He felt less constrained, poked with his stick here and there, approached the woman in the arm-chair, and noted that he was physically the biggest man in the room.

"To be sure," said K., "what use would you have for visitors? But still you need one now and then, me, for example, the Lane Surveyor."

"I don't know about that," replied the man slowly.

"If you've been asked to come you're probably needed, that's an exceptional case, but we small people stick to our tradition, and you can't blame us for that."

"No, no," said K., "I am only grateful to you and everybody here."

And taking them all by surprise he made an adroit turn and stood before the reclining woman. Out of weary blue eyes she looked at him, a transparent silk kerchief hung down to the middle of her forehead, die infant was asleep on her bosom. "Who are you?" asked K., and disdainfully - whether contemptuous of K. or her own answer was not clear - she replied:

"A girl from the Castle."

It had only taken a second or so, but already the two men were at either side of K. and were pushing him towards the door, as if there were no other means of persuasion, silently, but putting out all their strength. Something in this procedure delighted the old man, and he clapped his hands. The woman at the bath-tub laughed too, and the children suddenly shouted like mad. K. was soon out in the street, and from the threshold the two men surveyed him. Snow was again falling, yet the sky seemed a little brighter.

The bearded man cried impatiently:

"Where do you want to go? This is the way to the Castle, and that to the village."

K. made no reply to him, but turned to the other, who in spite of his shyness seemed to him the more amiable of the two, and said:

"Who are you? Whom have I to thank for sheltering me?"

"I am the tanner Lasemann," was the answer, "but you owe thanks to nobody."

"All right," said K., "perhaps we'll meet again."

"I don't suppose so," said the man.

At that moment the other cried, with a wave of his hand: "Good morning, Arthur; good morning, Jeremiah!"

K. turned round; so there were really people to be seen in the village streets. From the direction of the Castle came two young men of medium height, both very slim, in tight-fitting clothes, and like each other in their features. Although their skin was a dusky brown the blackness of their little pointed beards was actually striking by contrast. Considering the state of the road, they were walking at a great pace, their slim legs keeping time.

"Where are you off to?" shouted the bearded man.

One had to shout to them, they were going so fast and they would not stop.

"On business," they shouted back, laughing.

"Where?"

"At the inn." T

"Ìm going there too," yelled K. suddenly, louder than all the rest; he felt a strong desire to accompany them, not that he expected much from their acquaintance, but they were obviously good and jolly companions. They heard him, but only nodded, and were already out of sight. K. was still standing in the snow, and was little inclined to extricate his feet only for the sake of plunging them in again; the tanner and his comrade, satisfied with having finally got rid of him, edged slowly into the house through the door which was now barely ajar, casting backward glances at K., and he was left alone in the falling snow.

"A fine setting for a fit of despair," it occurred to him, "if I were only standing here by accident instead of design." Just then in the hut on his left hand a tiny window was opened, which had seemed quite blue when shut, perhaps from the reflexion of the snow, and was so tiny that when opened it did not permit the whole face of the person behind it to be seen, but only the eyes, old brown eyes.

"There he is," K. heard a woman's trembling voice say.

"It's the Land Surveyor," answered a man's voice.

Then the man came to the window and asked, not unamiably, but still as if he were anxious to have no complications in front of his house:

"Are you waiting for somebody?"

"For a sledge, to pick me up," said K.

"No sledges will pass here," said the man, "there's no traffic here."

"But it's the road leading to the Castle," objected K.

"All the same, all the same," said the man with a certain finality, "there's no traffic here."

Then they were both silent. But the man was obviously thinking of something, for he kept the window open.

"It's a bad road," said K., to help him out.

The only answer he got, however, was: "Oh yes."

But after a little the man volunteered: "If you like, I'll take you in my sledge."

"Please do,' said K. delighted, "what is your charge?"

"Nothing," said the man. K. was very surprised.

"Well, you're the Land Surveyor," explained the man, "and you belong to the Castle.

Where do you want to be taken?"

"To the Castle," returned K. quickly.

"I won't take you there," said the man without hesitation.

"But I belong to the Castle," said K., repeating the other's very words.

"Maybe," said the man shortly.

"Oh, well, take me to the inn," said K.

"All right," said the man, "Ì'll be out with the sledge in a moment"

His whole behaviour had the appearance of springing not from any special desire to be friendly but rather from a kind of selfish, worried, and almost pedantic insistence on shifting K. away from the front of the house. The gate of the courtyard opened, and a small light sledge, quite flat, without a seat of any kind, appeared, drawn by a feeble little horse, and behind it limped the man, a weakly stooped figure with a gaunt red snuffling face that looked peculiarly small beneath a tightly swathed woollen scarf. He was obviously ailing, and yet only to transport K. he had dragged himself out K. ventured to mention it, but the man waved him aside. All that K. elicited was that he was a coachman called Gerstacker, and that he had taken this uncomfortable sledge because it was standing ready, and to get out one of the others would have wasted too much time.

"Sit down," he said, pointing to the sledge.

"I'll sit beside you," said K.

"I'm going to walk," said Gerstacker.

"But why?" asked K.

"I'm going to walk," repeated Gerstacker, and was seized with a fit of coughing which shook him so severely that he had to brace his legs in the snow and hold on to the rim of the sledge. K. said no more, but sat down on the sledge, the man's cough slowly abated, and they drove off.

The Castle above them, which K. had hoped to reach that very day, was already beginning to grow dark, and retreated again into the distance. But as if to give him a parting sign till their next encounter a bell began to ring merrily up there, a bell which for at least a second made his heart palpitate for its tone was menacing, too, as if it threatened him with the fulfilment of his vague desire. This great bell soon died away, however, and its place was taken by a feeble monotonous little tinkle which might have come from the Castle, but might have been somewhere in the village. It certainly harmonized better with the slow-going journey, with the wretched-looking yet inexorable driver.

"I say," cried K. suddenly-they were already near the church, the inn was not far off, and K. felt he could risk something, "I'm surprised that you have the nerve to drive me round on your own responsibility; are you allowed to do that?"

Gerstacker paid no attention, but went on walking quietly beside the little horse.

"Hi " cried K., scraping some snow from the sledge and flinging a snowball which hit Gerstacker full in the ear. That made him stop and turn round; but when K. saw him at such close quarters- the sledge had slid forward a little-this stooping and somehow ill-used figure with the thin red tired face and cheeks that were different- one being flat and the other fallen instanding listening with his mouth open, displaying only a few isolated teeth, he found that what he had just said out of malice had to be repeated out of pity, that is, whether Gerstacker was likely to be penalized for driving him about.

"What do you mean?" asked Gerstacker uncomprehendingly, but without waiting for an answer he spoke to the horse and they moved on again.

When by a turn in the road K. recognized that they were near the inn, he was greatly surprised to see that darkness had already set in. Had he been gone for such a long time?

Surely not for more than an hour or two, by his reckoning. And it had been morning when he left. And he had not felt any need of food. And just a short time ago it had been uniform daylight, and now the darkness of night was upon them.

"Short days, short days," he said to himself, slipped off the sledge, and went towards the inn.

At the top of the little flight of steps leading into the house stood the landlord, a welcome figure, holding up a lighted lantern. Remembering his conductor for a fleeting moment K. stood still, there was a cough in the darkness behind him, that was he. Well, he would see him again soon. Not until he was level with the landlord, who greeted him humbly, did he notice two men, one on either side of the doorway. He took the lantern from his host's hand and turned the light upon them; it was the men he had already met, who were called Arthur and Jeremiah. They now saluted him. That reminded him of his soldiering days, happy days for him, and he laughed.

"Who are you?" he asked, looking from one to die other.

"Your assistants," they answered.

"It's your assistants," corroborated the landlord in a low voice.

"What?" said K., "are you my old assistants whom I told to follow me and whom I am expecting?"

They answered in the affirmative.

"That's good," observed K. after a short pause. "I'm glad you've come."

"Well," he said, after another pause, "you've come very late, you're very slack."

"It was a long way to come," said one of them.

"A long way?" repeated K., "but I met you just now coming from the Castle."

"Yes," said they without further explanation.

"Where is the apparatus?" asked K.

"We haven't any," said they.

"The apparatus I gave you?" said K.

"We haven't any,' they reiterated.

"Oh, you are fine fellows, " said K., "do you know anything about surveying?"

"No," said they.

"But if you are my old assistants you must know something about it, " said K.

They made no reply.

"Well, come in," said K., pushing them before him into the house.

They sat down then all three together over their beer at a small table, saying little, K. in the middle with an assistant on each side. As on the other evening, there was only one other table occupied by a few peasants.

"You're a difficult problem," said K., comparing them, as he had already done several times. "How am I to know one of you from the other? The only difference between you is your names, otherwise you're as like as ..."

He stopped, and then went on involuntarily, "You're as like as two snakes."

They smiled.

"People usually manage to distinguish us quite well," they said in self-justification.

"I am sure they do," said K., "I was a witness of that myself, but I can only see with my own eyes, and with them I can't distinguish you. So I shall treat you as if you were one man and call you both Arthur, that's one of your names, yours, isn't it?" he asked one of them.

"No," said the man, "I'm Jeremiah."

"It doesn't matter," said K. "I'll call you both Arthur. If I tell Arthur to go anywhere you must both go. If I give Arthur something to do you must both do it, that has the great disadvantage for me of preventing me from employing you on separate jobs, but the advantage that you will both be equally responsible for anything I tell you to do.

How you divide the work between you doesn't matter to me, only you're not to excuse yourselves by blaming each other, for me you're only one man."

They considered this, and said: "We shouldn't like that at all."

"I don't suppose so," said K., "of course you won't like it, but that's how it has to be."

For some little time one of the peasants had been sneaking round the table and K. had noticed him; now the fellow took courage and went up to one of the assistants to whisper something.

"Excuse me," said K., bringing his band down on the table and rising to his feet, "these are my assistants and we're discussing private business. Nobody is entitled to disturb us."

"Sorry, sir, sorry," muttered the peasant anxiously, retreating backwards towards his friends.

"And this is my most important charge to you," said K., sitting down again. "You're not to speak to anyone without my permission. I am a stranger here, and if you are my old assistants you are strangers too. We three strangers must stand by each other therefore, give me your hands on that."

All too eagerly they stretched out their hands to K.

"Never mind the trimming," said he, "but remember that my command holds good. I shall go to bed now and I recommend you to do the same. To-day we have missed a day's work, and to-morrow we must begin very early. You must get hold of a sleigh for taking me to the Castle and have it ready outside the house at six o'clock."

"Very well," said one.

But the other interrupted him. "You say "very well", and yet you know it can't be done."

"Silence," said K. "You're trying already to dissociate yourselves from each other."

But then the first man broke in: "He's right, it can't be done, no stranger can get into the Castle without a permit" "Where does one apply for a permit?"

"I don't know, perhaps to the Castellan."

"Then we'll apply by telephone, go and telephone to the Castellan at once, both of you."

They rushed to the instrument, asked for the connexion - how eager they were about it!

in externals they were absurdly docile - and inquired if K. could come with them next morning into the Castle. The "No" of the answer was audible even to K. at his table. But the answer went on and was still more explicit, it ran as follows:

"Neither to-morrow nor at any other time."

"I shall telephone myself," said K., and got up.

While K. and his assistants hitherto had passed nearly unremarked except for the incident with the one peasant, his last statement aroused general attention. They all got up when K. did, and although the landlord tried to drive them away, crowded round him in a close semicircle at the telephone. The general opinion among them was that K. would get no answer at all. K. had to beg them to be quiet, saying he did not want to hear their opinion. The receiver gave out a buzz of a kind that K. had never before heard on a telephone. It was like the hum of countless children's voices - but yet not a hum, the echo rather of voices singing at an infinite distance - blended by sheer impossibility into one high but resonant sound which vibrated on the ear as if it were trying to penetrate beyond mere hearing. K. listened without attempting to telephone, leaning his left arm on the telephone shelf. He did not know how long he had stood there, but he stood until the landlord pulled at his coat saying that a messenger had come to speak with him.

"Go away!" yelled K. in an access of rage, perhaps into the mouthpiece, for someone immediately answered from the other end. The following conversation ensued: "Oswald speaking, who's there?" cried a severe arrogant voice with a small defect in its speech, as seemed to K., which its owner tried to cover by an exaggerated severity. K. hesitated to announce himself, for he was at the mercy of the telephone, the other could shout him down or hang up the receiver, and that might mean the blocking of a not unimportant way of access. K.'s hesitation made the man impatient.

"Who's there?" he repeated, adding, "I should be obliged if there was less telephoning from down there, only a minute ago somebody rang up."

K. ignored this remark, and announced with sudden decision: "The Land Surveyor's assistant speaking"

"What Land Surveyor? What assistant?"

K. recollected yesterday's telephone conversation, and said briefly, "Ask Fritz."

This succeeded, to his own astonishment But even more than at his success he was astonished at the organization of the Castle service. The answer came: "Oh, yes. That everlasting Land Surveyor. Quite so. What about it? What assistant?" 'Joseph,' said K.

He was a little put out by the murmuring of the peasants behind his back, obviously they disapproved of his ruse. He had no time to bother about them, however, for the conversation absorbed all his attention.

"Joseph?" came the question. "But the assistants arc called ..." there was a short pause, evidently to inquire the names from somebody else, "Arthur and Jeremiah."

"These are the new assistants," said K.

"No, they are the old ones."

"They are the new ones, I am the old assistant; I came to-day after the Land Surveyor."

"No," was shouted back.

"Then who am I?" asked K. as blandly as before.

And after a pause the same voice with the same defect answered him, yet with a deeper and more authoritative tone: "You are the old assistant."

K. was listening to the new note, and almost missed the question: "What is it you want?"

He felt like laying down the receiver. He had ceased to expect anything from this conversation. But being pressed, he replied quickly: "When can my master come to the Castle?"

"Never," was the answer.

"Very well," said K., and hung the receiver up.

Behind him the peasants had crowded quite close. His assistants, with many side glances in his direction, were trying to keep them back. But they seemed not to take the matter very seriously, and in any case the peasants, satisfied with the result of the conversation, were beginning to give ground. A man came cleaving his way with rapid steps through the group, bowed before K., and handed him a letter. K. took it, but looked at the man, who for the moment seemed to him the more important. There was a great resemblance between this new-comer and the assistants, he was slim like them and clad in the same tightfitting garments, had the same suppleness and agility, and yet he was quite different. How much K. would have preferred him as an assistant. He reminded K. a little of the girl with the infant whom he had seen at the tanner's. He was clothed nearly all in white, not in silk, of course; he was in winter clothes like all the others, but the material he was wearing had the softness and dignity of silk. His face was clear and frank, his eyes larger than ordinary. His smile was unusually joyous; he drew his hand over his face as if to conceal the smile, but in vain.

"Who are you?" asked K.

"My name is Barnabas," said he, "I am a messenger." His lips were strong and yet gentle as he spoke.

"Do you approve of this kind of thing?" asked K., pointing to the peasants for whom he was still an object of curiosity, and who stood gaping at him with their open mouths, coarse lips, and literally tortured faces - their heads looked as if they had been beaten flat on top and their features as if the pain of the beating had twisted them to the present shape - and yet they were not exactly gaping at him, for their eyes often flitted away and studied some indifferent object in the room before fixing on him again, and then K. pointed also to his assistants who stood linked together, cheek against cheek, and smiling, but whether submissively or mockingly could not be determined. All these he pointed out as if presenting a train of followers forced upon him by circumstances, and as if he expected Barnabas - that indicated intimacy, it occurred to K. - always to discriminate between him and them. But Barnabas - quite innocently, it was clear - ignored the question, letting it pass as a well-bred servant ignores some remark of his master only apparently addressed to him, and merely surveyed the room in obedience to the question, greeting by a pressure of the hand various acquaintances among the peasants and exchanging a few words with the assistants, all with a free independence which set him apart from the others. Rebuffed but not mortified, K. returned to the letter in his hand and opened it.

Its contents were as follows: "My dear Sir, As you know, you have been engaged for the Count's service. Your immediate superior is the Superintendent of the village, who will give you all particulars about your work and the terms of your employment, and to whom you are responsible. I myself, however, will try not to lose sight of you. Barnabas, the bearer of this letter, will report himself to you from rime to time to learn your wishes and communicate them to me. You will find me always ready to oblige you, in so far as that is possible. I desire my workers to be contented."

The signature was illegible, but stamped beside it was "Chief of Department X."

"Wait a little!" said K. to Barnabas, who bowed before him, then he commanded the landlord to show him to his room, for he wanted to be alone with the letter for a while.

At the same time he reflected that Barnabas, although so attractive, was still only a messenger, and ordered a mug of beer for him. He looked to see how Barnabas would take it, but Barnabas was obviously quite pleased and began to drink the beer at once. Then K.

went off with the landlord.

The house was so small that nothing was available for K. but a little attic room, and even that had caused some difficulty, for two maids who had hitherto slept in it had had to be quartered elsewhere. Nothing indeed had been done but to clear the maids out, the room was otherwise quite unprepared, no sheets on the single bed, only some pillows and a horse-blanket still in the same rumpled state as in the morning. A few sacred pictures and photographs of soldiers were on the walls, the room had not even been aired; obviously they hoped that the new guest would not stay long, and were doing nothing to encourage him. K. felt no resentment, however, wrapped himself in the blanket, sat down at the table, and began to read the letter again by the light of a candle. It was not a consistent letter, in part it dealt with him as with a free man whose independence was recognized, the mode of address, for example, and the reference to his wishes. But there were other places in which he was directly or indirectly treated as a minor employee, hardly visible to the Heads of Departments; the writer would try to make an effort "not to lose sight" of him, his superior was only the village Superintendent to whom he was actually responsible, probably his sole colleague would be the village policeman. These were inconsistencies, no doubt about it. They were so obvious that they had to be faced.

It hardly occurred to K. that they might be due to indecision; that seemed a mad idea in connexion with such an organization. He was much more inclined to read into them a frankly offered choice, which left it to him to make what he liked out of the letter, whether he preferred to become a village worker with a distinctive but merely apparent connexion with the Castle, or an ostensible village worker whose real occupation was determined through the medium of Barnabas. K. did not hesitate in his choice, and would not have hesitated even had he lacked the experience which had befallen him since his arrival. Only as a worker in the village, removed as far as possible from the sphere of the Castle, could he hope to achieve anything in the Castle itself; the village folk, who were now so suspicious of him, would begin to talk to him once he was their fellow-citizen, if not exactly their friend; and if he were to become indistinguishable from Gerstacker or Lasemann - and that must happen as soon as possible, everything depended on that - then all kinds of paths would be thrown open to him, which would remain not only for ever closed to him but quite invisible were he to depend merely on the favour of the gentlemen in the Castle.

There was of course a danger, and that was sufficiently emphasized in the letter, even elaborated with a certain satisfaction, as if it were unavoidable. That was sinking to the workman's level - service, superior work, terms of employment, responsible workers -

the letter fairly reeked of it, and even though more personal messages were included they were written from the standpoint of an employer. If K. were willing to become a workman he could do so, but he would have to do it in grim earnest, without any other prospect.

K. knew that he had no real compulsory discipline to fear, he was not afraid of that, and in this case least of all, but the pressure of a discouraging environment, of a growing resignation to disappointment, the pressure of the imperceptible influences of every moment, these things he did fear, but that was a danger he would have to guard against.

Nor did the letter pass over the fact that if it should come to a struggle K. had had the hardihood to make the first advances; it was very subtly indicated and only to be sensed by an uneasy conscience - an uneasy conscience, not a bad one - it lay in the three words, "as you know", referring to his engagement in the Count's service. K. had reported his arrival, and only after that, as the letter pointed out, had he known that he was engaged. K. took down a picture from the wall and stuck the letter on the nail, this was the room he was to live in and the letter should hang there. Then he went down to the inn parlour. Barnabas was sitting at a table with the assistants.

"Oh, there you are," said K. without any reason, only because he was glad to see Barnabas, who jumped to his feet at once. Hardly had K. shown his face when the peasants got up and gathered round him - it had become a habit of theirs to follow him around.

"What are you always following me about for?" cried K.

They were not offended, and slowly drifted back to their seats again. One of them in passing said casually in apology, with an enigmatic smile which was reflected on several of the others' faces:

"There's always something new to listen to," and he licked his lips as if news were meat and drink to him.

K. said nothing conciliatory, it was good for them to have a little respect for him, but hardly had he reached Barnabas when he felt a peasant breathing down the back of his neck. He had only come, he said, for the salt-cellar, but K. stamped his foot with rage and the peasant scuttled away without the salt-cellar. It was really easy to get at K., all one had to do was to egg on the peasants against him, their persistent interference seemed much more objectionable to him than the reserve of the others, nor were they free from reserve either, for if he had sat down at their table they would not have stayed.

Only the presence of Barnabas restrained him from making a scene.

But he turned round to scowl at them, and found that they, too, were all looking at him. When he saw them sitting like that, however, each man in his own place, not speaking to one another and without any apparent mutual understanding, united only by the fact that they were all gazing at him, he concluded that it was not out of malice that they pursued him, perhaps they really wanted something from him and were only incapable of expressing it, if not that, it might be pure childishness, which seemed to be in fashion at the inn; was not the landlord himself childish, standing there stock-still gazing at K. with a glass of beer in his hand which he should have been carrying to a customer, and oblivious of his wife, who was leaning out of the kitchen hatch calling to him? With a quieter mind K. turned to Barnabas; he would have liked to dismiss his assistants, but could not think of an excuse. Besides, they were brooding peacefully over their beer.

"The letter," began K., "I have read it. Do you know the contents?"

"No," said Barnabas, whose look seemed to imply more than his words.

Perhaps K. was as mistaken in Barnabas's goodness as in the malice of the peasants, but his presence remained a comfort. "You are mentioned in the letter, too, you are supposed to carry messages now and then from me to the Chief, that's why I thought you might know the contents."

"I was only told," said Barnabas, "to give you the letter, to wait until you had read it, and then to bring back a verbal or written answer if you thought it needful."

"Very well," said K., "there's no need to write anything; convey to the Chief - by the way, what's his name? I couldn't read his signature."

"Klamm," said Barnabas.

"Well, convey to Herr Klamm my thanks for his recognition and for his great kindness, which I appreciate, being as I am one who has not yet proved his worth here. I shall follow his instructions faithfully. I have no particular requests to make for to-day."

Barnabas, who had listened with close attention, asked to be allowed to recapitulate the message. K. assented, Barnabas repeated it word for word. Then he rose to take his leave. K. had been studying his face the whole time, and now he gave it a last survey.

Barnabas was about the same height as K., but his eyes seemed to look down on K., yet that was almost in a kind of humility, it was impossible to think that this man could put anyone to shame. Of course he was only a messenger, and did not know the contents of the letters he carried, but the expression in his eyes, his smile, his bearing, seemed also to convey a message', however little he might know about it. And K. shook him by the hand, which seemed obviously to surprise him, for he had been going to content himself with a bow. As soon as he had gone - before opening the door he had leaned his shoulder against it for a moment and embraced the room generally in a final glance - K. said to the assistants: "I'll bring down the plans from my room, and then we'll discuss what work is to be done first."

They wanted to accompany him.

"Stay here," said K.

Still they tried to accompany him. K. had to repeat his command more authoritatively.

Barnabas was no longer in the hall. But he had only just gone out. Yet in front of the house - fresh snow was falling - K. could not see him either. He called out: "Barnabas!"

No answer.

Could he still be in the house?

Nothing else seemed possible. None the less K. yelled the name with the full force of his lungs. It thundered through the night. And from the distance came a faint response, so far away was Barnabas already. K. called him back, and at the same time went to meet him; the spot where they encountered each other was no longer visible from the inn.

"Barnabas," said K., and could not keep his voice from trembling, "I have something else to say to you. And that reminds me that it's a bad arrangement to leave me dependent on your chance comings for sending a message to the Castle. If I hadn't happened to catch you just now - how you fly along, I thought you were still in the house - who knows how long I might have had to wait for your next appearance."

"You can ask the Chief," said Barnabas, "to send me at definite times appointed by yourself."

"Even that would not suffice," said K., "I might have nothing to say for a year at a time, but something of urgent importance might occur to me a quarter of an hour after you had gone."

"Well," said Barnabas, "shall I report to the Chief that between him and you some other means of communication should be established instead of me?"

"No, no," said K., "not at all, I only mention the matter in passing, for this time I have been lucky enough to catch you."

"Shall we go back to the inn," said Barnabas, "so that you can give me the new message there?"

He had already taken a step in the direction of the inn.

"Barnabas," said K., "it isn't necessary, I'll go a part of the way with you."

"Why don't you want to go to the inn?" asked Barnabas.

"The people there annoy me," said K., "you saw for yourself how persistent the peasants are."

"We could go into your room," said Barnabas.

"It's the maids' room," said K., "dirty and stuffy - it's to avoid staying there that I

want to accompany you for a little, only," he added, in order finally to overcome Barnabas's reluctance, "you must let me take your arm, for you are surer of foot than I am."

And K. took his arm. It was quite dark, K. could not see Barnabas's face, his figure was only vaguely discernible, he had had to grope for his arm a minute or two. Barnabas yielded and they moved away from the inn. K. realized, indeed, that his utmost efforts could not enable him to keep pace with Barnabas, that he was a drag on him, and that even in ordinary circumstances this trivial accident might be enough to ruin everything, not to speak of side-streets like the one in which he had got stuck that morning, out of which he could never struggle unless Barnabas were to carry him. But he banished all such anxieties, and was comforted by Barnabas's silence; for if they went on in silence then Barnabas, too, must feel that their excursion together was the sole reason for their association.

They went on, but K. did not know whither, he could discern nothing, not even whether they had already passed the church or not. The effort which it cost him merely to keep going made him lose control of his thoughts. Instead of remaining fixed on their goal they strayed. Memories of his home kept recurring and filled his mind. There, too, a church stood in the marketplace, partly surrounded by an old graveyard which was again surrounded by a high wall. Very few boys had managed to climb that wall, and for some time K., too, had failed. It was not curiosity which had urged them on. The graveyard had been no mystery to them. They had often entered it through a small wicket-gate, it was only the smooth high wall that they had wanted to conquer. But one morning - the empty, quiet marketplace had been flooded with sunshine, when had K. ever seen it like that either before or since? - he had succeeded in climbing it with astonishing ease; at a place where he had already slipped down many a time he had clambered with a small flag between his teeth right to the top at the first attempt. Stones were still rattling down under his feet, but he was at the top. He stuck the flag in, it flew in the wind, he looked down and round about him, over his shoulder, too, at the crosses mouldering in the ground, nobody was greater than he at that place and that moment. By chance the teacher had come past and with a stern face had made K. descend. In jumping down he had hurt his knee and had found some difficulty in getting home, but still he had been on the top of the wall. The sense of that triumph had seemed to him then a victory for life, which was not altogether foolish, for now so many years later on the arm of Barnabas in the snowy night the memory of it came to succour him.

He took a firmer hold, Barnabas was almost dragging him along, the silence was unbroken. Of the road they were following all that K. knew was that to judge from its surface they had not yet turned aside into a by-street. He vowed to himself that, however difficult the way and however doubtful even the prospect of his being able to get back, he would not cease from going on. He would surely have strength enough to let himself be dragged. And the road must come to an end some time. By day the Castle had looked within easy reach, and, of course, the messenger would take the shortest cut. At that moment Barnabas stopped.

Where were they?

Was this the end?

Would Barnabas try to leave him?

He wouldn't succeed. K. clutched his arm so firmly that it almost made his hand ache.

Or had the incredible happened, and were they already in the Castle or at its gates? But they had not done any climbing so far as K. could tell. Or had Barnabas taken him up by an imperceptibly mounting road?

"Where are we?" said K. in a low voice, more to himself than to Barnabas.

"At home," said Barnabas in the same tone.

"At home?"

"Be careful now, sir, or you'll slip. We go down here."

"Down?"

"Only a step or two," added Barnabas, and was already knocking at a door. A girl opened it, and they were on the threshold of a large room almost in darkness, for there was no light save for a tiny oil lamp hanging over a table in the background.

"Who is with you, Barnabas?" asked the girl.

"The Land Surveyor," said he.

"The Land Surveyor," repeated the girl in a louder voice, turning towards the table.

Two old people there rose to their feet, a man and a woman, as well as another girl.

They greeted K. Barnabas introduced the whole family, his parents and his sisters Olga and Amalia. K. scarcely glanced at them and let them take his wet coat off to dry at the stove. So it was only Barnabas who was at home, not he himself. But why had they come here? K. drew Barnabas aside and asked:

"Why have you come here? Or do you live in the Castle precincts?"

"The Castle precincts?" repeated Barnabas, as if he did not understand.

"Barnabas," said K., "you left the inn to go to the Castle."

"No," said Barnabas, "I left it to come home, I don't go to the Castle till the early morning, I never sleep there." "Oh," said K., "so you weren't going to the Castle, but only here" - the man's smile seemed less brilliant, and his person more insignificant -

"Why didn't you say so?"

"You didn't ask me, sir," said Barnabas, "you only said you had a message to give me, but you wouldn't give it in the inn parlour, or in your room, so I thought you could speak to me quietly here in my parents' house. The others will all leave us if you wish - and, if you prefer, you could spend the night here. Haven't I done the right thing?"

K. could not reply. It had been simply a misunderstanding, a common, vulgar misunderstanding, and K. had been completely taken in by it. He had been bewitched by Barnabas's closefitting, silken-gleaming jacket, which, now that it was unbuttoned, displayed a coarse, dirty grey shirt patched all over, and beneath that the huge muscular chest of a labourer. His surroundings not only corroborated all this but even emphasized it, the old gouty father who progressed more by the help of his groping hands than by the slow movements of his stiff legs, and the mother with her hands folded on her bosom, who was equally incapable of any but the smallest steps by reason of her stoutness. Both of them, father and mother, had been advancing from their corner towards K. ever since he had come in, and were still a long way off. The yellow-haired sisters, very like each other and very like Barnabas, but with harder features than their brother, great strapping wenches, hovered round their parents and waited for some word of greeting from K. But he could not utter it. He had been persuaded that in this village everybody meant something to him, and indeed he was not mistaken, it was only for these people here that he could feel not the slightest interest. If he had been fit to struggle back to the inn alone he would have left at once. The possibility of accompanying Barnabas to the Castle early in the morning did not attract him. He had hoped to penetrate into the Castle unremarked in the night on the arm of Barnabas, but on the arm of the Barnabas he had imagined, a man who was more to him than anyone else, the Barnabas he had conceived to be far above his apparent rank and in the intimate confidence of the Castle. With the son of such a family, however, a son who integrally belonged to it, and who was already sitting at table with the others, a man who was not even allowed to sleep in the Castle, he could not possibly go to the Castle in the broad light of day, it would be a ridiculous and hopeless undertaking.

 K. sat down on a window-seat where he determined to pass the night without accepting any other favour. The other people in the village, who turned him away or were afraid of him, seemed much less dangerous, for all that they did was to throw him back on his own resources, helping him to concentrate his powers, but such ostensible helpers as these who on the strength of a petty masquerade brought him into their homes instead of into the Castle, deflected him, whether intentionally or not, from his goal and only helped to destroy him. An invitation to join the family at table he ignored completely, stubbornly sitting with bent head on his bench. Then Olga, the gentler of the sisters, got up, not without a trace of maidenly embarrassment, came over to K. and asked him to join the family meal of bread and bacon, saying that she was going to fetch some beer.

 "Where from?" asked K.

 "From the inn," she said.

 That was welcome news to K. He begged her instead of fetching beer to accompany him back to the inn, where he had important work waiting to be done. But the fact now emerged that she was not going so far as his inn, she was going to one much nearer, called the Herrenhof. None the less K. begged to be allowed to accompany her, thinking that there perhaps he might find a lodging for the night; however wretched it might be he would prefer it to the best bed these peqple could offer him. Olga did not reply at once, but glanced towards the table. Her brother stood up, nodded obligingly and said:

"If the gentleman wishes."

This assent was almost enough to make K. withdraw his request, nothing could be of much value if Barnabas assented to it. But since they were already wondering whether K. would be admitted into that inn and doubting its possibility, he insisted emphatically upon going, without taking the trouble to give a colourable excuse for his eagerness; this family would have to accept him as he was, he had no feeling of shame where they were concerned. Yet he was somewhat disturbed by Amalia's direct and serious gaze, which was unflinching and perhaps a little stupid.

On their short walk to the inn - K. had taken Olga's arm and was leaning his whole weight on her as earlier on Barnabas, he could not get along otherwise - he learned that it was an inn exclusively reserved for gentlemen from the Castle, who took their meals there and sometimes slept there whenever they had business in the village. Olga spoke to K. in a low and confidential tone; to walk with her was pleasant, almost as pleasant as walking with her brother. K. struggled against the feeling of comfort she gave him, but it persisted. From outside the new inn looked very like the inn where K. was staying. All the houses in the village resembled one another more or less, but still a few small differences were immediately apparent here; the front steps had a balustrade, and a fine lantern was fixed over the doorway. Something fluttered over their heads as they entered, it was a flag with the Count's colours. In the hall they were at once met by the landlord, who was obviously on a tour of inspection; he glanced at K. in passing with small eyes that were either screwed up critically, or half-asleep, and said:

"The Land Surveyor mustn't go anywhere but into the bar."

"Certainly," said Olga, who took K.'s part at once, "he's only escorting me."

But K. ungratefully let go her arm and drew the landlord aside. Olga meanwhile waited patiently at the end of the hall. "I should like to spend the night here," said K.

"I'm afraid that's impossible," said the landlord. "You don't seem to be aware that this house is reserved exclusively for gentlemen from the Castle."

"Well, that may be the rule," said K., "but it's surely possible to let me sleep in a corner somewhere."

"I should be only too glad to oblige you," said the landlord, "but besides the strictness with which the rule is enforced - and you speak about it as only a stranger could - it's quite out of the question for another reason; the Castle gentlemen are so sensitive that I'm convinced they couldn't bear the sight of a stranger, at least unless they were prepared for it; and if I were to let you sleep here, and by some chance or other - and chances are always on the side of the gentlemen - you were discovered, not only would it mean my ruin but yours too. That sounds ridiculous, but it's true."

This tall and closely-buttoned man who stood with his legs crossed, one hand braced against the wall and the other on his hip, bending down a little towards K. and speaking confidentially to him, seemed to have hardly anything in common with the village, even although his dark clothes looked like a peasant's finery.

"I believe you absolutely," said K., "and I didn't mean to belittle the rule, although I expressed myself badly. Only there's something I'd like to point out, I have some influence in the Castle, and shall have still more, and that secures you against any danger arising out of my stay here overnight, and is a guarantee that I am able fully to recompense any small favour you may do me."

"Oh, I know," said the landlord, and repeated again, "I know all that."

Now was the time for K. to state his wishes more clearly, but this reply of the landlord's disconcerted him, and so he merely asked: "Are there many of the Castle gentlemen staying in the house to-night?"

"As far as that goes, to-night is favourable," returned the landlord, as if in encouragement, "there's only one gentleman."

Still K. felt incapable of urging the matter, but being in hopes that he was as good as accepted, he contented himself by asking the name of the gentleman.

"Klamm," said the landlord casually, turning meanwhile to his wife who came rustling towards them in a remarkably shabby, old-fashioned gown overloaded with pleats and frills, but of a fine city cut. She came to summon the landlord, for the Chief wanted something or other. Before the landlord complied, however, he turned once more to K., as if it lay with K. to make the decision about staying all night. But K. could not utter a word, overwhelmed as he was by the discovery that it was his patron who was in the house.

Without being able to explain it completely to himself he did not feel the same freedom of action in relation to Klamm as he did to the rest of the Castle, and the idea of being caught in the inn by Klamm, although it did not terrify him as it did the landlord, gave him a twinge of uneasiness, much as if he were thoughtlessly to hurt the feelings of someone to whom he was bound by gratitude; at the same time, however, it vexed him to recognize already in these qualms the obvious effects of that degradation to an inferior status which he had feared, and to realize that although they were so obvious he was not even in a position to counteract them. So he stood there biting his lips and said nothing. Once more the landlord looked back at him before disappearing through a doorway, and K. returned the look without moving from the spot, until Olga came up and drew him away.

"What did you want with the landlord?" she asked.

"I wanted a bed for the night," said K.

"But you're staying with us!" said Olga in surprise.

In the bar, which was a large room with a vacant space in the middle, there were several peasants sitting by the wall on the tops of some casks, but they looked different from those in K.'s inn. They were more neatly and uniformly dressed in coarse yellowish-grey cloth, with loose jackets and tightly-fitting trousers. They were smallish men with at first sight a strong mutual resemblance, having flat bony faces, but rounded cheeks. They were all quiet, and sat with hardly a movement, except that they followed the newcomers with their eyes, but they did even that slowly and indifferently. Yet because of their numbers and their quietness they had a certain effect on K. He took Olga's arm again as if to explain his presence there. A man rose up from one corner, an acquaintance of Olga's, and made towards her, but K. wheeled her round by the arm in another direction. His action was perceptible to nobody but Olga, and she tolerated it with a smiling side-glance.

The beer was drawn off by a young girl called Frieda. An unobtrusive little girl with fair hair, sad eyes, and hollow cheeks, with a striking look of conscious superiority. As soon as her eye met K's it seemed to him that her look decided something concerning himself, something which he had not known to exist, but which her look assured him did exist. He kept on studying her from the side, even while she was speaking to Olga. Olga and Frieda were apparently not intimate, they exchanged only a few cold words. K. wanted to hear more, and so interposed with a question on his own account:

"Do you know Herr Klamm?"

Olga laughed out loud.

"What are you laughing at?" asked K. irritably.

"Ìm not laughing," she protested, but went on laughing.

"Olga is a childish creature," said K. bending far over the counter in order to attract Frieda's gaze again. But she kept her eyes lowered and laughed shyly.

"Would you like to see Herr Klamm?"

K. begged for a sight of him. She pointed to a door just on her left.

"There's a little peephole there, you can look through."

"What about the others?" asked K.

She curled her underlip and pulled K.. to the door with a hand that was unusually soft.

The little hole had obviously been bored for spying through, and commanded almost the whole of the neighbouring room. At a desk in the middle of the room in a comfortable arm-chair sat Herr Klamm, his face brilliantly lit up by an incandescent lamp which hung low before him. A middle-sized, plump, and ponderous man. His face was still smooth, but his cheeks were already somewhat flabby with age. His black moustache had long points, his eyes were hidden behind glittering pince-nez that sat awry. If he had been planted squarely before his desk K. would only have seen his profile, but since he was turned directly towards K. his whole face was visible. His left elbow lay on the desk, his right hand, in which was a Virginia cigar, rested on his knee. A beer-glass was standing on the desk, but there was a rim round the desk which prevented K. from seeing whether any papers were lying on it; he had the idea, however, that there were none. To make it certain he asked Frieda to look through the hole and tell him if there were any. But since she had been in that room a short time ago, she was able to inform him without further ado that the desk was empty. K. asked Frieda if his time was up, but she told him to go on looking as long as he liked. K. was now alone with Frieda. Olga, as a hasty glance assured him, had found her way to her acquaintance, and was sitting high on a cask swinging her legs.

"Frieda," said K. in a whisper, "do you know Herr Klamm well?"

"Oh, yes," she said, "very well."

She leaned over to K. and he became aware that she was coquettishly fingering the lowcut cream-coloured blouse which sat oddly on her poor thin body. Then she said:

"Didn't you notice how Olga laughed?"

"Yes, the rude creature," said K.

"Well," she said extenuatingly, "there was a reason for laughing. You asked if I knew Klamm, and you see I" - here she involuntarily lifted her chin a little, and again her triumphant glance, which had no connexion whatever with what she was saying, swept over K. - "I am his mistress."

"Klamm's mistress," said K.

She nodded.

"Then," said K. smiling, to prevent the atmosphere from being too charged with seriousness, "you are for me a highly respectable person."

"Not only for you," said Frieda amiably, but without returning his smile.

K. had a weapon for bringing down her pride, and he tried it: "Have you ever been in the Castle?"

But it missed the mark, for she answered: "No, but isn't it enough for me to be here in the bar?"

Her vanity was obviously boundless, and she was trying, it seemed, to get K. in particular to minister to it.

"Of course," said K., "here in the bar you're taking the landlord's place."

"That's so," she assented, "and I began as a barmaid at the inn by the bridge."

"With those delicate hands," said K. halfquestioningly, without knowing himself whether he was only flattering her or was compelled by something in her. Her hands were certainly small and delicate, but they could quite as well have been called weak and characterless.

"Nobody bothered about them then," she said, "and even now ..."

K. looked at her inquiringly. She shook her head and would say no more.

"You have your secrets, naturally," said K., "and you're not likely to give them away to somebody you've known for only half an hour, and who hasn't had the chance yet to tell you anything about himself."

This remark proved to be ill-chosen, for it seemed to arouse Frieda as from a trance that was favourable to him. Out of ihe leather bag hanging at her girdle she took a small piece of wood, stopped up the peephole with it, and said to K. with an obvious attempt to conceal the change in her attitude: "Oh, I know all about you, you're the Land Surveyor," and then adding: "but now I must go back to my work," she returned to her place behind the bar counter, while a man here and there came up to get his empty glass refilled. K.

wanted to speak to her again, so he took an empty glass from a stand and went up to her, saying:

"One thing more, Fraulein Frieda, it's an extraordinary feat and a sign of great strength of mind to have worked your way up from byre-maid to this position in the bar, but can it be the end of all ambition for a person like you? An absurd idea. Your eyes - don't laugh at me, Fraulein Frieda - speak to me far more of conquests still to come than of conquests past. But the opposition one meets in the world is great, and becomes greater the higher one aims, and it's no disgrace to accept the help of a man who's fighting his way up too, even though he's a small and uninfluential man. Perhaps we could have a quiet talk together sometime, without so many onlookers?"

"I don't know what you're after," she said, and in her tone this time there seemed to be, against her will, an echo rather of countless disappointments than of past triumphs.

"Do you want to take me away from Klamm perhaps? O heavens!" and she clapped her hands.

"You've seen through me," said K., as if wearied by so much mistrust, "that's exactly my real secret intention. You ought to leave Klamm and become my sweetheart. And now I can go. Olga!" he cried, "we're going home."

Obediently Olga slid down from her cask but did not succeed immediately in breaking through her ring of friends. Then Frieda said in a low voice with a hectoring look at K.:

"When can I talk to you?"

"Can I spend the night here?" asked K.

"Yes," said Frieda.

"Can I stay now?"

"Go out first with Olga, so that I can clear out all the others. Then you can come back in a little."

"Right," said K., and he waited impatiently for Olga.

But the peasants would not let her go; they made up a dance in which she was the central figure, they circled round her yelling all together and every now and then one of them left the ring, seized Olga firmly round the waist and whirled her round and round; the pace grew faster and faster, the yells more hungry, more raucous, until they were insensibly blended into one continuous howl. Olga, who had begun laughingly by trying to break out of the ring, was now merely reeling with flying hair from one man to the other.

"That's the kind of people I'm saddled with," said Frieda, biting her thin lips in scorn.

"Who are they?" asked K.

"Klamm's servants," said Frieda, "he keeps on bringing those people with him, and they upset me. I can hardly tell what I've been saying to you, but please forgive me if I've offended you, it's these people who are to blame, they're the most contemptible and objectionable creatures I know, and I have to fill their glasses up with beer for them.

How often I've implored Klamm to leave them behind him, for though I have to put up with the other gentlemen's servants, he could surely have some consideration for me; but it's all no use, an hour before his arrival they always come bursting in like cattle into their stalls. But now they've really got to get into the stalls, where they belong. If you weren't here I'd fling open this door and Klamm would be forced to drive them out himself."

"Can't he hear them, then?" asked K.

"No," said Frieda, "he's asleep."

"Asleep?" cried K. "But when I peeped in he was awake and sitting at the desk."

"He always sits like that," said Frieda, "he was sleeping when you saw him. Would I have let you look in if he hadn't been asleep? That's how he sleeps, the gentlemen do sleep a great deal, it's hard to understand. Anyhow, if he didn't sleep so much, he wouldn't be able to put up with his servants. But now I'll have to turn them out myself."

She took a whip from a corner and sprang among the dancers with a single bound, a little uncertainly, as a young lamb might spring. At first they faced her as if she were merely a new partner, and actually for a moment Frieda seemed inclined to let the whip fall, but she soon raised it again, crying:

"In the name of Klamm into the stall with you, into the stall, all of you!"

When they saw that she was in earnest they began to press towards the back wall in a kind of panic incomprehensible to K.., and under the impact of the first few a door shot open, letting in a current of night air through which they all vanished with Frieda behind them openly driving them across the courtyard into the stalls. In the sudden silence which ensued K. heard steps in the vestibule. With some idea of securing his position he dodged behind the bar counter, which afforded the only possible cover in the room. He had an admitted right to be in the bar, but since he meant to spend the night there he had to avoid being seen. So when the door was actually opened he slid under the counter. To be discovered there of course would have its dangers too, yet he could explain plausibly enough that he had only taken refuge from the wild licence of the peasants. It was the landlord who came in.

"Frieda !", he called, and walked up and down the room several times.

Fortunately Frieda soon came back, she did not mention K., she only complained about the peasants, and in the course of looking round for K. went behind the counter, so that he was able to touch her foot. From that moment he felt safe. Since Frieda made no reference to K., however, the landlord was cornpelled to do it.

"And where is the Land Surveyor?" he asked. He was probably courteous by nature, refined by constant and relatively free intercourse with men who were much his superior, but there was remarkable consideration in his tone to Frieda, which was all the more striking because in his conversation he did not cease to be an employer addressing a servant, and a saucy servant at that.

"The Land Surveyor - I forgot all about him," said Frieda, setting her small foot on K.'s chest. "He must have gone out long ago."

"But I haven't seen him," said the landlord, "and I was in the hall nearly the whole time."

"Well, he isn't in here," said Frieda coolly.

"Perhaps he's hidden somewhere," went on the landlord. "From the impression I had of him he's capable of a good deal." "He would hardly have the cheek to do that," said Frieda, pressing her foot down on K.

There was a certain mirth and freedom about her which K. had not previously remarked, and quite unexpectedly it took the upper hand, for suddenly laughing she bent down to K.

with the words: "Perhaps he's hidden underneath here," kissed him lightly and sprang up again saying with a troubled air: "No, he's not there."

Then the landlord, too, surprised K. when he said: "It bothers me not to know for certain that he's gone. Not only because of Herr Klamm, but because of the rule of the house. And the rule applies to you, Fraulein Frieda, just as much as to me. Well, if you answer for the bar, I'll go through the rest of the rooms. Good night! Sleep well!"

He could hardly have left the room before Frieda had turned out the electric light and was under the counter beside K. "My darling! My darling !", she whispered, but she did not touch him.

As if swooning with love she lay on her back and stretched out her arms; time must have seemed endless to her in the prospect of her happiness, and she sighed rather than sang some little song or other. Then as K. still lay absorbed in thought, she started up and began to tug at him like a child: "Come on, it's too close down here," and they embraced each other, her little body burned in K.'s hands, in a state of unconsciousness which K. tried again and again but in vain to master as they rolled a little way, landing with a thud on Klamm's door, where they lay among the small puddles of beer and other refuse gathered on the floor.

There, hours went past, hours in which they breathed as one, in which their hearts beat as one, hours in which K. was haunted by the feeling that he was losing himself or so strange that not even the air had anything in common with his native air, where one might die of strangeness, and yet whose enchantment was such that one could only go on and lose oneself further. So it came to him not as a shock but as a faint glimmer of comfort when from Klamm's room a deep, authoritative impersonal voice called for Frieda.

"Frieda," whispered K. in Frieda's ear, passing on the summons. With a mechanical instinct of obedience Frieda made as if to spring to her feet, then she remembered where she was, stretched herself, laughing quietly, and said:

"I'm not going, I'm never going to him again."

K. wanted to object, to urge her to go to Klamm, and began to fasten up her disordered blouse, but he could not bring himself to speak, he was too happy to have Frieda in his arms, too troubled also in his happiness, for it seemed to him that in letting Frieda go he would lose all he had. And as if his support had strengthened her Frieda clenched her fist and beat upon the door, crying:

"Im with the Land Surveyor!"

That silenced Klamm at any rate, but K. started up, and on his knees beside Frieda gazed round him in the uncertain light of dawn.

What had happened?

Where were his hopes?

What could he expect from Frieda now that she had betrayed everything?

Instead of feeling his way with the prudence befitting the greatness of his enemy and of his ambition, he had spent a whole night wallowing in puddles of beer, the smell of which was nearly overpowering.

"What have you done?" he said as if to himself. "We are both ruined."

"No," said Frieda, "it's only me that's ruined, but then I've won you. Don't worry. But just look how these two are laughing."

"Who?" asked K., and turned round.

There on the bar counter sat his two assistants, a little heavy-eyed for lack of sleep, but cheerful. It was a cheerfulness arising from a sense of duty well done.

"What are you doing here?" cried K. as if they were to blame for everything.

"We had to search for you," explained the assistants, "since you didn't come back to the inn; we looked for you at Barnabas's and finally found you here. We have been sitting here all night. Ours is no easy job."

"It's in the day-time I need you," said K., "not in the night, clear out."

"But it's day-time now," said they without moving.

It was really day, the doors into the courtyard were opened, the peasants came streaming in and with them Olga, whom K. had completely forgotten. Although her hair and clothes were in disorder Olga was as alert as on the previous evening, and her eyes flew to K. before she was well over the threshold.

"Why did you not come home with me?" she asked, almost weeping.

"All for a creature like that!" she said then, and repeated the remark several times.

Frieda, who had vanished for a moment, came back with a small bundle of clothing, and Olga moved sadly to one side.

"Now we can be off," said Frieda, it was obvious she meant that they should go back to the inn by the bridge.

K. walked with Frieda, and behind them the assistants; that was the little procession.

The peasants displayed a great contempt for Frieda, which was understandable, for she had lorded it over them hitherto; one of them even took a stick and held it as if to prevent her from going out until she had jumped over it, but a look from her sufficed to quell him.

When they were out in the snow K. breathed a little more freely. It was such a relief to be in the open air that the journey seemed less laborious; if he had been alone he would have got on still better. When he reached the inn he went straight to his room and lay down on the bed. Frieda prepared a couch for herself on the floor beside him. The assistants had pushed their way in too, and on being driven out came back through the window. K. was too weary to drive them out again. The landlady came up specially to welcome Frieda, who hailed her as "mother"; their meeting was inexplicably affectionate, with kisses and long embracings. There was little peace and quietness to be had in the room, for the maids too came clumping in with their heavy boots, bringing or seeking various articles, and whenever they wanted anything from the miscellaneous assortment on the bed they simply pulled it out from under K. They greeted Frieda as one of themselves.

In spite of all this coming and going K. stayed in bed the whole day through, and the whole night. Frieda performed little offices for him. When he got up at last on the following morning he was much refreshed, and it was the fourth day since his arrival.

He would have liked an intimate talk with Frieda, but the assistants hindered this simply by their importunate presence, and Frieda, too, laughed and joked with them from time to time. Otherwise they were not at all exacting, they had simply settled down in a corner on two old skirts spread out on the floor. They made it a point of honour, as they repeatedly assured Frieda, not to disturb the Land Surveyor and to take up as little room as possible, and in pursuit of this intention, although with a good deal of whispering and giggling, they kept on trying to squeeze themselves into a smaller compass, crouching together in the corner so that in the dim light they looked like one large bundle. From his experience of them by daylight, however, K. was all too conscious that they were acute observers and never took their eyes off him, whether they were fooling like children and using their hands as spyglasses, or merely glancing at him while apparently completely absorbed in grooming their beards, on which they spent much thought and which they were for ever comparing in length and thickness, calling on Frieda to decide between them.

From his bed K. often watched the antics of all three with the completest indifference.

When he felt himself well enough to leave his bed, they all ran to serve him. He was not yet strong enough to ward off their services, and noted that that brought him into a state of dependence on them which might have evil consequences, but he could not help it.

Nor was it really unpleasant to drink at the table the good coffee which Frieda had brought, to warm himself at the stove which Frieda had lit, and to have the assistants racing ten times up and down the stairs in their awkwardness and zeal to fetch him soap and water, comb and lookingglass, and eventually even a small glass of rum because he had hinted in a low voice at his desire for one. Among all this giving of orders and being waited on, K. said, more out of good humour than any hope of being obeyed:

"Go away now, you two, I need nothing more for the present, and I want to speak to Fraulein Frieda by herself."

And when he saw no direct opposition on their faces he added, by way of excusing them:

"We three shall go to the village Superintendent afterwards, so wait downstairs in the bar for me."

Strangely enough they obeyed him, only turning to say before going: "We could wait here."

But K. answered: "I know, but I don't want you to wait here."

It annoyed him, however, and yet in a sense pleased him when Frieda, who had settled on his knee as soon as the assistants were gone, said:

"What's your objection to the assistants, darling? We don't need to have any mysteries before them. They are true friends."

"Oh, true friends," said K., "they keep spying on me the whole time, it's nonsensical but abominable."

"I believe I know what you mean," she said, and she clung to his neck and tried to say something else but could not go on speaking, and since their chair was close to it they reeled over and fell on the bed. There they lay, but not in the forgetfulness of the previous night. She was seeking and he was seeking, they raged and contorted their faces and bored their heads into each other's bosoms in the urgency of seeking something, and their embraces and their tossing limbs did not avail to make them forget, but only reminded them of what they sought; like dogs desperately tearing up the ground they tore at each other's bodies, and often, helplessly baffled, in a final effort to attain happiness they nuzzled and tongued each other's face. Sheer weariness stilled them at last and brought them gratitude to each other. Then the maids came in. "Look how they're lying there," said one, and sympathetically cast a coverlet over them.

When somewhat later K. freed himself from the coverlet and looked round, the two assistants - and he was not surprised at that-were again in their corner, and with a finger jerked towards K. nudged each other to a formal salute, but besides them the landlady was sitting near the bed knitting away at a stocking, an infinitesimal piece of work hardly suited to her enormous bulk which almost darkened the room.

"I've been here a long time," she said, lifting up her broad and much furrowed face which was, however, still rounded and might once have been beautiful.

The words sounded like a reproach, an ill-timed reproach, for K. had not desired her to come. So he merely acknowledged them by a nod, and sat up. Frieda also got up, but left K. to lean over the landlady's chair.

"If you want to speak to me," said K. in bewilderment, "couldn't you put it off until after I come back from visiting the Superintendent? I have important business with him."

"This is important, believe me, sir," said the landlady, "your other business is probably only a question of work, but this concerns a living person, Frieda, my dear maid."

"Oh, if that's it," said K., "then of course you're right, but I don't see why we can't be left to settle our own affairs."

"Because I love her and care for her," said the landlady, drawing Frieda's head towards her, for Frieda as she stood only reached up to the landlady's shoulder.

"Since Frieda puts such confidence in you," cried K., "I must do the same, and since not long ago Frieda called my assistants true friends we are all friends together. So I can tell you that what I would like best would be for Frieda and myself to get married, the sooner the better. I know, oh, I know that I'll never be able to make up to Frieda for all she has lost for my sake, her position in the Herrenhof and her friendship with Klamm."

Frieda lifted up her face, her eyes were full of tears and had not a trace of triumph.

"Why? Why am I chosen out from other people?"

"What?" asked K. and the landlady simultaneously.

"She's upset, poor child," said the landlady, "upset by the conjunction of too much happiness and unhappiness."

And as if in confirmation of those words Frieda now flung herself upon K., kissing him wildly as if there were nobody else in the room, and then weeping, but still clinging to him, fell on her knees before him. While he caressed Frieda's hair with both hands K.

asked the landlady:

"You seem to have no objection?"

"You are a man of honour," said the landlady, who also had tears in her eyes.

She looked a little worn and breathed with difficulty, but she found strength enough to say: "There's only the question now of what guarantees you are to give Frieda, for great as is my respect for you, you're a stranger here; there's nobody here who can speak for you, your family circumstances aren't known here, so some guarantee is necessary. You must see that, my dear sir, and indeed you touched on it yourself when you mentioned how much Frieda must lose through her association with you."

"Of course, guarantees, most certainly," said K., "but they'll be best given before the notary, and at the same time other officials of the Count's will perhaps be concerned.

Besides, before I'm married there's something I must do. I must have a talk with Klamm."

"That's impossible," said Frieda, raising herself a little and pressing close to K.,

"what an idea!"

"But it must be done," said K., "if it's impossible for me to manage it, you must!"

"I can't, K., I can't," said Frieda. "Klamm will never talk to you. How can you even think of such a thing!"

"And won't he talk to you?" asked K.

"Not to me either," said Frieda, "neither to you nor to me, it's simply impossible."

She turned to the landlady with outstretched arms: "You see what he's asking for!"

"You're a strange person," said the landlady, and she was an awe-inspiring figure now that she sat more upright, her legs spread out and her enormous knees projecting under her thin skirt, "you ask for the impossible."

"Why is it impossible?" said K.

"That's what I'm going to tell you," said the landlady in a tone which sounded as if her explanation were less a final concession to friendship than the first item in a score of penalties she was enumerating, "that's what I shall be glad to let you know. Although I don't belong to the Castle, and am only a woman, only a landlady here in an inn of the lowest kind - it's not of the very lowest but not far from it - and on that account you may not perhaps set much store by my explanation, still I've kept my eyes open all my life and met many kinds of people and taken the whole burden of the inn on my own shoulders, for Martin is no landlord although he's a good man, and responsibility is a thing he'll never understand. It's only his carelessness, for instance, that you've got to thank - for I was tired to death on that evening - for being here in the village at all, for sitting here on this bed in peace and comfort."

"What?" said K., waking from a kind of absent-minded distraction, pricked more by curiosity than by anger.

"It's only his carelessness you've got to thank for it," cried the landlady again, pointing with her forefinger at K. Frieda tried to silence her.

"I can't help it," said the landlady with a swift turn of her whole body.

"The Land Surveyor asked me a question and I must answer it. There's no other way of making him understand what we take for granted, that Herr Klamm will never speak to him - will never speak, did I say? can never speak to him. Just listen to me, sir. Herr Klamm is a gentleman from the Castle, and that in itself, without considering Klamm's position there at all, means that he is of very high rank. But what are you, for whose marriage we are humbly considering here ways and means of getting permission? You are not from the Castle, you are not from the village, you aren't anything. Or rather, unfortunately, you are something, a stranger, a man who isn't wanted and is in everybody's way, a man who's always causing trouble, a man who takes up the maids' room, a man whose intentions are obscure, a man who has ruined our dear little Frieda and whom we must unfortunately accept as her husband. I don't hold all that up against you. You are what you are, and I have seen enough in my lifetime to be able to face facts. But now consider what it is you ask. A man like Klamm is to talk with you. It vexed me to hear that Frieda let you look through the peephole, when she did that she was already corrupted by you. But just tell me, how did you have the face to look at Klamm? You needn't answer, I know you think you were quite equal to the occasion. You're not even capable of seeing Klamm as he really is, that's not merely an exaggeration, for I myself am not capable of it either. Klamm is to talk to you, and yet Klamm doesn't talk even to people from the village, never yet has he spoken a word himself to anyone in the village. It was Frieda's great distinction, a distinction I'll be proud of to my dying day, that he used at least to call out her name, and that she could speak to him whenever she liked and was permitted the freedom of the peephole, but even to her he never talked. And the fact that he called her name didn't mean of necessity what one might think, he simply mentioned the name Frieda - who can tell what he was thinking of? - and that Frieda naturally came to him at once was her affair,] and that she was admitted without let or hindrance was an act] of grace on Klamm's part, but that he deliberately summoned her is more than one can maintain. Of course that's all over now for good. Klamm may perhaps call "Frieda" as before, that's possible, but she'll never again be admitted to his presence, a girl who has thrown herself away upon you. And there's one thing, one thing my poor head can't understand, that a girl who had the honour of being known as Klamm's mistress - a wild exaggeration in my opinion - should have allowed you even to lay a finger on her."

"Most certainly, that's remarkable," said K., drawing Frieda to his bosom - she submitted at once although with bent head "but in my opinion that only proves the possibility of your being mistaken in some respects. You're quite right, for instance, in saying that I'm a mere nothing compared with Klamm, and even though I insist on speaking to Klamm in spite of that, and am not dissuaded even by your arguments, that does not mean at all that I'm able to face Klamm without a door between us, or that I mayn't run from the room at the very sight of him. But such a conjecture, even though well founded, is no valid reason in my eyes for refraining from the attempt. If I only succeed in holding my ground there's no need for him to speak to me at all, it will be sufficient for me to see what effect my words have on him, and if they have no effect or if he simply ignores them, I shall at any rate have the satisfaction of having spoken my mind freely to a great man. But you, with your wide knowledge of men and affairs, and Frieda, who was only yesterday Klamm's mistress - I see no reason for questioning that tide - could certainly procure me an interview with Klamm quite easily; if it could be done in no other way I could surely see him in the Herrenhof, perhaps he's still there."

"It's impossible," said the landlady, "and I can see that you're incapable of understanding why. But just tell me what you want to speak to Klamm about?"

"About Frieda, of course," said K.

"About Frieda?" repeated the landlady, uncomprehendingly, and turned to Frieda. "Do you hear that, Frieda, it's about you that he, he, wants to speak to Klamm, to Klamm!"

"Oh," said K., "you're a clever and admirable woman, and yet every trifle upsets you.

Well, there it is, I want to speak to him about Frieda; that's not monstrous, it's only natural. And you're quite wrong, too, in supposing that from the moment of my appearance Frieda has ceased to be of any importance to Klamm. You underestimate him if you suppose that. I'm well aware that it's impertinence in me to lay down the law to you in this matter, but I must do it. I can't be the cause of any alteration in Klamm's relation to Frieda. Either there was no essential relationship between them - and that's what it amounts to if people deny that he was her honoured lover - in which case there is still no relationship between them, or else there was a relationship, and then how could I, a cipher in Klamm's eyes, as you rightly point out, how could I make any difference to it?

One flies to such suppositions in the first moment of alarm, but the smallest reflection must correct one's bias. Anyhow, let us hear what Frieda herself thinks about it"

With a far-away look in her eyes and her cheek on K.'s breast, Frieda said: "It's certain, as mother says, that Klamm will have nothing more to do with me. But I agree that it's not because of you, darling, nothing of that kind could upset him. I think on the other hand that it was entirely his work that we found each other under, the bar counter, we should bless that hour and not curse it."

"If that is so," said K. slowly, for Frieda's words were sweet, and he shut his eyes a moment or two to let their sweetness penetrate him, 'if that is so, there is less ground than ever to flinch from an interview with Klamm."

"Upon my word," said the landlady, with her nose in the air, "you put me in mind of my own husband, you're just as childish and obstinate as he is. You've been only a few days in the village and already you think you know everything better than people who have spent their lives here, better than an old woman like me, and better than Frieda who has seen and heard so much in the Herrenhof. I don't deny that it's possible once in a while to achieve something in the teeth of every rule and tradition. I've never experienced anything of that kind myself, but I believe there are precedents for it. That may well be, but it certainly doesn't happen in the way you're trying to do it, simply by saying

"no, no", and sticking to your own opinions and flouting the most well-meant advice. Do you think it's you I'm anxious about? Did I bother about you in the least so long as you were by yourself? Even though it would have been a good thing and saved a lot of trouble?

The only thing I ever said to my husband about you was: "Keep your distance where he's concerned." And I should have done that myself to this very day if Frieda hadn't got mixed up with your affairs. It's her you have to thank - whether you like it or not - for my interest in you, even for my noticing your existence at all. And you can't simply shake me off, for I'm the only person who looks after little Frieda, and you're strictly answerable to me. Maybe Frieda is right, and all that has happened is Klamm's will, but I have nothing to do with Klamm here and now. I shall never speak to him, he's quite beyond my reach. But you're sitting here, keeping my Frieda, and being kept yourself - I don't see why I shouldn't tell you - by me. Yes, by me, young man, for let me see you find a lodging anywhere in this village if I throw you out, even it were only a dog-kennel."

"Thank you," said K., "that's frank and I believe you absolutely. So my position is as uncertain as that, is it, and Frieda's position, too?"

"No!" interrupted the landlady furiously. "Frieda's position in this respect has nothing at all to do with yours. Frieda belongs to my house, and nobody is entitled to call her position here uncertain."

"All right, all right," said K., "I'll grant you that, too, especially since Frieda for some reason I'm not able to fathom seems to be too afraid of you to interrupt. Stick to me then for the present. My position is quite uncertain, you don't deny that, indeed you rather go out of your way to emphasize it. Like everything else you say, that has a fair proportion of truth in it, but it isn't absolutely true. For instance, I know where I could get a very good bed if I wanted it."

"Where? Where?" cried Frieda and the landlady simultaneously and so eagerly that they might have had the same motive for asking.

"At Barnabas's," said K.

"That scum!" cried the landlady. "That rascally scum I At Barnabas's! Do you hear -" and she turned towards the corner, but the assistants had long quitted it and were now standing arm-in-arm behind her. And so now, as if she needed support, sne seized one of them by the hand: "Do you hear where the man goes hobnobbing, with the family of Barnabas. Oh, certainly he'd get a bed there; I only wished he'd stay'd there overnight instead of in the Herrenhof. But where were you two?" '

"Madam," said K., before the assistants had time to answer, "these are my assistants. But you're treating them as if they were your assistants and my keepers. In every other respect I'm willing at least to argue the point with you courteously, but not where my assistants are concerned, that's too obvious a matter. I request you therefore not to speak to my assistants, and if my request proves ineffective I shall forbid my assistants to answer you."

"So I'm not allowed to speak to you," said the landlady, and they laughed all three, the landlady scornfully, but with less anger than K. had expected, and the assistants in their usual manner, which meant both much and little and disclaimed all responsibility.

"Don't get angry," said Frieda, "you must try to understand why we're upset. I can put it in this way, it's all owing to Barnabas that we belong to each other now. When I saw you for the first time in the bar - when you came in arm-in-arm with Olga - well, I knew something about you, but I was quite indifferent to you. I was indifferent not only to you but to nearly everything, yes, nearly everything. For at that time I was discontented about lots of things, and often annoyed, but it was a queer discontent and a queer annoyance. For instance, if one of the customers in the bar insulted me - and they were always after me - you saw what kind of creatures they were, but there were many worse than that, Klamm's servants weren't the worst - well, if one of them insulted me, what did that matter to me? I regarded it as if it had happened years before, or as if it had happened to someone else, or as if I had only heard tell of it, or as if I had already forgotten about it. But I can't describe it, I can hardly imagine it now, so different has everything become since losing Klamm."

And Frieda broke off short, letting her head drop sadly, folding her hands on her bosom.

"You see," cried the landlady, and she spoke not as if in her own person but as if she had merely lent Frieda her voice; she moved nearer, too, and sat close beside Frieda, "you see, sir, the results of your actions, and your assistants too, whom I am not allowed to speak to, can profit by looking on at them. You've snatched Frieda from the happiest state she had ever known, and you managed to do that largely because in her childish susceptibility she could not bear to see you arm-in-arm with Olga, and so apparently delivered hand and foot to the Barnabas family. She rescued you from that and sacrificed herself in doing. And now that it's done, and Frieda has given up all she had for the pleasure of sitting on your knee, you come out with this fine trump card that once you had the chance of getting a bed from Barnabas. That's by way of showing me that you're independent of me. I assure you, if you had slept in that house you would be so independent of me that in the twinkling of an eye you would be put out of this one."

"I don't know what sins the family of Barnabas have committed," said K., carefully raising Frieda - who drooped as if lifeless - setting her slowly down on the bed and standing up himself, "you may be right about them, but I know that I was right in asking you to leave Frieda and me to settle our own affairs. You talked then about your care and affection, yet I haven't seen much of that, but a great deal of hatred and scorn and forbidding me your house. If it was your intention to separate Frieda from me or me from Frieda it was quite a good move, but all the same I think it won't succeed, and if it does succeed - it's my turn now to issue vague threats you'll repent it. As for the lodging you favour me with - you can only mean this abominable hole - it's not at all certain that you do it of your own free will, it's much more likely that the authorities insist upon it I shall now inform them that I have been told to go - and if I am allotted other quarters you'll probably feel relieved, but not so much as I will myself. And now I'm going to discuss this and other business with the Superintendent, please be so good as to look after Frieda at least, whom you have reduced to a bad enough state with your so-called motherly counsel."

Then he turned to the assistants.

"Come along," he said, taking Klamm's letter from its nail and making for the door.

The landlady looked at him in silence, and only when his hand was on the latch did she say: "There's something else to take away with you, for whatever you say and however you insult an old woman like me, you're after all Frieda's future husband. That's my sole reason for telling you now that your ignorance of the local situation is so appalling that it makes my head go round to listen to you and compare your ideas and opinions with the real state of things. It's a kind of ignorance which can't be enlightened at one attempt, and perhaps never can be, but there's a lot you could learn if you would only believe me a little and keep your own ignorance constantly in mind. For instance, you would at once be less unjust to me, and you would begin to have an inkling of the shock it was to me - a shock from which I'm still suffering - when I realized that my dear little Frieda had, so to speak, deserted the eagle for the snake in the grass, only the real situation is much worse even than that, and I have to keep on trying to forget it so as to be able to speak civilly to you at all. Oh, now you're angry again! No, don't go away yet, listen to this one appeal; wherever you may be, never forget that you're the most ignorant person in the village, and be cautious; here in this house where Frieda's presence saves you from harm you can drivel on to your heart's content, for instance, here you can explain to us how you mean to get an interview with Klamm, but I entreat you, I entreat you, don't do it in earnest."

She stood up, tottering a little with agitation, went over to K., took his hand and looked at him imploringly.

"Madam," said K., "I don't understand why you should stoop to entreat me about a thing like this. If as you say, it's impossible for me to speak to Klamm, I won't manage it in any case whether I'm entreated or not. But if it proves to be possible, why shouldn't I do it, especially as that would remove your main objection and so make your other premises questionable. Of course, I'm ignorant, that's an unshaken truth and a sad truth for me, but it gives me all the advantage of ignorance, which is greater daring, and so I'm prepared to put up with my ignorance, evil consequences and all, for some time to come, so long as my strength holds out. But these consequences really affect nobody but myself, and that's why I simply can't understand your pleading. I'm certain you would always look after Frieda, and if I were to vanish from Frieda's side you couldn't regard that as anything but good luck. So what are you afraid of? Surely you're not afraid _ an ignorant man thinks everything possible" - here K. flung the door open - "surely you're not afraid for Klamm?"

The landlady gazed after him in silence as he ran down the staircase with the assistants following him.

To his own surprise K. had little difficulty in obtaining an interview with the Superintendent. He sought to explain this to himself by the fact that, going by his experience hitherto, official intercourse with the authorities for him was always very easy. This was caused on the one hand by the fact that the word had obviously gone out once and for all to treat his case with the external marks of indulgence, and on the other, by the admirable autonomy of the service, which one divined to be peculiarly effective precisely where it was not visibly present. At the mere thought of those facts, K. was often in danger of considering his situation hopeful; nevertheless, after such fits of easy confidence, he would hasten to tell himself that just there lay his danger.

Direct intercourse with the authorities was not particularly difficult then, for well organized as they might be, all they did was to guard the distant and invisible interests of distant and invisible masters, while K. fought for something vitally near to him, for himself, and moreover, at least at the very beginning, on his own initiative, for he was the attacker; and besides he fought not only for himself, but clearly for other powers as well which he did not know, but in which, without infringing the regulations of the authorities, he was permitted to believe.

But now by the fact that they had at once amply met his wishes in all unimportant matters - and hitherto only unimportant matters had come up - they had robbed him of the possibility of light and easy victories, and with that of the satisfaction which must accompany them and the well-grounded confidence for further and greater struggles which must result from them. Instead, they let K. go anywhere he liked - of course only within the village - and thus pampered and enervated him, ruled out all possibility of conflict, and transported him to an unofficial totally unrecognized, troubled, and alien existence.

In this life it might easily happen, if he were not always on his guard, until one day or other, in spite of the amiability of the authorities the scrupulous fulfilment of all his exaggeratedly light duties, might - deceived by the apparent favour shown him - conduc himself so imprudently that he might get a fall; and the authorities, still ever mild and friendly, and as it were against their wil but in the name of some public regulation unknown to hit might have to come and clear him out of the way. And what was it, this other life to which he was consigned? Never yet had K. seen vocation and life so interlaced as here, so interlaced sometimes one might think that they had exchanged places.

What importance, for example, had the power, merely formal up till now, which Klamm exercised over K.'s services, cor pared with the very real power which Klamm possessed in K.'s bedroom? So it came about that while a light and frivolous bearing, a certain deliberate carelessness was sufficient when one came in direct contact with the authorities, one needed in everything else the greatest caution, and had to look round on every side before one made a single step.

K. soon found his opinion of the authorities of the place confirmed when he went to see the Superintendent. The Superintendent, a kindly, stout, clean-shaven man, was laid up; he was suffering from a severe attack of gout, and received K. in bed.

"So here is our Land Surveyor," he said, and tried to sit up, failed in the attempt, and flung himself back again on die cushions, pointing apologetically to his leg. In the faint light of the room, where the tiny windows were still further darkened by curtains, a noiseless, almost shadowing woman pushed forward a chair for K. and placed it beside the bed.

"Take a seat, Land Surveyor, take a seat," said the Superintendent, "and let me know your wishes."

K. read out Klamm's letter and adjoined a few remarks to it. Again he had this sense of extraordinary ease in intercourse with the authorities. They seemed literally to bear every burden, one could lay everything on their shoulders and remain free and untouched oneself. As if he, too, felt this in his way, the Superintendent made a movement of discomfort on the bed. At length he said:

"You know about the whole business as, indeed, you have remarked. The reason why I've done nothing is, firstly, that I've been unwell, and secondly, that you've been so long in coming; I thought finally that you had given up the business. But now that you've been so kind as to look me up, really I must tell you the plain unvarnished truth of the matter. You've been taken on as Land Surveyor, as you say, but, unfortunately, we have no need of a Land Surveyor. There wouldn't be the least use for one here. The frontiers of our little state are marked out and all officially recorded. So what should we do with a Land Surveyor?"

Though he had not given the matter a moment's thought before, K. was convinced now at the bottom of his heart that he had expected some such response as this. Exactly for that reason he was able to reply immediately:

"This is a great surprise for me. It throws all my calculations out. I can only hope that there's some misunderstanding."

"No, unfortunately," said the Superintendent, "it's as I've said."

"But how is that possible?" cried K. "Surely I haven't made this endless journey just to be sent back again."

"That's another question," replied the Superintendent, "which isn't for me to decide, but how this misunderstanding became possible, I can certainly explain that. In such a large governmental office as the Count's, it may occasionally happen that one department ordains this, another that; neither knows of the other, and though the supreme control is absolutely efficient, it comes by its nature too late, and so every now and then a trifling miscalculation arises. Of course that applies only to the pettiest little affairs, as for example your case. In great matters I've never known of any error yet, but even little affairs are often painful enough. Now as for your case, I'll be open with you about its history, and make no official mystery of it - I'm not enough of the official for that, I'm a farmer and always will remain one. A long time ago - I had only been Superintendent for a few months - there came an order, I can't remember from what department, in which in the usual categorical way of the gentlemen up there, it was made known that a Land Surveyor was to be called in, and the municipality were instructed to hold themselves ready for the plans and measurements necessary for his work. This order obviously couldn't have concerned you, for it was many years ago, and I shouldn't have remembered it if I weren't ill just now and with ample time in bed to think of the most absurd things ..."

"Mizzi," he said, suddenly interrupting his narrative, to the woman who was still flitting about the room in incomprehensible activity, "please have a look in the cabinet, perhaps you'll find the order."

"You see, it belongs to my first months here," he explained to K., "at that time I still filed everything away."

The woman opened the cabinet at once. K. and the Superintendent looked on. The cabinet was crammed full of papers. When it was opened two large packages of papers rolled out, tied in round bundles, as one usually binds firewood; the woman sprang back in alarm.

"It must be down below, at the bottom," said the Superintendent, directing operations from the bed.

Gathering the papers in both arms the woman obediently threw them all out of the cabinet so as to read those at the bottom. The papers now covered half the floor.

"A great deal of work is got through here," said the Superintendent nodding his head, "and that's only a small fraction of it. I've put away the most important pile in the shed, but the great mass of it has simply gone astray. Who could keep it all together?

But there's piles and piles more in the shed."

"Will you be able to find the order?" he said, turning again to his wife, "you must look for a document with the word Land Surveyor underlined in blue pencil."

"It's too dark," said the woman, "I'll fetch a candle," and she stamped through the papers to the door.

"My wife is a great help to me," said the Superintendent, "in these difficult official affairs, and yet we can never quite keep up with them. True, I have another assistant for the writing that has to be done, the teacher, but all the same it's impossible to get things shipshape, there's always a lot of business that has to be left lying, it has been put away in that chest there," and he pointed to another cabinet.

"And just now, when I'm laid up, it has got the upper hand," he said, and lay back with a weary yet proud air.

"Couldn't I," asked K., seeing that the woman had now returned with the candle and was kneeling before the chest looking for the paper, "couldn't I help your wife to look for it?"

The Superintendent smilingly shook his head: "As I said before, I don't want to make any parade of official secrecy before you, but to let you look through these papers yourself - no, I can't go so far as that."

Now stillness fell in the room, only the rustling of the papers was to be heard. It looked, indeed, for a few minutes, as if the Superintendent were dozing. A faint rapping on the door made K. turn round. It was of course the assistants. All the same they showed already some of the effects of their training, they did not rush at once into the room, but whispered at first through the door which was slightly ajar:

"It's cold out here."

"Who's that?" asked the Superintendent, starting up.

"It's only my assistants," replied K. "I don't know where to ask them to wait for me, it's too cold outside and here they would be in the way."

"They won't disturb me," said the Superintendent indulgently. "Ask them to come in.

Besides I know them. Old acquaintances."

"But they're in my way," K. replied bluntly, letting his gaze wander from the assistants to the Superintendent and back again, and finding on the faces of all three the same smile.

"But seeing you're here as it is," he went on experimentally, "stay and help the Superintendent's lady there to look for a document with the word Land Surveyor underlined in blue pencil."

The Superintendent raised no objection. What had not been permitted to K. was allowed to the assistants. They threw themselves at once on the papers, but they did not so much seek for anything as rummage about in the heap, and while one was spelling out a document the other would immediately snatch it out of his hand. The woman meanwhile knelt before the empty chest, she seemed to have completely given up looking, in any case the candle was standing quite far away from her. "The assistants," said the Superintendent with a self-complacent smile, which seemed to indicate that he had the lead, though nobody was in a position even to assume this, "they're in your way then? Yet they're your own assistants."

"No," replied K. coolly, "they only ran into me here."

"Ran into you," said he, "you mean, of course, were assigned to you."

"All right then, were assigned to me," said K., "but they might as well have fallen from the sky, for all the thought that was spent in choosing them."

"Nothing here is done without taking thought," said the Superintendent, actually forgetting the pain in his foot and sitting up.

"Nothing!" said K., "and what about my being summoned here then?"

"Even your being summoned was carefully considered," said the Superintendent, "it was only certain auxiliary circumstances that entered and confused the matter. I'll prove it to you from the official papers."

"The papers will not be found," said K.

"Not be found?" said the Superintendent. "Mizzi, please hurry up a bit! Still I can tell you the story even without the papers. We replied with thanks to the order that I've mentioned already, saying that we didn't need a Land Surveyor. But this reply doesn't appear to have reached the original department - I'll call it A - but by mistake went to another department, B. So Department A remained without an answer, but unfortunately our full reply didn't reach B either. Whether it was that the order itself was not enclosed by us, or whether it got lost on the way - it was certainly not lost in my department, that I can vouch for - in any case all that arrived at Department B was the covering letter, in which was merely noted that the enclosed order, unfortunately an impracticable one, was concerned with the engagement of a Land Surveyor. Meanwhile Department A was waiting for our answer, they had, of course, made a memorandum of the case, but as excusably enough often happens and is bound to happen even under the most efficient handling, our correspondent trusted to the fact that we would answer him, after which he would either summon the Land Surveyor, or else if need be write us further about the matter. As a result he never thought of referring to his memorandum and the whole thing fell into oblivion. But in Department B the covering letter came into the hands of a correspondent, famed for his conscientiousness, Sordini by name, an Italian. It is incomprehensible even to me, though I am one of the initiated, why a man of his capacities is left in an almost subordinate position. This Sordini naturally sent the unaccompanied covering letter for completion.

Now months, if not years, had passed by this time since that first communication from Department A, which is understandable enough] for when - which is the rule - a document goes the proper rout it reaches the department at the outside in a day and is settled that day, but when it once in a while loses its way then in an organization so efficient as ours its proper destination must be sought for literally with desperation, otherwise it mightn't be found; and then, well then the search may last really for a long time.

Accordingly, when we got Sordini's note we had only a vague memory of the affair, there were only two of us to do the work at that time, Mizzi and myself, the teacher hadn't yet been assigned to us, we only kept copies in the most important instances, so we could only reply in the most vague terms that we knew nothing of this engagement of a Land Surveyor and that as far as we knew there was no need for one."

"But," here the Superintendent interrupted himself as if, carried on by his tale, he had gone too far, or as if at least it were possible that he had gone too far, "doesn't the story bore you?"

"No," said K., "it amuses me."

Thereupon the Superintendent said: "I'm not telling it to amuse you."

"It only amuses me," said K., "because it gives me an insight into the ludicrous bungling which in certain circumstances may decide the life of a human being."

"You haven't been given any insight into that yet," replied the Superintendent gravely, "and I can go on with my story. Naturally Sordini was not satisfied with our reply. I admire the man, although he is a plague to me. He literally distrusts everyone. Even if, for instance, he has come to know somebody, through countless circumstances, as the most reliable man in the world, he distrusts him as soon as fresh circumstances arise, as if he didn't want to know him, or rather as if he wanted to know that he was a scoundrel. I consider that right and proper, an official must behave like that. Unfortunately with my nature I can't follow out this principle; you see yourself how frank I am with you, a stranger, about those things, I can't act in any other way. But Sordini, on the contrary, was seized by suspicion when he read our reply. Now a large correspondence began to grow.

Sordini inquired how I had suddenly recalled that a Land Surveyor shouldn't be summoned.

I replied, drawing on Mizzi's splendid memory, that the first suggestion had come from the chancellery itself (but that it had come from a different department we had of course forgotten long before this).

Sordini countered: "Why had I only mentioned this official order now?"

I replied: "Because I had just remembered it."

Sordini: "That was very extraordinary."

Myself: "It was not in the least extraordinary in such a long-drawn-out business."

Sordini: "Yes, it was extraordinary, for the order that I remembered didn't exist."

Myself: "Of course it didn't exist, for the whole document had gone missing."

Sordini: "But there must be a memorandum extant relating to this first communication, and there wasn't one extant."

That drew me up, for that an error should happen in Sordini's department I neither dared to maintain nor to believe. Perhaps, my dear Land Surveyor, you'll make the reproach against Sordini in your mind, that in consideration of my assertion he should have been moved at least to make inquiries in the other departments about the affair. But that is just what would have been wrong; I don't want any blame to attach to this man, no, not even in your thoughts. It's a working principle of the Head Bureau that the very possibility of error must be ruled out of account. This ground principle is justified by the consummate organization of the whole authority, and it is necessary if the maximum speed in transacting business is to be attained. So it wasn't within Sordini's power to make inquiries in other departments, besides they simply wouldn't have answered, because they would have guessed at once that it was a case of hunting out a possible error."

"Allow me, Superintendent, to interrupt you with a question," said K. "Did you not mention once before a Control Authority? From your description the whole economy is one that would rouse one's apprehension if onecould imagine the control failing."

"You're very strict," said the Superintendent, "but multiply your strictness a thousand times and it would still be nothing compared with the strictness which the Authority imposes on itself. Only a total stranger could ask a question like yours. Is there a Control Authority? There are only control authorities. Frankly it isn't their function to hunt out errors in the vulgar sense, for errors don't happen, and even when once in a while an error does happen, as in your case, who can say finally that it's an error?"

"This is news indeed!" cried K.

"It's very old news to me," said the Superintendent. "Not unlike yourself I'm convinced that an error has occurred, and as a result Sordini is quite ill with despair, and the first Control Officials, whom we have to thank for discovering the source of error, recognize that there is an error. But who can guarantee that the second Control Officials will decide in the same way and the third lot and all the others?"

"That may be," said K. "I would much rather not mix in these speculations yet, besides this is the first mention I've heard of these Control Officials and naturally

I can't understand them yet. But I fancy that two things must be distinguished here: firstly, what is transacted in the offices and can be construed again officially this way or that, and secondly, my own actual person, me myself, situated outside of the offices and threatened by their encroachments, which are so meaningless that I can't even yet believe in the seriousness of the danger. The first evidently is covered by what you, Superintendent, tell me in such extraordinary and disconcerting detail. All the same I would like to hear a word now about myself."

"I'm coming to that too," said the Superintendent, "but you couldn't understand it without my giving a few more preliminary details. My mentioning the Control Officials just now was premature. So I must turn back to the discrepancies with Sordini. As I said, my defence gradually weakened. But whenever Sordini has in his hands even the slightest hold against anyone, he has as good as won, for then his vigilance, energy, and alertness are actually increased and it's a terrible moment for the victim, and a glorious one for the victim's enemies. It's only because in other circumstances I have experienced this last feeling that I'm able to speak of him as I do. All the same I have never managed yet to come within sight of him. He can't get down here, he's so overwhelmed with work. From the descriptions I've heard of his room every wall is covered with columns of documents tied together, piled on top of one another. Those are only the documents that Sordini is working on at the time, and as bundles of papers are continually being taken away and brought in, and all in great haste, those columns are always falling on the floor, and it's just those perpetual crashes, following fast on one another, that have come to distinguish Sordini's workroom. Yes, Sordini is a worker and he gives the same scrupulous care to the smallest case as to the greatest."

"Superintendent," said K., "you always call my case one of the smallest, and yet it has given hosts of officials a great deal of trouble, and if, perhaps, it was unimportant at the start, yet through the diligence of officials of Sordini's type it has grown into a great affair. Very much against my will, unfortunately, for my ambition doesn't run to seeing columns of documents, all about me, rising and crashing together, but to working quietly at my drawing-board as a humble Land Surveyor."

"No," said the Superintendent, "it's not at all a great affair, in. that respect you've no ground for complaint - it's one of the. Least important among the least important. The importance of a case is not determined by the amount of work it involves, you're far from understanding the authorities if you believe that. But even if it's a question of the amount of work, your case would remain one of the slightest. Ordinary cases, those without any so-called errors I mean, provide far more work and far more profitable work as well. Besides you know absolutely nothing yet of the actual work which was caused by your case. I'll tell you about that now. Well, presently Sordini left me out of count, but the clerks arrived, and every day a formal inquiry involving the most prominent members of the community was held in the Herrenhof. The majority stuck by me, only a few held back - the question of a Land Surveyor appeals to peasants - they scented secret plots and injustices and what not, found a leader, no less, and Sordini was forced by their assertions to the conviction that if I had brought the question forward in the Town Council, every voice wouldn't have been against the summoning of a Land Surveyor. So a commonplace - namely, a Land Surveyor wasn't needed - was turned after all into doubtful matter at least. A man called Brunswick distinguish himself especially, you don't know him, of course. Probably he's not a bad man, only stupid and fanciful, he's a son-in-law of Lasemann's."

"Of the Master Tanner?" asked K., and he described the fullbearded man whom he had seen at Lasemann's.

"Yes, that's the man," said the Superintendent.

"I know his wife, too," said K. a little at random.

"That's possible," replied the Superintendent briefly.

"She's beautiful," said K., "but rather pale and sickly. She comes, of course, from the Castle?"

It was half a question. The Superintendent looked at the clock, poured some medicine into a spoon, and gulped at it hastily.

"You only know the official side of the Castle?" asked K. bluntly.

"That's so," replied the Superintendent, with an ironical and yet grateful smile, "and it's the most important. And as for Brunswick, if we could exclude him from the Council we would almost all be glad, and Lasemann not least. But at that time Brunswick gained some influence, he's not an orator of course, but a shouter. But even that can do a lot.

And so it came about that I was forced to lay the matter before the Town Council.

However, it was Brunswick's only immediate triumph, for of course the Town Council refused by a large majority to hear anything about a Land Surveyor. That, too, was a long time ago, but the whole time since the matter has never been allowed to rest, partly owing to Sordini's conscientiousness, who by the most painful sifting of data sought to fathom the motives of the majority no less than the opposition, partly owing to Brunswick's stupidity and ambition, who had several personal acquaintances among the authorities whom he set working with fresh inventions of his fancy. Sordini, at any rate, didn't let himself be deceived by Brunswick - how could Brunswick deceive Sordini? - but simply to prevent himself from being deceived a new sifting of data was necessary, and long before it was ended Brunswick had already thought out something new. He's very, very versatile, no doubt of it, that goes with his stupidity. And now I come to a peculiar characteristic of our administrative apparatus. Along with its precision it's extremely sensitive as well. When an affair has been weighed for a very long time, it may happen, even before the matter has been fully considered, that suddenly in a flash the decision comes in some unforeseen place, that, moreover, can't be found any longer later on, a decision that settles the matter, if in most cases justly, yet all the same arbitrarily.

It's as if the administrative apparatus were unable any longer to bear the tension, the yearlong irritation caused by the same affair - probably trivial in itself - and had hit upon the decision by itself, without the assistance of the officials. Of course a miracle didn't happen and certainly it was some clerk who hit upon the solution or the unwritten decision, but in any case it couldn't be discovered by us, at least by us here, or even by the Head Bureau, which clerk had decided in this case and on what grounds. The Control Officials only discovered that much later, but we will never learn it. Besides by this time it would scarcely interest anybody.

Now, as I said, it's just these decisions that are generally excellent. The only annoying thing about them - it's usually the case with such things - is that one learns too late about them and so in the meantime keeps on still passionately canvassing things that were decided long ago. I don't know whether in your case a decision of this kind happened - some people say yes, others no - but if it had happened then the summons would have been sent to you and you would have made the long journey to this place, much time would have passed, and in the meanwhile Sordini would have been working away here all the time on the same case until he was exhausted. Brunswick would have been intriguing, and I would have been plagued by both of them. I only indicate this possibility, but I know the following for a fact: a Control Official discovered meanwhile that a query had gone out from the Department A to the Town Council many years before regarding a Land Surveyor, without having received a reply up till then. A new inquiry was sent to me, and now the whole business was really cleared up. Department A was satisfied with my answer that a|

Land Surveyor was not needed, and Sordini was forced to recognize that he had not been equal to this case and, innocently it is true, had got through so much nerveracking work for nothing.

And now imagine to yourself, Land Surveyor, my dismay when after the fortunate end of the whole business - and since then, too, a great deal of time had passed by suddenly you appear and it begins to look as if the whole thing must begin all over again. You'll understand of course that I'm firmly resolved, so far as I'm concerned, not to let that happen in any case?"

"Certainly," said K., "but I understand better still that a terrible abuse of my case, and probably of the law, is being carried on. As for me, I shall know how to protect myself against it."

"How will you do it?" asked the Superintendent.

"I'm not at liberty to reveal that," said K.

"I don't want to press myself upon you," said the Superintendent, "only I would like you to reflect that in me you have - I won't say a friend, for we're complete strangers of course - but to some extent a business friend. The only thing I will not agree to is that you should be taken on as Land Surveyor, but in other matters you can draw on me with confidence, frankly to the extent of my power, which isn't great."

"You always talk of the one thing," said K., "that I shan't be taken on as Land Surveyor, but I'm Land Surveyor already, here is Klamm's letter."

"Klamm's letter," said the Superintendent. "That's valuable and worthy of respect on account of Klamm's signature which seems to be genuine, but all the same - yet I won't dare to advance it on my own unsupported word. Mizzi," he called, and then: "But what are you doing?"

Mizzi and the assistants, left so long unnoticed, had clearly not found the paper they were looking for, and had then tried to shut everything up again in the cabinet, but on account of the confusion and superabundance of papers had not succeeded. Then the assistants had hit upon the idea which they were carrying out now. They had laid the cabinet on its back on the floor, crammed all the documents in, then along with Mizzi had knelt on the cabinet door and were trying now in this way to get it shut.

"So the paper hasn't been found," said the Superintendent. "A pity, but you know the story already. Really we don't need the paper now, besides it will certainly be found sometime yet. Probably it's at the teacher's place, there's a great pile of papers there too. But come over here now with the candle, Mizzi, and read this letter for me."

Mizzi went over and now looked still more grey and insignificant as she sat on the edge of the bed and leaned against the strong, vigorous man, who put his arm round her. In the candlelight only her pinched face was cast into relief, its simple and austere lines softened by nothing but age. Hardly had she glanced at the letter when she clasped her hands lightly and said:

"From Klamm."

Then they read the letter together, whispered for a moment, and at last, just as the assistants gave a "Hurrah!" for they had finally got the cabinet door shut which earned them a look of silent gratitude from Mizzi - then Superintendent said: "Mizzi is quite of my opinion and now I am at liberty to press it. This letter is in no sense an official letter, but only a private letter. That can be clearly seen in the very mode of address:

"My dear Sir." Moreover, there isn't a single word in it showing that you've been taken on as Land Surveyor. On the contrary it's all about state service in general, and even that is not absolutely guaranteed, as you know, that is, the task of proving that you are taken on is laid on you. Finally, you are officially and expressly referred to me, the Superintendent, as your immediate superior, for more detailed information, which, indeed, has in great part been given already. To anyone who knows how to read official communications, and consequently knows still better how to read unofficial letters, all this is only too clear. That you, a stranger, don't know it doesn't surprise me. In general the letter means nothing more than that Klamm intends to take a personal interest in you if you should be taken into the state service."

"Superintendent," said K., "you interpret the letter so well that nothing remains of it but a signature on a blank sheet of paper. Don't you see that in doing this you depreciate Klamm's name, which you pretend to respect?"

"You misunderstand me," said the Superintendent, 'I don't change the meaning of the letter, my reading of it doesn't disparage it, on the contrary. A private letter from Klamm has naturally far more significance than an official letter, but it hasn't precisely the kind of significance that you attach to it."

"Do you know Schwarzer?" asked K.

"No," replied the Superintendent.

"Perhaps you know him, Mizzi? You don't know him either? No, we don't know him."

"That's strange," said K., "he's a son of one of the undercastellans."

"My dear Land Surveyor," replied the Superintendent, "how on earth should I know all the sons of all the under-castellans?"

"Right," said K., "then you'll just have to take my word that he is one. I had a sharp encounter with this Schwarzer on the very day of my arrival. Afterwards he made a telephone inquiry of an under-castellan called Fritz and received the information that I was engaged as Land Surveyor. How do you explain that, Superintendent?"

"Very simply," replied the Superintendent. "You haven't once up till now come into real contact with our authorities. All those contacts of yours have been illusory, but owing to your ignorance of the circumstances you take them to be real. And as for the telephone. As you see, in my place, though I've certainly enough to do with the authorities, there's no telephone. In inns and suchlike places it may be of real use, as much use say as a penny in-the-slot musical instrument, but it's nothing more than that.

Have you ever telephoned here? Yes? Well, then perhaps you'll understand what I say. In the Castle the telephone works beautifully of course, I've been told it's going there all the time, that naturally speeds up the work a great deal. We can hear this continual telephoning in our telephones down here as a humming and singing, you must have heard it too. Now this humming and singing transmitted by our telephones is the only real and reliable thing you'll hear, everything else is deceptive. There's no fixed connexion with the Castle, no central exchange transmits our calls further. When anybody calls up the Castle from here the instruments in all the subordinate departments ring, or rather they would all ring if practically all the departments -1 know it for a certainty - didn't leave their receivers off. Now and then, however, a fatigued official may feel the need of a little distraction, especially in the evenings and at night and may hang the receiver on. Then we get an answer, but an answer of course that's merely a practical joke. And that's very understandable too. For who would take the responsibility of interrupting, in the middle of the night, the extremely important work up there that goes on furiously the whole time, with a message about his own little private troubles? I can't comprehend how even a stranger can imagine that when he calls up Sordini, for example, it's really Sordini that answers. Far more probably it's a little copying clerk from an entirely different department. On the other hand, it may certainly happen once in a blue moon that when one calls up the little copying clerk Sordini will answer himself.

Then finally the best thing is to fly from the telephone before the first sound comes through."

"I didn't know it was like that, certainly," said K. "I couldn't know of all these peculiarities, but I didn't put much confidence in those telephone conversations and I was always aware that tfo only things of real importance were those that happened in the
    Castle itself."

"No," said the Superintendent, holding firmly on to the words, "these telephone replies certainly have a meaning, why shouldn't they? How could a message given by an official from the Castld be unimportant? As I remarked before apropos Klamm's letter. All these utterances have no official significance. When you attach official significance to them you go astray. On the other hand, their private significance in a friendly or hostile sense is very great, generally greater than an official communication could ever be."

"Good." said K. "Granted that all this is so, I should have lots of good friends in the Castle. Looked at rightly the sudden inspiration of that department all these years ago -

saying that a Land Surveyor should be asked to come-was an act of friendship towards myself. But then in the sequel one act was followed by another, until at last, on an evil day, I was enticed here and then threatened with being thrown out again"

"There's a certain amount of truth in your view of the case," said the Superintendent, "you're right in thinking that the pronouncements of the Castle are not to be taken literally. But caution is always necessary, not only here, and always the more necessary the more important the pronouncement in question happens to be. But when you went on to talk about being enticed, I ceased to fathom you. If you had followed my explanation more carefully, then you must have seen that the question of your being summoned here is far too difficult to be settled here and now in the course of a short conversation."

"So the only remaining conclusion," said K., "is that everything is very uncertain and insoluble, including my being thrown out."

"Who would take the risk of throwing you out, Land Surveyor?" asked the Superintendent.

"The very uncertainty about your summons guarantees you the most courteous treatment, only you're too sensitive by all appearances. Nobody keeps you here, but that surely doesn't amount to throwing you out."

"Oh, Superintendent," said K., "now again you're taking far too simple a view of the case. I'll enumerate for your benefit a few of the things that keep me here: the sacrifice I made in leaving my home, the long and difficult journey, the wellgrounded hopes I built on my engagement here, my complete lack of means, the impossibility after this of finding some other suitable job at home, and last but not least my fiancee, who lives here."

"Oh, Frieda!" said the Superintendent without showing any surprise. "I know. But Frieda would follow you anywhere. As for the rest of what you've said, some consideration will be necessary and I'll communicate with the Castle about it. If a decision should be come to, or if it should be necessary first to interrogate you again, I'll send for you. Is that agreeable to you?"

"No, absolutely," said K., "I don't want any act of favour from the Castle, but my rights."

"Mizzi," the Superintendent said to his wife, who still sat pressed against him, and lost in a day-dream was playing with Klamm's letter, which she had folded into the shape of a little boat - K. snatched it from her in alarm.

"Mizzi, my foot is beginning to throb again, we must renew the compress." K. got up.

"Then I'll take my leave," he said.

"Hm," said Mizzi, who was already preparing a poultice, "the last one was drawing too strongly."

K. turned away.

At his last words the assistants with their usual misplaced zeal to be useful had thrown open both wings of the door. To protect the sickroom from the strong draught of cold air which was rushing in, K. had to be content with making the Superintendent a hasty bow. Then, pushing the assistants in front of him, he rushed out of the room and quickly closed the door.

Before the inn the landlord was waiting for him. Without being questioned he would not have ventured to address him, accordingly K. asked what he wanted.

"Have you found new lodgings yet?" asked the landlord, looking at the ground.

"You were told to ask by your wife?" replied K., "you're very much under her influence?"

"No," said the landlord, "I didn't ask because of my wife. But she's very bothered and unhappy on your account, can't work, lies in bed and sighs and complains all the time."

"Shall I go and see her?" asked K.

"I wish you would," said the landlord. "I've been to the Superintendent's already to fetch you. I listened at the door but you were talking. I didn't want to disturb you, besides I was anxious about my wife and ran back again. But she wouldn't see me, so there was nothing for it but to wait for you."

"Then let's go at once," said K., "I'll soon reassure her."

"If you could only manage it," said the landlord.

They went through the bright kitchen where three or four maids, engaged all in different corners at the work they were happening to be doing, visibly stiffened on seeing K. From the kitchen the sighing of the landlady could already be heard. She lay in a windowless annex separated from the kitchen by thin lath boarding. There was room in it only for a huge family bed and a chest. The bed was so placed that from it one could see over the whole kitchen and superintend the work. From the kitchen, on the other hand, hardly anything could be seen in the annex. There it was quite dark. Only the faint gleam of the upper bed-coverlet could be distinguished. Not until one's eyes become used to the darkness did one detach particular objects.

"You've come at last," said the landlady feebly.

She was lying stretched out on her back, she breathed with visible difficulty, she had thrown back the feather quilt. In bed she looked much younger than in her clothes, but a nightcap of delicate lacework which she wore, although it was too small and nodded on her head, made her sunk face look pitiable.

"Why should I have come?" asked K. mildly. "You didn't send for me."

"You shouldn't have kept me waiting so long," said the landlady with the capriciousness of an invalid. "Sit down," she went on, pointing to the bed, "and you others go away."

Meantime the maids as well as the assistants had crowded in.

"I'll go too, Gardana," said the landlord.

This was the first time that K. had heard her name.

"Of course," she replied slowly, and as if she were occupied with other thoughts she added absently: "Why should you remain any more than the others?"

But when they had all retreated to the kitchen-even the assistants this time went at once, besides, a maid was behind them - Gardana was alert enough to grasp that everything she said could be heard in there, for the annex lacked a door, and so she commanded everyone to leave the kitchen as well. It was immediately done.

"Land Surveyor," said Gardana, "there's a wrap hanging over there beside the chest, will you please reach me it? I'll lay it over me. I can't bear the feather quilt, my breathing is so bad."

And as K. handed her the wrap, she went on: "Look, this is a beautiful wrap, isn't it?"

To K. it seemed to be an ordinary woollen wrap. He felt it with his fingers again merely out of politeness, but did not reply.

"Yes, it's a beautiful wrap," said Gardana covering herself up.

Now she lay back comfortably, all her pain seemed to have gone, she actually had enough strength to think of the state of her hair which had been disordered by her lying position; she raised herself up for a moment and rearranged her coiffure a little round the nightcap. Her hair was abundant.

K. became impatient, and began: "You asked me, madam, whether I had found other lodgings yet."

"I asked you?" said the landlady, "no, you're mistaken."

"Your husband asked me a few minutes ago."

"That may well be," said the landlady, "I'm at variance with him. When I didn't want you here, he kept you here, now that I'm glad to have you here, he wants to drive you away. He's always like that."

"Have you changed your opinion of me so greatly, then?" asked K. "In a couple of hours?"

"I haven't changed my opinion," said the landlady more freely again, "give me your hand. There, and now promise to be quite frank with me and I'll be the same with you."

"Right," said K., "but who's to begin first?"

"I shall," said the landlady.

She did not give so much the impression of one who wanted to meet K. half-way, as of one who was eager to have the first word. She drew a photograph from under the pillow and held it out to K.

"Look at that portrait," she said eagerly.

To see it better K. stepped into the kitchen, but even there it was not easy to distinguish anything on the photograph, for it was faded with age, cracked in several places, crumpled, and dirty.

"It isn't in very good condition," said K.

"Unluckily no," said the landlady, "when one carries a thing about with one for years it's bound to be the case. But if you look at it carefully, you'll be able to make everything out, you'll see. But I can help you. Tell me what you see, I like to hear anyone talk about the portrait. Well, then?"

"A young man," said K.

"Right," said the landlady, "and what's he doing?"

"It seems to me he's lying on a board stretching himself and yawning."

The landlady laughed. "Quite wrong," she said.

"But here's the board and here he is lying on it," persisted K. on his side.

"But look more carefully," said the landlady in annoyance, "is he really lying down?"

"No," said K. now, "he's floating, and now I can see it, it's not a board at all, but probably a rope, and the young man is taking a high leap."

"You see," replied the landlady triumphantly, "he's leaping, that's how the I official messengers practise. I knew quite well that you would make it out. Can you make out his face, too?"

"I can only make out his face very dimly," said K., "he's obviously making a great leap. His mouth is open, his eyes tightly shut and his hair flutter."

"Well done," said the landlady appreciatively, "nobody who ever saw him could have made out more than that But he was a beautiful young man. I only saw him once for a second and I'll never forget him."

"Who was he then?" asked K.

"He was the messenger that Klamm sent to call me to him the first rime."

K could not hear properly, his attention was distracted by the rattling of glass. He immediately discovered the cause of the disturbance. The assistants were standing outside in the yard hopping from one foot to the other in the snow, behaving as if they were glad to see him again. In their joy they pointed each other out to him and kept tapping all the time on the kitchen window. At a threatening gesture from K. they stopped at once, tried to pull one another away, but the one would slip immediately from the grasp of the other and soon they were both back at the window again. K. hurried into the annex where the assistants could not see him from outside and he would not have to see them. But the soft and as it were beseeching tapping on the window-pane followed him there too for a long time.

"The assistants again," he said apologetically to the landlady and pointed outside.

But she paid no attention to him. She had taken the portrait from him, looked at it, smoothed it out, and pushed it again under her pillow. Her movements had become slower, but not with weariness, but with the burden of memory. She had wanted to tell K. the story of her life and had forgotten about him in thinking of the story itself. She was playing with the fringe of her wrap. A little time went by before she looked up, passed her hand over her eyes, and said:

"This wrap was given me by Klamm. And the nightcap, too. The portrait, the wrap, and the nightcap, these are the only three things of his I have as keepsakes. I'm not young like Frieda, I'm not so ambitious as she is, nor so sensitive either, she's very sensitive to put it bluntly, I know how to accommodate myself to life, but one thing I must admit, I couldn't have held out so long here without these three keepsakes. Perhaps these three things seem very trifling to you, but let me tell you, Frieda, who has had relations with Klamm for a long time, doesn't possess a single keepsake from him. I have asked her, she's too fanciful, and too difficult to please besides, I, on the other hand, though I was only three times with Klamm- after that he never asked me to come again, I don't know why I managed to bring three presents back with me all the same, having a premonition that my time would be short. Of course one must make a point of it. Klamm gives nothing of himself, but if one sees something one likes lying about there, one can get it out of him."

K. felt uncomfortable listening to these tales, much as they interested him.

"How long ago was all that, then?" he asked with a sigh.

"Over twenty years ago," replied the landlady, "considerably over twenty years."

"So one remains faithful to Klamm as long as that," said K. "But are you aware, madam, that these stories give me grave alarm when I think of my future married life?"

The landlady seemed to consider this intrusion of his own affairs unseasonable and gave him an angry sidelook.

"Don't be angry, madam," said K. "Ive nothing at all to say against Klamm. All the same, by force of circumstances I have come in a sense in contact with Klamm. That can't be gainsaid even by his greatest admirer. Well, then. As a result of that I am forced whenever Klamm is mentioned to think of myself as well, that can't be altered. Besides, madam," here K. took hold of her reluctant hand, "reflect how badly our last talk turned out and that this time we want to part in peace." "You're right," said the landlady, bowing her head, "but spare me. I'm not more touchy than other people. On the contrary, everyone has his sensitive spots, and I only have this one."

"Unfortunately it happens to be mine too," said K., "but promise to control myself. Now tell me, madam, how I am put up with my married life in face of this terrible fidelity granted that Frieda, too, resembles you in that?"

"Terrible fidelity !" repeated the landlady with a growl. "Is it a question of fidelity? I'm faithful to my husband but Klamm once chose me as his mistress, can I ever lose this honour? And you ask how you are to put up with Frieda? Land Surveyor, who are you after all that you dare ask such things?"

"j^fadam," said K. warningly.

"I know," said the landlady, controlling herself, "but my husband never put such questions. I don't know which to call the unhappier - myself then or Frieda now. Frieda who saucily left Klamm, or myself whom he stopped asking to come. Yet it is probably Frieda, though she hasn't even yet guessed the full extent of her unhappiness, it seems.

Still, my thoughts were more exclusively occupied by my unhappiness then, all the same, for I had always to be asking myself one question, and in reality haven't ceased to ask it to this day: Why did this happen? Three times Klamm sent for me, but he never sent a fourth time, no, never a fourth time. What else could I have thought of during those days? What else could I have talked about with my husband, whom I married shortly afterwards? During the day we had no time, we had taken over this inn in a wretched condition and had to struggle to make it respectable, but at night... For years all our nightly talks turned on Klamm and the reason for his changing his mind. And if my husband fell asleep during those talks I woke him and we went on again."

"Now," said K., "if you'll permit me, I'm going to ask a very rude question."

The landlady remained silent.

"Then I mustn't ask it," said K. "Well, that serves my purpose as well."

"Yes," replied the landlady, "that serves your purpose as well, and just that serves it best. You misconstrue everything, even a person's silence. You can't do anything else. I allow you to ask your question."

"If I misconstrue everything, perhaps I misconstrue my question as well, perhaps it's not so rude after all. I only want to know how you came to meet your husband and how this inn came into your hands."

The landlady wrinkled her forehead, but said indifferently: "That's a very simple story. My father was the blacksmith, and Hans, my husband, who was a groom at a big farmer's place, came often to see him. That was just after my last meeting with Klamm. I was very unhappy and really had no right to be so, for everything had gone as it should, and that I wasn't allowed any longer to see Klamm was Klamm's own decision. It was as it should be then, only the grounds for it were obscure. I was entitled to inquire into them, but I had no right to be unhappy. Still I was, all the same, couldn't work, and sat in our front garden all day. There Hans saw me, often sat down beside me. I didn't complain to him, but he knew how things were, and as he was a good young man, he wept with me. The wife of the landlord at that time had died and he had consequently to give up business, besides he was already an old man. Well once as he passed our garden and saw us sitting there, he stopped, and without more ado offered us the inn to rent, didn't ask for any money in advance, for he trusted us, and set the rent at a very low figure. I didn't want to be a burden on my father, nothing else mattered to me, and so thinking of the inn and of my new work that might perhaps help me to forget a little, I gave Hans my hand. That's the whole story."

There was silence for a little, then K. said: "The behaviour of the landlord was generous, but rash, or had he particular grounds for trusting you both?"

"He knew Hans well," said the landlady. "He was Hans's uncle."

"Well then," said K., "Hans's family must have been very anxious to be connected with you?"

"It may be so," said the landlady, "I don't know. I've never bothered about it."

"But it must have been so all the same," said K., "seeing that the family was ready to make such a sacrifice and to give the inn into your hands absolutely without security."

"It wasn't imprudent, as was proved later," said the landlady. "I threw myself into the work, I was strong, I was the blacksmith's daughter, I didn't need maid or servant. I was everywhere, in the taproom, in the kitchen, in the stables, in the yard. , I cooked so well that I even enticed some of the Herrenhof's customers away. You've never been in the inn yet at lunchtime, you don't know our day customers. At that time there were more of them, many of them have stopped coming since. And the consequence was that we were able not merely to pay the t regularly, but after a few years we bought the whole place. Today it's practically free of debt. The further consequence, I admit, was that I ruined my health, got heart disease, and am now an old woman. Probably you think that I'm much older than Hans, but the fact is that he's only two or three years younger than me and will never grow any older either, for at his work - smoking his pipe, listening to the customers, knocking out his pipe again, and fetching an occasional pot of beer.At that sort of work one doesn't grow old." "What you've done has been splendid," said K. "I don't doubt that for a moment, but we were speaking of the time before your marriage, and it must have been an extraordinary thing at that stage for Hans's family to press on the marriage - at a money sacrifice, or at least at such a great risk as the handing over of the inn must have been, and without trusting in anything but your powers of work, which besides nobody knew of then, and Hans's powers of work, which everybody must have known beforehand were nil."

"Oh, well," said the landlady wearily. "I know what you're getting at and how wide you are of the mark. Klamm had absolutely nothing to do with the matter. Why should he have concerned himself about me, or better, how could he in any case have concerned himself about me? He knew nothing about me by that time. The fact that he had ceased to summon me was a sign that he had forgotten me. When he stops summoning people, he forgets them completely. I didn't want to talk of this before Frieda. And it's not mere forgetting, it's something more than that. For anybody one has forgotten can come back to one's memory again, of course. With Klamm that's impossible. Anybody that he stops summoning he has forgotten completely, not only as far as the past is concerned, but literally for the future as well. If I try very hard I can of course think myself into your ideas, valid, perhaps, in the very different land you come from. But it's next thing to madness to imagine that Klamm could have given me Hans as a husband simply that I might have no great difficulty in going to him if he should summon me sometime again. Where is the man who could hinder me from running to Klamm if Klamm lifted his little finger? Madness, absolute madness, one begins to feel confused oneself when one plays with such mad ideas."

"No," said K., "I've no intention of getting confused. My thoughts hadn't gone so far as you imagined, though, to tell the truth, they were on that road. For the moment the only thing that surprises me is that Hans's relations expected so much from his marriage and that these expectations were actually fulfilled, at the sacrifice of your sound heart and your health, it is true. The idea that these facts were connected with Klamm occurred to me, I admit, but not with the bluntness, or not till now with the bluntness that you give it - apparently with no object but to have a dig at me, because that gives you pleasure. Well, make the most of your pleasure! My idea, however, was this: first of all Klamm was obviously the occasion of your marriage. If it hadn't been for Klamm you wouldn't have been unhappy and wouldn't have been sitting doing nothing in the garden, if it hadn't been for Klamm Hans wouldn't have seen you sitting there, if it hadn't been that you were unhappy a shy man like Hans would never have ventured to speak, if it hadn't been for Klamm Hans would never have found you in tears, if it hadn't been for Klamm the good old uncle would never have seen you sitting there together peacefully, if it hadn't been for Klamm you wouldn't have been indifferent to what life still offered you, and therefore would never have married Hans. Now in all this there's enough of Klamm already, it seems to me. But that's not all. If you hadn't been trying to forget, you certainly wouldn't have overtaxed your strength so much and done so splendidly with the inn. So Klamm was there too. But apart from that Klamm is also the root cause of your illness, for before your marriage your heart was already worn out with your hopeless passion for him. The only question that remains now is, what made Hans's relatives so eager for the marriage? You yourself said just now that to be Klamm's mistress is a distinction that can't be lost, so it may have been that that attracted them. But besides that, I imagine, they had the hope that the lucky star that led you to Klamm - assuming that it was a lucky star, but you maintain that it was - was your star and so would reinstant to you and not leave you quite so quickly and suddenly as Klamm did."

"Do you mean all this in earnest?" asked the landlady.

"Yes, in earnest," replied K. immediately, "only I consider Hans's relations were neither entirely right nor entirely wrong :n their hopes, and I think, too, I can see the mistake that they made. In appearance, of course, everything seems to have succeeded.

Hans is well provided for, he has a handsome wife, is looked up to, and the inn is free of debt. Yet in reality everything has not succeeded, he would certainly have been much happier with a simple girl who gave him her first love, and if he sometimes stands in the inn there as if lost, as you complain, and because he really feels as if he were lost - without being unhappy over it, I grant you, I know that much about him already - it's just as true that a handsome, intelligent young man like him would be happier with another wife, and by happier I mean more independent, industrious, manly. And you yourself certainly can't be happy, seeing you say you wouldn't be able to go on without these three keepsakes, and your heart is bad, too. Then were Hans's relatives mistaken in their hopes? I don't think so. The blessing was over you, but they didn't know how to bring it down."

"Then what did they miss doing?" asked the landlady.

She was lying outstretched on her back now gazing up at the ceiling.

"To ask Klamm," said K.

"So we're back at your case again," said the landlady.

"Or at yours," said K. "Our affairs run parallel."

"What do you want from Klamm?" asked the landlady.

She had sat up, had shaken out the pillows so as to lean her back against them, and looked K. full in the eyes.

"I've told you frankly about my experiences, from which you should have been able to learn something. Tell me now as frankly what you want to ask Klamm.

I've had great trouble in persuading Frieda to go up to her room and stay there, I was afraid you wouldn't talk freely enough in her presence."

"I have nothing to hide," said K. "But first of all I want to draw your attention to something. Klamm forgets immediately, you say. Now in the first place that seems very improbable to me, and secondly it is undemonstrable, obviously nothing more than legend, thought out moreover by the flappcrish minds of those who have been in Klamm's favour.

I'm surprised that you believe in such a banal invention."

"It's no legend," said the landlady, "it's much rather the result of general experience."

"I see, a thing then to be refuted by further experience," said K. "Besides there's another distinction still between your case and Frieda's. In Frieda's case it didn't happen that Klamm never summoned her again, on the contrary he summoned her but she didn't obey. It's even possible that he's still waiting for her."

The landlady remained silent, and only looked K. up and down with a considering stare.

At last she said: "Ìll try to listen quietly to what you have to say. Speak frankly and don't spare my feelings. I've only one request. Don't use Klamm's name. Call him "him" or something, but don't mention him by name."

"Willingly," replied K., "but what I want from him is difficult to express. Firstly, I want to see him at close quarters. Then I want to hear his voice. Then I want to get from him what his attitude is to our marriage. What I shall ask from him after that depends on the outcome of our interview. Lots of things may come up in the course of talking, but still the most important thing for me is to be confronted with him. You see I haven't yet spoken with a real official. That seems to be more difficult to manage than I had thought. But now I'm put under the obligation of speaking to him as a private person, and that, in my opinion, is much easier to bring about. As an official I can only speak to him in his bureau in the Castle, which may be inaccessible, or - and that's questionable, too - in the Herrenhof. But as a private person I can speak to him anywhere, in a house, in the street, wherever I happen to meet him. If I should find the official in front of me, then I would be glad to accost him as well, but that's not my primary object."

"Right," said the landlady pressing her face into the pillows as if she were uttering something shameful, "if by using my influence I can manage to get your request for an interview passed on to Klamm, promise me to do nothing on your own account until the reply comes back."

"I can't promise that," said K., "glad as I would be to fulfil ur wishes or your whims.

The matter is urgent, you see, specify after the unfortunate outcome of my talk with the Superintendent."

"That excuse falls to the ground," said the landlady, "the superintendent is a person of no importance. Haven't you found that out? He couldn't remain another day in his post if it weren't for his wife, who runs everything."

"Mizzi?" asked K.

The landlady nodded.

"She was present," said K.

"Did she express her opinion?" asked the landlady.

"No," replied K., "but I didn't get the impression that she could."

"There," said the landlady, "you see how distorted your view of everything here is. In any case the Superintendent's arrangements for you are of no importance, and I'll talk to his wife when I have time. And if I promise now in addition that Klamm's answer will come in a week at latest, you can't surely have any further grounds for not obliging me."

"All that is not enough to influence me," said K. "My decision is made, and I would try to carry it out even if an unfavourable answer were to come. And seeing that this is my fixed intention, I can't very well ask for an interview beforehand. A thing that would remain a daring attempt, but still an attempt in good faith so long as I didn't ask for an interview, would turn into an open transgression of the law after receiving an unfavourable answer. That frankly would be far worse."

"Worse?" said the landlady. "It's a transgression of the law in any case. And now you can do what you like. Reach me over my skirt."

Without paying any regard to K.'s presence she pulled on her skirt and hurried into the kitchen. For a long time already K. had been hearing noises in the dining-room. There was a tap ping on the kitchen-hatch. The assistants had unfastened it and were shouting that they were hungry. Then other faces appeared at it. One could even hear a subdued song being chanted by several voices. Undeniably K.'s conversation with the landlady had greatly delayed the cooking of the midday meal, it was not ready yet and the customers had assembled. Nevertheless nobody had dared to set foot in the kitchen after the landlady's order. But now when the observers at the hatch reported that the landlady was coming, the maids immediately ran back to the kitchen, and as K. entered the dining-room a surprisingly large company, more than twenty, men and women - all attired in provincial but not rustic clothes streamed back from the hatch to the tables to make sure of their seats. Only at one little table in the corner was a married couple seated already with a few children. The man, a kindly, blue-eyed person with disordered grey hair and beard, stood bent over the children and with a knife beat time to their singing, which he perpetually strove to soften. Perhaps he was trying to make them forget their hunger by singing. The landlady threw a few indifferent words of apology to her customers, nobody complained of her conduct. She looked round for the landlord, who had fled from the difficulty of the situation, however, long ago. When she went slowly into the kitchen, she did not take any more notice of K., who hurried to Frieda in her room.

At upstairs K. ran into the teacher. The room was improved by almost beyond recognition, so well had Frieda set to work. It was well aired, the stove amply stoked, the floor scrubbed, the bed put in order, the maids' filthy pile of things and even their photographs cleared away. The table, which had literally struck one in the eye before with its crust of accumulated dust, was covered with a white embroidered cloth. One was in a position to receive visitors now. K.'s small change of underclothes hanging before the fire - Frieda must have washed them early in the morning - did not spoil the impression much. Frieda and the teacher were sitting at the table, they rose at K.'s entrance. Frieda greeted K. with a kiss, the teacher bowed slightly. Distracted and still agitated by his talk with the landlady, K. began to apologize for not having been able yet to visit the teacher. It was as if he were assuming that the teacher had called on him finally because he was impatient at K.'s absence. On the other hand the teacher in his precise way only seemed now gradually remember that sometime or other there had been some matter between K. and himself of a visit.

"You must be, Land Surveyor," he said slowly, "the stranger I had a few words with he other day in the church square."

"I am," replied K. shortly.

The behaviour which he had submitted to when he felt homeless he did not intend to put up with now here in his room. He turned to Frieda and consulted with her about an important visit which he had to pay at once and for which he would need his best clothes.

Without further inquiry Frieda called over the assistants, who were already busy examining the new tablecloth, and commanded them to brush K.'s suit and shoes - which he had begun to take off - down in the yard. She herself took a shirt from the line and ran down to the kitchen to iron it. Now K. was left alone with the teacher, who was seated silently again at the table. K. kept him waiting for a little longer, drew off his shirt and began to wash himself at the tap. Only then, with his back to the teacher, did he ask him the reason for his visit.

"I have come at the instance of the Parish Superintendent," he said.

K. made ready to listen. But as the noise of the water made it difficult to catch what K. said, the teacher had to come nearer and lean against the wall beside him. K. excused his washing and his hurry by the urgency of his coming appointment. The teacher swept aside his excuses, and said: "You were discourteous to the Parish Superintendent, an old and experienced man who should be treated with respect."

"Whether I was discourteous or not I can't say," said K. while he dried himself, "but that I had other things to think of than polite behaviour is true enough, for my existence is at stake, which is threatened by a scandalous official bureaucracy whose particular failings I needn't mention to you, seeing that you're an acting member of it yourself. Has the Parish Superintendent complained about me?"

"Where's the man that he would need to complain of?" asked the teacher. "And even if there was anyone, do you think he would ever do it? I've only made out at his dictation a short protocol on your interview, and that has shown me clearly enough how kind the Superintendent was and what your answers were like."

While K. was looking for his comb, which Frieda must have cleared away somewhere, he said: "What? A protocol? Drawn up afterwards in my absence by someone who wasn't at the interview at all? That's not bad. And why on earth a protocol? Was it an official interview, then?"

"No," replied the teacher, "a semi-official one, the protocol too was only semi-official. It was merely drawn up because with us everything must be done in

187

strict order. In any case it's finished now, and it doesn't better your credit."

K., who had at last found the comb, which had been tucked into the bed, said more calmly: "Well, then, it's finished. Have you come to tell me that?"

"No," said the teacher, "but I'm not a machine and I had to give you my opinion. My instructions are only another proof of the Superintendent's kindness. I want to emphasize that his kindness in this instance is incomprehensible to me, and that I only carry out his instructions because it's my duty and out of respect to the Superintendent."

Washed and combed, K. now sat down at the table to wait for his shirt and clothes. He was not very curious to know the message that the teacher had brought, he was influenced besides by the landlady's low opinion of the Superintendent.

"It must be after twelve already, surely?" he said, thinking of the distance he had to walk. Then he remembered himself, and said: "You want to give me some message from the Superintendent."

"Well, yes," said the teacher, shrugging his shoulders as if he were discarding all responsibility. "The Superintendent is afraid that, if the decision in your case takes too long, you might do something rash on your own account. For my own part I don't know why he should fear that - my own opinion is that you should just be allowed to do what you like. We aren't your guardian angels and we're not obliged to run after you in all your doings. Well and good. The Superintendent, however, is of a different opinion. He can't of course hasten the decision itself, which is a matter for the authorities. But in his own sphere of jurisdiction he wants to provide a temporary and truly generous settlement. It simply lies with you to accept it. He offers you provisionally the post of school janitor."

At first K. thought very little of the offer made him, but the fact that an offer had been made seemed to him not without significance. It seemed to point to the fact that in the Superintendent's opinion he was in a hurry to look after himself, to carry out projects against the Town Council itself was preparing certain counter measures. And how seriously they were taking the matter !

The teacher, who had already been waiting for a while, and who before that, moreover, had made out the protocol, must of course have been told to run here by the Superintendent. When the teacher saw that he had made K. reflect at last, he went on: "I put my objections. I pointed out that up till now a janitor hadn't been found necessary.

The churchwarden's wife cleared up the place from time to time, and Fraulein Gisa, the second teacher, overlooked the matter. I had trouble enough with the children, I didn't want to be bothered by a janitor as well. The Superintendent pointed out that all the same the school was very dirty. I replied, keeping to the truth, that it wasn't so very bad. And, I went on, would it be any better if we took on this man as janitor? Most certainly not. Apart from the fact that he didn't know the work, there were only two big classrooms in the school, and no additional room. So the janitor and his family would have to live, sleep, perhaps even cook in one of the classrooms, which could hardly make for greater cleanliness. But the Superintendent laid stress on the fact that this post would keep you out of difficulties, and that consequently you would do your utmost to fill it creditably. He suggested further, that along with you we would obtain the services of your wife and your assistants, so that the school should be kept in first-rate order, and not only it, but the school-garden as well. I easily proved that this would not hold water. At last the Superintendent couldn't bring forward a single argument in your favour. He laughed and merely said that you were a Land Surveyor after all and so should be able to lay out the vegetable beds beautifully. Well, against a joke there's no argument, and so I came to you with the proposal."

"You've taken your trouble for nothing, teacher," said K. "I have no intention of accepting the post."

"Splendid!" said the teacher. "Splendid that you decline quite unconditionally," and he took his hat, bowed, and went. Immediately afterwards Frieda came rushing up the stairs an excited face, the shirt still unironed in her hand; she did not reply to K.'s inquiries. To distract her he told her about the teacher and the offer. She had hardly heard it when she flung the shirt on the bed and ran out again. She soon came back, but with the teacher, who looked annoyed and entered without any greeting. Frieda begged him to have a little patience - obviously she had done that already several times on the way up - then drew K. through a side door of which he had never suspected the existence, on to the neighbouring loft, and then at last, out of breath with excitement, told what had happened to her. Enraged that Frieda had humbled herself by making an avowal to K., and - what was still worse - had yielded to him merely to secure him an interview with Klamm, and after all had gained nothing but, so she alleged, cold and moreover insincere professions, the landlady was resolved to keep K. no longer in her house. If he had connections with the Castle, then he should take advantage of them at once, for he must leave the house that very day, that very minute, and she would only take him back again at the express order and command of the authorities; but she hoped it would not come to that, for she too had connexions with the Castle and would know how to make use of them.

Besides, he was only in the inn because of the landlord's negligence, and moreover he was not in a state of destitution, for this very morning he had boasted of a roof which was always free to him for the night. Frieda of course was to remain. If Frieda wanted to go with K. she, the landlady, would be very sorry.

Down in the kitchen she had sunk into a chair by the fire and cried at the mere thought of it. The poor, sick woman. But how could she behave otherwise, now that, in her imagination at any rate, it was a matter involving the honour of Klamm's keepsakes? That was how matters stood with the landlady. Frieda of course would follow him, K., wherever he wanted to go. Yet the position of both of them was very bad in any case, just for that reason she had greeted the teacher's offer with such joy. Even if it was not a suitable post for K., yet it was - that was expressly insisted on - only a temporary post. One would gain a little time and would easily find other chances, even if the final decision should turn out to be unfavourable.

"If it comes to the worst," cried Frieda at last, falling on K.'s neck, "we'll go away, what is there in the village to keep us? But for the time being, darling, we'll accept the offer, won't we? I've fetched the teacher back again, you've only to say to him

"Done", that's all, and we'll move over to the school."

"It's a great nuisance," said K. without quite meaning it, for ue was not much concerned about his lodgings, and in his underclothes he was shivering up here in the loft, which without wall or window on two sides was swept by a cold draught, "you've arranged the room so comfortably and now we must leave it. I would take up the post very, very unwillingly. The few snubs I've already had from the teacher have been painful enough, and now he's to become my superior, no less. If we could only stay here a little while longer, perhaps my position might change for the better this very afternoon. If you would only remain here at least, we could wait on for a little and give the teacher a non-committal answer. As for me, if it came to the worst, I could really always find a lodging for the night with gar -"

Frieda stopped him by putting her hand over his mouth.

"No, not that," she said beseechingly, "please never mention that again. In everything else I'll obey you. If you like I'll stay on here by myself, sad as it will be for me. If you like, we'll refuse the offer, wrong as that would seem to me. For look here, if you find another possibility, even this afternoon, why, it's obvious that we would throw up the post in the school at once. Nobody would object. And as for your humiliation in front of the teacher, let me see to it that there will be none. I'll speak to him myself, you'll only have to be there and needn't say anything, and later, too, it will be just the same, you'll never be made to speak to him if you don't want to, I - I alone - will be his subordinate in reality, and I won't be even that, for I know his weak points. So you see nothing will be lost if we take on the post, and a great deal if we refuse it.

Above all, if you don't wring something out of the Castle this very day, you'll never manage to find, even for yourself, anywhere at all in the village to spend the night in, anywhere, that is, of which I needn't be ashamed as your future wife. And if you don't manage to find a roof for the night, do you really expect me to sleep here in my warm room, while I know that you are wandering about out there in the dark and cold?"

K., who had been trying to warm himself all this time by clapping his chest with his arms like a carter, said: "Then there's nothing left but to accept, come along !"

When they returned to the room he went straight over to the fire. He paid no attention to the teacher. The latter, sitting at the table, drew out his watch and said: "It's getting late."

"I know, but we're completely agreed at last," said Frieda, "we accept the post."

"Good," said the teacher, "but the post is offered to the Land Surveyor. He must say the word himself."

Frieda came to K.'s help. "Really," she said, "he accepts the post. Don't you, K.?"

So K. could confine his declaration to a simple "Yes," which was not even directed to the teacher but to Frieda.

"Then," said the teacher, "the only thing that remains for me is to acquaint you with your duties, so that in that respect we can understand each other once and for all. You have, Land Surveyor, to clean and heat both classrooms daily, to make any small repairs in the house, further, to look after the class and gymnastic apparatus personally, to keep the garden path free of snow, run messages for me and the lady teacher, and look after all the work in the garden in the warmer seasons of the year. In return for that you have the right to live in whichever one of the classrooms you like. But, when both rooms are not being used at the same time for teaching, and you are in the room that is needed, you must of course move to the other room. You mustn't do any cooking in the school. In return you and your dependants will be given your meals here in the inn at the cost of the Town Council. That you must behave in a manner consonant with the dignity of the school, and in particular that the children during school hours must never be allowed to witness any unedifying matrimonial scenes, I mention only in passing, for as an educated man you must of course know that. In connection with that I want to say further that we must insist on your relations with Fraulein Frieda being legitimized at the earliest possible moment. About all this and a few other trifling matters, an agreement will be made out, which as soon as you move over to the school must be signed by you."

To K. all this seemed of no importance, as if it did not concern him or at any rate did not bind him. But the self-importance of the teacher irritated him, and he said carelessly: "I know, they're the usual duties."

To clear away the impression created by this remark Frieda inquired about the salary.

"Whether there will be any salary," said the teacher, "will only be considered after a month's trial service."

"But that is hard on us," said Frieda. "We'll have to marry on practically nothing, and have nothing to set up house on. Couldn't you make a representation to the Town Council, sir, to give us a small salary at the start? Couldn't you advise that?"

"No," replied the teacher, who continued to direct his words to K. "Representations to the Town Council will only be made if I give the word, and I shan't give it. The post has only been given to you as a personal favour, and one can't stretch a favour too far, if one has any consciousness of one's obvious responsibilities."

Now K. intervened at last, almost against his will. "As for the favour, teacher," he said, "it seems to me that you're mistaken. The favour is perhaps rather on my side."

"No," replied the teacher, smiling now that he had compelled K. to speak at last. "I'm completely grounded on that point. Our need for a janitor is just about as urgent as our need for a Land Surveyor. Janitor, Land Surveyor, in both cases it's a burden on our shoulders. I'll still have a lot of trouble thinking out how I'm to justify the post to the Town Council. The best thing and the most honest thing would be to throw the proposal on the table and not justify anything."

"That's just what I meant," replied K., "you must take me on against your will.

Although it causes you grave perturbation, you must take me on. But when one is compelled to take someone else on, and this someone else allows himself to be taken on, then he is the one who grants the favour."

"Strange," said the teacher. "What is it that compels us to take you on? The only thing that compels us is the Superintendent's kind heart, his too kind heart. I see, Land Surveyor, that you'll have to rid yourself of a great many illusions, before you can become a serviceable janitor. And remarks such as these hardly produce the right atmosphere for the granting of an eventual salary. I notice, too, with regret that your attitude will give me a great deal of trouble yet, all this time - I've seen it with my own eyes and yet can scarcely believe it - you've been talking to me in your shirt and drawers."

"Quite so," exclaimed K. with laugh, and he clapped his hands. "These terrible assistants, where have they been all this time?"

Frieda hurried to the door. The teacher, who noticed that K. was no longer to be drawn into conversation, asked her when she would move into the school.

"Today," said Frieda.

"Then tomorrow I'll come to inspect matters," said the teacher, waved a goodbye, and made to go out through the door, which Frieda had opened for herself, but ran into the maids, who already were arriving with their things to take possession of the room again.

And he, who made way for nobody, had to slip between them. Frieda followed him.

"You're surely in a hurry," said K., who this time was very pleased with the maids,

"had you to push your way in while we're still here?"

They did not answer, only twisted their bundles in embarrassment, from which K. saw the wellknown filthy rags projecting. "So you've never washed your things yet," said K.

It was not said maliciously, but actually with a certain indulgence. They noticed it, opened their hard mouths in concert, showed their beautiful animal-like teeth and laughed noiselessly, "Come along," said K., "put your things down, it's your room after all."

As they still hesitated, however - the room must have seemed to them all too well transformed - K. took one of them by the arm to lead her forward. But he let her go at once, so astonished was the gaze of both, which, after a brief glance between them, was now turned unflinchingly on K.

"But now you've stared at me long enough," he said, repelling a vague, unpleasant sensation, and he took up his clothes and boots, which Frieda, timidly followed by the assistants, had just brought, and drew them on. The patience which Frieda had with the assistants, always incomprehensible to him, now struck him again. After a long search she had found them below peacefully eating their lunch, the untouched clothes which they should have been brushing in the yard crumpled in their laps. Then she had had to brush everything herself, and yet she, who knew how to keep the common people in their places, had not even scolded them, and instead spoke in their presence of their grave negligence as if it were a trifling peccadillo, and even slapped one of them lightly, almost caressingly, on the cheek. K. would have to talk to her about this. But now it is time to be gone.

"The assistants will stay here to help you with the removing," he said.

They were not in the least pleased with this arrangement. Happy and full, they would have gladly skipped the exercise. Only when Frieda said, "Certainly, you stay here," did they yield.

"Do you know where I'm going?2 asked K.

"Yes," replied Frieda.

"And you don't want to hold me back any longer?" asked K.

"You'll find obstacles enough," she replied, "what does anything I say matter in comparison!"

She kissed K. good-bye, and as he had had nothing at lunch-time, she gave him a little packet of bread and sausage which she had brought for him from downstairs, reminded him that he must not return here again but to the school, and accompanied him, with her hand on his shoulder, to the door.

At first K. was glad to have escaped from the crush of the maids and the assistants in the warm room. It was freezing a little, the snow was firmer, the going easier. But already darkness was actually beginning to fall, and he hastened his steps. The Castle, whose contours were already beginning to dissolve, lay silent as ever. Never yet had K.

seen there the slightest sign of life - perhaps it was quite impossible to recognize anything at that distance, and yet the eye demanded it and could not endure that stillness. When K. looked at the Castle, often it seemed to him as if he were observing someone who sat quietly there in front of him - gazing, not lost in thought and so oblivious of everything, but free and untroubled, as if he were alone with nobody to observe him, and yet must notice that he was observed, and all the same remained with his calm not even slightly disturbed. And really - one did not know whether it was cause or effect - the gaze of the observer could not remain concentrated there, but slid away.

This impression today was strengthened still further by the early dusk. The longer he looked, the less he could make out and the deeper everything was lost in the twilight.

Just as K. reached the Herrenhof, which was still unlighted, a window was opened in the first storey, and a stout, smooth shaven young man in a fur coat leaned out and then remained at the window. He did not seem to make the slightest response to K.'s greeting.

Neither in the hall nor in the taproom did K. meet anybody. The smell of stale beer was still worse than last time. Such a state of things was never allowed even in the inn by the bridge. K. went straight over to the door through which he had observed Klamm, and lifted the latch cautiously, but the door was barred. Then he felt for the place where the peephole was, but the pin apparently was fitted so well that he could not find the place, so he struck a match. He was startled by a cry. In the corner between the door and the till, near the fire, a young girl was crouching and staring at him in the flare of the match, with partially opened sleep-drunken eyes. She was evidently Frieda's successor. She soon collected herself and switched on the electric light. Her expression was cross, then she recognized K.

"Ah, the Land Surveyor," she said smiling, held out her hand, and introduced herself.

"My name is Pepi."

She was small, redcheeked, plump. Her opulent reddish golden hair was twisted into a strong plait, yet some of it escaped and curled round her temples. She was wearing a dress of grey shimmering material, falling in straight lines, which did not suit her in the least. At the foot it was drawn together by a childishly clumsy silken band with tassels falling from it, which impeded her movements. She inquired after Frieda and asked whether she would come back soon. It was a question which verged on insolence.

"As soon as Frieda went away," she said next, "I was called here urgendy because they couldn't find anybody suitable at the moment. I've been a chambermaid till now, but this isn't a change for the better. There's lots of evening and night work in this job, it's very tiring, I don't think I'll be able to stand it. I'm not surprised that Frieda threw it up." "Frieda was very happy here," said K., to make her aware definitely of the difference between Frieda and herself, which she did not seem to appreciate.

"Don't you believe her," said Pepi. "Frieda can keep a straight face better than other people can. She doesn't admit what she doesn't want to admit, and so nobody noticed that she has anything to admit. I've been in service here with her several years already.

We've slept together all that time in same bed, yet I'm not intimate with her, and by now I'm rite out of her thoughts, that's certain. Perhaps her only 2>nd * ^ °^ lan

"I know," said Pepi, "that's just the reason why I've told you. Otherwise it wouldn't have any interest for you."

"I understand," said K. "You mean that I should be proud to have won such a reticent girl?"

"That's so," said she, laughing triumphantly, as if she had established a secret understanding with K. regarding Frieda. But it was not her actual words that troubled K. and deflected him for a little from his search, but rather her appearance and her presence in this place. Certainly she was much younger than Frieda, almost a child still, and her clothes were ludicrous. She had obviously dressed in accordance with the exaggerated notions which she had of the importance of a barmaid's position. And these notions were right enough in their way in her, for this position of which she was still incapable had come to her unearned and unexpectedly, and only for the time being. Not even the leather reticule which Frieda always wore on her belt had been entrusted to her.

And her ostensible dissatisfaction with the position was nothing but showing off. And yet, in spite of her childish mind, she too, apparently, had connections with the Castle.

If she was not lying, she had been a chambermaid. Without being aware of what she possessed she slept through the days here, and though if he took this tiny, plump slightly round-backed creature in his arms he could not extort from her what she possessed, yet that could bring him in contact with it and inspirit him for his difficult task. Then could her case now be much the same as Frieda's? Oh, no, it was different. One had only to think of Frieda's look to know that. K. would never have touched Pepi. All the same he had to lower his eyes tor a little now, so greedily was he staring at her.

"It's against orders for the light to be on," said Pepi, switching it off again. "I only turned it on because you gave me such a fright. What do you want here really? Did Frieda forget anything?"

"Yes," said K., pointing to the door, "a table-cover, a white embroidered table-cover, here in the next room."

"Yes, her table-cover," said Pepi. "I remember it, a pretty piece of work. I helped with it myself, but it can hardly be in that room."

"Frieda thinks it is. Who lives in it, then?" asked. K.

"Nobody," said Pepi, "it's the gentlemen's room. The gentlemen eat and drink there.

That is, it's reserved for that, but most of them remain upstairs in their rooms."

"If I knew," said K., "that nobody was in there just now, I would like very much to go in and have a look for the table-cover. But one can't be certain. Klamm, for instance, is often in the habit of sitting there."

"Klamm is certainly not there now," said Pepi. "He's making ready to leave this minute, the sledge is waiting for him in the yard."

Without a word of explanation K. left the taproom at once. When he reached the hall he returned, instead of to the door, to the interior of the house, and in a few steps reached the courtyard. How still and lovely it was here It was a four-square yard, bordered on three sides by the house buildings, and towards the street - a side-street which K. did not know - by a high white wall with a huge, heavy gate, open now. Here where the court was, the house seemed stiller than at the front. At any rate the whole first storey jutted out and had a more impressive appearance, for it was encircled by a wooden gallery closed in except for one tiny slit for looking through. At the opposite side from K. and on the ground floor, but in the corner where the opposite wing of the house joined the main building, there was an entrance to the house, open, and without a door. Before it was standing a dark, closed sledge to which a pair of horses was yoked.

Except for the coachman, whom at that distance and in the falling twilight K. guessed at rather than recognized, nobody was to be seen. Looking about him cautiously, his hands in his pockets, K. slowly coasted round two sides of the yard until he reached the sledge.

The coachman - one of the peasants who had been the other night in the taproom - smart in his fur coat, watched K. approaching non-committally, much as one follows the movements of a cat. Even when K. was standing beside him and had to move, and the horses were becoming a little restive at seeing a man coming out of the dusk, he remained completely detached. That exactly suited K.'s purpose. Leaning against the wall of the house he took out his lunch, thought gratefully of crieda and her solicitous provision for him, and meanwhile peered into the house. A very angular and broken stair led downwards and was crossed down below by a low but apparently deep passage. Everything was clean and whitewashed, sharply and distinctly defined. The wait lasted longer than K. had expected.

Long ago he had finished his meal, he was getting chilled, the twilight had changed into complete darkness, and still Klamm had not arrived.

"It might be a long time yet," said a rough voice suddenly, so near to him that K. started.

It was the coachman, who, as if waking up, stretched himself and yawned loudly.

"What might be a long time yet?" asked K., not ungrateful at being disturbed, for the perpetual silence and tension had already become a burden.

"Before you go away," said the coachman.

K. did not understand him, but did not ask further. He thought that would be the best means of making the insolent fellow speak. Not to answer here in this darkness was almost a challenge. And actually the coachman asked, after a pause: "Would you like some brandy?"

"Yes," said K. without thinking tempted only too keenly by the offer, for he was freezing.

"Then open the door of the sledge," said the coachman, "in the side pocket there are some flasks, take one and have a drink and then hand it up to me. With this fur coat it's difficult for me to get down."

K. was annoyed at being ordered about, but seeing that he had struck up with the coachman he obeyed, even at the possible risk of being surprised by Klamm in the sledge.

He opened the wide door and could without more ado have drawn a flask out of the side pocket which was fastened to the inside of the door. But now that it was open he felt an impulse which he could not withstand to go inside the sledge. All he wanted was to sit there for a minute. He slipped inside. The warmth within the sledge was extraordinary, and it remained although the door, which K. did not dare to close, was wide open. One could not tell whether it was a seat one was sitting on, so completely was one surrounded by blankets, cushions, and furs. One could turn and stretch on every side, and always one sank into softness and warmth. His arms spread out, his head supported on pillows which always seemed to be there, K. gazed out of the sledge into the dark house. Why was Klamm such a long time in coming? As if stupefied by the warmth after his long wait in the snow, K. began to wish that Klamm would come soon. The thought that he would much rather not be seen by Klamm in his present position touched him only vaguely as a faint disturbance of his comfort. He was supported in this obliviousness by the behaviour of the coachman, who certainly knew that he was in the sledge, and yet let him stay there without once demanding the brandy. That was very considerate, but still K. wanted to oblige him. Slowly, without altering his position, he reached out his hand to the side-pocket. But not the one in the open door, but the one behind him in the closed door.

After all, it didn't matter, there were flasks in that one too. He pulled one out, unscrewed the stopper, and smelt. Involuntarily he smiled, the perfume was so sweet, so caressing, like praise and good words from someone whom one likes very much, yet one does not know clearly what they are for and has no desire to know, and is simply happy in the knowledge that it is one's friend who is saying them.

"Can this be brandy?" K. asked himself doubtfully and took a taste out of curiosity.

Yes, strangely enough it was brandy, and burned and warmed him. How wonderfully it was transformed in drinking out of something which seemed hardly more than a sweet perfume into a drink fit for a coachman. "

Can it be?" K. asked himself as if self-reproachfully, and took another sip. Then - as K. was just in the middle of a long swig - everything became bright, the electric lights blazed inside on the stairs, in the passages, in the entrance hall, outside above the door. Steps could be heard coming down the stairs, the flask fell from K.'s hand, the brandy was spilt over a rug, K. sprang out of the sledge, he had just time to slam the door to, which made a loud noise, when a gentleman came slowly out of the house. The only consolation that remained was that it was not Klamm, or was not that rather a pity? It was the gentleman whom K. had already seen at the window on the first floor. A young man, very good looking, pink and white, but very serious. K., too, looked. thinking gravely, but his gravity was on his own account. Really it would have done better to have sent his assistants here, they oughtn't have behaved more foolishly than he had done. The gentleman still regarded him in silence, as if he had not enough breath in his overcharged bosom for what had to be said.

"This is unheard of," he said at last, pushing his hat a little back on his forehead.

What next? The gentleman knew nothing apparently of K.'s stay in the sledge, and yet found something that was unheard of? Perhaps that K. had pushed his way in as far as the courtyard?

"How do you come to be here?" the gentleman asked next, more softly now, breathing freely again, resigning himself to the inevitable.

What questions to ask!

And what could one answer?

Was K. to admit simply and flatly to this man that his attempt, begun with so many hopes, had failed?

Instead of replying, K. turned to the sledge, opened the door, and retrieved his cap, which he had forgotten there. He noticed with discomfort that the brandy was dripping from the footboard. Then he turned again to the gentleman, to show him that he had been in the sledge gave him no more compunction now, besides that wasn't the worst of it. When he was questioned, but only then, he would divulge the fact that the coachman himself had at least asked him to open the door of the sledge.

But the real calamity was that the gentleman had surprised him, that there had not been enough time left to hide from him so as afterwards to wait in peace for Klamm, or rather that he had not had enough presence of mind to remain in the sledge, close the door and wait there among the rugs for Klamm, or at least to stay there as long as this man was about. True, he couldn't know of course whether it might not be Klamm himself who was coming, in which case it would naturally have been much better to accost him outside the sledge. Yes, there had been many things here for thought, but now there was none, for this was the end.

"Come with me," said the gentleman, not really as a command, for the command lay not in the words, but in a slight, studiedly indifferent gesture of the hand which accompanied them.

"I'm waiting here for somebody," said K., no longer in the hope of any success, but simply on principle.

"Come," said the gentleman once more quite imperturbably, as if he wanted to show that he had never doubted that K. was waiting for somebody.

"But then I would miss the person I'm waiting for," said K. with an emphatic nod of his head.

In spite of everything that had happened he had the feeling that what he had achieved thus far was something gained, which it was true he only held now in seeming, but which^he must not relinquish all the same merely on account of a polite command.

"You'll miss him in any case, whether you go or stay," said the gentleman, expressing himself bluntly, but showing an unexpected consideration for K.'s line of thought.

"Then I would rather wait for him and miss him," said K. defiantly.

He would certainly not be driven away from here by the mere talk of this young man.

Thereupon with his head thrown back and a supercilious look on his face the gentleman closed his eyes for a few minutes, as if he wanted to turn from K's senseless stupidity to his own sound reason again, ran the tip of his tongue round his slightly parted lips, and said at last to the coachman: "Unyoke the horses."

Obedient to the gendeman, but with a furious sideglance at K., the coachman had now to get down in spite of his fur coat, and began very hesitatingly - as if he did not so much expect a counter-order from the gentleman as a sensible remark from K. - to back the horses and the sledge closer to the side wing, in which apparently, behind a big door, was the shed where the vehicles were kept. K. saw himself deserted, the sledge was disappearing in one direction, in the other, by the way he had come himself, the gentleman was receding, both it was true very slowly, as if they wanted to show K. that it was still in his power to call them back. Perhaps he had this power, but it would have availed him nothing. To call the sledge back would be to drive himself away. So he remained standing as one who held the field, but it was a victory which gave him no joy.

Alternately he looked at the backs of the gentleman and the coachman. The gentleman had already reached the door through which K. had first come into the courtyard. Yet once more he looked back, K. fancied he saw him shaking his head over such obstinacy, then with a short, decisive, final movement he turned away and stepped into the hall, where he immediately vanished. The coachman remained for a while still in the courtyard, he had a great deal of work with the sledge, he had to open the heavy door of the shed, back the sledge into its place, unyoke the horses, lead them to their stalls. All this he did gravely, with concentration, evidently without any hope of starting soon again, and this silent absorption which did not spare a single side-glance for K. seemed to the latter a far heavier reproach than the behaviour of the gentleman. And when now, after finishing his work in the shed, the coachman went across the courtyard in his slow, rolling walk, closed the huge gate and then returned, all very slowly, while he literally looked at nothing but his own footprints in the snow and finally shut himself into the shed. And now as all the electric lights went out too - for whom should they remain on? - and only up above the slit in the wooden gallery still remained bright, holding one's wandering gaze for a little, it seemed to K. as if at last those people had broken off all relations with him, and as if now in reality he were freer than he had ever been, and at liberty to wait here in this place usually forbidden to him as long as he desired, and had won a freedom such as hardly anybody else had ever succeeded in winning, and as if nobody could dare to touch him or drive him away, or even speak to him. But - this conviction was at least equally strong - as if at the same time there was nothing more senseless, nothing more hopeless, than this freedom, this waiting, this inviolability.

And he tore himself free and went back into the house - this time not along the wall but straight through the snow and met the landlord in the hall, who greeted him in silence and pointed towards the door of the taproom. K. followed the hint, for he was shivering, and wanted to see human faces. But he was greatly disappointed when he saw there, sitting at a little table - which must have been specially set out, for usually the customers put up with upturned barrels - the young gentleman and standing before him - an unwelcome sight for K. - the landlady from the Bridge Inn. Pepi, proud, her head thrown back and a fixed smile on her face, conscious of her incontestable dignity, her plait nodding with every movement, hurried to and fro, fetching beer and then pen and ink, for the gentleman had already spread out papers in front of him, was comparing dates which he looked up now in this paper, then again in a paper at the other end of the table, and was preparing to write. From her full height the landlady silently overlooked the gentleman and the papers, her lips pursed a little as if musing. It was as if she had already said everything necessary and it had been well received.

"The Land Surveyor, at last," said the gentleman at K.'s entrance, looking up briefly, then burying himself again in his papers. The landlady, too, only gave K. an indifferent

and not in the least surprised glance. But Pepi actually seemed to notice K. for the first time when he went up to the bar and ordered a brandy. K. leaned there, his hands pressed to his eyes, oblivious of everything. Then he took a sip of the brandy and pushed it back, saying it was undrinkable.

"All the gentlemen drink it," replied Pepi curdy, poured out the remainder, washed the glass and set it on the rack.

"The gentlemen have better stuff as well," said K.

"It's possible," replied Pepi, "but I haven't," and with that she was finished with K.

and once more at the gentleman's service, who, however, was in need of nothing, and behind whom she only kept walking to and fro in circles, making respectful attempts to catch a glimpse of the papers over his shoulder. But that was only her senseless curiosity and self-importance, which the landlady, too, reprehended with knitted brows.

Then suddenly the landlady's attention was distracted, she stared, listening intently, into vacancy. K. turned round, he could not hear anything in particular, nor did the others seem to hear anything. But the landlady ran on tiptoe and taking large steps to the door which led to the courtyard, peered through the keyhole, turned then to the others with wide, staring eyes and flushed cheeks, signed to them with her finger to near, and now they peered through the keyhole by turns. The landlady had, of course, the lion's share, but Pepi, too, was sidered. The gentleman was on the whole the most indifferent of the three. Pepi and the gentleman came away soon, but , landlady kept on peering anxiously, bent double, almost kneeling. One had almost the feeling that she was only imploring the keyhole now to let her through, for there had certainly been nothing more to see for a long time. When at last she got passed her hand over her face, arranged her hair, took a deep breath, and now at last seemed to be trying with reluctance to accustom her eyes again to the room and the people in it, K. said, not so much to get his suspicions confirmed, as to forestall the announcement, so open to attack did he feel now: "Has Klamm gone already then?"

The landlady walked past him in silence, but the gentleman answered from his table:

"Yes, of course. As soon as you gave up your sentry go, Klamm was able to leave. But it's strange how sensitive he is. Did you notice, landlady, how uneasily Klamm looked round him?"

The landlady did not appear to have noticed it, but the gentleman went on: "Well, fortunately there was nothing more to be seen, the coachman had effaced even the footprints in the snow."

"The landlady didn't notice anything," said K., but he said it without conviction, merely provoked by the gentleman's assertion, which was uttered in such a final and unanswerable tone.

"Perhaps I wasn't at the keyhole just then," said the landlady presently, to back up the gentleman, but then she felt compelled to give Klamm his due as well, and added: "All the same, I can't believe in this terrible sensitiveness of Klamm. We are anxious about him and try to guard him, and so go on to infer that he's terribly sensitive. That's as it should be and it's certainly Klamm's will. But how it is in reality we don't know.

Certainly, Klamm will never speak to anybody that he doesn't want to speak to, no matter how much trouble this anybody may take, and no matter how insufferably forward he may be.

But that fact alone, that Klamm will never speak to him, never allow him to come into his presence, is enough in itself. Why after all should it follow that he isn't able to endure seeing this anybody? At any rate, it can't be proved."

"That is essentially, of course," he said, "if I expressed myself a little to the test.

Then my opinion too, differently, it was to make myself comprehensible to the Land Surveyor. All the same it's a fact that when Klamm stepped out of the doorway he looked round him several times."

"Perhaps he was looking for me,' said K.

"Possibly," said the gentleman. "I hadn't thought of that."

They all laughed, Pepi, who hardly understood anything that was being said, loudest of all.

"Seeing we're all so happy here now," the gentleman went on, "I want to beg you very seriously, Land Surveyor, to enable me to complete my papers by answering a few questions."

"There's a great deal of writing there," said K. glancing at the papers from where he was standing.

"Yes, a wretched bore," said the gentleman laughing again, "but perhaps you don't know yet who I am. I'm Momus, Klamm's village secretary."

At these words seriousness descended on the room. Although the landlady and Pepi knew quite well who the gentleman was, yet they seemed staggered by the utterance of his name and rank. And even the gentleman himself, as if he had said more than his judgement sanctioned, and as if he were resolved to escape at least from any after-effects of the solemn import implicit in his own words, buried himself in his papers and began to write, so that nothing was heard in the room but the scratching of his pen.

"What is that: village secretary," asked K. after a pause.

The landlady answered for Momus, who now that he had introduced himself did not regard it seemly to give such explanations himself: "Herr Momus is Klamm's secretary in the same sense as any of Klamm's secretaries, but his official province, and if I'm not mistaken, his official standing" - still writing Momus shook his head decidedly and the landlady amended her phrase - "well, then, his official province, but not his official standing, is confined to the village. Herr Momus dispatches any clerical work of Klamm's which may become necessary in the village and as Klamm's deputy receives any petitions to Klamm which may be sent by the village."

As, still quite unimpressed by these facts, K. looked at the landlady with vacant eyes, she added in a halfembarrassed tone: "That's how it's arranged. All the gentlemen in the Castle have their village secretaries."

Momus, who had been listening far more attentively than K., supplied the landlady with a supplementary fact: "Most of the village seretaries work only for one gentleman, but I work for s for Klamm and for Vallabene."

"Yes," went on the landlady remembering now on her side too, and turning to K., "Herr Momus works for two gentlemen, for Klamm and for Vallabene, and so is twice a village secretary."

"Actually twice," said K., nodding to Momus - who now, leaning slightly forward, looked him full in the face - as one nods to a child whom one has just heard being praised. If there was a certain contempt in the gesture, then it was either unobserved or else actually expected. Precisely to ‚K., it seemed, who was not considered worthy even to be seen in passing by Klamm, these people had described in detail the services of a man out of Klamm's circle with the unconcealed intention of evoking K.'s recognition and admiration. And yet K. had no proper appreciation of it. He, who with all his powers strove to get a glimpse of Klamm, valued very little, for example, the post of a Momus who was permitted to live in Klamm's eye. For it was not Klamm's environment in itself that seemed to him worth striving for, but rather that he, K., he only and no one else, should attain to Klamm, and should attain to him not to rest with him, but to go on beyond him, farther yet, into the Castle. And he looked at his watch and said: "But now I must be going home."

Immediately the position changed in Momus's favour. "

Yes, of course," the latter replied, "the school work calls. But you must favour me with just a moment of your time. Only a few short questions."

"I don't feel in the mood for it," said K. and turned towards the door.

Momus brought down a document on the table and stood up: "In the name of Klamm I command you to answer my questions!"

"In the name of Klamm!" repeated K., "does he trouble himself about my affairs, then?"

"As to that," replied Momus, "I have no information and you certainly have still less.

We can safely leave that to him. All the same I cornmand you by virtue of my function granted by Klamm to stay here and to answer."

"Land Surveyor," broke in the landlady, "I refuse to advise you any further, my advice till now, the most well-meaning that you could have got, has been cast back at me in the most unheard-of manner. And I have come here to Momus - I have nothing to hide - simply to give the office adequate idea of your behaviour and your intentions and to protect myself for all time from having you quartered on me again. That's how we stand towards each other and that's how we'll always stand, and if I speak my mind accordingly now, I don't do it, I can tell you, to help you, but to ease a little the hard job which Herr Momus is bound to have in dealing with a man like you. All the same, just because of my absolute frankness and I couldn't deal otherwise than frankly with you even if I were to try - you can extract some advantage for yourself out of what I say, if you only take the trouble. In the present case I want to draw your attention to this, that the only road that can lead you to Klamm is through this protocol here of Herr Momus. But I don't want to exaggerate, perhaps that road won't get you as far as Klamm, perhaps it will stop long before it reaches him. The judgement of Herr Momus will decide that. But in any case that's the only road that will take you in the direction of Klamm. And do you intend to reject that road, for nothing but pride?"

"Oh, madam," said K., "that's neither the only road to Klamm, nor is it any better than the others. But you, Mr Secretary, decide this question, whether what I may say here can get as far as Klamm or not."

"Of course it can," said Momus, lowering his eyes proudly and gazing at nothing,

"otherwise why should I be secretary here?"

"Now you see, madam," said K., "I don't need a road to Klamm, but only to Mr Secretary."

"I wanted to throw open this road for you," said the landlady, "didn't I offer this morning to send your request to Klamm? That might have been done through Herr Momus. But you refused, and yet from now on no other way will remain for you but this one. But frankly, after your attempt on Klamm's privacy, with much less prospect of success. All the same this last, any, vanishing, yes, actually invisible hope, is your only one."

"How is it, madam," said K., "that originally you tried so hard to keep me from seeing Klamm, and yet now take my wish to see him quite seriously, and seem to consider me lost largely on account of the miscarrying of my plan? If at advise me sincerely from your heart against you not trying to see at how can you possibly drive me on the road to Klamm now, apparently just as sincerely, even though it's admitted that the road may not reach as far as him?"

"Am I driving you on?" asked the landlady. "Do you call it , driving you on when I tell you that your attempt is hopeless?. Would it really be the limit of audacity if you tried in that way push the responsibility on to me. Perhaps it's Herr Momus's presence that encourages you to do it. No, Land Surveyor, I'm not trying to drive you on to anything. I can admit only one mistake, that I overestimated you a little when I first saw you. Your immediate victory over Frieda frightened me, I didn't know what you might still be capable of. I wanted to prevent further damage, and thought that the only means of achieving that was to shake your resolution by prayers and threats. Since then I have learned to look on the whole thing more calmly. You can do what you like. Your actions may no doubt leave deep footprints in the snow out there in the courtyard, but they'll do nothing more."

"The contradiction doesn't seem to me to be quite cleared up," said K., "but I'm content with having drawn attention to it. But now I beg you, Mr Secretary, to tell me whether the landlady's opinion is correct, that is, that the protocol which you want to take down from my answers can have the result of gaining me admission to Klamm. If that's the case, I'm ready to answer all your questions at once. In that direction I'm ready, indeed, for anything."

"No," replied Momus, "that doesn't follow at all. It's simply a matter of keeping an adequate record of this afternoon's happenings for Klamm's village register. The record is already complete, there are only two or three omissions which you must fill in for the sake of order. There's no other object in view and no other object can be achieved."

K. gazed at the landlady in silence.

"Why are you looking at me?" asked she, "did I say anything else? He's always like that, Mr Secretary, he's always like that. Falsifies the information one gives him, and then maintains that he received false information. I've told him from the first and I tell him again to-day that he hasn't the faintest prospect of being received by Klamm.

Well, if there's no prospect in any case he won't alter that fact by means of this protocol. Could anything be clearer? I said further that this protocol is the only real official connection that he can have with Klamm. That too is surely clear and incontestable enough. But if in spite of that he won't believe me, and keeps on hoping -

I don't know why or with what idea - that he'll be able to reach Klamm, then so long as he remains in that frame of mind, the only thing that can help him is this one real official connection he has with Klamm, in other words, this protocol. That's all I have said, and whoever main, tains the contrary twists my words maliciously."

"If that is so, madam," said K., "then I beg your pardon, and I've misunderstood you.

For I thought - erroneously, as it turns out now - that I could take out of your former words that there was still some very tiny hope for me."

"Certainly," replied the landlady, "that's my meaning exactly. You're twisting my words again, only this time in the opposite way. In my opinion there is such a hope for you, and founded actually on this protocol and nothing else. But it's not of such a nature that you can simply fall on Herr Momus with the question: "Will I be allowed to see Klamm if I answer your questions?" When a child asks questions like that people laugh, when a grown man does it it is an insult to all authority. Herr Momus graciously concealed this under the politeness of his reply. But the hope that I mean consists simply in this, that through the protocol you have a sort of connection, a sort of connexion perhaps with Klamm. Isn't that enough? If anyone inquired for any service which might earn you the privilege of such a hope, could you bring forward the slightest one? For the last time, that's the best that can be said about this hope of yours, and certainly Herr Momus in his official capacity could never give even the slightest hint of it. For him it's a matter, as he says, merely of keeping a record of this afternoon's happenings, for the sake of order. More than that he won't say, even if you ask him this minute his opinion of what I've said."

"Will Klamm, then, Mr Secretary," asked K., "read the protocol?"

"No," replied Momus, "why should he? Klamm can't read every protocol, in fact he reads none. "Keep away from me with your protocols!" he usually says."

"Land Surveyor," groaned the landlady, "you exhaust me with such questions. Do you think it's necessary, or even simply desirable, that Klamm should read his protocol and become acquainted word for word with the curiousities of your life? Shouldn't you rather pray humbly that A,C protocol should be concealed from Klamm - a prayer, however, that would be just as unreasonable as the other, for who would hide anything from Klamm even though he has given many signs of his sympathetic nature? And is it even necessary for that you call your hope? Haven't you admitted yourself that you would be content if you only got the chance of speaking to Klamm, even if he never looked at you and never listened to you? And won't you achieve that at least through the protocol, perhaps much more?"

"Much more?" asked K. "In what way?"

"If you wouldn't always talk about things like a child, as if they were for eating. Who on earth can give any answer to such questions? The protocol will be put in Klamm's village register, you have heard that already, more than that can't be said with certainty. But do you know yet the full importance of the protocol, and of Herr Momus, and of the village register? Do you know what it means to be examined by Herr Momus?

Perhaps - to all appearances at least - he doesn't know it himself. He sits quietly there

and does his duty, for the sake of order, as he says. But consider that Klamm appointed him, that he acts in Klamm's name, that what he does, even if it never reaches Klamm, has yet Klamm's assent in advance. And how can anything have Klamm's assent that isn't filled by his spirit? Far be it from me to offer Herr Momus crude flattery besides he would absolutely forbid it himself - but I'm speaking of him not as an independent person, but as he is when he has Klamm's assent, as at present; then he's an instrument in the hand of Klamm, and woe to anybody who doesn't obey him."

The landlady's threats did not daunt K.. Of the hopes with which she tried to catch him he was weary. Klamm was far away. Once the landlady had compared Klamm to an eagle, and that had seemed absurd in K.'s eyes, but it did not seem absurd now. He thought of Klamm's remoteness, of his impregnable dwelling, of his silence, broken perhaps only by cries such as K. had never yet heard, of his downward-pressing gaze, which could never be proved or disproved, of his wheelings which could never be disturbed by anything that K.

did down below, which far above he followed at the behest of incomprehensibly laws and which only for instants were visible - all these things Klamm and the eagle had in common. But assuredly these had nothing to do with the protocol, over which just now Mornus was crumbling a roll dusted with salt, which he was eating with beer to help it out, in the process all the papers becoming covered with salt and caraway seeds.

"Good night," said K. "I've no objection to any kind of examination," and now he went at last to the door.

"He's going after all," said Momus almost anxiously to the landlady.

"He won't dare," said she.

K. heard nothing more, he was already in the hall. It was cold and a strong wind was blowing. From a door on the opposite side came the landlord, he seemed to have been keeping the hall under observation from behind a peephole. He had to hold the tail of his coat round his knees, the wind tore so strongly at him in the hall.

"You're going already, Land Surveyor?" he asked.

"You're surprised at that?" asked K.

"I am," said the landlord, "haven't you been examined then?"

"No," replied K. "I didn't let myself be examined."

"Why not?" asked the landlord.

"I don't know," said K., "why I should let myself be examined, why I should give in to a joke or an official whim. Perhaps some other time I might have taken it on my side too as a joke or as a whim, but not to-day." "

Why certainly, certainly," said the landlord, but he agreed only out of politeness, not from conviction. "I must let the servants into the taproom now," he said presently, "it's long past their time. Only I didn't want to disturb the examination."

"Did you consider it as important as all that?" asked K.

"Well, yes," replied the landlord.

"I shouldn't have refused," said K.

"No," replied the landlord, "you shouldn't have done that."

Seeing that K. was silent, he added, whether to comfort K. or to get away sooner:

"Well, well, the sky won't rain sulphur for all that."

"No," replied K., "the weather signs don't look like it."

K stepped out into the windswept street and peered into .. the darkness. Wild, wild weather. As if there were some connection between the two he reflected again how the landlady had striven to make him accede to the protocol, and how he had stood out. The landlady's attempt had of course not been a straightforward one, surreptitiously she had tried to put him against the protocol at the same time. In reality he could not tell whether he had stood out or given in. An intriguing nature, acting blindly, it seemed, like the wind, according to strange and remote behests which one could never guess at. He had only taken a few steps along the main street when he saw two swaying lights in the distance. These signs of life gladdened him and he hastened towards them, while they, too, made in his direction. He could not tell why he was so disappointed when he recognized the assistants. Still, they were coming to meet him, evidently sent by Frieda, and the lanterns which delivered him from the darkness roaring round him were his own; nevertheless he was disappointed, he had expected something else, not those old acquaintances who were such a burden to him. But the assistants were not alone. Out of the darkness between them Barnabas stepped out.

"Barnabas!" cried K. and he held out his hand, "have you come to see me?"

The surprise at meeting him again drowned at first all the annoyance which he had once felt at Barnabas.

"To see you," replied Barnabas unalterably friendly as before, "with a letter from Klamm."

"A letter from Klamm!" cried K. throwing back his head.

"Lights here!" he called to the assistants, who now pressed close to him on both sides holding up their lanterns. K. had to fold the large sheet in small compass to protect it from the wind while reading it. Then he read: "To the Land Surveyor at the Bridge Inn.

The surveying work which you have carried out thus far has ken appreciated by me. The work of the assistants, too, deserves Praise. You know how to keep them at their jobs. Do

not slacken in your efforts! Carry your work on to a fortunate contusion. Any interruption would displease me. For the rest be easy in your mind. The question of salary will presently be decided. I shall not forget you."

K. only looked up from the letter when the assistants, who read far more slowly than he, gave three loud cheers at the good news and waved their lanterns.

"Be quiet," he said, and to Barnabas: "There's been a misunderstanding."
Barnabas did not seem to comprehend.

"There's been a misunderstanding," K. repeated, and the weariness he had felt in the afternoon came over him again, the road to the schoolhouse seemed very long, and behind Barnabas he could see his whole family, and the assistants were still jostling him so closely that he had to drive them away with his elbows. How could Frieda have sent them to meet him when he had commanded that they should stay with her? He could quite well have found his own way home, and better alone, indeed, than in this company. And to make matters worse one of them had wound a scarf round his neck whose free ends flapped in the wind and had several times been flung against K.'s face. It is true, the other assistant had always disengaged the wrap at once with his long, pointed, perpetually mobile fingers, but that had not made things any better. Both of them seemed to have considered it an actual pleasure to walk here and back, and the wind and the wildness of the night threw them into raptures.

"Get out!" shouted K., "seeing that you've come to meet me, why haven't you brought my stick? What have I now to drive you home with?"

They crouched behind Barnabas, but they were not too frightened to set their lanterns on their protector's shoulders, right and left. However, he shook them off at once.

"Barnabas," said K., and he felt a weight on his heart when he saw that Barnabas obviously did not understand him, that though his tunic shone beautifully when fortune was there, when things became serious no help for to be found in him, but only dumb opposition, opposition against which one could not fight, for Barnabas himself was helpless, he could only smile, but that was of just as little help as the stars up there against this tempest down below.

"Look what Klamm has written!" said K., holding the letter before his face.
"He has been wrongly informed. I haven't done any surveying at all, and you see yourself how much the assistants are worth. And obviously, too, I can`t interrupt work which I've never begun. I can't even ° itc the gentleman's displeasure, so how can I have earned his preciation? As for being easy in my mind, I can never be hat"

"Ill see to it!" said Barnabas, who all the time had been eyeing past the letter, which he could not have read in any case if he was hiding it too close to his face.

"Oh," said K., "you promise me that you'll see to it, but can I really believe you? I'm in need of a trustworthy messenger, now more than ever."

K. bit his lip with impatience.

"Sir," replied Barnabas, with a gentle inclination of the head - K. almost allowed himself to be seduced by it again into believing Barnabas - Ill certainly see to it, and I'll certainly see to the message you gave me last time as well." "What!" cried K., "haven't you seen to that yet then? Weren't you at the Castle next day?"

"No," replied Barnabas, "my father is old, you've seen him yourself, and there happened to be a great deal of work just then, I had to help him, but now I'll be going to the Castle again soon."

"But what are you thinking of, you incomprehensible fellow?" cried K., beating his brow with his fist, "don't Klamm's affairs come before everything else, then? You're in an important position, you're a messenger, and yet you fail me in this wretched manner! What does your father's work matter? Klamm is waiting for this information, and instead of breaking your neck hurrying with it to him, you prefer to clean the stable!"

"My father is a cobbler," replied Barnabas calmly, "he had orders from Brunswick, and I'm my father's assistant"

"Cobbler, orders from Brunswick!" cried K. bitingly, as if he wanted to abolish the words for ever.

"And who can need boots here in these eternally empty streets? And what is all this cobbling to me? I entrusted you with a letter, not so that you might mislay it and crumple it on your bench, but that you might carry it at once to Klamm!"

K. became a little more composed now as he remembered that after all Klamm had apparently been all this time in the Herrenhof and not in the Castle at all. But Barnabas exasperated him again when, to prove that he had not forgotten K.'s first message, he now began to recite it.

"Enough! I don't want to hear any more," he said.

"Don't be angry with me, sir," said Barnabas, and as if unconsciously wishing to show disapproval of K. he withdrew his gaze from him and lowered his eyes, but probably he was only dejected by K.'s outburst.

"Im not angry," said K., and his exasperation turned now against himself, "with you, but it's a bad lookout for me only to have a messenger like you for important affairs."

"Look here," said Barnabas, and it was as if, to vindicate his honour as a messenger, he was saying more than he should, "Klamm is really not waiting for your message, he's actually cross when I arrive. "Another new message," he said once, and generally he gets up when he sees me coming in the distance and goes into the next room and doesn't receive me. Besides, it isn't laid down that I should go at once with every message. If it were laid down of course I would go at once. But it isn't laid down, and if I never went at all, nothing could be said to me. When I take a message it's of my own free will." "Well and good," replied K., staring at Barnabas and intentionally ignoring the assistants, who kept on slowly raising their heads by turns behind Barnabas's shoulder as from a trapdoor, and hastily disappearing again with a soft whistle in imitation of the whistling of the wind, as if they were terrified at K..

They enjoyed themselves like this for a long time.

"What it's like with Klamm I don't know, but that you can understand everything there properly I very much doubt, and even if you did, we couldn't better things there. But you can carry a message and that's all I ask you. A quite short message. Can you carry it for me to-morrow and bring me the answer to-morrow, or at least tell me how you were received? Can you do that and will you do that? It would be of great service to me. And perhaps I'll have a chance yet of rewarding you properly, or have you any wish now, perhaps, that I can fulfill?"

"Certainly I'll carry out your orders," said Barnabas.

"And will you do your utmost to carry them out as well as you can, to give the message to Klamm himself, to get a reply from Klamm himself, and immediately, all this immediately, to-morrow, in the morning, will you do that?"

"I'll do my best," replied Barnabas, "but I always do that."

"We won't argue any more about it now," said K.

This is the message: "The Land Surveyor begs the Director to grant him a personal interview. He accepts in advance any conditions which may be attached to the permission of this. He is driven to make this request because until now very intermediary has completely failed. In proof of this he advances the fact that till now he has not carried out any surveying at all, and according to the information given him by the village Superintendent will never carry out such work. Consenuently it is with humiliation and despair that he has read the last letter of the Director. Only a personal interview with the Director can be of any help here. The Land Surveyor knows how extraordinary his request is, but he will exert himself to make his disturbance of the Director as little felt as possible. He submits himself to any and every limitation of time, also any stipulation which may be considered necessary as to the number of words which may be allowed him during the interview, even with ten words he believes he will be able to manage. In profound respect and extreme impatience he awaits your decision."

K. had forgotten himself while he was speaking, it was as if he were standing before Klamm's door talking to the porter. "It has grown much longer than I had thought," he said, "but you must learn it by heart, I don't want to write a letter, it would only go the same endless way as the other papers."

So for Barnabas's guidance, K. scribbled it on a scrap of paper on the back of one of the assistants, while the other assistant held up the lantern. But already K. could take it down from Barnabas's dictation, for he had retained it all and spoke it out correctly without being put off by the misleading interpolations of the assistants.

"You've an extraordinary memory," said K., giving him the paper, "but now show yourself extraordinary in the other thing as well. And any requests? Have you none? It would reassure me a little - I say it frankly - regarding the fate of my message, if you had any."

At first Barnabas remained silent, then he said : "My sisters send you their greetings."

"Your sisters," replied K. "Oh, yes, the big strong girls."

"Both send you their greetings, but Amalia in particular," said Barnabas, "besides it was she who brought me this letter for you to-day from the Castle."

Struck by this piece of information, K. asked: "Couldn't she take my message to the Castle as well? Or Couldn't you both go and each of you try your luck?"

"Amalia is not allowed into the Chancellery," said Barnabas, "otherwise she would be very glad to do it."

"I'll come and see you perhaps to-morrow," said K., "only you come to me first with the answer. I'll wait for you in the school. Give my greetings to your sisters too."

K.'s promise seemed to make Barnabas very happy, and after they had shaken hands he could not help touching K. lightly on the shoulder. As if everything were once more as it had been when Barnabas first walked into the inn among the peasants in all his glory, K.

felt his touch on his shoulder as a distinction, though he smiled at it. In a better mood now, he let the assistants do as they pleased on the way home.

He reached the school chilled through and through, it was quite dark, the candles in the lanterns had burned down. Led by the assistants, who already knew their way here, he felt his road into one of the classrooms.

"Your first praiseworthy service," he said, remembering Klamm's letter.

Still half-asleep Frieda cried out from the corner: "Let K. sleep! Don't disturb him!" so entirely did K. occupy her thoughts, even though she had been so overcome with sleep that she had not been able to wait up for him. Now a light was got, but the lamp could not be turned up very far, for there was only a little paraffin left. The new household was still without many necessaries. The room had been heated, it was true, but it was a large one, sometimes used as the gymnasium - the gymnastic apparatus was standing about and hanging from the ceiling - and it had already used up all the supply of wood - had been very warm and cosy too, as K. was assured, but unfortunately had grown quite cold again. There was, however, a large supply of wood in a shed, but the shed was locked and the teacher had the key. He only allowed this wood to be used for heating the school during teaching hours. The room could have been endured if there had been beds where one might have taken refuge. But in that line there was nothing but one sack stuffed with straw, covered with praiseworthy tidiness by a woollen rug of Frieda's, but with no feather-bed and only two rough, stiff blankets, which hardly served to keep one warm. And it was precisely at this wretched bed of straw that the assistants were staring greedily, but of course without any hope of ever being allowed to lie on it.

Frieda looked anxiously at K.. That she knew how to make a room, even the most wretched, habitable, she had proved in the Bridge Inn, but here she had not been able to make any headway, quite without means as she was.

"Our only ornaments are the gymnastic contraptions," said she, trying to smile through her tears.

But for the chief deficiencies, the lack of sleeping accommodation and fuel, she promised absolutely to find help the very next day, and begged K. only to be patient till then. From no word, no hint, no sign could one have concluded that she harboured even the slightest trace of bitterness against K. in her heart, although, as he had to admit himself, he had torn her away first from the Herrenhof and now from the Bridge Inn as well. So in return K. did his best to find everything tolerable, which was not difficult for him, indeed, because in thought he was still with Barnabas repeating his message word for word, not however as he had given it to Barnabas, but as he thought it would sound before Klamm. After all, however, he was very sincerely glad of the coffee which Frieda had boiled for him on a spirit burner, and leaning against the almost cold stove followed the nimble, practised movements with which she spread the indispensable white table-cover on the teacher's table, brought out a flowered cup, then some bread and sausage, and actually a tin of sardines. Now everything was ready. Frieda, too, had not eaten yet, but had waited for K. Two chairs were available, there K. and Frieda sat down to their table, the assistants at their feet on the dais, but they could never stay quiet, even while eating they made a disturbance. Although they had received an ample store of everything and were not yet nearly finished with it, they got up from time to time to make sure whether there was still anything on the table and they could still expect something for themselves. K. paid no attention to them and only began to take notice when Frieda laughed at them. He covered her hand with his tenderly and asked softly why she was so indulgent to them and treated even their naughtiness so kindly. In this way one would never get rid of them, while through a certain degree of severity, which besides was demanded by their behaviour, one could manage either to curb them or, what was both more probable and more desirable, to make their position so hot for them that they would have finally to leave.

    The school here didn't seem to be a very pleasant place to live in for long, well, it wouldn't last very long in any case. But they would hardly notice all the drawbacks if the assist, ants were once gone and they two had the quiet house to themselves. And didn't she notice, too, that the assistants were becoming more impudent every day, as if they were actually encouraged now by Frieda's presence and the hope that K. wouldn't treat them with such firmness as he would have done in other circumstances? Besides, there were probably quite simple means of getting rid of them at once, without ceremony, perhaps Frieda herself knew of these, seeing that she was so well acquainted with all the circumstances. And from all appearances one would only be doing the assistants a favour if one got rid of them in some way, for the advantage they got by staying here couldn't be great, and besides the lazy spell which they must have enjoyed till now must cease here, to a certain extent at any rate, for they would have to work while Frieda spared herself after the excitements of the last few days, and he, K., was occupied in finding a way out of their painful position. All the same, if the assistants should go away, he would be so relieved that he felt he could quite easily carry out all the school work in addition to his other duties.

    Frieda, who had been listening attentively, stroked his arm and said that that was her opinion too, but that perhaps he took the assistants' mischief too seriously. They were mere lads, full of spirits and a little silly now that they were for the first time in strange service, just released from the strict discipline of the Castle, and so a little dazed and excited. And being in that state they of course committed lots of follies at which it was natural to be annoyed, but which it would be more sensible to laugh at.

    Often she simply couldn't keep from laughing. All the same she absolutely agreed with K. that it would be much better to send the assistants away and be by themselves, just the two of them. She pressed closer to K. and hid her face on his shoulder. And there she whispered something so low that K. had to bend his head to hear. It was that all the same she knew of no way dealing with the assistants and she was afraid that all that if had suggested would be of no avail. So far as she knew it. K. himself who had asked for them, and now he had them, would have to keep them. It would be best to treat them as a joke, which they certainly were. That would be the best way to put up with them. K. was displeased by her answer: half in jest, half in earnest, he replied that she seemed actually to be in league with them, or at least to have a strong inclination in their favour. Well, they were good-looking lads, but there was nobody who couldn't be got rid of if only one had the will, and he would show her that that was so in the case of the assistants. Frieda said that she would be very grateful to him if he could manage it. And from now on she wouldn't laugh at them any more, or have any unnecessary talk with them.

Besides she didn't find anything now to laugh at, it was really no joke always to be spied on by two men, she had learned to look at the two of them with K.'s eyes. And she actually shrank a little when the assistants got up again, partly to have a look at the food that was left, partly to get to the bottom of the continued whispering. K. employed this incident to increase Frieda's disgust for the assistants, drew her towards him, and so side by side they finished their supper.

Now it was time to go to bed, for they were all very sleepy. One of the assistants had actually fallen asleep over his food. This amused the other one greatly, and he did his best to get the others to look at the vacant face of his companion, but he had no success. K. and Frieda sat on above without paying any attention. The cold was becoming so extreme that they shirked going to bed. At last K. declared that the room must be heated, otherwise it would be impossible to get to sleep. He looked round to see if he could find an axe or something. The assistants knew of one and fetched it, and now they proceeded to the wood shed. In a few minutes the flimsy door was smashed and torn open.

As if they had never yet experienced anything so glorious, the assistants began to carry the wood into the classroom, hounding each other on and knocking against each other. Soon there was a great pile, the stove was set going, everybody lay down round it, the assistants were given a blanket to roll themselves in - it was quite ample for them, for it was decided that one of them should always remain awake and keep the fire going - and soon it was so hot round the stove that the blankets were no longer needed, the lamps were put out, and K. and Frieda happily stretched themselves out to sleep in the warm silence.

K. was awakened during the night by some noise or other, and in his first vague sleepy state felt for Frieda. He found that, instead of Frieda, one of the assistants was lying beside him. Probably because of the exacerbation which being suddenly awakened is sufficient in itself to cause, this gave him the greatest fright that he had ever had since he first came to the village. With a cry he sat up, and not knowing what he was doing he gave the assistant such a buffet that he began to cry. However the whole thing was cleared up in a moment. Frieda had been awakened - at least so it had seemed to her - by some huge animal, a cat probably, which had sprung on to her breast and then leapt away again. She had got up and was searching the whole room for the beast with a candle.

One of the assistants had seized the opportunity to enjoy the sack of straw for a little, an attempt which he was now bitterly repenting. Frieda could find nothing, however.

Perhaps it had only been a delusion, she went back to K. and on the way she stroked the crouching and whimpering assistant over the hair to comfort him, as if she had forgotten the evening's conversation. K. said nothing, but he asked the assistant to stop putting wood on the fire, for owing to almost all the heap having been squandered the room was already too hot.

Next morning nobody awoke until the school-children were there, standing with gaping eyes round the sleepers. This was unpleasant, for on account of the intense heat, which now towards morning had given way, however, to a coldness which could be felt, they had all taken off everything but their shirts, and just as they were beginning to put on their clothes, Gisa, the lady teacher, appeared at the door, a fair, tall, beautiful, but somewhat stiff young woman. She was evidently prepared for the new janitor, and seemed also to have been given her instructions by the teacher, for as soon as he appeared at the door, she began: "I can't put up with this. This is a fine state of affairs. You have permission to sleep in the classroom, but that's all. I am not obliged to teach in your bedroom. A janitor's family that loll in their beds far into the forenoon."

Well, something might be said about that, particularly as far as the family and the beds were concerned, thought K., while with Frieda's help - the assistants were of no use, lying on the floor they looked in amazement at the lady teacher and the children. He dragged across the parallel bars and the vaulting horse, threw the blanket over them, and so constructed a little room in which one could at least get on one's clothes protected from the children's gaze. He was not given a minute's peace, however, for the lady teacher began to scold because there was no fresh water in the washing basin-K. had just been thinking of fetching the basin for himself and Frieda to wash in, but he had at once given up the idea so as not to exasperate the lady teacher too much, but his renunciation was of no avail, for immediately afterwards there was a loud crash. Unfortunately, it seemed, they had forgotten to clear away the remains of the supper from the teacher's table, so she sent it all flying with her ruler and everything fell on the floor. She didn't need to bother about the sardine oil and the remainder of the coffee being spilt and the coffee-pot smashed to pieces, the janitor of course could soon clear that up.

Clothed once more, K. and Frieda, leaning on the parallel bars, witnessed the destruction of their few things. The assistants, who had obviously never thought of putting on their clothes, had stuck their heads through a fold of the blankets near the floor, to the great delight of the children. What grieved Frieda most was naturally the loss of the coffee-pot. Only when K. to comfort her assured her that he would go immediately to the village Superintendent and demand that it should be replaced, and see that this was done, was she able to gather herself together sufficiently to run out of their stockade in her chemise and skirt and rescue the table-cover at least from being stained any more. And she managed it, though the lady teacher to frighten her kept on hammering on the table with the ruler in the most nerve-racking fashion.

When K. and Frieda were quite clothed they had to compel the assistants - who seemed to be struck dumb by these events -to get their clothes on as well. Had not merely to order them and push them, indeed, but actually to put some of their clothes on for them. Then, when all was ready, K. shared out the remaining work. The assistants were to bring in wood and light the fire, but in the other classroom first, from which another and greater danger threatened, for the teacher himself was probably already there. Frieda was to scrub the floor and K. would fetch fresh water and set things to rights generally. For the time being breakfast could not be thought of. But so as to find out definitively the attitude of the lady teacher, K. decided to issue from their shelter himself first, the others were only to follow when he called them. He adopted this policy on the one hand because he did not want the position to be compromised in advance by any stupid act of the assistants, and on the other because he wanted Frieda to be spared as much as possible. For she had ambitions and he had none, she was sensitive and he was not, she only thought of the petty discomforts of the moment, while he was thinking of Barnabas and the future. Frieda followed all his instructions implicitly, and scarcely took her eyes from him. Hardly had he appeared when the lady teacher cried amid the laughter of the children, which from now on never stopped: "Slept well?" and as K. paid no attention - seeing that after all it was not a real question but began to clear up the washstand, she asked: "What have you been doing to my cat?"

A huge, fat old cat was lying lazily outstretched on the table, and the teacher was examining one of its paws which was evidently a little hurt. So Frieda had been right after all, this cat had not of course leapt on her, for it was past the leaping stage, but it had crawled over her, had been terrified by the presence of people in the empty house, had concealed itself hastily, and in its unaccustomed hurry had hurt itself. K. tried to explain this quietly to the lady teacher, but the only thing she had eyes for was the injury itself and she replied: "Well, then it's your fault through coming here.

Just look at thiss," and she called K. over to the table, showed him the paw, and before he could get a proper look at it, gave him a whack with the tawse over the back of his hand. The tails of the tawse were blunted, it was true, but, this time without any regard for the cat, she had brought them down so sharply that they raised bloody weals.

"And now go about your business," she said impatiently, bowing herself once more over the cat.

Frieda, who had been looking on with the assistants from behind the parallel bars, cried out when she saw the blood. K. held up his hand in front of the children and said:

"Look, that's what a sly, wicked cat has done to me."

He said it, indeed, not for the children's benefit, whose shouting and laughter had become continuous, so that it needed no further occasion or incitement, and could not be pierced or influenced by any words of his. But seeing that the lady teacher, too, only acknowledged the insult by a brief side-glance, and remained still occupied with the cat, her first fury satiated by the drawing of blood, K. called Frieda and the assistants, and then work began.

When K. had carried out the pail with the dirty water, fetched fresh water, and was beginning to turn out the classroom, a boy of about twelve stepped out from his desk, touched K.'s hand, and said something which was quite lost in the general uproar. Then suddenly every sound ceased and K. turned round. The thing he had been fearing all morning had come. In the door stood the teacher. In each hand the little man held an assistant by the scruff of the neck. He had caught them, it seemed, while they were fetching wood, for in a mighty voice he began to shout, pausing after every word: "Who has dared to break into the wood-shed? Where is the villain, so that I may annihilate him?"

Then Frieda got up from the floor, which she was trying to clean near the feet of the lady teacher, looked across at K. as if she were trying to gather strength from him, and said, a little of her old superciliousness in her glance and bearing: "I did it, Mr Teacher. I couldn't think of any other way. If the classrooms were to be heated in time, the wood-shed had to be opened. I didn't dare to ask you for the key in the middle of die

night, my fiance was at the Herrenhof, it was possible that he might stay there all night, so I had to decide for myself. If I have done wrongly, forgive my inexperience.

I've been scolded enough by my fiance, after he saw what had happened. Yes, he even forbade me to light the fires early, because he thought that you had shown by locking the wood-shed that you didn't want them to be put on before you came yourself. So it's his fault that the fires are not on, but mine that the shed has been broken into."

"Who broke open the door?" asked the teacher, turning to the assistants, who were still vainly struggling to escape from his grip.

"The gentleman," they both replied, and, so that there might be no doubt, pointed at K.

Frieda laughed, and her laughter seemed to be still more conclusive than her words.

Then she began to wring out in the pail the rag with which she had been scrubbing the floor, as if the episode had been closed with her declaration, and the evidence of the assistants were merely a belated jest. Only when she was at work on her knees again did she add: "Our assistants are mere children who in spite of their age should still be at their desks in school. Last evening I really did break open the door myself with the axe, it was quite easy, I didn't need the assistants to help me, they would only have been a nuisance. But when my fiand arrived later in the night and went out to see the damage and if possible put it right, the assistants ran out after him, likely because they were afraid to stay here by themselves, and saw my fiance working at the broken door, and that's why they say now - but they're only children - ." True, the assistants kept on shaking their heads during Frieda's story, pointed again at K. and did their best by means of dumb show to deflect her from her story. But as they did not succeed they submitted at last, took Frieda's words as a command, and on being questioned anew by the teacher made no reply.

"So," said the teacher, "you've been lying? Or at least you've groundlessly accused the janitor?"

They still remained silent, but their trembling and their apprehensive glances seemed to indicate guilt.

"Then I'll give you a sound thrashing straight away," he said, and he sent one of the children into the next room for his cane.

Then as he was raising it, Frieda cried: "The assistants have told the truth!" flung her scrubbing-cloth in despair into the pail, so that the water splashed up on every side, and ran behind the parallel bars, where she remained concealed.

"A lying crew!" remarked the lady teacher, who had just finished bandaging the pawr, and she took the beast into her lap, for which it was almost too big.

"So it was the janitor," said the teacher, pushing the assistants away and turning to K., who had been listening all the time leaning on the handle of his broom: "This fine janitor who out of cowardice allows other people to be falsely accused of his own villainies."

"Well," said K., who had not missed the fact that Frieda's intervention had appeased the first uncontrollable fury of the teacher, "if the assistants had got a little taste of the rod I shouldn't have been sorry. If they get off ten times when they should justly be punished, they can well afford to pay for it by being punished unjustly for once. But besides that it would have been very welcome to me if a direct quarrel between me and you, Mr Teacher, could have been avoided. Perhaps you would have liked it as well yourself too. But seeing that Frieda has sacrificed me to the assistants now-" here K. paused, and in the silence Frieda's sobs could be heard behind the screen - "of course a clean breast must be made of the whole business."

"Scandalous!" said the lady teacher.

"I am entirely of your opinion, Fraulein Gisa," said the teacher. "You, janitor, are of course dismissed from your post for these scandalous doings. Your further punishment I reserve meantime, but now clear yourself and your belongings out of the house at once. It will be a genuine relief to us, and the teaching will manage to begin at last. Now quick about it!" "I shan't move a foot from here," said K. "You're my superior, but not the person who engaged tne for this post. It was the Superintendent who did that, and I'll only accept notice from him. And he certainly never gave me this post so that I and my dependants should freeze here, but as you told me yourself - to keep me from doing anything thoughtless or desperate. To dismiss me suddenly now would therefore be absolutely against his intentions. Till I hear the contrary from his own mouth I refuse to believe it. Besides it may possibly be greatly to your own advantage, too, if I don't accept your notice, given so hastily."

"So you don't accept it?" asked the teacher.

K. shook his head.

"Think it over carefully," said the teacher, "your decisions aren't always for the best. You should reflect, for instance, on yesterday afternoon, when you refused to be examined."

"Why do you bring that up now?" asked K.

"Because it's my whim," replied the teacher, "and now I repeat for the last tune, get out!"

But as that too had no effect the teacher went over to the table and consulted in a whisper with Fraulefo Gisa. She said something about the police, but the teacher rejected it, finally they seemed in agreement, the teacher ordered the children to go into his classroom, they would be taught there along with the other children. This change delighted everybody, the room was emptied in a moment amid laughter and shouting, the teacher and Fraulein Gisa followed last. The latter carried the class register, and on it in all its bulk the perfectly indifferent cat. The teacher would gladly have left the cat behind, but a suggestion to that effect was negatived decisively by Fraulein Gisa with a reference to K.'s inhumanity. So, in addition to all his other annoyances, the teacher blamed K. for the cat as well. And that influenced his last words to K., spoken when he reached the door: "The lady has been driven by force to leave the room with her children, because you have rebelliously refused to accept my notice, and because nobody can ask of her, a young girl, that she should teach in the middle of your dirty household affairs.

So you are left to yourself, and you can spread yourself as much as you like, undisturbed by the disapproval of respectable people. But it won't last for long, I promise you that."

With that he slammed the door.

Hardly was everybody gone when K. said to the assistants: "Clear out!"

Disconcerted by the unexpectedness of the command, they obeyed, but when K. locked the door behind them they tried to get in again, whimpered outside and knocked on the door.

"You are dismissed," cried K., "never again will I take you into my service!"

But that, of course, was just what they did not want, and they kept hammering on the door with their hands and feet.

"Let us back to you, sir!" they cried, if they were being swept away by a flood and K. were dry wood.

But K. did not relent, he waited impatiently for the unbearable din to force the teacher to intervene.

That soon happened.

"Let your confounded assistants in!" he shouted.

"I've dismissed them," K. shouted back.

It had the incidental effect of showing the teacher what it was to be strong enough not merely to give notice but to enforce it. The teacher next tried to soothe the assistants by kindly assurances that they had only to wait quietly and K. would have to let them in sooner or later. Then he went away. And now things might have settled down if K. had not begun to shout at them again that they were finally dismissed once and for all, and had not the faintest chance of being taken back. Upon that they recommenced their din. Once more the teacher entered, but this time he no longer tried to reason with them, but drove them, apparently with his dreaded rod, out of the house. Soon they appeared in front of the windows of the gymnasium, rapped on the panes and cried something, but their words could no longer be distinguished.

They did not stay there long either, in the deep snow they could not be as active as their frenzy required. So they flew to the railings of the school garden and sprang on to the stone pediment, where, moreover, though only from a distance, they had a better view of the room. There they ran to and fro holding on to the railings, then remained standing and stretched out their clasped hands beseechingly towards K.. They went on like this for a long time, without thinking of the uselessness of their efforts. They were as if obsessed, they did not even stop when K. drew down the window blinds so as to rid himself of the sight of them.

In the now darkened room K. went over to the parallel bars to look for Frieda. On encountering his gaze she got up, put her hair in order, dried her tears and began in silence to prepare the coffee. Although she knew of everything, K. formally announced to her all the same that he had dismissed the assistants. She merely nodded. K. sat down at one of the desks and followed her tired movements. It had been her unfailing aliveliness.

A few days of living with K. had been enough to achieve this. Her work in the taproom had not been light, but apparently it had been more suited to her. Or was her separation from Klamm the real cause of her falling away? It was the nearness of Klamm that had made her so irrationally seductive. That was the seduction which had drawn K. to her, and now she was withering in his arms.

"Frieda," said K.

She put away the coffee-mill at once and went over to K. at his desk.

"You're angry with me?" asked she.

"No," replied K. "I don't think you can help yourself. You were happy in the Herrenhof.

I should have let you stay there."

"Yes," said Frieda, gazing sadly in front of her, "you should have let me stay there, I'm not good enough for you to live with. If you were rid of me, perhaps you would be able to achieve all that you want. Out of regard for me you've submitted yourself to the tyranny of the teacher, taken on this wretched post, and are doing your utmost to get an interview with Klamm. All for me, but I don't give you much in return."

"No, no," said K., putting his arm round her comfortingly. "All these things are trifles that don't hurt me, and it's not only on your account that I want to get to Klamm. And then think of all you've done for me! Before I knew you I was going about in a blind circle. Nobody took me up, and if I made up to anybody I was soon sent about my

business. And when I was given the chance of a little hospitality it was with people that I always wanted to run away from, like Barnabas's family -"

"You wanted to run away from them? You did? Darling!" cried Frieda eagerly, and after a hesitating "Yes," from K., sank back once more into her apathy.

But K. had no longer resolution enough to explain in what way everything had changed for the better for him through his connexion with Frieda. He slowly took away his arm and they sat for a little in silence, until - as if his arm had given her warmth and comfort, which now she could not do without - Frieda said: !I won't be able to stand this life here. If you want to keep me with you, we'll have to go away somewhere or other, to the south of France, or to Spain."

"I can't go away," replied K. "I came here to stay. I'll stay here."

And giving utterance to a self-contradiction which he made no effort to explain, he added as if to himself: "What could have enticed me to this desolate country except the wish to stay here?"

Then he went on: "But you want to stay here too, after all it's your own country. Only you miss Klamm and that gives you desperate ideas."

"I miss Klamm?" said Frieda. "I've all I want of Klamm here, too much Klamm. It's to escape from him that I want to go away. It's not Klamm that I miss, it's you. I want to go away for your sake, because I can't get enough of you, here where everything distracts me. I would gladly lose my pretty looks, I would gladly be sick and ailing, if I could be left in peace with you."

K. had only paid attention to one thing.

"Then Klamm is still in communication with you?" he asked eagerly, "he sends for you?"

"I know nothing about Klamm," replied Frieda, "I was speaking just now of others, I mean the assistants."

"Oh, the assistants," said K. in disappointment, "do they persecute you?"

"Why, have you never noticed it?" asked Frieda.

"No," replied K., trying in vain to remember anything, "they're certainly importunate and lascivious young fellows, but I hadn't noticed that they had dared to lift their eyes to you."

"No?" said Frieda, "did you never notice that they simply weren't to be driven out of our room in the Bridge Inn, that they jealously watched all our movements, that one of them finished up by taking my place on that sack of straw, that they gave evidence against you a minute ago so as to drive you out of this and ruin you, and so as to be left alone with me? You've never noticed all that?"

K. gazed at Frieda without replying. Her accusations against the assistants were true enough, but all the same they could be interpreted far more innocently as simple effects of the ludicrously childish, irresponsible, and undisciplined characters of the two. And didn't it also speak against their guilt that they had always done their best to go with K. everywhere and not to be left with Frieda? K. halfsuggested this.

"It's their deceit," said Frieda, "have you never seen through it? Well, why have you driven them away, if not for those reasons?"

And she went to the window, drew the blind aside a little, glanced out, and then called K. over. The assistants were still clinging to the railings. Tired as they must have been by now, they still gathered their strength together every now and then and stretched their arms out beseechingly towards the school. So as not to have to hold on all the time, one of them had hooked himself on to the railings behind by the tail of his coat.

"Poor things! Poor things!" said Frieda.

"You ask why I drove them away?" asked K. "You were the sole cause of that."

"I?" asked Frieda without taking her eyes from the assistants.

"Your much too kind treatment of the assistants," said K., "the way you forgave their offences and smiled at them and stroked their hair, your perpetual sympathy for them -

"Poor things! Poor things!" you said just now and finally this last thing that has happened, that you haven't scrupled even to sacrifice me to save the assistants from a beating."

"Yes, that's just it, that's what I've been trying to tell you, that's just what makes me unhappy, what keeps me from you even though I can't think of any greater happiness than to be with you all the time, without interruption, endlessly, even though I feel that here in this world there's no undisturbed place for our love, neither in the village nor anywhere else. And I dream of a grave, deep and narrow, where we could clasp each other in our arms as with iron bars, and I would hide my face in you and you would hide your face in me, and nobody would ever see us any more. But here - look, there are the assistants! It's not you they think of when they clasp their hands, but me."

"And it's not I who am looking at them," said K., "but you,"

"Certainly, me," said Frieda almost angrily, "that's what I've been saying all the time. Why else should they be always at my heels, even if they are messengers of Klamm's?"

"Messengers of Klamm's?" repeated K. extremely astonished by this designation, though it seemed natural enough at the same time.

"Certainly, messengers of Klamm's," said Frieda.

"Even if they are, still they're silly boys, too, who need to have more sense hammered into them. What ugly black young demons they are, and how disgusting the contrast is between their faces, which one would say belonged to grown-ups, almost to students, and their silly childish, behaviour. Do you think I don't see that? It makes me feel ashamed for them. Well, that's just it, they don't repel me, but I feel ashamed for them. I can't help looking at them. When one ought to be annoyed with them, I can only laugh at tem.

When people want to strike them, I can only stroke rheir hair. And when I'm lying beside you at night I can't sleep and must always be leaning across you to look at them, one of them lying rolled up asleep in the blanket and the other kneeling before the stove door putting in wood, and I have to bend forward so far that I nearly waken you. And it wasn't the cat that frightened me - oh, I've had experience of cats and I've bad experience as well of disturbed nights in the taproom - it wasn't the cat that frightened me, I'm frightened at myself. No, it didn't need that big beast of a cat to waken me, I start up at the slightest noise. One minute I'm afraid you'll waken and spoil everything, and the next I spring up and light the candle to force you to waken at once and protect me."

"I knew nothing of all this," said K., "it was only a vague suspicion of it that made me send them away. But now they're gone, and perhaps everything will be all right."

"Yes, they're gone at last," said Frieda, but her face was worried, not happy, "only we don't know who they are. Messengers of Klamm's I call them in my mind, though not seriously, but perhaps they are really that. Their eyes - those ingenuous and yet flashing eyes - remind me somehow of Klamm's. Yes, that's it, it's Klamm's glance that sometimes runs through me from their eyes. And so it's not true when I say that I'm ashamed for them. I only wish it were. I know quite well that anywhere else and in anyone else their behaviour would seem stupid and offensive, but in them it isn't. I watch their stupid tricks with respect and admiration. But if they're Klamm's messengers who'll rid us of them? And besides would it be a good thing to be rid of them? Wouldn't you have to fetch them back at once in that case and be happy if they were still willing to come?"

"You want me to bring them back again?" asked K.

"No, no!" said Frieda, "it's the last thing I desire. The sight of them, if they were to rush in here now, their joy at seeing me again, the way they would hop round like children and stretch out their arms to me like men. No, I don't I would be able to stand that. But all the same when I that if you keep on hardening your heart to them, it keep you, perhaps, from ever getting admittance to Klamm, I want to save you by any means at all from such consequences. In that case my only wish is for you to let them in. In that case let them in now at once. Don't bother about me. What do I matter? I'll defend myself as long as I can, but if I have to surrender, then I'll surrender with the consciousness that that, too, is for your sake."

"You only strengthen me in my decision about the assistants," said K. "Never will they come in with my will. The fact that I've got them out of this proves at least that in certain circumstances they can be managed, and therefore, in addition, that they have no real connexion with Klamm. Only last night I received a letter from Klamm from which it was clear that Klamm was quite falsely informed about the assistants, from which again one can only draw the conclusion that he is completely indifferent to them, for if that were not so he would certainly have obtained exact information about them. And the fact that you see Klamm in them proves nothing, for you're still, unfortunately, under the landlady's influence and see Klamm everywhere. You're still Klamm's sweetheart, and not my wife yet by a long chalk. Sometimes that makes me quite dejected, I feel then as if I had lost everything, I feel as if I had only newly come to the village, yet not full of hope, as I actually came, but with the knowledge that only disappointments await me, and that I will have to swallow them down one after another to the very dregs. But that is only sometimes," K. added smiling, when he saw Frieda's dejection at hearing his words, "and at bottom it merely proves one good thing, that is, how much you mean to me. And if you order me now to choose between you and the assistants, that's enough to decide the assistants' fate. What an idea, to choose between you and the assistants! But now I want to be rid of them finally, in word and thought as well. Besides who knows whether the weakness that has come over us both mayn't be due to the fact that we haven't had breakfast yet?"

"That's possible," said Frieda, smiling wearily and going about her work.

K., too, grasped the broom again. After a while there was a soft rap at the door.

"Barnabas!" cried K., throwing down the broom, and with a few steps he was at the door.

Frieda stared at him, more terrified at the man than anything else. With his trembling hands K.. could not turn the old lock immediately.

"I'll open in a minute," he kept on repeating instead of asking who was actually there.

And then he had to face the fact that through the wide-open door came not Barnabas, but the little boy who had tried to speak to him before. But K. had no wish to be reminded of him.

"What do you want here?" he asked. "The classes are being taught next door."

"I've come from there," replied the boy, looking up at K. quietly with his great brown eyes, and standing at attention, with his arms by his side.

"What do you want then? Out with it I" said K., bending a little forward, for the boy spoke in a low voice.

"Can I help you?" asked the boy.

"He wants to help us" said K. to Frieda, and then to the boy: "What's your name?"

"Hans Brunswick," replied the boy, "fourth standard, son of Otto Brunswick, master cobbler in Madeleinegasse."

"I see, your name is Brunswick," said K., now in a kinder tone.

It came out that Hans had been so indignant at seeing the bloody weals which the lady teacher had raised on K.'s hand, that he had resolved at once to stand by K. He had boldly slipped away just now from the classroom next door at the risk of severe punishment, somewhat as a deserter goes over to the enemy. It may indeed have been chiefly some such boyish fancy that had impelled him. The seriousness which he evinced in everything he did seemed to indicate it. Shyness held him back at the beginning, but he soon got used to K. and Frieda, and when he was given a cup of good hot coffee he became lively and confidential and began to question them eagerly and insistently, as if he wanted to know the gist of the matter as quickly as possible, to enable him to come to an independent decision about what they should do. There was something imperious in his character, but it was so mingled with childish innocence that they submitted to it without resistance, half-smilingly, half in earnest. In any case he demanded all their attention for himself. Work completely stopped, the breakfast lingered on unconscionably.

Although Hans was sitting at one of the scholars' desks and K. in a chair on the dais with Frieda beside him, it looked as if Hans were the teacher, and as if he were examining them and passing judgement on their answers. A faint smile round his soft mouth seemed to indicate that he knew quite well that all this was only a game, but that made him only the more serious in conducting it. Perhaps, too, it was not really a smile but the happiness of childhood that played round his lips. Strangely enough he only admitted quite late in the conversation that he had known K. ever since his visit to Lasemann's.

K. was delighted.

"You were playing at the lady's feet?" asked K.

"Yes," replied Hans, "that was my mother."

And now he had to tell about his mother, but he did so hesitatingly and only after being repeatedly asked. And it was clear now that he was only a child, out of whose mouth, it is true - especially in his questions - sometimes the voice of an energetic, far-seeing man seemed to speak. But then all at once, without transition, he was only a schoolboy again who did not understand many of the questions, misconstrued others, and in childish inconsiderateness spoke too low, although he had the fault repeatedly pointed out to him, and out of stubbornness silently refused to answer some of the other questions at all, quite without embarrassment, however, as a grown-up would have been incapable of doing. He seemed to feel that he alone had the right to ask questions, and that by the questions of Frieda and K. some regulation were broken and time wasted. That made him sit silent for a long time, his body erect, his head bent, his underlip pushed out. Frieda was so charmed by his expression at these moments that she sometimes put questions to him in the hope that they would evoke it. And she succeeded several times, but K. was only annoyed. All that they found out did not amount to much. Hans's mother was slightly unwell, but what her illness was remained indefinite. The child which she had had in her lap was Hans's sister and was called Frieda (Hans was not pleased by the fact that her name was the same as the lady's who was questioning him), the family lived in the village, but not with Lasemann - they had only been there on a visit and to be bathed, seeing that Lasemann had the big tub in which the younger children, to whom Hans didn't belong, loved to bathe and splash about. Of his father Hans spoke now with respect, now with fear, but only when his mother was not occupying the conversation.

Questions about Brunswick's family life remained, in spite of their efforts, unanswered.

K. learned that the father had the biggest shoemaker's business in the place, nobody could compete with him, a fact which quite remote questions brought again and again. He actually gave out work to the other shoemakers, for example to Barnabas's father. In this last case he had done it of course as a special favour - at least Hans's proud toss of the head seemed to hint at this, a gesture which made Frieda run over and give him a kiss. The question whether he had been in the Castle yet he only answered after it had been repeated several times, and with a "No." The same question regarding his mother he did not answer at all. At last K. grew tired. To him, too, these questions seemed useless, he admitted that the boy was right. Besides there was something humiliating in ferreting out family secrets by taking advantage of a child. Doubly humiliating, however, was the fact that in spite of his efforts he had learned nothing. And when to finish the matter he asked the boy what was the help he wanted to offer, he was no longer surprised to hear that Hans had only wanted to help with the work in the school, so that the teacher and his assistant might not scold K. so much. K. explained to Hans that help of that kind was not needed, scolding was part of the teacher's nature and one could scarcely hope to avoid it even by the greatest diligence, the work itself was not hard, and only because of special circumstances had it been so far behind that morning, besides scolding hadn't the same effect on K. as on a scholar, he shook it off, it was almost a matter of indifference to him, he hoped, too, to get quite clear of the teacher soon.

Though Hans had only wanted to help him in dealing with the teacher, however, he thanked him sincerely, but now Hans had better return to his class, with luck he would not be punished if he went back at once. Although K. did not emphasize and only involuntarily suggested that it was simply help in dealing with the teacher which he did not require, leaving the question of other kinds of help open, Hans caught the suggestion clearly and asked whether perhaps K. needed any other assistance. He would be very glad to help him, and if he were not in a position to help him himself, he would ask his mother to do so, and then it would be sure to be all right. When his father had difficulties, he, too, asked Hans's mother for help. And his mother had already asked once about K., she herself hardly ever left the house, it had been a great exception for her to be at Lasemann's that day. But he, Hans, often went there to play with Lasemann's children, and his mother had once asked him whether the Land Surveyor had ever happened to be there again. Only his mother wasn't supposed to talk too much, seeing she was so weak and tired, and so he had simply replied that he hadn't seen the Land Surveyor there, and nothing more had been said. But when he had found K. here in the school, he had had to speak to him, so that he might tell his mother the news. For that was what pleased his mother most, when without her express command one did what she wanted. After a short pause for reflection K. said that he did not need any help, he had all that he required, but it was very good of Hans to want to help him, and he thanked him for his good intentions. It was possible that later he might be in need of something and then he would turn to Hans, he had his address. In return perhaps he, K., might be able to offer a little help. He was sorry to hear that Hans's mother was ill and that apparently nobody in the village understood her illness. If it was neglected like that a trifling malady might sometimes lead to grave consequences. Now he, K., had some medical knowledge, and, what was of still more value, experience in treating sick people. Many a case which the doctors had given up he had been able to cure. At home they had called him "The Bitter Herb" on account of his healing powers. In any case he would be glad to see Hans's mother and speak with her.

Perhaps he might be able to give her good advice, for if only for Hans's sake he would be delighted to do it. At first Hans's eyes lit up at this offer, exciting K. to greater urgency, but the outcome was unsatisfactory, for to several questions Hans replied, without showing the slightest trace of regret, that no stranger was allowed to visit his mother, she had to be guarded so carefully. Although that day K. had scarcely spoken to her she had had to stay for several days in bed, a thing indeed that often happened. But his father had then been very angry with K. and he would certainly never K. to come to the house. He had actually wanted to seek out at the time to punish him for his impudence, only Hans's Bother had held him back. But in any case his mother never wanted to talk with anybody whatever, and her inquiry about K. was no exception to the rule. On the contrary, seeing he had been, mentioned, she could have expressed the wish to see him, but she hadn't done so, and in that had clearly made known her will. She only wanted to hear about K. but she did not want to speak to him. Besides it wasn't any real illness that she was suffering from, she knew quite well the cause of her state and often had actually indicated it.

Apparently it was the climate here that she could not stand, but all the same she would not leave the place, on account of her husband and children, besides, she was already better in health than she used to be. Here K. felt Hans's powers of thought visibly increasing in his attempt to protect his mother from K., from K. whom he had ostensibly wanted to help. Yes, in the good cause of keeping K. away from his mother he even contradicted in several respects what he had said before, particularly in regard to his mother's illness. Nevertheless K. remarked that even so Hans was still well disposed towards him, only when his mother was in question he forgot everything else. Whoever was set up beside his mother was immediately at a disadvantage. Just now it had been K., but it could as well be his father, for example. K. wanted to test this supposition and said that it was certainly thoughtful of Hans's father to shield his mother from any disturbance, and if he, K., had only guessed that day at this state of things, he would never have thought of venturing to speak to her, and he asked Hans to make his apologies to her now.

On the other hand he could not quite understand why Hans's father, seeing that the cause of her sickness was so clearly known as Hans said, kept her back from going somewhere else to get well. One had to infer that he kept her back, for she only remained on his account and the children's, but she could take the children with her, and she need not have to go away for any long time or for any great distance, even up on the Castle Hill the air was quite different. Hans's father had no need to fear the cost of the holiday, seeing he was the biggest shoemaker in the place, and it was pretty certain that he or she had relations or acquaintances in the Castle who would be glad to take her in.

Why did he not let her go?

He shouldn't underestimate an illness like this, K. had only seen Hans's mother for a minute, but it had actually been her striking pallor and weakness that had impelled him to speak to her. Even at that time he had been surprised that her husband had let her sit there in the damp steam of the washing and bathing when she was ill, and had put no restraint either on his loud talk with the others. Hans's father really did not know the actual state of things. Even if her illness had improved in the last few weeks, illnesses like that had ups and downs, and in the end, if one did not fight them, they returned with redoubled strength, and then the patient was past help. Even if K. could not speak to Hans's mother, still it would perhaps be advisable if he were to speak to his father and draw his attention to all this. Hans had listened intently, had understood most of it, and had been deeply impressed by the threat implicit in this dark advice.

Nevertheless he replied that K. could not speak to his father, for his father disliked him and would probably treat him as the teacher had done. He said this with a shy smile when he was speaking of K., but sadly and bitterly when he mentioned his father. But he added that perhaps K. might be able to speak to his mother all the same, but only without his father's knowledge. Then deep in thought Hans stared in front of him for a little - just like a woman who wants to do something forbidden and seeks an opportunity to do it without being punished - and said that the day after tomorrow it might be possible, his father was going to the Herrenhof in the evening, he had a conference there. Then he, Hans, would come in the evening and take K. along to his mother, of course, assuming that his mother agreed, which was however very improbable. She never did anything at all against the wishes of his father, she submitted to him in everything, even in things whose unreasonableness he, Hans, could see through. Long before this K. had called Hans up to the dais, drawn him between his knees, and had kept on caressing him cornfortingly.

The nearness helped, in spite of Hans's occasional reluctance, to bring about an understanding. They agreed finally to the following: Hans would first tell his mother the entire truth, but, so as to make her consent easier, add that K. wanted to speak to Brunswick himself as well, not about her at all but about his own affairs. Besides this was true. In the course of the conversation K. had remembered that Brunswick, even if he were a bad and dangerous man, could scarcely be his enemy now, if he had been, according to the information of the Superintendent, the leader of those who, even if only on political grounds, were in favour of engaging a Land Surveyor. K.'s arrival in the village must therefore have been welcomed by Brunswick. But in that case his morose greeting that first day and the dislike of which Hans spoke were almost incomprehensible - perhaps, however, Brunswick had been hurt simply because K. had not turned to him first for help, perhaps there existed some other misunderstanding which could be cleared up by a few words. But if that were done K. might very well secure in Brunswick a supporter against the teacher, yes and against the Superintendent as well. The whole official plot - for was it anything else really? - by means of which the Superintendent and the teacher were keeping him from reaching the Castle authorities and had driven him into taking a janitor's post, might be unmasked. If it came anew to a fight about K. between Brunswick and the Superintendent, Brunswick would have to include K. on his side, K. would become a guest in Brunswick's house, Brunswick's fighting resources would be put at his disposal in spite of the Superintendent. Who could tell what he might not be able to achieve by those means, and in any case he would often be in the lady's company - so he played with his dreams and they with him, while Hans, thinking only of his mother, painfully watched K.'s silence, as one watches a doctor who is sunk in reflexion while he tries to find the proper remedy for a grave case.

With K.'s proposal to speak to Brunswick about his post as Land Surveyor Hans was in agreement, but only because by means of this his mother would be shielded from his father, and because in any case it was only a last resort which with good luck might not be needed. He merely asked farther how K. was to explain to his father the lateness of the visit, and was content at last, though his face remained a little overcast, with the suggestion that K. would say that his unendurable post in the school and the teacher's humiliating treatment had made him in sudden despair forget all caution. Now that, so far as one could see, everything had been provided for, and the possibility of success at least conceded, Hans, freed from his burden of reflexion, became happier, and chatted for some time longer with K. and afterwards with Frieda

- who had sat for a long time as if absorbed by quite different thoughts, and only now began to take part in the conversation again. Among other things she asked him what he wanted to become; he did not think long but said he wanted to be a man like K. When he was asked next for his reasons he really did not know how to reply, and the question whether he would like to be a janitor he answered with a decided negative. Only through further questioning did they perceive by what roundabout ways he had arrived at his wish. K.'s present condition was in no way enviable, but wretched and humiliating. Even Hans saw this clearly without having to ask other people. He himself would have certainly preferred to shield his mother from K.'s slightest word, even from having to see him. In spite of this, however, he had come to K.

and had begged to be allowed to help him, and had been delighted when K. agreed. He imagined, too, that other people felt the same. And, most important of all, it had been his mother herself who had mentioned K.'s name. These contradictions had engendered in him the belief that though for the moment K. was wretched and looked down on, yet in an almost unimaginable and distant future he would excel everybody. And it was just this absurdly distant future and the glorious developments which were to lead up to it that attracted Hans. That was why he was willing to accept K. even in his present state. The peculiar childish' grown-up acuteness of this wish consisted in the fact that Hans looked on K. as on a younger brother whose future would reach further than his own, the future of a very little boy. And it was with an almost troubled seriousness that, driven into a corner by Frieda's questions, he at last confessed those things. K. only cheered him up again when he said that he knew what Hans envied him for. It was for his beautiful walking-stick, which Hans had been playing with constantly during the conversation. Now K. knew how to produce sticks like that, and if their plan were successful he would make Hans an even more beautiful one. It was no longer quite clear now whether Hans had not really meant merely the walkingstick, so happy was he made by K.'s promise. And he said goodbye with a glad face, not without pressing K.'s hand firmly and saying: "The day after to-morrow, then."

It had been high time for Hans to go, for shortly afterwards the teacher flung open the door and shouted when he saw K. and Frieda sitting idly at the table: "Forgive my intrusion, but will you tell me when this place is to be finally put in order? We have to sit here packed like herring, so that the teaching can't go on. And there are you lolling about in the big gymnasium, and you've even sent away the assistants to give yourselves more room. At least get on to your feet now and get a move on!"

Then to K.: "Now go and bring me my lunch from the Bridge Inn."

All this was delivered in a furious shout, though the words were comparatively inoffensive. K. was quite prepared to obey, but to draw the teacher he said: "But I've been given notice."

"Notice or no notice, bring me my lunch," replied the teacher.

"Notice or no notice, that's just what I want to be sure about," said K.

"What nonsense is this?" asked the teacher. "You know you didn't accept the notice."

"And is that enough to make it invalid?" asked K.

"Not for me," said the teacher, "you can take my word for that, but for the Superintendent, it seems, though I can't understand it. But take to your heck now, or else I'll fling you out in earnest."

K. was content the teacher then had spoken with the Superintendent, or perhaps he hadn't spoken after all, but had merely thought over carefully the Superintendent's probable intentions, and these had weighed in K.'s favour. Now K. was setting out hastily to get the lunch, but the teacher called him back from the very doorway, either because he wanted by this counter order to test K.'s willingness to serve, so that he might know how far he could go in future, or because a fresh fit of imperiousness had seized him, through too great compliance he would only become the teacher's slave and scapegoat, but within tain limits he decided for the present to give way to the fellow's caprices, for even if the teacher, as had been shown, had noted the power to dismiss him, yet he could certainly make the post so difficult that it could not be borne. And the post was more important in K.'s eyes now than ever before. The conversation with Hans had raised new hopes in him, improbable, he admitted, completely groundless even, but all the same not to be put out of his mind. They almost superseded Barnabas himself. If he gave himself up to them - and there was no choice - then he must husband all his strength, trouble about nothing else, food, shelter, the village authorities, no not even about Frieda and in reality the whole thing turned only on Frieda, for everything else only gave him anxiety in relation to her. For this reason he must try to keep this post which gave Frieda a certain degree of security, and he must not complain if for this end he were made to endure more at the teacher's hands than he would have had to endure in the ordinary course. All that sort of thing could be put up with, it belonged to the ordinary continual petty annoyances of life, it was nothing compared with what K. was striving for, and he had not come here simply to lead an honoured and comfortable life.

And so, as he had been ready to run over to the inn, he showed himself now willing to obey the second order, and first set the room to rights so that the lady teacher and her children could come back to it. But it had to be done with all speed, for after that K. had to go for the lunch, and the teacher was already ravenous. K. assured him that it would all be done as he desired. For a little the teacher looked on while K. hurried up, cleared away the sack of straw, put back the gymnastic apparatus in its place, and swept the room out while Frieda washed and scrubbed the dais. Their diligence seemed to appease the teacher, he only drew their attention to the fact that there was a pile of wood for the fire outside the door - he would not allow K. further access to the shed, of course - and then went back to his class with the threat that he would return soon and inspect.

After a few minutes of silent work Frieda asked K. why he submitted so humbly to the teacher now. The question was asked in a sympathetic, anxious tone, but K., who was thinking of little Frieda had succeeded in keeping her original promise to shield him from the teacher's orders and insults, merely replied shortly that since he was the janitor he must fulfil the janitor's duties. Then there was silence again until K., reminded vividly by this short exchange of words that Frieda had been for a long time lost in anxious thought - and particularly through almost the whole conversation with Hans - asked her bluntly while he carried in the firewood what had been troubling her.

Slowly turning her eyes upon him she replied that it was nothing definite, she had only been thinking of the landlady and the truth of much of what she said. Only when K.

pressed her did she reply more consecutively after hesitating several times, but without looking up from her work - not that she was thinking of it, for it was making no progress, but simply so that she might not be compelled to look at K. And now she told him that during his talk with Hans she had listened quietly at first, that then she had been startled by certain words of his, then had begun to grasp the meaning of them more dearly, and that ever since she had not been able to cease reading into his words a confirmation of a warning which the landlady had once given her, and which she had always refused to believe. Exasperated by all this circumlocution, and more irritated than touched by Frieda's tearful, complaining voice - but annoyed above all because the landlady was coming into his affairs again, though only as a recollection, for in person she had had little success up till now - K. flung the wood he was carrying in his arms on to the floor, sat down on it, and in tones which were now serious demanded the whole truth.

"More than once," began Frieda, "yes, since the beginning, the landlady has tried to make me doubt you, she didn't hold that you were lying, on the contrary she said that you were childishly open, but your character was so different from ours, she said, that, even when you spoke frankly, it was bound to be difficult for us to believe you. And if we did not listen to good advice he would have to learn to believe you through bitter experience.

Even she with her keen eye for people was almost taken in. But after her last talk with you in the Bridge Inn - I am only repeating her own words - she woke up to your tricks, she said and after that you couldn't deceive her even if you did your best to hide your intentions. But you hid nothing, she repeated that again and again, and then she said afterwards: "Try to listen to him carefully at the first favourable opportunity, not superficially, but carefully, carefully." That was all that she had done and your own words had told her all this regarding myself. That you made up to me - she used those very words - only because I happened to be in your way, because I did not actually repel you, and because quite erroneously you considered a barmaid the destined prey of any guest who chose to stretch out his hand for her. Moreover, you wanted, as the landlady learned at the Herrenhof, for some reason or other to spend that night at the Herrenhof, and that could in no circumstances be achieved except through me. Now all that was sufficient cause for you to become my lover for one night, but something more was needed to turn it into a more serious affair. And that something more was Klamm. The landlady doesn't claim to know what you want from Klamm, she merely maintains that before you knew me you strove as eagerly to reach Klamm as you have done since. The only difference was this, that before you knew me you were without any hope, but that now you imagine that in me youhave a reliable means of reaching Klamm certainly and quickly and even with advantage to yourself. How startled I was - but that was only a superficial fear without deeper cause when you said to-day that before you knew me you had gone about here in a blind circle. These might actually be the same words that the landlady used, she, too, says that it's only since you have known me that you've become aware of your goal. That's because you believe you have secured in me a sweetheart of Klamm's, and so possess a hostage which can only be ransomed at a great price. Your one endeavour is to treat with Klamm about this hostage. As in your eyes I am nothing and the price everything, so you are ready for any concession so far as I'm concerned, but as for the price you're adamant.

So it's a matter of indifference to you that I've lost my post at the Herrenhof and that I've had to leave the Bridge Inn as well, a matter of indifference that I have to endure the heavy work in the school. You have no tenderness to spare for me, you hardly even time for me, you leave me to the assistants, the idea of being jealous never comes into your mind, my only value for you is that I was old Klamm's sweetheart, in your ignorance you exert yourself to keep me from forgetting Klamm, so that when the decisive moment comes I should not make any resistance. Yet at the same time you carry on a feud with the landlady, the only one you think capable of separating me from you, and that's why you brought your quarrel with her to a crisis, so as to have to leave the Bridge Inn with me. But that, so far as I'm concerned, I belong to you whatever happens, you haven't the slightest doubt. You think of the interview with Klamm as a business deal, a matter of hard cash. You take every possibility into account.

Providing that you reach your end you're ready to do anything. Should Klamm want me you are prepared to give me to him, should he want you to suck to me you'll stick to me, should he want you to fling me out, you'll fling me out, but you're prepared to play a part too. If it's advantageous to you, you'll give out that you love me, you'll try to combat his indifference by emphasizing your own littleness, and then shame him by the fact that you're his successor, or you'll be ready to carry him the protestations of love for him which you know I've made, and beg him to take me on again, of course on your terms. And if nothing else answers, then you'll simply go and beg from him in the name of K. and wife.

But, the landlady said finally, when you see then that you have deceived yourself in everything, in your assumptions and in your hopes, in your ideas of Klamm and his relations with me, then my purgatory will begin, for then for the first time I'll be in reality the only possession you'll have to fall back on, but at the same time it will be a possession that has proved to be worthless, and you'll treat it accordingly, seeing that .you have no feeling for me but the feeling of ownership."

With his lips tightly compressed K. had listened intently, the wood he was sitting on had rolled asunder though he had not noticed it, he had almost slid on to the floor, and now at last he got up, sat down on the dais, took Frieda's hand, she feebly tried to pull away, and said: "In what you've haven't always been able to distinguish the landlady's thoughts from your own."

"They're the landlady's sentiment, purely," said Frieda, "I heard her out because I respected her but it was the first time in my life that I completely and wholly refused to accept her opinion. All that she said seemed to me so pitiful, so far from any understanding of how things stood between us. There seemed actually to be more truth to me at the direct opposite of what she said. I thought of that sad morning after our first night together. You kneeling beside me with a look as if everything were lost. And how it really seemed then that in spite of all I could do, I was not helping you but hindering you. It was through me that the landlady had become your enemy, a powerful enemy, whom even now you still undervalue. It was for my sake that you had to take thought, that you had to fight for your post, that you were at a disadvantage before the Superintendent, that you had to humble yourself before the teacher and were delivered over to the assistants, but worst of all for my sake you had perhaps lost your chance with Klamm.

That you still went on trying to reach Klamm was only a kind of feeble endeavour to propitiate him in some way. And I told myself that the landlady, who certainly knew far better than I, was only trying to shield me by her suggestions from bitter self-reproach.

A well-meant but superfluous attempt. My love for you had helped me through everything, and would certainly help you on too, in the long run, if not here in the village, then somewhere else. It had already given a proof of its power, it had rescued you from Barnabas's family."

"That was your opinion, then, at the time," said K., "and has it changed since?"

"I don't know," replied Frieda, glancing down at K.'s hand which still held hers, "perhaps nothing has changed. When you're so close to me and question me so calmly, then I think that nothing has changed. But in reality -" she drew her hand away from K., sat erect opposite him and wept without hiding her face. She held her tear-covered face up to him as if she were weeping not for herself and so had nothing to hide, but as if she were weeping over K.'s treachery and so the pain of seeing her tears was hidden. "But in reality everything has changed since I've listened to you talking with that boy. How innocently you began asking about the family, about this and that! To me you looked just due you did that night when you came into the taproom, impetuous and frank, trying to catch my attention with such a childlike eagerness. You were just the same as then, and all I wished was that the landlady had been here and could have listened to you, and then we should have seen whether she could soil stick to her opinion. But then quite suddenly - I don't know how it happened - I noticed that you were talking to him with a hidden intention. You won his trust - and it wasn't easy to win - by sympathetic words, simply so that you might with greater ease reach your end, which I began to recognize more and more clearly. Your end was that woman. In your apparently solkitous inquiries about her I could see quite nakedly your simple preoccupation with your own affairs. You were betraying that woman even before you had won her. In your words I recognized not only my past, but my future as well, it was as if the landlady were sitting beside me and explaining everything, and with all my strength I tried to push her away, but I saw clearly the hopelessness of my attempt, and yet it was not really myself who was going to be betrayed, it was not I who was really being betrayed, but that unknown woman. And then when I collected myself and asked Hans what he wanted to be and he said he wanted to be like you, and I saw that he had fallen under your influence so completely already, well what great difference was there between him, being exploited here by you, the poor boy, and myself that time in the taproom?"

"Everything," said K., who had regained his composure in listening. "Everything that you say is in a certain sense justifiable, it is not untrue, it is only partisan. These arc the landlady's ideas, my enemy's ideas, even if you imagine that they're your own.

And that comforts me. But they're instructive, one can learn a great deal from the landlady. She didn't express them to me personally, although she did not spare my feelings other ways. Evidently she put this weapon in your hands in the hope that you would employ it at a particularly bad or decisive point for me. If I am abusing you, then she is abusing you in the same way.

But, Frieda, just consider. Even if every, thing were just as the landlady says, it would only be shameful on one supposition, that is, that you did not love me. Then only then, would it really seem that I had won you through calculation and trickery, so as to profiteer by possessing you. In that case it might even have been part of my plan to appear before you arm-in-arm with Olga so as to evoke your pity, and the landlady has simply forgotten to mention that too in her list of my offences. But if it wasn't as bad as all that, if it wasn't a sly beast of prey that seized you that night, but you came to meet me, just as I went to meet you, and we found one another without a thought for ourselves, in that case, Frieda, tell me, how would things look? If that were really so, in acting for myself I was acting for you too, there is no distinction here, and only an enemy could draw it. And that holds in everything, even in the case of Hans.

Besides, in your condemnation of my talk with Hans your sensitiveness makes you exaggerate things morbidly, for if Hans's intentions and my own don't quite coincide, still that doesn't by any means amount to an actual antagonism between them, moreover our discrepancies were not lost on Hans, if you believe that you do grave injustice to the cautious little man, and even if they should have been all lost on him, still nobody will be any the worse for it, I hope."

"It's so difficult to see one's way, K.," said Frieda with a sigh. "I certainly had no doubts about you, and if I have acquired something of the kind from the landlady, I'll be only too glad to throw it off and beg you for forgiveness on my knees, as I do, believe me, all the time, even when I'm saying such horrible things. But the truth remains that you keep many things from me. You come and go, I don't know where or from where. Just now when Hans knocked you cried out Barnabas's name. I only wish you had once called out my name as lovingly as for some incomprehensible reason you called that hateful name. If you have no trust in me, how can I keep mistrust from rising? It delivers me completely to the landlady, whom you justify in appearance by your behaviour. Not in everything, I won't say that you justify her in everything, for was it not on my account alone that you sent the assistants packing? Oh, if you but knew ith what passion I try to find a grain of comfort for myself in all that you do and say, even when it gives me pain."

"Once and for all, Frieda," said K., "I conceal not the slightest thing from you. See how the landlady hates me, and how she does her best to get you away from me, and what despicable means she uses, and how you give in to her, Frieda, how you give in to her!

Tell me, now, in what way do I hide anything from you?

That I want to reach Klamm you know, that you can't help me to do it and that accordingly I must do it by my own efforts you know too. That I have not succeeded up till now you see for yourself. Am I to humiliate myself doubly, perhaps, by telling you of all the bootless attempts which have already humiliated me sufficiently? Am I to plume myself on having waited and shivered in vain all an afternoon at the door of Klamm's sledge? Only too glad not to have to think of such things any more, I hurry back to you, and I am greeted again with all those reproaches from you. And Barnabas? It's true I'm waiting for him. He's Klamm's messenger, it isn't I who made him that."

"Barnabas again!" cried Frieda. "I can't believe that he's a good messenger."

"Perhaps you're right," said K., "but he's the only messenger that's sent to me."

"All the worse for you," said Frieda, "all the more reason why you should beware of him."

"Unfortunately he has given me no cause for that till now," said K. smiling. "He comes very seldom, and what messages he brings are of no importance. Only the fact that they come from Klamm gives them any value."

"But listen to me," said Frieda, "for it is not even Klamm that's your goal now, perhaps that disturbs me most of all. That you always longed for Klamm while you had me was bad enough, but that you seem to have stopped trying to reach Klamm now is much worse, that's something which not even the landlady foresaw. According to the landlady your happiness, a questionable and yet very real happiness, would end on the day when you finally recognized that the hopes you founded on Klamm were in vain. But now you don't wait any longer even for that day, a young lad suddenly comes in and you begin to fight with him for his mother, as if you were fighting for your very life."

"You've understood my talk with Hans quite correctly," said K., "it was really so. But is your whole former life so completely from your mind - all except the landlady, of course, who allow herself to be wiped out - that you can't remember longer how one must fight to get to the top, especially when one begins at the bottom? How one must take advantage of every, thing that offers any hope whatever? And this woman comes from the Castle, she told me herself on my first day here, when I happened to stray into Lasemann's. What's more natural than to ask her for advice or even for help. If the landlady only knows the obstacles which keep one from reaching Klamm, then this woman probably knows the way to him, for she has come here by that way herself."

"The way to Klamm?" asked Frieda.

"To Klamm, certainly, where else?" said K.

Then he jumped up: "But now it's high time I was going for the lunch."

Frieda implored him to stay, urgently, with an eagerness quite disproportionate to the occasion, as if only his staying with her would confirm all the comforting things he had told her. But K. was thinking of the teacher, he pointed towards the door, which any moment might fly open with a thunderous crash, and promised to return at once, she was not even to light the fire, he himself would see about it. Finally Frieda gave in in silence.

As K. was stamping through the snow outside - the path should have been shovelled free long ago, strange how slowly the work was getting forward I - he saw one of the assistants, now dead tired, still holding to the railings. Only one, where was the other?

Had K. broken the endurance of one of them, then, at least? The remaining one was certainly still zealous enough, one could see that when, animated by the sight of K., he began more feverishly than ever to stretch out his arms and roll his eyes.

"His obstinacy is really wonderful," K. told himself, but had to add, "he'll freeze to the railings if he keeps it up." Outwardly, however, K. had nothing for the assistant but a threatening gesture with his fist, which prevented any nearer approach. Indeed the assistant actually retreated for an appreciable distance.

Just then Frieda opened one of the windows so as to air the room before putting on the fire, as she had promised K., immediately the assistant turned his attention from K., and crept as if irresistibly attracted to the window. Her face torn between a glance for the assistant and a beseeching helpless glance which she threw at K. Frieda put her hand out hesitatingly from the window, it was not clear whether it was a greeting or a cormmand to go away, nor did the assistant let it deflect him from resolve to come nearer. Then Frieda closed the outer window hastily, but remained standing behind it, her hand on the sash, with her head bent sideways, her eyes wide, and a fixed smile a her face. Did she know that standing like that she was more likely to attract the assistant than repel him?

But K. did not look back again, he thought he had better hurry as fast as he could and get back quickly.

At long last, late in the afternoon, when it was already dark, K. had cleared the garden path, piled the snow high on either side, beaten it down hard, and also accomplished his work for the day. He was standing by the garden gate in the middle of a wide solitude. He had driven off the remaining assistant hours before, and chased him a long way, but the fellow had managed to hide himself somewhere between the garden and the schoolhouse and could not be found, nor had he shown himself since. Frieda was indoors either starting to wash clothes or still washing Gisa's cat. It was a sign of great confidence on Gisa's part that this task had been entrusted to Frieda, an unpleasant and uncalled-for task, indeed, which K. would not have suffered her to attempt had it not been advisable in view of their various shortcomings to seize every opportunity of securing Gisa's goodwill. Gisa had looked on approvingly while K. brought down the little children's bath from the garret, heated water, and finally helped to put the cat carefully into the bath. Then she actually left the cat entirely in charge of Frieda, for Schwarzer, K.'s acquaintance of the first evening, had arrived, had greeted K. with a mixture of embarrassment - arising out of the events of that evening - and of unmitigated contempt such as one accords to a debtor, and had vanished with Gisa into the other schoolroom. The two of them were still there.

Schwarzer, K. had been told in the Bridge Inn, had been living in the village for some time, although he was a castellan's son, because of his love for Gisa, and through his influential connexions had got himself appointed as a pupil-teacher, a position which he filled chiefly by attending all Gisa's classes, either sitting on a school bench among the children, or preferably at Gisa's feet on the teacher's dais. His presence was no longer a disturbance, the children had got quite used to it, all the more easily, perhaps, because Schwarzer neither liked nor understood children and rarely spoke to them except when he took over the gymnastic lesson from Gisa, and was content merely to breathe the same air as Gisa and bask in her warmth and nearness. The only astonishing thing about it was that in the Bridge Inn at least Schwarzer was spoken of with a certain degree of respect, even if his actions were ridiculous rather than praiseworthy, and that Gisa was included in this respectful atmosphere. It was none the less unwarranted of Schwarzer to assume that his position as a pupil-teacher gave him a great superiority over K., for this superiority was non-existent. A school janitor was an important person to the rest of the staff - and should have been especially so to such an assistant as Schwarzer - a person not to be lightly despised, who should at least be suitably conciliated if professional considerations were not enough to prevent one from despising him. K. decided to keep this fact in mind, also that Schwarzer was still in his debt on account of their first evening, a debt which had not been lessened by the way in which events of succeeding days had seemed to justify Schwarzer's reception of him. For it must not be forgotten that this reception had perhaps determined the later course of events.

Because of Schwarzer the full attention of the authorities had been most unreasonably directed to K. at the very first hour of his arrival, while he was still a complete stranger in the village without a single acquaintance or an alternative shelter.

Overtired with walking as he was and quite helpless on his sack of straw, he had been at the mercy of any official action. One night later might have made all the difference, things might have gone quietly and been only half noticed. At any rate nobody would have known anything about him or have had any suspicions, there would have been no hesitation in accepting him at least for one day as a stray wanderer, his handiness and trustworthiness would have been recognized and spoken of in the neighbourhood, and probably he would soon have found accommodation somewhere as a servant. Of course the authorities would have found him out. But there would have been a big difference between having the Central Bureau, or whoever was on the telephone, disturbed on his account in the middle of the night by an insistent although ostensibly humble request for an immediate decision, made, too, by Schwarzer, who was probably not in the best odour up there, and a quiet visit by K. to the Superintendent on the next day during official hours to report himself in proper form as a wandering stranger who had already found quarters in a respectable house, and who would probably be leaving the place in another day's time unless the unlikely were to happen and he found some work in the village, only for a day or two, of course, since he did not mean to stay longer.

That, or something like that, was what would have happened had it not been for Schwarzer. The authorities would have pursued the matter further, but calmly, in the ordinary course of business, unharassed by what they probably hated most, the impatience of a waiting client. Well, all that was not K.'s fault, it was Schwarzer's fault, but Schwarzer was the son of a castellan, and had behaved with outward propriety, and so the matter could only be visited on K.'s head. And what was the trivial cause of it all?

Perhaps an ungracious mood of Gisa's that day, which made Schwarzer roam sleeplessly all night, and vent his annoyance on K. Of course on the other hand one could argue that Schwarzer's attitude was something K. had to be thankful for. It had been the sole precipitant of a situation K. would never by himself have achieved, nor have dared to achieve, and which the authorities themselves would hardly have allowed, namely, that from the very beginning without any dissimulation he found himself confronting the authorities face to face, in so fcur as that was at all possible. Still, that was a dubious gift, it spared K. indeed the necessity of lying and contriving, but it him almost defenceless, handicapped him anyhow in the struggle, and might have driven him to despair had he not been able to remind himself that the difference in strength between the authorities and himself was so enormous that all the guile of which he was capable would hardly have served appreciably to reduce the difference in his favour. Yet that was only a reflexion for his own consolation, Schwarzer was none the less in his debt, and having harmed K. then could be called upon now to help. K. would be in need of help in the quite trivial and tentative opening moves, for Barnabas seemed to have failed him again. On Frieda's account K. had refrained all day from going to Barnabas's house to make inquiries. In order to avoid receiving Barnabas in Frieda's presence he had laboured out of doors, and when his work was done had continued to linger outside in expectation of Barnabas, but Barnabas had not come. The only thing he could do now was to visit the sisters, only for a minute or two, he would only stand at the door and ask, he would be back again soon. So he thrust the shovel into the snow and set off at a run.

He arrived breathless at the house of Barnabas, and after a sharp knock flung the door open and asked, without looking to see who was inside: "Hasn't Barnabas come back yet?"

Only then did he notice that Olga was not there, that the two old people, who were again sitting at the far end of the table in a state of vacancy, had not yet realized what was happening at the door and were only now slowly turning their faces towards it, and finally that Amalia had been lying beside the stove under a blanket and in her alarm at K.'s sudden appearance had started up with her hand to her brow in an effort to recover her composure. If Olga had been there she would have answered immediately, and K.

could have gone away again, but as it was he had at least to take a step or two towards Amalia, give her his hand which she pressed in silence, and beg her to keep the startled old folks from attempting to meander through the room, which she did with a few words. K. learned that Olga was chopping wood in the yard, that Amalia, exhausted - for what reason she did not say - had had to lie down a short time before, and that Barnabas had not yet indeed returned, but must return very soon, for he never stayed overnight in the Castle.

K. thanked her for the information, wbich left him at liberty to go, but Amalia asked if he would not wait to see Olga. However, she added, he had already spoken to Olga during the day. He answered with surprise that he had not, and asked if Olga had something of particular importance to say to him. As if faintly irritated Amalia screwed Up her mouth silently, gave him a nod, obviously in farewell, and lay down again. From her recumbent position she let her eyes rest on him as if she were astonished to see him still there.

Her gaze was cold, clear, and steady as usual, it was never levelled exactly on the object she regarded but in some disturbing way always a little past it, hardly perceptibly, but yet unquestionably past it, not from weakness, apparently, nor from embarrassment, nor from duplicity, but from a persistent and dominating desire for isolation, which she herself perhaps only became conscious of in this way. K. thought he could remember being baffled on the very first evening by that look, probably even the whole hatefulness of the impression so quickly made on him by this family was traceable to that look, which in itself was not hateful but proud and upright in its reserve.

"You are always so sad, Amalia," said K., "is anything troubling you? Can't you say what it is? I have never seen a country girl at all like you. It never struck me before.

Do you really belong to this village? Were you born here?"

Amalia nodded, as if K. had only put the last of those questions, and then said: "So you'll wait for Olga?"

"I don't know why you keep on asking me that," said K. "I can't stay any longer because my fiancee's waiting for me at home."

Amalia propped herself on one elbow. She had not heard of the engagement. K. gave Frieda's name. Amalia did not know it. She asked if Olga knew of their betrothal. K. fancied she did, for she had seen him with Frieda, and news like that was quick to fly round in a village. Amalia assured him, however, that Olga knew nothing about it, and that it would make her very unhappy, for she seemed to be in love with K. She had not directly said so, for she was very reserved, but love betrayed itself involuntarily. K. was convinced that Amalia was mistaken. Amalia smiled, and this smile of hers, although sad, lit up her gloomy face, made her silence eloquent, her strangeness, intimate, and unlocked a mystery jealously guarded hitherto, a mystery which could indeed be concealed again, but never so completely. Amalia said that she was certainly not mistaken, she would even go further and affirm that K., too, had an in. clination for Olga, and that his visits, which were ostensibly concerned with some message or other from Barnabas, were really intended for Olga. But now that Amalia knew all about it he need not be so strict with himself and could come oftener to see them. That was all she wanted to say.

K. shook his head, and reminded her of his betrothal. Amalia seemed to set little store by this betrothal, the immediate impression she received from K., who was after all unaccompanied, was in her opinion decisive, she only asked when K. had made the girl's acquaintance, for he had been but a few days in the village. K. told her about his night at the Herrenhof, whereupon Amalia merely said briefly that she had been very much against his being taken to the Herrenhof. She appealed for confirmation to Olga, who had just come in with an armful of wood, fresh and glowing from the frosty air, strong and vivid, as if transformed by the change from her usual aimless standing about inside. She threw down the wood, greeted K. frankly, and asked at once after Frieda. K. exchanged a look with Amalia, who seemed, however, not at all disconcerted. A little relieved, K. spoke of Frieda more freely than he would otherwise have done, described the difficult circumstances in which she was managing to keep house in a kind of way in the school, and in the haste of his narrativ e- for he wanted to go home at once - so far forgot himself when bidding them goodbye as to invite the sisters to come and pay him a visit.

He began to stammer in confusion, however, when Amalia, giving him no time to say another word, interposed with an acceptance of the invitation. Then Olga was compelled to associate herself with it but K., still harassed by the feeling that he ought to go at once, and becoming uneasy under Amalia's gaze, did not hesitate any longer to confess that the invitation had been quite unpremeditated and had sprung merely from a personal impulse, but that unfortunately he could not confirm it since there was a great hostility, to him quite incomprehensible, between her who cried and their family.

"It's not hostility," said Amalia, getting off from her couch and flinging the blanket behind her, "it's nothing so big as that`s only a parrot repetition of what she hears everywhere. And now, go away, go to your young woman, I can see you're in a hurry. You needn't be afraid that we'll come, I only said it at first for fun, put of mischief. But you can come often enough to see us, there's nothing to hinder you, you can always plead Barnabas's messages as an excuse. I'll make it easier for you by telling you that Barnabas, even if he has a message from the Castle for you, can't go all the way up to the school to find you. He can't trail about so much, poor boy, he wears himself out in the service, you'll have to come yourself to get the news."

K. had never before heard Amalia utter so many consecutive sentences, and they sounded differently from her usual comments, they had a kind of dignity which obviously impressed not only K. but Olga too, although she was accustomed to her sister. She stood a little to one side her arms folded, in her usual stolid and somewhat stooping posture once more, with her eyes fixed on Amalia, who on the other hand looked only at K.

"It's an error," said K., "a gross error to imagine that I'm not in earnest in looking for Barnabas, it's my most urgent wish, really my only wish, to get my business with the authorities properly settled. And Barnabas has to help me in that, most of my hopes are based on him. I grant he has disappointed me greatly once as it is, but that was more my fault than his. In the bewilderment of my first hours in the

village I believed that everything could be settled by a short walk in the evening, and when the impossible proved impossible I blamed him for it. That influenced me even in my opinion of your family and of you. But that is all past, I think I understand you better now, you are even -"

K. tried to think of the exact word, but could not find it immediately, so contented himself with a makeshift - "You seem to be the most good-natured people in the village so far as my experience goes. But now, Amalia, you're putting me off the track again by your depreciation - if not of your brother's service - then of the importance he has for me.

Perhaps you aren't acquainted with his affairs, in which case it doesn't matter, but perhaps you are acquainted with both of them - and that's the impression I incline to have - in which case it's a bad thing, for that would indicate that your brother is deceiving me."

"Calm yourself," cried Amalia, "I'm not acquainted with them, nothing could induce me to become acquainted with them, nothing at all, not even my consideration for you, which would move me to do a great deal, for, as you say, we are good-natured people. But my brother's affairs are his own business, I know nothing about them except what I hear by chance now and then against my will. On the other hand Olga can tell you all about them, for she's in his confidence."

And Amalia went away, first to her parents, with whom she whispered, then to the kitchen. She went without taking leave of K., as if she knew that he would stay for a long time yet and that no good-bye was necessary.

Seeing that with a somewhat astonished face K. remained standing where he was, Olga laughed at him and drew him towards the settle by the stove, she seemed to be really happy at the prospect of sitting there alone with him, but it was a contented happiness without a single hint of jealousy. And precisely this freedom of hers from jealousy and therefore from any kind of claim upon him did K. good, he was glad to look into her blue eyes which were not cajoling, nor hectoring, but shyly simple and frank. It was as if the warning of Frieda and the landlady had made him, not more susceptible to all those things, but more observant and more discerning. And he laughed with Olga when she expressed her wonder at his calling Amalia good-natured, of all things, for Amalia had many qualities, but good-nature was certainly not one of them. Whereupon K. explained that of course his praise had been meant for Olga, only Amalia was so masterful that she not only took to herself whatever was said in her presence, but induced other people of their own free will to include her in everything. "That's true," said Olga becoming more serious, "truer than you think. Amalia's younger than me, and younger than Barnabas, but hers is the final, decisive voice in the family for good or for ill, of course she has the burden of it more than anybody, the good as well as the bad."

K.. thought that an exaggeration, for Amalia had just said that she paid no attention, for instance, to her brother's flairs, while Olga knew all about them.

"How can I make it clear?" said Olga, "Amalia bothers neither about Barnabas nor about me, she really bothers about nobody but the old people whom she tends day and night. Now she has just asked them again if they want anything and has gone into the kitchen to cook them something, and for their sakes she has overcome her indisposition, for she's been ill since midday and been lying here on the settle. But although she doesn't bother about us we're as dependent on her as if she were the eldest, and if she were to advise us in our affairs we should certainly follow her advice, only she doesn't do it, she's different from us. You have experience of people, you come from a strange land, don't you think, too, that she's extraordinarily clever?"

"Extraordinarily unhappy is what she seems to me," said K., "but how does it go with your respect for her that Barnabas, for example, takes service as a messenger, in spite of Amalia's evident disapproval, and even her scorn?"

"If he knew what else to do he would give up being a messenger at once, for it doesn't satisfy him."

"Isn't he an expert shoemaker?" asked K.

"Of course he is," said Olga, "and in his spare time he does work for Brunswick, and if he liked he could have enough work to keep him going day and night and earn a lot of money."

"Well then," said K., "that would be an alternative to his services as a messenger."

"An alternative?" asked Olga in astonishment. "Do you think he does it for money?"

"Maybe he does," said K., "but didn't you say he was discontented?"

"He's discontented, and for various reasons," said Olga, "but it's Castle service, anyhow a kind of Castle service, at least one would suppose so."

"What!" said K., "do you even doubt that?"

"Well," said Olga, "not really, Barnabas goes into the bureaux and is accepted by the attendants as one of themselves, he sees various officials, too, from the distance, is entrusted with relatively important letters, even with verbally delivered messages, that's a good deal, after all, and we should be proud of what he has achieved for a young man of his years."

K. nodded and no longer thought of going home.

"He has a uniform of his own, too?" he asked.

"You mean the jacket?" said Olga. "No, Amalia made that for him long before he became a messenger. But you're touching on a sore spot now. He ought long ago to have had, not a uniform, for there aren't many in the Castle, but a suit provided by the department, and he has been promised one, but in things of that kind the Castle moves slowly, and the worst of it is that one never knows what this slowness means. It can mean that the matter's being considered, but it can also mean that it hasn't yet been taken up, that Barnabas for instance is still on probation, and in the long run it can also mean that the whole thing has been settled, that for some reason or other the promise has been cancelled, and that Barnabas will never get his suit. One can never find out exactly what is happening, or only a long time afterwards. We have a saying here, perhaps you've heard it: Official decisions are as shy as young girls."

"That's a good observation," said K., he took it still more seriously than

Olga, "a good observation, and the decisions may have other characteristics in common with young girls."

"Perhaps," said Olga. "But as far as the official suit's concerned, that's one of Barnabas's great sorrows, and since we share all our troubles, it's one of mine too. We ask ourselves in vain why he doesn't get an official suit. But the whole affair is not just so simple as that. The officials, for instance, apparently have no official dress.

So far as we know here, and so far as Barnabas tells us, the officials go about in their ordinary clothes, very fine clothes, certainly. Well, you've seen Klamm. Now, Barnabas is certainly not an official, not even one in the lowest category, and he doesn't overstep his limitations so far as to want to be one. But according to Barnabas, the highergrade servants, whom one certainly never sees down here in the village, have no official dress.

That's a kind of comfort, one might suppose, but it's deceptive comfort, for is Barnabas a high-grade servant? Not he.

However partial one might be towards him one couldn't maintain that, the fact that he comes to the village and even lives here is sufficient proof of the contrary, for the higher-grade servants are even more inaccessible than the officials, perhaps rightly so, perhaps they are even of higher rank than many an official, there's some evidence of that, they work less, and Barnabas says it's a marvellous sight to see these tall and distinguished men slowly walking through the corridors, Barnabas always gives them a wide berth. Well, he might be one of the lower-grade servants, then, but these always have an official suit, at least whenever they come down into the village, it's not exactly a uniform, there are many different versions of it, but at any rate one can always tell Castle servants by their clothes, you've seen some of them in the Herrenhof. The most noticeable thing about the clothes is that they're mostly closefitting, a peasant or a handworker couldn't do with them. Well, a suit like that hasn't been given to Barnabas and it's not merely the shame of it or the disgrace - one could put up with that but the fact that in moments of depression - and we often have such moments, none too rarely, Barnabas and I - it makes us doubt everything. Is it really Castle service Barnabas is doing, we ask ourselves then. Granted, he goes into the bureaux, but are the bureaux part of the real Castle? And even if there are bureaux actually in the Castle, are they the bureaux that Barnabas is allowed to enter? He's admitted into certain rooms, but they're only a part of the whole, for there are barriers behind which there are more rooms. Not that he's actually forbidden to pass the barriers, but he can't very well push past them once he has met his chiefs and been dismissed by them.

Besides, everybody is watched there, at least so we believe. And even if he did push on farther what good would it be to him, if he had no official duties to carry out and were a mere intruder? And you mustn't imagine that these barriers are a definite dividing-line. Barnabas is always impressing that on me. There are barriers even at the entrance to the rooms where he's admitted, so you see there are barriers he can pass, and they're just the same as the ones he's never yet passed, which looks as if one oughtn't to suppose that behind the ultimate barriers the bureaux are any different from those Barnabas has already seen. Only that's what we do suppose in moments of depression.

And the doubt doesn't stop there, we can't keep it within bounds. Barnabas sees officials, Barnabas is given messages. But who are those officials, and what are the messages? Now, so he says, he's assigned to Klamm, who gives him his instructions in person. Well, that would be a great favour, even higher-grade servants don't get so far as that, it's almost too much to believe, almost terrifying. Only think, directly assigned to Klamm, speaking with him face to face! But is it really the case? Well, suppose it is so, then why does Barnabas doubt that the official who is referred to as Klamm is really Klamm?"

"Olga," said K., "you surely must be joking. How can there be any doubt about Klamm's appearance, everybody knows what he looks like, even I have seen him."

"Of course not, K.," said Olga. "Ìm not joking at all, I'm desperately serious. Yet I'm not telling you all this simply to relieve my own feelings and burden yours, but because Amalia charged me to tell you, since you were asking for Barnabas, and because I think too that it would be useful for you to know more about it. I'm doing it for Barnabas's sake as well, so that you won't pin too many hopes upon him, and suffer disappointment, and make him suffer too because of your disappointment. He's very sensitive, for instance he didn't sleep all night because you were displeased with him yesterday evening. He took you to say that it was a bad lookout for you to have only a messenger like him. These words kept him off his sleep. I don't suppose that you noticed how upset he was, for Castle messengers must keep themselves well under control.

But he hasn't an easy time, not even with you, although from your point of view you don't ask too much of him, for you have your own prior conception of a messenger's powers and make your demands accordingly. But in the Castle they have a different conception of a messenger's duties, which couldn't be reconciled with yours, even if Barnabas were to devote himself entirely to the task, which, unfortunately, he often seems inclined to do.

Still, one would have to submit to that and raise no objections if it weren't for the question whether Barnabas is really a messenger or not. Before you, of course, he can't express any doubt of it whatever, to do that would be to undermine his very existence and to offend grievously against laws which he believes himself still plighted to, and even to me he doesn't speak freely, I have to cajole him and kiss his doubts out of him, and even then he rarely likes to admit that his doubts are doubts. He has something of a man in him. And I'm sure that he doesn't tell me everything, although I'm his sole confidante. But we do often speak about Klamm, whom I've never seen. You know Frieda doesn't like me and has never let me look at him, still his appearance is well known in the village, some people have seen him, everybody has heard of him, and out of glimpses and rumours and through various distorting factors an image of Klamm has been constructed which is certainly true in fundamentals. But only in fundamentals. In detail it fluctuates, and yet perhaps not so much as Klamm's real appearance. For he's reported as having one appearance when he comes into the village and another on leaving it. After having his beer he looks different from what he does before it, when he's awake he's different from when he's asleep, when he's alone he's different from when he's talking to people, and - what is incomprehensible after all that - he's almost another person up in the Castle. And even within the village there are considerable differences in the accounts given of him, differences as to his height, his bearing, his size, and the cut of his beard.

Fortunately there's one thing in which all the accounts agree, he always wears the same clothes, a black morning coat with long tails. Now of course all these differences aren't the result of magic, but can be easily explained. They depend on the mood of the observer, on the degree of his excitement, on the countless graduations of hope or despair which are possible for him when he sees Klamm, and besides, he can usually see Klamm only for a second or two. I'm telling you all this just as Barnabas has often told it to me, and, on the whole, for anyone not personally interested in the matter, it would be a sufficient explanation. Not for us, however. It's a matter of life or death for Barnabas whether it's really Klamm he speaks to or not."

"And for me no less," said K., and they moved nearer to each other on the settle.

All this depressing information of Olga's certainly affected K., but he regarded it as a great consolation to find other people who were at least externally much in the same situation as him with whom he could join forces and whom he could touch at many points, not merely at a few points as in Frieda's case. He was indeed gradually giving up all hope of achieving success through Barnabas, but the worse it went with Barnabas in the Castle the nearer he felt drawn to him down here; never would K. have believed that in the village itself such a despaired struggle could go on as Barnabas and his sister were involved in. Of course it was as yet far from being adequately explained and might turn out to be quite the reverse, one shouldn't let Olga's unquestionable innocence mislead one into taking Barnabas's uprightness for granted. "Barnabas is familiar with all those accounts of Klamm's appearance," went on Olga, "he has collected and compared a great many, perhaps too many he even saw Klamm once through a carriage window in the village, or believed he saw him, and so was sufficiently prepared to recognize him again, and yet - how can you explain this? - when he entered a bureau in the Castle and had one of several officials pointed out to him as Klamm he didn't recognize him, and for a long time afterwards couldn't accustom himself to the idea that it was Klamm. But if you ask Barnabas what was the difference between that Klamm and the usual description given of Klamm, he can't tell you, or rather he tries to tell you and describes the official of the Castle, but his description coincides exactly with the descriptions we usually hear of Klamm. Well then, Barnabas, I say to him, why do you doubt it, why do you torment yourself?

Whereupon in obvious distress he begins to reckon up certain characteristics of the Castle official, but he seems to be thinking them out rather than describing them, and besides that they are so trivial - a particular way of nodding the head, for instance, or even an unbuttoned waistcoat - that one simply can't take them seriously. Much more important seems to me the way in which Klamm receives Barnabas. Barnabas has often described it to me, and even sketched the room. He's usually admitted into a large room, but the room isn't Klamm's bureau, nor even the bureau of any particular official. It's a room divided into two by a single reading-desk stretching all its length from wall to wall. One side is so narrow that two people can hardly squeeze past each other, and that's reserved for the officials, the other side is spacious, and that's where clients wait, spectators, servants, messengers. On the desk there are great books lying open, side by side, and officials stand by, most of them reading. They don't always stick to the same book, yet it isn`t the books that they change but their places, and it always astounds Barnabas to see how they have to squeeze oast each other when they change places, because there's so little room. In front of the desk and close to it there are small low tables at which clerks sit ready to write from dictation, whenever the officials wish it. And the way that is done always amazes Barnabas. There's no express command given by the official, nor is the dictation given in a loud voice, one could hardly tell that it was being given at all, the official just seems to go on reading as before, only whispering as he reads, and the clerk hears the whisper. Often it's so low that the clerk can't hear it at all in his seat, and then he has to jump up, catch what's being dictated, sit down again quickly and make a note of it, then jump up once more, and so on.

What a strange business! It's almost incomprehensible. Of course Barnabas has time enough to observe it all, for he's often kept standing in the big room for hours and days at a time before Klamm happens to see him. And even if Klamm sees him and he springs to attention, that needn't mean anything, for Klamm may turn away from him again to the book and forget all about him. That often happens. But what can be the use of a messenger-service so casual as that? It makes me quite doleful to hear Barnabas say in the early morning that he's going to the Castle. In all likelihood a quite useless journey, a lost day, a completely vain hope. What's the good of it all? And here's cobbler's work piled up which never gets done and which Brunswick is always asking for."

"Oh, well," said K., "Barnabas has just to hang on till he gets a commission. That's understandable, the place seems to be over-staffed, and everybody can't be given a job every day, you needn't complain about that, for it must affect everybody. But in the long run even a Barnabas gets commissions, he has brought two letters already to me."

"It's possible, of course," answered Olga, "that we're wrong in complaining, especially a girl like me who knows things only from hearsay and can't understand it all so well as Barnabas, who certainly keeps many things to himself. But let me tell you how the letters are given out, your letters, for example. Barnabas doesn't get these directly from Klamm, but from a clerk. On no particular ay at no particular hour - that's why the service, however easy it appears, is really very exhausting, for Barnabas must be always on the alert - a clerk suddenly remembers about him and gives him a sign, without any apparent instructions from Klamm who merely goes on reading in his book. True, sometimes Klamm is polishing his glasses when Barnabas comes up, but he often does that, anyhow - however, he may take a look at Barnabas then, supposing, that is, that he can see anything at all without his glasses, which Barnabas doubts. For Klamm's eyes are almost shut, he generally seems to be sleeping and only polishing his glasses in a kind of dream.

Meanwhile the clerk hunts among the piles of manuscripts and writings under his table and fishes out a letter for you, so it's not a letter newly written, indeed, by the look of the envelope, it's usually a very old letter, which has been lying there a long time.

But if that is so, why do they keep Barnabas waiting like that? And you too? And the letter too, of course, for it must be long out of date. That's how they get Barnabas the reputation of being a bad and slow messenger. It's all very well for the clerk, he just gives Barnabas the letter, saying: "From Klamm for K." and so dismisses him. But Barnabas comes home breathless, with his hardly won letter next to his bare skin, and then we sit here on the settle like this and he tells me about it and we go into all the particulars and weigh up what he has achieved and find ultimately that it's very little, and questionable at that until Barnabas lays the letter down with no longer any inclination to deliver it, yet doesn't feel inclined to go to sleep either, and so sits cobbling on his stool all night. That's how it is, K., and now you have all my secrets and you can't be surprised any longer at Amalia's indifference to them."

"And what happens to the letter?" asked K.

"The letter?" said Olga. "Oh, some time later when I've plagued Barnabas enough about it, it may be days or weeks later, he picks it up again and goes to deliver it. In such practical matters he's very dependent on me. For I can usually pull myself together after I've recovered from the first impression of what he has told me, but he can't, probably because he knows more. So I always find something or other to to him, such as -

"What are you really aiming at Barnabas?

What kind of career, what ambition are you dreaming of?

Are you thinking of climbing so high that you'll have to leave or to leave me, completely behind you?

Is that what you're aiming at?

How can I help believing so when it's, the only possible explanation why you're so dreadfully discontented with all you've done already?

Only take a look round and see whether any of our neighbours has got on so well as you.

I admit their situation is different from ours and they have no grounds for ambition beyond their daily work, but even without making comparisons it's easy to see that you're all right. Hindrances there may be, doubts and disappointments, but that only means, what we all knew beforehand, that you get nothing without paying for it, that you have to fight for every trivial point. All the more reason for being proud instead of downcast.

And aren't you fighting for us as well?

Doesn't that mean anything to you?

Doesn't that put new strength into you?

And the fact that I'm happy and almost conceited at having such a brother, doesn't that give you any confidence?

It isn't what you've achieved in the Castle that disappoints me, but the little that I'm able to achieve with you. You're allowed into the Castle, you're a regular visitor in the bureaux, you spend whole days in the same room as Klamm, you're an officially recognized messenger, with a claim on an official suit, you're entrusted with important commissions, you have all that to your credit, and then you come down here and instead of embracing me and weeping for joy you seem to lose all heart as soon as you set eyes on me, and you doubt everything, nothing interests you but cobbling, and you leave the letter, the pledge of our future, lying in a corner."

That's how I speak to him, and after I've repeated the same words day after day he picks up the letter at last with a sigh and goes off. Yet probably it's not the effect of what I say that drives him out, but a desire to go to the Castle again, which he dare not do without having delivered his message."

"But you're absolutely right in everything you say," said K., "it's Dazing how well you grasp it all. What an extraordinarily clear mind you have!"

"No,' said Olga, "it takes you in, and perhaps it takes him in too. For what has he really achieved? He's allowed into a bureau, but it doesn't seem to be even a bureau. He speaks to Klamm, but is it Klamm? Isn't it rather someone who's a little like Klamm? A secretary, perhaps, at the most, who resembles Klamm a little and takes pains to increase the resemblance and poses a little in Klamm's sleepy and dreamy style. That side of his nature is the easiest to imitate there are many who try it on, although they have sense enough not to attempt anything more. And a man like Klamm who is so much sought after and so rarely seen is apt to take different shapes in people's imagination. For instance, Klamm has a village secretary here called Momus. You know him, do you? He keeps well in the background too, but I've seen him several times. A stoutly-built young man, isn't he?

And so evidently not in the least like Klamm. And yet you'll find people in the village who swear that Momus is Klamm, he and no other. That's how people work their own confusion. Is there any reason why it should be different in the Castle? Somebody pointed out that particular official to Barnabas as Klamm, and there is actually a resemblance that Barnabas has always questioned. And everything goes to support his doubt. Are we to suppose that Klamm has to squeeze his way among other officials in a common room with a pencil behind his ear? It's wildly improbable. Barnabas often says, somewhat like a child and yet in a child's mood of trustfulness: "The official is really very like Klamm, and if he were sitting in his own office at his own desk with his name on the door I would have no more doubt at all." That's childish, but reasonable.

Of course it would be still more reasonable of Barnabas when he's up there to ask a few people about the truth of things, for judging from his account there are plenty of men standing round. And even if their information were no more reliable than that of the man who pointed out Klamm of his own accord, there would be surely some common ground, some ground for comparison, in the various things they said. That's not my idea, but Barnabas's, yet he doesn't dare to follow it out, he doesn't venture to speak to anybody for fear of offending in ignorance against some unknown rule and so losing his job. You see how uncertain he feels. And this miserable uncertainty of his shows a clearer light on his position there than all his descriptions. How ambiguous and threatening everything must appear to him when he won't even risk opening his mouth to put an innocent question!

When I reflect on that I blame myself for letting him into those unknown rooms, which have such an effect on him that, though he's daring rather than cowardly, he apparently trembles with fright as he stands there."

"Here I think you've touched on the essential point," said K. "That's it! After all you've told me, I believe I can see the matter clearly. Barnabas is too young for this task. Nothing he tells you is to be taken seriously at its face value. Since he's beside himself with fright up there, he's incapable of observing, and when you force him to give an account of what he has seen you get simply confused fabrications. That doesn't surprise me. Fear of the authorities is born in you here, and is further suggested to you all your lives in the most various ways and from every side, and you yourselves help to strengthen it as much as possible. Still, I have no fundamental objection to that. If an authority is good why should it not be feared? Only one shouldn't suddenly send an inexperienced youngster like Barnabas, who has never been farther than this village, into the Castle, and then expect a truthful account of everything from him, and interpret each single word of his as if it were a revelation, and base one's own life's happiness on the interpretation. Nothing could be more mistaken. I admit that I have let him mislead me in exactly the same way and have set hopes upon him and suffered disappointments through him, both based simply on his own words, that is to say, with almost no basis."

Olga was silent.

"It won't be easy for me," went on K., "to talk you out of your confidence in your brother, for I see how you love him and how much you expect from him. But I must do it, if only for the sake of that very love and expectation.

For let me point out that there's always something - I don't know what it is - that hinders you from seeing clearly how much Barnabas has - I'll not say achieved - but has had bestowed on him. He's permitted to go into the bureaux, or if you prefer, into an antechamber, well let it be an antechamber, it has doors that lead on , barriers which can be passed if one has the courage.

To me, for instance, even this antechamber is utterly inaccessible for the present at least. Who it is that Barnabas speaks to there I have no idea, perhaps the clerk is the lowest in the whole staff but even if he is the lowest he can put one in touch with the next man above him, and if he can't do that he can at least give the other's name, and if he can't even do that he can refer to somebody who can give the name. This so-called Klamm may not have the smallest trait in common with the real one, the resemblance may not exist except in the eyes of Barnabas, half, blinded by fear, he may be the meanest of the officials, he may not even be an official at all, but all the same he has work of some kind to perform at the desk, he reads something or other in his great book, he whispers something to the clerk, he thinks something when his eye falls on Barnabas once in a while, and even if that isn't true and he and his acts have no significance whatever he has at least been set there by somebody for some purpose.

All that simply means that something is there, something which Barnabas has the chance of using, something or other at the very least. And that it is Barnabas's own fault if he can't get any further than doubt and anxiety and despair. And that's only on the most unfavourable interpretation of things, which is extremely improbable. For we have the actual letters which I certainly set no great store on, but more than on what Barnabas says. Let them be worthless old letters, fished at random from a pile of other such worthless old letters, at random and with no more discrimination than the love-birds show in the fairs when they pick one's fortune out of a pile; let them be all that, still they have some bearing on my fate. They're evidently meant for me, although perhaps not for my good, and, as the Superintendent and his wife have testified, they arc written in Klamm's own hand, and, again on the Superintendent's evidence, they have a significance which is only private and obscure, it is true, but still great."

"Did the Superintendent say that?" asked Olga.

"Yes, he did," replied K.

"I must tell Barnabas that," said Olga quickly, "that will encourage him greatly."

"But he doesn't need encouragement," said K., "to encourage him amounts to telling him that he's right, that he has only to go on as he is doing now, but that is just the way he will never achieve anything by. If a man has his eyes bound you can encourage him as much as you like to stare through the bandage, but he'll never see anything. He'll be able to see only when the bandage is removed. It's help Barnabas needs, not encouragement. Only think, up there you have all the inextricable complications of a great authority - I imagined that I had an approximate conception of its nature before I came here, but how childish my ideas were! - up there, then, you have the authorities and over against them Barnabas, nobody more, only Barnabas, pathetically alone, where it would be enough honour for him to spend his whole life cowering in a dark and forgotten corner of some bureau."

"Don't imagine, K., that we underestimate the difficulties Barnabas has to face," said Olga, "we have reverence enough for the authorities, you said so yourself."

"But it's a mistaken reverence," said K., "a reverence in the wrong place, the kind of reverence that dishonours its object. Do you call it reverence that leads Barnabas to abuse the privilege of admission to that room by spending his time there doing nothing, or makes him when he comes down again belittle and despise the men before whom he has just been trembling, or allows him because he's depressed or weary to put off delivering letters and fail in executing commissions entrusted to him? That's far from being reverence. But I have a further reproach to make, Olga. I must blame you too, I can't exempt you. Although you fancy you have some reverence for the authorities, you sent Barnabas into the Castle in all his youth and weakness and forlornness, or at least you didn't dissuade him from going."

"This reproach that you make," said Olga, "is one I have made myself from the beginning. Not indeed that I sent Barnabas to the Castle, I didn't send him, he went himself, but I ought to have prevented him by all the means in my power, by force, by craft, by persuasion. I ought to have prevented him, but if I had to decide again this very day, and if I were to feel as keenly as I did then and still do the straits Barnabas is in, and our whole family, and if Barnabas, fully conscious of the responsibility and danger ahead of him, were once more to free himself from me with a smile and set off, I wouldn't hold him back even to-day, in spite of all that has happened in between, and I believe that in my place you would do exactly the same. You don't know the plight we are in, that's why you're unfair to all of us, and especially to Barnabas. At that time we had more hope than now, but even then our hope wasn't great, but our plight was great, and is so still. Hasn't Frieda told you anything about us?"

"Mere hints," said K., "nothing definite, but the very mention of your name exasperates her."

"And has the landlady told you nothing either?"

"No, nothing."

"Nor anybody else?"

"Nobody."

"Of course. How could anybody tell you anything? Everyone knows something about us, either the truth, so far as it is accessible, or at least some exaggerated rumour, mostly invention, and everybody thinks about us more than need be, but nobody will actually speak about it, people are shy of putting these things into words. And they're quite right in that. It's difficult to speak of it even before you, K., and when you've heard it all it's possible - isn't it? - that you'll go away and not want to have anything more to do with us, however little it may seem to concern you. Then we should have lost you, and I confess that now you mean almost more to me than Barnabas's service in the Castle.

But yet - and this argument has been distracting me all the evening - you must be told, otherwise you would have no insight into our situation, and, what would vex me most of all, you would go on being unfair to Barnabas. Complete accord would fail between us, and you could neither help us, nor accept our additional help. But there is still one more question: Do you really want to be told?"

"Why do you ask?" said K., "if it's necessary, I would rather be told, but why do you ask me so particularly?" "Superstition," said Olga. "You'll become involved in our affairs, innocent as you are, almost as innocent as Barnabas."

"Tell me quickly," said K., "I'm not afraid. You're certainly making it much worse than it is with such womanish fussing."

Amaliàs secret "Judge for yourself," said Olga, "I warn you it sounds quite simple, one can't comprehend at first why it should be of any importance. There's a great official in the Castle called Sortini."

"I've heard of him already" said K., "he had something to do with bringing me here."

"I don't think so," said Olga, "Sortini hardly ever comes into the open. Aren't you mistaking him for Sordini, spelt with a "d"?"

"You're quite right," said K., "Sordini it was."

"Yes," said Olga, "Sordini is well known, one of the most industrious of the officials, he's often mentioned. Sortini on the other hand is very retiring and quite unknown to most people. More than three years ago I saw him for the first and last time. It was on the third of July at a celebration given by the Fire Brigade, the Castle too had contributed to it and provided a new fire-engine. Sortini, who was supposed to have some hand in directing the affairs of the Fire Brigade, but perhaps he was only deputizing for someone else - the officials mostly hide behind each other like that, and so it's difficult to discover what any official is actually responsible for - Sortini took part in the ceremony of handing over the fire-engine. There were of course many other people from the Castle, officials and attendants, and true to his character Sortini kept well in the background. He's a small, frail, reflective-looking gentleman, and one thing about him struck all the people who noticed him at all, the way his forehead was furrowed. All the furrows - and there were plenty of them although he's certainly not more than forty - were spread fanwise over his forehead, running towards the root of his nose. I've never seen anything like it.

Well then, we had that celebration. Amalia and I had been excited about it for weeks beforehand, our Sunday clothes had been done up for the occasion and were partly new, Amalia's dress was specially fine, a white blouse foaming high in front with one row of lace after the other, our mother had taken every bit of her lace for it. I was jealous, and cried half the night before the celebration. Only when the Bridge Inn landlady came to see us in the morning-"

"The Bridge Inn landlady?" asked K.

"Yes," said Olga, "she was a great friend of ours, well, she came and had to admit that Amalia was the finer, so to console me she lent me her own necklace of Bohemian garnets.

When we were ready to go and Amalia was standing beside me and we were all admiring her, my father said: "To-day, mark my words, Amalia will find a husband". Then, I don't know why, I took my necklace, my great pride, and hung it round Amalia's neck, and wasn't jealous any longer. I bowed before her triumph and I felt that everyone must bow before her, perhaps what amazed us so much was the difference in her appearance, for she wasn't really beautiful, but her sombre glance, and it has kept the same quality since that day, was high over our heads and involuntarily one had almost literally to bow before her.

Everybody remarked on it, even Lasemann and his wife who came to fetch us."

"Lasemann?" asked K.

"Yes, Lasemann," said Olga, "we were in high esteem, and the celebration couldn't well have begun without us, for my father was the third in command of the Fire Brigade."

"Was your father still so active?" asked K.

"Father?" returned Olga, as if she did not quite comprehend, "three years ago he was still relatively a young man, for instance, when a fire broke out at the Herrenhof he carried an official, Galater, who is a heavy man, out of the house on his back at a run.

I was there myself, there was no real danger, it was only some dry wood near a stove which had begun to smoke, but Galater was terrified and cried for help out of the window, and the Fire Brigade turned out, and father had to carry him out although the fire was already extinguished. Of course Galater finds it difficult to move and has to be careful in circumstances like that. I'm telling you this only on father's account. Not much more than three years have passed since then, and look at him now."

Only then did K. become aware that Amalia was again in the room, but she was a long way off at the table where her parents sat, she was feeding her mother who could not move her rheumaticky arms, and admonishing her father meanwhile to wait in patience for a little, it would soon be his turn. But her admonition was in vain, for her father, greedily desiring his soup, overcame his weakness and tried to drink it first out of the spoon and then out of the bowl, and grumbled angrily when neither attempt succeeded. The spoon was empty long before he got it to his lips, and his mouth never reached the soup, for his drooping moustache dipped into it and scattered it everywhere except into his mouth.

"And have three years done that to him?" asked K., yet he could not summon up any sympathy for the old people, and for that whole corner with the table in it he felt only repulsion.

"Three years," replied Olga slowly, "or, more precisely, a few hours at that celebration. The celebration was held on a the village, at the brook. There was already a large crowd there when we arrived, many people had come in from eighbouring villages, and the noise was bewildering. Of course my father took us first to look at the fire-engine, he laughed with delight when he saw it, the new fire-engine made him happy. He began to examine it and explain it to us, he wouldn't hear of any opposition or holding back, but made every one of us stoop and almost crawl under the engine if there was something there he had to show us, and he smacked Barnabas for refusing. Only Amalia paid no attention to the engine, she stood upright beside it in her fine clothes and nobody dared to say a word to her, I ran up to her sometimes and took her arm, but she said nothing.

Even to-day I cannot explain how we came to stand for so long in front of the fire-engine without noticing Sortini until the very moment my father turned away, for he had obviously been leaning on a wheel behind the fire-engine all the time. Of course there was a terrific racket all round us, not only the usual kind of noise, for the Castle had presented the Fire Brigade with some trumpets as well as the engine, extraordinary instruments on which with the smallest effort - a child could do it - one could produce the wildest blasts. To hear them was enough to make one think the Turks were there, and one could not get accustomed to them, every fresh blast made one jump.

And because the trumpets were new everybody wanted to try them, and because it was a celebration, everybody was allowed to try. Right at our ears, perhaps Amalia had attracted them, were some of these trumpet blowers. It was difficult to keep one's wits about one, and obeying fadier and attending to the fire-engine was the utmost we were capable of, and so it was that Sortini escaped our notice for such a long time, and besides we had no idea who he was.

"There is Sortini," Lasemann whispered at last to my father - I was beside him - and father, greatly excited, made a deep bow, and signed to us to do the same. Without having met till now father had always honoured Sortini as an authority in Fire Brigade matters, and had often spoken of him at home, so it was a very astonishing and important matter for us actually to see Sortini with our own eyes. Sortini, however, paid no attention to us, and in that he wasn't peculiar, for most of the officials hold themselves aloof in public besides he was tired, only his official duty kept him there. It', not the worst officials who find duties like that particularly try. And anyhow there were other officials and attendants mingling with the people. But he stayed by the fire-engine and discouraged by his silence all those who tried to approach him with some request or piece of flattery.

So it happened that he didn't notice us until long after we had noticed him. Only as we bowed respectfully and father was making apologies for us did he look our way and scan us one after another wearily, as if sighing to find that there was still another and another to look at, until he let his eyes rest on Amalia, to whom he had to look up, for she was much taller than he. At the sight of her he started and leapt over the shaft to get nearer to her, we misunderstood him at first and began to approach him, father leading the way, but he held us off with uplifted hand and then waved us away. That was all. We teased Amalia a lot about having really found a husband, and in our ignorance we were very merry the whole of that afternoon. But Amalia was more silent than usual.

"She's fallen head over ears in love with Sortini," said Brunswick, who is always rather vulgar and has no comprehension of natures like Amalia's. Yet this time we were inclined to think that he was right, we were quite mad all that day, and all of us, even Amalia, were as if stupefied by the sweet Castle wine when we came home about midnight."

"And Sortini?" asked K.

"Yes, Sortini," said Olga, "I saw him several times during the afternoon as I passed by, he was sitting on the engine shaft with his arms folded, and he stayed there till the Castle carriage came to fetch him. He didn't even go over to watch the fire-drill at which father, in the very hope that Sortini was watching, distinguished himself beyond all the other men of his age."

"And did you hear nothing more from him?" asked K. "You seem to have a great regard for Sortini."

"Oh, yes, regard," said Olga, "oh, yes, and hear from him we certainly did. Next morning we were roused from our heavy sleep by a scream from Amalia. The others rolled back into their beds again, but I was completely awake and ran to her. She was standing by the window holding a letter in her hand which had just been given her from the window by a man who was still waiting for an answer. The letter was short, and Amalia had already read it, add held it in her drooping hand. How I always loved her when she was tired like that I I knelt down beside her and read the letter. Hardly had I finished it when Amalia after a brief glance at me took it back, but she couldn't bring herself to read it again, and tearing it in pieces she threw the fragments in the face of the man outside and shut the window. That was the morning which decided our fate. I say "decided", but every minute of the previous afternoon was just as decisive."

"And what was in the letter?" asked K.

"Yes, I haven't told you that yet," said Olga, "the letter was from Sortini addressed to the girl with the garnet necklace. I can't repeat the contents. It was a summons to come to him at the Herrenhof, and to come at once, for in half an hour he was due to leave. The letter was couched in the vilest language, such as I have never heard, and I could only half guess its meaning from the context. Anyone who didn't know Amalia and saw this letter must have considered a girl who could be written to like that as dishonoured, even if she had never had a finger laid on her. And it wasn't a love letter, there wasn't a tender word in it, on the contrary Sortini was obviously enraged because the sight of Amalia had disturbed him and distracted him in his work.

Later on we pieced it all together for ourselves. Evidently Sortini had intended to go straight to the Castle that evening, but on Amalia's account had stayed in the village instead, and in the morning, being very angry because even overnight he hadn't succeeded in forgetting her, had written the letter. One couldn't but be furious on first reading a letter like that, even the most cold-blooded person might have been, but though with anybody else fear at its threatening tone would soon have got the upper hand, Amalia only felt anger, fear she doesn't know, neither for herself nor for others. And while I crept into bed again repeating to myself the closing sentence, which broke off in the middle, "See that you come, at once, or else - I" Amalia remained on the windowscat looking out, as if she were expecting further messengers and were prepared to treat them all as she had done the first."

"So that's what the officials are like," said K. reluctantly, "that's the kind of type one finds among them. What did your father do? I hope he protested energetically in the proper quarter, if For didn't prefer a shorter and quicker way of doing it at the Herrenhof. The worst thing about the story isn't the insult to Amalia, that could easily have been made good, I don't know why you lay such exaggerated stress upon it. Why should such a letter from Sortini shame Amalia for ever? - which is what one would gather from your story, but that's a sheer impossibility, it would have been easy to make up for it to Amalia, and in a few days the whole thing might have blown over, it was himself that Sortini shamed, and not Amalia.

It's Sortini that horrifies me, the possibility of such an abuse of power. The very thing that failed this one time because it came naked and undisguised and found an effective opponent in Amalia, might very well succeed completely on a thousand other occasions in circumstances just a little less favourable, and might defy detection even by its victim."

"Hush," said Olga, "Amalia's looking this way."

Amalia had finished giving food to her parents and was now busy taking off her mother's clothes. She had just undone the skirt, hung her mother's arms round her neck, lifted her a little, while she drew the skirt off, and now gently set her down again. Her father, still affronted because his wife was being attended to first, which obviously only happened because she was even more helpless than he, was attempting to undress himself.

Perhaps, too, it was a reproach to his daughter for her imagined slowness. Yet although he began with the easiest and least necessary thing, the removal of the enormous slippers in which his feet were loosely stuck, he could not get them pulled off at all, and wheezing hoarsely was forced to give up trying, and leaned back stiffly in his chair again.

"But you don't realize the really decisive thing," said Olga, "you may be right in all you say, but the decisive thing was Amalia's not going to the Herrenhof. Her treatment of the messenger might have been excused, it could have been passed over. But it was because she didn't go that the curse was laid upon our family, and that turned her treatment of the messenger into an unpardonable offence, yes, it was even brought forward openly later as the chief offence."

"What!" cried K. at once, lowering his voice again, as Olga raised her hands imploringly, "do you, her sister, actually say that Amalia should have run to the Herrenhof after Sortini?"

"No'" said Olga, "Heaven preserve me from such a suspicion, how can you believe that? I don't know anybody who's so right as Amalia in everything she does. If she had gone to the Herrenhof I should of course have upheld her just the same. But her not going was heroic. As for me, I confess it frankly, had I received a letter like that I should have gone. I shouldn't have been able to endure the fear of what might happen, only Amalia could have done that. For there were many ways of getting round it. Another girl, for instance, might have decked herself up and wasted some time in doing it and then gone to the Herrenhof only to find that Sortini had left, perhaps to find that he had left immediately after sending the messenger, which is very probable, for the moods of the gentlemen are fleeting. But Amalia neither did that nor anything else, she was too deeply insulted, and answered without reserve. If she had only made some pretence of compliance, if she had but crossed the threshold of the Herrenhof at the right moment, our punishment could have been turned aside, we have very clever advocates here who can make a great deal out of a mere nothing, but in this case they hadn't even the mere nothing to go on, there was, on the contrary, the disrespect to Sortini's letter and the insult to his messenger."

"But what is all this about punishment and advocates?" said K. "Surely Amalia couldn't be accused or punished because of Sortini's criminal proceedings?"

"Yes," said Olga, "she could, not in a regular suit at law, of course. And she wasn't punished directly, but she was punished all right in other ways, she and the whole family, and how heavy the punishment has been you are surely beginning to understand. In your opinion it's unjust and monstrous, but you're the only one in the village of that opinion, it's an opinion favourable to us, and ought to comfort us, and would do that if it weren't so obviously based on error. I can easily prove that, and you must forgive me if I mention Frieda by the way, but between Frieda and Klamm, leaving aside the final outcome of the two affairs, the first preliminaries were much the same as between Amalia and Sortini, and yet, although that might have shocked you at the beginning you accept it now as quite natural. And that's not merely because you're accustomed to it, custom alone couldn't blunt one's plain judgement, it's simply that you've freed yourself from prejudice."

"No, Olga," said K., "I don't see why you drag in Frieda, her case wasn't the same, don't confuse two such different things, and now go on with your story."

"Please don't be offended," said Olga, "if I persist in the comparison, it's a lingering trace of prejudice on your part, even in regard to Frieda that makes you feel you must defend her from a comparison. She's not to be defended, but only to be praised.

In comparing the two cases, I don't say they're exactly alike, they stand in the same relation as black to white, and the white is Frieda. The worst thing one can do to Frieda is to laugh at her, as I did in the bar very rudely - and I was sorry for it later - but even if one laughs it's out of envy or malice, at any rate one can laugh. On the other hand, unless one is related to her by blood, one can only despise Amalia. Therefore the two cases are quite different, as you say, but yet they are alike."

"They're not at all alike," said K., and he shook his head stubbornly, "leave Frieda out of it, Frieda got no such fine letter as that of Sortini's, and Frieda was really in love with Klamm, and, if you doubt that, you need only ask her, she loves him still."

"But is that really a difference?" asked Olga. "Do you imagine Klamm couldn't have written to Frieda in the same tone? That's what the gentlemen are like when they rise from their desks, they feel out of place in the ordinary world and in their distraction they say the most beastly things, not all of them, but many of them. The letter to Amalia may have been the thought of a moment, thrown on the paper in complete disregard for the meaning to be taken out of it. What do we know of the thoughts of these gentlemen?

Haven't you heard of, or heard yourself, the tone in which Klamm spoke to Frieda? Klamm's notorious for his rudeness, he can apparently sit dumb for hours and then suddenly bring out something so brutal that it makes one shiver. Nothing of that kind is known of Sortini, but then very little is known of him. All that's really known about him is that his name is like Sordini's. If it weren't for that resemblance between the two names problably he wouldn't be known at all. Even as the Fire Brigade uthority apparently he's confused with Sordini, who is the real authority, and who exploits the resemblance in name to push things on to Sortini's shoulders, especially any duties falling on him as a deputy, so that he can be left undisturbed to his work. When a man so unused to society as Sortini suddenly felt himself in love with a village girl, he'll naturally take it quite differently from, say, the joiner's apprentice next door.

And one must remember, too, that between an official and a village cobbler's daughter there's a great gulf fixed which has to be somehow bridged over, and Sortini tried to do it in that way, where someone else might have acted differently. Of course we're all supposed to belong to the Castle, and there's supposed to be no gulf between us, and nothing to be bridged over, and that may be true enough on ordinary occasions, but we've had grim evidence that it's not true when anything really important crops up.

At any rate, all that should make Sortini's methods more comprehensible to you, and less monstrous. Compared with Klamm's they're comparatively reasonable, and even for those intimately affected by them much more endurable. When Klamm writes a loving letter it's much more exasperating than the most brutal letter of Sortini's. Don't mistake me, I'm not venturing to criticize Klamm, I'm only comparing the two, because you're shutting your eyes to the comparison. Klamm's a kind of tyrant over women, he orders first one and then another to come to him, puts up with none of them for long, and orders them to go just as he ordered them to come. Oh, Klamm wouldn't even give himself the trouble of writing a letter first. And in comparison with that is it so monstrous that Sortini, who's so retiring, and whose relations with women are at least unknown, should condescend for once to write in his beautiful official hand a letter, however abominable? And if there's no distinction here in Klamm's favour, but the reverse, how can Frieda's love for him establish one? The relation existing between the women and the officials, believe me, is very difficult, Or rather very easy to determine. Love always enters into it. There's no such thing as an official's unhappy love affair. So in respect it's no praise to say of a girl - I'm referring to many others besides Frieda - that she gave herself to an official only out of love. She loved him and gave herself to him, that was all there's nothing praiseworthy in that. But you'll object that Amalia didn't love Sortini. Well, perhaps she didn't love him, but then after all perhaps she did love him, who can decide?

Not even she herself. How can she fancy she didn't love him when she rejected him so violently, as no official has ever been rejected? Barnabas says that even yet she sometimes trembles with the violence of the effort of closing the window three years ago.

That is true, and therefore one can't ask her anything.

She has finished with Sortini, and that's all she knows. Whether she loves him or not she does not know. But we do know that women can't help loving the officials once they give them any encouragement, yes, they even love them beforehand, let them deny it as much as they like, and Sortini not only gave Amalia encouragement, but leapt over the shaft when he saw her. Although his legs were stiff from sitting at desks he leapt right over the shaft. But Amalia's an exception, you will say. Yes, that she is, that she has proved in refusing to go to Sortini, that's exception enough, but if in addition she weren't in love with Sortini, she would be too exceptional for plain human understanding.

On that afternoon, I grant you, we were smitten with blindness, but the fact that in spite of our mental confusion we thought we noticed signs of Amalia's being in love, showed at least some remnants of sense. But when all that's taken into account, what difference is left between Frieda and Amalia? One thing only, that Frieda did what Amalia refused to do."

"Maybe," said K., "but for me the main difference is that I'm engaged to Frieda, and only interested in Amalia because she's a sister of Barnabas's, the Castle messenger, and because her destiny may be bound up with his duties. If she had suffered such a crying injustice at the hands of an official as your tale seemed to infer at the beginning, I should have taken the matter up seriously, but more from a sense of public duty than from any personal sympathy with Amalia. But what you say has changed the aspect of the situation for me in a way I don't quite understand, but am prepared to accept, since it's you who tell me, and therefore I want to drop the whole affair.

I'm no member of the Fire Brigade, Sortini means nothing to me. But Frieda means something to me, I have trusted her completely and want to go on trusting her, and it surprises me that you go out of your way, while discussing Amalia, to attack Frieda and try to shake my confidence in her. I'm not assuming that you're doing it with deliberate intent, far less with malicious intent, for in that case I should have left long ago.

You're not doing it deliberately, you're betrayed into it by circumstances, impelled by your love for Amalia you want to exalt her above all other women, and since you can't find enough virtue in Amalia herself you help yourself out by belittling the others.

Amalia's act was remarkable enough, but the more you say about it the less clearly can it be decided whether it was noble or petty, clever or foolish, heroic or cowardly. Amalia keeps her motives locked in her own bosom and no one will ever get at them. Frieda, on the other hand, has done nothing at all remarkable, she has only followed her own heart, for anyone who looks at her actions with goodwill that is clear, it can be substantiated, it leaves no room for slander.

However, I don't want either to belittle Amalia or to defend Frieda, all I want is to let you see what my relation is to Frieda, and that every attack on Frieda is an attack on myself. I came here of my own accord, and of my own accord I have settled here, but all that has happened to me since I came, and, above all, any prospects I may have - dark as they are, they still exist - I owe entirely to Frieda, and you can't argue that away.

True, I was engaged to come here as a Land Surveyor, yet that was only a pretext, they were playing with me, I was driven out of everybody's house, they're playing with me still to-day. But how much more complicated die game is now that I have, so to speak, a larger circumference - which means something, it may not be much - yet I have already a home, a position and real work to do, I have a promised wife who takes her share of my professional duties when I have other business, I'm going to her and become a member of the community, and besides official connexion I have also a personal connexion with Klamm, although as yet I haven't been able to make use of it. That's surely quite a lot?

And when I come to you, why do you me welcome? Why do you confide the history of your family to me? Why do you hope that I might possibly help you? Certainly not because I'm 'the Land Surveyor whom Lasemann and Brunswick, for instance, turned out of their house a week ago, but because I'm a man with some power at my back. But that I owe to Frieda, to Frieda who is so modest that if you were to ask her about it, she wouldn't know it existed. And so, considering all this, it seems that Frieda in her innocence has achieved more than Amalia in all her pride, for may I say that I have the impression that you're seeking help for Amalia. And from whom? In the last resort from no one else but Frieda."

"Did I really speak so abominably of Frieda?" asked Olga, "I certainly didn't mean to, and I don't think I did, still, it's possible. We're in a bad way, our whole world is in ruins, and once we begin to complain we're, carried farther than we realize. You're quite right, there's a big difference now between us and Frieda, and it's a good thing to emphasize it once in a while. Three years ago we were respectable girls and Frieda an outcast, a servant in the Bridge Inn, we used to walk past her without looking at her, I admit we were too arrogant, but that's how we were brought up. But that evening in the Herrenhof probably enlightened you about our respective positions to-day. Frieda with the whip in her hand, and I among the crowd of servants. But it's worse even than that Frieda may despise us, her position entitles her to do so, actual circumstances compel it. But who is there who doesn't despise us? Whoever decides to despise us will find himself in good company. Do you know Frieda's successor? Pepi, she's called. I met her for the first time the night before last, she used to be a chambermaid. She certainly outdoes Frieda in her contempt for me. She saw me through the window as I was coming for beer, and ran to the door and locked it, so that I had to beg and pray for a long time and promise her the ribbon from my hair before she would let me in. But when I gave it to her she threw it into a corner. Well, I can't help it if she despises me, I'm partly dependent on her goodwill, and she's the barmaid in the Herrenhof. Only for the time being, it's true, for she certainly hasn't the qualities needed for permanent employment there. One only has to overhear how the landlord speaks to Pepi and compare it with his tone to Frieda. But that doesn't hinder Pepi from despising even Amalia, Amalia, whose glance alone would be enough to drive pepi with all her plaits and ribbons out of the room much faster than her own fat legs would ever carry her. I had to listen again yesterday to her infuriating slanders against Amalia until the customers took my part at last, although only in the kind of way you have seen already."

"How touchy you are," said K. "I only put Frieda in her right place, but I had no intention of belittling you, as you seem to think. Your family has a special interest for me, I have never denied it. But how this interest could give me cause for despising you I can't understand."

"Oh, and," said Olga, "I'm afraid that even you will understand it yet. Can't you even understand that Amalia's behaviour to Sortini was the original cause of our being despised?"

"That would be strange indeed," said K., "one might admire or condemn Amalia for such an action, but despise her? And even if she is despised for some reason I can't comprehend, why should the contempt be extended to you others, her innocent family? For Pepi to despise you, for instance, is a piece of impudence, and I'll let her know it if ever I'm in the Herrenhof again."

"If you set out, K.," said Olga, "to convert all the people who despise us you'll have your work cut out for you, for it's all engineered from the Castle. I can still remember every detail of that day following the morning I spoke of. Brunswick, who was our assistant then, had arrived as usual, taken his share of the work and gone home, and we were sitting at breakfast, all of us, even Amalia and myself, very gay, father kept on talking about the celebration and telling us his plans in connection with the Fire Brigade, for you must know that the Castle has its own Fire Brigade which had sent a deputation to the celebration, and there had been much discussion about it, the gentlemen present, from the Castle had seen that performance of our Fire Brigade, had expressed great approval, and compared the Castle Brigade unfavourably with ours, so there had been some talk of reorganizing the Castle Brigade with the help of instructors from the village. There were several possible candidates, but father had hopes that he would be chosen. That was what he was discussing, and in his usual delightful way had sprawled over the table until he embraced half of it in his arms, and as he gazed through the open window at the sky his face was young and shining with hope, and that was the last time I was to see it like that. Then Amalia, with a calm conviction we had never noticed in her before, said that too much trust shouldn't be placed in what the gentlemen said, they were in the habit of saying pleasant things on such occasions, but it meant little or nothing, the words were hardly out of their mouths before they were forgotten, only of course people were always ready to be taken in again next time. Mother forbade her to say things like that, but father only laughed at her precocious air of wisdom, then he gave a start, and seemed to be looking round for something he had only just missed - but there was nothing missing - and said that Brunswick had told him some story of a messenger and a torn-up letter, did we know anything of it, who was concerned in it, and what it was all about? We kept silent. Barnabas, who was as youthful then as a spring lamb, said something particularly silly or cheeky, the subject was changed, and the whole affair forgotten."

Amaliàs Punishment

"But not long afterwards we were overwhelmed with questions from all sides about the story of the letter, we were visited by friends and enemies, acquaintances and complete strangers. Not one of them stayed for any length of time, and our best friends were the quickest to go. Lasemann, usually so slow and dignified, came in hastily as if only to see the size of the room, one look round it and he was gone, it was like a horrible kind of children's game when he fled, and father, shaking himself free from some other people, ran after him to the very door and then gave it up. Brunswick came and gave notice, he said quite honestly that he wanted to set up in business for himself, a shrewd man, he knew how to seize the right moment. Customers came and hunted round father's store-room for the boots they had left to be repaired, at first father tried to persuade them to change their minds - and we all backed him up as much as we could - but later he gave it up, and without saying a word helped them to find their belongings, line after line in the order-book was cancelled, the pieces of leather people had left with us were handed back. All debts owing us were paid, everything went smoothly without the slightest trouble, they asked for nothing better than to break every connexion with us quickly and completely, even if they lost by it. That counted for nothing. And finally, as we might have foreseen, Seemann appeared, the Captain of the Fire Brigade. I can still see the scene before me, Seemann, tall and stout, but with a slight stoop from weakness in the lungs, a serious man who never could laugh, standing in front of my father whom he admired, whom he had promised in confidence to make a deputy Captain, and to whom he had now to say that the Brigade required his services no longer and asked for the return of his diploma.

All the people who happened to be in our house left their business for the moment and crowded round the two men, Seemann found it difficult to speak and only kept on tapping father on the shoulder, as if he were trying to tap out of him the words he ought to say and couldn't find. And he kept on laughing, probably to cheer himself a little and everybody else, but since he's incapable of laughing and no one had ever heard him laugh, it didn't occur to anybody that he was really laughing. But father was too tired and desperate after the day he'd had to help anybody out, he looked even too tired to grasp what was happening. We were all in despair, too, but being young didn't believe in the completeness of our ruin, and kept on expecting that someone in the long procession of visitors would arrive and put a stop to it all and make everything swing the other way again. In our foolishness we thought that Seemann was that very man. We were all keyed up waiting for his laughter to stop, and for the decisive statement to come out at last.

What could he be laughing at, if not at the stupid injustice of what had happened to us?

Oh, Captain, Captain, tell them now at last, we thought, and pressed close to him, but that only made him recoil from us in the most curious way.

At length, however, he did begin to speak, in response not to our secret wishes, but to the encouraging or angry cries of the crowd. Yet still we had hopes. He began with great praise for our father. Called him an ornament to the Brigade, an inimitable model to Posterity, an indispensable member whose removal must reduce the Brigade almost to ruin.

That was all very fine, had he stopped there. But he went on to say that since in spite of that the Brigade had decided, only as a temporary measure of course, to ask for his resignation, they would all understand the seriousness of the reason which forced the Brigade to do so. Perhaps if father had not distinguished himself so much at the celebration of the previous day it would not have been necessary to go so far, but his very superiority had drawn official attention to the Brigade, and brought it into such prominence that the spotlessness of its reputation was more than ever a matter of honour to it. And now that a messenger had been insulted, the Brigade couldn't help itself, and he, Seemann, found himself in the difficult position of having to convey its decision. He hoped that father would not make it any more difficult for him. Seemann was glad to have got it out. He was so pleased with himself that he even forgot his exaggerated tact, and pointed to the diploma hanging on the wall and made a sign with his finger. Father nodded and went to fetch it, but his hands trembled so much that he couldn't get it off the hook. I climbed on a chair and helped him. From that moment he was done for, he didn't even take the diploma out of its frame, but handed the whole thing over to Seemann. Then he sat down in a corner and neither moved nor spoke to anybody, and we had to attend to the last people there by ourselves as well as we could."

"And where do you see in all this the influence of the Castle?" asked K. "So far it doesn't seem to have come in. What you've told me about is simply the ordinary senseless fear of the people, malicious pleasure in hurting a neighbour, specious friendship, things that can be found anywhere, and, I must say, on the part of your father - at least, so it seems to me - a certain pettiness, for what was the diploma? Merely a testimonial to his abilities, these themselves weren't taken from him, if they made him indispensable so much the better, and the one way he could have made things difficult for the Captain would have been by flinging the diploma at his feet before he had said two words. But the significant thing to me is that you haven't mentioned Amalia at all.

Amalia, who was to blame for everything, apparently stood quietly in the background and watched the whole house collapse."

"No," said Olga, "nobody ought to be blamed, nobody could have done anything else, all that was already due to the influence of the castle."

"Influence of the Castle," repeated Amalia, who had hopped in unnoticed from the courtyard. "The old people had been sitting with Castle gossip you're at? Still sitting with their heads together? And yet you wanted to go away immediately you came, K., and it's nearly ten now. Are you really interested in that kind of gossip? There are people in the village who live on it, they stick their heads together just like you two and entertain each other by the hour. But I didn't think you were one of them."

"On the contrary," said K., "that's exactly what I am, and moreover people who don't care for such gossip and leave it all to others don't interest me particularly."

"Indeed," said Amalia, "well, there are many different kinds of interest, you know. I heard once of a young man who thought of nothing but the Castle day and night, he neglected everything else and people feared for his reason, his mind was so wholly absorbed by the Castle. It turned out at length, however, that it wasn't really the Castle he was thinking of, but the daughter of a charwoman in the offices up there, so he got the girl and was all right again."

"I think I would like that man," said K.

"As for your liking the man, I doubt it," said Amalia, "it's probably his wife you would like. Well, don't let me disturb you, I've got to go to bed, and I must put out the light for the old folks' sake. They're sound asleep now, but they don't really sleep for more than an hour, and after that the smallest glimmer disturbs them. Goodnight."

And actually the light went out at once, and Amalia bedded herself somewhere on the floor near her parents.

"Who's the young man she mentioned?" asked K.

"I don't know," said Olga, "perhaps Brunswick although it doesn't fit him exactly, but it might have been somebody else. It's not easy to follow her, for often one can't tell whether she's speaking ironically or in earnest. Mostly she's in earnest but sounds ironical."

"Never mind explaining," said K. "How have you come to be so dependent on her? Were things like that before the catastrophe? Or did it happen later? And do you never feel that you want to be independent of her? And is there any sense in your dependence? She's the youngest, and should give way to you. Innocently or not, she was the person who brought ruin on the family. And instead of begging your pardon for it every day she carries her head higher than anybody else, bother herself about nothing except what she chooses to do for your parents, nothing would induce her to become acquainted with your affairs, to use her own expression, and then if she docs speak to you at all she's mostly in earnest, but sounds ironical. Does she queen it over you on account of her beauty, which you've mentioned more than once? Well, you're all three very like each other, but Amalia's distinguishing mark is hardly a recommendation, and repelled me the first time I saw it, I mean her cold hard eye. And although she's the youngest she doesn't look it, she has the ageless look of women who seem not to grow any older, but seem never to have been young either. You see her every day, you don't notice the hardness of her face.

That's why, on reflection, I can't take Sortini's passion for her very seriously, perhaps he sent the letter simply to punish her, but not to summon her."

"I won't argue about Sortini," said Olga, "for the Castle gentlemen everything is possible, let a girl be as pretty or as ugly as you like. But in all the rest you're utterly mistaken so far as Amalia is concerned. I have no particular motive for winning you over to Amalia's side, and if I try to do it it's only for your own sake. Amalia in some way or other was the cause of our misfortunes, that's true, but not even my father, who was the hardest hit, and who was never very sparing of his tongue, particularly at home, not even my father has ever said a word of reproach to Amalia even in our very worst times. Not because he approved of her action, he was an admirer of Sortini, and how could he have approved of it? He couldn't understand it even remotely, for Sortini he would have been glad to sacrifice himself and all that was his, although hardly io the way things actually happened, as an outcome apparendy of Sortini's anger. I say apparently, for we never heard another word from Sortini. If he was reticent before then, from that day on he might as well have been dead. Now you should have seen Amalia at that time. We all knew that no definite punishment would be visited on us. We were only

shunned. By the village and by the Castle.

But while we couldn't help noticing the ostracism of the village, the Castle gave us no sign. Of course we heard of The Land Surveyor from the Castle in the past, so how could you notice the reverse? This blankness was the worst of all. It as far worse than the withdrawal of the people down here, for they hadn't deserted us out of conviction, perhaps they had nothing very serious against us, they didn't despise us then as you do to-day, they only did it out of fear, and were waiting to see what would happen next. And we weren't afraid of being, stranded, for all our debtors had paid us, the settling-up had keen entirely in our favour, and any provisions we didn't have were sent us secretly by relations, it was easy enough for us, it was harvest time - though we had no fields of pur own and nobody would take us on as workers, so that for the first time in our lives we were condemned to go nearly idle. So there we sat all together with the windows shut in the heats of July and August. Nothing happened. No invitations, no news, no callers, nothing."

"Well," said K., "since nothing happened and you had no definite punishment hanging over you, what was there to be afraid of? What people you are!"

"How am I to explain it?" said Olga. "We weren't afraid of anything in the future, we were suffering under the immediate present, we were actually enduring our punishment. The others in the village were only waiting for us to come to them, for father to open his workshop again, for Amalia, who could sew the most beautiful clothes, fit for the best families, to come asking for orders again, they were all sorry to have had to act as they did. When a respected family is suddenly cut out of village life it means a loss for everybody, so when they broke with us they thought they were only doing their duty, in their place we should have done just the same. They didn't know very clearly what was the matter, except that the messenger had returned to the Herrenhof with a handful of torn paper. Frieda had seen him go out and come back, had exchanged a few words with him, and then spread what she had learned everywhere. But not in the least from enmity to us, simply from a sense of duty which anybody would have felt in the same circumstances. And, as I've said, a happy ending to the whole story would have pleased everybody else. If we had suddenly put in an appearance with the news that everything was that it had only been a misunderstanding, say, which was now quite cleared up, or that there had been actually cause for offence which had now been made good, or else - and even this would have satisfied people - that through our fluency in the Castle the affair had been dropped, we should certainly have been received again with open arms, there would have been kissings and congratulations, I have seen that kind of thing happen to others once or twice already. And it wouldn't have been necessary to say even as much as that. If we had only come out in the open and shown ourselves, if we had picked up our old connections without letting fall a single word about the affair of the letter, it would have been enough, they would all have been glad to avoid mentioning the matter. It was the painfulness of the subject as much as their fear that made them draw away from us, simply to avoid hearing about it or speaking about it or thinking about it or being affected by it in any way.

When Frieda gave it away it wasn't out of mischief but as a warning, to let the parish know that something had happened which everybody should be careful to keep clear of. It wasn't our family that was taboo, it was the affair, and our family only in so far as we were mixed up in the affair. So if we had quietly come forward again and let bygones be bygones and shown by our behaviour that the incident was closed, no matter in what way, and reassured public opinion that it was never likely to be mentioned again, whatever its nature had been, everything would have been made all right in that way, too, we should have found friends on all sides as before, and even if we hadn't completely forgotten what had happened people would have understood and helped us to forget it completely.

Instead of that we sat in the house.

I don't know what we were expecting, probably some decision from Amalia, for on that morning she had taken the lead in the family and she still maintained it. Without any particular contriving or commanding or imploring, almost by her silence alone. We others, of course, had plenty to discuss, there was a steady whispering from morning till evening, sometimes father would call me to him in sudden panic and I would have to spend half the night on the edge of his bed. Or we would often creep away together, I and Barnabas, who did nothing about it all at first, and was always in a fever for some explanation, always the same, for he realized well enough that the carefree years that others of his age looked forward to were now out of the question for him, so we used to put our heads together, K., just like we two now, and forget that it was night, and that morning had come again.

Our mother was the feeblest of us all, probably because she had not only endured our common sorrows but the private sorrow of each of us, and so we were horrified to see changes in her which, as we guessed, lay in wait for all of us. Her favourite seat was the corner of the sofa, it's long since we parted with it, it stands now in Brunswick's big living-room, well, there she sat and - we couldn't tell exactly what was wrong - used to doze or carry on long conversations with herself, we guessed it from the moving of her lips. It was so natural for us to be always discussing the letter, to be always turning it over in all its known details and unknown potentialities, and to be always outdoing each other in thinking out plans for restoring our fortunes. It was natural and unavoidable, but not good, we only plunged deeper and deeper into what we wanted to escape from. And what good were these inspirations, however brilliant? None of them could be acted on without Amalia, they were all tentative, and quite useless because they stopped short of Amalia, and even if they had been put to Amalia they would have met with nothing but silence.

Well, I'm glad to say I understand Amalia better now than I did then. She had more to endure than all of us, it's incomprehensible how she managed to endure it and still survive. Mother, perhaps, had to endure all our troubles, but that was because they came pouring in on her. And she didn't hold out for long. No one could say that she's holding out against them to-day, and even at that time her mind was beginning to go. But Amalia not only suffered, she had the understanding to see her suffering clearly, we saw only the effects, but she knew the cause, we hoped for some small relief or other, she knew that everything was decided, we had to whisper, she had only to be silent. She stood face to face with the truth and went on living and endured her life then as now.

In all our straits we were better off than she. Of course, we had to leave our house.

Brunswick toot it on, and we were given this cottage, we brought our things over in several journeys with a handcart, Barnabas and I pulling father and Amalia pushing behind, mother was already sitting here on a chest, for we had brought her here first, and she whimpered softly all the time. Yet I remember that even during those toilsome journeys - they were painful, too, for we often met harvest wagons, and the people became silent when they saw us and turned away their faces - even during those journeys Barnabas and I couldn't stop discussing our troubles and our plans, so that we often stood stock still in the middle of pulling and had to be roused by father's "Hallo" from behind.

But all our talking made no difference to our life after the removal, except that we began gradually to feel the pinch of poverty as well. Our relatives stopped sending us things, our money was almost done, and that was the time when people first began to despise us in the way you can see now. They saw that we hadn't the strength to shake ourselves clear of the scandal, and they were irritated. They didn't underestimate our difficulties, although they didn't know exactly what they were, and they knew that probably they wouldn't have stood up to them any better themselves, but that made it only all the more needful to keep clear of us - if we had triumphed they would have honoured us correspondingly, but since we failed they turned what had only been a temporary measure into a final resolve, and cut us off from the community for ever. We were no longer spoken of as ordinary human beings, our very name was never mentioned, if they had to refer to us they called us Barnabas's people, for he was the least guilty. Even our cottage gained an evil reputation, and you yourself must admit, if you're honest, that on your first entry into it you thought it justified its reputation. Later on, when people occasionally visited us again, they used to screw up their noses at the most trivial things, for instance, because the little oil-lamp hung over the table. Where should it hang if not over the table? and yet they found it insupportable. But if we hung the lamp somewhere else they were still disgusted. Whatever we did, whatever we had, it was all despicable."

Petitions

"What were we doing meanwhile?

The worst thing we could have done, something much more deserving of contempt than our original offence - we betrayed Amalia, we shook off her silent restraint, we couldn't go on living like that, without hope of any kind we could not live, and we began each in his or her own fashion with prayers or blustering to beg the Castle's forgiveness. We knew, of course, that we weren't in a position to make anything good, and we knew too that the only likely connexion we had with the Castle-through Sortini, who had been father's superior and had approved of him - was destroyed by what had happened, and yet we buckled down to the job.

Father began it, he started making senseless petitions to the Village Superintendent, to the secretaries, the advocates, the clerks, usually he wasn't received at all, but if by guile or chance he managed to get a hearing - and how we used to exult when the news came, and rub our hands! - he was always thrown out immediately and never admitted again.

Besides, it was only too easy to answer him, the Castle always has the advantage.

What was it that he wanted?

What had been done to him?

What did he want to be forgiven for?

When and by whom had so much as a finger been raised against him in the Castle?

Granted he had become poor and lost his customers, etc., these were all chances of everyday life, and happened in all shops and markets. Was the Castle to concern itself about things of that kind? It concerned itself about the common welfare, of course, but it couldn't simply interfere with the natural course of events for the sole purpose of serving the interest of one man. Did he expect officials to be sent out to run after his customers and force them to come back? But, father would object - we always discussed the whole interview both before and afterwards, sitting in a corner as if to avoid Amalia, who knew well enough what we were doing, but paid no attention - well, father would object, he wasn't complaining about his poverty, he could easily make up again for all he had lost, that didn't matter if only he were forgiven. But what was there to forgive?

Then came the answer. An accusation had come in against him, at least there was none in the registers, not in those registers anyhow which were accesible to the public advocates, consequently, so far as could be established, there was neither any accusation standing again him, nor one in process of being taken up. Could he perhance refer to some official decree that had been issued against him? Father couldn't do that.

Well then, if he knew of nothing and nothing had happened, what did he want?

What was there to forgive him?

Nothing but the way he was aimlessly wasting official time, but that was just the unforgivable sin. Father didn't give in, he was still very strong in those days, and his enforced leisure gave him plenty of time. "I'll restore Amalia's honour, it won't take long now,'" he used to say to Barnabas and me several times a day, but only in a low voice in case Amalia should hear, and yet he only said it for her benefit, for in reality he wasn't hoping for the restoration of her honour, but only for forgiveness. Yet before he could be forgiven he had to prove his guilt, and that was denied in all the bureaux.

He hit upon the idea - and it showed that his mind was already giving way - that his guilt was being concealed from him because he didn't pay enough. Until then he had paid only the established taxes, which were at least high enough for means like ours. But now he believed that he must pay more, which was certainly a delusion, for, although our officials accept bribes simply to avoid trouble and discussion, nothing is ever achieved in that way. Still, if father had set his hopes on that idea, we didn't want them upset.

We sold what we had left to sell - nearly all things we couldn't do without - to get father the money for his efforts and for a long time every morning brought us the satisfaction of knowing that when he went on his day's rounds he had at least a few coins to rattle in his pocket. Of course we simply starved all day, and the only thing the money really did was to keep father fairly hopeful and happy. That could hardly be called an advantage, however. He wore himself out on these rounds of his, and the money only made them drag on and on instead of coming to a quick and natural end.

Since in reality nothing extra could be done for him in return for those extra payments, clerks here and there tried to make a pretence ot giving something in return, promising to look the matter up, hinting that they were on the track of something, and that as a favour to father, and not as a duty, they would follow it up - and father, instead of growing sceptical, only became more and more credulous. He used to bring home such obviously worthless promises as if they were great triumphs, and it was a torment to see him behind Amalia's back twisting his face in a smile and opening his eyes wide as he pointed to her and made signs to us that her salvation, which would have surprised nobody so much as herself, was coming nearer and nearer through his efforts, but that it was still a secret and we mustn't tell. Things would certainly have gone on like this for a long time if we hadn't finally been reduced to the position of having oo more money to give him.

Barnabas, indeed, had been taken on meanwhile by Brunswick, after endless imploring, as an assistant, on condition that he fetched his work in the dusk of the evening and brought it back again in the dark - it must be admitted that Brunswick was taking a certain risk in his business for our sake, but in exchange he paid Barnabas next to nothing, and Barnabas is a model workman - yet his wages were barely enough to keep us from downright starvation. Very gently and after much softening of the blow we told our father that he could have no more money, but he took it very quietly. He was no longer capable of understanding how hopeless were his attempts at intervention, but he was wearied out by continual disappointments. He said, indeed-and he spoke less clearly than before, he used to speak almost too clearly - that he would have needed only a very little more money, for to-morrow or that very day he would have found out everything, and now it had all gone for nothing, ruined simply for lack of money, and so on, but the tone in which he said it showed that he didn't believe it all.

Besides, he brought out a new plan immediately of his own accord. Since he had failed in proving his guilt, and consequently could hope for nothing more through official channels, he would have to depend on appeals alone, and would to move the officials personally. There must certainly be among them who had good sympathetic hearts, which couldn't give way to in their official capacity, but out of office hours, if one caught them at the right time, they surely listen."

Here K., who had listened with absorption hitherto, interrupted Olga's narrative with the question: "And don't you think he was right?"

Although his question would have answered itself in the course of the narrative he wanted to know at once.

"No," said Olga, "there could be no question of sympathy or anything of the kind. Young and inexperienced as we were, we knew that, and father knew it too, of course, but he had forgotten it like nearly everything else. The plan he had hit on was to plant himself on the main road near the Castle, where the officials pass in their carriages, and seize any opportunity of putting up his prayer for forgiveness. To be honest, it was a wild and senseless plan, even if the impossible should have happened, and his prayer have really reached an official's ear. For how could a single official give a pardon? That could only be done at best by the whole authority, and apparently even the authority can only condemn and not pardon.

And in any case even if an official stepped out of his carriage and was willing to take up the matter, how could he get any clear idea of the affair from the mumblings of a poor, tired, ageing man like father? Officials are highly educated, but one-sided. In his own department an official can grasp whole trains of thought from a single word, but let him have something from another department explained to him by the hour, he may nod politely, but he won't understand a word of it. That's quite natural, take even the small official affairs that concern the ordinary person - trifling things that an official disposes of with a shrug - and try to understand one of them, through and through, and you'll waste a whole lifetime on it without result.

But even if father had chanced on a responsible official, no official can settle anything without the necessary documents, and certainly not on the main road. He can't pardon anything, he can only settle it officially, and he would simply refer to the official procedure, which had already been a complete failure for father. What a pass father must have been in to think of insisting on such a plan! If there were even the faintest possibility of getting pardon in that way, that part of the road would be packed with petitioners. But since it's sheer impossibility the road is absolutely empty. But maybe that strengthened father in his hopes, he found food for them everywhere. He had great need to find it, for a sound wouldn't have had to make such complicated calculations, he would have realized from external evidence that the thing was impossible.

When officials travel to the village or back to the Castle it's not for pleasure, but because there's work wailing for them in the village or in the Castle, and so they travel at a neat pace. It's not likely to occur to them to look out of the carriage windows in search of petitioners, for the carriages are crammed with papers which they study on the way."

"But," said K., "I've seen the inside of an official sledge in which there weren't any papers."

Olga's story was opening for him such a great and almost incredible world that he could not help trying to put his own small experiences in relation to it, as much to convince himself of its reality as of his own existence.

"That's possible," said Olga, "but in that case it's even worse, for that means that the official's business is so important that the papers are too precious or too numerous to be taken with him, and those officials go at a gallop. In any case, none of them can spare time for father. And besides, there are several roads to the Castle. Now one of them is in fashion, and most carriages go by that, now it's another and everything drives pell-mell there. And what governs this change of fashion has never yet been found out.

At eight o'clock one morning they'll all be on another road, ten minutes later on a third, and half an hour after that on the first road again, and then they may stick to that road all day, but every minute there's the possibility of a change. Of course all the roads join up near the village, but by that tune all the carriages are racing like mad, while nearer the Castle the pace isn't quite so fast. And the amount of traffic varies just as widely and incomprehensibly as the choice of roads. There are often days when there's not a carriage to be seen, and others when they travel in crowds.

Now, just think of all that in relation to father. In his best suit, which soon becomes his only suit, off he goes every morning from the house with our best wishes. He takes with him a small Fire badge, which he has really no business to keep, to stick ia coat once he's out of the village, for in the village itself he is afraid to let it be seen, although it's so small that it can hardly be seen two paces away, but father insists that it's just the thing to draw a passing official's attention. Not far from the Castle entrance there's a market garden, belonging to a man called Bertuch who sells vegetables to the Castle, and there on the narrow stone ledge at the foot of the garden fence father took up his post.

Bertuch made no objection because he used to be very friendly with father and had been one of his most faithful customers - you see, he has a lame foot, and he thought that nobody but father could make him a boot to fit it. Well there sat father day after day, it was a wet and stormy autumn but the weather meant nothing to him. In the morning at his regular hour he had his hand on the latch and waved us goodbye, in the evening he came back soaked to the skin, every day, it seemed, a little more bent, and flung himself down in a corner. At first he used to tell us all his little adventures, such as how Bertuch for sympathy and old friendship's sake had thrown him a blanket over the fence, or that in one of the passing carriages he thought he had recognized this or the other official, or that this or the other coachman had recognized him again and playfully flicked him with his whip. But later he stopped telling us these things, evidently he had given up all hope of ever achieving anything there, and looked on it only as his duty, his dreary job, to go there and spend the whole day.

That was when his rheumatic pains began, winter was coming on, snow fell early, the winter begins very early here. Well, so there he sat sometimes on wet stones and at other times in the snow. In the night he groaned with pain, and in the morning he was many a time uncertain whether to go or not, but always overcame his reluctance and went. Mother clung to him and didn't want to let him go, so he, apparently grown timid because his limbs wouldn't obey him, allowed her to go with him, and so mother began to get pains too. We often went out to them, to take them food, or merely to visit them, or to try to persuade them to come back home. How often we found them crouching together against each other on their narrow seat, huddled up under a thin blanket which scarcely covered them, and round them nothing but the grey of snow and mist, and far away for days at a time not a soul to be seen, not a carriage. Sight that was, K., a sight to be seen.

Until one morning father couldn't move his stiff legs out of bed at all, he wasn't to be comforted, in a slight delirium he thought he could see an official stopping his carriage beside Bertuch's just at that moment, hunting all along the fence for him and then climbing angrily into his carriage again with a shake of his head. At that father shrieked so loudly that it was as if he wanted to make the official hear him at all that distance, and to explain how blameless his absence was. And it became a long absence, he never went back again, and for weeks he never left his bed. Amalia took over the nursing, the attending, the treatment, did everything he needed, and with a few intervals has kept it up to this day. She knows healing herbs to soothe his pain, she needs hardly any sleep, she's never alarmed, never afraid, never impatient, she does everything for the old folks. While we were fluttering around uneasily without being able to help in anything she remained cool and quiet whatever happened. Then when the worst was past and father was able again to struggle cautiously out of bed with one of us supporting him on each side, Amalia withdrew into the background again and left him to us."

Olgàs plans

"Now it was necessary again to find some occupation for father that he was still fit for, something that at least would make him believe that he was helping to remove the burden of guilt from our family. Something of the kind was not hard to find, anything at all in fact would have been as useful for the purpose as sitting in Bertuch's garden, but I found something that actually gave me a little hope. Whenever there had been any talk of our guilt among officials or clerks or anybody else, it was truly the insult to Sortini's messenger that had always been brought up, further than that nobody dared to go.

Now, I said to myself, since public opinion, even if only ostensibly, recognise nothing but the insult to the messenger, then, even if it were still only ostensibly, everything might be put right if you could propitiate the messenger. No charge had actually been made, we were told, no department therefore had taken upth affair yet, and so the messenger was at liberty, as far as he was concerned - and there was no question of anything more - in forgive the offence.

All that of course couldn't have any decisiy importance, was mere semblance and couldn't produce in turn, anything but semblance, but all the same it would cheer up my father and might help to harass the swarm of clerks who had been tormenting him, and that would be a satisfaction. First of course one had to find the messenger. When I told father of my plan, at first he was very annoyed, for to tell the truth he had become terribly self-willed. For one thing he was convinced - this happened during his illness - that we had always held him back from final success, first by stopping his allowance and then by keeping him in his bed. And for another he was no longer capable of completely understanding any new idea. My plan was turned down even before I had finished telling him about it, he was convinced that his job was to go on waiting in Bertuch's garden, and as he was in no state now to go there every day himself, we should have to push him there in a handbarrow. But I didn't give in, and gradually he became reconciled to the idea, the only thing that disturbed him was that in this matter he was quite dependent on me, for I had been the only one who had seen the messenger, he did not know him. Actually one messenger is very like another, and I myself was not quite certain that I would know this one again. Presently we began to go to the Herrenhof and look around among the servants.

The messenger of course had been in Sortini's service and Sortini had stopped coming to the "village, but the gentlemen are continually changing their servants, one might easily find our man among the servants of another gentleman, and even if he himself was not to be found, still one might perhaps get news of him from the other servants. For this purpose it was of course necessary to be in the Herrenhof every evening, and people weren't very pleased to see us anywhere, far less in a place like that. And we couldn't appear either as paying customers. But it turned out that they could put us to some use all the same.

You know what a trial the servants were to Frieda. Bottom they are mostly quiet people, but pampered by too little work - "May you be as well off as a servant" is a favourite toast among the officials - and really, as far as an easy work goes servants seem to be the real masters in the Castle, they know their own dignity too, and in the Castle, there they have to behave in accordance with their regulations, they're quiet and dignified, several times I've been assured of that, and one can find even among the servants down here some faint signs of that, but only faint signs, for usually, seeing that the Castle regulations aren't fully binding on them in the village, they seem quite changed. A wild unmanageable lot, ruled by their insatiable impulses instead of by their regulations.

Their scandalous behaviour knows no limits, it's lucky for the village that they can't leave the Herrenhof without permission, but in the Herrenhof itself one must try to get on with them somehow. Frieda, for instance, felt that very hard to do and so she was very glad to employ me to quieten the servants.

For more than two years, at least twice a week, I've spent the night with the servants in the stalls. Earlier, when father was still able to go to the Herrenhof with me, he slept somewhere in the taproom, and in that way waited for the news that I would bring in the morning. There wasn't much to bring. We've never found the messenger to this day, he must be still with Sortini who values him very highly, and he must have followed Sortini when Sortini retired to a more remote bureau. Most of the servants haven't seen him since we saw him last ourselves, and when one or other claims to have seen him it's probably a mistake. So my plan might have actually failed, and yet it hasn't failed completely. It's true we haven't found the messenger, and going to the Herrenhof and spending the night there - perhaps his pity for me, too, any pity that he's still capable of - has unfortunately ruined my father, and for two years now he has ken in the state you've seen him in, and yet things are perhaps better with him than with my mother, for we're waiting daily for her death. It has only been put off thanks to Amalia's superhuman efforts.

But what I've achieved in the Herrenhof is a certain connection with the Castle. Don't despise me when I that I don't repent what I've done. What conceivable sort a connexion with the Castle can this be, you'll no doubt be thinking. And you're right, it's not much of a connection. I know a great many of the servants now, of course, almost all the gentlemen's servants who have come to the village during the last two years, and if I should ever get into the Castle, I shan't be a stranger there. Of course, they're servants only in the village. In the Castle they're quite different, and probably wouldn't know me or anybody else there that they've had dealings with in the village, that's quite certain, even if they have sworn a hundred times in the stall that they would be delighted to see me again in the Castle. Besides, I've already had experience of how little all these promises are worth. But still that's not the really important thing.

It isn't only through the servants themselves that I have a connection with the Castle, for apart from that I hope and trust that what I'm doing is being noticed by someone up there - and the management of the staff of servants is really an extremely important and laborious official function - and that finally whoever is noticing me may perhaps arrive at a more favourable opinion of me than the others, that he may recognize that I'm fighting for my family and carrying on my father's efforts, no matter in how poor a way.

If he should see it like that, perhaps he'll forgive me too for accepting money from the servants and using it for our family. And I've achieved something more yet, which even you, I'm afraid, will blame me for. I learned a great deal from the servants about the ways in which one can get into the Castle service without going through the difficult preliminaries of official appointment lasting sometimes for years. In that case, it's true, one doesn't become an actual official employee, but only a private and semi-official one, one has neither rights nor duties - and the worst is not to have any duties - but one advantage one does have, that one is on the spot, one can watch for favourable opportunities and take advantage of them, one may not be an employee, but by good luck some work may come one's way, perhaps no real employee is handy, there's a call, one flies to answer it, and one has become the very thing that one wasn't a minute before. An employee. Only, when is one likely to get a chance like that?

At once, one has hardly arrived, one has hardly had to look round before the chance is there, and many a one hasn't even the presence of mind, being quite new to the job, seize the opportunity. But in another case one may have to wait for even more years than the official employees, and after being a semi-official servant for so long one can never be lawfully taken on afterwards as an official employee.

So there's enough here to make one pause, but it sinks to nothing when one takes into account that the test for the official appointments is very stringent and that a member of any doubtful family is turned down in advance. Let us say someone like that goes in for the examination, for years he waits in fear and trembling for the result, from the very first day everybody asks him in amazement how he could have dared to do anything so wild, but he still goes on hoping - how else could he keep alive? Then after years and years, perhaps as an old man, he learns that he has been rejected, learns that everything is lost and that all his life has been in vain. Here, too, of course there are exceptions, that's how one is so easily tempted. It happens sometimes that really shady customers are actually appointed, there are officials who, literally in spite of themselves, are attracted by those outlaws. At the entrance examinations they can't help sniffing the air, smacking their lips, and rolling their eyes towards an entrant like that, who seems in some way to be terribly appetizing to them, and they have to stick close to their books of regulations so as to withstand him.

Sometimes, however, that doesn't help the entrant to an appointment, but only leads to an endless postponement of the preliminary proceedings, which are never terminated, but only broken off by the death of the poor man. So official appointment no less than the other kind is full of obvious and concealed difficulties, and before one goes in for everything of the kind it's highly advisable to weigh everything carefully. Now, we didn't fail to do that, Barnabas and I. Every time that I came back from the Herrenhof we sat down together and I told the latest news that I had gathered, for days we talked it over, and Barnabas's work lay idle for longer spells than was good for it. And here I may be to blame in your opinion. I knew quite well that much reliance was n to be put on the servants' stories. I knew that they never had much inclination to tell me things about the Castle, that the always changed the subject, and that every word had to be dragged out of them, and then, when they were well started that they let themselves go, talked nonsense, bragged, tried to surpass one another in inventing improbable lies, so that in the continuous shouting in the dark stalls, one servant beginning where the other left off, it was clear that at best only a few scanty scraps of truth could be picked up. But I repeated everything to Barnabas again just as I had heard it, though he still had no capacity whatever to distinguish between what was true and what was false, and on account of the family's position was almost famishing to hear all these things. And he drank in everything and burned with eagerness for more. And as a matter of fact the cornerstone of my new plan was Barnabas. Nothing more could be done through the servants. Sortini's messenger was not to be found and would never be found, Sortini and his messenger with him seemed to be receding farther and farther, by many people their appearance and names were already forgotten, and often I had to describe them at length and in spite of that learn nothing more than that the servant I was speaking to could remember them with an effort, but except for that could tell nothing about them. And as for my conduct with the servants, of course I had no power to decide how it might be looked on and could only hope that the Castle would judge it in the spirit I did it in, and that in return a little of the guilt of our family would be taken away, but I've received no outward sign of that.

Still I stuck to it, for so far as I was concerned I saw no other chance of getting anything done for us in the Castle. But for Barnabas I saw another possibility. From the tales of the servants - if I had the inclination, and I had only too much inclination - I could draw the conclusion that anyone who was taken into the Castle service could do a great deal for his family. But then what was there that was worthy or belief in these tales? It was impossible to make certain of that, but that there was very little was clear. For when, say, a servant that I would never see again, or that I would hardly recognize were I to see him again, solemnly promised me to help to get my brother a post in the Castle, or at least, if Barnabas should to the Castle on other business, to support him, or at least to back him up - for according to the servants' stories it sometimes happens that candidates for posts become unconscious or deranged during the protracted waiting and then they're lost if some friend doesn't look after them - when things like that and a great many more were told to me, they were probably justified as warnings, but the promises that accompanied them were quite baseless. But not to Barnabas. It's true I warned him not to believe them, but my mere telling of them was enough to enlist him for my plan. The reasons I advanced for it myself impressed him less, the thing that chiefly influenced him was the servants' stories. And so in reality I was completely thrown back upon myself. Amalia was the only one who could make herself understood to my parents, and the more I followed, in my own way, the original plans of father, the more Amalia shut herself off from me, before you or anybody else she talks to me, but not when we're alone.

To the servants in the Herrenhof I was a plaything which in their fury they did their best to wreck, not one intimate word have I spoken with any of them during those two years, I've had only cunning or lying or silly words from them, so only Barnabas remained for me, and Barnabas was still very young. When I saw the light in his eyes as I told him those things, a light which has remained in them ever since, I felt terrified and yet I didn't stop, the things at stake seemed too great. I admit I hadn't my father's great though empty plans. I hadn't the resolution that men have. I confined myself to making good the insult to the messenger, and only asked that the actual modesty of my attempt should be put to my credit. But what I had failed to do by myself I wanted now to achieve in a different way and with certainty through Barnabas. We had insulted a messenger and driven him into a more remote bureau. What was more natural than for us to offer a new messenger in the person of Barnabas, so that the other messenger's work might be carried on by him, and the other messenger might remain quietly in retirement as long as he for as long a time as he needed to forget the insult? I was quite aware, of course, that in spite of all its modesty ther was a hint of presumption in my plan, that it might give way to the impression that we wanted to dictate to the authorities how they should decide a personal question, or that we doubted their ability to make the best arrangements, which they might have made long before we had struck upon the idea that something could be done.

But then, I thought again that it was in fact possible that the authorities should misunderstand me so grossly or if they should, that they should do so intentionally, that in other words all that I did should be turned down in advance without further examination. So I did not give in and Barnabas's ambition kept him from giving in. In this term of preparation Barnabas became so uppish that he found that cobbling was far too menial work for him, a future bureau employee, yes, he even dared to contradict Amalia, and flatly, on the few occasions that she spoke to him about it. I didn't grudge him this brief happiness, for with the first day that he went to the Castle his happiness and his arrogance would be gone, a thing easy enough to foresee.

And now began that parody of service of which I've told you already. It was amazing with what little difficulty Barnabas got into the Castle that first time, or more correctly into the bureau which in a manner of speaking has become his workroom. This success drove me almost frantic at the time, when Barnabas whispered the news to me in the evening after he came home. I ran to Amalia, seized her, drew her into a corner, and kissed her so wildly that she cried with pain and terror. I could explain nothing for excitement, and then it had been so long since we had spoken to each other, so I put off telling her until the next day or the day after. For the next few days, however, there was really nothing more to tell. After the first quick success nothing more happened. For two long years Barnabas led this heart-breaking life. The servants failed us completely, I gave Barnabas a short note to take with him recommending him to their consideration, reminding them at the same time of their promises, and Barnabas, as often as he saw a servant, drew out the note and held it up, and even if I sometimes may have presented it to someone who didn't know me, and even if those who did know me were irritated by his hand holding out the note in silence - for he didn't dare to speak up there - yet all the same it was a shame that nobody helped him, and it was a relief-which we could have secured, I must admit, by our own action and much earlier - when a servant who had probably been pestered several times already took the note, crushed it up and flung it into the wastepaper basket. Almost as if he had said: "That's just what you yourselves do with letters", it occurred to me.

But barren of results as all this time was in other ways, it had a good effect on Barnabas, if one can call it a good thing that he grew prematurely old, became a man before his time, yes, even in some ways more grave and sensible than most men. Often it makes me sad to look at him and compare him with the boy that he was only two years ago.

And with it all I'm quite without the comfort and support that, being a man, he could surely give me. Without me he could hardly have got into the Castle, but since he is there, he's independent of me. I'm his only intimate friend, but I'm certain that he only tells me a small part of what he has on his mind. He tells me a great many things about the Castle, but from his stories, from the trifling details that he gives, one can't understand in the least how those things could have changed him so much. In particular I can't understand how the daring he had as a boy - it actually caused us anxiety - how he can have lost it so completely up there now that he's a man. Of course all that useless standing about and waiting all day, and day after day, and going on and on without any prospect of a change, must break a man down and make him unsure of himself and in the end actually incapable of anything - else but this hopeless standing about.

But why didn't he put up a fight even at the beginning?

Especially seeing that he soon recognized that I had been right and that there was no opportunity there for his ambition, though there might be some hope perhaps for the betterment of our family's condition. For up there, in spite of the servants' whims, everything goes on very soberly, ambition seeks its sole satisfaction in work, and as in this way the work itself gains the ascendancy, ambition ceases to have any place at all, for childish desires there's no room up there. Nevertheless Barnabas fancied, so he has told me, that he could clearly see how great the power and knowledge even of those very mentionable officials were into whose bureau he is allowed. How fast they dictated, with half-shut eyes and brief gestures, merely by raising a finger quelling the surly servants, and making them smile with happiness even when they were checked. Or perhaps rinding an important passage in one of the books and becoming quite absorbed in it, while the others would crowd round as near as the cramped space would allow them, and crane their necks to see it. These things and other things of the same kind gave Barnabas a great idea of those men, and he had the feeling that if he could get the length of being noticed by them and could venture to address a few words to them, not as a stranger, but as a colleague - true a very subordinate colleague - in the bureau, incalculable things might be achieved for our family.

But things have never got that length yet, and Barnabas can't venture to do anything that might help towards it, although he's well aware that, young as he is, he's been raised to the difficult and responsible position of chief breadwinner in our family on account of this wholt unfortunate affair.

And now for the final confession. It was a week after your arrival. I heard somebody mentioning it in the Herrenhof, but didn't pay much attention. A Land Surveyor had come and I didn't even know what a Land Surveyor was. But next evening Barnabas - at an agreed hour I usually set out to go a part of the way to meet him - came home earlier than usual, saw Amalia in the sittingroom, drew me out into the street, laid his head on my shoulder, and cried for several minutes. He was again the little boy he used to be.

Something had happened to him that he hadn't been prepared for. It was as if a whole new world had suddenly opened to him, and he could not bear the joy and the anxieties of all this newness. And yet the only thing that had happened was that he had been given a letter for delivery to you. But it was actually the first letter, the first commission, that he had ever been given."

Olga stopped.

Everything was still except for the heavy, occasionally disturbed breathing of the old people.

K. merely said casually, as if to round off Olga's story: "You've all been playing with me. Barnabas brought me the letter with the air of an old much occupied messenger, and you as well as Amalia - who at that time must have been in with you - behaved as if carry - messages and the letter itself were matters of indifference."

"You must distinguish between us," said Olga. "Barnabas had in made a happy boy again by the letter, in spite of all the doubts that he had about his capability. He confined those doubts to himself and me, but he felt it a point of honour to look like a real messenger, as according to his ideas real messengers looked. So although his hopes were now rising to an official uniform I had to alter his trousers, and in two hours, so that they would have some resemblance at least to the close-fitting trews of the official uniform, and he might appear in them before you, knowing, of course, that on this point you could be easily taken in.

So much for Barnabas.

But Amalia really despises his work as a messenger, and now that he seemed to have had a little success - as she could easily guess from Barnabas and myself and our talking and whispering together - she despised it more than ever. So she was speaking the truth, don't deceive yourself about that. But if I, K., have seemed to slight Barnabas's work, it hasn't been with any intention to deceive you, but from anxiety. These two letters that have gone through Barnabas's hands are the first signs of grace, questionable as they are, that our family has received for three years. This change, if it is a change and not deception - deceptions are more frequent than changes - is connected with your arrival here, our fate has become in a certain sense dependent on you, perhaps these two letters are only a beginning, and Barnabas's abilities will be used for other things than these two letters concerning you - we must hope that as long as we can - for the time being, however, everything centres on you.

Now up in the Castle we must rest content with whatever our lot happens to be, but down here we can, it may be, do something ourselves, that is, make sure of your goodwill, or at least save ourselves from your dislike, or, what's more important, protect you as far as our strength and experience go, so that your connexion with the Castle - by which we might perhaps be helped too - might not be lost.

Now what was our best way of bringing that about?

To prevent you from having any suspicion of us when we appealed - I preached you - for you're a stranger here and because of the certain to be full of suspicion, full of justifiable suspicion. And besides, we're despised by everybody and you must be influence by the general opinion, particularly through your fiancee how could we put ourselves forward without quite unintentionally setting ourselves up against your fiancee, and so offering you?

And the messages, which I had read before you got them - Barnabas didn't read them, as a messenger he couldn't allow himself to do that - seemed at the first glance obsolete and not of much importance, yet took on the utmost importance in as much as they referred you to the Superintendent. Now in these circumstances how were we to conduct ourselves towards you? If we emphasized the letters' importance, we laid ourselves under suspicion by overestimating what was obviously unimportant, and in pluming ourselves as the vehicle of these messages we should be suspected of seeking our own ends, not yours.

More, in doing that we might depreciate the value of the letter itself in your eyes and so disappoint you sore against our will. But if we didn't lay much stress on the letters we should lay ourselves equally under suspicion, for why in that case should we have taken the trouble of delivering such an unimportant letter, why should our actions and our words be in such clear contradiction, why should we in this way disappoint not only you, the addressee, but also the sender of the letter, who certainly hadn't handed the letter to us so that we should belittle it to the addressee by our explanations? And to hold the mean, without exaggeration on either side, in other words to estimate the just value of those letters, is impossible, they themselves change in value perpetually, the reflections they give rise to are endless, and chance determines where one stops reflecting, and so even our estimate of them is a matter of chance.

And when on the top of that there came anxiety about you, everything became confused, and you mustn't judge whatever I said too severely. When, for example - as once happened

- Barnabas arrived with the news that you were dissatisfied with his work, and in his first distress - his professional vanity was wounded too I must admit - resolved to retire from the service altogether, then to make good the mistake I was certainly ready to deceive, to lie, to do anything, no matter how if it would only . But even then I would have been doing it, at least in my opinion, as much for your sake as for ours."

There was a knock.

Olga ran to the door and unfastened it.

A strip of light from a dark lantern fell across the threshold. The late visitor put questions in a whisper and was answered in the same way, but was not satisfied and tried to force his way to the room. Olga found herself unable to hold him back any longer and called to Amalia, obviously hoping that to keep the old people from being disturbed in their sleep Amalia would do anything to eject the visitor. And indeed she hurried over at once, pushed Olga aside, and stepped into the street and closed the door behind her. She only remained there for a moment, almost at once she came back again, so quickly had she achieved what had proved impossible for Olga. K. then learned from Olga that the visit was intended for him. It had been one of the assistants, who was looking for him at Frieda's command. Olga had wanted to shield K. from the assistant. If K. should confess his visit here to Frieda later, he could, but it must not be discovered through the assistant.

K. agreed.

But Olga's invitation to spend the night there and wait for Barnabas he declined, for himself he might perhaps have accepted for it was already late in the night and it seemed to him that now, whether he wanted it or not, he was bound to this family in such a way that a bed for the night here, though for many reasons painful, nevertheless, when one considered this common bond, was the most suitable for him in the village.

All the same he declined it, the assistant's visit had alarmed him, it was incomprehensible to him how Frieda, who knew his wishes quite well, and the assistants, who had learned to fear him, had come together again like this, so that Frieda didn't scruple to send an assistant for him, only one of them, too, while the other had probably remained to keep her company. He asked Olga whether she had a whip, she hadn't one, but she had a good hazel switch, and he took it. Then he asked whether were was any other way out of the house, there was one through the yard, only one had to clamber over the wall of the neighbouring garden and walk through it before one reached the street.

K. decided to do this.

While Olga was conducting through the yard, K. tried hastily to reassure her fears, told her that he wasn't in the least angry at the small artifices she had told him about, but understood them very well, thanked her for the confidence she had shown in him in telling him her story and asked her to send Barnabas to the school as soon as he arrived, even if it were during the night. It was true, the messages which Barnabas brought were not his only hope, otherwise things would be bad indeed with him, but he didn't by any means leave them out of account, he would hold to them and not forget Olga either, for still more important to him than the messages themselves was Olga, her bravery, her prudence, if he had to choose between Olga and Amalia it wouldn't cost him much reflection. And he pressed her hand cordially once more as he swung himself on to the wall of the neighbouring garden.

When he reached the street he saw indistinctly in the darkness that a little farther along the assistant was still walking up and down before Barnabas's house. Sometimes he stopped and tried to peep into the room through the drawn blinds. K. called to him.

Without appearing visibly startled he gave up his spying on the house and came towards K.

"Who are you looking for?" asked K., testing the suppleness of the hazel switch on his leg.

"You," replied the assistant as he came nearer.

"But who are you?" asked K. suddenly, for this did not appear to be the assistant.

He seemed older, wearier, more wrinkled, but fuller in the face, his walk too was quite different from the brisk walk of the assistants, which gave an impression as if their joints were charged with electricity. It was slow, a little halting, elegantly valetudinarian.

"You don't recognize me?" asked the man, "Jeremiah, your old assistant."

"I see," said K. tentatively producing the hazel switch again, which he had concealed behind his back. "But you look quite different."

"It's because I'm by myself," said Jeremiah. "When I'm by myself then all my youthful spirits are gone."

"But where is Arthur?" asked K.

"Arthur?" said Jeremiah. "The little dear? He has left the service. You were rather hard and rough on us, you know, and the gentle soul couldn't stand it. He's gone back to the Castle to put oa a complaint."

"And you?" asked K.

"Im able to stay here," said Jeremiah, "Arthur is putting in a complaint for me too."

"What have you to complain about, then?" asked K.

"That you can't understand a joke. What have we done? Jested a little, laughed a little, teased your fiancee a little. And all according to our instructions, too. When Galater sent us to you -"

"Galater?" asked K.

"Yes, Galater," replied Jeremiah, "he was deputizing for Klamm himself at the time.

When he sent us to you he said: "I took a good note of it, for that's our business.

You're to go down there as assistants to the Land Surveyor."

We replied: "But we don't know anything about the work."

Thereupon he replied: "That's not the main point. If it's necessary, he'll teach you it The main thing is to cheer him up a little. According to the reports I've received he takes everything too seriously. He has just got to the village, and starts off thinking that a great experience, whereas in reality it's nothing at all. You must make him see that."

"Well?" said K., "was Galater right, and have you carried out your task?"

"That I don't know," replied Jeremiah. "In such a short time it was hardly possible. I only know that you were very rough on us, and that's what we're complaining of. I can't understand how you, an employee yourself and not even a Castle employee, aren't able to see that a job like that is very hard work, and that it's very wrong to make the work harder for the poor workers, and wantonly, almost childishly, as you have done. Your total lack of consideration in letting us freeze at the railings, and almost felling Arthur with your fist on the straw sack - Arthur, a man who feels a single cross word for

days - and in chasing me up and down in the snow all afternoon, so that it was an hour before I could recover from it t And I'm no longer young!"

"My dear Jeremiah," said K., "you're quite right about all this, only it's Galater you should complain to. He sent you here of his own accord, I didn't beg him to send you. And as I hadn't asked you it was at my discretion to send you back again, and like you, I would much rather have done it peacefully than with violence, but evidently you wouldn't have it any other way. Besides, why didn't you speak to me when you came first as frankly as you've done just now?"

"Because I was in the service," said Jeremiah, "surely that's obvious"

"And now you're in the service no longer?" asked K.

"That's so" said Jeremiah, "Arthur has given notice in the Castle that we're giving up the job, or at least proceedings have been set going that will finally set us free from it."

"But you're still looking for me just as if you were in the service," said K.

"No," replied Jeremiah, "I was only looking for you to reassure Frieda. When you forsook her for Barnabas's sister she was very unhappy, not so much because of the loss, as because of your treachery, besides she had seen it coming for a long time and had suffered a great deal already on that account. I only went up to the schoolwindow for one more look to see if you mightn't have become more reasonable. But you weren't there.

Frieda was sitting by herself on a bench crying. So then I went to her and we came to an agreement. Everything's settled. I'm to be waiter in the Herrenhof, at least until my business is settled in the Castle, and Frieda is back in the taproom again. It's better for Frieda. There was no sense in her becoming your wife. And you haven't known how to value the sacrifice that she was prepared to make for you either. But the good soul had still some scruples left, perhaps she was doing you an injustice, she thought, perhaps you weren't with the Barnabas girl after all. Although of course there could be no doubt where you were, I went all the same so as to make sure of it once and for all. For after all this worry Frieda deserved to sleep peacefully for once, not to mention myself. So I went and not only found you there, but was able to see incidentally as well that you had the girls on a string. The black one especially - a real wild-cat - she's set her cap at you. Well, everyone to his taste. But all the same it wasn't necessary for you to take the roundabout way through the next-door garden, I know that way."

So now the thing had come after all which he had been able to foresee, but not to prevent.

Frieda had left him.

It could not be final, it was not so bad as that, Frieda could be won back, it was easy for any stranger to influence her, even for those assistants who considered Frieda's position much the same as their own, and now that they had given notice had prompted Frieda to do the same, but K. would only have to show himself and remind her of all that spoke in his favour, and she would come back to him, especially if he should be in a position to justify his visit to those girls by some success due entirely to them. Yet in spite of those reflexions, by which he sought to reassure himself on Frieda's account, he was not reassured. Only a few minutes ago he had been praising Frieda up to Olga and calling her his only support. Well, that support was not of the firmest, no intervention of the mighty ones had been needed to rob K. of Frieda - even this not very savoury assistant had been enough - this puppet which sometimes gave one the impression of not being properly alive.

Jeremiah had already begun to disappear.

K. called him back.

"Jeremiah," he said, "I want to be quite frank with you. Answer one question of mine too in the same spirit. We're no longer in the position of master and servant, a matter of congratulation not only to you but to me too. We have no grounds, then, for deceiving each other. Here before your eyes I snap this switch which was intended for you, for it wasn't for fear of you that I chose the back way out, but so as to surprise you and lay it across your shoulders a few times. But don't take it badly, all that is over. If you hadn't been forced on me as a servant by the bureau, but had been simply an acquaintance, we would certainly have got on splendidly, even if your appearance might have disturbed me occasionally. And we can make up now for what we have missed in that way."

"Do you think so?" asked the assistant, yawning and closing his eyes wearily. "I could of course explain the matter more at length, but I have no time, I must go to Frieda, the poor child is waiting for me, she hasn't started on her job yet, at my request the landlord has given her a few hours' grace - she wanted to fling herself into the work at once probably to help her to forget - and we want to spend that little time at least together. As for your proposal, I have no cause, certainly, to deceive you, but I have just as little to confide anything to you. My case, in other words, is different from yours. So long as my relation to you was that of a servant, you were naturally a very important person in my eyes, not because of your own qualities, but because of my office, and I have done anything for you that you wanted, but now you're of no importance to me.

Even your breaking the switch doesn't affect me, it only reminds me what a rough master I had, it is not calculated to prejudice me in your favour."

"You talk to me," said K, "as if it were quite certain that you'll never have to … anything from me again. But that isn't really so. From all appearances you're not free from me, things aren't settled here so quickly as that -"

"Sometimes even more quickly," Jeremiah threw in.

"Sometimes," said K, "but nothing points to the fact that it's so this time, at least neither you nor I have anything that we can show in black and white. The proceedings are only started, it seems, and I haven't used my influence yet to intervene, but I will. If the affair turns out badly for you, you'll find that you haven't exactly endeared yourself to your master, and perhaps it was superfluous after all to break the hazel switch. And then you have abducted Frieda, and that has given you an inflated notion of yourself, but with all the respect that I have for your person, even if you have none for me any longer, a few words from me to Frieda will be enough - I know it - to smash up the lies that you've caught her with. And only lies could have estranged Frieda from me."

"These threats don't frighten me," replied Jeremiah, "you don't in the least want me as an assistant, you were afraid of me even as an assistant, you're afraid of assistants in any case, it was only fear that made you strike poor Arthur."

"Perhaps," said K., "but did it hurt the less for that? Perhaps I'll be able to show my fear of you in that way many times yet. Once I see that you haven't much joy in an assistant's work, it'll give me great satisfaction again, in spite of all my fear, to keep you at it. And moreover I'll do my best next time to see that you come by yourself, without Arthur, I'll be able then to devote more attention to you."

"Do you think," asked Jeremiah, "that I have even the slightest fear of all this?"

"I do think so," said K., "you're a little afraid, that's certain, and if you're wise, very much afraid. If that isn't so why didn't you go straight back to Frieda? Tell me, are you in love with her, then?"

"In love!" said Jeremiah. "She's a nice clever girl, a former sweetheart of Klamm's, so respectable in any case. And as she kept on asking me to save her from you. Why shouldn't I do her the favour, particularly as I wasn't doing you any harm, seeing that you've consoled yourself with these damned Barnabas girls?"

"Now I can see how frightened you are," said K., "frightened out of your wits. You're trying to catch me with lies. All that Frieda asked for was to be saved from those filthy swine of assistants, who were getting past bounds, but unfortunately I hadn't time to fulfil her wish completely, and now this is the result of my negligence."

"Land Surveyor, Land Surveyor!" someone shouted down the street.

It was Barnabas.

He came up breathless with running, but did not forget to greet K. with a bow. "It's done!" he said.

"What's done?" asked K. "You've laid my request before Klamm?"

"That didn't come off," said Barnabas, "I did my best, but it was impossible, I was urgent, stood there all day without being asked and so close to the desk that once a clerk actually pushed me away, for I was standing in his light, I reported myself when Klamm looked up - and that's forbidden - by lifting my hand, I was the last in the bureau, was left alone there with only the servants, but had the luck all the same to see Klamm coming back again, but it was not on my account, he only wanted to have another hasty glance at something in a book and went away immediately. Finally, as I still made no move, the servants almost swept me out of the door with the broom. I tell you all this so that you need never complain of my efforts again."

"What good is all your zeal to me, Barnabas," said K., "when it hasn't the slightest success?"

"But I have had success!" replied Barnabas. "As I was leaving my bureau - I call it my bureau - I saw a gentleman coming slowly towards me along one of the passages, which were quite empty except for him. By that time in fact it was very late. I decided to wait for him. It was a good pretext to wait longer, indeed I would much rather have waited in any case, so as not to have to bring you news of failure. But apart from that it was worth while waiting, for it was Erlanger.

You don't know him?

He's one of Klamm's chief secretaries. A weakly little gentleman, he limps a little. He recognized me at once, he's famous for his splendid memory and his knowledge of people, he just draws his brows together and that's enough for him to recognize anybody, often people even that he's never seen before, that he's only heard of or read about.

For instance, he could hardly ever have seen me. But although he recognizes everybody immediately, he always asks first as if he weren't quite sure.

"Aren't you Barnabas?" he asked me.

And then he went on: "You know the Land Surveyor, don't you?"

And then he said: "That's very lucky. I'm just going to the Herrenhof. The Land Surveyor is to report to me there. I'll be in room number 15. But he must come at once.

I've only a few things to settle there and I leave again for the Castle at 5 o'clock in the morning. Tell him that it's very important that I should speak to him.'"

Suddenly Jeremiah set off at a run.

In his excitement Barnabas had scarcely noticed his presence till now and asked:

"Where's Jeremiah going?"

"To forestall me with Erlanger," said K., and set off after Jeremiah, caught him up, hung on to his arm, and said: "Is it a sudden desire for Frieda that's seized you? I've got it as well, so we'll go together side by side."

Before the dark Herrenhof a little group of men were standing, two or three had lanterns with them, so that a face here and there could be distinguished. K. recognized only one acquaintance, Gerstacker the carrier. Gerstacker greeted him with the inquiry:

"You're still in the village?"

"Yes," replied K. "I've come here for good."

"That doesn't matter to me," said Gerstacker, breaking out into a fit of coughing and turning away to the others.

It turned out that they were all waiting for Erlanger. Erlanger had already arrived, but he was consulting first with Momus before he admitted his clients. They were all complaining at not being allowed to wait inside and having to stand out there in the snow. The weather wasn't very cold, but still it showed a lack of consideration to keep them standing there in front of the house in the darkness, perhaps for hours. It was certainly not the fault of Erlanger, who was always very accommodating. He knew nothing about it, and would certainly be very annoyed if reported to him. It was the fault of the Herrenhof landlady, who in her positively morbid determination to be refined, couldn't suffer a lot of people to come into the Herrenhof at the same time.

"If it absolutely must be and they must come," she used to say, "then in Heaven's name let them come one at a time."

And she managed to arrange that the clients, who at first had waited simply in a passage, later on the stairs, then in the hall, and finally in the taproom, were at last pushed out into the street. But even that had not satisfied her. It was unendurable for her to be always "besieged", as she expressed herself, in her own house. It was incomprehensible to her why there should need to be clients waiting at all.

"To dirty the front-door steps," an official had once told her, obviously in annoyance, but to her this pronouncement had seemed very illuminating, and she was never tired of quoting it. She tried her best - and she had the approval in this case of the clients too - to get a building set up opposite the Herrenhof where the clients could wait. She would have liked best of all if the interviews and examinations could have taken place outside the Herrenhof altogether, but the officials opposed that, and when the officials opposed her seriously the landlady naturally enough was unable to gainsay them, though in lesser matters she exercised a kind of petty tyranny, thanks to her indefatigable, yet femininely insinuating zeal.

And the landlady would probably have to endure those interviews and examinations in the Herrenhof in perpetuity, for the gentlemen from the Castle refused to budge from the place whenever they had official business in the village. They were always in a hurry, they came to the village much against their will, they had not the slightest intention of prolonging their stay beyond the time absolutely necessary, and so they could not be asked, simply for the sake of making things more pleasant in the Herrenhof, to waste time by transferring themselves with all their papers to some other house. The officials preferred indeed to get through their business in the taproom or in their rooms, if possible while they were at their food, or in bed before retiring for the night, or in the morning when they were too weary to get up and wanted to stretch themselves for a little longer.

Yet the question of the erection of a waiting-room outside seemed to be nearing a favourable solution. But it was really a sharp blow for the landlady - people laughed a little over it - that this matter of a waiting-room should itself make innumerable interviews necessary, so that the lobbies of the house were hardly ever empty. The waiting group passed the time by talking in half-whispers about those things."

K. was struck by the fact that, though their discontent was general, nobody saw any objection to Erlanger's summoning his clients in the middle of the night. He asked why this was so and got the answer that they should be only too thankful to Erlanger. It was only his goodwill and his high conception of his office that induced him to come to the village at all, he could easily if he wished - and it would probably be more in accordance with the regulations too - he could easily send an under-secretary and let him draw up statements.

Still, he usually refused to do this, he wanted to see and hear everything for himself, but for this purpose he had to sacrifice his nights, for in his official time-table there was no time allowed for journeys to the village. K. objected that even Klamm came to the village during the day and even stayed for several days. Was Erlanger, then, a mere secretary, more indispensable up there? One or two laughed good-humouredly, others maintained an embarrassed silence, the latter gained the ascendancy, and K. received hardly any reply. Only one man replied hesitatingly, that of course Klamm was indispensable, in the Castle as in the village.

Then the front door opened and Momus appeared between two attendants carrying lamps.

"The first who will be admitted to Herr Erlanger," he said, "are Gerstacker and K., are these two men here?"

They reported themselves, but before they could step forward Jeremiah slipped in with an "I'm a waiter here," and, greeted by Momus with a smiling slap on the shoulder, disappeared inside.

"I'll have to keep a sharper eye on Jeremiah," K. told himself, though he was quite aware at the same time that Jeremiah was probably far less dangerous than Arthur who was working against him in the Castle. Perhaps it would actually have been wiser to let himself be annoyed by them as assistants, than to have them prowling about without supervision and allow them to carry on their intrigues in freedom, jntrigues for which they seemed to have special facilities.

As K. was passing Momus the latter started as if only now did he recognize in him the Land Surveyor.

"Ah, the Land Surveyor?" he said. "The man who was so unwilling to be examined and now is in a hurry to be examined. It would have been simpler to let me do it that time. Well, really it's difficult to choose the right time for a hearing."

Since at these words K. made to stop, Momus went on: "Go in, go in! I needed your answers then, I don't now."

Nevertheless K. replied, provoked by Momus's tone: "You only think of yourselves. I would never and will never answer merely because of someone's office, neither then nor now."

Momus replied: "Of whom, then, should we think? Who else is there here? Look for yourself?"

In the hall they were met by an attendant who led them the old way, already known to K., across the courtyard, then into the entry and through the low, somewhat downward-sloping passage. The upper storeys were evidently reserved only for higher officials, the secretaries, on the other hand, had their rooms in this passage, even Erlanger himself, although he was one of the highest among them.

The servant put out his lantern, for here it was brilliant with electric light.

Everything was on a small scale, but elegantly finished. The space was utilized to the best advantage. The passage was just high enough for one to walk without bending one's head. Along both sides the doors almost touched each other. The walls did not quite reach to the ceiling, probably for reasons of ventilation, for here in the low cellar-like passage the tiny rooms could hardly have windows. The disadvantage of those incomplete walls was that the passage, and necessarily the rooms as well, were noisy. Many of the rooms seemed to be occupied, in most the people were still awake, one could hear voices, hammering, the clink of glasses. But the impression was not one of particular gaiety. The voices were muffled, only a word here and there could be indistinctly made out, it did not seem to be conversation either, probably someone was only dictating something or reading something aloud.

And precisely from the rooms where there was a sound of glasses and plates no word was to be heard, and the mering reminded K. that he had been told some time or that certain of the officials occupied themselves occasionally with carpentry, model engines, and so forth, to recuperate from the continual strain of mental work. The passage itself was empty except for a pallid, tall, thin gentleman in a fur coat, under which his night-clothes could be seen, who was sitting before one of the doors. Probably it had become too stuffy for him in the room, so he had sat down outside and was reading a newspaper, but not very carefully. Often he yawned and left off reading, then bent forward and glanced along the passage, perhaps he was waiting for a client whom he had invited and who had omitted to come.

When they had passed him the servant said to Gerstacker: "That's Pinzgauer."

Gerstacker nodded: "He hasn't been down here for a long time now," he said.

"Not for a long time now," the servant agreed.

At last they stopped before a door which was not in any way different from the others, and yet behind which, so the servant informed them, was Erlanger. The servant got K. to lift him on to his shoulders and had a look into the room through the open slit.

"He's lying down," said the servant climbing down, "on the bed, in his clothes, it's true, but I fancy all the same that he's asleep. Often he's overcome with weariness like that, here in the village, what with the change in his habits. We'll have to wait. When he wakes up he'll ring. Besides, it has happened before this for him to sleep away all his stay in the village, and then when he woke to have to leave again immediately for the Castle. It's voluntary, of course, the work he does here."

"Then it would be better if he just slept on," said Gerstacker, "for when he has a little time left for his work after he wakes, he's very vexed at having fallen asleep, and tries to get everything settled in a hurry, so that one can hardly get a word in."

"You've come on account of the contract for the carting for the new building?" asked the servant.

Gerstacker nodded, drew the servant aside, talked to him in a low voice, but the servant hardly listened, gazed away over Gerstacker, whom he overtopped by more than a head, and stroked his hair slowly and seriously.

Then, as he was looking round aimlessly, K. saw Frieda far away at a turn of the passage.

She behaved as if she did not recognize him and only stared at him expressionlessly.

She was carrying a tray with some empty dishes in her hand. He said to the servant, who, however, paid no attention whatever to him the more one talked to the servant the more absent-minded he seemed to become - that he would be back in a moment, and ran off to Frieda.

Reaching her he took her by the shoulders as if he were seizing his own property again, and asked her a few unimportant questions with his eyes holding hers. But her rigid bearing hardly as much as softened, to hide her confusion she tried to rearrange the dishes on the tray and said: "What do you want from me? Go back to the others - oh, you know whom I mean, you've just come from them, I can see it."

K. changed his tactics immediately.

The explanation mustn't come so suddenly, and mustn't begin with the worst point, the point most unfavourable to himself. "I thought you were in the taproom," he said.

Frieda looked at him in amazement and then softly passed her free hand over his brow and cheeks. It was as if she had forgotten what he looked like and were trying to recall it to mind again, even her eyes had the veiled look of one who was painfully trying to remember.

"I've been taken on in the taproom again," she said slowly at last, as if it did not matter what she said, but as if beneath her words she were carrying on another conversation with K. which was more important - "this work here is not for me, anybody at all could do it. Anybody who can make beds and look good-natured and doesn't mind the advances of the boarders, but actually likes them. Anybody who can do that can be a chambermaid. But in the taproom, that's quite different. I've been taken on straight away for the taproom again, in spite of the fact that I didn't leave it with any great distinction, but, of course, I had a word put in for me. But landlord was delighted that I had a word put in for me to it easy for him to take me on again. It actually ended by the having to press me to take on the post.

When you reflect what the taproom reminds me of you'll understand that. Finally I decided to take it on. I'm only here temporarily. Pepi begged not to put her to the shame of having to leave the taproom at once, and seeing that she has been willing and has done everything to the best of her ability, we have given her a twenty-four hours' extension."

"That's all very nicely arranged," said K., "but once you left the taproom for my sake, and now that we're soon to be married are you going back to it again?"

"There will be no marriage," said Frieda.

"Because I've been unfaithful to you?" asked K.

Frieda nodded.

"Now, look here, Frieda," said K. "we've often talked already about this alleged unfaithfulness of mine, and every time you've had to recognize finally that your suspicions were unjust. And since then nothing has changed on my side, all I've done has remained as innocent as it was at first and as it must always remain. So something must have changed on your side, through the suggestions of strangers or in some way or other.

You do me an injustice in any case, for just listen to how I stand with those two girls.

The one, the dark one I'm almost ashamed to defend myself on particular points like this, but you give me no choice - the dark one, then, is probably just as displeasing to me as to you. I keep my distance with her in every way I can, and she makes it easy, too, no one could be more retiring than she is."

"Yes," cried Frieda, the words slipped out as if against her will, K. was delighted to see her attention diverted, she was not saying what she had intended - "Yes, you may look upon her as retiring, you tell me that the most shameless creature of them all is retiring, and incredible as it is, you mean it honestly, you're not shamming, I know. The Bridge Inn landlady once said of you : "I can't abide him, but I can't let him alone, either, one simply can't control oneself when one sees a child that can hardly walk trying to go too far for it, one simply has to interfere."

"Pay attention to her advice for this once," said K. smiling, "but that girl - whether she's retiring or shameless doesn't matter - I don't want to hear any more about her."

"But why do you call her retiring?" asked Frieda obdurtely - K. considered this interest of hers a favourable sign "have you found her so, or are you simply casting a reflexion on somebody else?"

"Neither the one nor the other," said K., "I call her that out of gratitude, because she makes it easy for me to ignore her, and because if she said even a word or two to me I couldn't bring myself to go back again, which would be a great joss to me, for I must go there for the sake of both our futures, as you know. And it's simply for that reason that I have to talk with the other girl, whom I respect, I must admit, for her capability, prudence, and unselfishness, but whom nobody could say was seductive."

"The servants are of a different opinion," said Frieda.

"On that as on lots of other subjects," said K. "Are you going to deduce my unfaithfulness from the tastes of the servants?"

Frieda remained silent and suffered K. to take the tray from her, set it on the floor, and put his arm through hers, and walk her slowly up and down in the corner of the passage.

"You don't know what fidelity is," she said, his nearness putting her a little on the defensive, "what your relations with the girl may be isn't the most important point. The fact that you go to that house at all and come back with the smell of their kitchen on your clothes is itself an unendurable humiliation for me. And then you rush out of the school without saying a word. And stay with them, too, the half of the night. And when you're asked for, you let those girls deny that you're there, deny it passionately, especially the wonderfully retiring one. And creep out of the house by a secret way, perhaps actually to save the good name of the girls, the good name of those girls. No, don't let us talk about it any more."

"Yes, don't let us talk of this," said K., "but of something else, Frieda. Besides, there's nothing more to be said about it. You know why I have to go there. It isn't easy for me, but I overcome my feelings. You shouldn't make it any harder for me than it is.

To-night I only thought of dropping in there for a minute to see whether Barnabas had come at last, for he had an important message which he should have brought long before.

He hadn't come, but he was bound to come very soon, so I was assured, and it seemed very probable too. I didn't want to let him come after me, for you to be insulted by his presence.

The hours passed and unfortunately he didn't. But another came all right, a man whom I hate. I had no insention of letting myself be spied on by him, so I left through the neighbour's garden, but I didn't want to hide from him either and I went up to him frankly when I reached the street, with a very good and supple hazel switch, I admit.

That is all, so there's nothing more to be said about it.

But there's plenty to say about something else.

What about the assistants, the very mention of whose name is as repulsive to me as that family is to yours. Compare your relations with them with my relations with that family.

I understand your antipathy to Barnabas's family and I can share it. It's only for the sake of my affairs that I go to see them, sometimes it almost seems to me that I'm abusing and exploiting them.

But you and the assistants!

You've never denied that they persecute you, and you've admitted that you're attracted by them. I wasn't angry with you for that, I recognized that powers were at work which you weren't equal to, I was glad enough to see that you put up a resistance at least, I helped to defend you, and just because I left off for a few hours, trusting in your constancy, trusting also, I must admit, in the hope that the house was securely locked and the assistants finally put to flight - I still underestimate them, I'm afraid - just because I left off for a few hours and this Jeremiah - who is, when you look at him closely, a rather unhealthy elderly creature had the impudence to go up to the window.

Just for this, Frieda, I must lose you and get for a greeting: "There will be no marriage."

Shouldn't I be the one to cast reproaches?

But I don't, I have never done so."

And once more it seemed advisable to K. to distract Frieda's mind a little, and he begged her to bring him something to eat, for he had had nothing since midday. Obviously relieved by the request, Frieda nodded and ran to fetch something, not farther along the passage, however, where K. conjectured the kitchen was, but down a few steps to the left.

In a little she brought a plate with slices of meat and a bottle of wine, but they were clearly only the remains of a meal, the scraps of meat had been hastily ranged out anew so as to hide the fact, yet whole sausage skins had been overlooked, and the bottle was three-quarters empty. However, K. said nothing and fell on the food with a good appetite.

"You were in the kitchen?" he asked.

"No, in my own room," she said. "I have a room down there."

"You might surely have taken me with you," said K. "I'll go down now, so as to sit down for a little while I'm eating."

"I'll bring you a chair," said Frieda already making to go.

"Thanks," replied K. holding her back, "I'm neither going down there, nor do I need a chair any longer."

Frieda endured his hand on her arm defiantly, bowed her head and bit her lip.

"Well, then, he is down there," she said, "did you expect anything else? He's lying on my bed, he got a cold out there, he's shivering, he's hardly had any food. At bottom it's all your fault, if you hadn't driven the assistants away and run after those people, we might be sitting comfortably in the school now. You alone have destroyed our happiness.

Do you think that Jeremiah, so long as he was in service, would have dared to take me away? Then you entirely misunderstood the way things are ordered here. He wanted me, he tormented himself, he lay in watch for me, but that was only a game, like the play of a hungry dog who nevertheless wouldn't dare to leap up on the table. And just the same with me. I was drawn to him, he was a playmate of mine in my childhood - we played together on the slope of the Castle Hill, a lovely time, you've never asked me anything about my past - but all that wasn't decisive as long as Jeremiah was held back by his service, for I knew my duty as your future wife.

But then you drove the assistants away and plumed yourself on it besides, as if you had done something for me by it. Well, in a certain sense it was true. Your plan has succeeded as far as Arthur is concerned, but only for the moment, he's delicate, he hasn't Jeremiah's passion that nothing can daunt, besides you almost shattered his health for him by the buffet you gave him that night - it was a blow at my happiness as well - he fled to the Castle to complain, and even if he comes back soon, he's gone now all the same.

But Jeremiah stayed.

When he's in service he fears the slightest look of his master, but when he's not in service there's nothing he's afraid of. He came and took me. Forsaken by you, commanded by him, my old friend, I couldn't resist. I didn't unlock the school door. He smashed the window and lifted me out. We flew here, the landlord looks up to him, nothing could be more welcome to the guests, either, than to have such a waiter, so we were taken on, he isn't living with me, but we are staying in the same room."

"In spite of everything," said K., "I don't regret having driven the assistants from our service. If things stood as you say and your faithfulness was only determined by the assistants being in the position of servants, then it was a good thing that it came to an end. The happiness of a married life spent with two beasts of prey, who could only be kept under by the whip wouldn't have been very great. In that case I'm even thankful to this family who have unintentionally had some part in separating us."

They became silent and began to walk backwards and forwards again side by side, though neither this time could have told who had made the first move. Close beside him, Frieda seemed annoyed that K. did not take her arm again.

"And so everything seems in order," K. went on, "and we might as well say good-bye, and you go to your Jeremiah, who must have had this chill, it seems, ever since I chased him through the garden, and whom you've already left by himself too long in that case, and I to the empty school, or, seeing that there's no place for me there without you, anywhere else where they'll take me in. If I hesitate still in spite of this, it's because I have still a litde doubt about what you've told me, and with good reason. I have a different impression of Jeremiah. So long as he was in service, he was always at your heels and I don't believe that his position would have held him back permanently from making a serious attempt on you.

But now that he considers that he's absolved from service, it's a different case.

Forgive me if I have to explain myself in this way. Since you're no longer his master's fiancee, you're by no means such a temptation for him as you used to be. You may be the friend of his childhood, but - I only got to know him really from a short talk to-night - in my opinion he doesn't lay much weight on such sentimental considerations. I don't know why he should seem a passionate person in your eyes. His mind seems to me on the contrary to be particularly cold. He received from Galater certain instructions relating to me, instructions probably not very much in my favour, he exerted himself to carry them out, with a certain passion for service, I'll admit - it's not so uncommon here - one of them was - he should wreck our relationship. Probably he tried to do it by several means, one of them was to tempt you by his evil languishing glances, another - here the landlady supported him - was to invent fables about my unfaithfulness.

His attempt succeeded, some memory or other of Klamm that clung to him may have helped, he has lost his position, it is true, but probably just at the moment when he no longer needed it, then he reaped the fruit of his labours and lifted you out through the school window, with that his task was finished, and his passion for jervice having left him now, he'll feel bored, he would rather be in Arthur's shoes, who isn't really complaining up there at all, but earning praise and new commissions, but someone had to stay behind to follow the further developments of the affair.

It's rather a burdensome task to him to have to look after you. Of love for you he hasn't a trace, he frankly admitted it to me. As one of Klamm's sweethearts he of course respects you, and to insinuate himself into your bedroom and feel himself for once a little Klamm certainly gives him pleasure, but that is all, you yourself mean nothing to him now, his finding a place for you here is only a supplementary part of his main job.

So as not to disquieten you he has remained here himself too, but only for the time being, as long as he doesn't get further news from the Castle and his cooling feelings towards you aren't quite cured."

"How you slander him," said Frieda, striking her little fists together.

"Slander?" said K., "no, I don't wish to slander him. But I may quite well perhaps be doing him an injustice, that is certainly possible. What I've said about him doesn't lie on the surface for anybody to see, and it may be looked at differently too. But slander?

Slander could only have one object, to combat your love for him. If that were necessary and if slander were the most fitting means, I wouldn't hesitate to slander him. Nobody could condemn me for it, his position puts him at such an advantage as compared with me that, thrown back solely on my own resources, I could even allow myself a little slander.

It would be a comparatively innocent, but in the last resort a powerless, means of defence. So put down your fists."

And K. took Frieda's hand in his.

Frieda tried to draw it away, but smilingly and not with any great earnestness.

"But I don't need slander," said K., "for you don't love him, you only think you do, and you'll be thankful to me for ridding you of your illusion. For think, if anybody wanted to take you away from me without violence, but with the most careful calculation, he could only do it through the two assistants. In appearance, for childish, merry, irresponsible youths, fallen from the sky, from the Castle, a dash of childhood's memories with them too.

That of course must have seemed very nice, especially when I was the antithesis of it all, and was always running after affairs moreover which were scarcely comprehensible, which were exasperating to you, and which threw me together with people whom you considered deserving of your hate - something of which you carried over to me too, in spite of all my innocence. The whole thing was simply a wicked but very clever exploitation of the failings in our relationship. Everybody's relations have their blemishes, even ours, we came together from two very different worlds, and since we have known each other the life of each of us has had to be quite different, we still feel insecure, it's all too new. I don't speak of myself, I don't matter so much, in reality I've been enriched from the very first moment that you looked on me, and to accustom oneself to one's riches isn't very difficult. But - not to speak of anything else - you were torn away from Klamm, I can't calculate how much that must have meant, but a vague idea of it I've managed to arrive at gradually, you stumbled, you couldn't find yourself, and even if I was always ready to help you, still I wasn't always there, and when I was there you were held captive by your dreams or by something more palpable, the landlady, say - in short there were times when you turned away from me, longed, poor child, for vague inexpressible things, and at those periods any passable man had only to come within your range of vision and you lost yourself to him, succumbing to the illusion that mere fancies of the moment, ghosts, old memories, things of the past and things receding ever more into the past, life that had once been lived that all this was your actual present-day life.

A mistake, Frieda, nothing more than the last and, properly regarded, contemptible difficulties attendant on our final reconciliation. Come to yourself, gather yourself together. Even if you thought that the assistants were sent by Klamm - it's quite untrue, they come from the plater - and even if they did manage by the help of this illusion to charm you so completely that even in their disreputable nicks and their lewdness you thought you found traces of them, just as one fancies one catches a glimpse of some precious stone that one has lost in a dung heap, while in reality one couldn't be able to find it even if it were there - all the same they're only hobbledehoys like the servants in the stall, except that they're not healthy like them, and a little fresh air makes them ill and compels them to take to their beds, which I must say that they know how to snuffle out with a servant's true cunning."

Frieda had let her head fall on K.'s shoulder.

Their arms round each other, they walked silently up and down.

"If we had only," said Frieda after a while, slowly, quietly, almost serenely, as if she knew that only a quite short respite of peace on K.'s shoulder were reserved for her, and she wanted to enjoy it to the utmost, "if we had only gone away somewhere at once that night, we might be in peace now, always together, your hand always near enough for mine to grasp.

Oh, how much I need your companionship, how lost I have felt without it ever since I've known you, to have your company, believe me, is the only dream that I've had, that and nothing else."

Then someone called from the side passage, it was Jeremiah, he was standing there on the lowest step, he was in his shirt, but had thrown a wrap of Frieda's round him. As he stood there, his hair rumpled, his thin beard lank as if dripping with wet, his eyes painfully beseeching and wide with reproach, his sallow cheeks flushed, but yet flaccid, his naked legs trembling so violently with cold that the long fringes of the wrap quivered as well, he was like a patient who had escaped from hospital, and whose appearance could only suggest one thought, that of getting him back in bed again. This in fact was the effect that he had on Frieda, she disengaged herself from K., and was down beside Jeremiah in a second. Her nearness, the solicitude with which she drew the wrap closer round him, the haste with which she tried to force him back into the room, seemed to give him new strength, it was as if he only recognized K. now.

"Ah, the Land Surveyor!" he said, stroking Frieda's cheek to propitiate her, for she did not want to let him talk any "forgive the interruption. But I'm not at all well, that must be my excuse. I think I'm feverish, I must drink some tea and get a sweat. Those damned railings in the school garden, they'll give me something to think about yet, and then, already chilling to the bone, I had to run about all night afterwards. One sacrifices one's health for things not really worth it, without noticing it at the time.

But you, Land Surveyor, mustn't let yourself be disturbed by me, come into the room here with us, pay me a sick visit, and at the same time tell Frieda whatever you have still to say to her. When two who are accustomed to one another say goodbye, naturally they have a great deal to say to each other at the last minute which a third party, even if he's lying in bed waiting for his tea to come, can't possibly understand. But do come in, I'll be perfectly quiet."

"That's enough, enough!" said Frieda pulling at his arm. "He's feverish and doesn't know what he's saying. But you, K., don't you come in here, I beg you not to. It's my room and Jeremiah's, or rather it's my room and mine alone, I forbid you to come in with us. You always persecute me. Oh, K., why do you always persecute me? Never, never will I go back to you, I shudder when I think of the very possibility. Go back to your girls.

They sit beside you before the fire in nothing but their shifts, I've been told, and when anybody comes to fetch you they spit at him. You must feel at home there, since the place attracts you so much. I've always tried to keep you from going there, with little success, but all the same I've tried. All that's past now, you are free. You've a lovely life in front of you. For the one you'll perhaps have to squabble a little with the servants, but as for the other, there's nobody in heaven or earth that will grudge you her. The union is blessed beforehand. Don't deny it, I know you can disprove anything, but in the end nothing is disproved. Only think, Jeremiah, he has disproved everything!"

They nodded with a smile of mutual understanding.

"But," Frieda went on, "even if everything were disproved, what would be gained by that, what would it matter to me? What happens in that house is purely their business and his business, not mine. Mine is to nurse you till you're well again, as you were at one time, before K. tormented you for my sake."

"So you're not coming in after all, Surveyor?" asked Jeremiah, but was now definitely away by Frieda, who did not even turn to look at K. in.

There was a little door down there, still lower than the joors in the passage - not Jeremiah only, even Frieda had to stoop on entering - within it seemed to be bright and warm, a few whispers were audible, probably loving cajolements to get Jeremiah to bed, then the door was closed.

****

The text of the first German edition of The Castle ends. It has been translated by Willa and Edwin Muir. What follows is the continuation of the text together with additional material (different versions, fragments, passages deleted by the author, etc.) as found among Kafka's papers after the publication of the first edition and included by the editor, Max Brod, in the definitive German edition. The translation is by Eithne Willins and Ernst

****

Only now did K. notice how quiet it had become in the passage, not only here in this part of the passage wher he had been with Frieda, and which seemed to belong to the public rooms of the inn, but also in the long passage with the rooms that had earlier been so full of bustle. So the gentlemen had gone to sleep at last after all K. too was very tired, perhaps it was from fatigue that he had not stood up to Jeremiah as he should have. It would perhaps have been more prudent to take his cue from Jeremiah, who was obviously exaggerating how bad his chill was - his woefulness was not caused by his having a chill, it was congenital and could not be relieved by any herbal tea - to take his cue entirely from Jeremiah, make a similar display of his own really great fatigue, sink down here in the passage, which would in itself afford much relief, sleep a little, and then perhaps be nursed a little too. Only it would not have worked out as favourably as with Jeremiah, who would certainly have won this competition for sympathy, and rightly so, probably, and obviously every other fight too. K. was so tired that he wondered whether he might not try to go into one of these rooms, some of which were sure to be empty, and have a good sleep in a luxurious bed. In his view this might turn out to be recompense for many things. He also had a night-cap handy. On the tray that Frieda had left on the floor there had been a small decanter of rum. K, did not shrink from the exertion of making his way back, and he drained the little bottle to the dregs. Now he at least felt strong enough to go before Erlanger. He looked for the door of Erlanger's room, but since the servant and Gerstacker were no longer to be seen and all the doors looked alike, he could not find it. Yet he believed he remembered more or less in what part of the passage the door had been, and decided to open a door that in his opinion was probably the one he was looking for.

The experiment could not be so very dangerous. If it was Erlanger's room Erlanger would doubtless receive him, if it was somebody else's room it would be possible to apologize and go away again, and if he was asleep, which was what was probable, then K.'s visit not be noticed at all. It could turn out badly only if the was empty, for then K. would scarcely be able to resist the teptation to get into the bed and sleep for ages.

He once more glanced along the passage to right and to left, to see whether after all there might not be somebody coming who would be able to give him some information and make the venture unnecessary, but the long passage was quiet and empty. Then K. listened at the door. Here too was no inmate. He knocked so quietly that it could not have wakened a sleeper, and when even now nothing happened he opened the door very cautiously indeed.

But now he was met with a faint scream. It was a small room, more than half filled by a wide bed, on the night-table the electric lamp was burning, beside it was a travelling handbag. In the bed, but completely hidden under the quilt, someone stirred uneasily and whispered through a gap between quilt and sheet: "Who is it?"

Now K. could not withdraw again so easily, discontentedly he surveyed the voluptuous but unfortunately not empty bed, then remembered the question and gave his name. This seemed to have a good effect, the man in the bed pulled the quilt a little off his face, anxiously ready, however, to cover himself up again completely if something was not quite all right out there. But then he flung back the quilt without qualms and sat up. It was certainly not Erlanger. It was a small, well-looking gentleman whose face had a certain contradictoriness in that the cheeks were chubby as a child's and the eyes merry as a
child's, but that the high forehead, the pointed nose, the narrow mouth, the lips of which would scarcely remain closed, the almost vanishing chin, were not like a child's at all, but revealed superior intellect. It was doubtless his satisfaction with this, his satisfaction with himself, that had preserved him a marked residue of something healthily childlike.

"Do you know Friedrich?" he asked.

K. said he did not.

"But he knows you," the gentleman said, smiling.

K. nodded, there was no lack of people who knew him, this was indeed one of the main obstacles in his way.

"I am his secretary,' the gentleman said, "my name is Burgel."

"Excuse me," K. said, reaching for the door-handle, "I am sorry, I mistook your door for other. The fact is I have been summoned to Secretary Erlanger`s"

"What a pity," Burgel said. "Not that you are summoned here, but that you made a mistake about the doors. The fact is once I am wakened I am quite certain not to go to sleep again. Still, that need not sadden you so much, it's my personal misfortune. Why, anyway, can't these doors be locked, eh? There's a reason for that, of course. Because, according to an old saying the secretaries' doors should always be open. But that, again need not be taken quite so literally."

Burgel looked queryingly and merrily at K., in contrast to his lament he seemed thoroughly well rested. Burgel had doubtessly never in his life been as tired as K. was now.

"Where do you think of going now?" Burgel asked. "It's four o'clock. Anyone to whom you might think of going you would have to wake, not everybody is as used to being disturbed as I am, not everyone will put up with it as tolerantly, the secretaries are a nervous species. So stay for a little while. Round about five o'clock people here begin to get up, then you will be best able to answer your summons. So please do let go of the door-handle now and sit down somewhere, granted there isn't overmuch room here, it will be best if you sit here on the edge of the bed. You are surprised that I should have neither chair nor table here? Well, I had the choice of getting either a completely furnished room with a narrow hotel bed, or this big bed and nothing else except the washstand. I chose the big bed, after all, in a bedroom the bed is undoubtedly the main thing! Ah, for anyone who could stretch out and sleep soundly, for a sound sleeper, this bed would surely be truly delicious. But even for me, perpetually tired as I am without being able to sleep, it is a blessing, I spend a large part of the day in it, deal with all my correspondence in it, here conduct all the interviews with applicants. It works quite well. Of course the applicants have nowhere to sit, but they get over that, and after all it's more agreeable for them too if they stand and the recorder is at ease than if they sit cornfortably and get barked at. So the only place I have to offer is this here on the edge of the bed, but that is not an official place and is only intended for nocturnal conversations. But you are quiet, Land Surveyor?"

"I am very tired," said K., who on receiving the invitation had instantly, rudely, without respect, sat down on the bed and leaned against the post.

"Of course," Burgelsaid, laughing, "everybody is tired here. The work, for instance, that I got through yesterday and have already got through even to-day is no small matter.

It's completely out of the question of course that I should go to sleep now, but if this most utterly unprobable thing should happen after all and I should go to sleep while you are still here, then please stay quiet and don't open the door, either. But don't worry, I shall certainly not go to sleep or at best only for a few minutes. The way it is with me is that probably because I am so very used to dealing with applicants I do actually find it easiest to go to sleep when I have company."

"Do go to sleep, please do, Mr Secretary," K. said, pleased at this announcement, "I shall then, with your permission, sleep a little too."

"No, no," Burgel said, laughing again, "unfortunately I can't go to sleep merely on being invited to do so, it's only in the course of conversation that the opportunity may arise, it's most likely to be a conversation that puts me to sleep. Yes, one's nerves suffer in our business. I, for instance, am a liaison secretary. You don't know what that is? Well, I constitute the strongest liaison" - here he hastily rubbed his hands in involuntary merriment - "between Friedrich and the village, I constitute the liaison between his Castle and village secretaries, am mostly in the village, but not permanently. At every moment I must be prepared to drive up to the Castle. You see the travelling-bag - a restless life, not suitable for everyone. On the other hand it is true that now I could not do without this kind of work, all other work would seem insipid to me. And how do things stand with the land-surveying?"

"I am not doing any such work, I am not being employed as a Land Surveyor," K. said, he was not really giving his mind to the matter, actually he was only yearning for Burgel to fall asleep, but even this was only out of a certain sense of duty towards himself, in his heart of hearts he was sure that the moment when Burgel would go to sleep was still infinitely remote.

"That is amazing,' Burgel said with a lively jerk of his head, and pulled a note-pad out from under the quilt in order to make a note.

"You are a Land Surveyor and have no land-surveying to do."

K. mechanically, he had stretched out his left arm along the top the bed-post and laid his head on it, he had already tried various ways of making himself comfortable, but this position was th most comfortable of all, and now, too, he could attend a little better to what Burgel was saying.

"I am prepared," Burgel continued, "to follow up this matter further. With us here things are quite certainly not in such a way that an expert employee should be left unused. And it must after all be painful to you too. Doesn't it cause you distress?"

"It causes me distress," K. said slowly and smiled to himself, for just now it was not distressing him in the least. Besides, Burgel's offer made little impression on him. It was utterly dilettante. Without knowing anything of the circumstances under which K.'s appointment had come about, of the difficulties that it encountered in the community and at the Castle, of the complications that had already occurred during K.'s sojourn here or had been foreshadowed, without knowing anything of all this, indeed without even showing, what should have been expected of a secretary as a matter of course, that he had at least an inkling of it all, he offered to settle the whole affair up there in no time at all with the aid of his little note-pad.

"You seem to have had some disappointments," Burgel said, by this remark showing that he had after all some knowledge of human nature, and indeed, since entering the room, K. had from time to time reminded himself not to underestimate Burgel but in his state it was difficult to form a fair judgement of anything but his own weariness.

"No," Burgel said, as if he were answering a thought of K.'s and were considerately trying to save him the effort of formulating it aloud.

"You must not let yourself be frightened off by disappointments. Much here does seem to be arranged in such a way as to frighten people off, and when one is newly arrived here the obstacles do appear to be completely insurmountable. I don't want to inquire into what all this really amounts to, perhaps the appearance does really correspond to the reality, in my position I lack the right detachment to come to a conclusion about that, but pay attention, there are sometimes after all opportunities that are almost not in accord with the general situation, opportunities in which by means of a glance, a sign of trust, more can be achieved than by means of lifelong exhausting efforts.

Indeed, that is how it is.

Good, then again, of course, these opportunities are in accord with the general situation in so far as they are never made use of. But why then are they never made use of? I ask time and again."

K. did not know why.

He did certainly realize that what Burgel was talking about probably concerned him closely, but he now felt a great dislike of everything that concerned him, he shifted his head a little to one side as though in this manner he were making way for Burgel's questions and could no longer be touched by them.

"It is," Burgel continued, stretching his arms and yawning, which was in bewildering contradiction to the gravity of his words, "it is a constant complaint of the secretaries that they are compelled to carry out most of the village interrogations by night.

But why do they complain of this?

Because it is too strenuous for them?

Because they would rather spend the night sleeping?

No, that is certainly not what they complain of.

Among the secretaries there are of course those who are hardworking and those who are less hard-working, as everywhere. But none of them complains of excessive exertion, and least of all in public. That is simply not our way. In this respect we make no distinction between ordinary time and working time. Such distinctions are alien to us.

But what then have the secretaries got against the night interrogations? Is it perhaps consideration for the applicants? No, no, it is not that either. Where the applicants are concerned, the secretaries are ruthless, admittedly not a lot more ruthless than towards themselves, but merely precisely as ruthless. Actually this ruthlessness is, when you come to think of it, nothing but a rigid obedience to and execution of their duty, the greatest consideration that the applicants can really wish for.

And this is at bottom - granted, a superficial observer does not notice this - completely recognized. Indeed, it is, for instance in this case, precisely the night interrogations that are welcomed by the applicants, no objections in principle come in regarding the night interrogations. Why nevertheless the secretaries' dislike?"

This K. did not know , he knew so little, he could not even distinguish where Burgel was seriously or only apparently expecting an answer.

"You let me lie down in your bed," he thought, "I shall answer all your questions for you at noon to-morrow or, better still tomorrow evening."

But Burgel did not seem to be paying attention to him, he was far too much occupied with the question that he had put to himself: "So far as I can see and so far as my own experience takes me, the secretaries have the following qualms regarding the night interrogations: the night is suitable for negotiations with applicants for the reason that by night it is difficult or positively impossible completely to preserve the official character of the negotiations. This is not a matter of externals, the forms can of course, if desired, be just as strictly observed by night as by day. So it is not that, on the other hand the official power of judgement suffers at night. One tends involuntarily to judge things from a more private point of view at night, the allegations of the applicants take on more weight than is due to them, the judgement of the case becomes adulterated with quite irrelevant considerations of the rest of the applicants' situation, their sufferings and anxieties, the necessary barrier between the applicants and the officials, even though externally it may be impeccably maintained, weakens, and where otherwise, as is proper, only questions and answers are exchanged, what sometimes seems to take place is an odd, wholly unsuitable changing of places between the persons.

This at least is what the secretaries say, and they are of course the people who, through their vocation, are endowed with a quite extraordinary subtlety of feeling in such matters. But even they - and this has often been discussed hi our circles - notice little of those unfavourable influences during the night interrogations. On the contrary, they exert themselves right from the beginning to counteract them and end up by believing they have achieved quite particularly good results. If, however, one reads the records through afterwards one is often amazed at their obvious and glaring weaknesses. And these are defects, and, what is more, ever and again mean half-unjustified gains for the applicants, which at least according to our regulations cannot be repaired by the usual direct method. Quite certainly they will at some later time be corrected by a control-officer, but this will only profit the law, but will not be able to damage that applicant more. Are the complaints of the secretaries under such circumstances not thoroughly justified?"

K. had already spent a little while sunk in half-sleep, but now he was roused again.

"Why all this? Why all this?" he wondered, and from under lowered eyelids considered Burgel not like an official discussing difficult questions with him, but only like something that was preventing him from sleeping and whose further meaning he could not discover.

But Burgel, wholly abandoned to the pursuit of his thoughts, smiled, as though he had just succeeded in misleading K. a little. Yet he was prepared to bring him back on to the right road immediately.

"Well," he said, "on the other hand one cannot simply go and call these complaints quite justified, either. The night interrogations are, indeed, nowhere actually prescribed by the regulations, so one is not offending against any regulation if one tries to avoid them, but conditions, the excess of work, the way the officials are occupied in the Castle, how indispensable they are, the regulation that the interrogation of applicants is to take place only after the final conclusion of all the rest of the investigation, but then instantly, all this and much else has after all made the night interrogations an indispensable necessity. But if now they have become a necessity - this is what I say - this is nevertheless also, at least indirectly, a result of the regulations, and to find fault with the nature of the night interrogations would then almost mean - I am, of course, exaggerating a little, and only since it is an exaggeration can I utter it, as such - would then indeed mean finding fault with the regulations.

On the other hand it may be conceded to the secretaries that they should try as best they can to safeguard themselves, within the terms of the regulations, against the night interrogations and their perhaps only apparent disadvantages. This is in fact what they do, and indeed to the greatest extent. They permit only subjects of negotiation from which there is in every sense as litde as possible to be feared, test themselves closely prior to negotiations and, if the result of the test demands it, even at the very last moment cancel all examinations, strengthen their hand by summoning an applicant often as many as ten times before really dealing with him, have a liking for sending away - to deputize for them colleagues who are not competent to deal with the given case and who can, therefore, handle it with greater ease, schedule the negotiations at least for the beginning or the end of the night, avoiding the middle hours, there ar many more such measures, the secretaries are not the people to let anyone get the better of them so easily, they are almost a resilient as they are vulnerable."

K. was asleep, it was not real sleep, he could hear Burgel's words perhaps better than during his former dead-tired state of waking, word after word struck his ear, but the tiresome consciousness had gone, he felt free it was no longer Burgel who held him, only he still sometimes groped towards Burgel, he was not yet in the depths of sleep but immersed in it he certainly was. No one should deprive him of that now. And it seemed to him as though with this he had achieved a great victory and already there was a party of people there to celebrate it, and he or perhaps someone else raised the champagne glass in honour of this victory. And so that all should know what it was all about the fight and the victory were repeated once again or perhaps not repeated at all, but only took place now and had already been celebrated earlier and there was no leaving off celebrating it, because fortunately the outcome was certain.

A secretary, naked, very like the statue of a Greek god, was hard pressed by K. in the fight. It was very funny and K. in his sleep smiled gently about how the secretary was time and again startled out of his proud attitude by K,'s assaults and would hastily have to use his raised arm and clenched fist to cover unguarded parts of his body and yet was always too slow in doing so. The fight did not last long. Step for step, and they were very big steps, K. advanced.

Was it a fight at all?

There was no serious obstacle, only now and then a squeak from the secretary.

This Greek god squeaked like a girl being tickled. And finally he was gone,

K. was alone in the large room, ready for battle he turned round, looking for his opponent. But there was no longer anyone there, the company had also scattered, only the champagne glass lay broken on the floor. K. trampled it to smithereens. But the splinters pricked him, with a start he woke once again, he felt sick, like a small child being woken up.

Nevertheless, at the sight of Burgel`s chest a thought that was part of his dream brushed his awareness: "Here you have your Greek god! Go on, haul him out of bed!"

"There is, however," Burgel said, his face thoughtfully tilted towards the ceiling, as though he were searching his memory for examples, but without being able to find any, "there is however, nevertheless, in spite of all precautionary measures, a way in which it is possible for the applicants to exploit this nocturnal weakness of the secretaries - always assuming that it is a weakness - to their own advantage.

Admittedly, a very rare possibility, or, rather, one that almost never occurs. It consists in the applicant's coming unannounced in the middle of the night. You marvel, perhaps, that this, although it seems to be so obvious, should happen so very seldom.

Well, yes, you are not familiar with conditions here. But even you must, I suppose, have been struck by the foolproofness of the official organization. Now from this foolproofness it does result that everyone who has any petition or who must be interrogated in any matter for other reasons, instantly, without delay, usually indeed even before he has worked the matter out for himself, more, indeed, even before he himself knows of it, has already received the summons. He is not yet questioned this time, usually not yet questioned, the matter has usually not yet reached that stage, but he has the summons, he can no longer come unannounced, at best he can come at the wrong time, well, then all that happens is that his attention is drawn to the date and the hour of the summons, and if he then comes back at the right time he is as a rule sent away, that no longer causes any difficulty.

Having the summons in the applicant's hand and the case noted in the files are, it is true, not always adequate, but, nevertheless, powerful defensive weapons for the secretaries. This refers admittedly only to the secretary in whose competence the matter happens to lie. It would still, of course, be open to everyone to approach the others in the night, taking them by surprise. Yet this is something scarcely anyone will do, it is almost senseless.

First of all it would mean greatly annoying the competent secretary.

We secretaries are, it is true, by no means jealous of each other with regard to work, as everyone carries far too great a burden of work, a burden that is piled on him truly stint, but in dealing with the applicants we simply must not tolerate any interference with our sphere of competence. An applicant, one before now, has lost the game because, thinking he would not be making progress with the competent authority, he tried to slip through by approaching some other, one not competent. Such attempts must, besides, fail also because of the fact that a non-competent secretary, even when he is taken unawares at dead of night and has die best will to help, precisely as a consequence of his non-competence can scarcely intervene any more effectively than the next best lawyer, indeed at bottom much less so, for what he lacks, of course - even if otherwise he could do something, since after all he knows the secret paths of the law better than all these legal gentry - concerning things with regard to which he is not competent, what he lacks is quite simply time, he hasn't a moment to spare for it.

So who then, the prospects being such, would spend his nights playing the non-competent secretary?

Indeed, the applicants are in any case fully occupied if, besides carrying out their normal duties, they wish to respond to the summonses and hints from the competent authorities, "fully occupied" that is to say in the sense in which it concerns the applicants, which is, of course, far from being the same as "fully occupied" in the sense in which it concerns the secretaries."

K. nodded, smiling, he believed he now understood everything perfectly. Not because it concerned him, but because he was now convinced he would fall fast asleep in the next few minutes, this time without dreaming or being disturbed. Between the competent secretaries on the one hand and the non-competent on the other, and confronted with the crowd of fully occupied applicants, he would sink into deep sleep and in this way escape everything.

Burgel's quiet, self-satisfied voice, which was obviously doing its best to put its owner to sleep, was something he had now become so used to that it would do more to put him to sleep than to disturb him.

"Clatter, mill, clatter on and on," he thought, "you clatter just for me."

"Where then, now," Burgel said, fidgeting at his underlip with two fingers, with widened eyes, craning neck, rather as though after a strenuous long walk he were approaching a delightful view, "where now is that previously mentioned, rare possibility that never occurs? The secret lies in the regulations regardjug competence. The fact is things are not so constituted, and so such a large living organization cannot be so constituted, that there is only one definite secretary competent to deal with each case.

It is rather that one is competent above all others, but partly others are in certain respects, even though to a smaller degree - also competent.

Who, even if he were the hardest of workers, could keep together on his desk, single-handed, all the aspects of even the most minor incident? Even what I have been saying about the competence above all others is saying too much. For is not the whole competence contained even in the smallest? Is not what is decisive here the passion with which the case is tackled? And is this not always the same, always present in full intensity? In all things there may be distinctions among the secretaries, and there are countless such distinctions, but not in the passion. None of them will be able to restrain himself if it is demanded of him that he shall concern himself with a case in regard to which he is competent if only in the smallest degree. Outwardly, indeed, an orderly mode of negotiation must be established, and so it comes about that a particular secretary comes into the foreground for each applicant, one they have, officially, to keep to.

This, however, does not even need to be the one who is in the highest degree competent in regard to the case, what is decisive here is the organization and its particular needs of the moment. That is the general situation.

And now, Land Surveyor, consider the possibility that through some circumstances or other, in spite of the obstacles already described to you, which are in general quite sufficient, an applicant does nevertheless, in the middle of the night, surprise a secretary who has a certain degree of competence with regard to the given case. I dare say you have never thought of such a possibility? I am quite prepared to believe it. Nor is it at all necessary to think of that for it does, after all, practically never occur.

What sort of and quite specially constituted, small, skilful grain would an applicant have to be in order to slip through the incomparable sieve?

You think it cannot happen at all?

You are right, it cannot happen at all.

But some night - for who can vouch for everything? - it does happen.

Admittedly, I don't know anyone among my acquaintances to whom it has ever happened, well, it is true that proves very little, the circle of those acquaintances is restricted in comparison to the number involved here, and besides it is by no means certain that a secretary to whom such a thing has happened will admit it, since it is, after all, a very personal affair and one that in a sense gravely touches the official sense of shame.

Nevertheless my experience does perhaps prove that what we are concerned with is a matter so rare, actually only existing by way of rumour, not confirmed by anything else at all, that there is, therefore, really no need to be afraid of it. Even if it were really to happen, one can - one would think - positively render it harmless by proving to it, which is very easy, that there is no room for it in this world.

In any case it is morbid to be so afraid of it that one hides, say, under the quilt and does not dare to peep out. And even if this perfect improbability should suddenly have taken on shape, is then everything lost? On the contrary. That everything should be lost is yet more improbable than the most improbable thing itself. Granted, if the applicant is actually in the room things are in a very bad way. It constricts the heart.

"How long will you be able to put up resistance?" one wonders.

But it will be no resistance at all, one knows that. You must only picture the situation correctly. The never-beheld, always-expected applicant, truly thirstingly expected and always reasonably regarded as out of reach - there this applicant sits. By his mute presence, if by nothing else, he constitutes an invitation to penetrate into his poor life, to look around there as in one's own property and there to suffer with him under the weight of his futile demands. This invitation in the silent night is beguiling.

One gives way to it, and now one has actually ceased to function in one's official capacity. It is a situation in which it very soon becomes impossible to refuse to do a favour.

To put it precisely, one is desperate.

To put it still more precisely, one is very happy for the defenceless position in which one sits here waiting for the applicant to utter his plea and knowing that once it is uttered one must grant it, even if, at least in so far as one has oneself a general view of the situation, it positively tears the official organization to shreds: this is, I suppose, the worst thing that can happen to one in the fulfilment of one's duties, above all - apart from everything else - because it is also a promotion, one surpassing all conceptions, that one here for the pioment usurps. For it is inherent in our position that we are not empowered to grant pleas such as that with which we are here concerned, yet through the proximity of this nocturnal applicant our official powers do in a manner of speaking grow, we pledge ourselves to do things that are outside our scope.

Indeed, we shall even fulfil our pledges.

The applicant wrings from us in the night, as the robber does in the forest, sacrifices of which we should otherwise never be capable.

Well, all right, that is the way it is now when the applicant is still there, strengthening us and compelling us and spurring us on, and while everything is still half unconsciously under way. But how it will be afterwards, when it is all over, when, sated and carefree, the applicant leaves us and there we are, alone, defenceless in the face of our misuse of official power - that does not bear thinking of.

Nevertheless, we are happy.

How suicidal happiness can be!

We might, of course, exert ourselves to conceal the true position from the applicant.

He himself will scarcely notice anything of his own accord. He has, after all, in his own opinion probably only for some indifferent, accidental reasons -being overtired, disappointed, ruthless and indifferent from over-fatigue and disappointment - pushed his way into a room other than the one he wanted to enter, he sits there in ignorance, occupied with his thoughts, if he is occupied at all, with his mistake or with his fatigue.

Could one not leave him in that situation?

One cannot.

With the loquacity of those who are happy one has to explain everything to him. Without being able to spare oneself in the slightest one must show him in detail what has happened and for what reasons this has happened, how extraordinarily rare and how uniquely great the opportunity is, one must show how the applicant, though he has stumbled into this opportunity in utter helplessness such as no other being is capable of than precisely an applicant, can, however, now, if he wants to, Land Surveyor, dominate everything and to that end has to do nothing but in some way or other put forward his plea, for which fulfilment is already what which indeed it is already coming to meet, all this one tn show.

It is the official's hour of travail. But when one has do even that, then, Land Surveyor, all that is essential has been done, then one must resign oneself and wait."

K. was asleep, impervious to all that was happening, his head, which had at first been lying on his left arm on top of the bedpost, had slid down as he slept and now hung unsupported, slowly dropping lower. The support of the arm above was no longer sufficient. Involuntarily K. provided himself with new support by planting his right hand firmly against the foot of the bed whereby he accidentally took hold of Burgel's foot, which happened to be sticking up under the quilt. Burgel looked down and abandoned the foot to him, tiresome though this might be.

Now there came some vigorous knocking on the partition wall.

K. started up and looked at the wall.

"Isn't the Land Surveyor there?" a voice asked.

"Yes," Burgel said, freed his foot from K.'s hold and suddenly stretched wildly and wantonly like a little boy.

"Then tell him it's high time for him to come over here," the voice continued.

There was no consideration shown for Burgel or for whether he might still require K.'s presence.

"It's Erlanger," Burgel said in a whisper, seeming not at all surprised that Erlanger was in the next room.

"Go to him at once, he's already annoyed, try to conciliate him. He's a sound sleeper.

But still, we have been talking too loudly. One cannot control oneself and one's voice when one is speaking of certain things.

Well, go along now, you don't seem able to shake yourself out of your sleep.

Go along, what are you still doing here?

No, you don't need to apologize for being sleepy, why should you?

One's physical energies last only to a certain limit. Who can help the fact that precisely this limit is significant in other ways too?

No, nobody can help it That is how the world itself corrects the deviations in its course and maintains the balance. This is indeed an excellent, time and again unimaginably excellent arrangement, even if in other respects dismal and cheerless. Well, go along, I don't know why you look at me like that. If you delay much longer Erlanger will be down on roe, and that is something I should very much like to avoid."

"Go along now.

Who knows what awaits you over there?

Everything here is full of opportunities, after all. Only there are, of course, opportunities that are, in a manner of speaking, too great to be , made use of, there are things that are wrecked on nothing but themselves.

Yes, that is astonishing.

For the rest, I hope I shall now be able to get to sleep for a while after all. Of course, it is five o'clock by now and the noise will soon be beginning. If you would only go!"

Stunned by suddenly being woken up out of deep sleep, still boundlessly in need of sleep, his body aching all over from having been in such an uncomfortable position, K. could for a long time not bring himself to stand up, but held his forehead and looked down at his lap. Even Burgel's continual dismissals would not have been able to make him go, it was only a sense of the utter uselessness of staying any longer in this room that slowly brought him to it. How indescribably dreary this room seemed to him. Whether it had become so or had been so all the time, he did not know. Here he would not even succeed in going to sleep again. This conviction was indeed the decisive factor. Smiling a little at this, he rose supporting himself wherever he found any support, on the bed, on the wall, on the door, and, as though he had long ago taken leave of Burgel, left without saying good-bye.

Problaly he would have walked past Erlanger's room just as indifferently if Erlanger had not been standing in the open door, beckoning to him.

One short sign with the forefinger.

Erlanger was already completely dressed to go out, he wore a black fur coat with a tight collar buttoned up high. A servant was just handing him his gloves and was still holding a fur cap.

"You should have come long ago," Erlanger said.

K. tried to apologize.

Wearily shutting his eyes, Erlanger indkated that ne was not interested in hearing apologies.

"The matter is as follows," he said. "Formerly a certain Frieda was employed in toe taproom. I only know her name, I don't know the girl herself, she is no concern of mine.

This Frieda sometimes served Klamm with beer.

Now there seems to be another girl. Well, this change is, of course, probably of no importance anyone, and quite certainly of none to Klamm. But the bigger a job is, and Klamm's job is, of course, the biggest, the less strength is left over for protecting oneself against the external world, and as a result any unimportant alteration in the most unimportant things can be a serious disturbance. The smallest alteration on the writing-desk, the removal of a duty spot that has been there ever since anyone can remember, all this can be disturbing, and so, in the same way, can a new barmaid.

Well of course, all of this, even if it would disturb anyone else and in any given job, does not disturb Klamm. That is quite out of the question. Nevertheless we are obliged to keep such a watch over Klamm's comfort that we remove even disturbances that are not such for him - and probably there are none whatsoever for him - if they strike us as being possible disturbances.

It is not for his sake, it is not for the sake of his work, that we remove these disturbances, but for our sake, for the sake of our conscience and our peace of mind. For this reason this Frieda must at once return to the taproom. Perhaps she will be disturbing precisely through the fact of her return. Well, then we shall send her away again, but, for the time being, she must return. You are living with her, as I am told, therefore arrange immediately for her return. In this no consideration can be given to personal feelings, that goes without saying, of course, hence I shall not enter into the least further discussion of the matter. I am already doing much more than is necessary if I mention that if you show yourself reliable in this trivial affair it may on some occasion be of use to you in improving your prospects. That is all I have to say to you."

He gave K. a nod of dismissal, put on the fur cap handed to him by the servant, and, followed by the servant, went down the passage, rapidly, but limping a little.

Sometimes orders that were given here were very easy to carry out, but this case did not please K. Not only because the order affected Frieda and, though intended as an order, sounded to K. like scornful laughter, but above all because what it confronted K. with was the futility of all his endeavours and orders, the unfavourable and the favourable, disregarded him, and even the most favourable probably had an ultimate unfavourable core, but in any case they all disregarded him, and he was in much too lowly a position to be able to intervene or, far less, to silence them and to gain a hearing for his own voice.

If Erlanger waves you off, what are you going to do?

And if he were not to wave you off, what could you say to him?

True, K. remained aware that his weariness had to-day done him more harm than all the unfavourableness of circumstances, but why could he, who had believed he could rely on his body and who would never have started out on his way without that conviction, why could he not endure a few bad nights and one sleepless night, why did he become so unmanageably tired precisely here where nobody was tired or, rather, where everyone was tired all the time, without this, however, doing any damage to the work, indeed, even seeming to promote it?

The conclusion to be drawn from this was that this was in its way a quite different sort of fatigue from K.'s. Here it was doubtless fatigue amid happy work, something that outwardly looked like fatigue and was actually indestructable repose, indestructable peace. If one is a little tired at noon, that is part of the happy natural course of the day.

"For the gentlemen here it is always noon," K. said to himself.

And it was very much in keeping with this that now, at five o'clock, things were beginning to stir everywhere on each side of the passage. This babel of voices in the rooms had something extremely merry about it. Once it sounded like the jubilation of children getting ready for a picnic, another time like daybreak in a hen-roost, like the joy of being in complete accord with the awakening day.

Somewhere indeed a gentleman imitated the crowing of a cock. Though the passage itself was still empty, the doors were already in motion, time and again one would be opened a little and quickly shut again, the passage buzzed with this opening and shutting of doors, now and then, too, in the space above the partition walls, which did not quite reach to the ceiling, K. saw towsled early-morning heads appear and instantly vanish again.

From far off there slowly came a little barrow pushed by a servant, containing files. A second servant walked beside it, with a catalogue in his hand, obviously comparing the numbers on the doors with those on the file. The little barrow stopped outside most of the doors, usually then, too, the door would open and the appropriate riles, sometimes, however, only a small sheet of paper - in such cases a little conversation came about between the room and the passage, probably the servant was being reproached - would be handed into the room. If the door remained shut, the files were carefully piled up on the threshold. In such cases it seemed to K. as though the movement of the doors round about did not diminish, even though there the files had already been distributed, but as though it were on the contrary increasing. Perhaps the others were yearningly peering out at the files incomprehensibly left lying on the threshold, they could not understand how anyone should only need to open the door in order to gain possession of his files and yet should not do so.

Perhaps it was even possible that files that were never picked up at all might later be distributed among the other gentlemen, who were even now seeking to make sure, by frequent peering out, whether the files were still lying on the threshold and whether there was thus still hope for them. Incidentally, these files that remained lying were for the most part particularly big bundles. And K. assumed that they had been temporarily left lying out of a certain desire to boast or out of malice or even out of justifiable pride that would be stimulating to colleagues. What strengthened him in this assumption was the fact that sometimes, always when he happened not to be looking, the bag, having been exposed to view for long enough, was suddenly and hastily pulled into the room and the door then remained as motionless as before, the doors round about then also became quiet again, disappointed or, it might be, content that this object of constant provocation had at last been removed, but then, however, they gradually came into motion again.

K. considered all this not only with curiosity but also with sympathy. He almost enjoyed the feeling of being in the midst of this bustle, looked this way and that, following - even though at an appropriate distance - the servants, who, admittedly, had already more than once turned towards him with a severe glance, with lowered head and pursed lips, while he watched their work of distribution. The further it progressed the less smoothly it went, either the catalogue was not quite correct, of the files were not always clearly identifiable for the servants, or the gentlemen were raising objections for other reasons.

At any rate it would happen that some of the distributions had to be withdrawn, then the little barrow moved back, and through the chink of the door negotiations were conducted about the return of files. These negotiations in themselves caused great difficulties, but it happened frequently enough that if it was a matter of return precisely those doors that had earlier on been in the most lively motion now remained inexorably shut, as though they did not wish to know anything more about the matter at all.

Only then did the actual difficulties begin.

He who believed he had a claim to the files became extremely impatient, made a great din inside his room, clapping his hands, stamping his feet, ever and again shouting a particular file-number out into the passage through the chink of the door. Then the little barrow was often left quite unattended. The one servant was busy trying to appease the impatient official, the other was outside the shut door battling for the return. Both had a hard time of it. The impatient official was often made still more impatient by the attempts to appease him, he could no longer endure listening to the servant's empty words, he did not want consolation, he wanted files.

Such a gentleman once poured the contents of a whole wash-basin through the gap at the top, on to the servant. But the other servant, obviously the higher in rank, was having a much harder time of it if the gentleman concerned at all deigned to enter into negotiations, there were matter-of-fact discussions during which the servant referred to his catalogue, the gentleman to his notes and to precisely those files that he was supposed to return, which for the time being, however, he clutched tightly in his hand, so that scarcely a corner of them remained visible to the servant's longing eyes. Then, too, the servant would have to run back for fresh evidence to the little barrow, which had by itself rolled a little further along the slightly sloping passage, or he would have to go to the gentleman claiming the files and there report the objections raised by the gentleman now in possession, receiving in return fresh counter-objections. Such negotiations lasted a very long time sometimes agreement was reached, the gentleman would haps hand over part of the files or get other files as compensation, since all that had happened was that a mistake had been made.

But it also happened sometimes that someone simply had to abandon all the files demanded, either because he had been driven into a corner by the servant's evidence or because he was tired of the prolonged bargaining, but then he did not give the files to the servant, but with sudden resolution flung them out into the passage, so that the strings came undone and the papers flew about and the servants had a great deal of trouble getting everything straight again. But all this was still relatively simple compared with what happened when the servant got no answer at all to his pleading for the return of the files. Then he would stand outside the closed door, begging, imploring, citing his catalogue, referring to regulations, all in vain, no sound came from inside the room, and to go in without permission was obviously something the servant had no right to do. Then even this excellent servant would sometimes lose his self-control, he would go to his barrow, sit down on the files, wipe the sweat from his brow, and for a little while do nothing at all but sit there helplessly swinging his feet. All round there was very great interest in the affair, everywhere there was whispering going on, scarcely any door was quiet, and up above at the top of the partition wall faces queerly masked almost to the eyes with scarves and kerchiefs, though for the rest never for an instant remaining quiet in one place, watched all that was going on.

In the midst of this unrest K. had been struck by the fact that Burgel's door had remained shut the whole time and that the servant had already passed along this part of the passage, but no files had been allotted to Burgel.

Perhaps he was still asleep, which would indeed, in all this din, have indicated that he was a very sound sleeper, but why had he not received any files?

Only very few rooms, and these probably unoccupied ones, had been passed over in this manner.

On the other hand there was already a new and particularly restless occupant of Erlanger's room, Erlanger must positively have been driven out in the night by him, this was not much in keeping with Erlanger's cool, distant nature, but the fact that he had had to wait on the threshold for K. did after all indicate that it was so.

Ever and again K. would then soon return from all distracting observations to watching the servant. Truly, what K. had otherwise been told about servants in general, about their slackness, their easy life, their arrogance, did not apply to this servant, there were doubtless exceptions among the servants too or, what was more probable, various groups among them, for here, as K.. noticed, there were many nuances of which he had up to now scarcely had as much as a glimpse. What he particularly liked was this servant's inexorability. In his struggle with these stubborn little rooms - to K. it often seemed to be a struggle with the rooms, since he scarcely ever caught sight of the occupants - the servant never gave up. His strength did sometimes fail - whose strength would not have failed? - but he soon recovered, slipped down from the little barrow and, holding himself straight, clenching his teeth, returned to the attack against the door that had to be conquered.

And it would happen that he would be beaten back twice or three times, and that in a very simple way, solely by means of that confounded silence, and nevertheless was still not defeated. Seeing that he could not achieve anything by frontal assault, he would try another method, for instance, if K. understood righdy, cunning.

He would then seemingly abandon the door, so to speak allowing it to exhaust its own taciturnity, turned his attention to other doors, after a while returned, called the other servant, all this ostentatiously and noisily, and began piling up files on the threshold of the shut door, as though he had changed his mind, and as though there were no justification for taking anything away from this gentleman, but, on the contrary, something to be allotted to him. Then he would walk on, still, however, keeping an eye on the door, and then when the gentleman, as usually happened, soon cautiously opened the door in order to pull the files inside, in a few leaps the servant was there, thrust his foot between the door and the doorpost, so forcing the gentleman at least to negotiate with him face to face, which then usually led after all to a more or less satisfactory result.

And if this method was not successful or if at one door this seemed to him not the right approach, he would try another method. He would then transfer his attention to the gendeman who was claiming the files. Then he pushed aside the other servant, who worked always only in a mechanical way, a fairly useless assistant to him, and himself began talking persuasively to the gentleman, whisperingly, furtively, pushing his head right round the door, probably making promises to him and assuring him that at the next distribution the other gentleman would be appropriately punished, at any rate he would often point towards the opponent's door and laugh, in as far as his fatigue allowed.

Then, however, there were cases, one or two, when he did abandon all attempts, but even here K. believed that it was only an apparent abandonment or at least an abandonment for justifiable reasons, for he quietly walked on, tolerating, without glancing round, the din made by the wronged gentleman, only an occasional, more prolonged closing of the eyes indicating that the din was painful to him. Yet then the gentleman would gradually quieten down, and just as a child's ceaseless crying gradually passes into ever less frequent single sobs, so it was also with his outcry. But even after it had become quite quiet there, there would, nevertheless, sometimes be a single cry or a rapid opening and slamming of that door. In any case it became apparent that here, too, the servant had probably acted in exactly the right way. Finally there remained only one gentleman who would not quieten down, he would be silent for a long period, but only in order to gather strength, then he would burst out again, no less furiously than before. It was not quite clear why he shouted and complained in this way, perhaps it was not about the distribution of files at all.

Meanwhile the servant had finished his work. Only one single file, actually only a little piece of paper, a leaf from a note-pad, was left in the little barrow, through his helper's fault, and now they did not know whom to allot it to.

"That might very well be my file," it flashed through K.'s mind.

The Mayor had, after all, constantly spoken of this smallest of small cases. And, arbitrary and ridiculous though he himself at bottom regarded his assumption as being, K. tried to get closer to the servant, who was thoughtfully glancing over the little piece of paper.

This was not altogether easy, for the servant ill repaid K.'s sympathy, even in the midst of his most strenuous work he had always still found time to look round at K., angrily or impatiently, with nervous jerks of his head. Only now, after finishing the distribution, did he seem to have somewhat forgotten K., as indeed he had altogether become more indifferent, this being understandable as a result of his great exhaustion, nor did he give himself much trouble with the little piece of paper, perhaps not even reading it through, only pretending to do so, and although here in the passage he would probably have delighted any occupant of a room by allotting this piece of paper to him, he decided otherwise, he was now sick and tired of distributing things, with his forefinger on his lips he gave his companion a sign to be silent, tore - K. was still far from having reached his side - the piece of paper into shreds and put the pieces into his pocket.

It was probably the first irregularity that K. had seen in the working of the administration here, admittedly it was possible that he had misunderstood this too. And even if it was an irregularity, it was pardonable. Under the conditions prevailing here the servant could not work unerringly, some time the accumulated annoyance, the accumulated uneasiness, must break out, and if it manifested itself only in the tearing up of a little piece of paper it was still comparatively innocent. For the yells of the gentleman who could not be quieted by any method were still resounding through the passage, and his colleagues, who in other respects did not adopt a very friendly attitude to each other, seemed to be wholly of one mind with respect to this uproar.

It gradually began to seem as if the gentleman had taken on the task of making a noise for all those who simply by calling out to him and nodding their heads encouraged him to keep it up. But now the servant was no longer paying any further attention to the master, he had finished his job, he pointed to the handle of the little barrow, indicating that the other servant should take hold of it, and so they went away again as they had come, only more contentedly and so quickly that the little barrow bounced along ahead of them.

Only once did they start and glance back again, when the gentleman who was ceaselessly screaming and shouting, and outside whose door K. was now hanging about because he would have liked to discover what it really was that the gentleman wanted, evidently found shouting no longer adequate, probably had discovered the button of an electric bell and, doubtless enraptured at being relieved in this way, instead of shouting now began an uninterrupted ringing of the bell.

Hereupon a great muttering began in the other rooms, which seemed to indicate approval, the gentleman seemed to be doing something that all would have liked to do long ago and only for some unknown reason had had to leave undone.

Was it perhaps attendance, perhaps Frieda for whom the gentleman was ringing?

If that was so, he could go on ringing for a long time. For Frieda was busy wrapping Jeremiah up in wet sheets, and even supposing he were well again by now, she had no time, for then she was in his arms.

But the ringing of the bell did instantly have an effect. Even now the landlord of the Herrenhof himself came hastening along from far off, dressed in black and buttoned up as always. But it was as though he were forgetful of his dignity, he was in such a hurry.

His arms were half outspread, just as if he had been called on account of some great disaster and were coming in order to take hold of it and instantly smother it against his chest, and at every little irregularity in the ringing he seemed briefly to leap into the air and hurry on faster still.

Now his wife also appeared, a considerable distance behind him, she too running with outspread arms, but her steps were short and affected, and K. thought to himself that she would come too late, the landlord would in the meantime have done all that was necessary.

And in order to make room for the landlord as he ran K. stood close back against the wall. But the landlord stopped straight in front of K., as though K. were his goal, and the next instant the landlady was there too, and both overwhelmed him with reproaches, which in the suddenness and surprise of it he did not understand, especially since the ringing of the gentleman's bell was also mixed up with it and other bells also began ringing, now no longer indicating a state of emergency, but only for fun and in excess of delight. Because he was very much concerned to understand exactly what his fault was, K.

was entirely in agreement with the landlord's taking him by the arm and walked away with him out of this uproar, which was continually increasing, for behind them - K. did not turn round at all, because the landlord, and even more, on the other side, the landlady, was talking to him urgently - the doors were now opening wide, the passage was becoming animated, traffic seemed to be beginning there as in a lively narrow little alley, the doors ahead of them were evidently waiting impatiently for K. to go past them at long last so that they could release the gentlemen, and in the midst of all this, pressed again and again, the bells kept on ringing as though celebrating a victory.

Now at last - they were by now again in the quiet white courtyard, where some sledges were waiting - K. gradually learnt what it was all about.

Neither the landlord nor the landlady could understand how K. could have dared to do such a thing.

But what had he done?

K. asked time and again, but for a long time could not get any answer because his guilt was all too much a matter of course to the two of them and hence it simply did not occur to them that he asked in good faith. Only very slowly did K. realize how everything stood. He had had no right to be in the passage. In general it was at best the taproom, and this only by way of privilege and subject to revocation, to which he had entry. If he was summoned by one of the gentlemen, he had, of course, to appear in the place to which he was summoned, but had to remain always aware - surely he at least had some ordinary common sense? - that he was in a place where he actually did not belong, a place whither he had only been summoned by one of the gentlemen, and that with extreme reluctance and only because it was necessitated by official business.

It was up to him, therefore, to appear quickly, to submit to the interrogation, then, however, to disappear again, if possible even more quickly.

Had he then not had any feeling at all of the grave impropriety of being there in the passage?

But if he had had it, how had he brought himself to roam about there like cattle at pasture?

Had he not been summoned to attend a night interrogation and did He not know why the night interrogations had been introduced?

The night interrogations - and here K. was given a new explanation of their meaning - had after all only the purpose of examining applicants. The sight of whom by day would be able to the gentlemen, and this quickly, at night, with the possibility of, immediately after the unendurable artificial interrogation, forgetting all the ugliness of it in sleep. K.'s behaviour, however, had been a mockery of precautionary measures. Even ghosts vanish towards morning, but K. had remained there, his hands in his pockets, as though he were expecting that, since he did not take himself off, the whole passage with all the rooms and gentlemen would take itself off. And this - he could be sure of it - would quite certainly have happened if it had been in any way possible, for the delicacy Of the gentlemen was limitless. None of them would drive K. away, or even say, what went after all without saying, that he should at long last go away. None of them would do that, although during the period of K.'s presence they were probably trembling with agitation and the morning, their favourite time, was being ruined for them. Instead of taking any steps against K., they preferred to suffer, in which, indeed, a certain part was probably played by the hope that K. would not be able to help gradually, at long last, coming to realize what was so glaringly obvious and, in accord with the gentlemen's anguish, would himself begin to suffer, to the point of unendurability, from his own standing there in the passage in the morning, visible to all, in that horribly unfitting manner.

A vain hope.

They did not know or in their kindness and condescension did not want to admit there also existed hearts that were insensitive, hard, and not to be softened by any feeling of reverence. Does not even the nocturnal moth, the poor creature, when day comes seek out a quiet cranny, flatten itself out there, only wishing it could vanish and being unhappy because it cannot?

K. on the other hand planted himself precisely where he was most visible, and if by doing so he had been able to prevent day from breaking, he would have done so. He could not prevent it, but, alas, he could delay it and make it more difficult. Had he not watched the distribution of the files? Something that nobody was allowed to watch except the people most closely involved. Something that neither the landlord nor his wife had been allowed to see in their own house. Something of which they had only heard tell and in allusions, as for instance to-day from the servants. Had he then not noticed under what difficulties the distribution of files had proceeded, something in itself incomprehensible, since after all each of the gentlemen served only the cause, never thinking of his personal advantage and hence being obliged to exert all his powers to seeing that the distribution of the files, this important, fundamental, preliminary work, should proceed quickly and easily and without any mistakes?

And had K. then not been even remotely struck by the notion that the main cause of all the difficulties was the fact that the distribution had had to be carried out with the doors almost quite shut, without any chance of direct dealings between the gentlemen, who among each other naturally could come to an understanding in a twinkling, while the mediation through the servants inevitably dragged on almost for hours, never could function smoothly, and was a lasting torment to the gentlemen and the servants and would probably have damaging consequences in the later work?

And why could the gentlemen not deal with each other?

Well, did K. still not understand?

The like of it had never occurred in the experience of the landlady - and the landlord for his part confirmed this - and they had, after all, had to deal with many sorts of difficult people. Things that in general one would not dare to mention in so many words one had to tell him frankly, for otherwise he would not understand the most essential things. Well, then, since it had to be said: it was on his account, solely and exclusively on his account, that the gentlemen had not been able to come forth out of their rooms, since in the morning, so soon after having been asleep, they were too bashful, too vulnerable, to be able to expose themselves to the gaze of strangers.

They literally felt, however completely dressed they might be, too naked to show themselves. It was admittedly difficult to say why they felt this shame, perhaps these everlasting workers felt shame merely because they had been asleep. But what perhaps made them feel even acuter shame than showing themselves was seeing strangers. What they had successfully disposed of by means of the night interrogations, namely the sight of the applicants they found so hard to endure, they did not want now in the morning to have suddenly, without warning, in all its truth to nature, obtruding itself upon them all over again. That was the two gentlemen for the first time and had also had to answer their questions, into the bargain. Everything, so far as he knew had worked out pretty well, but then that misfortune had occurred, which, after what had gone before, he could scarcely be blamed for.

Unfortunately only Erlanger and Burgel had realized what a condition he was in and they would certainly have looked after him and so prevented all the rest, but Erlanger had had to go away immediately after the interrogation, evidently in order to drive up to the Castle, and Burgel, probably himself tired after that interrogation - and how then should K. have been able to come out of it with his strength unimpaired? - had gone to sleep and had indeed slept through the whole distribution of files.

If K. had had a similar chance he would have been delighted to take it and would gladly have done without all the prohibited insight into what was going on there, and this all the more lightheartedly since in reality he had been quite incapable of seeing anything, for which reason even the most sensitive gentlemen could have shown themselves before him without embarrassment.

The mention of the two interrogations - particularly of that with Erlanger - and the respect with which K. spoke of the gentlemen inclined the landlord favourably towards him. He seemed to be prepared to grant K.'s request to be allowed to lay a board across the barrels and sleep there at least till dawn, but the landlady was markedly against it, twitching ineffectively here and there at her dress, the slovenly state of which she seemed only now to have noticed, she kept on shaking her head. A quarrel obviously of long standing with regard to the orderliness of the house was on the point of breaking out afresh. For K. in his fatigued state the talk between the couple took on exaggeratedly great significance. To be driven out from here again seemed to him to be a misfortune surpassing all that had happened to him hitherto. This must not be allowed to happen, even if the landlord and the landlady should unite against him.

Crumpled up on the barrel, he looked in eager expectancy at the two of them until the landlady, with her abnormal touchiness, which had long ago struck K., suddenly stepped aside and probably she had by now been discussing other things with the landlord, exclaimed: "How he stares at me! Do send him away now!"

But K., seizing the opportunity and now utterly, almost to the point of indifference, convinced that he would stay said: "I'm not looking at you, only at your dress."

"Why my dress?" the landlady asked agitatedly.

K. shrugged his shoulders.

"Come on!" the landlady said to the landlord. "Don't you see he's drunk, the lout?

Leave him here to sleep it off!"

And she even ordered Pepi, who on being called by her emerged out of the dark, towsled, tired, idly holding a broom in her hand, to throw K. some sort of a cushion.

When K. woke up he at first thought he had hardly slept at all. The room was as empty and warm as before, all the walls in darkness, the one bulb over the beer-taps extinguished, and outside the windows was the night. But when he stretched, and the cushion fell down and the bed and the barrels creaked, Pepi instantly appeared, and now he learnt that it was already evening and that he had slept for well over twelve hours.

The landlady had asked after him several times during the day, and so had Gerstacker, who had been waiting here in the dark, by the beer, while K. had been talking to the landlady in the morning, but then he had not dared to disturb K., had been here once in the meantime to see how K. was getting on, and finally, so at least it was alleged, Frieda had also come and had stood for a moment beside K., yet she had scarcely come on K.'s account but because she had had various things to make ready here, for in the evening she was to resume her old duties after all.

"I suppose she doesn't like you any more?" Pepi asked, bringing coffee and cakes.

But she no longer asked it maliciously, in her old way, but sadly, as though in the meantime she had come to know the malice of the world, compared with which all one's own malice fails and becomes senseless. She spoke to K. as to a fellow sufferer, and when he tasted the coffee and she thought she saw that it was not sweet enough for him, she ran and brought him the full sugar-bowl. Her sadness had, indeed, not prevented her from tricking herself out to-day if anything even more than the last time. She wore an abundance of bows and ribbons plaited into her hair, along her forehead and on her temples the hair had been carefully curled with the tongs, and round her neck she had a little chain that hung down into the low-cut opening of her blouse.

When, in his contentment at having at last slept his fill and now being permitted to drink a good cup of coffee, K. furtively stretched his hand out towards one of the bows and tried to untie it, Pepi said wearily: "Do leave me alone," and sat down beside him on a barrel.

And K. did not even need to ask her what was the matter, she at once began telling the story herself, rigidly staring into K.'s coffeemug, as though she needed some distraction, even while she was talking, as though she could not quite abandon herself to her suffering even when she was discussing it, as that would be beyond her powers.

First of all K. learnt that actually he was to blame for Pepi's misfortunes, but that she did not bear him any grudge. And she nodded eagerly as she talked, in order to prevent K. from raising any objection. First he had taken Frieda away from the taproom and thus made Pepi's rise possible. There was nothing else that could be imagined that could have brought Frieda to give up her situation, she sat tight there in the taproom like a spider in its web, with all the threads under her control, threads of which no one knew but she.

It would have been quite impossible to winkle her out against her will, only love for some lowly person, that is to say, something that was not in keeping with her position, could drive her from her place.

And Pepi?

Had she ever thought of getting the situation for herself?

She was a chambermaid, she had an insignificant situation with few prospects, she had dreams of a great future like any other girl, one can't stop oneself from having dreams, but she had never seriously thought of getting on in the world, she had resigned herself to staying in the job she had.

And now Frieda suddenly vanished from the taproom, it had happened so suddenly that the landlord had not had a suitable substitute on hand at the moment, he had looked round and his glance had fallen on Pepi, who had, admittedly, pushed herself forward in such a way as to be noticed. At that time she had loved K. as she had never loved anyone before.

Month after month she had been down there in her tiny dark room, prepared to spend years there, or, if the worst came to the worst, to spend her whole life here, ignored by everyone, and now suddenly K. had appeared, a hero, a rescuer of maidens in distress, and had opened up the way upstairs for her. Admittedly he did not know anything about her, he had not done it for her sake, but that did not diminish her gratitude, in the night preceding her appointment - the appointment was not yet definite, but still, it was now very probable - she spent hours talking to him, whispering her thanks in his ear. And in her eyes it exalted what he had done still more that it should have been Frieda, of all people, with whom he had burdened himself.

There was something incomprehensibly selfless in his making Frieda his mistress in order to pave the way for Pepi - Frieda, a plain, oldish, skinny girl with short, thin hair, a deceitful girl into the bargain, always having some sort of secret, which was probably connected, after all, with her appearance. If her wretchedness was glaringly obvious in her face and figure, she must at least have other secrets that nobody could inquire into, for instance her alleged affair with Klamm. And even thoughts like the following had occurred to Pepi at that time: is it possible that K. really loves Frieda, isn't he deceiving himself or is he perhaps deceiving only Frieda, and will perhaps the sole outcome of the whole thing after all be nothing but Pepi's rise in the world, and will K. then notice the mistake, or not want to cover it up any more, and no longer see Frieda, but only Pepi, which need not even be a crazy piece of conceit on Pepi's part, for so far as Frieda was concerned she was a match for her, one girl against another, which nobody would deny, and it had, after all, been primarily Frieda's position and the glory that Frieda had been able to invest it with that had dazzled K. at the moment.

And so then Pepi had dreamed that when she had the position K. would come to her, pleading, and she would then have the choice of either granting K.'s plea and losing her situation or of rejecting him and rising further. And she had worked out for herself that she would renounce everything and lower herself to him and teach him what true love was, which he would never be able to learn from Frieda and which was independent of her positions of honour in the world.

But then everything turned out differently.

And what was to blame for this?

Above all, K. and then, of course, Frieda's artfulness.

Above all, K.

For what was he after, what sort of strange person was he?

What was he trying to get, what were these important things that kept him busy and made him forget what was nearest of all, best of all most beautiful of all?

Pepi was the sacrifice and everything was stupid and everything was lost. And anyone who had the strength to set fire to the whole Herrenhof and burn it down, burn it to the ground, so that not a trace of it was left, burn it up like a piece of paper in the stove, he would to-day be Pepi's chosen love.

Well, so Pepi came into the taproom, four days ago to-day, shortly before lunch-time.

The work here was far from easy, it was almost killingly hard work, but there was a good deal to be got out of it too. Even previously Pepi had not lived only for the day, and even if she would never have aspired to this situation even in her wildest dreams, still, she had made plenty of observations, she knew what this situation involved, she had not taken on the situation without being prepared. One could not take it on without being prepared, otherwise one lost it in the first few hours. Particularly if one were to behave here the way the chambermaids did.

As a chambermaid one did in time come to feel one was quite lost and forgotten. It was like working down a mine, at least that was the way it was in the secretaries' passage, for days on end there. Except for a few daytime applicants who flitted in and out without daring to look up one didn't see a soul but two or three other chambermaids, and they were just as embittered.

In the morning one wasn't allowed to leave the room at all, that was when the secretaries wished to be alone among themselves, their meals were brought to them from the kitchen by the men-servants, the chambermaids usually had nothing to do with that, and during meal-times, too, one was not allowed to show oneself in the passage.

It was only while the gentlemen were working that the chambermaids were allowed to do the rooms, but naturally not those that were occupied, only those that happened to be empty at the time, and the work had to be done quite quietly so that the gentlemen were not disturbed at their work.

But how was it possible to do the cleaning quietly when the gentlemen occupied their rooms for several days on end, and the men-servants, dirty lot that they were, pottered about there into the bargain, and when the chambermaid was finally allowed to go into the room, it was in such a state that not even the flood could wash it clean?

Truly, they were exalted gentlemen, but one had to make a great effort to overcome one's disgust so as to be able to clean up after them. It wasn't that the chambermaids had such a great amount of work, but it was pretty tough. And never a kind word, never anything but reproaches, in particular the following, which was the most tormenting and the most frequent: that files had got lost during the doing of the rooms. In reality nothing ever got lost, every scrap of paper was handed over to the landlord, but in fact of course files did get lost, only it happened not to be the fault of the maids.

And then commissions came, and the maids had to leave their rooms, and the members of the commission rummaged through the beds, the girls had no possessions, of course, their few things could be put in a basket, but still, the commission searched for hours all the same. Naturally they found nothing. How should files come to be there? What did the maids care about files? But the outcome was always the same, abuse and threats uttered by the disappointed commission and passed on by the landlord. And never any peace, neither by day nor by night, noise going on half through the night and noise again at the crack of dawn. If at least one didn't have to live in, but one had to, for it was the chambermaids' job to bring snacks from the kitchen as they might be ordered, in between times, particularly at night. Always suddenly the first thumping on the chambermaids' door, the order being dictated, the running down to the kitchen, shaking the sleeping scullery-lads, the setting down of the tray with the things ordered outside the chambermaids' door, from where the men-servants fetched it how sad all that was.

But that was not the worst.

The worst was when no order came, that was to say, when, at dead of night, when everyone ought to be asleep and most of them really were asleep at last, sometimes a tiptoeing around began outside the chambermaids' door. Then the girls got out of bed - the bunks were on top of each other, for there was very little space there, the whole room the maids had being actually nothing more than a large cupboard with three shelves in it - listened at the door, knelt down, put their arms round each other in fear and whoever was tiptoeing outside the door could be heard all the time. They would all be thankful if only he would come right in and be done with it, but nothing happened, nobody came in. And at the same time one had to admit to oneself that it need not necessarily be some danger threatening, perhaps it was only someone walking up and down outside the door, trying to make up his mind to order something, and then not being able to bring himself to it after all. Perhaps that was all it was, but perhaps it was something quite different. For really one didn't know the gentlemen at all, one had hardly set eyes on them.

Anyway, inside the room the maids were fainting in terror, and when at last it was quiet again outside they leant against the wall and had not enough strength left to get back into bed. This was the life that was waiting for Pepi to return to it, this very evening she was to move back to her place in the maids' room.

And why?

Because of K. and Frieda.

Back again into that life she had scarcely escaped from, which she escaped from, it is true, with K.'s help, but also, of course, through very great exertions of her own. For in that service there the girls neglected themselves, even those who were otherwise the most careful and tidy. For whom should they smarten themselves? Nobody saw them, at best the staff in the kitchen. Anyone for whom that was enough was welcome to smarten herself.

But for the rest they were always in their little room or in the gentlemen's rooms, which it was madness and a waste so much as to set foot in with clean clodies on. And always by artificial light and in that stuffy air - with the heating always on - and actually always tired. The one free afternoon in the week was best spent sleeping quietly and without fear in one of the cubby-holes in the kitchen.

So what should one smarten oneself up for?

Yes, one scarcely bothered to dress at all.

And now Pepi had suddenly been transferred to the taproom, where, if one wanted to maintain one's position there, exactly the opposite was necessary, where one was always in full view of people, and among them very observant gentlemen, used to the best of everything, and where one therefore always had to look as smart and pleasant as possible.

Well, that was a change. And Pepi could say of herself that she had not failed to rise to the occasion. Pepi was not worrying about how things would turn out later. She knew she had the abilities necessary in this situation, she was quite certain of it, she had this conviction even now and nobody could take it away from her, not even to-day, on the day of her defeat. The only difficulty was how she was to stand the test in the very beginning, because she was, after all, only a poor chambermaid, with nothing to wear and no jewellery, and because the gentlemen had not the patience to wait and see how one would develop, but instantly, without transition, wanted a barmaid of the proper kind, or else they turned away. One would think they didn't expect so very much since, after all, Frieda could satisfy them.

But that was not right.

Pepi had often thought about this, she had, after all, often been together with Frieda and had for a time even slept together with her. It wasn't easy to find Frieda out, and anyone who was not very much on the look-out - and which of the gentlemen was very much on the look-out, after all? - was at once misled by her. No one knew better than Frieda herself how miserable her looks were, for instance when one saw her for the first time with her hair down, one clasped one's hands in pity, by rights a girl like that shouldn't even be a chambermaid. And she knew it, too, and many a night she had spent crying about it, pressing tight against Pepi and laying Pepi's hair round her own head. But when she was on duty all her doubts vanished, she thought herself better-looking than anyone, and she had the knack of getting everyone to think the same. She knew what people were like, and really that was where her art lay. And she was quick with a lie, and cheated, so that people didn't have time to get a closer look at her. Naturally that wouldn't do in the long run, people had eyes in their heads and sooner or later their eyes would tell them what to think.

But the moment she noticed the danger of that she was ready with another method, recently, for instance, her affair with Klamm.

Her affair with Klamm!

If you don't believe it, you can go and get proof.

Go to Klamm and ask him.

How cunning, how cunning.

And if you don't happen to dare to go to Klamm with an inquiry like that, and perhaps wouldn't be admitted to him with infinitely more important inquiries, and Klamm is, in fact, completely inaccessible to you only to you and your sort, for Frieda, for instance, pops in to see him whenever she likes - if that's how it is, you can still get proof of the thing, you only need to wait. After all, Klamm won't be able to tolerate such a false rumour for long, he's certain to be very keen to know what stories go round about him in the taproom and in the public rooms, all this is of the greatest importance to him, and if it's wrong he will refute it at once.

But he doesn't refute it.

Well, then there is nothing to be refuted and it is sheer truth. What one sees, indeed, is only that Frieda takes the beer into Klamm's room and comes out again with the money.

But what one doesn't see Frieda tells one about, and one has to believe her. And she doesn't even tell it, after all, she's not going to let such secrets out. No, the secrets let themselves out wherever she goes and, since they have been let out once and for all, she herself, it is true, no longer shrinks from talking about them herself, but modestly, without asserting anything, only referring to what is generally known anyway.

Not to everything.

One thing, for instance, she does not speak of, namely that since she has been in the taproom Klamm drinks less beer than formerly, not much less, but still perceptibly less beer, and there may indeed be various reasons for this, it may be that a period has come when Klamm has less taste for beer or that it is Frieda who causes him to forget about beer-drinking. Anyway, however amazing it may be, Frieda is Klamm's mistress. But how should the others not also admire what is good enough for Klamm? And so, before anyone knows what is happening, Frieda has turned into a great beauty, a girl of exactly the kind that the taproom needs. Indeed, almost too beautiful, too powerful, even now the taproom is hardly good enough for her any more.

And, in fact, it does strike people as odd that she is still in the taproom. Being a barmaid is a great deal, and from that point of view the liaison with Klamm seems very credible, but if the taproom girl has once become Klamm's mistress, why does he leave her in the taproom, and so long? Why does he not take her up higher?

One can tell people a thousand times that there is no contradiction here, that Klamm has definite reasons for acting as he does, or that some day, perhaps even at any moment now, Frieda's elevation will suddenly come about. All this does not make much impression.

People have definite notions and in the long run will not let themselves be distracted

from them by any talk, however ingenious. Nobody any longer doubted that Frieda was Klamm's mistress, even those who obviously knew better were by now too tired to doubt it.

"Be Klamm's mistress, and to hell with it," they thought, "but if you are, we want to see signs of it in your getting on too."

But one saw no signs of it and Frieda stayed in the taproom as before and secretly was thoroughly glad that things remained the way they were. But she lost prestige with people, that, of course, she could not fail to notice, indeed she usually noticed things even before they existed. A really beautiful, lovable girl, once she has settled down in the taproom, does not need to display any arts. As long as she is beautiful, she will remain taproom maid, unless some particularly unfortunate accident occurs. But a girl like Frieda must be continually worried about her situation, naturally she has enough sense not to show it, on the contrary, she is in the habit of complaining and cursing the situation. But in secret she keeps a weather-eye open all the time. And so she saw how people were becoming indifferent, Frieda's appearance on the scene was no longer anything that made it worth anyone's while even to glance up, not even the menservants bothered about her any more, they had enough sense to stick to Olga and girls of that sort, from the landlord's behaviour, too, she noticed that she was becoming less and less indispensable, one could not go on for ever inventing new stories about Klamm, everything has its limits, and so dear Frieda decided to try something new.

If anyone had only been capable of seeing through it immediately!

Pepi had sensed it, but unfortunately she had not seen through it.

Frieda decided to cause a scandal, she, Klamm's mistress, throws herself away on the first comer, if possible on the lowest of the low. That will make a stir, that will keep people talking for a long time, and at last, at last, people will remember what it means to be Klamm's mistress and what it means to throw away this honour in the rapture of a new love.

The only difficulty was to find the suitable man with whom the clever game could be played. It must not be an acquaintance of Frieda's, not even one of the menservants for he would probably have looked at her askance and have walked on, above all he would not have remained serious enough about it and for all her ready tongue it would have been impossible to spread the story that she, Frieda, had been attacked by him, had not been able to defend herself against him and in an hour when she did not know what she was doing had submitted to him. And although it had to be one of the lowest of the low, it nevertheless had to be one of whom it could be made credible that in spite of his crude, coarse nature he longed for nobody but Frieda herself and had no loftier desire than heavens above! - to marry Frieda.

But although it had to be a common man, if possible even lower than a servant, much lower than a servant, yet it must be one on whose account one would not be laughed to scorn by every girl, one in whom another girl, a girl of sound judgement, might also at some time find something attractive.

But where does one find such a man?

Another girl would probably have spent her whole life looking for him. Frieda's luck brought the Land Surveyor into the taproom to her, perhaps on the very evening when the plan had come into her mind for the first time.

The Land Surveyor!

Yes, what was K. thinking of?

What special things had he in mind?

Was he going to achieve something special?

A good appointment, a distinction?

Was he after something of that sort?

Well, then he ought to have set about things differendy from the very beginning. After all, he was a nonentity, it was heart-rending to see his situation. He was a Land Surveyor, that was perhaps something, so he had learnt something, but if one didn't know what to do with it, then again it was nothing after all. And at the same time he made demands, without having the slightest backing, made demands not outright, but one noticed that he was making some sort of demands, and that was, after all, infuriating.

Did he know that even a chambermaid was lowering herself if she talked to him for any length of time? And with all these special demands he tumbled headlong into the most obvious trap on the very first evening. Wasn't he ashamed of himself? What was it about Frieda that he found so alluring? Could she really appeal to him, that skinny, sallow thing?

Ah no, he didn't even look at her, she only had to tell him she was Klamm's mistress, for him that was still a novelty, and so he was lost! But now she had to move out, now, of course, there was no longer any room for her in the Herrenhof. Pepi saw her the very same morning before she moved out, the staff all came running up, after all, everyone was curious to see the sight.

And so great was her power even then that she was pitied, she was pitied by everyone, even by her enemies. So correct did her calculations prove to be from the very start.

Having thrown herself away on such a man seemed incomprehensible to everyone and a blow of fate, the little kitchenmaids, who, of course, admire every barmaid, were inconsolable. Even Pepi was touched, not even she could remain quite unmoved, even though her attention was actually focused on something else. She was struck by how little sad Frieda actually was. After all it was at bottom a dreadful misfortune that had come upon her, and indeed she was behaving as though she were very unhappy, but it was not enough, this acting could not deceive Pepi. So what was it that was keeping her going? Perhaps the happiness of her new love? Well, this possibility could not be considered. But what else could it be? What gave her the strength to be as coolly pleasant as ever even to Pepi, who was already regarded as her successor?

Pepi had not then had the time to think about it, she had had too much to do getting ready for the new job. She was probably to start on the job in a few hours and still had not had her hair done nicely, had no smart dress, no fine underclothes, no decent shoes.

All this had to be procured in a few hours. If one could not equip oneself properly, then it was better to give up all thought of the situation, for then one was sure of losing it in the very first half-hour.

Well, she succeeded partly.

She had a special gift for hair-dressing, once, indeed, the landlady had sent for her to do her hair, it was a matter of having a specially light hand, and she had it, of course, her abundant hair was the sort you could do anything you like with. There was help forthcoming in the matter of the dress too. Her two colleagues kept faith with her, it was after all a sort of honour for them, too, if a girl out of their own group was chosen to be barmaid, and then later on, when she had come to power, Pepi would have been able to provide them with many advantages. One of the girls had for a long time been keeping some expensive material, it was her treasure, she had often let the others admire it, doubtless dreaming of how some day she would make magnificent use of it and - this had been really very nice of her - now, when Pepi needed it, she sacrificed it. And both girls had very willingly helped her with the sewing, if they had been sewing it for themselves they could not have been keener.

That was indeed a very merry, happy job of work. They sat, each on her bunk, one over the other, sewing and singing, and handed each other the finished parts and the accessories, up and down. When Pepi thought of it, it made her heart ever heavier to think that it was all in vain and that she was going back to her friends with empty hands. What a misfortune and how frivolously brought about, above all by K.

How pleased they had all been with the dress at that time, it seemed a pledge of success and when at the last moment it turned out that there was still room for another ribbon, the last doubt vanished. And was it not really beautiful, this dress? It was crumpled now and showed some spots, the fact was, Pepi had no second dress, had to wear this one day and night, but it could still be seen how beautiful it was, not even that accursed Barnabas woman could produce a better one. And that one could pull it tight and loosen it again as one liked, on top and at the bottom, so that although it was only one dress, it was so changeable - this was a particular advantage and was actually her invention.

Of course it wasn't so difficult to make clothes for her, Pepi didn't boast of it, there it was - everything suited young, healthy girls. It was much harder to get hold of underclothing and boots, and here was where the failure actually began. Here, too, her girl friends helped out as best they could, but they could not do much. It was, after all, only coarse underclothing that they got together and patched up, and instead of high-heeled little boots she had to make do with slippers, of a kind one would rather hide than show.

They comforted Pepi. After all, Frieda was not dressed so very beautifully either, and sometimes she went round looking so sluttish that the guests preferred to be served by the cellarmen rather than by her. This was in fact so, but Frieda could afford to do that, she already enjoyed favour and prestige. When a lady for once makes an appearance looking besmirched and carelessly dressed, that is all the more alluring - but in the case of a novice like Pepi?

And besides, Frieda could not dress well at all, she was simply devoid of all taste. If a person happened to have a sallow skin, then, of course, she must put up with it, but she needn't go around, like Frieda, wearing a low-cut cream blouse to go with it, so that one's eyes were dazzled by all that yellow. And even if it hadn't been for that, she was too mean to dress well. Everything she earned, she hung on to, nobody knew what for. She didn't need any money in her job, she managed by means of lying and trickery, this was an example Pepi did not want to and could not imitate, and that was why it was justifiable that she should smarten herself up like this in order to get herself thoroughly noticed right at the beginning. Had she only been able to do it by stronger means, she would, in spite of all Frieda's cunning, in spite of all K.'s foolishness, have been victorious.

After all, it started very well.

The few tricks of the trade and things it was necessary to know she had found out about well beforehand. She was no sooner in the taproom than she was thoroughly at home there.

Nobody missed Frieda at the job. It was only on the second day that some guests inquired what had become of Frieda.

No mistake was made, the landlord was satisfied, on the first day he had been so anxious that he spent all the time in the taproom, later he only came in now and then, finally, since the money in the till was correct - the takings were on the average even a little higher than in Frieda's time - he left everything to Pepi.

She introduced innovations.

Frieda had even supervised the men-servants, at least partly, particularly when anyone was looking, and this not out of keenness for the work, but out of meanness, out of a desire to dominate, out of fear of letting anyone else invade her rights, Pepi on the other hand allotted this job entirely to the cellarmen, who, after all, are much better at it. In this way she had more time left for the private rooms, the guests got quick service; nevertheless she was able to chat for a moment with everyone, not like Frieda, who allegedly reserved herself entirely for Klamm and regarded every word every approach, on the part of anyone else as an insult to Klamm.

This was, of course, quite clever of her, for, if for once she did allow anyone to get near her, it was an unheard-of favour. Pepi, however, hated such arts, and anyway they were no use at the beginning. Pepi was kind to everyone and every, one requited with her kindness. All were visibly glad of the change. When the gentlemen, tired after their work, were at last free to sit down to their beer for a little while, one could positively transform them by a word, by a glance, by a shrug of the shoulders. So eagerly did all hands stroke Pepi's curls that she had to do her hair again quite ten times a day, no one could resist the temptation offered by these curls and bows, not even K., who was otherwise so absent-minded.

So exciting days flew past, full of work, but successful. If only they had not flown past so quickly, if only there had been a little more of them! Four days were too little even if one exerted oneself to the point of exhaustion, perhaps the fifth day would have been enough, but four days were too little. Pepi had, admittedly, gained wellwishers and friends even in four days, if she had been able to trust all the glances she caught, when she came along with the beer-mugs, she positively swam in a sea of friendliness, a clerk by the name of Bartmeier was crazy about her, gave her this little chain and locket, putting his picture into the locket, which was, of course, brazen of him.

This and other things had happened, but it had only been four days, in four days, if Pepi set about it, Frieda could be almost, but still not quite, forgotten. And yet she would have been forgotten, perhaps even sooner, had she not seen to it by means of her great scandal that she kept herself talked about, in this way she had become new to people, they might have liked to see her again simply for the sake of curiosity.

What they had come to find boring to the point of disgust had, and this was the doing of the otherwise entirely uninteresting K., come to have charm for them again. Of course they would not have given up Pepi as long as she was there in front of them and exerting influence by her presence, but they were mostly elderly gentlemen, slow and heavy in their habits, it took some time for them to get used to a new barmaid, and however advantageous the exchange might be, it still took a few days, took a few days against the gentlemen's own will, only five days perhaps, but four days were not enough, in spite of everything Pepi still counted only as the temporary barmaid.

And then what was perhaps the greatest misfortune: in these four days, although he had been in the village during the first two, Klamm did not come down into the saloon. Had he come, that would have been Pepi's most decisive test, a test, incidentally, that she was least afraid of, one to which she was more inclined to look forward.

She would - though it is, of course, best not to touch on such things in words at all - not have become Klamm's mistress, nor would she have promoted herself to that position by telling lies, but she would have been able to put the beer-glass on the table at least as nicely as Frieda, have said good-day and good-bye prettily without Frieda's officiousness, and if Klamm did look for anything in any girl's eyes at all, he would have found it to his entire satisfaction in Pepi's eyes. But why did he not come? Was it chance? That was what Pepi had thought at the time, too. All those two days she had expected him at any moment, and in the night she waited too.

"Now Klamm is coming," she kept on thinking, and dashed to and fro for no other reason than the restlessness of expectation and the desire to be the first to see him, immediately on his entry.

This continual disappointment made her very tired.

Perhaps that was why she did not get so much as she could have got done. Whenever she had a little time she crept up into the passage that the staff was strictly forbidden to enter, there she would squeeze into a recess and wait.

"If only Klamm would come now," she thought, "if only I could take the gentleman out of his room and carry him down into the saloon on my arms. I should not collapse under that burden, however great it might be."

But he did not come.

In that passage upstairs it was so quiet that one simply couldn't imagine it if one hadn't been there. It was so quiet that one couldn't stand being there for very long, the quietness drove one away.

But over and over again: driven away ten times, ten times again Pepi went up there.

It was senseless, of course. If Klamm wanted to come, he would come, but if he did not want to come, Pepi would not lure him out, even if the beating of her heart half suffocated her there in the recess. It was senseless, but if he did not come, almost everything was senseless.

And he did not come.

To-day Pepi knew why Klamm did not come.

Frieda would have found it wonderfully amusing if she had been able to see Pepi up there in the passage, in the recess, both hands on her heart.

Klamm did not come down because Frieda did not allow it.

It was not by means of her pleading that she brought this about, her pleading did not penetrate to Klamm. But - spider that she was - she had connections of which nobody knew.

If Pepi said something to a guest, she said it openly, the next table could hear it too.

Frieda had nothing to say, she put the beer on the table and went. There was only the rustling of her silk petticoat, the only thing on which she spent money. But if she did for once say something, then not openly, then she whispered it to the guest, bending low so that people at the next table pricked up their ears. What she said was probably quite trivial, but still, not always, she had connections, she supported the ones by means of the others, and if most of them foiled - who would keep on bothering about Frieda? - still, here and there one did hold firm.

These connections she now began to exploit.

K. gave her the chance to do this.

Instead of sitting with her and keeping a watch on her, he hardly stayed at home at all, wandering, having discussions here and there, paying attention to everything, only not to Frieda, and finally, in order to give her still more freedom, he moved out of the Bridge Inn into the empty school.

A very nice beginning for a honeymoon all this was.

Well, Pepi was certainly the last person to reproach K. for not having been able to stand living with Frieda. Nobody could stand living with her. But why then did he not leave her entirely, why did he time and again return to her, why did he cause the impression, by his roaming about, that he was fighting for her cause?

It really looked as though it were only through his contact with Frieda that he had discovered what a nonentity he in fact was, that he wished to make himself worthy of Frieda, wished to make his way up somehow, and for that reason was for the time being sacrificing her company in order to be able later to compensate himself at leisure for these hardships.

Meanwhile Frieda was not wasting her time, she sat tight in the school, where she had probably led K., and kept the Herrenhof and K. under observation.

She had excellent messengers at her disposal: K.'s assistants, whom - one couldn't understand it, even if one knew K. one couldn't understand it - K. left entirely to her.

She sent them to her old friends, reminded people of her existence, complained that she was kept a prisoner by a man like K., incited people against Pepi, announced her imminent arrival, begged for help, implored them to betray nothing to Klamm, behaved as if Klamm's feelings had to be spared and as if for this reason he must on no account be allowed to come down into the taproom. What she represented to one as a way of sparing Klamm's feelings she successfully turned to account where the landlord was concerned, drawing attention to the fact that Klamm did not come any more. How could he come when downstairs there was only a Pepi serving?

True, it wasn't the landlord's fault, this Pepi was after all the best substitute that could be found, only the substitute wasn't good enough, not even for a few days. All this activity of Frieda's was something of which K. knew nothing, when he was not roaming about he was lying at her feet, without an inkling of it, while she counted the hours still keeping her from the taproom. But this running of errands was not the only thing the assistants did, they also served to make K. jealous, to keep him interested in Frieda had known the assistants since her childhood, they certainly had no secrets from each other now, but in K.'s honour they were beginning to have a yearning for each other, and for K. there arose the danger that it would turn out to be a great love. And K. did everything Frieda wanted, even what was contradictory and senseless, he let himself be made jealous by the assistants, at the same time allowing all three to remain together while he went on his wanderings alone. It was almost as though he were Frieda's third assistant.

And so, on the basis of her observations, Frieda at last decided to make her great coup: she made up her mind to return. And it was really high time, it was admirable how Frieda, the cunning creature, recognized and exploited this fact. This power of observation and this power of decision were Frieda's inimitable art. If Pepi had it, how different the course of her life would be. If Frieda had stayed one or two days longer in the school, it would no longer be possible to drive Pepi out, she would be barmaid once and for all, loved and supported by all, having earned enough money to replenish her scanty wardrobe in the most dazzling style, only one or two more days and Klamm could not be kept out of the saloon by any intrigues any longer, would come, drink, feel comfortable and, if he noticed Frieda's absence at all, would be highly satisfied with the change, only one or two more days and Frieda, with her scandal, with her connections, with the assistants, with everything, would be utterly and completely forgotten, never would she come out into the open again. Then perhaps she would be able to cling all the more tightly to K. and, assuming that she were capable of it, would really learn to love him?

No, not that either.

For it didn't take even K. more than one day to get tired of her, to recognize how infamously she was deceiving him, with everything, with her alleged beauty, her alleged constancy, and most of all with Klamm's alleged love, it would only take him one day more, and no longer, to chase her out of the house, and together with her the whole dirty setup with the assistants.

Just think, it wouldn't take even K. any longer than that.

And now, between these two dangers, when the grave was positively beginning to close over her - K. in his simplicity was still keeping the last narrow road open for her - she suddenly bolted. Suddenly - hardly anyone expected such a thing, it was against nature-suddenly it was she who drove away K., the man who still loved her and kept on pursuing her, and, aided by the pressure of her friends and'the assistants, appeared to the landlord as the rescuer, as a result of the scandal associated with her much more alluring than formerly, demonstrably desired by the lowest as by the highest, yet having fallen a prey to the lowest only for a moment, soon rejecting him as was proper, and again inaccessible to him and to all others, as formerly. Only that formerly all this was quite properly doubted, whereas now everyone was again convinced.

So she came back, the landlord, with a sidelong glance at Pepi, hesitated - should he sacrifice her, after she had proved her worth so well? - but he was soon talked over, there was too much to be said for Frieda, and above all, of course, she would bring Klamm back to the saloon again.

That is where we stand, this evening.

Pepi is not going to wait till Frieda comes and makes a triumph out of taking over the job. She has already handed over the till to the landlady, she can go now. The bunk downstairs in the maids' room is waiting for her, she will come in, welcomed by the weeping girls, her friends, will tear the dress from her body, the ribbons from her hair, and stuff it all into a corner where it will be thoroughly hidden and won't be an unnecessary reminder of times better forgotten. Then she will take the big pail and the broom, clench her teeth, and set to work.

In the meantime, however, she had to tell K. everything so that he, who would not have realized this even now without help, might for once see clearly how horridly he had treated Pepi and how unhappy he had made her. Admittedly, he, too, had only been made use of and misused in all this.

Pepi had finished.

Taking a long breath, she wiped a few tears from her eyes and cheeks and then looked at K., nodding, as if meaning to say that at bottom what mattered was not her misfortune at all, she would bear it all right, for that she needed neither help nor comfort from anyone at all, least of all from K., even though she was so young she knew something about life, and her misfortune was only a confirmation of what she knew already, but what mattered was K., she had wanted to show him what he himself was like, even after the collapse of all her hopes she had thought it necessary to do that.

"What a wild imagination you have, Pepi," K. said. "For it isn't true at all that you have discovered all these things only now. All this is, of course, nothing but dreams out of that dark, narrow room you chambermaids have downstairs, dreams that are in their place there, but which look odd here in the freedom of the taproom. You couldn't maintain your position here with such ideas, that goes without saying. Even your dress and your way of doing your hair, which you make such a boast of, are only freaks born of that darkness and those bunks in your room, there they are very beautiful, I am sure, but here everyone laughs at them, secretly or openly.

And the rest of your story?

So I have been misused and deceived, have I?

No, my dear Pepi, I have not been misused and deceived any more than you have. It is true, Frieda has left me for the present or has, as you put it, run away with one of the assistants, you do see a glimmer of the truth, and it is really very improbable that she will ever become my wife, but it is utterly and completely untrue that I have grown tired of her and still less that I drove her out the very next day or that she deceived me, as other women perhaps deceive a man.

You chambermaids are used to spying through keyholes, and from that you get this way of thinking, of drawing conclusions, as grand as they are false, about the whole situation from some little thing you really see. The consequence of this is that I, for instance, in this case know much less than you.

I cannot explain by any means as exactly as you can why Frieda left me. The most probable explanation seems to me to be that you have touched on but not elaborated, which is that I neglected her. That is unfortunately true, I did neglect her, but there were special reasons for that, which have nothing to do with this discussion.

I should be happy if she were to come back to me, but I should at once begin to neglect her all over again. This is how it is. While she was with me I was continually out on those wanderings that you make such a mock of. Now that she is gone I am almost unemployed, am tired, have a yearning for a state of even more complete unemployment.

Have you no advice to give me, Pepi?"

"Oh yes, I have," Pepi said, suddenly becoming animated and seizing K. by the shoulders, "we have both been deceived, let us stick together. Come downstairs with me to the maids!"

"So long as you complain about being deceived," K. said, "I cannot come to an understanding with you. You are always claiming to have been deceived because you find it flattering and touching. But the truth is that you are not fitted for this job. How obvious your unfittedness must be when even I, who in your view know less about things than anyone can see that.

You are a good girl, Pepi. But it is not altogether easy to realize that, I for instance at first took you to be cruel and haughty, but you are not so, it is only this job that confuses you because you are not fitted for it, I am not going to say that the job is too grand for you. It is, after all not a very splendid job, perhaps, if one regards it closely, it is somewhat more honourable than your previous job, on the whole, however, the difference is not great, both are indeed so similar one can hardly distinguish between them. Indeed, one might almost assert that being a chambermaid is preferable to the taproom, for there one is always among secretaries, here, on the other hand, even though one is allowed to serve the secretaries' chiefs in the private rooms, still, one also has to have a lot to do with quite common people, for instance with me.

Actually I am not really supposed to sit about anywhere but right here in the taproom - and is it such a great and glorious honour to associate with me? Well, it seems so to you, and perhaps you have your reasons for thinking so. But precisely that makes you unfitted. It is a job like any other, but for you it is heaven, consequently you set about everything with exaggerated eagerness, trick yourself out as in your opinion the angels are tricked out - but in reality they are different - tremble for the job, feel you are constantly being persecuted, try by means of being excessively pleasant to win over everyone who in your opinion might be a support to you, but in this way bother them and repel them, for what they want at the inn is peace and quiet and not the barmaid's worries on top of their own.

It is just possible that after Frieda left none of the exalted guests really noticed the occurrence, but to-day they know of it and are really longing for Frieda, for Frieda doubtless did manage everything quite differently. Whatever she may be like otherwise and however much she valued her job, in her work she was greatly experienced, cool, and composed, you yourself stress that, though admittedly without learning anything from it.

Did you ever notice the way she looked at things?

That was not merely a barmaid's way of looking at things, it was almost the way a landlady looks around. She saw everything, and every individual person into the bargain, and the glance that was left for each individual person was still intense enough to subdue him.

What did it matter that she was perhaps a little skinny, a little oldish, that one could imagine cleaner hair?

Those are trifles compared with what she really had, and anyone whom these deficiencies disturbed would only have shown that he lacked any appreciation of greater things. One can certainly not charge Klamm with that, and it is only the wrong point of view of a young, inexperienced girl that makes you unable to believe in Klamm's love for Frieda.

Klamm seems to you - and this rightly - to be out of reach, and that is why you believe Frieda could not have got near to him either.

You are wrong.

I should take Frieda's own word for this, even if I had not infallible evidence for it.

However incredible it seems to you and however little you can reconcile it with your notions of the world and officialdom and gentility and the effect a woman's beauty has, still, it is true, just as we are sitting here beside each other and I take your hand between my hands, so too, I dare say, and as though it were the most natural thing in the world, did Klamm and Frieda sit beside each other, and he came down of his own free will, indeed he came hurrying down, nobody was lurking in the passage waiting for him and neglecting the rest of the work, Klamm had to bestir himself and come downstairs, and the faults in Frieda's way of dressing, which would have horrified you, did not disturb him at all.

You won't believe her!

And you don't know how you give yourself away by this, how precisely in this you show your lack of experience!

Even someone who knew nothing at all about the affair with Klamm could not fail to see from her bearing that someone had moulded her, someone who was more than you and I and all the people in the village and that their conversations went beyond the jokes that are usual between customers and waitresses and which seem to be your aim in life.

But I am doing you an injustice. You can see Frieda's merits very well for yourself, you notice her power of observation, her resolution, her influence on people, only you do, of course, interpret it all wrongly, believing she turns everything self-seekingly to account only for her own benefit and for evil purposes, or even as a weapon against you.

No, Pepi, even if she had such arrows, she could not shoot them at such short range.

And self-seeking?

One might rather say that by sacrificing what she had and what she was entitled to expect she has given us both the opportunity to prove our worth in higher positions, but that we have both disappointed her and are positively forcing her to return here. I do not know whether it is like this, and my own guilt is by no means clear to me, only when I compare myself with you something of this kind dawns on me: it is as if we had both striven too intensely, too noisily, too childishly, with too little experience, to get something that for instance with Frieda's calm and Frieda's matter-of-factness can be got easily and without much ado.

We have tried to get it by crying, by scratching, by tugging-just as a child tugs at the tablecloth, gaining nothing, but only bringing all the splendid things down on the floor and putting them out of its reach for ever. I don't know whether it is like that, but what I am sure of is that it is more likely to be so than the way you describe it as being."

"Oh well," Pepi said, "you are in love with Frieda because she's run away from you, it isn't hard to be in love with her when she's not there. But let it be as you like, and even if you are right in everything, even in making me ridiculous, what are you going to do now? Frieda has left you, neither according to my explanation nor according to your own have you any hope of her coming back to you, and even if she were to come back, you have to stay somewhere in the meantime, it is cold, and you have neither work nor a bed, come to us, you will like my girl friends, we shall make you comfortable, you will help us with our work, which is really too hard for girls to do all by themselves, we girls will not have to rely only on ourselves and won't be frightened any more in the night!

Come to us!

My girl friends also know Frieda, we shall tell you stories about her till you are sick and tired of it.

Do come!

We have pictures of Frieda too and we'll show them to you. At that time Frieda was more modest than she is to-day, you will scarcely recognize her, only perhaps by her eyes, which even then had a suspicious, watchful expression.

Well now, are you coming?"

"But is it permitted? Only yesterday there was that great scandal because I was caught in your passage."

"Because you were caught, but when you are with us you won't be caught. Nobody will know about you, only the three of us. Oh, it will be jolly. Even now life there seems much more bearable to me than only a little while ago. Perhaps now I shall not lose so very much by having to go away from here.

Listen, even with only the three of us we were not bored, one has to sweeten the bitterness of one's life, it's made bitter for us when we're still young, well, the three of us stick together, we live as nicely as is possible there, you'll like Henriette particularly, but you'll like Emilie too, I've told them about you, there one listens to such tales without believing them, as though outside the room nothing could really happen, it's warm and snug and tight there, and we press together still more tightly.

No, although we have only each other to rely on, we have not become tired of each other. On the contrary, when I think of my girl friends, I am almost glad that I am going back. Why should I get on better than they do? For that was just what held us together, the fact that the future was barred to all three of us in the same way, and now I have broken through after all and was separated from them. Of course I have not forgotten them, and my first concern was how I could do something for them. My own position was still insecure - how insecure it was, I did not even realize - and I was already talking to the landlord about Henriette and Emilie. So far as Henriette was concerned the landlord was not quite unrelenting, but for Emilie, it must be confessed, who is much older than we are, she's about as old as Frieda, he gave me no hope.

But only think, they don't want to go away, they know it's a miserable life they lead there, but they have resigned themselves to it, good souls, I think their tears as we said goodbye were mostly because they were sad about my having to leave our common room, going out into the cold - to us there everything seems cold that is outside the room - and having to make my way in the big strange rooms with big strange people, for no other purpose than to earn a living, which after all I had managed to do up to now in the life we led together. They probably won't be at all surprised when now I come back, and only in order to indulge me will they weep a little and bemoan my fate. But then they will see you and notice that it was a good thing after all that I went away. It will make them happy that now we have a man as a helper and protector, and they will be absolutely delighted that it must all be kept a secret and that through this secret we shall be still more tightly linked with each other than before.

Come, oh please come to us!

No obligation will arise so far as you are concerned, you will not be bound to our room for ever, as we are. When the spring comes and you find a lodging somewhere else and if you don't like being with us any more, then you can go if you want to.

Only, of course, you must keep the secret even then and not go and betray us, for that would mean our last hour in the Herrenhof had come, and in other respects too, naturally, you must be careful when you are with us, not showing yourself anywhere unless we regard it as safe, and altogether take our advice. That is the only thing that ties you, and this must count just as much with you as with us, but otherwise you are completely free, the work we shall share out to you will not be too hard, you needn't be afraid of that."

Well then, are you coming?"

"How much longer is it till spring?" K. asked.

"Till spring?" Pepi repeated. "Winter is long here, a very long winter, and monotonous.

But we don't complain about that down there, we are safe from the winter. Well yes, some day spring comes too, and summer, and there's a time for that too, I suppose. But in memory, now, spring and summer seem as short as though they didn't last much longer than two days, and even on those days, even during the most beautiful day, even then sometimes snow falls."

At this moment the door opened.

Pepi started, in her thoughts she had gone too far away from the taproom, but it was not Frieda, it was the landlady. She pretended to be amazed at finding K. still here. K. excused himself by saying that he had been waiting for her, and at the same time he expressed his thanks for having been allowed to stay here overnight. The landlady could not understand why K. had been waiting for her. K. said he had had the impression that she wanted to speak to him again, he apologized if that had been a mistake, and for the rest he must go now anyway, he had left the school, where he was a caretaker, to itself much, too long, yesterday's summons was to blame for everything, he still had too little experience of these matters, it would certainly not happen again that he would cause the landlady such inconvenience and bother as yesterday.

And he bowed, on the point of going.

The landlady looked at him as though she were dreaming. This gaze kept K. longer than was his intention. Now she smiled a little, and it was only the amazement on K.'s face that, as it were, woke her up. It was as though she had been expecting an answer to her smile and only now, since none came, did she wake up.

"Yesterday, I think, you had the impudence to say something about my dress."

K. could not remember.

"You can't remember? Then it's not only impudence, but afterwards cowardice into the bargain."

By way of excuse K. spoke of his fatigue of the previous day, saying it was quite possible that he had talked some nonsense, in any case he could not remember now. And what could he have said about the landlady's clothes? That they were more beautiful than any he had ever seen in his life. At least he had never seen any landlady at her work in such clothes.

"That's enough of these remarks!" the landlady said swiftly. "I don't want to hear another word from you about my clothes. My clothes are none of your business. Once and for all, I forbid you to talk about them."

K. bowed again and went to the door.

"What do you mean," the landlady shouted after him, "by saying you've never before seen any landlady at work in such clothes? What do you mean by making such senseless remarks?

It's simply quite senseless. What do you mean by it?"

K. turned round and begged the landlady not to get excited.

Of course the remark was senseless. After all, he knew nothing at all about clothes. In his situation any dress that happened to be clean and not patched seemed luxurious. He had only been amazed at the landlady's appearing there, in the passage, at night, among all those scantily dressed men, in such a beautiful evening-dress, that was all.

"Well now," the landlady said, "at last you seem to have remembered the remark you made yesterday, after all. And you put the finishing touch to it by some more nonsense. It's quite true you don't know anything about clothes. But then kindly refrain - this is a serious request I make to you - from setting yourself up as a judge of what are luxurious dresses or unsuitable evening-dresses, and the like ... And let me tell you" -here it seemed as if a cold shudder went through her - "you've no business to interfere with my clothes in any way at all, do you hear?"

And as K. was about to turn away again in silence, she asked: "Where did you get your knowledge of clothes, anyway?"

K. shrugged his shoulders, saying he had no knowledge.

"You have none," the landlady said. "Very well then, don't set up to have any, either.

Come over to the office, I'll show you something, then I hope you'll stop your impudent remarks for good."

She went through the door ahead of him. Pepi rushed forward to K., on the pretext of settling the bill. They quickly made their plans, it was very easy, since K. knew the courtyard with the gate opening into the side-street, beside the gate there was a little door behind which Pepi would stand in about an hour and open it on hearing a threefold knock.

The private office was opposite the taproom, they only had to cross the hall, the landlady was already standing in the lighted office and impatiently looking towards K.

But there was yet another disturbance. Gerstacker had been waiting in the hall and wanted to talk to K. It was not easy to shake him off, the landlady also joined in and rebuked Gerstacker for his intrusiveness.

"Where are you going? Where are you going?" Gerstacker could still be heard calling out even after the door was shut, and the words were unpleasantly interspersed with sighs and coughs. It was a small, over-heated room. Against the end-walls were a standing-desk and an iron safe, against the side-walls were a wardrobe and an ottoman. It was the wardrobe that took up most room. Not only did it occupy the whole of the longer wall, its depth also made the room very narrow, it had three slidingdoors by which it could be opened completely. The landlady pointed to the ottoman, indicating that K. should sit down, she herself sat down on the revolving chair at the desk.

"Didn't you once learn tailoring?" the landlady asked.

"No, never," K. said.

"What actually is it you are?"

"Land Surveyor."

"What is that?"

K. explained, the explanation made her yawn.

"You're not telling the truth. Why won't you tell the truth?"

"You don't tell the truth either."

"I? So now you're beginning your impudent remarks again? And if I didn't tell the truth - do I have to answer for it to you? And in what way don't I tell the truth then?"

"You are not only a landlady, as you pretend."

"Just listen to that! All the things you discover! What else am I then? But I must say, your impudence is getting thoroughly out of hand."

"I don't know what else you are. I only see that you are a landlady and also wear clothes that are not suitable for a landlady and of a kind that to the best of my knowledge nobody else wears here in the village."

"Well, now we're getting to the point. The fact is you can't keep it to yourself, perhaps you aren't impudent at all, you're only like a child that knows some silly thing or other and which simply can't, by any means, be made to keep it to itself. Well, speak up! What is so special about these clothes?"

"You'll be angry if I say."

"No, I shall laugh about it, it'll be some childish chatter. What sort of clothes are they then?"

"You insist on hearing. Well, they're made of good material, pretty expensive, but they are old-fashioned, fussy, often renovated, worn, and not suitable either for your age or for your figure or for your position. I was struck by them the very first time I saw you, it was about a week ago, here in the hall."

"So there now we have it! They are old-fashioned, fussy, and what else did you say? And what enables you to judge all this?"

"I can see for myself, one doesn't need any training for that.'"

"You can see it without more ado. You don't have to inquire anywhere, you know at once what is required by fashion. So you're going to be quite indispensable to me, for I must admit I have a weakness for beautiful clothes. And what will you say when I tell you that this wardrobe is full of dresses?"

She pushed the sliding doors open, one dress could be seen tightly packed against the next, filling up the whole length and breadth of the wardrobe, they were mostly dark, grey, brown, black dresses, all carefully hung up and spread out.

"These are my dresses, all old-fashioned, fussy, as you think. But they are only the dresses for which I have no room upstairs in my room, there I have two more wardrobes full, two wardrobes, each of them almost as big as this one. Are you amazed?"

"No. I was expecting something of the sort. Didn't I say you're not only a landlady, you're aiming at something else.'

"I am only aiming at dressing beautifully, and you are either a fool or a child or a very wicked, dangerous person. Go, go away now!"

K. was already in the hall and Gerstacker was clutching at his sleeve again, when the landlady shouted after him: "I am getting a new dress to-morrow, perhaps I shall send for you."

THE END